NEW GEPT

新制全民英檢

10回試題完全掌握最新內容與趨勢！

初級 聽力&閱讀 題庫大全

── ○ 題本＋解答 ○ ──

U0050493

CONTENTS

目錄

NEW GEPT
新制全民英檢初級聽力 & 閱讀題庫大全

聽力測驗答對題數與分數對照表

答對題數	分數	答對題數	分數	答對題數	分數
30	120	20	80	10	40
29	116	19	76	9	36
28	112	18	72	8	32
27	108	17	68	7	28
26	104	16	64	6	24
25	100	15	60	5	20
24	96	14	56	4	16
23	92	13	52	3	12
22	88	12	48	2	8
21	84	11	44	1	4

閱讀測驗答對題數與分數對照表

答對題數	分數	答對題數	分數	答對題數	分數
30	120	20	80	10	40
29	116	19	76	9	36
28	112	18	72	8	32
27	108	17	68	7	28
26	104	16	64	6	24
25	100	15	60	5	20
24	96	14	56	4	16
23	92	13	52	3	12
22	88	12	48	2	8
21	84	11	44	1	4

TEST 01

GEPT
全民英檢

初級初試

題目本

本測驗分四個部分,全部都是單選題,共 30 題,作答時間約 20 分鐘。作答說明為中文,印在試題冊上並經由光碟放音機播出。

第一部分 看圖辨義

共 5 題。每題請聽光碟放音機播出題目和三個英文句子之後,選出與所看到的圖畫最相符的答案。每題只播出一遍。

例:(看)

(聽)

Look at the picture. What does the man do?

(A) He is a doctor.

(B) He is a teacher.

(C) He is a cook.

正確答案為 (A)。

聽力測驗第一部分試題從這裡開始。

A. Question 1

B. Question 2 and 3

C. Question 4 and 5

第二部分 問答

共 10 題。每題請聽光碟放音機播出的英文句子，再從試題冊上三個回答中，選出一個最適合的答案。每題只播出一遍。

例：（聽）May I use your bathroom?

（看）(A) Sure. This way, please.

(B) You're welcome.

(C) I'd like two hamburgers.

正確答案為 (A)。

現在開始聽力測驗第二部分。

6. (A) I'm late. Sorry.
   (B) Pretty good. Thank you.
   (C) Thank you very much.

7. (A) No, but I can help you.
   (B) Yes, please. I'm looking for the restroom.
   (C) You're welcome.

8. (A) Just a minute, please.
   (B) No, I'm fine.
   (C) I'm afraid not.

9. (A) Who are you?
   (B) This is Mr. Lin speaking.
   (C) Thank you for calling.

10. (A) You're welcome.
    (B) No problem.
    (C) Thank you.

11. (A) He is very tall.
    (B) He is 170 centimeters tall.
    (C) He is the tallest in his family.

12. (A) It is August 8.
    (B) It is Tuesday.
    (C) It is my birthday.

13. (A) I'd love to.
    (B) This cup of coffee is too strong for me.
    (C) No sugar, please.

14. (A) Oops! I'm going to be late.
    (B) Mmm... Let me think about it.
    (C) That's right. I can't wait.

15. (A) Oh, really?
    (B) I'd want another.
    (C) Here comes the bus.

第三部分 簡短對話

共 10 題。每題請聽光碟放音機播出的一段對話和一個相關的問題後,再從試題冊上三個選項中,選出一個最適合的答案。每段對話和問題播出一遍。

例:(聽)(男)What a nice-looking skirt. Is it expensive?

　　　(女)No, I got it at the night market last night. I bought three at once.

　　　(男)Well, but it really looks nice and expensive.

　　　(女)You wanna get one for your girlfriend?

　　　(男)Good idea. Where's the night market?

Question: What are the speakers mainly discussing?

(看)(A) Where the woman bought the skirt

　　　(B) What the woman bought last night

　　　(C) How much the skirt cost

正確答案為 (B)。

現在開始聽力測驗第三部分。

16. (A) Two.
    (B) Three.
    (C) We don't know.

17. (A) The woman went to a movie last night.
    (B) The man went to a movie last night.
    (C) Neither of them went to a movie last night.

18. (A) He's driving.
    (B) He's cooking.
    (C) He's sweeping the floor.

19. (A) Yes, they are in the same class.
    (B) Yes, Mary is their classmate.
    (C) No, they just met for the first time.

20. (A) Bill is younger.
    (B) Mary is younger.
    (C) Mary is about the same age as Bill.

21. (A) They are in a convenience store.
    (B) They are at a fast food restaurant.
    (C) They are in a department store.

22. (A) She didn't get anything on her birthday.
    (B) Her boyfriend has gone to Japan.
    (C) Something bad happened to her.

23. (A) Yes, they studied together for the GEPT exam recently.
    (B) No, they haven't seen each other for years.
    (C) No, she's not been in contact with her for years.

24. (A) Alice was absent from their high school reunion.
    (B) Their high school reunion will be held this weekend.
    (C) They forgot about an activity.

25. (A) Get something to drink.
    (B) Buy some stamps.
    (C) See a doctor.

第四部分 短文聽解

共 5 題，每題有 3 個圖片選項。請聽光碟放音機播出的題目，並選出一個最適當的圖片。每題只播出一遍。

例：（看）

(A)　　　　　　　　　　(B)　　　　　　　　　　(C)

（聽）

Listen to the following message. What will Steve probably buy after work?

　　Hi, Mom. This is Steve. I just made a call to you, but you didn't answer your phone. I will have a meeting with Mr. Roberts at the office tonight. I won't go home until 8 o'clock, so I can't have dinner with you tonight. I will buy some fast food on my way home. Don't worry about me.

正確答案為 (C)。

現在開始聽力測驗第四部分。

Question 26

(A)　　　　　　　　　　(B)　　　　　　　　　　(C)

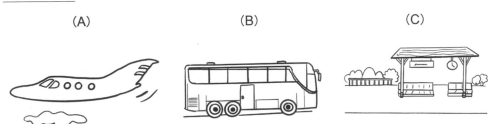

Question 27

(A)  (B)  (C)

Question 28

(A)  (B)  (C)

Question 29

(A)  (B)  (C)

Question 30

(A)  (B)  (C)

未經指示前請勿翻頁

本測驗分三個部分，全部都是單選題，共 30 題，作答時間 35 分鐘。

第一部分：詞彙

共 10 題，每個題目裡有一個空格。請由四個選項中選出一個最適合題意的字或詞作答。

1. Don't go out on a typhoon day. _____ home is better.
   (A) Stay
   (B) Staying
   (C) To stay
   (D) Stayed

2. I like to listen to some _____ when I take a shower.
   (A) activity
   (B) building
   (C) music
   (D) calendar

3. Julia was rushed to hospital after she had a car _____.
   (A) problem
   (B) society
   (C) question
   (D) accident

4. It's an ice block. I can feel the _____ over my head.
   (A) heat
   (B) goal
   (C) coldness
   (D) warm

5. She _____ a diary in English to practice her writing ability.
   (A) writes
   (B) keeps
   (C) holds
   (D) draws

6. My son is _____ a helpful kid that everyone in the class likes him.
   (A) what
   (B) so
   (C) such
   (D) some

7. David can do the job by _____. He said he won't need help.
   (A) himself
   (B) herself
   (C) themselves
   (D) myself

8. Mother has _____ housework to do every day.
   (A) many
   (B) several
   (C) a lot of
   (D) few

9. I'm about to get off at the next exit, and _____ be there very soon.
   (A) would
   (B) will
   (C) won't
   (D) are going to

10. There are beautiful flowers and trees on _____ sides of the road.
   (A) each
   (B) both
   (C) all
   (D) three

第二部分 段落填空

共 8 題，包括二個段落，每個段落各含有四個空格。每格均有四個選項，請依照文意選出最適合的答案。

Questions 11-14

　　Mary was doing the dishes when there was a power failure. She had to find a flashlight, but she 　(11)　. What's worse, she had to comfort her little daughter, who was then screaming terribly because she was afraid of the 　(12)　. After Mary spent much effort making her daughter fall asleep, and when she was ready to go to bed, an ambulance rushed near and woke the little girl up. Then, 　(13)　, so her daughter cried loudly again, when it was already 4:30 A.M. And of course, she had to calm down her baby again, and this took her almost an hour. Then at 6:00 A.M., her alarm clock went off; it was time 　(14)　 up and go to work.

◢ power failure 停電

11. (A) can
　　(B) can't
　　(C) could
　　(D) couldn't

12. (A) light
　　(B) dark
　　(C) noise
　　(D) cold

13. 【新題型】(A) Mary tried to sing a song to her daughter
　　(B) the thunder was heard from the sky
　　(C) luckily, nobody got hurt
　　(D) the rain stopped suddenly

14. (A) to get
　　(B) get
　　(C) getting
　　(D) got

Questions 15-18

Dozens of years ago, we could find many different kinds of maps of our towns. For example, there were some maps which ___(15)___ all the electrical lines in your town. If you had lived in a city ___(16)___ bus service, you could have found a map of bus routes. Besides, there were also street maps that might be more useful to you. ___(17)___ If you do not know ___(18)___ to find street maps, you might try gas stations, visitor centers, or bookstores.

15. (A) show
    (B) showed
    (C) shows
    (D) has showed

16. (A) for
    (B) from
    (C) with
    (D) without

17. (A) To get a street map of your city should not be too difficult.

新題型

    (B) You can also choose to use a cellphone.
    (C) There's actually no way to find a useful map.
    (D) Or else, you can ask for directions from local people.

18. (A) where
    (B) what
    (C) how
    (D) whether

第三部分 閱讀理解

共 12 題，包括 4 個題組，每個題組含 1 至 2 篇短文，與數個相關的四選一的選擇題。請由試題冊上的選項中選出最適合的答案。

Questions 19-21

From:	Service@fashionsop.com.tw
To:	Undisclosed-Recipient
Subject:	Try Fashion Shop

To whom it may concern,

　　Fashion Shop tells you how easy it is to start your own business. Maybe you want to sell fashionable goods such as hats, dresses, pants, watches, rings, etc. You're able to make it just by joining us in about one minute, and it takes no more than 10 minutes to open your online store.

Only $5 per month, and free for a limited time!
Click the button below to have a fantastic experience!

Join Now

Please e-mail us at Service@fashionsop.com.tw for any more questions.
Sincerely,
Custumer Service
August 1

After clicking the "JOIN NOW" button, you'll see the following web page.

← → C ↑ 🔍 www.fashionshop.com/register   ⊟ ⧠ ⊠

Try Fashion Shop for Free

Start a 7-day free trial before the end of this month to begin doing business with customers around the world right now! You need to pay by credit card.

Already a member? Log in here.

Name

Email address

Company Name

Credit Card No.

SPECIAL NOTE

1. A new member needs to first pay a three-month membership fee before his/her new store can be opened.
2. Refund is available and please contact us at 5523-21688 if you do not want to continue to use within the 7 days of trial.

19. What is the email aimed at?
    (A) Telling members about some good news
    (B) Inviting people to join
    (C) Reminding members of an important event
    (D) Sharing a fantastic experience

20. What does "a limited time" mean in the email?
    (A) There will be no free trial seven days from now.
    (B) There will be free trial from now until August 31.
    (C) New members can enjoy 7 additional days of membership.
    (D) New members need to type in their credit card numbers after seven days
        of free trial.

21. How much should a new member need to pay at first?
    (A) $5
    (B) $10
    (C) $15
    (D) $20

From:	david_chang@yourmail.com
To:	john_hsu@@yourmail.com
Subject:	Re: Mid-Autumn Festival Acvivity

Dear John,

I hope you have enjoyed your BBQ party during the Mid-Autumn Festival holidays. We did not have a BBQ party, though, because our balcony is too small to do that activity, and I couldn't find another good place.

By the way, the Moon Festival this year happened to be the birthday of my wife, Mary. We went out for dinner together. We decided to go out to a restaurant to celebrate such a special day. I had booked a table. After we arrived at the restaurant, I ordered a steak and a bottle of beer. Mary ordered a chicken cutlet and a glass of champagne. Each meal came with a salad. The food was delicious!

Wish you all the best and look forward to see you soon.

David

22. What is the purpose of David email?
    (A) To accept an invitation
    (B) To offer advice
    (C) To tell about a recent life event
    (D) To make a future plan

23. Why did the couple go out for dinner?
    (A) To talk about looking for a babysitter
    (B) To celebrate their kids' birthday
    (C) Because there was a new restaurant nearby
    (D) Because it was a special day

24. What did the couple NOT order in the restaurant?
    (A) steak
    (B) chicken outlet
    (C) drinks
    (D) salad

Questions 25-27

Andy was a single old man but he led a happy life. Every day there were many friends visiting his place. They would drink some tea and chat, or play chess the whole afternoon. One thing is, he was very forgetful. For example, he often forgot which piece he had moved.

One day, he was hit by a flying ball when he went out to go jogging around a park. He did not know where it came from. He felt a headache the following day, so he decided to see a doctor. In a small hospital, the doctor asked him, "How old are you?" Andy replied, "I can't remember, Dr. Wang. But let me try to think." After a few minutes, he said, "I remember now, doctor! When I got married, I was thirty years old, and my wife was twenty. Now my wife is forty, and that is twice twenty. So I am twice thirty. I am sixty years old now, am I?"

The doctor gave him a smile and asked him, "Where's your wife? Didn't she come here with you?" Andy said, "Oh, Dr. Wang. I forgot my wife had died last year."

25. What is the story mainly about?
    (A) An old man and his wife
    (B) A friendly doctor
    (C) A chess lover
    (D) An old man of bad memory

26. When did Andy get married?
    (A) Thirty years ago
    (B) Twenty years ago
    (C) At the age of twenty
    (D) When he was forty

27. Which of the following is correct?
    (A) Andy's wife is ten years younger than him.
    (B) Andy is twenty years older than his wife.
    (C) Andy is twice thirty now.
    (D) Andy's wife was forty when they got married.

Questions 28-30

The Wang family was very busy last Saturday. For them, it was a big day, because a wholly new living environment was awaiting them. Before the big truck arrived on 3:00 p.m., they had to put all things into boxes, such as clothes, toys, books, photo albums and other items they did not want to throw away. Besides, they needed to clear and clean all the floors and take away, or throw away all the old food out of the kitchen.

Of course, they did not have to move large furniture on their own. Mr. Wang spent NT$8,000 hiring movers to do that. When the truck arrived, two men got out and moved the washing machine, the refrigerator, the clothes closet, the beds and other large furniture onto the truck. And then, they carefully carried all the boxes out and place them in the back of the truck.

At last, Mr. Wang got into the truck with his son David, while Mrs. Wang drove a car with Sandy and Mary. Kevin, aged 16 and their oldest son, was already in the new apartment waiting for them.

28. How many children do the couple have?
    (A) Two
    (B) Three
    (C) Four
    (D) Five

29. What did the family NOT do?
    (A) Pack boxes
    (B) Clean the floors
    (C) Move the refrigerator
    (D) Drive to their new place

30. What does the first word "big" in the first paragraph mean?
    (A) Large
    (B) Heavy
    (C) Busy
    (D) Important

—結束—

TEST 02

GEPT
全民英檢
初級初試

題目本

本測驗分四個部分，全部都是單選題，共 30 題，作答時間約 20 分鐘。作答說明為中文，印在試題冊上並經由光碟放音機播出。

第一部分 看圖辨義

共 5 題。每題請聽光碟放音機播出題目和三個英文句子之後，選出與所看到的圖畫最相符的答案。每題只播出一遍。

例：（看）

（聽）

Look at the picture. What does the man do?

(A) He is a doctor.

(B) He is a teacher.

(C) He is a cook.

正確答案為 (A)。

聽力測驗第一部分試題從這裡開始。

A. Question 1

B. Question 2 and 3

C. Question 4 and 5

第二部分 問答

共 10 題。每題請聽光碟放音機播出的英文句子，再從試題冊上三個回答中，選出一個最適合的答案。每題只播出一遍。

例：（聽）May I use your bathroom?

（看）(A) Sure. This way, please.

(B) You're welcome.

(C) I'd like two hamburgers.

正確答案為 (A)。

6. (A) I'm Judy.
   (B) I'm twelve years old.
   (C) I'm from Taiwan.

7. (A) Yes, I have a pen.
   (B) Pen.
   (C) P-e-n

8. (A) Yes, she is cooking in the kitchen.
   (B) No, she is in her room.
   (C) Yes, she is in her office.

9. (A) No, we are not.
   (B) No, they are not classmates.
   (C) Yes, we are not.

10. (A) I'm not ready.
    (B) Yes, I think I am a bit drunk.
    (C) No, but I can give it a try.

11. (A) I go to school at seven thirty in the morning.
    (B) I had no time to watch it.
    (C) It's ten after eleven.

12. (A) I'm going to do my homework.
    (B) I'm going to the library.
    (C) I'm going on a diet.

13. (A) It's Friday.
    (B) I didn't go to school today.
    (C) It's September 15.

14. (A) Sounds good.
    (B) Yes, I can see many trees.
    (C) Lunch isn't ready.

15. (A) Oh, is it still open?
    (B) It's my pleasure.
    (C) OK. Just take care.

第三部分 簡短對話

共 10 題。每題請聽光碟放音機播出的一段對話和一個相關的問題後，再從試題冊上三個選項中，選出一個最適合的答案。每段對話和問題播出一遍。

TEST 02

例：（聽）（男）What a nice-looking skirt. Is it expensive?

（女）No, I got it at the night market last night. I bought three at once.

（男）Well, but it really looks nice and expensive.

（女）You wanna get one for your girlfriend?

（男）Good idea. Where's the night market?

Question: What are the speakers mainly discussing?

（看）(A) Where the woman bought the skirt

(B) What the woman bought last night

(C) How much the skirt cost

正確答案為 (B)。

現在開始聽力測驗第三部分。

16. (A) She is sick.
    (B) She shouldn't wear blue
        clothes.
    (C) She has no idea.

17. (A) The man's new hairstyle
    (B) A barber shop
    (C) What hairstyle suits the man

18. (A) In a company
    (B) In a classroom
    (C) In a barber shop

19. (A) He has one brother and one
        sister.
    (B) He has only one brother.
    (C) He doesn't have any brothers
        or sisters.

20. (A) She ate them last night.
    (B) Because she caught a cold.
    (C) Because she eats them very
        often recently.

21. (A) Go fishing.
    (B) Draw some money.
    (C) Get something to eat.

22. (A) They're standing in line buy
        some drinks.
    (B) They're buying tickets.
    (C) They're eating lunch.

23. (A) On a train
    (B) In the living room
    (C) Outside a house

24. (A) She's feeling unhappy.
    (B) She doesn't want to go to work
        today.
    (C) She doesn't make much effort
        on the project.

25. (A) 2:00 p.m.
    (B) 2:30 p.m.
    (C) 3:30 p.m.

第四部分 短文聽解

共 5 題，每題有 3 個圖片選項。請聽光碟放音機播出的題目，並選出一個最適當的圖片。**每題只播出一遍**。

例：（看）

(A)　　　　　　　(B)　　　　　　　(C)

（聽）

Listen to the following message. What will Steve probably buy after work?

　　Hi, Mom. This is Steve. I just made a call to you, but you didn't answer your phone. I will have a meeting with Mr. Roberts at the office tonight. I won't go home until 8 o'clock, so I can't have dinner with you tonight. I will buy some fast food on my way home. Don't worry about me.

正確答案為 (C)。

Question 26

(A)　　　　　　　(B)　　　　　　　(C)

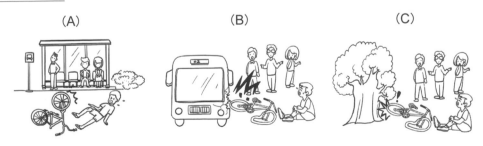

Question 27

(A)

(B)

(C)

  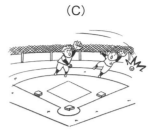

Question 28

(A)

(B)

(C)

Question 29

(A)

(B)

(C)

Question 30

(A)

(B)

(C)

未經指示前請勿翻頁

本測驗分三個部分，全部都是單選題，共 30 題，作答時間 35 分鐘。

第一部分 詞彙

共 10 題，每個題目裡有一個空格。請由四個選項中選出一個最適合題意的字或詞作答。

1. I do not have a motorcycle, _____.
   (A) too
   (B) either
   (C) neither
   (D) only

2. Miss Wang asked her students _____ their books.
   (A) opened
   (B) to open
   (C) opening
   (D) and opened

3. Jerry has one brother, but he doesn't have _____ sisters.
   (A) some
   (B) many
   (C) no
   (D) any

4. It's hard to say how to get there. Let me draw a _____ for you.
   (A) sight
   (B) map
   (C) photo
   (D) line

5. David was not _____ to the party last weekend.
   (A) invited
   (B) invented
   (C) interested
   (D) increased

6. I work in a _____ , where a lot of furniture is made every day.
   (A) factory
   (B) garden
   (C) hospital
   (D) museum

7. After that accident, he didn't work _____ .
   (A) anyway
   (B) anymore
   (C) anything
   (D) anytime

8. _____ the help of each of you, we're not able to finish the task in time.
   (A) With
   (B) Without
   (C) For
   (D) From

9. The basketball player is taller than _____ of us.
   (A) that
   (B) these
   (C) much
   (D) any

10. She's always willing to help _____ people with the same problems.
    (A) other
    (B) the other
    (C) others
    (D) the others

第二部分 段落填空

共 8 題，包括二個段落，每個段落各含有四個空格。每格均有四個選項，請依照文意選出最適合的答案。

Questions 11-14

Grace does not like to read, (11) she enjoys listening to music, especially when she takes a bath every night. Her favorite song goes like this: "Oh, I like (12) around the world, but I'm just a passing traveller to the world. I'll tell you where I'm from, what I like to eat and that I'm very happy to be here."

One day, however, she found that she was bored with listening to the same music over and over (13) . She wanted to listen to different styles of songs. So, she went online to search for rock music. But it sounded too noisy. (14) She thought it might help her fall asleep, but actually she dislikes such a style.

11. (A) and
    (B) but
    (C) or
    (D) when

12. (A) travel
    (B) traveled
    (C) to travel
    (D) to traveling

13. (A) more
    (B) than
    (C) often
    (D) again

14. (A) So she tried to read some interesting books.
    (B) Then she continued to look for some country music.
    (C) Besides, she always has a lot of new clothes to try on.
    (D) Nowadays music is easy to download from many web sites.

新題型

Questions 15-18

Yesterday my nephew Sam visited me. He told me that his mother   (15)   be away for a while, and he didn't know where to spend his boring afternoon. So he decided to come to my place to kill time. Actually I knew that he only wanted to play the video games that I had just bought last week.

I took him to my room and showed him   (16)   to play the newest games. He looked so excited that he almost forgot it was time to go home.   (17)   and she asked me to   (18)   his son home. Anyway, I always like to help people. But the problem is, Sam was still unwilling to leave my room.

15. (A) will
　　(B) will not
　　(C) would
　　(D) would not

16. (A) what
　　(B) how
　　(C) where
　　(D) when

17. (A) Then his mother made a call to me
　　(B) So I was very happy to have him here
　　(C) I thought his mother hasn't come
　　(D) Maybe I should call his mother

18. (A) take
　　(B) ask
　　(C) call
　　(D) bring

新題型

TEST 02

第三部分 閱讀理解

共 12 題，包括 4 個題組，每個題組含 1 至 2 篇短文，與數個相關的四選一的選擇題。請由試題冊上的選項中選出最適合的答案。

Questions 19-21

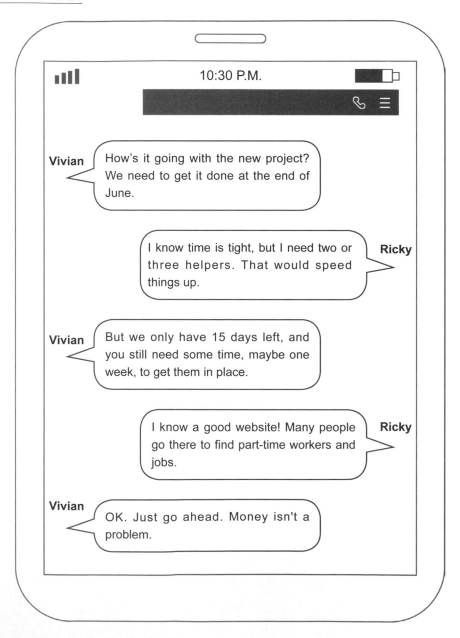

Vivian
How's it going with the new project? We need to get it done at the end of June.

Ricky
I know time is tight, but I need two or three helpers. That would speed things up.

Vivian
But we only have 15 days left, and you still need some time, maybe one week, to get them in place.

Ricky
I know a good website! Many people go there to find part-time workers and jobs.

Vivian
OK. Just go ahead. Money isn't a problem.

Ricky went to the site the following day and filled in the form below.

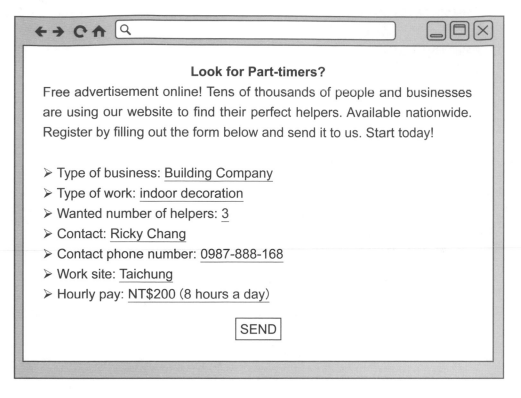

Look for Part-timers?

Free advertisement online! Tens of thousands of people and businesses are using our website to find their perfect helpers. Available nationwide. Register by filling out the form below and send it to us. Start today!

➢ Type of business: Building Company
➢ Type of work: indoor decoration
➢ Wanted number of helpers: 3
➢ Contact: Ricky Chang
➢ Contact phone number: 0987-888-168
➢ Work site: Taichung
➢ Hourly pay: NT$200 (8 hours a day)

SEND

19. What is the purpose of this advertisement?
    (A) To help people find a part-time job.
    (B) To help companies or stores advertise for their products.
    (C) To guide companies to write about a part-time job.
    (D) To encourage people or business to join a website.

20. When did Ricky go to the web site to find helpers?
    (A) On June 14.   (B) On June 15.
    (C) On June 16.   (D) On June 17.

21. How much will they need to pay for the short-time hired workers a day?
    (A) NT$ 200   (B) NT$ 1600
    (C) NT$ 4800   (D) It's totally free.

Questions 22-24

(The telephone is ringing...)

Julia: Good afternoon, Dr. Chou's office. How may I help you?

Mrs. Hu: This is Mrs. Hu calling. I would like to make an appointment for my health checkup.

Julia: Let me check the appointment records I've made. Hold on, please.

(After a few seconds...) Hello, Mrs. Hu? Thank you for waiting.

Mrs. Hu: Yes. You're welcome.

Julia: Your checkup is arranged for Friday, July 15. You should be in the hospital before 9:00 a.m. Is this time convenient for you?

Mrs. Hu: No problem.

Julia: May I have your number, please?

Mrs. Hu: Sure. *0-9-7-2-3-4-9-1-7-6

Julia: Thanks. By the way, I'd like to remind you that, from 12:00 a.m. of that date on, do not eat or drink anything.

Mrs. Hu: I know that. Thanks for your reminder.

Julia: And if you want to change the appointment, please give me a call as soon as possible.

Mrs. Hu: Okay. Thank you very much.

Julia: See then. Bye.

Mrs. Hu: Goodbye.

22. Why did Mrs. Hu make this phone call?
    (A) She wanted to talk to Julia.
    (B) She wanted to pay a visit to Dr. Chou.
    (C) She'd like to know what's going on with her health.
    (D) She wanted to cancel her appointment.

23. What does Julia probably do?
    (A) She is a housewife.
    (B) She is a nurse.
    (C) She is a hotel employee.
    (D) She is a restaurant waitress.

24. What is Mrs. Hu advised to do?
    (A) Pay the bill as soon as possible.
    (B) Cancel her appointment if it is needed.
    (C) Call Dr. Chou if she wants to make any changes.
    (D) Remember the rule of keeping from taking food.

Questions 25-27

Nowadays smartphones has become something necessary in our daily life. We use it to watch TV and movies, pay the bill, know about the latest news and information, and we won't get lost any longer thanks to the Google Maps. So it is difficult for young people now to imagine such a story as follows.

Mr. Jones was an honest countryman and usually worked on the farm. He did not like to use too many 3C products. He did not have a smartphone. He thought it is too complex. He had an old mobile phone, though. Anyway, he was satisfied with his own simple life. One day, he wanted to go to a department store in a city. Then he found the address on the newspaper, got into his car and drove to the city. He drove for a long time, but he got lost so he stopped and asked somebody to help him.

"Go straight along this road for one kilometer," a lady told him. "Then turn right when you see a post office on the corner. And you need to take the second road on the left." After half an hour, Mr. Jones arrived at the department store finally, but it was closed.

◢ complex 複雜的

25. What title should be given to short article?
    (A) How Smartphone Can Help You
    (B) 3C Products Found Bad to Your Health
    (C) Not Everybody Uses a Smartphone
    (D) Google Maps Help You A Lot

26. Why did Mr. Jones ask somebody to help him?
    (A) Because he didn't know the address.
    (B) He got hurt in an accident.
    (C) His car broke down on the road.
    (D) He got lost.

27. What should Mr. Jones do when he saw a post?
    (A) Take a right turn.
    (B) Turned left.
    (C) Stopped his car.
    (D) Keep going straight.

From:	janet_chen@tpa.edu.gov
To:	grace_liu@goodmail.com
Subject:	Re: How's it going?

TEST 02

Dear Grace,

I'm so sorry that I reply to your last letter this late. These days I've been busy preparing for the entrance exam and have been always coming home late from the library. I stay there to study until 9:30 every evening. The entrance exam will be held on July 2, and there is only about one month left. I will know how much I have learned and studied during the past year after that.

In fact, I have been under much pressure. My parents hope I can enter the No.1 school and they expect me to be a doctor. They said they are confident I will make it. That may be encouraging to me, but I doubt what I take the exam for. The college degree doesn't mean anything to me, even though most of my classmates decided to get it anyway.

Well, I will get back to you as soon as the exam is over. By then we can have a good chat about anything. I know a great coffee shop near my apartment. We can also enjoy the great sea view there.

Cheers,
Janet

28. What is the purpose of Janet's email?
    (A) To decide on a get-together date
    (B) To cancel an important date
    (C) To tell about current situation
    (D) To plan an overseas trip

29. Who could Janet mostly be?
    (A) A teacher
    (B) A student
    (C) A librarian
    (D) An office worker

30. Which of the following is **NOT** true about Janet?
    (A) She's worried about an upcoming exam.
    (B) Her parents hope she can enter the best school.
    (C) She just wants to make money now.
    (D) A college degree means a lot to her.

一結束一

TEST 03

GEPT
全民英檢
初級初試

題目本

本測驗分四個部分，全部都是單選題，共 30 題，作答時間約 20 分鐘。作答說明為中文，印在試題冊上並經由光碟放音機播出。

第一部分 看圖辨義

共 5 題。每題請聽光碟放音機播出題目和三個英文句子之後，選出與所看到的圖畫最相符的答案。每題只播出一遍。

例：（看）

（聽）

Look at the picture. What does the man do?

(A) He is a doctor.

(B) He is a teacher.

(C) He is a cook.

正確答案為 (A)。

聽力測驗第一部分試題從這裡開始。

A. Question 1

⚠ DANGER

ELECTRIC SHOCK
Turn power off when doing repairs

B. Question 2 and 3

C. Question 4 and 5

第二部分 問答

共 10 題。每題請聽光碟放音機播出的英文句子，再從試題冊上三個回答中，選出一個最適合的答案。每題只播出一遍。

例：（聽）May I use your bathroom?
　　（看）(A) Sure. This way, please.
　　　　 (B) You're welcome.
　　　　 (C) I'd like two hamburgers.

正確答案為 (A)。

6.　(A) I think I did a great job.
　　(B) I did many things.
　　(C) I don't agree with you.

7.　(A) There are still other movies.
　　(B) It sure looks bad.
　　(C) But I don't like it.

8.　(A) Maybe in the future.
　　(B) Of course. This way, please.
　　(C) You're welcome.

9.　(A) It's twelve o'clock.
　　(B) Thanks. I will.
　　(C) I'm fine. Thank you.

10.　(A) It is my luggage.
　　(B) That's very kind of you.
　　(C) Never mind.

11.　(A) I like to drink hot tea.
　　(B) Milk and sugar, please.
　　(C) Well-done.

12.　(A) Yes, that's right.
　　(B) No, that's nothing to do with me.
　　(C) That's all right.

13.　(A) Thanks.
　　(B) May I help you?
　　(C) How much is it?

14.　(A) Nice to meet you, David.
　　(B) Let's go, David.
　　(C) How are you today?

15.　(A) Jack is a doctor.
　　(B) Yes, I had a good time.
　　(C) No, I haven't.

第三部分 簡短對話

共 10 題。每題請聽光碟放音機播出的一段對話和一個相關的問題後,再從試題冊上三個選項中,選出一個最適合的答案。每段對話和問題播出一遍。

例:(聽)(男)What a nice-looking skirt. Is it expensive?

(女)No, I got it at the night market last night. I bought three at once.

(男)Well, but it really looks nice and expensive.

(女)You wanna get one for your girlfriend?

(男)Good idea. Where's the night market?

Question: What are the speakers mainly discussing?

(看)(A) Where the woman bought the skirt

(B) What the woman bought last night

(C) How much the skirt cost

正確答案為 (B)。

現在開始聽力測驗第三部分。

16. (A) The woman's new style.
    (B) A skirt is on hot sale.
    (C) The weather becomes cool.

17. (A) Once a week.
    (B) Every day.
    (C) Every other day.

18. (A) They are studying in a
        classroom.
    (B) They are talking on the phone.
    (C) They are eating dinner in a
        restaurant.

19. (A) She is going to buy some new
        clothes.
    (B) She is going to have dinner
        with two friends.
    (C) She is going to book a hotel
        room.

20. (A) It's raining.
    (B) It's a cloudy day.
    (C) It's windy.

21. (A) Preparing for a birthday party.
    (B) Studying for an entrance
        exam.
    (C) Cooking for dinner.

22. (A) Their bus just left five minutes
        ago.
    (B) They have missed an
        important meeting.
    (C) They didn't have money to
        take a taxi.

23. (A) She dislikes young kids.
    (B) She doesn't feel any pain.
    (C) She feels tired.

24. (A) A concert.
    (B) A famous book.
    (C) A film.

25. (A) 2:30 p.m.
    (B) 2:45 p.m.
    (C) 3:00 p.m.

第四部分 短文聽解

共 5 題，每題有 3 個圖片選項。請聽光碟放音機播出的題目，並選出一個最適當的圖片。每題只播出一遍。

例：（看）

(A)　　　　　　　　(B)　　　　　　　　(C)

（聽）

Listen to the following message. What will Steve probably buy after work?

Hi, Mom. This is Steve. I just made a call to you, but you didn't answer your phone. I will have a meeting with Mr. Roberts at the office tonight. I won't go home until 8 o'clock, so I can't have dinner with you tonight. I will buy some fast food on my way home. Don't worry about me.

正確答案為 (C)。

Question 26

(A)　　　　　　　　(B)　　　　　　　　(C)

Question 27

(A)

(B)

(C)

  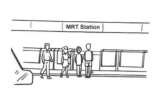

Question 28

(A)

(B)

(C)

Question 29

(A)

(B)

(C)

 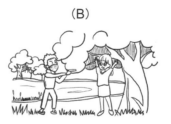 

Question 30

(A)

(B)

(C)

 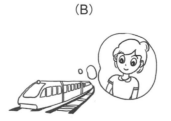 

未經指示前請勿翻頁

本測驗分三個部分，全部都是單選題，共 30 題，作答時間 35 分鐘。

第一部分 詞彙

共 10 題，每個題目裡有一個空格。請由四個選項中選出一個最適合題意的字或詞作答。

1. We are going to have a picnic _____ Saturday.
   (A) on the
   (B) last
   (C) next
   (D) on next

2. Look at the _____! It's the last day of this month.
   (A) clock
   (B) channel
   (C) calendar
   (D) computer

3. My father did not go home early _____ he worked late.
   (A) so
   (B) because
   (C) before
   (D) after

4. I want _____ of you to listen carefully. This is quite important.
   (A) all
   (B) every
   (C) much
   (D) none

5. Is the world safer _____ it was a year ago?
   (A) after
   (B) than
   (C) and
   (D) then

6. If you want your English to be better, just _____ practicing.
   (A) keep
   (B) to keep
   (C) keeping
   (D) keeps

7. My mom cooks dinner sometimes, but _____ my dad does it.
   (A) ever
   (B) never
   (C) usually
   (D) seldom

8. I saw her parents at the school fair, but I didn't see _____.
   (A) them
   (B) his
   (C) that
   (D) it

9. Andrew grew up in Taiwan, but he _____ born in Japan.
   (A) is
   (B) was
   (C) has been
   (D) will be

10. The fried chicken is so _____ that so many people are willing to stand in line for it.
    (A) amazed
    (B) foreign
    (C) expensive
    (D) delicious

第二部分 段落填空

共 8 題，包括二個段落，每個段落各含有四個空格。每格均有四個選項，請依照文意選出最適合的答案。

Questions 11-14

Susan was an office worker a few years ago. Although she was always busy, she kept the habit of learning some languages. After Susan got off ___(11)___ at six o'clock, she went to an evening class to study English three days a week. It was such a wonderful course that she enjoyed learning English more and more. Besides, she had wished her GEPT grades could improve a lot ___(12)___.

However, sometimes she forgot to do her homework and she did not remember to bring her textbooks needed for the class. She wanted to avoid making such mistakes, which ___(13)___ her much trouble. As a result, she always tried to remind herself ___(14)___ putting the textbooks in her bag before she went to bed every night. Besides, she would do her homework right after arriving home.

11. (A) class   (B) school   (C) office   (D) work

12. (A) because she could speak better English
    (B) so that she might get a pay raise
    (C) and she could make a lot of good friends
    (D) but she still couldn't like English

13. (A) cause   (B) will cause   (C) are causing   (D) had caused

14. (A) to   (B) for   (C) of   (D) with

Questions 15-18

    (15)   You will be considered out-of-fashion if you do not know how to buy things online. Just by a click of the mouse, you can buy whatever you're interested in   (16)   going outdoors. You can avoid getting tired and being trapped in the crowds or busy traffic. You can save a lot of time. Besides, you can choose from more varieties of goods whose prices are generally lower.

    Every coin has its two sides. Shopping online could cause some troubles or unhappy experiences, because you could buy things   (17)   from the pictures you see on the Internet.   (18) , it may cause people to buy goods that are not badly needed. That's a waste of money.

15. (A) Sometimes you need to be careful when shopping online.
    (B) Nowadays many people are used to shopping online.
    (C) Online shopping has its strong and weak points.
    (D) Some aged people may not know about online shopping.

16. (A) before
    (B) after
    (C) when
    (D) without

17. (A) different
    (B) difference
    (C) differently
    (D) differ

18. (A) First of all
    (B) Furthermore
    (C) In short
    (D) As a result

第三部分 閱讀理解

共 12 題，包括 4 個題組，每個題組含 1 至 2 篇短文，與數個相關的四選一的選擇題。請由試題冊上的選項中選出最適合的答案。

Questions 19-21

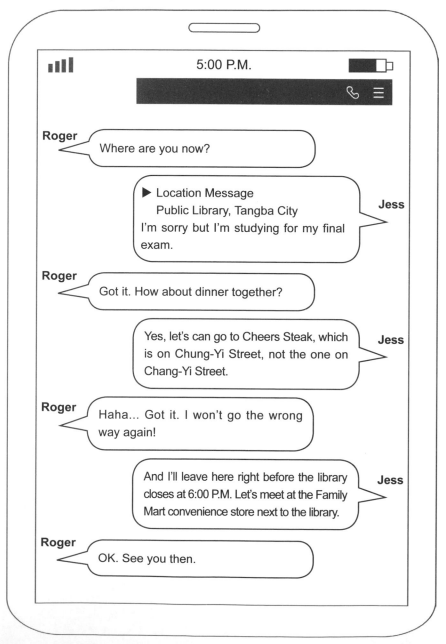

Roger went to the library's web site to make sure of its address.

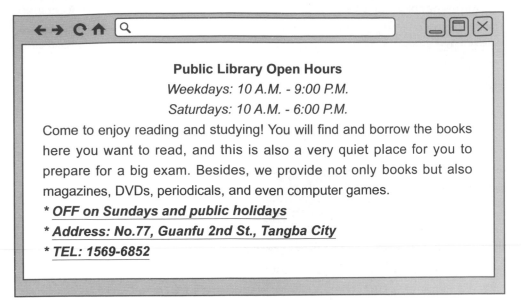

Public Library Open Hours
Weekdays: 10 A.M. - 9:00 P.M.
Saturdays: 10 A.M. - 6:00 P.M.
Come to enjoy reading and studying! You will find and borrow the books here you want to read, and this is also a very quiet place for you to prepare for a big exam. Besides, we provide not only books but also magazines, DVDs, periodicals, and even computer games.
* *OFF on Sundays and public holidays*
* *Address: No.77, Guanfu 2nd St., Tangba City*
* *TEL: 1569-6852*

19. On what day did the LINE message take place?
    (A) On Monday
    (B) On Friday
    (C) On Saturday
    (D) On Sunday

20. What is true about the time people can use the library?
    (A) People can go to the library 24/7.
    (B) The library is open until 6 P.M. on Sundays.
    (C) The library is open from 10:00 A.M. on Mondays.
    (D) The library is closed after 9:00 P.M on Saturdays.

21. According to the message, where is the Family Mart?
    (A) On Chung-Yi Street.
    (B) On Chang-Yi Street.
    (C) On No.77, Guanfu 2nd Street.
    (D) On No.75, Guanfu 2nd Street.

Questions 22-24

Many people, especially at the age of over 40, have difficulty falling asleep. There can be quite different reasons for each person to experience this trouble. But for me, that is because there was someone in my family who snores while he is sleeping. Sometimes this problem can be quite serious, because no one can sleep well except the one who is snoring.

So what can we do to avoid snoring when we slept? One way is to <u>resist</u> eating a big meal before going to bed. Changing the position when sleeping also helps. For people like me who can't fall asleep with noise, wearing earplugs is another way. But if it doesn't work, you need to wake up the one who is snoring. Tell him/her it is time for them to watch you sleep.

22. Why couldn't the speaker fall asleep?
    (A) Because he hears someone breathe noisily.
    (B) Because he usually keeps snoring while falling asleep.
    (C) Because he ate too much before going to bed.
    (D) Because he doesn't know how to wear earplugs.

23. The word "resist" in the first line of the second paragraph is close to _____ in meaning.
    (A) take easy
    (B) keep away from
    (C) think nothing of
    (D) be good at

24. Which of the following is NOT true?
    (A) People can wear earplugs to avoid noise.
    (B) People can change their position to stop snoring.
    (C) If you hear someone snoring, you will have a bad dream.
    (D) If you eat too much before sleeping, you may breathe noisily when you sleep.

Questions 25-27

David was brought up in Italy and he had studied English there since he was an elementary school student. However, he did not study hard in English classes. He often forgot to do his homework and got bad grades in this subject. As time passed by, he was being afraid of speaking English.

At the age of 25, he left for the United States to work for an international company. On his first day of work, he took a bus to his company and he needed to know which stop was his destination. The lady sitting next to him was a beautiful American, who had long blonde hair and wore a fashionable hat. When he spoke to her in his broken English, she answered him in Italian instead. She had studied Italian for 2 years when she was a university student. And they fell in love at first sight. They got married one year later.

Now David can speak English much better – and more confidently, almost better than his five-year-old son.

25. What should be a good title for this story?
    (A) Love at First Sight: David and His Wife
    (B) Importance of the English Language
    (C) How David Met His Wife
    (D) How David's English Improved

26. When did David start to learn English?
    (A) At the age of 25.
    (B) When he met his wife.
    (C) When he went to primary school.
    (D) After he went to the U.S. for work

27. Which of the following is True?
    (A) David's son can't speak better English than his father.
    (B) David got married at the age of 26.
    (C) David's wife spoke better Italian than English.
    (D) David is an Italian and his wife is an American.

Questions 28-30

From:	Jason Fried Chicken@surmail.com
To:	Undisclosed-Recipient
Subject:	Celebration and Special Offer

Dear customers,

   To celebrate our first successful year in business, we are going to offer you some special deals on September 1.

   To give our regular customers a big surprise, if you take one numbered fried chiecken meal, you can get a free vegetable sandwich and a corn soup. Besides, if you buy three fried drumsticks or three chicken wings, you can get another one free. Please note that the free fried drumstick or fried wing has to be of the same price of the one bought or lower. Simply show us your membership card to enjoy these offers.

   First-time customers will receive 10% discount on all fried chicken meals during this whole day.

PS. Place an order of at least NT$250, and you'll get a 12% discount and
    free delivery when you order through UberEats or Foodpanda application
    at any time.

                                                  Jason Fried Chicken Shop

28. What is the purpose of this email?
    (A) To invite customers to join an activity
    (B) To increase the number of members
    (C) To advertise online ordering and delivery services
    (D) To encourage customers to buy something

29. Who possibly wrote this email?
    (A) A restaurant employee   (C) A club member
    (B) A regular customer   (D) A delivery man

30. What is true about the special offer?
    (A) Customers can enjoy free delivery only on September 1.
    (B) First-time customers cannot enjoy the "buy-three-get-one" offer.
    (C) Customers can only buy fried chicken meals at the shop.
    (D) First-time customers can enjoy a 20% discount on all fried chicken meals.

一結束一

TEST 04

GEPT
全民英檢
初級初試

題目本

本測驗分四個部分，全部都是單選題，共 30 題，作答時間約 20 分鐘。作答說明為中文，印在試題冊上並經由光碟放音機播出。

第一部分 看圖辨義

共 5 題。每題請聽光碟放音機播出題目和三個英文句子之後，選出與所看到的圖畫最相符的答案。每題只播出一遍。

例：（看）　　　　　　　　　　（聽）

Look at the picture. What does the man do?

(A) He is a doctor.

(B) He is a teacher.

(C) He is a cook.

正確答案為 (A)。

聽力測驗第一部分試題從這裡開始。

A. Question 1

B. Question 2 and 3

C. Question 4 and 5

第二部分 問答

共 10 題。每題請聽光碟放音機播出的英文句子，再從試題冊上三個回答中，選出一個最適合的答案。每題只播出一遍。

例：（聽）May I use your bathroom?

（看）(A) Sure. This way, please.

(B) You're welcome.

(C) I'd like two hamburgers.

正確答案為 (A)。

6. (A) I got it.
   (B) Don't drink and drive.
   (C) It sure tastes good.

7. (A) There are two cats running and playing.
   (B) Her cats are beautiful and smart.
   (C) She doesn't have any.

8. (A) Same here.
   (B) Hi, I'm Sean. Nice to meet you.
   (C) Oh, I'm so sorry.

9. (A) Thanks.
   (B) That's too bad.
   (C) How much is it?

10. (A) Yes, this way please.
    (B) Brian Chang is my father.
    (C) Brian Chang.

11. (A) Yes, he was here a moment ago.
    (B) No, I wasn't very busy.
    (C) No, thanks.

12. (A) It's been ten years.
    (B) Usually about 45 minutes.
    (C) It won't be long.

13. (A) Here you go.
    (B) Thanks a lot.
    (C) Good idea.

14. (A) He is a writer.
    (B) He lives in New York.
    (C) Not very well.

15. (A) Not at all.
    (B) Why not?
    (C) Good luck.

第三部分 簡短對話

共 10 題。每題請聽光碟放音機播出的一段對話和一個相關的問題後，再從試題冊上三個選項中，選出一個最適合的答案。每段對話和問題播出一遍。

例：（聽）（男）What a nice-looking skirt. Is it expensive?

（女）No, I got it at the night market last night. I bought three at once.

（男）Well, but it really looks nice and expensive.

（女）You wanna get one for your girlfriend?

（男）Good idea. Where's the night market?

Question: What are the speakers mainly discussing?

（看）(A) Where the woman bought the skirt

(B) What the woman bought last night

(C) How much the skirt cost

正確答案為 (B)。

現在開始聽力測驗第三部分。

16. (A) He hurt his foot.
    (B) He hurt his hand.
    (C) He couldn't find the vegetables to cook dinner.

17. (A) In a movie theater
    (B) On an airplane
    (C) On a bus

18. (A) A new shoe shop
    (B) How the woman got a good deal
    (C) The woman's new shoes

19. (A) Buy some furniture
    (B) Surf the Internet
    (C) Sell a closet

20. (A) Have some tea
    (B) Speak to Mr. Wang
    (C) Have a meeting with Mr. Hsu

21. (A) He is a waiter.
    (B) He is a taxi driver.
    (C) He is a policeman.

22. (A) Eating something
    (B) Making a hamburger
    (C) Ordering a meal

23. (A) A doctor
    (B) A nurse
    (C) A waitress

24. (A) Cold
    (B) Warm
    (C) Hot

25. (A) Before 6:30 p.m.
    (B) Between 6:30 and 7:00 p.m.
    (C) After 7:00 p.m.

第四部分：短文聽解

共 5 題，每題有 3 個圖片選項。請聽光碟放音機播出的題目，並選出一個最適當的圖片。每題只播出一遍。

例：（看）

(A)   (B)   (C)

（聽）

Listen to the following message. What will Steve probably buy after work?

    Hi, Mom. This is Steve. I just made a call to you, but you didn't answer your phone. I will have a meeting with Mr. Roberts at the office tonight. I won't go home until 8 o'clock, so I can't have dinner with you tonight. I will buy some fast food on my way home. Don't worry about me.

正確答案為 (C)。

Question 26

(A)   (B)   (C)

 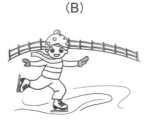 

Question 27

(A)

(B)

(C)

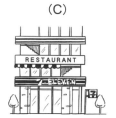

Question 28

(A)

(B)

(C)

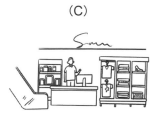

Question 29

(A)

(B)

(C)

Question 30

(A)

(B)

(C)

未經指示前請勿翻頁

本測驗分三個部分，全部都是單選題，共 30 題，作答時間 35 分鐘。

第一部分 詞彙

共 10 題，每個題目裡有一個空格。請由四個選項中選出一個最適合題意的字或詞作答。

1. I can't read the _____ . I need to find someone to ask for directions.
   - (A) picture
   - (B) list
   - (C) map
   - (D) newspaper

2. Although Rebecca has a wide _____ , she is unable to spell many words.
   - (A) knowledge
   - (B) activity
   - (C) vocabulary
   - (D) information

3. John did not _____ a college in the country after graduating from senior high school.
   - (A) meet
   - (B) prepare
   - (C) imagine
   - (D) enter

4. George's favorite _____ is collecting coins and stamps.
   - (A) habit
   - (B) hobby
   - (C) housework
   - (D) health

5. It was raining so hard that we couldn't go _____.
   (A) anything
   (B) anyway
   (C) anyone
   (D) anywhere

6. My aunt is busy _____ in the kitchen.
   (A) cook
   (B) to cook
   (C) cooking
   (D) for cooking

7. Tom speaks good English, _____ John doesn't.
   (A) and
   (B) when
   (C) while
   (D) before

8. David looked so excited because he _____ get a ticket to the concert.
   (A) has
   (B) should
   (C) could
   (D) won't

9. John studied hard. He thought getting good grades _____ very important.
   (A) was
   (B) were
   (C) will be
   (D) is

10. It is sure _____. Remember to bring an umbrella.
    (A) of raining
    (B) to rain
    (C) raining
    (D) rains

第二部分：段落填空

共 8 題，包括二個段落，每個段落各含有四個空格。每格均有四個選項，請依照文意選出最適合的答案。

Questions 11-14

　　Once upon a time when people gathered and lived together in a common society, they ___(11)___ different rules and laws. Some jobs they had done were aimed at keeping the people in the same society safe, ___(12)___, and orderly. In addition, people had to have some basic things, such as food, clothes, and houses. ___(13)___ They needed streets, sidewalks, streetlights, hospitals, shops, markets, and even garbage areas. So they elected their government to provide ___(14)___ with what they would need in the future. We can say that the government is a group of people whom these people chose to run their society.

▲ sidewalk 人行道

11. (A) made　　　(B) broke　　　(C) decided　　　(D) took

12. (A) health　　(B) healthier　　(C) healthy　　(D) healthily

13. (A) They had other needs, too.
　　(B) Those are what they needed most.
　　(C) They have spent much time making those basic things.
　　(D) At that time, life was difficult.

14. (A) they　　　(B) them　　　(C) themselves　　(D) theirs

Questions 15-18

When the sun rises and ___(15)___ in the early morning, it produces a bright light and we usually feel the warmth. weather. ___(16)___ Later, it will come together to form clouds. Some clouds form as the air warms up near the Earth's surface and ___(17)___ . When the warmed air rises, its pressure and temperature would drop, causing very small water drops to stay in the air.

Several types of clouds form in this way. And then the water in the clouds falls down again, like rain or snow, to the ground and the sea. All this water will turn into springs, rivers and lakes, and at last runs ___(18)___ into the sea.

15. (A) falls
    (B) shines
    (C) heats
    (D) passes

16. (A) Some hot air would stay above
        the sea level.
    (B) The clouds can take many
        different kinds of shape.
    (C) Usually we know the hot
        summer is around the corner.
    (D) Then part of the sea water
        travels into the air in very small
        drops.

17. (A) rising
    (B) rise
    (C) rises
    (D) rose

18. (A) out
    (B) up
    (C) back
    (D) over

第三部分：閱讀理解

共 12 題，包括 4 個題組，每個題組含 1 至 2 篇短文，與數個相關的四選一的選擇題。請由試題冊上的選項中選出最適合的答案。

Questions 19-21

Helen clicked on the photo Mary sent and see this.

PLEASE COME & CELEBRATE WITH US
the freshness of **new life** and **new love** as we,

HELEN PARKEN

AND

STEPHEN GATES

are getting married!
Our wedding reception will be held
on Sunday, July 25, 2021
TWELVE O'CLOCK AT NOON
Grand Hotel (Taipei)
1, Chungshan N. Rd., Sec.4

19. Why did Helen send messages to Mary?
    (A) To ask her for a favor
    (B) To make an apology for a past mistake
    (C) To invite her to join an event
    (D) To treat her to a big meal

20. Which of the following is true about Helen?
    (A) She is married.
    (B) She congratulates on Mary's upcoming wedding.
    (C) July 25 is her birthday.
    (D) Parken is her family name.

21. What did Helen mean by writing "One never goes to the temple for nothing."?
    (A) She won't be available on July 25, 2021.
    (B) She might be complaining about something.
    (C) She's happy about their friendship.
    (D) They used to go to a temple together to pray for love.

Questions 22-24

From:	library_service@surmail.com
To:	Undisclosed-Recipient
Subject:	Please note

Dear library users,

The library will be CLOSED during the upcoming 4-day Mid-Autumn Festival holidays, and will re-open on Sept.24. For return of books during the period, please use the Return box at the front door of Holiday Room. If the book(s) you borrowed will be overdue during this period, you can return it/ them later on Sept.24 at the latest without any fines caused.

For the late return of books, magazines or periodicals, we have set new rules. You will be fined NT$10 for each overdue day being until all publications are returned. Besides, your borrowing right will be cancelled for the time being 3 days after you fail to return your borrowed items and pay the fines. So please make sure you keep your borrowed item(s) to be returned before its/their due date. We will also send you a notice 3 days before a borrowed item is overdue.

Happy holidays from all the staff of Central Library.

Central Library Service Center

22. What is the main purpose of this notice?
  (A) To tell library users about a special activity
  (B) To let library users know a new rule
  (C) To ask library users to follow up overdue items
  (D) To inform library staff of the upcoming days off

23. What is NOT true about the Central Library?
  (A) It is closed now.
  (B) It will be open after Sept. 24.
  (C) Library staff do not work during this period.
  (D) You can return your borrowed items during this period.

24. What does "an overdue book" mean?
  (A) It means a book you should return.
  (B) It means a book you can borrow from the library.
  (C) It means a book that's been out of print.
  (D) It means a book that can't be borrowed.

Questions 25-27

　　　Lisa went on a tour group in Europe last summer. One day, after they checked in at a hotel, the tour guide allowed them to take a free break so that they can go anywhere nearby, but she asked them to be back to the hotel before dinner time.

　　　Dinner was served from six to eight. Lisa went out alone for a walk. She saw an old-style building and felt very excited. She wanted to go inside to look around, but some locals told her it wasn't open to the public that day. So she could just take some photos of herself in front of the building.

　　　When she looked at the time shown on her smart phone, she said to herself, "Oops! It's fifteen to six thirty. Time to have dinner! I'd better go back right now."

25. When should Lisa come back to the hotel?
　　(A) Before six
　　(B) Before eight
　　(C) After six fifteen
　　(D) Before bedtime

26. What did Lisa NOT do during their free time?
　　(A) She took a walk around.
　　(B) She talked with some locals.
　　(C) She took some selfies with her smart phone.
　　(D) She went inside an old building and took some photos.

27. Which of the following is true?
　　(A) Lisa went out for a walk in the afternoon that day.
　　(B) The old-style building closed before six that day.
　　(C) She asked some locals to take photos of herself.
　　(D) Lisa went back to the hotel before dinner time.

Questions 28-30

When you are prepared to travel far, what kind of places do you usually choose to stay at? Have you ever stayed in an expensive hotel but you don't think it's worth the money you paid? Or have you stayed in a cheap hostel where you share a room with other strangers? If both experiences are terrible to you, here is one recommended choice: holiday apartments.

Compared with general hotels or hostels, holiday apartments can give you more space. You can use everything in such an apartment, including the living room, kitchen, study, and of course, the bathroom. Some apartments even have lovely gardens, gyms, swimming pools, KTVs, table tennis rooms, etc. You'll feel at home in the holiday apartment.

The best thing is, stay in holiday apartments is generally affordable. It is priced in the unit of the entire apartment, not per person. Therefore, it is basically suitable for a family or friends traveling in a group of 3 to 5 persons. Of course, there are also holiday apartments designed for couples or lovers, and they are cheaper than ordinary hotels. If you travel with friends or your family, a holiday apartment will be your best choice!

28. What can we learn about from the reading?
    (A) Where to find a nice holiday apartment
    (B) How to choose a nice holiday apartment
    (C) Why we should choose a holiday apartment
    (D) How to change a house into a holiday apartment

29. Which of the following is true about holiday apartments?
    (A) They are mainly designed for people who travel in two or more.
    (B) You need to pay extra fees for gyms or swimming pools.
    (C) People can make new friends when living in holiday apartments.
    (D) They are mostly found in the countryside.

30. What does it mean to say that stay in holiday apartments is "affordable"?
    (A) You can have more personal space.
    (B) You can find them everywhere.
    (C) You don't have to spend much on them.
    (D) You can use everything in them.

—結束—

TEST 04

83

TEST 05

GEPT
全民英檢
初級初試

題目本

本測驗分四個部分，全部都是單選題，共 30 題，作答時間約 20 分鐘。作答說明為中文，印在試題冊上並經由光碟放音機播出。

第一部分 看圖辨義

共 5 題。每題請聽光碟放音機播出題目和三個英文句子之後，選出與所看到的圖畫最相符的答案。每題只播出一遍。

例：（看）

（聽）

Look at the picture. What does the man do?

(A) He is a doctor.

(B) He is a teacher.

(C) He is a cook.

正確答案為 (A)。

聽力測驗第一部分試題從這裡開始。

A. Question 1

B. Question 2 and 3

C. Question 4

C. Question 5

第二部分 問答

共 10 題。每題請聽光碟放音機播出的英文句子，再從試題冊上三個回答中，選出一個最適合的答案。每題只播出一遍。

例：（聽）May I use your bathroom?
　　（看）(A) Sure. This way, please.
　　　　　(B) You're welcome.
　　　　　(C) I'd like two hamburgers.

正確答案為 (A)。

6. (A) You look so cool.
　　(B) Just enjoy yourselves.
　　(C) Very funny.

7. (A) I wear it only once a week.
　　(B) Thanks. It's a present from my
　　　　boyfriend.
　　(C) I got a headache yesterday.

8. (A) Nothing. I just stayed home.
　　(B) How about you?
　　(C) I need to make an important
　　　　call.

9. (A) She's going to turn up.
　　(B) You're welcome.
　　(C) Not at all.

10. (A) You can try it on in the
　　　　dressing room.
　　(B) Turn around, and let me take a
　　　　look.
　　(C) Go straight ahead, and you'll
　　　　find it.

11. (A) Yes, I like it.
　　(B) Yes, if you like.
　　(C) This is Henry speaking.

12. (A) What's wrong with you?
　　(B) I must be catching a cold.
　　(C) How much does it cost?

13. (A) He's coming here soon.
　　(B) I don't care.
　　(C) I have no idea.

14. (A) I haven't seen you for a long
　　　　time.
　　(B) Not anymore.
　　(C) Neither am I.

15. (A) I cut my finger.
　　(B) I caught a cold.
　　(C) That's a good idea.

第三部分 簡短對話

共 10 題。每題請聽光碟放音機播出的一段對話和一個相關的問題後，再從試題冊上三個選項中，選出一個最適合的答案。每段對話和問題播出一遍。

例：（聽）（男）What a nice-looking skirt. Is it expensive?

（女）No, I got it at the night market last night. I bought three at once.

（男）Well, but it really looks nice and expensive.

（女）You wanna get one for your girlfriend?

（男）Good idea. Where's the night market?

Question: What are the speakers mainly discussing?

（看）(A) Where the woman bought the skirt

(B) What the woman bought last night

(C) How much the skirt cost

正確答案為 (B)。

現在開始聽力測驗第三部分。

16. (A) A kind of fruit
    (B) Several strawberry ice cream
    (C) A phone

17. (A) In a classroom
    (B) At a bus stop
    (C) In a park

18. (A) Buy some drinks
    (B) Walk to Taipei 101
    (C) Take a bus

19. (A) A taxi driver and a passenger
    (B) A clerk and a customer
    (C) A manager and her employee

20. (A) She is ill.
    (B) She needs to study.
    (C) A friend will visit her later.

21. (A) She thinks it's so-so.
    (B) She couldn't believe it's so bad.
    (C) It's well done.

22. (A) Give the woman a ride
    (B) Have a late night meal with the woman
    (C) Ask the woman to drive him home

23. (A) Sunny
    (B) Cloudy
    (C) Rainy

24. (A) Worried
    (B) Confident
    (C) Excited

25. (A) A friend of the woman
    (B) Someone the woman doesn't know
    (C) A person who is sitting next to the man

第四部分：短文聽解

共 5 題，每題有 3 個圖片選項。請聽光碟放音機播出的題目，並選出一個最適當的圖片。每題只播出一遍。

例：（看）

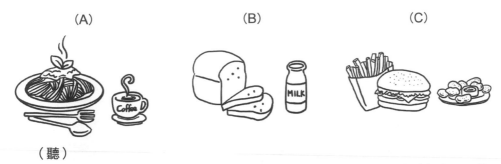

（聽）

Listen to the following message. What will Steve probably buy after work?

    Hi, Mom. This is Steve. I just made a call to you, but you didn't answer your phone. I will have a meeting with Mr. Roberts at the office tonight. I won't go home until 8 o'clock, so I can't have dinner with you tonight. I will buy some fast food on my way home. Don't worry about me.

正確答案為 (C)。

Question 26

Question 27

(A)   (B)   (C)

Question 28

(A)   (B)   (C)

Question 29

(A)   (B)   (C)

Question 30

(A)   (B)   (C)

未經指示前請勿翻頁

本測驗分三個部分，全部都是單選題，共 30 題，作答時間 35 分鐘。

第一部分 詞彙

共 10 題，每個題目裡有一個空格。請由四個選項中選出一個最適合題意的字或詞作答。

1. I didn't have a _____ to eat my soup with.
   (A) teapot
   (B) dish
   (C) plate
   (D) spoon

2. I use the electronic _____ if I don't know how to spell a word.
   (A) dictionary
   (B) typewriter
   (C) newspaper
   (D) magazine

3. Each hand has one thumb and four _____.
   (A) feet
   (B) teeth
   (C) fingers
   (D) toes

4. I can't find my keys. Did you see where I put _____?
   (A) they
   (B) theirs
   (C) it
   (D) them

5. Madonna used to be one of the _____ famous singers in the world. Almost everybody knew her.
   (A) every
   (B) more
   (C) much
   (D) most

6. I can't hear you! Please _____.
   (A) help me
   (B) speak up
   (C) go away
   (D) lend me some money

7. The thief raised _____ of his hands after he was caught by the policeman.
   (A) each
   (B) both
   (C) all
   (D) two

8. _____ going, and you'll become better and better.
   (A) Keep
   (B) Kept
   (C) Keeping
   (D) To keep

9. I'm about to get off at the next exit, and _____ be there very soon.
   (A) would
   (B) will
   (C) won't
   (D) are going to

10. I lost my pencil. Can you lend me _____?
    (A) it
    (B) itself
    (C) one
    (D) yours

第二部分：段落填空

共 8 題，包括二個段落，每個段落各含有四個空格。每格均有四個選項，請依照文意選出最適合的答案。

Questions 11-14

　　Everybody knows that doing exercise is good to health, and there are quite a few ways to do that. Sport games, for some people who like to seek ___(11)___ or championship, may be a choice. Some people, however, do not like sports or team games ___(12)___ there must be losers or someone who falls behind or stay in the last place. In my opinion, you can do and enjoy many things in life, and ___(13)___. Sometimes you feel unhappy after you play a sport game. You can just go roller-skating, jogging, swimming, hiking, ___(14)___, or even take a walk with friends along a riverside. Of course, if you are used to staying under pressure, sports might be better to you.

> ◢ compete 競爭，對抗

11. (A) result   (B) friendship
　　(C) victory   (D) pleasure

12. (A) because   (B) so
　　(C) before   (D) after

13. (A) it is not necessary for you to compete with anybody
　　(B) you always need to compete for the first place
　　(C) sports games may be a good choice
　　(D) you need to take more care of your health

14. (A) bike   (B) to bike
　　(C) biking   (D) biked

Questions 15-18

Working as a doctor ___(15)___ my first wish even since I was an elementary school student. Every time when I told my parents about this, they just laughed and said, "Keep up the good work and just try your best." With several years ___(16)___ passed, however, my goal has never changed. Doctors can save people's lives and help patients recover their health. ___(17)___ Whether you are rich or poor, and whether you are a famous or an ordinary person, sometimes you get sick. Now I am studying medicine in a university. I feel ___(18)___ than ever that I have made a very correct decision to do something meaningful for my future career.

15. (A) is
    (B) was
    (C) has been
    (D) will be

16. (A) have
    (B) had
    (C) are
    (D) having

17. 新題型 (A) You need to keep early hours to stay healthy.
    (B) Time and tide wait for no man.
    (C) God helps those who help themselves.
    (D) What else is more important than helping others keep healthy?

18. (A) stronger
    (B) more strongly
    (C) very strong
    (D) strongest

第三部分 閱讀理解

共 12 題，包括 4 個題組，每個題組含 1 至 2 篇短文，與數個相關的四選一的選擇題。請由試題冊上的選項中選出最適合的答案。

Questions 19-21

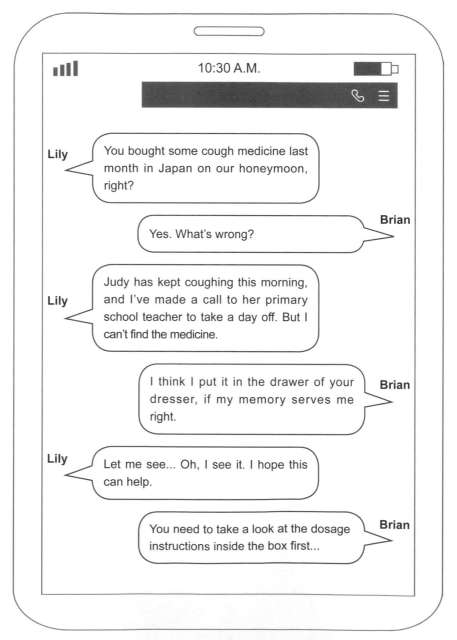

Lily: You bought some cough medicine last month in Japan on our honeymoon, right?

Brian: Yes. What's wrong?

Lily: Judy has kept coughing this morning, and I've made a call to her primary school teacher to take a day off. But I can't find the medicine.

Brian: I think I put it in the drawer of your dresser, if my memory serves me right.

Lily: Let me see... Oh, I see it. I hope this can help.

Brian: You need to take a look at the dosage instructions inside the box first...

Lily opened the medicine box and saw this:

Dosage Instructions

- Adults and children over 12: 2 spoonfuls every 4 hours, and no more than 12 spoonfuls within 24 hours.
- Children 6 to under 12: 1 spoonful every 4 hours, and no more than 6 spoonfuls within 24 hours.
- Children under 6: ask for advice from your doctor.

19. Why did Lily send this message to Brian?
    (A) To tell a secret
    (B) To make a phone call
    (C) To find medicine
    (D) To know how to take medicine

20. What can we learn from the cough medicine?
    (A) It was given as a present.
    (B) It is suitable only for adults.
    (C) Children can't take this medicine without a doctor's advice.
    (D) Lily found it in the bedroom.

21. How many spoonfuls can Judy take at one time?
    (A) One
    (B) Two
    (C) Six
    (D) It depends on the doctor's advice.

From:	Purchasing Manager
To:	All staff
Subject:	Quick Note
Date:	February 10

Hello everyone,

Please remember to follow the office rules and fill in the <u>request</u> form when asking for office supplies you need. It allows us to keep a record of how many we could use on a regular basis. So please make sure you have done this before you take away the items you want. Besides, if the items you need are unavailable, and you wish the company to buy them, you can fill out the Office Supplies purchase form and they must be signed by your supervisor and by me. Please keep this in mind or else you'll be punished next time.

Thanks,
Biob Jesso
Purchasing manager

22. Why did the purchasing manager write this E-mail?
    (A) To remind employees of getting to work on time.
    (B) To remind employees not to make a mistake again.
    (C) To ask for return of office supplies
    (D) To teach employees how to fill in certain forms.

23. What does the manager say about asking for office supplies?
    (A) There are rules to follow.
    (B) Pay attention to certain time.
    (C) It's become easier and easier.
    (D) It's important to ask for signature.

24. What does the word "request" mean in the first sentence of the letter?
    (A) How the form should be filled in.
    (B) How employees keep a record.
    (C) What employees ask for.
    (D) What employees sign with.

TEST 05

Questions 25-27

After we take a shower, we usually dry ourselves with a towel. But when you finish bathing your dog, it just needs to shake its body quickly. According to a study, when dogs get wet, they can naturally shake off more than half of the water on their bodies within less than a second.

The study has found that animals will shake from "head" to "tail," when they get wet. To get water off, smaller animals must shake faster than larger ones. Besides, within one second, rats can shake 18 times, dogs 6 times, and bears 4 times. Larger animals, though shaking fewer times, can also quickly dry their bodies.

For some animals, shaking the body is not just to dry themselves. This move has something to do with whether they can live. If their bodies are too wet, it may be not easy for them to walk, jump or run. In fact, they could be in danger. If they can't move or run fast, they could be shot dead by a hunter, for example. This is why "wet dog shaking" has become a common habit of many animals.

25. What is the article mainly about?
    (A) How fast animals can dry themselves
    (B) Why animals need to dry themselves
    (C) What animal can shake themselves fastest
    (D) Whether smaller or larger animals can live longer

26. What is true about shaking?
    (A) Different animals have different ways of shaking.
    (B) Some animals scare away their enemies by shaking.
    (C) Pet animals can shake better than wild animals.
    (D) Shaking themselves dry help animals run away from their enemies.

27. What is explained in this reading?
    (A) An animal's tail may stop them from running away.
    (B) Some animals shake too many times and hurt their heads.
    (C) Larger animals need fewer shakes than smaller ones.
    (D) Most animals learn shaking from dogs.

Questions 28-30

Adam's favorite hobby is reading. When he was still a high school student, he liked to read under a big tree, while most of his classmates and friends play cellphone video games. He likes the story of *Zeroun Lost His Horse* most, because he is touched by the old man who always keeps calm and hopeful about the future. From the story, Adam knows that every cloud has a silver lining.

Adam's father did not work and was a heavy drinker. Every time when he got drunk, there would be a big fight in his home. Adam's mother, to protect him, sadly made up her mind to leave his father. At that time, life was difficult for this mother and her son because she needed to work and rent a place. Even so, she bought Adam any books he was interested in. She believed that reading would be good for her son.

Adam liked to read some stories about famous people and he was surprised by how they succeeded. In fact, he hoped to be a writer in the future so he can write touching stores that can help poor people change their lives.

28. What is the main idea of this story?
    (A) Drinking will ruin your family at last.
    (B) Reading helps you become a famous person.
    (C) Bad things may happen, but will get better at last.
    (D) Clouds are sometimes beautiful to watch.

29. Adam likes the story of *Zeroun Lost His Horse* because _____.
    (A) it is about a smart horse that saves an old man's life
    (B) it is closer to what happens in real life
    (C) he can imagine beautiful clouds from the story
    (D) it has a wonderful ending

30. What is true about Adam's mother?
    (A) She is a heavy drinker but she took much care of her son.
    (B) She is poor but generous to Adam.
    (C) She lived a happy family life and her husband loved her much.
    (D) She hoped to be a writer in the future.

—結束—

TEST 06

GEPT
全民英檢
初級初試

題目本

本測驗分四個部分，全部都是單選題，共 30 題，作答時間約 20 分鐘。作答說明為中文，印在試題冊上並經由光碟放音機播出。

第一部分 看圖辨義

共 5 題。每題請聽光碟放音機播出題目和三個英文句子之後，選出與所看到的圖畫最相符的答案。每題只播出一遍。

例：（看）

（聽）

Look at the picture. What does the man do?

(A) He is a doctor.

(B) He is a teacher.

(C) He is a cook.

正確答案為 (A)。

聽力測驗第一部分試題從這裡開始。

A. Question 1

B. Question 2 and 3

C. Question 4

C. Question 5

第二部分 問答

共 10 題。每題請聽光碟放音機播出的英文句子，再從試題冊上三個回答中，選出一個最適合的答案。每題只播出一遍。

例：（聽）May I use your bathroom?
　　（看）(A) Sure. This way, please.
　　　　　(B) You're welcome.
　　　　　(C) I'd like two hamburgers.

正確答案為 (A)。

6. (A) No, her voice is too low.
   (B) Not for a long time.
   (C) Yes, I've heard about this girl.

7. (A) It'll take a few months.
   (B) For one year.
   (C) About 10 meters long.

8. (A) I may just stay at home.
   (B) I'm doing the dishes now.
   (C) That's a good idea.

9. (A) I'm so happy.
   (B) It's really nice of you.
   (C) You're welcome.

10. (A) I'm glad you like it.
    (B) No, it'll be getting colder.
    (C) It is yours.

11. (A) No, I don't care.
    (B) OK. Thank you.
    (C) Just help yourself.

12. (A) My name is David.
    (B) I usually walk home after
        school.
    (C) I don't have one.

13. (A) No, I didn't take any seats.
    (B) Yes, you can take it away.
    (C) Yes, my friend will be back
        soon.

14. (A) My name is David.
    (B) My cousin.
    (C) I'll be there soon.

15. (A) Here you are.
    (B) Today is not my day.
    (C) That's a good idea.

第三部分 簡短對話

共 10 題。每題請聽光碟放音機播出的一段對話和一個相關的問題後，再從試題冊上三個選項中，選出一個最適合的答案。每段對話和問題播出一遍。

例：（聽）（男）What a nice-looking skirt. Is it expensive?

（女）No, I got it at the night market last night. I bought three at once.

（男）Well, but it really looks nice and expensive.

（女）You wanna get one for your girlfriend?

（男）Good idea. Where's the night market?

Question: What are the speakers mainly discussing?

（看）(A) Where the woman bought the skirt

(B) What the woman bought last night

(C) How much the skirt cost

正確答案為 (B)。

現在開始聽力測驗第三部分。

16. (A) It's hot.
    (B) It's cool.
    (C) It's warm.

17. (A) He'll be busy with his project.
    (B) He'll go on a trip to relax a bit.
    (C) He hasn't had any plans yet.

18. (A) The man's income.
    (B) A motorbike.
    (C) A highway.

19. (A) In an office.
    (B) At school.
    (C) At a train station.

20. (A) Because she wanted some sweet taste.
    (B) Because she was sick.
    (C) Because she was not thirsty.

21. (A) Asking for directions.
    (B) Taking a written test.
    (C) Learning to drive.

22. (A) On an express train.
    (B) On an airplane.
    (C) On a boat.

23. (A) She feels tired.
    (B) She feels bored.
    (C) She feels excited.

24. (A) At 2:20 p.m.
    (B) At 2:40 p.m.
    (C) At 2:45 p.m.

25. (A) A manager and a secretary.
    (B) A doctor and a nurse.
    (C) A clerk and a customer.

第四部分 短文聽解

共 5 題，每題有 3 個圖片選項。請聽光碟放音機播出的題目，並選出一個最適當的圖片。<u>每題只播出一遍</u>。

例：（看）

(A)   (B)   (C)

（聽）

Listen to the following message. What will Steve probably buy after work?

Hi, Mom. This is Steve. I just made a call to you, but you didn't answer your phone. I will have a meeting with Mr. Roberts at the office tonight. I won't go home until 8 o'clock, so I can't have dinner with you tonight. I will buy some fast food on my way home. Don't worry about me.

正確答案為 (C)。

Question 26

(A)   (B)   (C)

Question 27

(A)

(B)

(C)

Question 28

(A)

(B)

(C)

Question 29

(A)

(B)

(C)

Question 30

(A)

(B)

(C)

未經指示前請勿翻頁

本測驗分三個部分，全部都是單選題，共 30 題，作答時間 35 分鐘。

第一部分 詞彙

共 10 題，每個題目裡有一個空格。請由四個選項中選出一個最適合題意的字或詞作答。

1. Is this the answer _____ the question?
   (A) to
   (B) of
   (C) for
   (D) from

2. Both of the girls are really good. I can't make _____ my mind.
   (A) it
   (B) up
   (C) ready
   (D) for

3. It makes me _____ to sit there without doing anything.
   (A) bore
   (B) boring
   (C) bored
   (D) to bore

4. Mike _____ live with his family when he studied at the university.
   (A) doesn't
   (B) didn't
   (C) hasn't
   (D) hadn't

5. The meeting will begin as soon as the manager _____ in.
    (A) comes
    (B) came
    (C) will come
    (D) is coming

6. We agreed that Mary _____ on the exam.
    (A) cheats
    (B) will cheat
    (C) cheated
    (D) is cheating

7. Please _____ the lamp and _____ your book to do your homework.
    (A) open; close
    (B) turn on; turn off
    (C) open; turn on
    (D) turn on; open

8. I'm very surprised that this young little girl is not afraid of _____.
    (A) something
    (B) everything
    (C) anything
    (D) nothing

9. David _____ lots of English magazines when he was a university student.
    (A) read
    (B) reads
    (C) was reading
    (D) has read

10. Hurry up, or we _____ miss the train.
    (A) do
    (B) will
    (C) would
    (D) are going to

第二部分 段落填空

共 8 題，包括二個段落，每個段落各含有四個空格。每格均有四個選項，請依照文意選出最適合的答案。

Questions 11-14

　　Titan was brought up in the mountains. Every morning, he ___(11)___ to walk down the mountain to a lake where he could collect water. Then he carried two buckets of water on his shoulders and went back up. In this way, he had to go back and forth 4 times a day, before there was enough water needed in a day. In other words, ___(12)___. One day, his cow was injured. So he carried it on his shoulder to a doctor for animals. Everyone in town was ___(13)___ by what they saw. On the return trip, he noticed a piece of paper on a street wall, which read "Superman Match". He said to himself, "Looks interesting." So he led his cow to the match site. He saw several men lifting large rocks, and others pushing forward very ___(14)___ objects. When the winner was announced, he clapped loudly and walked to the site.

▲ announce 宣布，公告

11. (A) needed   (B) hoped   (C) forgot   (D) finished

12. (A) he often fell down and got injured
　　(B) sometimes he would be lazy to do that
　　(C) he had very strong arms and legs
　　(D) he became tired of this kind of life

13. (A) surprised   (B) kicked   (C) knocked   (D) lifted

14. (A) light   (B) cheap   (C) heavy   (D) strange

Questions 15-18

Do you like meat? If yes, you may be interested in the following study results. According to this study, the world's population's need for meat has been ___(15)___. In 1960, a total of 64 million tons of meat were eaten. At that time, each person ate about 21 kilograms of meat each year. By 2007, this number had climbed to 268 million tons, or about 40 kg per person. Besides, ___(16)___. In the 1960s, people's favorite meat was beef. Of the meat being eaten, 40% is beef. In 2007, pork was the most popular. However, because people are more concerned about health issues in recent years, poultry meat has increased from 12% to 32%. By the way, do you know which ___(17)___ is the largest meat eater in the world? The answer is Luxembourg! In 2007, every Luxembourger ate about 137 kg of meat! Second only to Luxembourgers are Americans. Every American eats about 126 kilograms! ___(18)___, let's not talk about the numbers. I will play a song for you. Its title is Currywurst. The singer sang his love for this kind of meat food.

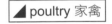 poultry 家禽

TEST 06

15. (A) falling
    (B) growing
    (C) serious
    (D) similar

16. (A) we have changed our way of cooking meat
    (B) new kinds of meat have hit the market
    (C) people's favorite meat also experienced some changes
    (D) doctors have been worried that we eat too much meat

新題型

17. (A) nation
    (B) company
    (C) area
    (D) race

18. (A) Besides
    (B) Therefore
    (C) Next
    (D) For example

第三部分：閱讀理解

共 12 題，包括 4 個題組，每個題組含 1 至 2 篇短文，與數個相關的四選一的選擇題。請由試題冊上的選項中選出最適合的答案。

Questions 19-21

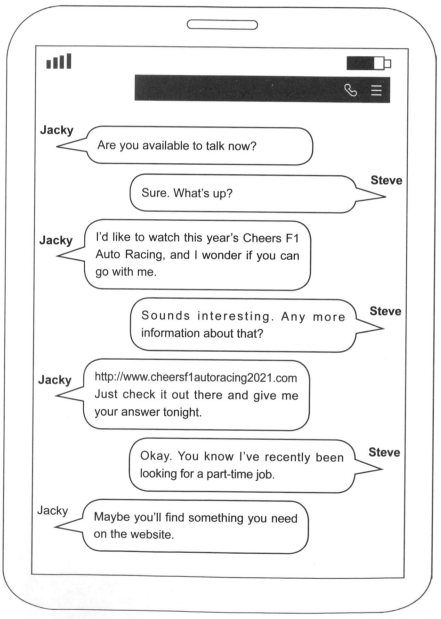

Q http://www.cvheersf1autoracing2021.com

Remember how exciting Cheers F1 Auto Racing is last year in Agogo City? Now it's time to get ready for this year's Cheers F1 Auto Racing in Trivago City. Check it out now!

➢ About Cheers F1 Auto Racing
   ◎ The history ◎ 2021 game programs ◎ 2021 race teams
➢ About Trivago City
   ◎ The history ◎ How to get here   ◎ Where to watch the races
   ◎ Find hotels ◎ Eat in the city   ◎ Shop in the city
➢ More
   ◎ Watch past recorded videos   ◎ Join our work team
   ◎ Buy tickets now   ◎ Email us

19. Why did Jacky send the messages to Steve?
    (A) To tell him about a good news
    (B) To say thanks to him
    (C) To invite him to an activity
    (D) To make a complaint

20. Where would Steve click on the webpage for the information he needed?
    (A) Where to watch the races
    (B) Join our work team
    (C) 2021 race teams
    (D) 2021 game programs

21. What information may Not be interesting to Jacky?
    (A) How much the ticket prices are
    (B) Where to go shopping in Agogo City
    (C) What happened in the past about Trivago City
    (D) The race teams in 2021

From:	Peter Piper
To:	Mandy Minor
Subject:	David's reading
Attachment:	Special Program.pdf

Dear Mrs. Minor,

I am writing to let you know that I am really concerned about your son's ability to read. He has been in this class for three months, and in trouble with the words in all kinds of stories and books.

Most of his classmates can read at Level 7, but he is only able to do Level 2. To assist him in making more progress, I suggest he take a special reading course. Please open the file <u>attached</u> and you'll see the link to a website. This course helps students learn and read the sounds of words in traditional teaching methods. He only has to spend twenty to thirty minutes on this every day.

Please email or call me directly after class if you have any questions about this.

Regards,
Peter Piper
Reading Trainer

22. What is the purpose of Mr. Piper email?
    (A) To tell about the issue of David's speaking ability
    (B) To let the mother know her child's learning
    (C) To offer the latest news of the school
    (D) To suggest the mother takes a course

23. Which of the following is true about the special reading course?
    (A) It is designed for beginners in learning English.
    (B) Parents can also use it.
    (C) Students can use it every day.
    (D) All children are required to use it.

24. The word "attached" here is closest in meaning to _____?
    (A) collected
    (B) decided
    (C) included
    (D) invited

TEST 06

Questions 25-27

Marcel Proust (1871-1922) is a great French writer and is considered one of the most influential thinkers in the 20th century. His most famous book is *À la Recherche du Temps Perdu*, which is generally named "Remembrance of Things Past."

In this book, Proust shows us some rich people who are always unhappy. These rich people have always believed that they should be reasonably welcomed or loved. When they find that they are not as popular as they thought they should be, they feel disappointed, so they try hard to make themselves look important to others. That is why they always lose themselves and have never enjoyed a happy life.

Compared with the lives of these people in his book, in the last fifteen years of Proust's life, although life was still difficult, he could still find happiness. During those years, he became seriously ill. He had to spend most of his time in the hospital bed. He started writing "*À la Recherche du Temps Perdu*" in the ward. He was very happy with writing this book, and finally became a great writer because of this book.

25. Which of the following is NOT true about Proust?
    (A) He wrote about rich but unhappy people in his work.
    (B) He had much pleasure from writing in his later life.
    (C) He lived a difficulty life in his later years.
    (D) He started writing *À la Recherche du Temps Perdu* when he was fifteen.

26. What can we learn about the rich people in Proust's book?
    (A) They learn lessons from their past.
    (B) They try to get what they do not have.
    (C) Most of them are always healthy and live happily.
    (D) Some of them are often sick but feel still happy.

27. What is the closest meaning of "disappointed" in paragraph 2, line 4?
    (A) angry   (B) funny
    (C) sad   (D) strange

Questions 28-30

It was almost twelve, and Mrs. Lee felt a bit worried. What happened? Mary said she would be back home before eleven. Mrs. Lee kept calling her on her cellphone, but still no one answered. She put on a coat and went out from her bedroom to the living room. She stood at a window and look out. David walked out of his room and asked his mom, "Hasn't Sister come back yet?" "Not yet, but I think she's now on the way home." David went back to his room and studied. He had a very important exam the next day.

"David is always a well-behaved boy," Mrs. Lee thought. "He's five years younger, but he seldom makes me worried." Ten minutes later, her cellphone rang. "What's wrong with you? You made me so worried again! Where are you? ... What? OK. Just stay in front of the theater with Helen. I'll go there and drive you and Helen home. I'll be there in about ten minutes." Mrs. Lee took the car key and went out right away.

28. What does the story mainly tell us?
    (A) You should not turn off your cellphones when you are out.
    (B) Children should not come home too late.
    (C) Parents shouldn't let their children go out before an important exam.
    (D) Children should not leave their parents worried.

29. Which of the following is true?
    (A) Mary would come home ten minutes later.
    (B) Mrs. Lee cannot drive a car.
    (C) Helen is David's sister.
    (D) Mary is five years older than David.

30. Where did Mary go?
    (A) She went to a shopping mall with Helen.
    (B) She went to a movie with Helen.
    (C) She had a date with her boyfriend.
    (D) She went to the beach alone.

—結束—

TEST 07

GEPT 全民英檢
初級初試

題目本

本測驗分四個部分，全部都是單選題，共 30 題，作答時間約 20 分鐘。作答說明為中文，印在試題冊上並經由光碟放音機播出。

第一部分 看圖辨義

共 5 題。每題請聽光碟放音機播出題目和三個英文句子之後，選出與所看到的圖畫最相符的答案。每題只播出一遍。

例：（看）

（聽）

Look at the picture. What does the man do?

(A) He is a doctor.

(B) He is a teacher.

(C) He is a cook.

正確答案為 (A)。

聽力測驗第一部分試題從這裡開始。

A. Question 1

> **!** **Next train does not stop**
> Please stand behind the yellow platform line.

B. Question 2 and 3

C. Question 4 and 5

第二部分：問答

共 10 題。每題請聽光碟放音機播出的英文句子，再從試題冊上三個回答中，選出一個最適合的答案。每題只播出一遍。

例：（聽）May I use your bathroom?
（看）(A) Sure. This way, please.
　　　(B) You're welcome.
　　　(C) I'd like two hamburgers.

正確答案為 (A)。

6. (A) Sit down, please.
　　(B) I'm sorry.
　　(C) Yes, please.

7. (A) It's very cheap.
　　(B) I'm fine. Thank you.
　　(C) It went sour. When did you buy it?

8. (A) This is Mr. Lin speaking.
　　(B) Yes, I'll send messages to him.
　　(C) OK. I'll get back to him.

9. (A) I'm so glad to see you again.
　　(B) Cheer up.
　　(C) Much better. Thanks.

10. (A) You're welcome.
　　(B) OK. Sure.
　　(C) Here it is.

11. (A) That's okay.
　　(B) Medium, please.
　　(C) I want a large box.

12. (A) Let's call it a day.
　　(B) How are you lately?
　　(C) Would you like to go?

13. (A) I think so.
　　(B) Sorry. I made a mistake.
　　(C) Ok. There you go.

14. (A) No, I've been in the U.S. for a year.
　　(B) Yes, that's a good idea.
　　(C) Yes, a few times.

15. (A) Can you give me a hand?
　　(B) Give me the menu, please.
　　(C) Just help yourself.

第三部分：簡短對話

共 10 題。每題請聽光碟放音機播出的一段對話和一個相關的問題後，再從試題冊上三個選項中，選出一個最適合的答案。每段對話和問題播出一遍。

例：（聽）（男）What a nice-looking skirt. Is it expensive?

（女）No, I got it at the night market last night. I bought three at once.

（男）Well, but it really looks nice and expensive.

（女）You wanna get one for your girlfriend?

（男）Good idea. Where's the night market?

Question: What are the speakers mainly discussing?

（看）(A) Where the woman bought the skirt

(B) What the woman bought last night

(C) How much the skirt cost

正確答案為 (B)。

現在開始聽力測驗第三部分。

16. (A) In a parking lot.
    (B) At a train station.
    (C) In a supermarket.

17. (A) Buy some food and drinks
    (B) Take the order
    (C) Invite some friends

18. (A) How to talk happily
    (B) A girl
    (C) The woman's boyfriend

19. (A) He was late.
    (B) He had a car accident.
    (C) He lost his cellphone.

20. (A) At about 1:30 p.m.
    (B) At about 1:45 p.m.
    (C) At about 2:00 p.m.

21. (A) See a doctor for his knees.
    (B) Take a taxi.
    (C) Walk to the Urban Park.

22. (A) A doctor and a patient.
    (B) A shop assistant and a
        customer.
    (C) A judge and a lawyer.

23. (A) Make Mary feel comfortable.
    (B) Do nothing.
    (C) Ask what happened.

24. (A) A factory worker
    (B) A principal
    (C) A tour guide

25. (A) It'll be rainy and cold.
    (B) It'll be cold.
    (C) It'll be hot and dry.

第四部分 短文聽解

共 5 題，每題有 3 個圖片選項。請聽光碟放音機播出的題目，並選出一個最適當的圖片。每題只播出一遍。

例：（看）

     (A)   (B)   (C)

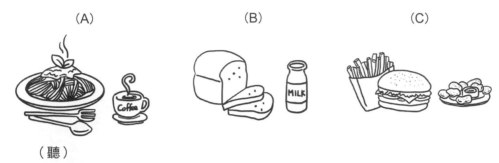

（聽）

Listen to the following message. What will Steve probably buy after work?

    Hi, Mom. This is Steve. I just made a call to you, but you didn't answer your phone. I will have a meeting with Mr. Roberts at the office tonight. I won't go home until 8 o'clock, so I can't have dinner with you tonight. I will buy some fast food on my way home. Don't worry about me.

正確答案為 (C)。

Question 26

     (A)   (B)   (C)

 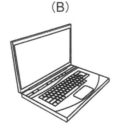 

Question 27

(A)

(B)

(C)

Question 28

(A)

(B)

(C)

Question 29

(A)

(B)

(C)

Question 30

(A)

(B)

(C)

未經指示前請勿翻頁

本測驗分三個部分，全部都是單選題，共 30 題，作答時間 35 分鐘。

第一部分　詞彙

共 10 題，每個題目裡有一個空格。請由四個選項中選出一個最適合題意的字或詞作答。

1. Kate was sick yesterday, _____ she didn't go to school.
   (A) so
   (B) because
   (C) that
   (D) but

2. Sam's dog always _____ loudly at strangers.
   (A) answers
   (B) barks
   (C) jumps
   (D) fears

3. My brother helped me _____ my homework.
   (A) for
   (B) no
   (C) with
   (D) in

4. There are six boys _____ soccer in the park.
   (A) play
   (B) played
   (C) playing
   (D) to play

5. Kevin goes jogging _____ .
   (A) every two day
   (B) each two days
   (C) each other day
   (D) every other day

6. He is the _____ child in his family.
   (A) each
   (B) only
   (C) one
   (D) just

7. Tim often eats in McDonald's because he is _____ lazy to cook.
   (A) so
   (B) very
   (C) such
   (D) too

8. I couldn't find _____ to stay, because all the hotels nearby were full.
   (A) anything
   (B) anywhere
   (C) anybody
   (D) anytime

9. I got many gifts at the party. Is this the _____ you gave me?
   (A) other
   (B) another
   (C) one
   (D) all

10. My uncle is a policeman. He _____ a lot of thieves and robbers.
    (A) catch
    (B) will have caught
    (C) has caught
    (D) is catching

第二部分 段落填空

共 8 題，包括二個段落，每個段落各含有四個空格。每格均有四個選項，請依照文意選出最適合的答案。

Questions 11-14

    In the dark corner, there was a baby mouse hiding around some grasses. His mother collected some dry ___(11)___ and covered him with them. He lay in this secret place alone, and his mother went to look for some food. He did not move at ___(12)___, during the silent night.

    A big cat showed up. The little mouse didn't dare to move his head, and even one of his feet. He was shaken with fear. Luckily, the cat didn't see him and walked past. Shortly after that, a hungry dog came along. ___(13)___ The dog only caught sight of these dead leaves and walked by.

    The mother mouse came back to the secret place. And ___(14)___ was safe now for the baby mouse to move and enjoy some food.

> ◢ dare v. 膽敢 still adj. 靜止的

11. (A) air   (B) leaves   (C) tanks   (D) trunks

12. (A) all   (B) least   (C) once   (D) last

13. (A) The leaves on the ground looked strange to him.
    (B) It felt so happy because there was food ahead.
    (C) The baby mouse still dared not move.
    (D) The cat suddenly came back to fight for food.

新題型

14. (A) there
    (B) he
    (C) it
    (D) something

Questions 15-18

Jennifer once thought that the __(15)__ old man who lived across from her place was very poor and lonely. She often saw him __(16)__ in his same old clothes and sitting alone in the park.

Last Christmas, Jennifer was out for a jog. When passing the park, she saw the old man carrying a big bag on his shoulder. She guessed that he would come over and ask her for money or help. But she was surprised to find that many children followed him. The old man came to her, took out a gift box from the bag and smiled and said to her, "Merry Christmas! I bought gifts for everyone. This is for you." __(17)__ She changed her __(18)__ about the old man. Since then, she has no longer judged people by how they look. Now she is learning to appreciate others from points of view.

15. (A) curious
    (B) favorite
    (C) childish
    (D) skinny

16. (A) dress
    (B) dressed
    (C) dressing
    (D) to dress

17. (A) At that moment, Jennifer felt so moved.
    (B) Jennifer had doubts about this.
    (C) Then a kid came along to complain about his gift.
    (D) However, things are not so simple.

18. (A) mind
    (B) life
    (C) hope
    (D) story

新題型

第三部分：閱讀理解

共 12 題，包括 4 個題組，每個題組含 1 至 2 篇短文，與數個相關的四選一的選擇題。請由試題冊上的選項中選出最適合的答案。

Questions 19-21

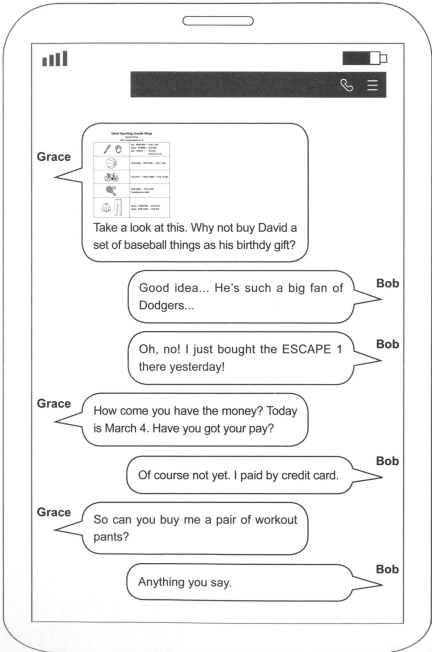

Bob clicked on the photo Grace sent.

Giant Sporting Goods Shop

Special Prices
ONLY during March 8~15

	bat：~~NT$1,800~~ → NT$ 1,350 glove：~~NT$800~~ → NT$ 600 ball：~~NT$70~~ →　　NT$ 60 　　　　　　　　NT$ 55 (≧10)
	SPALDING：~~NT$ 1300~~ → NT$ 1,000
	ESCAPE 1：~~NT$ 13,800~~ → NT$ 10,000
	~~NT$ 4,800~~ → NT$ 3,600 (Including two balls)
	jacket：~~NT$2,500~~ → NT$2,000 pants：~~NT$ 1,200~~ → NT$ 800

NOTE：We offer better prices for large orders. Please call us for more details.

19. Why did Grace send the messages to Bob?
    (A) To suggest what to buy David for his birthday.
    (B) To ask him when he gets his pay.
    (C) To tell him what's on sale.
    (D) To invite him to go shopping.

20. How much did it cost Bob to purchase the ESCAPE 1?
    (A) NT$ 10,000
    (B) NT$ 13,800
    (C) NT$ 1,000
    (D) NT$ 4,800

21. What is true about the sporting goods shop?
    (A) It mainly sells baseball goods.
    (B) Grace bought a pair of sports pants in this shop yesterday.
    (C) Bob will need to pay NT$ 1200 for a pair of pants.
    (D) It has better prices if you buy more.

Questions 22-24

Guo-hui grew up in a small village in Pingtung. He and his elder sister came to Tainan last month. Both of them lived in their uncle's house. Their house in Pingtung was damaged in an earthquake. Their parents had to stay in Pingtung to take care of their little brother because he was then hit and hurt by the fallen bookshelf.

Guo-hui and his elder sister went to the same school in Tainan. The teachers and classmates in the school were very kind to them, but Guo-hui did not feel happy because they had to stay in Tainan for a long time until their house was completely repaired. He missed his classmates and friends in Pingtung very much. They were friends, and they could talk about everything with him. They would contact him via email, LINE or video call. This made him feel much better. Guo-hui looked forward to living with his parents and little brother as soon as possible. He also hoped to return to Pingtung to study.

22. Which of the following is true about Guo-hui?
    (A) His parents sold their house.
    (B) The house of his family was damaged in an earthquake.
    (C) He got hurt and needed better medical care.
    (D) He went alone to Tainan to study.

23. Where are Guo-hui's parents?
    (A) In a big city.
    (B) In the countryside.
    (C) In a foreign country.
    (D) In a hospital.

24. Who are "They" as underlined in the second paragraph?
    (A) Guo-hui and his family members.
    (B) Guo-hui and his friends in Tainan.
    (C) Guo-hui's classmates and friends in Pingtung.
    (D) Guo-hui and his classmates and friends in Pingtung.

TEST 07

Questions 25-27

Among many stories about those who are unable to use part of their body because of different causes, we see many artists with "weak" bodies show "strong" power in their great works of art.

Take Frida Kahlo as an example. She was a girl with good hands and feet. She was hit heavily by a bus when she was eighteen years old. Most of her body was badly injured, but she still tried hard to live well. She loved to paint and allowed us to appreciate many great works. Another example is Christy Brown. When he was born, the only part of his body that could be moved was his left foot. However, he was still able to write and draw wonderfully. Brown wrote in his autobiography what happened in his life and how he started painting with his left foot. At last, don't forget Steve Wonder. He went blind shortly after he was born, but later he became a famous singer and songwriter.

These artists whose physical condition is worse than that of ordinary people, with their strong willpower, bring us many beautiful things, and hope for life. Their stories tell us that the most important thing in life is not what we have, but what we can create in our own conditions.

25. What should be the main idea of this article?
   (A) History always repeats itself.
   (B) Art is able to protect a weak mind.
   (C) Try to make the most use of your lives.
   (D) Many great artists have strong mind.

26. What is true about the three artists in this article?
   (A) They were all not in good health when they were born.
   (B) They all had problems with their bodies.
   (C) They are all popular painters.
   (D) They were all born into poor family.

27. What does the underlined "autobiography" mean?
   (A) A movie about a famous person
   (B) A picture of a person himself/herself
   (C) A book of a person's life by that person
   (D) A book on a person's childhood

From:	sarah1210@yahoo.com
To:	alicechnag@yahoo.com
Subject:	Re: How's the new life?

Dear Alice,

It's not easy, to tell the truth. Being the oldest kid at Little Angels isn't something you'd be proud of. Those who go there usually want very young kids, or babies at best, because they remember little about their birth parents or even they've never seen them. This makes them easy to be close to their new parents. I felt happy for those who left with their new families. Really, I did, though I might have a sense of loss.

I never thought Mr. and Mrs. Lin would pick me. They said they felt as if they had known me for many years. After a few afternoons of talking with me, they decided to take me home. But it's not easy to live with a stranger, at least now. David is nice, but he's too polite. It seems I'm just a guest in his family. We seldom talk, and just say good morning or good night to each other. Betty deals with this better than her older brother. I have my own room, and this is the only place now where I can make myself at home.

I have tried to make them feel easier with me, because, for the first time in my life, I feel that I belong somewhere.

All the best,
Sarah

28. What is the purpose of Sarah's email?
    (A) To complain about life at Little Angels
    (B) To tell about her new life
    (C) To explain why the couple took her home
    (D) To show regret about leaving Little Angels

29. What is true about the kids at Little Angels?
    (A) They do not live with their parents.
    (B) They are often not treated well.
    (C) Most of them have health problems.
    (D) They were born there.

30. What does "this" in the 3rd paragraph mean?
    (A) Being polite to a stranger
    (B) Living with a stranger
    (C) Making oneself at home
    (D) Feeling happy for the kids at Little Angels

                    ―結束―

TEST 08

GEPT
全民英檢

初級初試

題目本

本測驗分四個部分，全部都是單選題，共 30 題，作答時間約 20 分鐘。作答說明為中文，印在試題冊上並經由光碟放音機播出。

第一部分 看圖辨義

共 5 題。每題請聽光碟放音機播出題目和三個英文句子之後，選出與所看到的圖畫最相符的答案。每題只播出一遍。

例：（看）

（聽）

Look at the picture. What does the man do?

(A) He is a doctor.
(B) He is a teacher.
(C) He is a cook.

正確答案為 (A)。

聽力測驗第一部分試題從這裡開始。

A. Question 1

B. Question 2 and 3

C. Question 4 and 5

第二部分 問答

共 10 題。每題請聽光碟放音機播出的英文句子，再從試題冊上三個回答中，選出一個最適合的答案。每題只播出一遍。

例：（聽）May I use your bathroom?
（看）(A) Sure. This way, please.
(B) You're welcome.
(C) I'd like two hamburgers.

正確答案為 (A)。

6. (A) Once a week.
   (B) It's a long story.
   (C) It's warm.

7. (A) I felt much better. Thanks.
   (B) I love fall, too.
   (C) I didn't pass, either.

8. (A) By airplane.
   (B) I went there yesterday.
   (C) I felt bad.

9. (A) Speaking.
   (B) Have fun.
   (C) I am not she.

10. (A) I am good at playing basketball.
    (B) Only once.
    (C) I am fifteen years old.

11. (A) She's my sister.
    (B) She's sad.
    (C) She's doing her homework.

12. (A) Good idea.
    (B) You're welcome.
    (C) Oh, sorry!

13. (A) He's very old.
    (B) He is still a puppy.
    (C) He's almost 10.

14. (A) Neil loves it very much.
    (B) It's my favorite.
    (C) About NT$ 2000

15. (A) Sounds great.
    (B) I will pick him up later.
    (C) Today isn't my day.

第三部分 簡短對話

共 10 題。每題請聽光碟放音機播出的一段對話和一個相關的問題後,再從試題冊上三個選項中,選出一個最適合的答案。每段對話和問題播出一遍。

例:(聽)(男)What a nice-looking skirt. Is it expensive?
　　　　(女)No, I got it at the night market last night. I bought three at once.
　　　　(男)Well, but it really looks nice and expensive.
　　　　(女)You wanna get one for your girlfriend?
　　　　(男)Good idea. Where's the night market?

Question: What are the speakers mainly discussing?
　　　　(看)(A) Where the woman bought the skirt
　　　　　　(B) What the woman bought last night
　　　　　　(C) How much the skirt cost

正確答案為 (B)。

現在開始聽力測驗第三部分。

16. (A) In a classroom
    (B) In an office
    (C) On a bus

17. (A) She is waiting for the bus.
    (B) She is taking an order in a
        restaurant.
    (C) She is asking for directions.

18. (A) An office worker
    (B) A restaurant waitress
    (C) A supermarket clerk

19. (A) It will be cloudy.
    (B) It will be sunny.
    (C) It will be snowy.

20. (A) She's a clerk.
    (B) She's a waitress.
    (C) She's a coach.

21. (A) Board an airplane
    (B) Send a letter
    (C) Receive a mail

22. (A) She's feeling excited.
    (B) She's feeling tired.
    (C) She's feeling bored.

23. (A) Yes, he likes noodles.
    (B) No, he wants to take a break
        before dinner.
    (C) No, he isn't.

24. (A) How to make use of their free
        time
    (B) Their hobbies
    (C) Their favorite sports

25. (A) Why the man bought the shirt
    (B) What the man wears today
    (C) A very expensive shirt

第四部分 短文聽解

共 5 題，每題有 3 個圖片選項。請聽光碟放音機播出的題目，並選出一個最適當的圖片。<u>每題只播出一遍</u>。

例：（看）

（聽）

Listen to the following message. What will Steve probably buy after work?

　　Hi, Mom. This is Steve. I just made a call to you, but you didn't answer your phone. I will have a meeting with Mr. Roberts at the office tonight. I won't go home until 8 o'clock, so I can't have dinner with you tonight. I will buy some fast food on my way home. Don't worry about me.

正確答案為 (C)。

Question 26

(A)　　　　　　　(B)　　　　　　　(C)

Question 27

(A)

(B)

(C)

Question 28

(A)

(B)

(C)

Question 29

(A)

(B)

(C)

Question 30

(A)

(B)

(C)

未經指示前請勿翻頁

TEST 08

本測驗分三個部分，全部都是單選題，共 30 題，作答時間 35 分鐘。

第一部分 詞彙

共 10 題，每個題目裡有一個空格。請由四個選項中選出一個最適合題意的字或詞作答。

1. The restaurant has many delicious dishes. Jack often _____ there on weekends.
   (A) go
   (B) went
   (C) has gone
   (D) goes

2. Can you _____ me the way to the train station?
   (A) give
   (B) tell
   (C) keep
   (D) take

3. The teacher won't _____ her students come in if they are late.
   (A) put
   (B) order
   (C) let
   (D) need

4. Her mother is the _____ of a clothes shop.
   (A) teacher
   (B) baker
   (C) sailor
   (D) manager

5. Last night, Helen was hit by a car. She was taken to the _____.
    (A) restaurant
    (B) hospital
    (C) apartment
    (D) museum

6. The movie was so _____ that many people fell asleep.
    (A) bored
    (B) to bore
    (C) boring
    (D) bores

7. The manager _____ a lot of time holding meetings every day.
    (A) costs
    (B) spends
    (C) pays
    (D) takes

8. Lisa _____ in the U.S. since 1998.
    (A) lives
    (B) lived
    (C) has lived
    (D) will live

9. Vicky's daughter is not always early to school. She is _____ late.
    (A) usually
    (B) sometimes
    (C) often
    (D) never

10. Either you or your sister _____ to wash the dishes tonight.
    (A) have
    (B) has
    (C) had
    (D) having

TEST 08

第二部分 段落填空

共 8 題，包括二個段落，每個段落各含有四個空格。每格均有四個選項，請依照文意選出最適合的答案。

Questions 11-14

    Stanley and William have been good friends for many years. Stanley is planning a trip to Seattle with William. Stanley's uncle lives there, so they will __(11)__ at his uncle's place. In fact, Stanley __(12)__ to Seattle for three times. He really loves this city. There are many __(13)__ places, such as Pike Market and the first Starbucks. When they visit the market, they might also have a good chat at a coffee shop while enjoying the fantastic view. Seattle is a beautiful city. __(14)__ William can't wait to go there after hearing about what Stanley said.

11. (A) stay
    (B) celebrate
    (C) remember
    (D) visit

12. (A) went
    (B) has been
    (C) has gone
    (D) is going

13. (A) boring
    (B) new
    (C) famous
    (D) glad

14. (A) They will probably cancel this trip.
    (B) Stanley left for the airport yesterday.
    (C) William has run out of his money.
    (D) They are sure they will have fun.

新題型

Questions 15-18

Alan is a senior high school student. He studies hard and does his homework after dinner on weekdays. But on weekends, __(15)__ . Sometimes he __(16)__ fishing with his father on Sundays. Still, basketball is his favorite hobby. Maybe that's __(17)__ he likes to move and run, not always to sit somewhere and think about something. When he shoots a layup and scores, he feels so excited and happy. Even if he gets a grade that is not so satisfactory, or he has a fight with his girlfriend, he will feel very relaxed and forget about anything unpleasant __(18)__ leaving the basketball court.

15. (A) he likes to play video games at home
    (B) he always gets up very late
    (C) he plays basketball with some good friends
    (D) he goes to a library with a good friend

16. (A) goes
    (B) plays
    (C) takes
    (D) makes

17. (A) what
    (B) when
    (C) because
    (D) how

18. (A) before
    (B) for
    (C) after
    (D) when

TEST 08

第三部分 閱讀理解

共 12 題，包括 4 個題組，每個題組含 1 至 2 篇短文，與數個相關的四選一的選擇題。請由試題冊上的選項中選出最適合的答案。

Questions 19-21

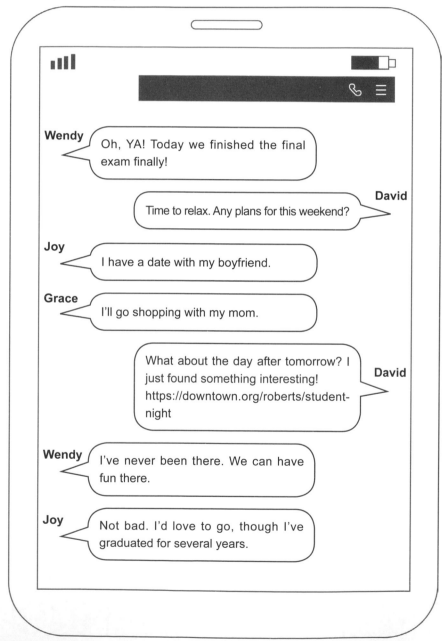

Wendy
Oh, YA! Today we finished the final exam finally!

David
Time to relax. Any plans for this weekend?

Joy
I have a date with my boyfriend.

Grace
I'll go shopping with my mom.

David
What about the day after tomorrow? I just found something interesting! https://downtown.org/roberts/student-night

Wendy
I've never been there. We can have fun there.

Joy
Not bad. I'd love to go, though I've graduated for several years.

They clicked on the link David sent and see this.

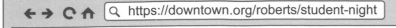

https://downtown.org/roberts/student-night

Students' Night at Robert's!!
Every Thursday, 7:00 P.M.-10:00 P.M.

Show your student card to come in free,
and enjoy half price for everything on the menu.

(For a table of four or more, we treat each to a drink of your choice!)

Not a student? Find out your old school uniform and wear it to Robert's Restaurant on Students' Night. We also offer you a special free drink.

Hotline for booking: 0960-333-888
LINE: @roberts
FB: Robert's Restanrant
      Business hours: 5:00P.M. - 10:00P.M. Closed on Mondays.

19. What do we know about the Students' Night at Robert's?
    (A) You need to wear school uniform to be there.
    (B) Every student will get a free drink of his/her choice.
    (C) Robert's will be open later on Students' Night than on other days.
    (D) You can enjoy a free drink there even if you're not a student.

20. On what day did they finish their final exam?
    (A) On Monday   (B) On Tuesday
    (C) On Wednesday   (D) On Thursday

21. Which is NOT true about the talkers?
    (A) David suggested going to Robert's on Students' Night.
    (B) Joy and Grace can enjoy a free drink of his/her choice.
    (C) Wendy found Students' Night interesting.
    (D) Joy is not a student now.

Questions 22-24

Emily stayed up late last night because she needed to prepare a quarterly report for an important sales meeting today. She could have done with it earlier if John, the assistant sales manager, had provided her with necessary information yesterday morning as he had promised.

She didn't go to bed until 2:00 A.M. When she woke up this morning, it was already fifteen to nine and she found her alarm clock failed to work. She was almost late for work, so she decided to go to work by taxi. But she found she had left her cellphone home. When she arrived at the office, it was already nine twenty. The meeting already started twenty minutes ago. The sales manager pulled a long face when Emily walked into the meeting room. What's worse, she found she forgot to bring the report she had finished last night. What Emily could say is "Today is really not my day."

22. What is the best title for this passage?
    (A) Emily's Daily Life
    (B) Don't Stay Up Too Often
    (C) Nothing Going Right Today for Emily
    (D) Don't Trust Others Too Much

23. When did the sales meeting start?
    (A) It started at nine.
    (B) It started at fifteen to nine.
    (C) It started after Emily walked into the meeting room.
    (D) It started twenty minutes before John arrived.

24. Which of the following is true?
    (A) Emily goes to work by taxi every day.
    (B) Emily made a phone call to the sales manager on her way to work.
    (C) The sales manager looked unhappy when Emily walked into the meeting room.
    (D) John gave necessary information to Emily on time.

Questions 25-27

Almost everybody has experienced nightmares, or bad dreams. Usually, a person will wake up during or just after having a nightmare and he or she will be able to remember all or part of the bad dream clearly. They are a type of dream that causes you to feel worried, fearful or scared.

Many people may have a dream of failing from a height, while some may also dream of failing a test, losing their jobs, missing their money or seeing their friends or family members die. If you see a car accident in the morning, you may have nightmares of that accident later. Because you have bad dreams, you can't sleep well. Sometimes, nightmares can be more than just bad dreams. They can be so serious that they cause a person to be in distress or they may trouble a person's work, family or social life.

If you want to get a good night's sleep, you can listen to music, drink a glass of milk or watch some funny TV programs before going to bed. That can help you sleep well.

25. Where does this passage probably come from?
    (A) A travel guide
    (B) A user's manual
    (C) A health magazine
    (D) A diary

26. Which word can the underlined "distress" be changed to?
    (A) Safety
    (B) Doubt
    (C) Worry
    (D) Silence

27. Which of the following is NOT correct?
    (A) Not many people dream about failing from a height.
    (B) If you see something terrible in the morning, you may have bad dreams.
    (C) If you want to get a good night's sleep, you can listen to some good music before sleep.
    (D) Bad dreams can influence your social life.

Questions 28-30

From:	Kelly_huang@gmail.com
To:	lisa_chen@msn.com
Subject:	Re: Planned Trip to Vancouver

Dear Lisa,

How are you doing lately? I heard that a strong typhoon hit your country recently and it caused serious damages to some houses and buildings. I hope you and your family members are safe and sound.

You said in your last E-mail that you are planning a trip to Canada and you asked whether you can stay with me. More than welcome! There's a guest room available now. Besides, I can give you some suggestions on where to go. So, after you deciding how long you will stay, list some interesting or popular places of scenery you want to visit. Also, find out some indoor or outdoor activities that may interest you. Finally, don't forget to get an idea of how much to tip waiters or waitresses, or you might feel embarrassed.

Please let me know as soon as possible if your have set the date of your trip. Keep in touch.

Yours,
Kelly
June 20, 2021

28. What is the purpose of this email?
    (A) To complain about a strong typhoon
    (B) To offer ideas of taking a trip
    (C) To know about recent life events
    (D) To invite a friend home

29. What does "sound" at the end of the 1st paragraph mean?
    (A) Voice
    (B) Energetic
    (C) Healthy
    (D) Free

30. Which of the following is correct?
    (A) Lisa is going on a trip.
    (B) Kelly will go to Canada and visit Lisa in summer.
    (C) It'll be convenient for Lisa to stay at Kelly's place.
    (D) Lisa has decided on when to visit Kelly.

一結束一

TEST 09

GEPT
全民英檢
初級初試

題目本

本測驗分四個部分，全部都是單選題，共 30 題，作答時間約 20 分鐘。作答說明為中文，印在試題冊上並經由光碟放音機播出。

第一部分 看圖辨義

共 5 題。每題請聽光碟放音機播出題目和三個英文句子之後，選出與所看到的圖畫最相符的答案。每題只播出一遍。

例：（看）

（聽）

Look at the picture. What does the man do?

(A) He is a doctor.
(B) He is a teacher.
(C) He is a cook.

正確答案為 (A)。

聽力測驗第一部分試題從這裡開始。

A. Question 1

B. Question 2 and 3

C. Question 4 and 5

第二部分 問答

共 10 題。每題請聽光碟放音機播出的英文句子，再從試題冊上三個回答中，選出一個最適合的答案。每題只播出一遍。

例：（聽）May I use your bathroom?
　　（看）(A) Sure. This way, please.
　　　　　(B) You're welcome.
　　　　　(C) I'd like two hamburgers.

正確答案為 (A)。

6. (A) Yes, she is late.
　 (B) I hope so.
　 (C) We'll celebrate it at a fancy restaurant.

7. (A) It tastes better than chicken.
　 (B) It is terrible.
　 (C) Well done, please.

8. (A) No, this Friday.
　 (B) Next Tuesday.
　 (C) My uncle lives nearby.

9. (A) This an old color TV.
　 (B) I like both.
　 (C) Yes, pink is better.

10. (A) I like the movie so much.
　 (B) Yes, I won the basketball game.
　 (C) I failed the exam again.

11. (A) The Happy Bank is in front of the supermarket.
　 (B) I go to the Happy Restaurant once a week.
　 (C) It's near my school.

12. (A) It looks big enough.
　 (B) Do you want to try a smaller one?
　 (C) Sorry. We don't have a fitting room.

13. (A) What's that?
　 (B) Sorry. I don't have one.
　 (C) You're welcome.

14. (A) No, I've lost my watch.
　 (B) Yes, I have.
　 (C) Yes, I've heard of the film.

15. (A) Cooking is my favorite hobby.
　 (B) Some French fries
　 (C) Thanks for your praise.

第三部分 簡短對話

共 10 題。每題請聽光碟放音機播出的一段對話和一個相關的問題後,再從試題冊上三個選項中,選出一個最適合的答案。每段對話和問題播出一遍。

例:(聽)(男)What a nice-looking skirt. Is it expensive?

(女)No, I got it at the night market last night. I bought three at once.

(男)Well, but it really looks nice and expensive.

(女)You wanna get one for your girlfriend?

(男)Good idea. Where's the night market?

Question: What are the speakers mainly discussing?

(看)(A) Where the woman bought the skirt

(B) What the woman bought last night

(C) How much the skirt cost

正確答案為 (B)。

現在開始聽力測驗第三部分。

16. (A) The woman
    (B) His friends
    (C) The woman's friends

17. (A) In a convenience store
    (B) In a restaurant
    (C) In a farm

18. (A) A shopkeeper and an employee
    (B) A manager and an assistant
    (C) A clerk and a customer

19. (A) Give the man her cellphone number
    (B) Show the man her new cellphone
    (C) Order some food

20. (A) Go running
    (B) Lose weight
    (C) Go shopping

21. (A) Eat lunch
    (B) Buy a movie ticket
    (C) Go to the bus stop

22. (A) Advising a patient
    (B) Taking some medicine
    (C) Seeing a doctor

23. (A) She wants to save money.
    (B) She wanted to live with her sister.
    (C) She moved to Taipei to work.

24. (A) How to be popular with people
    (B) Their friend
    (C) Their own plans

25. (A) By taxi
    (B) By bus
    (C) On foot

第四部分 短文聽解

共 5 題，每題有 3 個圖片選項。請聽光碟放音機播出的題目，並選出一個最適當的圖片。每題只播出一遍。

例：（看）

(A)　　　　　　　　　(B)　　　　　　　　　(C)

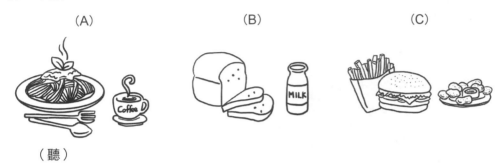

（聽）

Listen to the following message. What will Steve probably buy after work?

　　Hi, Mom. This is Steve. I just made a call to you, but you didn't answer your phone. I will have a meeting with Mr. Roberts at the office tonight. I won't go home until 8 o'clock, so I can't have dinner with you tonight. I will buy some fast food on my way home. Don't worry about me.

正確答案為 (C)。

Question 26

(A)　　　　　　　　　(B)　　　　　　　　　(C)

Question 27

(A)

(B)

(C)

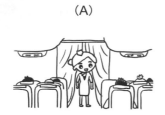 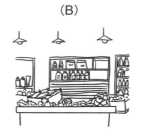 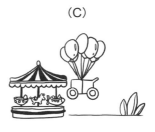

Question 28

(A)

(B)

(C)

  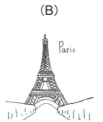 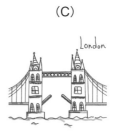

Question 29

(A)

(B)

(C)

Question 30

(A)

(B)

(C)

未經指示前請勿翻頁

本測驗分三個部分，全部都是單選題，共 30 題，作答時間 35 分鐘。

第一部分 詞彙

共 10 題，每個題目裡有一個空格。請由四個選項中選出一個最適合題意的字或詞作答。

1. Neil didn't go home until 11 p.m. His parents were _____ about him.
   (A) worried
   (B) embarrassed
   (C) glad
   (D) sad

2. Christmas is _____ the corner. Let's buy some presents this weekend.
   (A) about
   (B) on
   (C) around
   (D) at

3. The manager looked very serious. He had to make a difficult _____.
   (A) decision
   (B) experience
   (C) wish
   (D) example

4. Wendy used to be _____ when she was little. She looks a lot slimmer now.
   (A) slender
   (B) chubby
   (C) strange
   (D) attractive

5. He thinks eating vegetables _____ good for health.
   (A) has
   (B) have
   (C) is
   (D) are

6. The Art Museum _____ soon. We look forward to visiting it.
   (A) will build
   (B) is building
   (C) has been built
   (D) will be built

7. Frank looks very happy. He's been _____ by the University of Seattle.
   (A) allowed
   (B) quit
   (C) arrived
   (D) accepted

8. The writer _____ name is Beth just bought a new apartment.
   (A) who
   (B) whose
   (C) what
   (D) that

9. Rita lost her money. She borrowed money _____ her classmate.
   (A) to
   (B) from
   (C) for
   (D) by

10. Vicky found her bicycle _____ this morning.
    (A) stolen
    (B) stealing
    (C) stole
    (D) steal

第二部分 段落填空

共 8 題，包括二個段落，每個段落各含有四個空格。每格均有四個選項，請依照文意選出最適合的答案。

Questions 11-14

　　Stanley took a three-day trip alone to eastern Taiwan. He ___(11)___ an early train at 8:00 o'clock. When he arrived at his first station, it was already 11:30 A.M. The weather was pretty good. ___(12)___ Then he took a walk to a very famous street vendor and enjoy his ___(13)___ lunch. It tasted so good and cost only one hundred dollars. After that, he rented a bicycle and rode it carefreely to a hot spot where rice fields were around. There were not many people ___(14)___ it wasn't a holiday. He decided to spend the whole afternoon hiding himself in such a beautiful nature.

▲ carefreely 悠閒地

11. (A) drove
　　(B) caught
　　(C) kept
　　(D) bought

12. (A) He saw many people go cycling there.
　　(B) But he just wanted to take a rest.
　　(C) But it rained suddenly.
　　(D) It was a sunny day.

13. (A) delicious
　　(B) expensive
　　(C) important
　　(D) terrible

14. (A) although
　　(B) when
　　(C) because
　　(D) if

Questions 15-18

Many people like to go shopping. It makes them   (15)   good, but sometimes there might be bad experience. Some people feel bored during the holidays, so they decide to go shopping in a department store, hypermarket..., etc.   (16)   She is a housewife and in fact, she has no hobbies, except window shopping. Sometimes Brad goes with her. Usually he buys things he wants quickly, but his wife spends much time   (17)   about whether to buy something or not. It wastes a lot of time to Brad. Since Brad's wife can't make a   (18)   decision, sometimes they argue with each other on the street.

15. (A) feeling
    (B) to feel
    (C) feel
    (D) felt

16. (A) But Brad's wife loves shopping
        very much.
    (B) Take Brad's wife for example.
    (C) They can get some good deals
        there.
    (D) Sometimes shopping is a good
        hobby.

17. (A) thinking
    (B) think
    (C) to think
    (D) thought

18. (A) thoughtful
    (B) similar
    (C) slow
    (D) quick

新題型

第三部分 閱讀理解

共 12 題，包括 4 個題組，每個題組含 1 至 2 篇短文，與數個相關的四選一的選擇題。請由試題冊上的選項中選出最適合的答案。

Questions 19-21

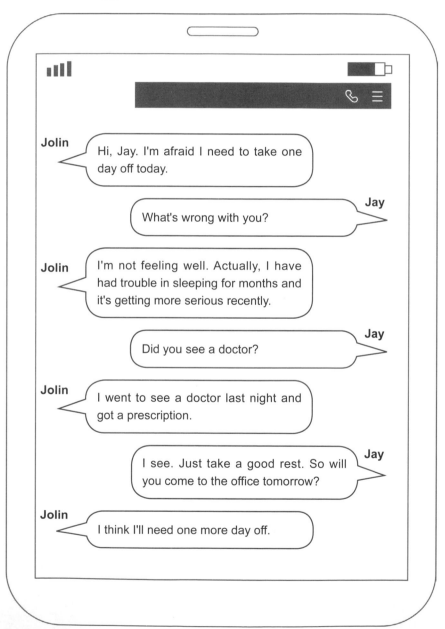

Dr. Chen gave Jolin this piece of one-week prescription.

Health Hospital

✧ Name: Jolin Wang
✧ Age: 28
✧ Problem: insomnia
✧ Medicine: Xychelin
✧ Two pills before going to bed every day for a week
  Take only with water
  Do not drive after taking the medicine
✧ Doctor: Chen Yo-Wei
✧ Date: October 13

◢ pill 藥片

19. Why did Jolin send this message?
  (A) To see a doctor
  (B) To quit a job
  (C) To ask for leave
  (D) To tell a secret

20. When will Jolin probably go to work?
  (A) On October 13
  (B) On October 14
  (C) On October 15
  (D) On October 16

21. How many pills of Xychelin did Jolin get?
  (A) 2
  (B) 7
  (C) 14
  (D) 28

Questions 22-24

Tommy loves old songs very much, and he still used audio tapes to listen to music, even though nowadays many people have learned how to download MP3 files on the Internet.

He bought a radio tape recorder from a flea-market store last week. He thought the sound quality was terrible, so he brought it back to the store. He told the clerk he wanted a <u>refund</u>. However, the clerk said, "I'm afraid we are not able to make it, but I can give you another one." Tommy was so mad that he shouted at her. Then, Tommy asked to see the shopkeeper. The shopkeeper was polite and patient with him. "I'm sorry to hear that. We can't give your money back, but I'd like to offer you a lamp as a gift," said the shopkeeper.

Tommy took the lamp home and found it didn't work a few days later.

22. Why did Tommy go to the store?
    (A) He wanted to buy a radio.
    (B) He wanted to see the shopkeeper.
    (C) He worked there.
    (D) He wanted to return a radio tape recorder and got his money back.

23. What does the word "refund" underlined in the second paragraph mean?
    (A) Pay more money
    (B) Get money back
    (C) Buy another product
    (D) Find out the problem

24. Which of the following is true?
    (A) The manager was very friendly.
    (B) The clerk shouted at Tommy.
    (C) Tommy finally got his money back.
    (D) Tommy bought a new lamp.

Losing weight is never easy, because many diet plans make you feel hungry or even easily angry. This is the major reason why many dieters might find it hard to make it at the end.

Here are three tips for weight loss that won't make you feel you are torturing yourself. At first, try to cut back on sugar in your diet plan. This won't feel hungry that easily. The second tip is getting a good night's sleep. And if you often stay up late, you will have difficulty cutting weight. The last, you should exercise every day. You can choose to go jogging, play tennis, etc. It's important to exercise very often. If you just exercise once a week, you will find you become heavier during your weight-losing plan.

By the way, don't skip breakfast. Try to eat breakfast every day. Skipping breakfast is not good for health. If you eat nothing in the morning, you will be tired easily.

25. What is the best title of the passage?
    (A) Use Your Time Well
    (B) Three tips for Exercise
    (C) How to Lose Weight Healthily
    (D) Importance of Eating Breakfast

26. What can "torturing" in the second paragraph be changed to?
    (A) Paying attention to
    (B) Bringing pain to
    (C) Causing injury to
    (D) Turning back on

27. According to the passage, which of the following is correct?
    (A) Avoid too much sugar can help.
    (B) To do exercise, if you're hungry during your diet plan.
    (C) Staying up late easily makes you tired.
    (D) If you do exercise once a week, you can lose weight easily.

TEST 09

Questions 28-30

From:	dora_hills@gmail.com
To:	dennis88@msn.com
Subject:	Sally's birthday party

Dear Dennis,

How's everything? I'm writing to ask if you are available on June 25th at 7 p.m. when there will be an important event. That's right. We are going to celebrate the birthday of Sally. She's going to turn 18. This is a milestone in life, and it needs each of us to get together and have fun. We are sincere to invite you to join us.

There will be many kinds of delicious food, drinks, and desserts at the party. You are one of Sally's old and best friends, so you must not miss this party and it will be special with you here. If you have any question, please contact me by replying to this e-mail.

Your family members or friends will be very welcome to this evening party. By the way, don't forget to bring a present. You know, a thoughtful gift will be better than an expensive one.

Yours,
Dora Hills
June 18

28. What is Dora's e-mail mostly about?
    (A) Sally will cancel the party.
    (B) Sally will hold a party for Dora.
    (C) Dora wants to invite Dennis to the party.
    (D) Dennis will refuse the invitation.

29. What does "milestone" in the 1st paragraph mean?
    (A) Big surprise
    (B) Great experience
    (C) Important event
    (D) Excellent news

30. Which of the following is correct?
    (A) Sally invites Dennis to the party.
    (B) The party offers drinks only.
    (C) Dora asks Dennis to leave Sally alone.
    (D) Sally will be 18 years old soon.

—結束—

TEST 10

GEPT
全民英檢
初級初試

題目本

本測驗分四個部分，全部都是單選題，共 30 題，作答時間約 20 分鐘。作答說明為中文，印在試題冊上並經由光碟放音機播出。

第一部分 看圖辨義

共 5 題。每題請聽光碟放音機播出題目和三個英文句子之後，選出與所看到的圖畫最相符的答案。每題只播出一遍。

例：（看）

（聽）

Look at the picture. What does the man do?

(A) He is a doctor.

(B) He is a teacher.

(C) He is a cook.

正確答案為 (A)。

聽力測驗第一部分試題從這裡開始。

A. Question 1

B. Question 2 and 3

C. Question 4 and 5

第二部分 問答

共 10 題。每題請聽光碟放音機播出的英文句子，再從試題冊上三個回答中，選出一個最適合的答案。每題只播出一遍。

例：（聽）May I use your bathroom?
　　（看）(A) Sure. This way, please.
　　　　 (B) You're welcome.
　　　　 (C) I'd like two hamburgers.

正確答案為 (A)。

6. (A) Yes, since 2019.
   (B) Yes, next week.
   (C) Yes, a couple of times.

7. (A) That means she went to the U.S. last year.
   (B) Where does she go to the elementary school?
   (C) So she's a junior high school student, right?

8. (A) It is 23 inches.
   (B) It's been long time.
   (C) Its only 50 dollars.

9. (A) Nice to meet you.
   (B) I bought this dress a couple of days ago.
   (C) It's a nice day.

10. (A) The look is nice.
    (B) Take this umbrella with you.
    (C) It's a nice deal.

11. (A) Yes, I've been there once.
    (B) I've been great.
    (C) I'm never late.

12. (A) Your check, please.
    (B) They are sold out.
    (C) I need your library card, please.

13. (A) Oh, couldn't be better.
    (B) I am doing it well.
    (C) I am doing my homework.

14. (A) Did you go swimming?
    (B) What day are you taking a trip?
    (C) That sounds like fun.

15. (A) I like to sing and dance.
    (B) It's very kind of you.
    (C) Everything will be fine.

第三部分 簡短對話

共 10 題。每題請聽光碟放音機播出的一段對話和一個相關的問題後，再從試題冊上三個選項中，選出一個最適合的答案。每段對話和問題播出一遍。

例：（聽）（男）What a nice-looking skirt. Is it expensive?

（女）No, I got it at the night market last night. I bought three at once.

（男）Well, but it really looks nice and expensive.

（女）You wanna get one for your girlfriend?

（男）Good idea. Where's the night market?

Question: What are the speakers mainly discussing?

（看）(A) Where the woman bought the skirt

(B) What the woman bought last night

(C) How much the skirt cost

正確答案為 (B)。

現在開始聽力測驗第三部分。

16. (A) Going to the airport
    (B) Buying an airplane ticket
    (C) Boarding a flight

17. (A) He is a booking clerk.
    (B) He is a doctor.
    (C) He is a waiter.

18. (A) He's going to play computer games.
    (B) He's going to play tennis.
    (C) He's going to visit Mary.

19. (A) Change a shirt
    (B) Have a refund
    (C) Make some money

20. (A) At an airport
    (B) At a train station
    (C) At a movie theater

21. (A) By cash
    (B) With a credit card
    (C) With an Easy Card

22. (A) Rent an apartment
    (B) Look around an apartment
    (C) Buy an apartment

23. (A) The woman's parents
    (B) A famous singer
    (C) When to go to a concert

24. (A) In New York
    (B) In Boston
    (C) In Seattle

25. (A) She quit her job.
    (B) She was let go by her boss.
    (C) She argued with her boss and was fired.

第四部分 短文聽解

共 5 題，每題有 3 個圖片選項。請聽光碟放音機播出的題目，並選出一個最適當的圖片。<u>每題只播出一遍</u>。

例：（看）

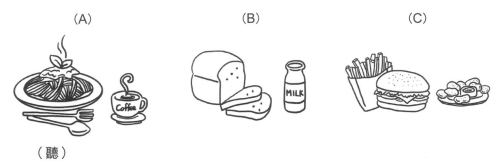

（A）　　　　　　　　　（B）　　　　　　　　　（C）

（聽）

Listen to the following message. What will Steve probably buy after work?

　　Hi, Mom. This is Steve. I just made a call to you, but you didn't answer your phone. I will have a meeting with Mr. Roberts at the office tonight. I won't go home until 8 o'clock, so I can't have dinner with you tonight. I will buy some fast food on my way home. Don't worry about me.

正確答案為（C）。

Question 26

（A）　　　　　　　　　（B）　　　　　　　　　（C）

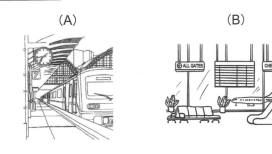
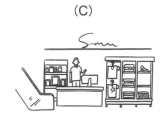

Question 27

(A)

(B)

(C)

Question 28

(A)

(B)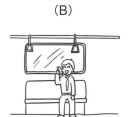

(C)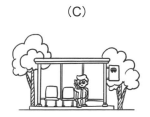

Question 29

(A)

(B)

(C)

Question 30

(A)

(B)

(C)

未經指示前請勿翻頁

本測驗分三個部分,全部都是單選題,共 30 題,作答時間 35 分鐘。

第一部分 詞彙

共 10 題,每個題目裡有一個空格。請由四個選項中選出一個最適合題意的字或詞作答。

1. Mrs. Thomas is very busy. She decides to _____ someone as a secretary to help her.
   (A) employ
   (B) embarrass
   (C) encourage
   (D) examine

2. Alan is only _____ for collecting suggestions. The manager will make the final decision.
   (A) responsible
   (B) regular
   (C) relative
   (D) recent

3. Rose has her teeth checked by a(n) _____ once a month.
   (A) journalist
   (B) artist
   (C) dentist
   (D) scientist

4. Helen paid NT$2,000 _____ the brown jacket.
   (A) from
   (B) by
   (C) of
   (D) for

5. I apologized for interrupting your talk, _____ I have something important to say.
    (A) and
    (B) but
    (C) or
    (D) when

6. This reminds me _____ a story I have ever read.
    (A) with
    (B) of
    (C) from
    (D) for

7. Molly is _____ at his decision to move to Seattle.
    (A) surprising
    (B) surprised
    (C) surprises
    (D) surprise

8. Dr. Potter was the smartest man _____ Sally has ever known.
    (A) which
    (B) that
    (C) whose
    (D) who

9. Someone knocked at the door _____ he was watching TV.
    (A) because
    (B) after
    (C) while
    (D) although

10. Larry is _____ taller than his neighbor, Peter.
    (A) more
    (B) most
    (C) very
    (D) much

第二部分 段落填空

共 8 題，包括二個段落，每個段落各含有四個空格。每格均有四個選項，請依照文意選出最適合的答案。

Questions 11-14

Frank was looking for a new job, and he had an interview this morning. However, He got up too late. When he arrived at the company, the ___(11)___ looked at him unhappily and asked him many questions he did not know how to answer. ___(12)___ After that, he decided to have lunch near the company. He got a call while he was ___(13)___ his food. A stranger said on the phone that his son was kidnapped by them. He asked Frank to prepare one million dollars. Then Frank shouted at him, "Are you kidding? I don't have a kid. I am still ___(14)___."

▲ kidnap 綁架

11. (A) professor
    (B) policeman
    (C) interviewer
    (D) shopkeeper

12. (A) He knew he had done it badly.
    (B) The interview seemed very successful.
    (C) He asked for a second interview.
    (D) They talked about many interesting things.

13. (A) waiting for
    (B) shouting at
    (C) proud of
    (D) mad at

14. (A) skinny
    (B) single
    (C) sincere
    (D) skillful

Questions 15-18

Everyone has a dream or many dreams. Do you remember what your dream was when you were an elementary school student? (15) Everyone can be successful (16) what they are or where they come from, even though some people try their best just to earn a living. It may take a lot of courage to (17) them come true. Although some dreams may look difficult, never say (18) . As an old saying goes, "Men are great for the dreams they have."

15. (A) Sometimes you may have trouble falling asleep.
    (B) Are you interested in what you have dreamed?
    (C) Do you still insist on your past dreams?
    (D) Have you dreamed of a ghost?

16. (A) in case of
    (B) according to
    (C) as if
    (D) no matter

17. (A) make
    (B) take
    (C) bring
    (D) do

18. (A) yes
    (B) hello
    (C) die
    (D) bye

第三部分 閱讀理解

共 12 題，包括 4 個題組，每個題組含 1 至 2 篇短文，與數個相關的四選一的選擇題。請由試題冊上的選項中選出最適合的答案。

Questions 19-21

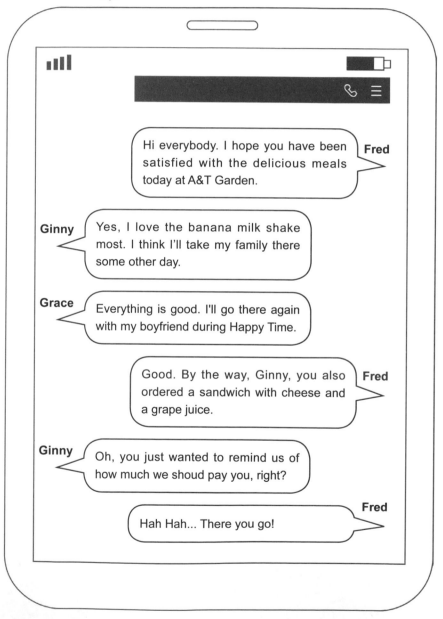

Here are their order and the poster of the restaurant.

A&T Garden			
Table: 2	__3__ person(s)	Order taken by Fred	13:30 | Dec.14
1	Apple Pie		NT$250 x3
2	Ice Cream		NT$100 x1
3	Milk Shake (chocolate) (large)		NT$180 x2
4	Milk Shake (banana)		NT$150 x2
5	Chicken Sandwich		NT$80 x1
6	Chicken Sandwich (with cheese)		NT$90 x1
7	Orange Juice		NT$100 x1
8	Grape Juice		NT$100 x1
Total Price: NT$ 1,880			
Thank you & expect to see you again! TEL: 2882-5252			

A&T Garden
Open Hours:
11:00 A.M. – 11:00 P.M.
Tues. to Sun.

Happy Time: 25% OFF
2:30 – 4:30 P.M.
9:00-11:00 P.M.

19. Why did Fred send this message to his friends?
    (A) To invite them to a restaurant
    (B) To ask them for money
    (C) To treat them to lunch
    (D) To tell them something interesting

20. How much should Ginny pay for her food?
    (A) NT$300
    (B) NT$320
    (C) NT$340
    (D) NT$350

21. When will Grace possibly go there with her boyfriend?
    (A) 11:00 A.M. on Wednesday
    (B) 3:00 P.M. on Monday
    (C) 8:00 P.M. on Friday
    (D) 10:00 P.M. on Thursday

Questions 22-24

My mother was <u>awful</u> at cooking. To her, cooking was more like an exciting experience. You put some of this and some of that in a pot, and you wait and see what will happen. "No tries, no results." is what she would say when her result did not turn out good, and I heard that many times.

My father was a good cook, and he loved to cook, too. He often said that he got my mother to marry him with a table of delicious food, not with an expensive ring. "A family needs only one good cook," he said.

Now I am a cook myself. And I have my own restaurant. I learned how to cook from my father, of course. From him, I learned the art of cooking. But I did learn one thing from my mother. It's her famous saying: "No tries, no results."

22. What can be a good title for this reading?
    (A) Tried Your Best
    (B) How to Be a Good Cook
    (C) Be Brave to Give It a Try
    (D) The Art of Cooking

23. What can the word "awful" underlined in the first paragraph be changed to _____.
    (A) fantastic
    (B) favorite
    (C) general
    (D) stupid

24. Which of the following is true?
    (A) You need to try many times to be a good cook.
    (B) The writer complained about his mother's cooking.
    (C) The husband should help his wife to cook.
    (D) The writer learned the art of cooking from his father.

Questions 25-27

Studying is never what you do at the night before a quiz. It's impossible to do all your studying the night before an examination. Everyone is different, and different habits work for different students. Hence, it is important to develop good habits. Here are some important tips for study.

First of all, try to do preview and review. Preview your lessons before class. It makes you understand well in class. Also, review your lessons after school. The second, keep the habit of studying every day. You should spend at least one hour studying after school. Don't just study before the test because you're not likely to get good grades this way. The third, take notes during a class. Don't fall asleep or talk to your classmates in class. On the other hand, pay attention to what your teachers say in class. The last, plan your learning time well. Making a plan will save you a lot of time.

It is never too late to study well. If you want to improve your grades, you should follow these <u>effective</u> skills. They are useful. Trust yourself and you can make it.

25. What is the reading mainly about?
    (A) The advantages of studying hard
    (B) Some tips for studying well
    (C) How to develop good hobbies
    (D) Tips for doing your homework

26. The underlined word "effective" is closest in meaning to _____?
    (A) useful
    (B) easy
    (C) special
    (D) famous

27. In what kind of magazine would you probably read this passage?
    (A) Music magazine
    (B) Fashion magazine
    (C) Travel magazine
    (D) Education magazine

Questions 28-30

Dear Sir/Madam,

I am writing to complain about the poor service I received from your store last Saturday. I am not satisfied with the bad behavior of your store clerk, Lisa. In fact, I am a regular customer of your store. I've had made a big purchase at your store for many times.

I caught a fancy of several dresses yesterday. The clerk was busy on the phone while I was trying them on. I thought I didn't look good in some of the dresses I picked, so I only took one. The clerk, however, looked at me coldly and impolitely while she put the dresses back in place. She was so rude that I didn't want to visit your store anymore. I would like an apology for how I was treated.

I look forward to hearing from you within the next week.

Sincerely,
Meg Pitt
December 12

28. Why did Meg Pitt send this letter?
    (A) To thank for kindness
    (B) To return purchased items
    (C) To praise a store clerk
    (D) To complain about poor service.

29. What is true about Meg?
    (A) She bought some clothes.
    (B) She made a big purchase.
    (C) She only purchased a dress.
    (D) She bought nothing.

30. Which of the following is correct?
    (A) Meg went to the store on December 12.
    (B) Meg wanted someone to say sorry to her.
    (C) The clerk treated her friendly.
    (D) Meg wrote this letter to Lisa.

一結束一

國際學村

全民英語能力分級檢定測驗
初級初試答案紙（第二回）

聽 力 測 驗

	A B C
1	A B C
2	A B C
3	A B C
4	A B C
5	A B C
6	A B C
7	A B C
8	A B C
9	A B C
10	A B C
11	A B C
12	A B C
13	A B C
14	A B C
15	A B C
16	A B C
17	A B C
18	A B C
19	A B C
20	A B C
21	A B C
22	A B C
23	A B C
24	A B C
25	A B C
26	A B C
27	A B C
28	A B C
29	A B C
30	A B C

閱 讀 能 力 測 驗

	A B C
1	A B C
2	A B C
3	A B C
4	A B C
5	A B C
6	A B C
7	A B C
8	A B C
9	A B C
10	A B C
11	A B C
12	A B C
13	A B C
14	A B C
15	A B C
16	A B C
17	A B C
18	A B C
19	A B C
20	A B C
21	A B C
22	A B C
23	A B C
24	A B C
25	A B C
26	A B C
27	A B C
28	A B C
29	A B C
30	A B C

考生姓名：_____

注意事項：

1. 限用 2B 鉛筆作答，否則不予計分。
2. 劃記要粗黑、清晰，不可出格，擦拭要清潔，若劃記過輕或污損不清，不為機器所接受，考生自行負責。
3. 作答樣例：
正確方式 ■   錯誤方式 ☑ ⊠ ▢ ◑

國際學村

全民英語能力分級檢定測驗
初級初試答案紙（第一回）

聽 力 測 驗

	A B C
1	A B C
2	A B C
3	A B C
4	A B C
5	A B C
6	A B C
7	A B C
8	A B C
9	A B C
10	A B C
11	A B C
12	A B C
13	A B C
14	A B C
15	A B C
16	A B C
17	A B C
18	A B C
19	A B C
20	A B C
21	A B C
22	A B C
23	A B C
24	A B C
25	A B C
26	A B C
27	A B C
28	A B C
29	A B C
30	A B C

閱 讀 能 力 測 驗

	A B C
1	A B C
2	A B C
3	A B C
4	A B C
5	A B C
6	A B C
7	A B C
8	A B C
9	A B C
10	A B C
11	A B C
12	A B C
13	A B C
14	A B C
15	A B C
16	A B C
17	A B C
18	A B C
19	A B C
20	A B C
21	A B C
22	A B C
23	A B C
24	A B C
25	A B C
26	A B C
27	A B C
28	A B C
29	A B C
30	A B C

考生姓名：_____

注意事項：

1. 限用 2B 鉛筆作答，否則不予計分。
2. 劃記要粗黑、清晰，不可出格，擦拭要清潔，若劃記過輕或污損不清，不為機器所接受，考生自行負責。
3. 作答樣例：
正確方式 ■   錯誤方式 ☑ ⊠ ▢ ◑

國際學村　全民英語能力分級檢定測驗 初級初試答案紙（第四回）

聽　力　測　驗

	A B C		A B C
1	A B C	16	A B C
2	A B C	17	A B C
3	A B C	18	A B C
4	A B C	19	A B C
5	A B C	20	A B C
6	A B C	21	A B C
7	A B C	22	A B C
8	A B C	23	A B C
9	A B C	24	A B C
10	A B C	25	A B C
11	A B C	26	A B C
12	A B C	27	A B C
13	A B C	28	A B C
14	A B C	29	A B C
15	A B C	30	A B C

閱　讀　能　力　測　驗

	A B C		A B C
1	A B C	16	A B C
2	A B C	17	A B C
3	A B C	18	A B C
4	A B C	19	A B C
5	A B C	20	A B C
6	A B C	21	A B C
7	A B C	22	A B C
8	A B C	23	A B C
9	A B C	24	A B C
10	A B C	25	A B C
11	A B C	26	A B C
12	A B C	27	A B C
13	A B C	28	A B C
14	A B C	29	A B C
15	A B C	30	A B C

考生姓名：

注意事項：

1. 限用 2B 鉛筆作答，否則不予計分。
2. 劃記要粗黑、清晰、不可出格，擦拭要清潔，若劃記過輕或污損不清，不為機器所接受，考生自行負責。
3. 作答樣例：

正確方式　■

錯誤方式　☑ ☒ □ ●

國際學村　全民英語能力分級檢定測驗 初級初試答案紙（第三回）

聽　力　測　驗

	A B C		A B C
1	A B C	16	A B C
2	A B C	17	A B C
3	A B C	18	A B C
4	A B C	19	A B C
5	A B C	20	A B C
6	A B C	21	A B C
7	A B C	22	A B C
8	A B C	23	A B C
9	A B C	24	A B C
10	A B C	25	A B C
11	A B C	26	A B C
12	A B C	27	A B C
13	A B C	28	A B C
14	A B C	29	A B C
15	A B C	30	A B C

閱　讀　能　力　測　驗

	A B C		A B C
1	A B C	16	A B C
2	A B C	17	A B C
3	A B C	18	A B C
4	A B C	19	A B C
5	A B C	20	A B C
6	A B C	21	A B C
7	A B C	22	A B C
8	A B C	23	A B C
9	A B C	24	A B C
10	A B C	25	A B C
11	A B C	26	A B C
12	A B C	27	A B C
13	A B C	28	A B C
14	A B C	29	A B C
15	A B C	30	A B C

考生姓名：

注意事項：

1. 限用 2B 鉛筆作答，否則不予計分。
2. 劃記要粗黑、清晰、不可出格，擦拭要清潔，若劃記過輕或污損不清，不為機器所接受，考生自行負責。
3. 作答樣例：

正確方式　■

錯誤方式　☑ ☒ □ ●

聽 力 測 驗

1	A B C
2	A B C
3	A B C
4	A B C
5	A B C
6	A B C
7	A B C
8	A B C
9	A B C
10	A B C
11	A B C
12	A B C
13	A B C
14	A B C
15	A B C
16	A B C
17	A B C
18	A B C
19	A B C
20	A B C
21	A B C
22	A B C
23	A B C
24	A B C
25	A B C
26	A B C
27	A B C
28	A B C
29	A B C
30	A B C

閱 讀 能 力 測 驗

1	A B C
2	A B C
3	A B C
4	A B C
5	A B C
6	A B C
7	A B C
8	A B C
9	A B C
10	A B C
11	A B C
12	A B C
13	A B C
14	A B C
15	A B C
16	A B C
17	A B C
18	A B C
19	A B C
20	A B C
21	A B C
22	A B C
23	A B C
24	A B C
25	A B C
26	A B C
27	A B C
28	A B C
29	A B C
30	A B C

考生姓名：

注意事項：
1. 限用 2B 鉛筆作答，否則不予計分。
2. 劃記要粗黑、清晰，不可出格、擦拭要清潔，若劃記過輕或污損不清，不為機器所接受，考生自行負責。
3. 作答樣例：
   正確方式 ■ 錯誤方式 ☑ ⊠ ◐ ▢

聽 力 測 驗

1	A B C
2	A B C
3	A B C
4	A B C
5	A B C
6	A B C
7	A B C
8	A B C
9	A B C
10	A B C
11	A B C
12	A B C
13	A B C
14	A B C
15	A B C
16	A B C
17	A B C
18	A B C
19	A B C
20	A B C
21	A B C
22	A B C
23	A B C
24	A B C
25	A B C
26	A B C
27	A B C
28	A B C
29	A B C
30	A B C

閱 讀 能 力 測 驗

1	A B C
2	A B C
3	A B C
4	A B C
5	A B C
6	A B C
7	A B C
8	A B C
9	A B C
10	A B C
11	A B C
12	A B C
13	A B C
14	A B C
15	A B C
16	A B C
17	A B C
18	A B C
19	A B C
20	A B C
21	A B C
22	A B C
23	A B C
24	A B C
25	A B C
26	A B C
27	A B C
28	A B C
29	A B C
30	A B C

考生姓名：

注意事項：
1. 限用 2B 鉛筆作答，否則不予計分。
2. 劃記要粗黑、清晰，不可出格、擦拭要清潔，若劃記過輕或污損不清，不為機器所接受，考生自行負責。
3. 作答樣例：
   正確方式 ■ 錯誤方式 ☑ ⊠ ◐ ▢

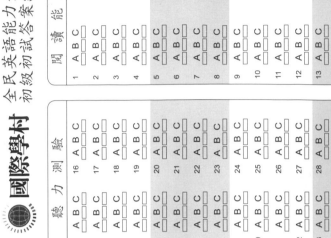

國際學村 全民英語能力分級檢定測驗
初級初試答案紙（第八回）

聽 力 測 驗

閱 讀 能 力 測 驗

考生姓名：＿＿＿＿＿＿＿

注意事項：

1. 限用 2B 鉛筆作答，否則不予計分。
2. 劃記要粗黑、清晰，不可出格，擦拭要清潔，若劃記過
   輕或污損不清，不為機器所接受，考生自行負責。
3. 作答樣例：
   正確方式　■　錯誤方式　

國際學村 全民英語能力分級檢定測驗
初級初試答案紙（第七回）

聽 力 測 驗

閱 讀 能 力 測 驗

考生姓名：＿＿＿＿＿＿＿

注意事項：

1. 限用 2B 鉛筆作答，否則不予計分。
2. 劃記要粗黑、清晰，不可出格，擦拭要清潔，若劃記過
   輕或污損不清，不為機器所接受，考生自行負責。
3. 作答樣例：
   正確方式　■　錯誤方式

國際學村　全民英語能力分級檢定測驗　初級初試試答案紙（第十回）

閱　讀　能　力　測　驗

	A B C D		A B C D
1	A B C D	16	A B C D
2	A B C D	17	A B C D
3	A B C D	18	A B C D
4	A B C D	19	A B C D
5	A B C D	20	A B C D
6	A B C D	21	A B C D
7	A B C D	22	A B C D
8	A B C D	23	A B C D
9	A B C D	24	A B C D
10	A B C D	25	A B C D
11	A B C D	26	A B C D
12	A B C D	27	A B C D
13	A B C D	28	A B C D
14	A B C D	29	A B C D
15	A B C D	30	A B C D

聽　力　測　驗

	A B C D		A B C D
1	A B C D	16	A B C D
2	A B C D	17	A B C D
3	A B C D	18	A B C D
4	A B C D	19	A B C D
5	A B C D	20	A B C D
6	A B C D	21	A B C D
7	A B C D	22	A B C D
8	A B C D	23	A B C D
9	A B C D	24	A B C D
10	A B C D	25	A B C D
11	A B C D	26	A B C D
12	A B C D	27	A B C D
13	A B C D	28	A B C D
14	A B C D	29	A B C D
15	A B C D	30	A B C D

考生姓名：

注意事項：

1. 限用 2B 鉛筆作答，否則不予計分。
2. 劃記要粗黑、清晰，不可出格，擦拭要清潔，若劃記過輕或污損不清，不為機器所接受，考生自行負責。
3. 作答樣例：
   正確方式　　　　錯誤方式

國際學村　全民英語能力分級檢定測驗　初級初試試答案紙（第九回）

閱　讀　能　力　測　驗

	A B C D		A B C D
1	A B C D	16	A B C D
2	A B C D	17	A B C D
3	A B C D	18	A B C D
4	A B C D	19	A B C D
5	A B C D	20	A B C D
6	A B C D	21	A B C D
7	A B C D	22	A B C D
8	A B C D	23	A B C D
9	A B C D	24	A B C D
10	A B C D	25	A B C D
11	A B C D	26	A B C D
12	A B C D	27	A B C D
13	A B C D	28	A B C D
14	A B C D	29	A B C D
15	A B C D	30	A B C D

聽　力　測　驗

	A B C D		A B C D
1	A B C D	16	A B C D
2	A B C D	17	A B C D
3	A B C D	18	A B C D
4	A B C D	19	A B C D
5	A B C D	20	A B C D
6	A B C D	21	A B C D
7	A B C D	22	A B C D
8	A B C D	23	A B C D
9	A B C D	24	A B C D
10	A B C D	25	A B C D
11	A B C D	26	A B C D
12	A B C D	27	A B C D
13	A B C D	28	A B C D
14	A B C D	29	A B C D
15	A B C D	30	A B C D

考生姓名：

注意事項：

1. 限用 2B 鉛筆作答，否則不予計分。
2. 劃記要粗黑、清晰，不可出格，擦拭要清潔，若劃記過輕或污損不清，不為機器所接受，考生自行負責。
3. 作答樣例：
   正確方式　　　　錯誤方式

NEW
GEPT

新制全民英檢

10回試題完全掌握最新內容與趨勢！

初級 聽力&閱讀 題庫大全

○─── 解析本 ───○

全民英語能力分級檢定測驗的問與答

　　財團法人語言訓練中心（LTTC）自 2000 年全民英檢（General English Proficiency Test, GEPT）推出至今，持續進行該測驗可信度及有效度的研究，以期使測驗品質最佳化。

　　因此，自 2021 年一月起，GEPT 調整部分初級、中級及中高級的聽讀測驗題數與題型內容，並提供成績回饋服務。另一方面，此次調整主要目的是要反映 108 年國民教育新課綱以「素養」及「學習導向評量（Learning Oriented Assessment）」為中心的教育理念，希望可以透過適當的測驗內容與成績回饋，有效促進國人的英語溝通能力。而調整後的題型與內容將更貼近日常生活，且更能符合各階段英文學習的歷程。透過適當的測驗內容與回饋，使學生更有效率地學習與應用。

Q 2021 年起，初級測驗的聽力與閱讀（初試）在題數與題型上有何不同？

初級的聽力測驗維持不變，而閱讀測驗部分調整如下：

調整前	調整後
■ 第一部分 詞彙與結構 15 題	■ 第一部分 詞彙 10 題
■ 第二部分 段落填空 10 題	■ 第二部分 段落填空 8 題
■ 第一部分 閱讀理解 10 題	■ 第一部分 閱讀理解 12 題
共 35 題	共 30 題

調整重點：

1. 第一部分「詞彙和結構」，改為「詞彙」。
2. 第二部分「段落填空」增加選項為句子或子句類型。
3. 第三部分「閱讀理解」增加多文本、圖片類型。

Q 考生可申請單項合格證書

另外，證書核發也有新制，除了現在已經有的「聽讀證書」與「聽讀說寫證書」外，也可以申請口說或寫作的單項合格證書，方便考生證明自己的英語強項，更有利升學、求職。

Q 何謂 GEPT 聽診室 ── 個人化成績服務？

「GEPT 聽診室」成績服務，提供考生個人化強弱項診斷回饋和實用的學習建議，更好的是，考生在收到成績單的一個月內即可自行上網免費閱覽下載，非常便利。其中的內容包括：

1. **能力指標的達成率**─以圖示呈現您（考生）當次考試的能力表現
2. **強弱項解析與說明**─以例題說明各項能力指標的具體意義。
3. **學習指引**─下一階段的學習方法與策略建議。
4. **字彙與句型**─統計考生該次考試表現中，統整尚未掌握的關鍵字彙與句型。

※ 以上內容整理自全民英檢官方網站。

Q 英檢初級的聽力需要達到什麼程度及其運用範圍為何？

初級考生須具備基礎英文能力，並能理解與使用淺易的日常用語，其參考單字範圍以「教育部基礎 1200-2000 字」為主，而聽力測驗考生必須聽出這 1200 字以內，並能聽懂母與人士語速慢且清晰的對話，並大致掌握談話主題。透過視覺輔助，理解人、事、時、地、物的簡單描述，例如簡單的問路與方向指示。考生應能大致聽懂日常生活相關的對話，例如簡短的公共場所廣播、體育賽事、天氣狀況播報、電話留言等。

Q 英檢初級的聽力需要達到什麼程度及其運用範圍為何？

閱讀測驗考生必須可以認出並理解 2000 單字以內，與個人生活、家庭、朋友及學校生活相關的的基本詞彙與用語。並能看懂與日常生活相關的淺易英文、閱讀標示／公告／廣告／個人書信／簡訊／文字對話訊息／故事／說明文／簡單菜單（menu）／行程表／時刻表／賀卡…等。

考生應能掌握短文主旨與部分細節、釐清上下文關係與短文結構，並整合與歸納兩篇文本的多項訊息。

Q 英檢初級初試的通過標準為何？

級數	測驗項目	通過標準
初級	聽力測驗 閱讀測驗	兩項測驗成績總和達 160 分，且其中任何一項成績不得低於 72 分。

本書特色與使用說明

1

依 2021 年最新改版英檢初級題型編排設計，精心撰寫 10 回聽力&閱讀模擬試題，可以作為準備全民英檢初級以及會考使用，也適合在家自修，老師課堂測驗與練習使用！

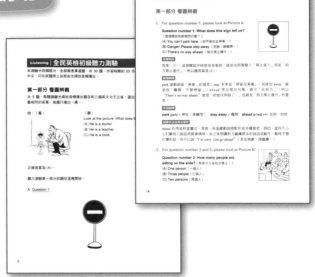

2

可剪下作答紙，方便考生實際練習，並檢視與記錄自己的測驗結果。將你得到的成績，用黑點（●）標示在表格上，就能感受到自己分數的進步。

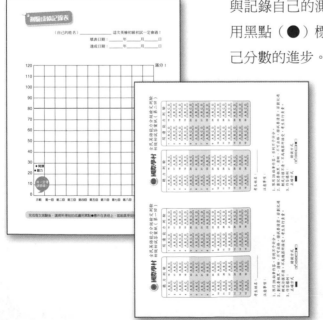

3

依 2021 年最新改版英檢初級題型編排設計，新調整的題型會以「NEW」標記。

13. (A) Mary tried to sing a song to her daughter
    (B) the thunder was heard from the sky
    (C) luckily, nobody got hurt
    (D) the rain stopped suddenly

14. (A) to get
    (B) get
    (C) getting
    (D) got

13. 答案：(B)。這是要挑選一個句子、子句或句子的一部分放入空格，前後和空格句之間的連接關係，是否讓句意顯得自然通順，所以要或根據整段文章的意旨。空格後面句子提到「『所以』她女兒又顯然應填入一個讓她女兒又放聲大哭的「原因」，正確答案應為一陣雷聲」。(A)、(C) 與 (D) 明顯不會是讓小孩放聲大哭的原因項句子的翻譯：
(A) 瑪麗試著唱首歌給她女兒聽
(C) 所幸，沒有人受傷
(D) 雨突然停了

14. 答案：(A)。四個選項是同一個動詞的不同形態，應直接根據斷。「it + be 動詞 + time + 不定詞（to-V）」為固定句型，意時候了。」故正確答案為 (A)。

破題關鍵
11. 看到對等連接詞必須立即想到：結構、時態對等，然後用「(A)、(B) 兩個選項後，根據句意選出正確答案。
12. 當選項都是相同詞類時，要選出正確答案的話，只能透過

想報名參加英檢初級的考生們，一定要先熟悉題型調整後的測驗內容，以降低實際測驗時的焦慮感。

第三部分 閱讀理解

共 12 題，包括 4 個題組，每個題組含 1 至 2 篇短文，與數個相關的題。請由試題冊上的選項中選出最適合的答案。

Questions 19-21

From:	Service@fashionsop.com.tw
To:	Undisclosed-Recipient
Subject:	Try Fashion Shop

To whom it may concern,
　　Fashion Shop tells you how easy it is to start your own busine you want to sell fashionable goods such as hats, dresses, pants rings, etc. You're able to make it just by joining us in about one mi takes no more than 10 minutes to open your online store.

Only $5 per month, and free for a limited time!
Click the button below to have a fantastic experience!

4

史上最詳盡！「答題解說」＋「破題關鍵」＋「字詞解釋」＋「相關文法或用法補充」。每一題的解析讓你從這道題目中學習相關的必考重點文法或句型，真正讓你培養實力，為下一級數與階段做準備！

★「答題解說」給你最正確的解題觀念與步驟，且讓你了解錯誤選項錯在哪裡！

★「破題關鍵」讓你知道這一題只要抓到哪個關鍵字詞，答案就出來了！

---

4. **It's an ice cube. I can feel the _____ over my head.** （那是冰塊。我可以感覺到頭上寒意。）

(A) heat　(B) goal　(C) coldness　(D) warm

答題解說

答案：(C)。如果單就「feel the _____ 」來看，四個名詞的選項似乎都是正確答案，所以還是必須根據整體句意來判斷。句子大意是「這東西是冰塊，因為可以感覺到 _____ 在頭上」。顯然答案應該是「寒冷（coldness）」，才能符合 ice cube（冰塊）的意思。其餘選項均不符句意。

破題關鍵

本題關鍵是「ice 與 coldness 的連結」。其餘的 heat（熱）、goal（目標）以及 warm（溫）都與 ice（冰）沒有任何關係。

字詞解釋

cube [kjub] n. 塊，立方體　　**heat** [hit] n. 熱　　**goal** [gol] n. 目標　　**coldness** [ˋkoldnɪs] n. 冷，寒冷　　**warm** [wɔrm] n. 暖和的狀態

相關文法或用法補充

文法裡有所謂「連綴動詞」，feel 就是其中之一，常用於「連綴動詞＋形容詞」的結構。不過 feel 也可以當及物動詞，後面接名詞作為其受詞，表示「觸摸看看」，例如 feel the cloth to see its quality（摸看看這布料，看它品質好不好）。

★「相關文法或用法補充」是從這一題的答題關鍵點再進行延伸學習，讓你不僅沒有輸在起跑點，還能為下一階段超前佈署！

★符號說明

n. 名詞｜v. 動詞｜adj. 形容詞

adv. 副詞｜prep. 介系詞｜conj. 連接詞

phr. 片語

sb. = somebody｜sth. = something

＊初級程度外的字詞

5

提供一整回的 QR 碼線上音檔，沒有光碟播放器也能練習聽力測驗。

Listening｜全民英檢初級聽力測驗　　🎧 Round 1

本測驗分四個部分，全部都是單選題，共 30 題，作答時間約 20 分鐘。作答說明為中文，印在試題冊上並經由光碟放音機播出。

第一部分 看圖辨義

共 5 題。每題請聽光碟放音機播出題目和三個英文句子之後，選出與所看到的圖畫最相符的答案。每題只播出一遍。

例：（看）　　　　　　　　　　（聽）

Look at the picture. What does the man do?

(A) He is a doctor.

(B) He is a teacher.

(C) He is a cook.

6

書中所附的 MP3 分為三種版本：整回分割、同題型分割、單題分割。方便考生們的任何運用。用電腦打開光碟片中的檔案時，你會看見以下 3 個資料夾：

1. **整回分割**：內容是 Test_01.mp3、Test_02.mp3 ...

    有 10 個「整回分割」的音檔。此音檔可供實際模擬測驗使用，播放時從第一題到最後一題，中間不會切割。模擬測驗時可嘗試用手提播放器播放「整回分割」音檔，以確實模擬實際考試狀況。

2. **同題型分割**：

    每一回測驗都有四種題型個部分：「看圖辨義」、「問答」、「簡短對話」、「短文聽解」，此版本每個音檔即代表一個題型（檔名是 Test_01_part_1.mp3、Test_01_part_2.mp3 …）。若考生想針對特定的題型來訓練則可使用此版本。

3. **單題分割**

    也就是一題一個檔案，每一回有 30 個檔案（檔名是 Test_01_part_1_01.mp3、Test_01_part_1_02.mp3 …）。此版本方便考生針對單題不斷練習。使用此版本的音檔，就不需要為了找特定題目按快轉鍵或倒退鍵按來按去，或是用滑鼠在時間軸上面點來點去、拉來拉去，直接按到那個音檔就是那個題目，高興重複練幾次都可以。

CONTENTS

目錄

NEW GEPT
新制全民英檢初級聽力 & 閱讀題庫大全

測驗成績記錄表

（自己的姓名）＿＿＿＿＿＿＿＿ 這次英檢初級初試一定會過！

填表日期：＿＿＿＿年＿＿＿＿月＿＿＿＿日

達成日期：＿＿＿＿年＿＿＿＿月＿＿＿＿日

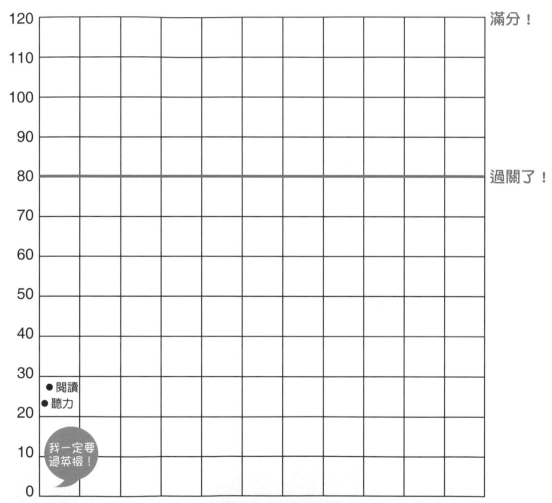

滿分！

過關了！

120											
110											
100											
90											
80											
70											
60											
50											
40											
30											

●閱讀
●聽力

我一定要過英檢！

示範　第一回　第二回　第三回　第四回　第五回　第六回　第七回　第八回　第九回　第十回

完成每次測驗後，請將所得到的成績用黑點●標示在表格上，就能感受到自己分數的進步。

1

GEPT
全民英檢

初級初試
中譯＋解析

第一部分 看圖辨義

1. **For question number 1, please look at Picture A.**

Question number 1: What does this sign tell us?
（這個標誌告訴我們什麼？）
(A) You can't park here.（你不能在此停車。）
(B) Danger! Please stay away.（危險！請離開。）
(C) There's no way ahead.（前方禁止通行。）

答題解說

答案：(C)。這個標誌平時很容易看到，就是告訴駕駛人「禁止進入」或是「前方禁止通行」，所以確答案是 (C)。

破題關鍵

park 當動詞是「停車」的意思；stay 本來是「停留在某處」，其後加 away，就是指「離開，不要停留」；ahead 常出現在句尾，表示「在前方」，所以 "There's no way ahead." 就是「前面沒有路了。」也就是「前方禁止通行」的意思。

字詞解釋

park [pɑrk] v. 停放（車輛等）　　**stay away** v. 離開　　**ahead** [ə`hɛd] adv. 在前，向前

相關文法或用法補充

ahead 的用途相當廣泛，常與一些基礎動詞搭配形成各種意思。例如，當你不小心打斷別人說話或做事情時，但之後想讓對方繼續原本的談話或動作，暫時不想打擾的話，你可以說 "I'm sorry. Just go ahead!"（真是抱歉。請繼續。）

2. **For question number 2 and 3, please look at Picture B.**

Question number 2: How many people are sitting on the sofa?（有多少人坐在沙發上？）
(A) One person（一個人）
(B) Three people（三個人）
(C) Two persons（兩個人）

答題解說

答案：(C)。即使沒聽出一開始的 How many，單從三個選項也可以知道是在問「有多少人」，再來還是得仔細聽完整句才能夠正確答題，別看到圖片中有三個人，就直接選(B)了。注意只有兩個人坐在沙發上。

破題關鍵

俗話說「不要看到黑影就開槍。」本題要問的是「多少人坐在沙發上？」雖然圖中明顯有三個人，但關鍵在題目最後的 sofa（沙發）這個字，這是個很簡單且容易聽出來的單字。

字詞解釋

people [ˋpipl] n. 人，人們　**sofa** [ˋsofə] n. 沙發　**person** [ˋpɝsn̩] n. 人，個人

相關文法或用法補充

問對方「有多少～」可以用 How many... 或 How much...，many 後面必須接「可數名詞」，而 much 後面接「不可數名詞」。例如：How many pens do you have?（你有幾枝筆？）、How much water do you drink every day?（你每天喝多少水？）

3. **Question number 3: Please look at Picture B again.**

What are they doing?（他們正在做什麼？）
(A) They are watching a movie.（他們正在看一部電影。）
(B) They are repairing the TV（他們正在修理電視。）
(C) They are sleeping.（他們正在睡覺。）

答題解說

答案：(A)。本題取材自居家生活中的場景，只要聽懂並理解各選項的意思，即可選出正確答案。題目問的是「正在做什麼？（What... doing?）」，從圖片中可以清楚看見這三個人坐在電視機前看電視（也許是看電影、看綜藝節目、看球賽），雖然沒有「看電視」的選項，但 (A) They are watching a movie. 就是在「看電視中播放的電影」，所以答案是 (A)。選項 (B) 刻意用 TV 來誤導答題，應注意 repair 是「修理」的意思。

破題關鍵

"watch a move" 是「在家看電視播放的電影」，而 "see a movie"「是到電影院去看電影」的意思，請務必釐清兩者的不同。

repair [rɪ`pɛr] v. 修理

現在進行式（be + Ving）除了表示「正在做什麼」，也可以用來表示「不久的未來」即將要發生的事情或動作。例如：Hurry up! The bus is arriving.（快一點。公車就要到了。）另外，也可以表示「某段特定時間」將進行的事、動作或趨勢，可能持續一個星期、幾個月、甚至一年。例如：Mary is writing another book this year.（Mary 今年會再寫一本書。）

4. **For question number 4 and 5, please look at Picture C.**

   Question number 4: What is true about the picture?
   （關於這張圖何者正確？）
   (A) People are buying movie tickets.
      （人們正在買電影票。）
   (B) They are in a movie theater.（他們在電影院裡。）
   (C) People are leaving the theater.（人們正在離開電影院。）

答案：(A)。圖片中一群人在一個窗口前排隊，明顯是在買票進場看電影。所以正確答案是(A)。其餘選項的敘述皆與圖片不符。

只要看懂圖片中的物品及人物動作，就能了解圖片中的場景。接著就是要能夠聽得出來選項中的關鍵字詞，包括 buying movie tickets（購買電影票）、movie theater（電影院）、leaving（離開）等。

following [`fɑləwɪŋ] adj. 以下的　**wait** [wet] v. 等候　**ticket** [`tɪkɪt] n. 票　**theater** [`θɪətə] n. 電影院　**leave** [liv] v. 離開

在英文裡，表示「電影」的單字，最簡單的就是 movie 以及 film，movie 和 film 在意思上雖然沒有太大差別，但確切來說，前者是「電影」，後者是「影片」。主要必須注意固定搭配用語。比方說，「電影業」的英文是 film industry，而不說 movie industry；「拍片」是 shoot a film，而不用 shoot a movie；「電影明星」是 movie star，而不會說 film star；filmmaker 是指「電影製片」或「導演」，但 movie maker 常用來指某種可製作影片的應用程式或工具。另外，英式英語的

cinema（電影院）這個字也很常出現在文章或報導中，但在美式英語中主要還是以 movie theater 來表示。

5. **Question number 5: Please look at Picture C again.**

   What information is given in this picture?
   （圖片中提供了什麼資訊？）
   (A) How much the movie ticket prices are（電影票價多少）
   (B) Where the theater is（電影院的地點）
   (C) What is showing now（正在上映什麼）

   答題解說
   答案：(C)。題目是在問圖片右上方 STAR WARS 的文字要提供的是什麼樣的資訊。STAR WARS（星際大戰）是電影名稱，所以正確答案是 (C)。

   破題關鍵
   也許你知道 STAR WARS 是電影片名，但也別一聽到 movie 就選了 (A)，後面還有個 prices 呢。另外 "showing now" 就是「正在上映」的意思。

   字詞解釋
   price [praɪs] n. 價格　　**theater** [ˋθɪətɚ] n. 劇場；電影院　　**movie** [ˋmuvɪ] n. 電影

   相關文法或用法補充
   我們中文講的「價格很貴／便宜」常常被說成 The price is expensive/cheap.，其實這是錯誤的表達，因為在英文裡，expensive 或 cheap 通常是指「物品、東西」本身的貴或便宜，而不是「價位、價格」。如果要表示「價格昂貴／便宜」要用 high 或 low 來表示。例如：The price is too high for me.（這價格對我來說太高了。）

第二部分 問答

6. **How's it going lately?**（最近如何？）

   (A) I'm late. Sorry.（我遲到了。抱歉。）
   (B) Pretty good. Thank you.（很好。謝謝你。）
   (C) Thank you very much.（非常感謝你。）

   答題解說
   答案：(B)。以 How 開頭的問句就是問對方「～如何？」。而這裡的 how 作為問

第 1 回
第 2 回
第 3 回
第 4 回
第 5 回
第 6 回
第 7 回
第 8 回
第 9 回
第 10 回

候語的開頭（相當於 How are you?），因此即使聽不出題目最後的 lately，其實也不影響作答。對於他人的問好，最直接、簡單的回答就是先回答「好」或「不好」。如果要感謝對方的關心可以再補上 Thank you.。

破題關鍵

聽到句首的 How，就知道不可能直接回答 Thank you；而選項（A）刻意用 late 與題目的 lately 造成混淆。

字詞解釋

lately [`letlɪ] adv. 最近　　**pretty** [`prɪtɪ] adv. 非常

相關文法或用法補充

how 也常用來詢問對方對於某事物的感覺（例如 How was your party?），或者問對方做某件事情的過程與方法（例如：How do you come to school every day?）。

7. **May I help you?**（有什麼我可以為您效勞的嗎？）

(A) No, but I can help you.（沒有，但我可以幫你。）
(B) Yes, please. I'm looking for the restroom.（是的，麻煩一下。我在找洗手間。）
(C) You're welcome.（不用客氣。）

答題解說

答案：（B）。什麼情況下會聽到 "May I help you?"？像是大樓管理處、大賣場服務台、百貨公司專櫃，或是店家接起電話的第一句，都可能是這句話。了解它的意思是「有什麼我可以為您效勞的嗎？」以及它的使用場合，就可以輕易選出正確答案。

破題關鍵

也可以直接從 3 個選項來分析。(A) 是用來表達「可以提供協助」，但完全與題目問句不相關。(C) 通常用來回應對方所表達的感謝。

字詞解釋

look for 找尋　　**restroom** [`rɛstˌrum] 洗手間　　**welcome** [`wɛlkəm] adj. 受歡迎的

相關文法或用法補充

與 May I help you? 這句話相同意思的是 Can I help you?，但其實 May I help you? 會比 Can I help you? 更加有禮貌。此外，很多人以為也可以說 What can I help you?，但這句話在文法上是錯誤的，正確說法是 What can I help you with?，或是 What can I do for you?。至於在回覆時，可以說 Yes, please.、Yes, I hope so.、Thank you.、Great.、That's very kind / nice of you, thanks. 等等。

第 1 回
第 2 回
第 3 回
第 4 回
第 5 回
第 6 回
第 7 回
第 8 回
第 9 回
第 10 回

8. **Are you available this weekend?**（你這個週末有空嗎？）

(A) Just a minute, please.（請稍候一下。）
(B) No, I'm fine.（不，我沒事。）
(C) I'm afraid not.（我恐怕沒空。）

答題解說

答案：(C)。這是以 be 動詞開頭的疑問句，基本上來說是要以 Yes/No... 來回答，不過通常考題不會出得這麼直接且呆板，較常見的正確答案都是屬於「間接性」的回答。就三個選項來分析，題目是問「你有空嗎？」(A) 選項的「請稍候」顯然沒有針對問題來回答，而 (B) 選項雖然以 No 開頭，但後面卻說「我沒事」，這也是答非所問。選項 (C) 的 I'm afraid not. 可以還原成 I'm afraid I won't be available.，這是正確答案。

破題關鍵

本題的破題關鍵就在 available 這個形容詞，它表示「可行的；有空的」，只要聽懂這個字，就知道在問對方「是否有空」，或是想和對方約會之類的，但千萬別一聽到 Are you...? 就以為回答 No, ... 的答案一定是正確的喔！

字詞解釋

available [əˋveləbl] **adj.** 有空的　　**minute** [ˋmɪnɪt] 分鐘；短暫的時間
afraid [əˋfred] **adj.** 害怕的

相關文法或用法補充

詢問對方是否有空，當然還有很多說法，比方說 Are you free?、Do you have a minute (to talk)?、Can you spare some time?、What time is OK for you?、When are you not occupied? 等等。

9. **May I speak to Mr. Lin?**（請問林先生在嗎？）

(A) Who are you?（你是誰？）
(B) This is Mr. Lin speaking.（我就是林先生。）
(C) Thank you for calling.（謝謝您的來電。）

答題解說

答案：(B)。本題考的是電話用語。「May I speak to + 人?」通常是打電話要找某人時，開頭的第一句話。如果接電話的人正好就是對方要找的人，就可以說「This is...（某人）speaking.」或是 This is he/she.。所以正確答案就是 (B) 了，不可以說 I am...。如果對方要找的人不在，可以回答 I am sorry but he/she is out/

unavailable now.，或是要請對方稍等時，可以說 Hold on, please. 等。當然，有時為了過濾對方的身分，你也可以反問對方是誰，但是電話用語與一般日常對話不同，不可以說 Who are you?，而是 Who is this?，所以 (A) 是錯誤的。至於 (C) 的回答完全是雞同鴨講，可直接排除掉。

關鍵當然就在能否聽出 May I speak to... 並了解其意思，但假如不知道這是電話用語，其實如果早先一步看過 3 個選項，尤其是 (B) 及 (C)，大概也猜得出來這題要考什麼。

字詞解釋

May I speak to...? 請問～在嗎？　　**Thank you for calling**. 謝謝您的來電。

相關文法或用法補充

❶ 接／打電話問候語
  ① Hello? → 非正式用語，通常用於準備接熟識親友的來電。
  ② 人 + speaking → 接電話時千萬別說 Hello, I'm Jack. 而要說 Hello, (This is/It's) Jack speaking. 或是 Hello, it's/This is Jack.。
  ③ 如果是打電話給對方，要先表明自己的身分時，可以說： It's/This is Jack calling。
❷ 指名要找某人時
  ① Is Jack there?/Jack, please. → 非正式用法，通常用於打電話給熟識的親友。
  ② May/Could/Can I speak to Jack, please? 或是 I'd like to speak to B, please. → 正式用法，通常用於公務往來通話的第一句。

10. Have a nice trip.（旅途愉快。）

(A) You're welcome.（不客氣。）
(B) No problem.（沒問題。）
(C) Thank you.（謝謝你。）

答題解說

答案：(C)。問題句是祝福對方旅途愉快的常見用法。對於別人給予的祝福，最直接、簡單的回答當然就是 Thank you. 了。選項 (A) 是對於別人感謝你時的回答，而 (B) 除了也可以用來回應對方的感謝（也可以解釋成「不客氣」），通常是用來請對方放心、問題不大等等。

第 1 回

第 2 回

第 3 回

第 4 回

第 5 回

第 6 回

第 7 回

第 8 回

第 9 回

第 10 回

破題關鍵

英文裡的祝福用語往往都看不到主詞。比方說，「祝你幸福。」（Wish you happiness.）、「祝你幸運。」（Good luck.）、「玩得愉快！」（Have a good time!）……等，聽到這樣的祝福話語，說聲感謝應該算是反射動作了吧！

字詞解釋

trip [trɪp] n. 旅途　　**welcome** [ˋwɛlkəm] adj. 歡迎的　　**problem** [ˋprɑbləm] n. 問題

相關文法或用法補充

「祈使句」在英文的文法中扮演一個相當重要的角色，通常會出現在口語會話中。基本上，祈使句省略主詞 you，以原形動詞開頭。現在就來看看哪些時候可以使用祈使句吧！

❶ 命令或要求
  ① Turn off the radio, please.（請關掉收音機。）
  ② Pass me the spoon and chopsticks, please.（請遞給我湯匙和筷子。）
❷ 邀請：Just make yourself at home.（就當作是在自己家吧！）
❸ 給予忠告、建議或指示
  ① Don't drink cold water when you are sick.（生病時別喝冷水。）
  ② First, turn left at traffic lights. Then, keep going straight. And, you will see the coffee shop on the right side.（首先，在紅綠燈的地方左轉。接著，繼續直走。然後，你會看到咖啡店在你的右手邊。）
❹ 警告：Mind the gap between the train and the platform!（小心車廂與月台間隙！）
❺ 祝福：Have a nice weekend!（祝你有個愉快的週末。）

11. **How tall is John?**（約翰多高？）

(A) He is very tall.（他很高。）
(B) He is 170 centimeters tall.（他 170 公分高 。）
(C) He is the tallest in his family.（他是家裡最高的。）

答題解說

答案：(B)。how tall... 是用來問某人的身高，回答時要有具體的「數字」，不能含糊回答。因此本題正確答案是(B)。

破題關鍵

回答「多高、多長」時，應有具體的數字，後面再加單位名稱，記得要用複數。

tall [tɔl] adj. 高的　　**centimeter** [ˋsɛntəˌmitə] n. 公分　　**family** [ˋfæməlɪ] n. 家庭

相關文法或用法補充

詢問對方身高、體重等，也是日常生活會話裡很常聽到的。身高的部分，最簡單的說法就是 How tall are you? 也可以用 What's your height? 來問。那麼在回答時，可以說 I am 160 cm tall. 或是 I am 160 cm in height.。至於體重的部分，可以問對方：How heavy are you?、How much do you weigh? 或是 What's your weight?

12. **What day is it today?**（今天星期幾？）

(A) It is August 8.（今天是 8 月 8 日。）
(B) It is Tuesday.（今天是星期二。）
(C) It is my birthday.（今天是我的生日。）

答題解說

答案：(B)。以 What day 開頭的問句是在問「星期幾」，所以選項 (B) 回答今天是週二，就是正確答案。選項 (A) 回答的是「日期」，選項 (C) 最後也有個 -day 的音，讓你覺得好像也是針對問題在回答，但根本是答非所問。

破題關鍵

關鍵當然在於聽出且聽懂 What day...? 的意思，但要是不確定是 What day 還是 What date 呢？其實只要稍微有點文法概念的話，就會知道，英文裡沒有 what date is (it) today...? 的說法，為什麼呢？請繼續往下看「相關文法或用法補充」吧！

字詞解釋

August [ɔˋgəst] n. 八月　　**Tuesday** [ˋtjuzde] n. 週二　　**birthday** [ˋbɝθˌde] n. 生日

相關文法或用法補充

大家可能都學過 what time、what day、what year... 這些用來問時間的問句，其中 What day...? 是用來問「星期幾」。而 date 因為是「日期（幾月幾日）」的意思，所以很多人很自然地認為可以「比照辦理」。只要把 day 換成 date，就可以用 What date...? 來問日期是幾月幾日。但是 day 和 date 兩字發音太接近了，連老外也聽不出來你在問哪一個吧！所以為了避免混淆，當要問日期時，習慣上不會用同一個句型。所以「今天是幾月幾日？」要說 What's today's date? 或是 What's the date today?，而不是 What date is (it) today?。即使不是要問今天的日期，而是要問其他日期，也要說 What's the date of...?，而不是 What date is...?。雖然說 What date is (it) today? 或是 What date is the party? 的句子，嚴格說起來並不是錯

誤的，但在溝通上容易造成困擾或誤解，而語言主要的目的就是溝通，這也是為了避免使用不利於溝通的說法。

13. Why not join us for a cup of coffee?（何不跟我們一起去喝杯咖啡？）

(A) I'd love to.（我很樂意。）

(B) This cup of coffee is too strong for me.（這杯咖啡對我來說太濃了。）

(C) No sugar, please.（不加糖，謝謝。）

答題解說

答案：(A)。Why not...? 常用來表達「提議、建議」，題目這句是向對方提議一起去喝咖啡，所以 (A) 選項就是正確的回答，可以還原成 I would love to join you for a cup of coffee.（我很樂意和你們一起去喝杯咖啡。）其餘兩個選項的敘述雖然也都跟 coffee 有關，但純粹是為了混淆聽者的辨別能力，其實是答非所問。

破題關鍵

關鍵在於聽出且了解 Why not...? 不是一般問句，而是向對方提出建議或邀請的表達方式，接著就可以只憑直覺反應選出 I'd love to. 的答案了。或者如果有先看過三個選項，也可以馬上判斷出 (B)、(C) 的回答應該是在咖啡廳中或是已經在喝咖啡的場合了。

字詞解釋

join [dʒɔɪn] v. 加入　　**coffee** [ˋkɔfɪ] n. 咖啡　　**strong** [strɔŋ] adj.（味道、氣味）濃的，強烈的　　**sugar** [ˋʃʊgɚ] n.（食用）糖

相關文法或用法補充

如何用英文提出「邀請或建議」？除了「Why not + 原形動詞」的句型，還有「What/How about + Ving」喔！以下整理三個比較簡單且常用的句型：

❶ Let's + 原形動詞

　→ 表示「我們去～（做某事）吧」，例如：

　　Let's go for a biking trip.（我們騎腳踏車出去逛逛吧。）

❷ What/How about + Ving

　→ 表示「～（做某事）如何？」，例如：

　　What/How about going for a biking trip?（我們騎腳踏車出去逛逛如何？）

❸ Why not + 原形動詞（= Why don't you + 原形動詞）

　→ 表示「何不～（去做某事）」，例如：

　　Why don't you go for a biking trip with me? =Why not go for a biking trip with me?（何不跟我出去騎腳踏車？）

14. The Chinese New Year is coming soon!（農曆新年就快到了！）

(A) Oops! I'm going to be late.（糟糕！我快遲到了。）
(B) Mmm... Let me think about it.（嗯⋯讓我考慮一下。）
(C) That's right. I can't wait.（沒錯。我等不及了。）

答題解說

答案：(C)。Chinese New Year 就是指「農曆新年」，也可以用 Lunar（Chinese）New Year 表示，是每年很多人都期待的佳節，因此聽到這件「好事」快要來了，會有什麼正常的反應呢？選項 (C) 的「我等不及了」就是最正確的回應，其他兩個選項都是不相關的回答。

破題關鍵

Chinese New Year 對於許多初學英文的人來說，相信不會太陌生，就算聽不出來，至少 coming soon（快到了）也是可以經常聽到的吧，本題只要掌握住這兩個關鍵詞，再與選項中的 can't wait 作連結，就可以確定答案了。

字詞解釋

soon [sun] adv. 不久，快　　**late** [let] adj. 遲到的　　**think about** 考慮，思考　　**wait** [wet] v. 等待

相關文法或用法補充

日常生活對話中，難免都會聊到各種佳節或節日，有時候也會出現在聽力的考題中，如果聽不出來會讓答題自信度降低不少喔！以下就來看看一些重要節日的說法：

New Year's Day（新年、元旦）、Chinese（Lunar）New Year's Eve（除夕）、Lantern Festival（元宵節）、Valentine's Day（情人節）、Tomb Sweeping Day（清明節）、Mother's Day（母親節）、Dragon Boat Festival（端午節）、Father's Day（父親節）、Mid-Autumn Festival（中秋節）、Teacher's Day/ Confucius' Birthday（教師節）、Double Tenth Day（雙十節）、Halloween（萬聖節前夕）、All Saints' Day（萬聖節）、Thanksgiving Day（感恩節）、Christmas Eve/Xmas Eve（聖誕夜）、Christmas（Day)/Xmas（聖誕節）

15. Let's take a break. It's still early.（我們休息一下。現在還早。）

(A) Oh, really?（噢，真的嗎？）
(B) I'd want another.（我要再一份。）
(C) Here comes the bus.（公車來了。）

第 1 回
第 2 回
第 3 回
第 4 回
第 5 回
第 6 回
第 7 回
第 8 回
第 9 回
第 10 回

答題解說

答案：(A)。本題有兩句話。第一句（Let's take a break.）要表達的是提出建議，而第二句是單純在陳述一個事實（「現在時間還很早」）。選項中沒有一句可以用來回應對方提議，只有 (A) 反問對方「是真的嗎？」，可以用來作為回應。

破題關鍵

就本題來說，在尚未聽到錄音播放前，即使先看過三個選項也無法預測題目會怎麼問，只能在聽過並了解播放的題目句之後，才能正確作答。基本上題目與選項的用字，在發音上辨識度都很高，只要可以了解 Let's...、take a break、another、Here comes... 這幾個關鍵字詞的意思，就能輕鬆答題。

字詞解釋

break [brek] n. 休息　**take a break** 休息一下　**really** [ˋrɪəlɪ] adv. 真正地，非常　**another** [əˋnʌðɚ] pron. 另一個　**Here comes...** ～來了

相關文法或用法補充

❶ 很多人認為 take a break 和 take a rest 沒有任何差別，其實 Take a break 是指「暫停手邊的工作，去做別的事」。也許是出去吃飯、出去走走放鬆一下之類的。但是 take a rest 就是要「休息一下」，小睡一下，什麼都不做，所以別搞混了喔！

❷ another 當代名詞時，指「再一個，另一個」的意思。例如：He doesn't want this one, please show him another.（他不想要這個，請再給他看別的。）

第三部分 簡短對話

16. M: The watches on the table are so nice-looking. Where did you get them?
    W: I bought them both in a department store.
    M: They are not cheap, right?
    W: I spent almost my whole monthly income!

    Question: How many watches did the woman buy?
    (A) Two　(B) Three　(C) We don't know.

英文翻譯

男：桌上的這些手錶真是好看。你在哪裡買到這些手錶的？
女：我這兩支錶都是在百貨公司買的。
男：它們不便宜吧，是嗎？

女：我花了幾乎整整一個月的薪水呢！

問題：女子買了幾支錶？

(A) 兩支　　(B) 三支　　(C) 我們不知道。

答案：(A)。題目問的是女子買了幾支錶，所以應注意聽女子的發言部分：I bought them both...（我買的這兩支錶……），只要聽到這裡，答案就出來了。

從選項來看，題目要問的是一個數字（How many...?），所以要特別注意對話中出現與數字有關的關鍵字（both）。

nice-looking [`naɪs`lʊkɪŋ] **adj.** 好看的，漂亮的　　**bought** [bɔt] **v.** 買（buy 的過去式及 P.P.）　　**department store** [dɪ`pɑrtmənt] [stor] **n.** 百貨公司　　**whole** [hol] **adj.** 全部的　　**monthly** [`mʌnθlɪ] **adj.** 每月的　　**income** [`ɪn͵kʌm] **n.** 收入，所得

nice-looking 如其字面意思，就是「好看的」意思。She looks nice. = She is nice-looking.。像這樣由兩個字組成的形容詞，稱為「複合形容詞」。「複合形容詞」在英文裡有多種形式，例如： man-eating（吃人的）、snow-covered（被雪覆蓋著的）、good-looking（好看的）、never-ending（永無休止的）、well-done（做得好的）……等。

17. **W: I didn't go to a movie last night.**

　　M: I didn't, either.

　　W: So are you still busy with your paper?

　　M: That's right. Professor Lee asked me to hand it in next Monday.

Question: Who went to a movie last night?

(A) The woman went to a movie last night.

(B) The man went to a movie last night.

(C) Neither of them went to a movie last night.

女：我昨天晚上沒有去看電影。

男：我也沒去。

女：所以你還在忙你的報告嗎？

男：沒錯。李教授要求我下週一交報告。

問題：昨晚誰去看了電影？
(A) 女子昨晚去看電影了。
(B) 男子昨晚去看了電影。
(C) 兩人昨晚上都沒去看電影。

答題解說

答案：(C)。本題的答題關鍵就在於是否聽出 either 這個字。either 表示「也不～」，用於否定句，男子表示，他昨晚「也」沒有去看電影。對話裡面只有兩個人，而其中一人說出「..., either.」（也不～），這就表示「兩個人都沒去」，那麼答案就出來了。反之，如果聽到的是 So... 或 ..., too，那就表示「兩個人都有去」。

破題關鍵

如果有先瞄過三個選項內容，大概就會發現題目一定是跟「有沒有去看電影」這件事有關。而從錄音中一女一男的發言，應該不難聽出兩人都說了 didn't 吧！所以就算聽不懂 either，應該也選得出答案就是 (C) 了。

字詞解釋

either [ˋiðɚ] adv. 也不⋯　　**busy** [ˋbɪzɪ] adj. 忙碌的　　**paper** [ˋpepɚ] n. 報告
professor [prəˋfɛsɚ] n. 教授　　**hand in** v. 繳交

相關文法或用法補充

對話中的 I didn't, either. 在文法中稱為「附和句」，分成肯定與否定附和句兩種用法：

❶ 肯定用法：
　① A: I'm Taiwanese.（我是台灣人。）B: Me too. / I am, too. / So am I.（我也是。）
　② A: I like tea.（我喜歡茶。）B: I do, too. / So do I.（我也是。）
　　而如果第一句用助動詞（will / would / can / could / may / might / should / shall...）或是完成式（have / had + V-pp）時，則附和句就要使用同樣的時態做回覆。例如：A: I have been to Japan.（我去過日本。）B: I have, too. / So have I.（我也去過。）

❷ 否定用法：
　① A: I'm not Taiwanese.（我不是台灣人。）B: Me either. / I am not, either. / Neither am I.（我也不是。）
　② A: I don't like tea.（我不喜歡茶。）B: I don't, either. / Neither do I.（我也不喜歡。）

③ A: I haven't been to Japan.（我沒去過日本。）B: I haven't, either. / Neither have I.（我也沒去過。）

18. M: What is that noise?

W: It's from the ambulance behind.

M: Well, I have to give way for it, right?

W: You can say that again.

Question: What is the man probably doing?

(A) He's driving.　(B) He's cooking.　(C) He's sweeping the floor.

英文翻譯

男：那是什麼噪音？

女：是從後面的救護車傳來的。

男：嗯，我得讓道吧，是嗎？

女：那當然。

問題：這名男子可能正在做什麼？

(A) 他在開車。(B) 他在煮東西。(C) 他在掃地。

答題解說

答案：(A)。本題的對話內容雖然有點複雜，但是三個選項都很容易看懂意思，且還沒聽到錄音播放之前，應該也可以知道這題是要問「男子正在做什麼？」，因此，先看過選項的話，絕對可以更容易掌握對話中的關鍵字詞。而本題主要關鍵就在於是否聽出且聽懂 give way（讓道）這個片語，因為它不可能用在煮飯或看雜誌等情境之中。

破題關鍵

如果沒聽懂 give way 呢？其實從 ambulance behind（後面的救護車）一樣可以知道，這對男女應該是「車子裡」，所以不可能是 (B) 或 (C) 的答案了。

字詞解釋

noise [nɔɪz] **n.** 噪音　**ambulance** [ˋæmbjələns] **n.** 救護車　**behind** [bɪˋhaɪnd] **adv.** 在後面　**give way for** 為～讓路，為～讓道　**You can say that again.** 你說得沒錯。

相關文法或用法補充

after 和 behind 都有「在～之後」的意思，但兩者用法有很大的差別：

❶ after 當介系詞時，通常指「時間」的「之後」。例如：

We're going to leave at half after ten.（我們打算十點半離開。）

After you, please.（您先請。）

❷ after 當作副詞時表示「之後，以後」，主要是指時間的先後。此時 after 通常會與其他字構成副詞片語。例如：

Tom left at ten o'clock and Sam did so soon after.（Tom 在十點時離開，隨後不久 Sam 也離席了。）

❸ behind 當介系詞或副詞時，通常指「位置」的「之後」。例如：

Don't hide behind the door.（別躲在門後。）

The policeman seize the thief from behind.（警察從背後抓住了小偷。）

❹ after 和 behind 只有在當介系詞表示「隨～之後」時，才可劃上等號：

I came in after/behind John.（我在約翰後面進來。）

19. M: Hey Mary! Welcome to my birthday party.

W: Hi, John. Happy Birthday!

M: Thank you. By the way, who are the pretty girls?

W: Joy and Lily. They are my classmates.

M: Nice to meet you, Joy and Lily.

Question: Does the man know Joy and Lily?

(A) Yes, they are in the same class.

(B) Yes, Mary is their classmate.

(C) No, they just met for the first time.

英文翻譯

男：嘿，瑪麗！歡迎來我的生日派對。

女：嗨，約翰。生日快樂。

男：謝謝。對了，這些美女是誰？

女：喬和莉莉。她們是我的同學。

男：很高興認識妳們，喬和莉莉。

問題：男子認識喬和麗麗嗎？

(A) 是的，他們在同個班級中。

(B) 是的，瑪麗是她們的同學。

(C) 不，他們才第一次見面。

答題解說

答案：(C)。本題是問男子是否認識女子（Mary）帶來的兩位朋友（Joy and Lily），關鍵之處在於，男子的第二句問說 "... who are the pretty girls?"（這些美女是誰？）表示他之前沒見過 Joy 及 Lily。所以 (C) 的答案顯然是最正確的

了。至於最後男子說 Nice to meet you, Joy and Lily.，其實也可以用來判斷出他們是第一次見面。另外，本題刻意用選項 (A) 的 in the same class 和對話中女子所說的 classmates 來誤導聽者，必須注意問題句的主詞是該名男子。

本題也可用「刪除法」來作答。因為題目問的是男子是否認識 Joy 及 Lily，但對話中提到她們是女子（Mary）的同學，顯然 (A)、(B) 都不可能是答案。

welcome [ˈwɛlkəm] **adj.** 受歡迎的　　**birthday** [ˈbɝθˌde] **n.** 生日　　**pretty** [ˈprɪtɪ] **adj.** 漂亮的　　**classmate** [ˈklæsˌmet] **n.** 同班同學　　**for the first time** 第一次

初次見面時的打招呼用語，通常會說　Nice to meet/see you.，但如果是再次遇見對方就不能說 Nice to meet you.，否則對方心裡可能會 O.S.：你忘了我們見過面嗎？。第二次以上見到對方的場合，可以說 Nice to see you again.。另外，當彼此初次見面後要道別時，可以說 Nice meeting you. 或 Nice to have met you.。

20. **W: My name is Mary, and I'm twenty-six years old.**
    M: I'm Bill. I'm 8 years older than you.
    W: Wow, I can't believe it! You look younger than me.

    Question: Who's younger?
    (A) Bill is younger.
    (B) Mary is younger.
    (C) Mary is about the same age as Bill.

女：我的名字叫瑪麗，我現在 26 歲。
男：我叫比爾。我大你八歲。
女：哇噢，我真不敢相信！你看起來比我年輕。
問題：誰比較年輕？
(A) 比爾比較年輕。
(B) 瑪麗比較年輕。
(C) 瑪麗與比爾差不多年紀。

答案：(B)。本題是問年齡大小的問題，就文法觀點來說，是在考比較級的用法。比爾說「我大你八歲。」所以瑪麗年紀比較輕，答案當然就是 (B) 了。

第 1 回
第 2 回
第 3 回
第 4 回
第 5 回
第 6 回
第 7 回
第 8 回
第 9 回
第 10 回

破題關鍵

本題屬於自然命中法。首先，可以根據選項內容來反推出題目是針對年齡大小來提問的。確定了這一點之後，在聽錄音播放時就可以集中注意力來聽錄音中的比較用語（older than you），這樣問題就迎刃而解了。

字詞解釋

believe [brˋliv] v. 相信　**younger** [ˋjʌŋɚ] adj. 更年輕的（young 的比較級）　**the same age as** 和～一樣年紀

相關文法或用法補充

形容詞比較級的結構：帶有形容詞比較級的主要子句 + than 引導的從屬子句。而從屬子句會省略掉和主要子句相同的部分。例如：

❶ Mary is older than Jane (is). （瑪麗比簡年紀大一點。）

❷ There are more parks in Beijing than (there are parks) in Shanghai. （北京的公園比上海多。）

但有時候，當被比較的對象是很清楚明瞭或可以忽略時，其後可以不需要 than。例如：

❶ I am feeling better today. （今天我感覺好多了。）

❷ She said she will be more careful next time. （她說她下次會更加小心。）

另外，比較級前面可以加上表示「程度」的副詞。例如：My sister is two years older than me. （我姐姐比我大兩歲。）

21. W: What can I help you with, sir?

M: I'm looking for a pair of jeans for my daughter.

W: OK, this way, please. Let me show you.

Question: Where did the conversation take place?

(A) They are in a convenience store.

(B) They are at a fast food restaurant.

(C) They are in a department store.

英文翻譯

女：先生，有什麼我可以為您效勞的？

男：我在幫我女兒找一件牛仔褲。

女：好的，這邊請。我拿給您看看。

問題：這則對話可能發生在什麼地方？

(A) 他們在便利商店。

(B) 他們在速食餐廳。

(C) 他們在百貨公司。

答案：(C)。本題是問兩位說話者在什麼地方，但對話中完全沒提到與地點有關的名詞，所以必須聽懂對話中男女的交談內容。一開始女子說 What can I help you, sir?，而男子回答說 I'm looking for a pair of jeans...（我在找一件牛仔褲…），顯然這不會是在「便利商店」與「速食店」進行的情境對話。

本題其實可以用「刪除法」來解題，因為從一開始女子說 What can I help you with, sir? 可知，「便利商店」與「速食店」應可直接排除，接著男子說要找一件牛仔褲，那就更確定答案一定是 (C) 了。

look for 找尋　**a pair of** 一對，一雙　**jeans** [dʒinz] **n.** 牛仔褲　**convenience store** [kən`vinjəns] [stor] **n.** 便利商店　**fast food** [fæst] [fud] **n.** 速食　**department store** [dɪ`partmənt] [stor] **n.** 百貨公司

英文裡有不少特殊名詞只有複數形式，且有其固定搭配的「數量詞」，特別是一些「成雙成對的名詞」，例如 trousers（褲子）、clothes（衣服）、pants（長褲）、glasses（眼鏡）、shoes（鞋子）、sunglasses（太陽眼鏡）、scissors（剪刀）……這些單字可以用 a pair of / pairs of 等來修飾。另外，也有一些字看起來是複數名詞，但其實並不是，例如 news（消息）、means（手段）……等。

22. **M: How come you look so upset?**

W: Today is not my day.

M: Come on. What's wrong?

W: My boyfriend is "missing."

Question: What's wrong with the woman?
(A) She didn't get anything on her birthday.
(B) Her boyfriend has gone to Japan.
(C) Something bad happened to her.

男：你怎麼看起來這麼不高興？
女：我今天很倒楣。
男：別這樣。怎麼了？

女：我男朋友「不見了」。

問題：女子發生了什麼事？

(A) 她生日當天沒收到任何東西。

(B) 她男朋友已經去了日本。

(C) 她發生了不好的事。

答題解說

答案：(C)。本題問的是女子發生了什麼事，就對話內容來說，這類問題的答案通常會在說話者本身的言談當中。男子問女子說，「怎麼了？（What's wrong?）」女子回答說「我男朋友找不到人。（My boyfriend is missing.）」表示「不好的事（Something bad）」發生在她身上，所以答案是 (C)。選項 (A) 刻意用 birthday 來混淆對話中的 day。

破題關鍵

如果有先看過三個選項，在聽到題目問 What's wrong... 時，基本上選項 (C) 的 Something bad happened... 就一定是正確答案，甚至對話內容完全聽不懂也不影響答題。

字詞解釋

how come 何以…，為什麼…　**upset** [ʌpˋsɛt] **adj.** 心煩的，苦惱的　**wrong** [rɔn] **adj.** 錯誤的，不對的　**missing** [ˋmɪsɪŋ] **adj.** 失蹤的，找不到的

相關文法或用法補充

❶ How come 其實就是 Why（為什麼）的意思，屬於較為不正式或口語上的慣用語。若在商務、正式社交或公開場合，還是避開如此口語的用法較為妥當。另外，必須注意的是，How come 後面要接「直述句」，而 Why 後面須接疑問句。例如：Why do you take the bus? = How come you take the bus?。

❷ 不定代名詞 something 一般用於肯定句中。例如：Let's get something to drink.（我們去弄點東西喝。）但如果要用形容詞修飾 something，必須放在它的後面，在文法上也稱為「後位修飾」。比方說：There is something interesting in this film.（這部電影有些地方蠻有趣的。）

23. M: Where's Amy?

W: She told me she's been busy with her GEPT exam recently, so we might not see her today.

M: What a pity! I haven't seen her for years.

W: Neither have I.

Question: Did the woman see Amy recently?

(A) Yes, they studied together for the GEPT exam recently.

(B) No, they haven't seen each other for years.

(C) No, she's not been in contact with her for years.

男：Amy 人呢？

女：她告訴我她最近忙著英檢的考試，所以我們今天可能沒辦法見到她。

男：真是可惜！我已經好幾年沒看到她了。

女：我也是。

問題：女子最近見過 Amy 嗎？

(A) 是的，他們最近一起唸書準備考全民英檢。

(B) 不，她們已經多年未曾見面。

(C) 不，她已經多年沒有聯繫她了。

答題解說

答案：(B)。本題是 Yes-No 的問題。題目問的是女子最近是否與 Amy 見過面。這是在一個聚會的情境，男子問女子 Amy 在哪，女子回答他說，因為 Amy 最近在準備考試，不克前來。接下來才是重點：男子說「我已經好幾年沒看到她了」，而女子回答他 Neither have I.，這是所謂的「附和句」，等於 I haven't seen her for years, either.。所以答案就是 (B) 了。選項 (A) 是刻意提到 GEPT 來混淆答題，而選項 (B)、(C) 句尾都有 for years，讓人感覺 (C) 好像也可能是答案，但要注意的是，女子一開始就說 " She told me she's been busy..."，所以 (C) 是錯誤選項。

破題關鍵

關於「女子最近是否見過 Amy」的問題，只要注意聽出男子說的 "haven't seen her" 以及最後女子說 Neither haven't I 時，答案應該就很清楚了，但別被 (C) 選項的 in contact（有聯繫）誤導了。

字詞解釋

recently [ˈrisntlɪ] **adv.** 最近　　**pity** [ˈpɪtɪ] **n.** 可惜；同情　　**contact** [ˈkɑntækt] **n.** 聯繫，接觸

相關文法或用法補充

busy 雖然是個很基本的形容詞，但是與它搭配的介系詞經常是各大考試會考的，也是日常生活中經常用到的詞語：

❶ be busy + Ving（忙於做某事）

They are busy doing their homework.（他們正忙於做家庭作業。）

❷ be busy with/at/about + N.（忙於某事）

They are busy with their homework.（他們忙於做家庭作業。）

He is busy at work.（他忙著工作。）

What are you being busy about recently?（你最近都在忙些什麼？）

另外，如果要跟別人說「今天很忙」，千萬別說成 Today is busy.，因為 Today 不是「人」，沒辦法表現出「忙」的樣子，而應該說 I'm busy today.。如果要用 busy 來形容事物，也不是不行，但意思會變成「活動很多的、熱鬧的」。例如，It's been a busy day.（真是忙碌的一天。）、busy schedule（忙碌的行程）、busy highway（擁擠的公路）。

24. M: Alice, we missed you last Saturday night.

W: Last Saturday night...?

M: At our high school get-together.

W: Oops! I made a mistake. I thought it was this weekend.

M: Maybe you're really too busy. That's OK. Let's expect the next time.

Question: What are they talking about?

(A) Alice was absent from their high school reunion.

(B) Their high school reunion will be held this weekend.

(C) They forgot about an activity.

英文翻譯

男：Alice，我們上週六晚上沒看到妳。

女：上週六晚上……？

男：在我們高中的聚會上。

女：哎喲！我記錯了。我以為是這個週末。

男：也許妳真的太忙了。沒關係。我們期待下次吧！

問題：他們在討論什麼？

(A) Alice 沒有出席他們的高中同學會。

(B) 他們的高中同學會將於本週末舉辦。

(C) 他們忘了一場活動。

答題解說

答案：(A)。題目問的是對話內容為何，所以最好是先看過選項再仔細聆聽對話，才能正確作答。首先，男子第一句話就說，上週六晚上沒看到妳，而女子回答她記錯時間了，這表示她沒有去參加同學會，所以 (A) 是正確的答案。選項

（B）用 this weekend 來混淆對話中出現過的同一字詞，但事實上同學會已經過了；選項（C）是明顯錯誤的敘述。另外，雖然 get-together 是「動詞片語轉為名詞使用」的例子，意思是「相聚，聚會」，但即使不知道這件事，因為前面有 high school 當作修飾語，基本上可以猜得出來這指的是一場「活動」（activity），其實是不影響作答的。

男子第一句話中的 missed 就是最大的關鍵點，它可不是「思念」的意思，在這裡表示「錯過」。We missed you... 表示「我們沒有看到你…」，也就是「你人不在」的意思，而（A）選項的 absent（不在的，未出席的）正呼應了 missed 這個字，因此聽完（A）的敘述，大概心裡有個底：「這就是答案了。」順道一提，We missed you 當然也有可能是「我們思念你」的意思，但英文裡往往一個字詞有多重解釋，必須視前後文或對話的情境來判別。

miss [mɪs] v. 錯過；思念　**reunion** [ri`junjən] n. （親友等）重相聚　**mistake** [mɪ`stek] n. 錯誤　**hold** [hold] v. 舉行　**activity** [æk`tɪvətɪ] n. 活動

miss 這個動詞有三種意思：

❶ 錯過：可以用來表示「沒有參加」、「沒有注意到」、「沒有趕上」等。例如：

① A: Did you watch the baseball game last night? B: Oops! I miss it. （A：你昨晚有看棒球比賽嗎？B：糟糕！我錯過了。）

② Sorry, but I missed what you're saying. Would you please say again?（抱歉，我沒聽清楚你在說什麼。可以麻煩你再說一次嗎？）

❷ 思念：通常帶有悲傷的心情，思念的對象可能是「人」、「事情」、「物品」、「過去某一時刻」等。例如：I'm missing the days we got together.（我思念我們在一起的日子。）

❸ 漏掉：通常表示失去一次好機會。例如：I think you've missed the point.（我想你沒有了解重點在哪。）

25. M: How much time does it take to go to the post office?

W: It's about a 10-minute walk away.

M: That's not too far. Where could I find it?

W: Just turn left at the street corner, keep walking straight and you'll see it next to a 24-hour convenience store.

第 1 回

第 2 回

第 3 回

第 4 回

第 5 回

第 6 回

第 7 回

第 8 回

第 9 回

第 10 回

M: Thanks for your kindness.

Question: What might the man want to do?

(A) Get something to drink.　(B) Buy some stamps.　(C) See a doctor.

英文翻譯

男：到郵局要花多久時間？

女：走路大概 10 分鐘。

男：那不會太遠。哪裡可以找得到？

女：就在那街角左轉、一直直走，然後你會在一間 24 小時的便利商店旁邊看到它。

男：感謝妳的善心。

問題：男子可能要去做什麼？

(A) 買東西喝。(B) 買一些郵票。(C) 看醫生。

答題解說

答案：(B)。題目問的是男子「可能要做」的事情，雖然問題的答案顯然不會直接出現在對話中，但是可以很容易地從對話內容去判斷，屬於「推論」的題型。所以答案的線索通常會出現在男子的發言中。他一開始就問說去郵局要花多久時間，而從三個選項來看，去郵局可以做什麼，答案已經很明顯了，不會是「買飲料喝」或是「看醫生」吧！答案就是 (B) 的買郵票。stamp 是英檢初級範圍的字彙，應該要可以聽得懂。但須注意的是，別因為對話中出現 convenience store（便利商店），就選了 (A) 喔！

破題關鍵

本題關鍵字有兩個：post office 以及 stamp。只要有先看過三個選項，知道 stamp 的意思，也聽得懂對話中的 post office，基本上答案就出來了，而接下來的對話內容就跟答案沒什麼關係了。

字詞解釋

post office n. 郵局　**walk** [wɔk] n. 步行距離　**corner** [ˋkɔrnɚ] n. 轉角　**straight** [stret] adv. 直接地，一直地　**convenience store** n. 便利商店　**stamp** [stæmp] n. 郵票

相關文法或用法補充

take 用於花費「時間」，主詞都是花時間做的「某事」，其後若有第二個動詞，則只能用「不定詞」形式。其慣用句型為：

❶ It + takes + 人 + 時間 + to-V → 做（某事）花了（某人）（多久時間）

❷ V-ing（動名詞當主詞）+ takes + 人 + 時間 → 做（某事）花了（某人）（多久時間）

例如：It took me 3 hours to get home last night.
= Getting home took me 3 hours last night.
（我昨晚花了三小時才回到家。）

但若要以人為主詞，則動詞要改成 spend，且其後的第二個動詞要改為 Ving 形式。例如：

I spent 3 hours getting home last night.
（我昨晚花了三小時才回到家。）

第四部分 短文聽解

For question number 26, please look at the three pictures.

Question number 26: Listen to the following announcement. Where does it take place?

 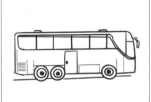 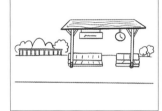

Ladies and gentlemen. Now we're close to the airport. The local time is 4:15 P.M. Because we start to go down, you should be in your seat, with your seatbelt firmly fixed. Besides, please make sure all electronic devices are turned off. Thanks.

英文翻譯

請看以下三張圖。並仔細聆聽接下來的廣播內容。這段廣播是在哪裡播出的？
各位女士及先生們。現在我們已接近機場了。當地時間是下午四點十五分。因為我們要開始下降了，您應坐在您的位置上，且繫緊您的安全帶。此外，請確認所有電子產品的電源已關閉。謝謝。

答題解說

答案：(A)。首先，題目句一定要聽懂，這是個 Where 開頭的問句，所以即使聽不出 take place（發生），看看三張圖，大概也知道要問的是「這裡的背景是在哪裡？」接著，仔細看過三張圖之後，在錄音播放內容裡，你只要可以聽出一開

始的關鍵字 airport，答案就出來了。airport 可是英檢初級單字表中的單字喔！

第
1
回

第
2
回

第
3
回

第
4
回

第
5
回

第
6
回

第
7
回

第
8
回

第
9
回

第
10
回

破題關鍵

這則廣播內容的關鍵字詞，除了一開始最基本的 airport 之外，其實接下來還有 local time（當地時間）、start to go down（開始下降）以及 electronic devices are turned off（關閉電子產品）等，都是在飛機上才會聽到的內容。只要可以聽出其中一部分，就會知道這是在飛機上的廣播。

字詞解釋

airport [ˈɛrˌport] **n.** 機場　　**local** [ˈlokl] **adj.** 當地的　　**seatbelt** [ˈsitbɛlt] **n.** 安全帶　　**firmly** [ˈfɝmlɪ] **adv.** 堅固地　　**fix** [fɪks] **v.** 固定　　**electronic** [ɪlɛkˈtrɑnɪk] **adj.** 電子的　　**device** [dɪˈvaɪs] **n.** 裝置　　**turn off** 關閉

相關文法或用法補充

這裡的 with your seatbelt firmly fixed 有個相當常見且很重要的文法：with 引導表「附帶條件或說明」的副詞片語。雖然更精確的說法是「獨立分詞構句」，但這對於英檢初級的考生來說是難了點，因此現階段您只要記住「with + 名詞」的後面可能會再接 V-ing（表主動）或 P.P.（表被動）。例如：

She felt surprised, <u>with</u> her mouth <u>wide open</u>.（她感到驚奇，且嘴巴張得開開的。）

He took a break on the sofa, <u>with</u> his eyes <u>closed</u>.（他在沙發上休息，眼睛閉著。）

For question number 27, please look at the three pictures.

Question number 27: Listen to the following message. What is Patty probably going to do later?

Hi, Patty. I just made a call to you, but you didn't answer your phone. I guess you're riding your motorcycle on the way home. I've e-mailed you three photos of the sample you asked for yesterday. Please let me know which one you would like to pick no later than this weekend. Thank you.

請看以下三張圖。並仔細聆聽以下訊息內容。Patty 晚些時候可能會去做什麼？

嗨，Patty。我剛打電話給妳，不過妳沒有接電話。我想妳正在騎車回家的路上。我已將妳昨天要求的 3 張樣品照片用電子郵件寄給妳了。請在本週末結束之前讓我知道妳想挑哪一張。謝謝妳。

答案：(C)。這則訊息的留言者表示，他將 3 張樣品照片用電子郵件寄給了受話者 Patty，並請她本週末結束前做出選擇，所以 Patty 接下來要做的事，就如同圖 (C) 所示，坐在電腦前收 E-mail 並檢視樣品照片。圖 (A) 刻意用挑選「實體」樣本，而圖 (B) 則用收到實體信件的圖來誤導答題。

題目要問的是受話者（Patty）未來或即將會去做什麼，所以關鍵就在播放內容中提及有關「計畫」、「（被）要求、指示、拜託……要去做的事情」。解題關鍵是 I've e-mailed you... Please let me know which one you pick... → 要收電子郵件 + 選擇樣本。

later [ˋletɚ] adv. 較晚地，後來　**make a call to**... 打電話給～　**sample** [ˋsæmpl] n. 樣品，樣本　**pick** [pɪk] v. 挑選

no later than 後面接一個「時間點」，表示「不超過某個時間點」，但須注意的是，這跟「by + 時間點」是不一樣的。以這則訊息留言內容中的 no later than this weekend 來說，意思很清楚：「不晚於這個週末」，亦即包含週六與週日，所以 Patty 最晚在週日午夜 12:00 之前回覆即可。但如果改成 by 或 before this weekend，則 Patty 最晚要在週五午夜 12:00 之前回覆了。

For question number 28, please look at the three pictures.

Question number 28: Listen to the following talk. What did Jerry eat for dinner last night?

Hi, my name is Jerry. I'd like to tell you all that I really enjoyed my dinner last night. Mommy cooked a big pot of everything, including many kinds of meat and vegetables. Daddy said we can eat it for several days so that Mommy doesn't have to cook every day.

中文翻譯

請看以下三張圖。並仔細聆聽播放的談話內容。Jerry 昨晚的晚餐吃什麼？

嗨，我的名字叫 Jerry。我想告訴大家，我真的好享受我昨晚的晚餐。媽咪煮了一大鍋包括多種肉類與蔬菜的各種食物。爹地說我們可以吃個好幾天，那麼媽咪就不必每天煮飯了。

答題解說

答案：(B)。談話內容中表示，說話者很喜歡昨晚的晚餐（dinner）。他母親煮了一大鍋（a big pot of）各種食物，就如同圖 (B) 的火鍋一樣，非常豐盛的晚餐。所以顯然答案就是 (B) 了。雖然圖 (A) 中也有肉（meat）有菜（vegetables），但 Jerry 昨晚並非吃烤肉。而談話內容完全沒有提到圖 (C) 所示的披薩（pizza）。

破題關鍵

題目要問的是昨晚吃什麼，所以要注意聽播放內容中提及有關「食物」、「食物容器」等有關的字詞。解題關鍵只有一個字：pot。雖然這個字是初級程度的單字，但在聽的時候往往不容易聽得出來（也可能聽成 part）。雖然會去選 (C) 的機會不大，但有可能被誤導去選 (A)，這時候只要注意到題目音檔裡有 cook（這個字出現了兩次，不應該忽略掉喔）這個動詞就不致於去選 (A) 了。

字詞解釋

pot [pɑt] n. 鍋子　**meat** [mit] n. 肉　**vegetable** [ˋvɛdʒətəbl̩] n. 蔬菜

相關文法或用法補充

既然本題關鍵字是 pot 那麼就再多認識一些「餐具」的英文吧！
fork（叉子）、spoon（湯匙）、dish/plate（盤子）、bowl（碗）、cup（帶把手的杯子）、glass（玻璃杯）、napkin（餐巾）、straw（吸管）、chopsticks（筷子）

第 1 回
第 2 回
第 3 回
第 4 回
第 5 回
第 6 回
第 7 回
第 8 回
第 9 回
第 10 回

For question number 29, please look at the three pictures.

Question number 29: Listen to the following story. Which picture best describes the short story?

Long ago, there was a single sheep living on a wide farm, and she had to eat a lot of grass every day. One day, it rained very hard, and she just wanted to stay in her small house. However, her owner didn't think so, so she still had to go outside to eat grass.

英文翻譯

請看以下三張圖。並仔細聆聽播放的故事內容。哪一張圖最能夠描述這則小故事的內容？

很久以前，在一個寬闊的農場上只住著一隻綿羊，而她每天必須吃很多草。有一天，雨下得很大，所以她只想待在她的小屋裡。然而，她的主人不這麼認為，所以她還是得到外面去吃草。

答題解說

答案：(B)。播放的內容提到，雨下得很大（it rained very hard），雖然羊兒想待在室內，但主人不肯（her owner didn't think so）。所以羊兒最終還是得在下雨天中去外面吃草（she still had to go outside to eat grass）。正確答案當然就是(B)了。

破題關鍵

題目要問的是故事內容符合哪一張圖。從三張圖可以看出一樣的地方是：一隻綿羊在吃草，而不一樣之處：室內或室外、下雨還是沒下雨。所以關鍵在於是否可以聽出「不同之處」。

字詞解釋

single [ˋsɪŋgl] **adj.** 單一的 **sheep** [ʃip] **n.** 綿羊 **grass** [græs] **n.** 草，牧草 **outside** [ˋaʊtˋsaɪd] **adv.** 在外面，在室外

相關文法或用法補充

There be... 的意思為「有～」，但真正的主詞是 be 動詞後的名詞，所以單複數變化也是由該名詞決定。此外，「There + be + N + Ving」的句型表示「主動」進行

某個動作，這個句型乃簡化自形容詞子句。例如：

There is a sheep which lives on a wide farm.（在一個寬闊的農場上住有一隻綿羊。）= There is a sheep living on a wide farm.（可省略 which + be 動詞）

另外，「There + be + N + P.P.」表示被動進行某個動作。例如：There were some cakes which were eaten by the kid.（有幾塊蛋糕被這小孩給吃掉了。）= There were some cakes eaten by the kid.

For question number 30. Please look at the three pictures.

Question number 30: Listen to the following weather report. What will the weather look like tomorrow?

Now, let's take a look at the weather forecast for tomorrow. It's going to be mostly cloudy in most cities and the temperatures will drop sharply in the evening, but there won't be rain, except in some mountain areas. So please remember to bring a coat if you're getting home late from work.

英文翻譯

請看以下三張圖。並仔細聆聽播放的氣象報導。明天的天氣會如何？
現在，我們來看看明天的天氣預報。大部分城市將是多雲時陰且傍晚氣溫將驟降，不過不會下雨，除了部分山區之外。所以，請記得帶件外套，如果你從工作場所晚歸的話。

答題解說

答案：(C)。播放的內容提到，明日大部分城市多雲時陰（mostly cloudy），但是不會下雨（there won't be rain），雖然也有提到部分山區會下雨，但這三張圖片看不出來是否在山區，所以正確答案當然就是 (C) 了。

破題關鍵

從三張圖來看，還沒聽到題目句也知道要注意聽播放內容中有關「天氣狀況」的語句，例如 mostly cloudy 以及 there won't be rain。

weather [ˋwɛðɚ] n. 天氣　　**forecast** [ˋforˌkæst] n. 預報，預測　　**cloudy** [ˋklaʊdɪ] adj. 多雲的，陰天的　　**temperature** [ˋtɛmprətʃɚ] n. 溫度　　**drop** [drɑp] v. 掉下，下降　**sharply** [ˋʃɑrplɪ] adv. 突然，猛烈地　　**except** [ɪkˋsɛpt] prep. 除～之外　　**coat** [kot] n. 外套，大衣

相關文法或用法補充

「天氣」的話題通常會在不知道要聊什麼時出現吧！但別只會說 good、bad、hot、cold、sunny... 這些沒什麼程度的英文喔！以下就來看看「關於天氣狀況，還有什麼字可以說」：

clear 晴朗的、mostly clear 晴時多雲、partly clear 多雲時晴、partly cloudy 多雲、mostly cloudy 多雲時陰、cloudy 陰天、dark clouds 烏雲、foggy 有霧、windy 颳風。

Reading | 全民英檢初級閱讀測驗　　　Round 1

第一部分 詞彙

1. **Don't go out on a typhoon day. _____ home is better.**（颱風天別外出。待在家比較好。）

   (A) Stay　(B) Staying　(C) To stay　(D) Stayed

   答題解說

   答案：(B)。四個選項是 stay 這個動詞的不同形態，因此應先就文法結構的觀點看。空格所在的這個句子已經有動詞（is）了，所以不可能填入動詞，故 (A) 可直接排除。本題要表達的意思是勸告的語意，所以應選擇動名詞的 (B) Staying；雖然不定詞也可以當主詞，但選 (C) To stay 的話，會形成「為了待在家比較好」的奇怪句意。另外，stay 是不及物動詞，沒有被動式（stayed）的用法。

   破題關鍵

   這題主要是考你區分「不定詞」與「動名詞」不同的概念。只要記住一個觀念：「不定詞」要表達的是兩個動作或兩件事「不同時」，而「動名詞」要表達的是兩個動作或兩件事「同時」發生。所以就本題來看，「不要出門」與「待在家」是兩個同時發生的事，所以要選動名詞的 Staying。

   字詞解釋

   typhoon [taɪˋfun] n. 颱風

   相關文法或用法補充

   颱風的英文是 typhoon，颱風天則是 typhoon day，但「颱風假」可不能說成 typhoon day off 喔！正確的說法是 day off due to the typhoon。例如：We're going to have a day off due to the typhoon.（我們明天將有個颱風假。）

2. **I like to listen to some _____ when I take a shower.**（我沖澡時喜歡聽一些音樂。）

   (A) activity　(B) building　(C) music　(D) calendar

   答題解說

   答案：(C)。句子大意是「洗澡時喜歡聽些 _____」，將各個選項套入空格中時，很容易了解「聽活動」、「聽建築物」、「聽日曆」都是不符合句意與邏輯

的說法。因此，「聽音樂」才是正確的說法。

本題關鍵就是 listen 這個動詞，listen to 後面必須接「與聲音有關」的名詞。選項中只有 (C) music（音樂）是與聲音有關的名詞。

shower [ˈʃaʊə] n. 淋浴　　**activity** [ækˈtɪvətɪ] n. 活動　　**calendar** [ˈkæləndə] n. 日曆

表示「聽」的 listen 與 hear 是很容易令人混淆的動詞。有人會問，英文裡的「聽力測驗」為什麼不是 hearing test，而是 listening test？其實，英文裡的 hearing test 是做健檢時的「聽力測驗」。另外，hear 是及物動詞，而 listen 是不及物動詞，後面通常搭配 to。

3. **Julia was rushed to hospital after she had a car ＿＿＿＿.**（Julia 出了一場車禍意外之後被緊急送往醫院去。）

(A) problem　　(B) society　　(C) question　　(D) accident

答案：(D)。句子大意是「在發生車子 ＿＿＿＿ 之後被緊急送到醫院去」。如果單就「she had a car ＿＿＿＿」來看，car society（汽車社團）是最不符合句意的說法。此外，為前面有「被火速送醫」的句子，顯然「車子問題」不會導致「送醫治療」吧！因此 car accident 才正確答案。

本題關鍵是「hospital 與 accident 的連結」。從一開始的 rushed to a hospital（火速送醫），可直接聯想到是「車禍意外」的結果。

rush [rʌʃ] v. 急送，急派　　**accident** [ˈæksədənt] n. 意外事故　　**society** [səˈsaɪətɪ] n. 社會，社團　　**problem** [ˈprɑbləm] n. 問題

rush 可以當動詞及名詞用，有「趕」的意思，常用於 in a rush（急忙地）、rush into the scene of an accident（衝進事故現場）、rush someone to hospital（將某人緊急送醫）、rush to answer the phone（急忙接電話）……等情境中。另外，「趕飛機／火車」千萬別說成 rush a plane/train，而要用 catch 這個動詞：have a plane/train to catch。（必須趕飛機／火車）。

第 1 回
第 2 回
第 3 回
第 4 回
第 5 回
第 6 回
第 7 回
第 8 回
第 9 回
第 10 回

4. **It's an ice cube. I can feel the _____ over my head.**（那是冰塊。我可以感覺到頭上寒意。）

   (A) heat　(B) goal　(C) coldness　(D) warm

   答題解說

   答案：(C)。如果單就「feel the _____」來看，四個名詞的選項似乎都是正確答案，所以還是必須根據整體句意來判斷。句子大意是「這東西是冰塊，因為可以感覺到 _____ 在頭上」。顯然答案應該是「寒冷（coldness）」，才能符合 ice cube（冰塊）的意思。其餘選項均不符句意。

   破題關鍵

   本題關鍵是「ice 與 coldness 的連結」。其餘的 heat（熱）、goal（目標）以及 warm（溫）都與 ice（冰）沒有任何關係。

   字詞解釋

   cube [kjub] n. 塊，立方體　**heat** [hit] n. 熱　**goal** [gol] n. 目標　**coldness** [ˋkoldnɪs] n. 冷，寒冷　**warm** [wɔrm] n. 暖和的狀態

   相關文法或用法補充

   文法裡有所謂「連綴動詞」，feel 就是其中之一，常用於「連綴動詞 + 形容詞」的結構。不過 feel 也可以當及物動詞，後面接名詞作為其受詞，表示「觸摸看看」，例如 feel the cloth to see its quality（摸看看這布料，看它品質好不好）。

5. **She _____ a diary in English to practice her writing ability.**（她寫英文日記來練習她的寫作能力。）

   (A) writes　(B) keeps　(C) holds　(D) draws

   答題解說

   答案：(B)。四個選項都是不同意思的及物動詞，其後均可接名詞作為其受詞，所以還是必須根據整體句意來判斷。句子大意是「_____ 英文日記來練習寫作能力」。顯然，應該是「『寫』日記～」的意思，而英文裡寫日記的「寫」可不是用 write，而是用 keep，因為「寫日記」是一種「習慣、持續性的行為」。

   破題關鍵

   「寫日記」的英文說法就是 "keep a diary" 為常見固定用語，沒有 "write a diary" 的說法。因此本題看到空格後面的 diary 時，應該要直接想到 keep 這個動詞。

diary [ˋdaɪərɪ] n. 日記　　**practice** [ˋpræktɪs] v. 練習　　**ability** [əˋbɪlətɪ] n. 能力　　**draw** [drɔ] v. 畫

相關文法或用法補充

其實學英文，最難的一點就是「搭配詞」（collocation）。為什麼「寫日記」是 keep a diary 而不是 write a diary？為什麼「開支票」是 write a check 而不是 open a check？為什麼我們常常會「搭配錯誤」呢？主要原因之一就是受到中文的影響！以下是幾個常見受中文干擾的搭配用語，讓你擺脫中文思維：

「喝湯」是 eat soup，不是 drink soup；「擦香水」是 wear perfume，不是 wipe/rub perfume；「濃茶」是 strong tea，不是 thick tea；「趕飛機」是 have a plane to catch，不是 rush a plane；「接電話」是 take/answer a call，不是 accept/receive a call；「參加考試」是 take an exam，不是 attend/join an exam。

6. **My son is _____ a helpful kid that everyone in the class likes him.**
（我兒子是個如此樂於助人的小孩，所以班上每個人都喜歡他。）

⒜ what　　⒝ so　　⒞ such　　⒟ some

答題解說

答案：⒞。空格前是 be 動詞 is，後面是不定冠詞 a。英文裡沒有 "so a…" 以及 "some a..." 的用法，所以 ⒝、⒟ 可直接排除。接下來要注意的是 kid 後面的 that，such... that... 是很常見的固定用語，表示「如此～以致於～」，所以 ⒜ 也是錯的。

破題關鍵

看到 so 和 such 兩個選項，再看到後面的 that 時，大概就知道這題要考的是「如此～以致於～」的表達，只要掌握住「so + adj + N. + that」以及「such a + adj. + N.」的不同句型結構，就可以迎刃而解了。

字詞解釋

helpful [ˋhɛlpfəl] adj. 樂於助人的，有幫助的

相關文法或用法補充

helpful 來自 help 加上形容詞字尾 -ful，它可以用來修飾「事物」表示「有用的，有幫助的」，也可以用來形容「人」，表示「樂於助人的」。例如：helpful advisor（樂於助人的顧問）、give helpful advice（給予有用的建議）。

7. **David can do the job by _____. He said he won't need help.**（David 可以自己做這份工作。他說他不需要幫忙。）

(A) himself　(B) herself　(C) themselves　(D) myself

答題解說

答案：(A)。從四個選項來看，這是考「反身代名詞」的題目。因為主詞是 David，所以要表達「靠他自己」時要用 by himself。

破題關鍵

有些題目可以直接看選項，判斷「考點」為何，然後掌握與它連結的關鍵字，答案就出來了。本題的連結關係是：David → himself。

字詞解釋

by oneself 靠某人自己

相關文法或用法補充

反身代名詞的字尾是 -self（單數）或 -selves（複數）：

人稱	單數	複數
第 1 人稱	myself	ourselves
第 2 人稱	yourself	yourselves
第 3 人稱	himself、herself、itself	themselves

8. **Mother has _____ housework to do every day.**（母親每天都有許多家務事要做。）

(A) many　(B) several　(C) a lot of　(D) few

答題解說

答案：(C)。空格後面是 housework 這個不可數名詞，再從四個選項來看，可以判斷這是考「修飾不可數名詞的形容詞」的題目。many（許多的）、several（幾個的）以及 few（很少的）後面都必須接複數可數名詞。a lot of 後面可接可數或不可數名詞。

破題關鍵

「知道 housework 是不可數名詞」是主要關鍵，但如果不知道也沒關係，看到它後面沒有加 -s，且前面也沒有冠詞（a/the），基本上也很容易判斷是不可數名詞。

第 1 回
第 2 回
第 3 回
第 4 回
第 5 回
第 6 回
第 7 回
第 8 回
第 9 回
第 10 回

housework [ˋhaʊsˏwɝk] **n.** 家務事

修飾可數或不可數名詞的形容詞，整理如下：

❶ 修飾可數名詞：many、a few、few、a/the number of、dozens of

❷ 修飾不可數名詞：little、a little of、much、a bit of、an amount of、a great deal of

❸ 修飾可數及不可數名詞：some/any、more、most、all、enough、a lot of / lots of、no、plenty of

9. **I'm about to get off at the next exit, and _____ be there very soon.**（我就要下匝道了，很快就會抵達那裡。）

(A) would　　(B) will　　(C) won't　　(D) are going to

答案：(B)。四個選項都是助動詞，但因為主詞是 I，所以 (D) are going to 可直接先排除掉。句子大意是「就快要下匝道，且即將抵達」，所以 (C) won't 不符句意。而助動詞 would 除了是 will 的過去式，也帶有不確定的臆測意味，也不符句意。

本題的主要參考指標是前面的 I'm about to...，"be about to-V" 的意思與 be going to 很接近，但是更強調「就要⋯，即將⋯」，當然也表示「未來」的時態。

be about to-V 即將　　**get off** 駛離　　**exit** [ˋɛksɪt] **n.** 出口，（快速道路的）匝道

「be about to」和「will」與「be going to」一樣都是用來表示未來即將、將要做某些事，但又有些不同。比方說，如果你正要打電話給某人，正好這時候對方打電話來問「你怎麼沒打給我？」這時候你就可以說 "Oh! I'm about to call you."，這會比 I'm going to call you." 所表現的時間差距更短。當然，如果你只是想敷衍對方，也可以說 I will call you.。

10. There are beautiful flowers and trees on _____ sides of the road.（這道路的兩邊都有美麗的花與樹。）

(A) each (B) both (C) all (D) three

> 答題解說

答案：（B）。句子大意是「路的『兩邊』有花與樹」，所以正確答案應為 both。空格後面的名詞為複數（sides），因此不可能用 each 來修飾。至於 all 與 three 雖可修飾複數名詞，但不符合語意與邏輯。

> 破題關鍵

這題要考的是關鍵字 road 的連結關係。「道路」本來就只有「兩側」、「兩邊」，所以只能用 both 來修飾。

> 字詞解釋

beautiful [`bjutəfəl] **adj.** 美麗的　　**flower** [`flaʊɚ] **n.** 花

> 相關文法或用法補充

both 可當形容詞或限定詞，也可以當代名詞、副詞用，意思是「兩者都」：

❶ Both her parents are doctors. → 形容詞用法
❷ Both of her parents are doctors. → 代名詞用法
❸ I like orange and apple both. → 副詞用法

第二部分 段落填空

Questions 11-14

Mary was doing the dishes when there was a power failure. She had to find a flashlight, but she **couldn't**. What's worse, she had to comfort her little daughter, who was then screaming terribly because she was afraid of the **dark**. After Mary spent much effort making her daughter fall asleep, and when she was ready to go to bed, an ambulance rushed near and woke the little girl up. Then, **the thunder was heard from the sky**, so her daughter cried loudly again, when it was already 4:30 A.M. And of course, she had to calm down her baby again, and this took her almost an hour. Then at 6:00 A.M., her alarm clock went off; it was time **to get** up and go to work.

> 中文翻譯　瑪麗在洗碗盤時，突然停電了。她得找支手電筒，不過她卻找不到。更糟的是，她還得安慰她的小女兒，停電的當時她因為怕黑而放聲尖叫。在瑪

麗花了好大力氣才讓女兒睡著之後，且當她準備要去睡覺時，一輛救護車急駛而近，且把她女兒吵醒了。然後，天空響起一陣雷聲，所以她女兒又放聲大哭了，而當時已經凌晨四點半了。而且當然，她又得再次讓她女兒安靜下來了，而這又耗了她將近一個小時的時間。到了早上六點，她的鬧鐘響起；是她該起床去上班的時候了。

答題解說

11. 答案：(D)。空格前有對等連接詞 but，而前面是用過去式的動詞（had to），所以空格所在的這個句子當然也必須是過去式。選項中 (C) 與 (D) 都是過去式的助動詞。根據後面的連接性副詞（What's worse 更糟的是），表示前面發生的這件事不是什麼好事，所以「無法找到手電筒」是比較符合前後文句意的答案。

12. 答案：(B)。四個選項是不同意思的名詞，所以應根據前後文句意判斷。前面提到了 power failure（停電）、look for a flashlight（找手電筒），因此空格所在的這個句子要表達的應該是「小孩子怕黑」，因此正確答案為 (B)。

13. 答案：(B)。這是要挑選一個句子、子句或句子的一部分放入空格後，確認空格前後和空格句之間的連接關係，是否讓句意顯得自然通順，所以必須對照上下文或根據整段文章的意旨。空格後面句子提到「『所以』她女兒又放聲大哭了」，顯然應填入一個讓她女兒又放聲大哭的「原因」，正確答案應為 (B)「天空響起一陣雷聲」。(A)、(C) 與 (D) 明顯不會是讓小孩放聲大哭的原因。以下是其餘選項句子的翻譯：

(A) 瑪麗試著唱首歌給她女兒聽

(C) 所幸，沒有人受傷

(D) 雨突然停了

14. 答案：(A)。四個選項是同一個動詞的不同形態，應直接根據文法與句構來判斷。「it + be 動詞 + time + 不定詞（to-V）」為固定句型，意思是「是該……的時候了。」故正確答案為 (A)。

破題關鍵

11. 看到對等連接詞必須立即想到：結構、時態對等，然後用「刪除法」排除掉 (A)、(B) 兩個選項後，根據句意選出正確答案。

12. 當選項都是相同詞類時，要選出正確答案的話，只能透過理解句意了。但如果對於前後文還是一知半解，可以從其中的關鍵字詞去聯想正確答案。看到前面有「停電」（power failure）的話，就可以肯定答案是「怕黑」（afraid of the dark）了。

13. 這個適當的句子主詞是 the thunder（雷聲，打雷），要表達的是「可以聽見天空中傳來的雷聲」，因此雷聲是「被聽到」的，動詞應用被動式，故正確答案為 (B)。動詞 hear 的變化形為 hear → heard → heard。動詞 hear 的主詞一定是「活

生生」的人或動物等，但是當主詞不是「人」而是「物」時，那一定要用被動式了。

14. 基本上這題只要看到 "it was time"，答案就出來了。「it's time to-V / that...」是很基礎且常見的句型喔！

字詞解釋

do the dishes 洗碗盤　**power failure** n. [ˋpaʊɚ] [ˋfeljɚ] 斷電　**flashlight** [ˋflæʃ͵laɪt] n. 手電筒　**what's worse** adv. 更糟的是　**comfort** [ˋkʌmfɚt] v. 安撫　**scream** [skrim] v. 尖叫　**terribly** [ˋtɛrəblɪ] adv. 可怕地，非常　**be afraid of** 害怕～　**dark** [dɑrk] n. 黑暗　**effort** [ˋɛfɚt] n. 努力　**fall asleep** 睡著　**ambulance** [ˋæmbjələns] n. 救護車　**rush** [rʌʃ] v. 趕忙　**loudly** [ˋlaʊdlɪ] adv. 大聲地　**calm down** 使安靜下來　**go off** （鈴聲、鬧鐘等）響起　**terrible** [ˋtɛrəbl] adj. 可怕的　**accident** [ˋæksədənt] n. 意外　**suddenly** [ˋsʌdn̩lɪ] adv. 突然地

相關文法觀念補充

11. 「對等連接詞」用來連接兩個「對等的」單字（可能是動詞、名詞、形容詞或副詞）、片語或子句。對等連接詞主要有 and、but 以及 or 這三個。

12. dark 與 black 雖然都有「黑」的意思，但兩者意思差異很大。dark 表示「黑暗的、暗色的」，例如「天快變黑了。」可以說 It's getting dark。而 black 專指顏色的「黑」，例如「黑色的長褲」是 black pants。

13. 表示「聽」的 listen 與 hear 是很容易令人混淆的動詞。有人會問，英文裡的「聽力測驗」為什麼不是 hearing test，而是 listening test？其實，英文裡的 hearing test 是做健檢時的「聽力測驗」。另外，hear 是及物動詞，而 listen 是不及物動詞，後面通常搭配 to。

14. It's time 後面接子句的話，要注意子句中的動詞必須用「過去簡單式」。例如：It's time (that) you pulled yourself together.（是你該振作起來的時候了。）

Questions 15-18

Dozens of years ago, we could find many different kinds of maps of our towns. For example, there were some maps which **showed** all the electrical lines in your town. If you had lived in a city **with** bus service, you could have found a map of bus routes. Besides, there were also street maps that might be more useful to you. **To get a street map of your city should not be too difficult.** If you do not know **where** to find street maps, you might try gas stations, visitor centers, or bookstores.

中文翻譯 數十年前，我們可以找到很多不同種類的我們城鎮的地圖。例如，有一些地圖呈現了你城鎮裡所有的電路管線。假如你住在一個有公車服務的城市

裡，你就可能可以找到公車路線圖。此外，還有可能對你來說更有用的街道圖。要取得一張城市的街道圖應該不會太難。假如你不知道哪裡可以找到街道圖，你可以試著到加油站、遊客中心或書店找找看。

答題解說

15. 答案：(B)。本句是考動詞時態的問題，整篇一開始就看到 Dozens of years ago...（數十年前…），而且主要子句的時態是過去式（were），因此 which 引導的形容詞子句也必須用過去式，故正確答案為(B)。

16. 答案：(C)。在 If 引導的這個條件句中，空格前後都是名詞，顯然應填入一個介系詞。而句意是，「假如你住在一個城市 ＿＿＿＿＿ 公車服務，你可以找到公車路線圖。」所以應該是「住在一個有公車服務的城市裡」，表示「帶有」的 with 才是正確答案。

17. 答案：(A)。這是要挑選一個句子、子句或句子的一部分放入空格後，確認空格前後和空格句之間的連接關係，是否能讓句意顯得自然通順。空格前一句提到「還有街道圖，可能對你來說更有用。」而後面這句也提到「街道圖」（...to find street maps, you might try...），因此空格這句一定是跟街道圖相關，故 (A) To get a street map of your city should not be too difficult.（要取得一張城市的街道圖應該不會太難。）是正確答案。以下是其餘選項句子的翻譯：
(B) 你也可以選擇使用手機。
(C) 實際上沒有辦法找到一張有用的地圖。
(D) 否則，你可以找當地人問路。

18. 答案：(A)。首先，就文法結構而言，選項中的 what 可直接排除，因為空格後面 to find 已經有受詞了。接著應從句意去判斷。後面主要子句的意思是「你可以試著到加油站、遊客中心或書店找找看」，所以前面條件句應該是「假如你不知道『哪裡』找街道圖」的意思。故正確答案是(A)。

破題關鍵

15. 答題關鍵是：在解題時，要一直記住這整篇都是在描述過去的事情，所以動詞必須用過去式。

16. 介系詞的用法。表示「一個有～的城市」，要用 with 來表示。翻譯時，with 常被翻成「有，帶有，附帶」。

17. 此類題型一樣要找關鍵字詞。這裡的關鍵是 street maps 以及最後提到可以去哪些地方取得地圖，而且一開始就提到場景是「數十年前」，所以不會是用手機，而其他兩個選項也都是不相關的。

18. 首先，刪去最不可能的答案 (B) what 之後，只要再看到後面有三個「地點」（gas stations, visitor centers, or bookstores），答案就出來了。

字詞解釋

several [`sɛvərəl] **adj.** 數個的　**different** [`dɪfərənt] **adj.** 不同的　**map** [mæp] **n.** 地圖　**electrical** [ɪ`lɛktrɪkl] **adj.** 電的　**route** [rut] **n.** 路線，航線　**difficult** [`dɪfə͵kəlt] **adj.** 困難的　**gas station** 加油站　**direction** [də`rɛkʃən] **n.** 方向　**local** [`lokl] **adj.** 當地的，本地的

相關文法觀念補充

15. 關係代名詞當主詞時，關係子句的動詞單複數，必須跟隨關係代名詞所代替的先行詞。

16. 這裡的 with 用法是「有～的」的意思。例如：a girl with long hair（長髮的女孩）、a room with a high ceiling（天花板很高的房間）

17. To get a street map... 這句話是以不定詞當作主詞，視為單數，此時句子的動詞必須用第三人稱單數。

18. 「疑問詞 + 不定詞（to-V）」= 名詞片語，它簡化自「疑問詞引導的名詞子句」，這樣的文法觀念要記起來喔！

第三部分 閱讀理解

Questions 19-21

中文翻譯

寄件人	Service@fashionsop.com.tw
收件人	不公開收件者
主旨	嘗試 Fashion Shop

敬啟者：

　　Fashion Shop 告訴您展開自己的事業是多麼容易的事。也許你會想賣時尚物品，像是帽子、洋裝、長褲、手錶、戒指……等。您只要花大約一分鐘的時間加入我們，就可以做得到，而開設您的網路商店只要花不到十分鐘。

每個月只要 5 美元，限時免費。
按下面的按鈕，來取得絕佳體驗！

現在就加入

如有任何疑問，請寄電子郵件至 Service@fashionsop.com.tw 。
謹啟
客服部
八月一日

按下「現在就加入」按鈕之後，您會看到以下網頁畫面。

Q www.fashionshop.com/register

免費試用 Fashion Shop
本月底前開始七天免費試用，馬上就可以開始和全世界的顧客做生意！您
必須透過信用卡支付。
已經是會員了嗎？在此登入。
姓名

電子郵件地址

公司名稱

信用卡號碼

特別注意
1. 新會員在開設自己的商店前，須預先支付三個月的會員費。
2. 如果您在七天試用期內不想繼續使用，請撥打 5523-21688 與我們聯
   絡，以取得退款。

19. 這封電子郵件的目的為何？
    (A) 告知會員一些好消息
    (B) 邀請人們加入
    (C) 提醒會員一個重要事件
    (D) 分享美好的經驗

20. 電子郵件中的「a limited time」所指為何？
    (A) 從現在起的七天沒有免費試用。
    (B) 從現在起到八月三十一日都可以免費試用。
    (C) 新會員可多享有七天的會員。
    (D) 新會員在七天免費試用之後需要輸入信用卡號碼。

21. 新會員一開始必須支付多少費用？
    (A) $5　(B) $10　(C) $15　(D) $20

答題解說

19. 答案：(B)。第三句提到 "You're able to make it just by joining us..."，顯然這則廣告的目的就是「邀請人們加入（Fashion Shop）」，一起展開新的事業。

20. 答案：(C)。本題需要整合與歸納兩篇文本的資訊才能夠得到正確的答案。題目中的 a limited time 出現在電子郵件裡：Only $5 per month, and free for a limited time!（每個月只要 5 美元，限時免費。）接著在第二篇的網頁一開始也提到 free 的部分："Start a 7-day free trial before the end of this month to begin..."（本月底前開始七天免費試用，馬上就可以開始…）所以這裡的「限時」其實有兩層意思：一個是「七天」，一個是「八月底前」。因此，選項中只有 (C) 的「新會員可多享有七天的會員期。」符合答案。

21. 答案：(C)。本題需要整合與歸納兩篇文本的資訊才能夠得到正確的答案。第一篇的廣告電郵中提到價錢的部分是：Only $5 per month, and...。接著要看到第二篇的網頁中 SPECIAL NOTE 底下的文字提到，A new member needs to first pay a three-month membership fee before his/her new store can be opened.（新會員在開始自己的商店前，須預先支付三個月的會員費。）所以新會員一開始必須先支付 15 美元才能開始使用 Fashion Shop。

破題關鍵

19. 這一題比較快速且關鍵的解題方式，就是找到「關鍵字詞（Fashion Shop）」之後，通常下一句或下下一句就會告訴你答案了。

20. (A) 的敘述看似正確，但它的意思是「從現在 8 月 1 日起的七天，也就是說到 8 月 7 日間註冊的新會員沒有免費試用期，這是不正確的說法。

21. limit 當動詞時表示「限制」，過去分詞 limited 可當形容詞用，表示「受到限制

57

的」，雖然本題要看懂題目不難，不過底下四個選項也都跟時間限制有關，必須每一句仔細看清楚才行。這裡的「免費試用」其實就是一開始七天免費，但必須先支付費用，如果七天之內不想繼續使用，可以退費的機制。

字詞解釋

business [`bɪznɪs] n. 事業，公司  **fashionable** [`fæʃənəbl] adj. 流行的，時尚的
goods [gʊdz] n. 商品，貨物 **customer** [`kʌstəmɚ] n. 顧客，買主 **click** [klɪk] n. 點擊
（連結、按鈕等） **button** [`bʌtn] n. 按鈕  **fantastic** [fæn`tæstɪk] adj. 極好的
experience [ɪk`spɪrɪəns] n. 經驗，體驗  **be aimed at**... 以～為目標  **invite** [ɪn`vaɪt] v.
邀請 **remind** [rɪ`maɪnd] v. 提醒  **event** [ɪ`vɛnt] n. 事件，大事 **trial** [`traɪəl] n. 試用，
試驗 **credit** [`krɛdɪt] n. 信用；賒帳  **membership** [`mɛmbɚˌʃɪp] n. 會員身分（或資
格） **fee** [fi] n. 費用 **contact** [`kɑntækt] v. 接觸；聯絡  **continue** [kən`tɪnjʊ] v. 繼續
additional [ə`dɪʃənl] adj. 附加的，額外的 **type in** 輸入，鍵入 **at first** 一開始時

相關文法或用法補充

❶ "make it" 讓人想到一句很有名的廣告詞：Trust me. You can make it!。所以它的意思就是「做得到」。值得一提的是，這裡的 it 其實沒有指前文中的任何一個事物，只要記住 "make it" 就是「做到；趕上」的意思。例如：She made it in films.（她在電影界很成功。）、We just made it in time for the train.（我們正好趕上火車。）

❶ 「in + 一小段時間」，很多人都會以為是「在～時間之內」，但其實是「在～（一段時間）之後」的意思。例如，I'll be back in 5 minutes.，不是「我 5 分鐘之內回來。」而是「我 5 分鐘之後回來。」

Questions 22-24

中文翻譯

寄件人	david_chang@yourmail.com
收件人	john_hsu@@yourmail.com
主旨	回覆：中秋節活動

親愛的約翰：

　　希望你在中秋假期時的烤肉派對中玩得愉快。不過，我們沒有烤肉，因為我們的陽台太小，無法做這樣的活動，而且我無法找到另外一個好地方。

第 1 回
第 2 回
第 3 回
第 4 回
第 5 回
第 6 回
第 7 回
第 8 回
第 9 回
第 10 回

對了，今年的中秋節正好是我太太瑪麗的生日。我們一起出去吃了晚餐。我們決定去餐廳慶祝這樣一個特別的日子。我訂好了位子。在我們抵達餐廳之後，我點了一份牛排及一瓶啤酒。瑪麗點了雞排及一杯香檳。每一份餐點都附有沙拉。食物非常美味！

祝你一切順利，並期待很快與你見面。

大衛

22. 大衛這封電子郵件的目的為何？
    (A) 接受一項邀請
    (B) 提供建議
    (C) 告知生活近況
    (D) 進行未來計畫

23. 這對夫婦為何外出吃晚餐？
    (A) 為了討論找褓姆的事　　　(B) 為了慶祝他們小孩的生日
    (C) 因為附近有一家新的餐廳　(D) 因為那是個特別的日子

24. 這對夫婦在餐廳裡沒有點什麼？
    (A) 牛排　(B) 雞排　(C) 飲料　(D) 沙拉

答題解說

這個題組是一封電子郵件，內容主要關於 David 回覆 John 中秋節當天在做什麼。

22. 答案：(C)。題目要問的是這封電子郵件的目的（或主旨），可以先從第一段找線索：從「我們沒有烤肉，因為我們的陽台太小…」這部分可以得知，要告訴寄件者中秋節當天他們沒有烤肉，所以下面這一段既要告訴對方中秋節當天他們（夫妻倆）在做什麼。也就是很久不見的朋友來信問候，於是告知對方生活近況。所以正確答案是 (C) To tell about a recent life event。

23. 答案：(D)。第二段第二句就是與題目相關的句子：「我們一起出去吃了晚餐。」通常接著就會對於第一句進行說明（也就是外出吃飯的原因）：「中秋節是瑪麗的生日。所以我們決定去餐廳慶祝這樣一個特別的日子。」選項 (A)、(B)、(C) 分別用文章中出現過的褓姆（babysitter）、生日（birthday）、餐廳（restaurant）來誤導答題。

24. 答案：(D)。文章中提到說話者「我點了一份牛排及一瓶啤酒」，而他的太太則「點了雞排及一杯香檳」，但「沙拉（salad）」是「每一份餐點都有附的」，並非「點餐」來的，故正確答案應為 (D)。

22. 信件的主旨通常看完第一段,或是再加上第二段前一、兩句就可以得知,因此從第一段告知對方中秋節沒有烤肉,以及第二段一開始提到當天去慶祝太太生日,就能夠知道主旨是「告知近況」。

23. 題目是問「這對夫婦外出吃晚餐」的原因,首先找到第一句的 "went out for dinner" 之後,答案通常會在下一句或下下一句出現:the Moon Festival... happened to be.... Mary's birthday...

24. 這題要問的「點餐」的問題,關鍵字是 order。可以從 "I ordered... Mary ordered..." 這部分找答案。隨後的 Each meal came with... 是「每份餐附有…」的意思。

字詞解釋

usually [ˋjuʒʊəlɪ] adv. 通常   **though** [ðo] adv. 然而,不過   **decide** [dɪˋsaɪd] v. 決定 **celebrate** [ˋsɛlə͵bret] v. 慶祝   **babysitter** [ˋbebɪsɪtɚ] n. 褓姆   **for the time being** adv. 暫時   **arrive** [əˋraɪv] v. 抵達   **cutlet** [ˋkʌtlɪt] n. 肉片,肉排   **champagne** [ʃæmˋpen] n. 香檳   **delicious** [dɪˋlɪʃəs] adj. 美味的   **have a good time** 玩得快樂

相關文法或用法補充

❶ 書本(book)這個字當動詞可以表示「預訂」(另一個常見的動詞是 reserve),它的受詞可能是旅館房間、車票、機票、餐廳座位等。這裡要特別一提的是,同學朋友要聚餐時,通常要「訂餐廳」,但千萬別說成 book a restaurant,那會變成要把整家餐廳「包下來」了,你要訂的是「桌子」。比方說,打電話去餐廳時,可以說「我要訂位子,5 個人」,英文是 I'd like to book/reserve a table of five.。

❷ order 當動詞本來有「命令」的意思,但去餐廳吃飯要點餐時,也可以拿來用喔!比方說,服務生可能會對你說「您準備要點餐了嗎?」英文就是 Are you ready to order (any food/dishes)?。不過,如果吃完飯後要去 KTV 唱歌,要表達「點一首歌」的話,就不是用 order 了,而是 request a song。request 是「要求」的意思。

Questions 25-27

中文翻譯

　　安迪是個單身的老人家,不過他過得很快樂。每天都有許多朋友到他的住處。他們會喝些茶以及聊天,或是一整個下午在下棋。有件事是,他很健忘。例如,他常常忘記走了哪一步棋。

　　有一天,他外出繞著公園慢跑時,他被一顆飛來的球擊中頭部。他不知道球是從哪裡飛來的。隔天他覺得頭痛,於是他決定去看醫生。在一間小醫院中,醫生問他:「你幾歲了?」安迪回答,「王醫生,我不記得了。但是讓我試著想想看。」

幾分鐘後，他說「醫生，我現在想起來了！在我結婚的時候，我 30 歲，而我太太 20 歲。現在我太太是 40 歲，是 20 歲的兩倍，所以我是 30 歲的兩倍。我現在是 60 歲了，對不對？」

醫師給了他一個微笑，然後問他，「你太太呢？她沒跟你一起來嗎？」安迪說，「噢，王醫師。我忘了我太太去年就過世了。」

25. 這個故事主要關於什麼？
　　(A) 一個老人家與他太太　　　　(B) 一位友善的醫師
　　(C) 一個愛下棋的人　　　　　　(D) 一個記性很差的老人

26. 安迪什麼時候結婚？
　　(A) 三十年前　　　　　　　　　(B) 二十年前
　　(C) 二十歲時　　　　　　　　　(D) 在他四十歲時

27. 以下何者是正確的？
　　(A) 安迪的太太比他年輕十歲。
　　(B) 安迪比他太太大二十歲。
　　(C) 安迪現在是三十歲的兩倍。
　　(D) 他們結婚時，安迪的太太是四十歲。

答題解說

這是一則現實生活中的人物介紹故事。內容敘述一個單身的老人家，從容易健忘到幾乎要得了老年癡呆症的過程。

25. 答案：(D)。題目問的是本篇故事的主旨，第一段第一句說，安迪是個單身的老人家。顯然這個故事就是在講這個老人家，故選項 (B) 可直接排除。雖然第一段有提到老人家常和一些朋友下棋，但只要稍微掃一下後面兩段的內容，都沒有繼續提到下棋的事，顯然 (C) 也不會是正確答案。接下來二、三段提到他太太的部分，只是醫生在診斷時提到，也不是故事重點。所以我們可從第一段提到「有件事是，他很健忘。」以及整篇的最後一句「我忘了我太太去年就過世了。」了解，這個老人記性很差的狀況。

26. 答案：(B)。題目要問的是 Andy 結婚時是幾年前或是他幾歲時。當醫生問 Andy「你現在幾歲？」時，他想了一下，然後說 When I married, I was thirty years old, and my wife was twenty.（在我結婚的時候，我 30 歲，而我太太 20 歲。）不過選項中看不到「在他 30 歲時」的答案，但是我們知道 Andy 的太太現在 40 歲（Now my wife is forty...），因此，他們已經結婚 20 年了，故正確答案應為 (B)。

27. 答案：(A)。這是個「何者為是／非」的題型，基本上，應通盤了解整段內容之後，以「刪去法」的方式一一核對每一個選項的敘述。內容中提到「在我結婚的時候，我 30 歲，而我太太 20 歲。」因此 (A) 就是正確的答案，那麼，(B)、(D)

就可以直接排除了。接著提到「Andy 的太太現在 40 歲」，那就表示，Andy 現在是 50 歲，所以 (C) 也是錯誤的。

25. 文章或故事主旨的部分，只要從各段主題句下手，即可大致掌握全篇的主要內容。這篇故事其實在第一段的 "One thing is, he was very forgetful." 就點出全篇重點了。另外，這裡選項用 bad memory（記性差）與故事中的 forgetful（健忘的）做連結。

26. 在內容中找到 get married 的相關字詞：When I married...。可以看到兩個重要資訊：I was thirty 以及 my wife was twenty。但這樣還不夠，下一句才點出答案所在：Now my wife is forty...。所以結婚已經 20 年了。

27. 這一題的答案，其實是屬於「承上題」的題型。也就是說，這種「何者為是／非」的題型，可以留到最後再做，因為它的解題線索往往會在解其他題時出現。

single [ˋsɪŋgl] **adj.** 單身的；單一的　　**led** [lɛd] **v.** 過著（某種生活），lead 的過去式　**chess** [tʃɛs] **n.** 西洋棋　**forgetful** [fəˋgɛtfəl] **adj.** 健忘的　**piece** [pis] **n.**（棋子的）一顆　**headache** [ˋhɛdˌek] **n.** 頭痛　**hit** [hɪt] **v,** 打，擊中　**decide** [dɪˋsaɪd] **v.** 決定　**hospital** [ˋhɑspɪtl] **n.** 醫院　**reply** [rɪˋplaɪ] **v.** 回答　**remember** [rɪˋmɛmbɚ] **v.** 記得　**twice** [twaɪs] **adv.** 兩倍（= **double**）

❶「身體部位 + -ache」表示「～痛」，常見的有 headache（頭痛）、toothache（牙痛）、heartache（心痛）、backache（背痛，腰痛）、stomachache（胃痛）、earache（耳痛）等。不過，也不是所有身體部位都可以這樣用，但 ache 可以當不及物動詞，所以你可以說 My hand/nose/lip... is aching.（我的手／鼻子／嘴唇…正在痛。）。另外 achy 是形容詞，表示「疼痛的」，所以你也可以用「身體部位 + be 動詞 + achy」來表示「～痛」喔！

❷ 年齡的表達方式。最簡單的就是「be 動詞 + 數字 + years old」，在口語中，甚至也會把 year(s) old 省略掉。那如果要用到 age 這個字呢？以「我」當主詞來舉例，最常見的就是「I'm at the age of / at age + 數字」、「My age is + 數字」。但是沒有 My age is 20 years old. 這種說法喔！

❸ twice（兩倍）是「倍數詞」的一種，相當於 double 這個字。舉凡 once, twice, thrice, double, triple, four times, ... 都是倍數詞。例如：「6 是 2 的三倍。」可以說 "Six is thrice two."；「這本書是那本的兩倍厚。」是 "This book is double as thick as that one."。

Questions 28-30

中文翻譯

　　上週六王家的人很忙碌。對他們來說，那是個重要的日子，因為一個全新的生活環境正等著他們。在大貨車於下午三點抵達之前，他們必須將所有東西放進箱子中，像是衣服、玩具、書籍、相簿以及其他他們不想丟掉的東西。此外，他們得清空及清潔所有地板，並帶走或扔掉廚房的全部舊食物。

　　當然，他們不需要自己搬大型傢俱。王先生花了八千元雇用搬家工人做這件事。當載貨車抵達時，兩名男子下了車並將洗衣機、冰箱、衣櫥、床及其他大型傢具搬上貨車。接著，他們小心翼翼地將所有箱子搬了出來，並放在貨車後面。

　　最後，王先生和他兒子大衛上了載貨車，而王太太開車載仙蒂與瑪麗。凱文，他們 16 歲的大兒子已經在他們的新公寓等他們了。

28. 這對夫婦有幾個小孩？
　　(A) 兩個。(B) 三個。(C) 四個。(D) 五個。

29. 這家人沒有做什麼？
　　(A) 打包箱子　　　　　　　　(B) 清潔地板
　　(C) 搬冰箱　　　　　　　　　(D) 開車到新的住處

30. 第一段第一個 big 這個字的意思是？
　　(A) 大型的　(B) 重的　(C) 忙碌的　(D) 重要的

答題解說

這是一段日常生活中的家庭故事。內容敘述一家人即將搬遷至新住所的故事。

28. 答案：(C)。第三段提到：王先生和他兒子大衛上了載貨車，而王太太開車載仙蒂與瑪麗（Mr. Wang got into the truck with his son David, while Mrs. Wang drove a car with Sandy and Mary.）。接著又說，凱文，他們 16 歲的大兒子已經在他們的新公寓等他們了（Kevin, aged 16 and their oldest son, was already in the new apartment waiting for them.）。所以，王先生與王太太共有 4 個孩子。

29. 答案：(C)。可以就四個選項來一一檢視。(A) 的部分可以從 "Before the big truck arrived on 3:00 p.m., they had to put all things into boxes..." 的內容看到；(B) 的部分是在 "...they needed to clear and clean all the floors..."；(C) 的部分可以從 "Of course, they did not have to move large furniture... two men got out and moved the washing machine, the refrigerator..." 得知，他們沒有做「搬冰箱」這件事；(D) 的部分呼應 "Mrs. Wang drove a car with Sandy and Mary." 這句話。所以答案是 (C)。

30. 答案：(D)。第一段第一個 big 所在的句子是 "For them, it was a big day..."（對他們來說，那是個重要的日子…），之所以解釋為「重要的」是因為，他們要搬新家，至於選項 (C) 的 busy 套入句中似乎也可以，但 big 本身沒有「忙碌」的意思，所以正確答案應為 (D) important。

28. 題目要問的是這對夫妻有幾個孩子，屬於內容細節問題，可以從開始提到其子女的部分開始找尋線索，包括 his son、their oldest son，以及這中間的 Sandy and Mary。

29. 題目問這家人「沒有」做什麼，也就是指在搬家過程中，有什麼事情是由搬運工人來做的。以一般常識來說，大型傢俱肯定是由搬家公司來處理，所以答案是 (C) Move the refrigerator（搬冰箱）

30. 一般小學生也知道 big 是「大的」，所以這邊問 big 是什麼意思時，肯定不會是小學生也知道的那個意思。可以參考後面 because 子句的 "a wholly new living environment was awaiting them"（一個全新的生活環境正等著他們），顯然這是個「重要的」日子。

字詞解釋

big [bɪg] **adj.** 重大的　　**wholly** [ˋholɪ] **adv.** 完全地　　**environment** [ɪnˋvaɪrənmənt] **n.** 環境
await [əˋwet] **v.** 等候　　**album** [ˋælbəm] **n.** 相簿，專輯　　**throw** [θro] **v.** 投，擲，拋，扔
furniture [ˋfɝnɪtʃɚ] **n.** 傢俱　　**on one's own** 靠自己　　**washing machine** 洗衣機
refrigerator [rɪˋfrɪdʒəˏretɚ] **n.** 冰箱　　**closet** [ˋklɑzɪt] **n.** 衣櫥

相關文法或用法補充

❶ big 有很多種意思，不能只知道它是「大的」意思。這裡的「重要的」也可以用來修飾「人」，所謂「大人物」，也可以用 "big man/woman" 來表示。另外，形容一個人「寬宏大量」，可以用 big heart 來表示。如果要說一個人所說的話是「吹牛」可以用 big talk 來表示喔！

❷ 所謂「不可數名詞」主要是指一些物質名詞、抽象名詞和專有名詞。例如：news（新聞）、advice（建議、忠告）、information（資訊）、work（工作）、travel（旅遊）、weather（天氣）、luggage（行李）、progress（進展）、love（愛）、money（金錢）、furniture（傢俱）、homework（作業）、water（水）、bread（麵包）、milk（牛奶）、wealth（財富）、attention（注意力）、electricity（電）……等。

❸ 在說明某人的特定年齡時，除了用 "years old" 表示之外，aged 是個常用的字，它是個形容詞，意為「（某人）… 歲的」，如：A woman aged 50 has given birth to twins.（一名 50 歲婦女產下了一對雙胞胎）；They've got two children, aged 3 and 7.（他們有兩個孩子，一個 3 歲，一個 7 歲）。

2

GEPT
全民英檢

初級初試
中譯＋解析

第一部分 看圖辨義

1. **For question number 1, please look at Picture A.**

Question number 1: What does this sign tell us?
（這個標誌告訴我們什麼？）
(A) Stop walking here.（別在此走動。）
(B) Do not enter.（禁止進入。）
(C) Show your I.D. please.（請出示您的識別證。）

答題解說

答案：(B)。Stop 的字眼表示「禁止」做某事。而下方的文字 Staff Only 表示「只有員工才能進入」，這是寫給一般民眾看的，所以 (B) 是正確答案。

字詞解釋

enter [ˋɛntɚ] v. 進入　　**I.D.** (= identification) 識別證，身分證

相關文法或用法補充

enter 可以當及物動詞（後面要有受詞），也可以當不及物動詞，常與介系詞 into 連用。其區別在：

1. 若表示進入某一「具體的」場所、建築物等，是及物動詞用法。例如「我一進屋大家就安靜了下來。」：

   誤：Silence fell as I entered into the room.
   正：Silence fell as I entered the room.

2. 若表示開始進入或從事某一「狀態」或「活動」，或用於較「抽象」的概念，則可後接 into。如：

   (1) Let's enter into this topic.（我們來開始討論這個主題。）
   (2) He entered into partnership with his brother.（他和弟弟合夥做生意。）

2. **For question number 2 and 3, please look at Picture B.**

Question number 2: What does the boy have for lunch?
（這男孩中餐吃什麼？）
(A) Fried noodles（炒麵）
(B) Hamburger, fries and Coke（漢堡、薯條及可樂）
(C) Pizza and Coke（比薩及可樂）

第 1 回
第 2 回
第 3 回
第 4 回
第 5 回
第 6 回
第 7 回
第 8 回
第 9 回
第 10 回

答題解說

答案：(B)。本題是問「吃什麼」（what），只要看清楚男孩手上拿的，以及他桌上放的食物，就可以選出正確答案了。

破題關鍵

雖然從三個選項來看，知道題目要問的是什麼食物，但圖的右上方有食物，男孩的桌上也有食物，所以一定要聽出 have sth. for lunch（吃～當作午餐）這個用語。這裡的 lunch 也可以替換成 breakfast 或 dinner 等。

字詞解釋

fried [fraɪd] **adj.** 油炸的　　**noodle** [`nudl] **n.** 麵條　　**hamburger** [`hæmbɝɡɚ] **n.** 漢堡
pizza [`pitsə] **n.** 披薩

相關文法或用法補充

講到「吃」，你知道 eat 與 have 這兩個動詞差別在哪裡嗎？其實 eat 比較強調「吃」的動作，而且其後可以不接受詞，過去式是 ate，過去分詞是 eaten。而 have 比較偏「進食」等陳述一件事情的感覺，「吃」的動作感沒那麼強，也可以用來表示喝飲料，後面要有名詞作為其受詞。過去式和過去分詞都是 had。

3. **Question number 3: Please look at Picture B again.**

Where is the boy?（這男孩在哪裡？）
(A) In a fast food restaurant（在一家速食店）
(B) In the dining room（在飯廳）
(C) At a street food stand（在一個路邊小吃攤）

答題解說

答案：(A)。本題是問「在哪裡」（where）。雖然三個選項都是「吃東西的地方」，但右上方有標示價錢，顯然不會是在家裡的 dining room，而左方有一個標示 PUSH 的門，所以男孩應該在「室內」用餐，不會是在路邊攤。故 (A) 的速食店是正確答案。

掌握 fast food（速食）、dining room（飯廳）以及 street food（路邊小吃）三個關鍵字詞即可選出正確答案。

字詞解釋

dining [ˋdaɪnɪŋ] **n.** 進餐（**dine** 的現在分詞）　　**stand** [stænd] **n.** 攤子，小販賣部

相關文法或用法補充

「食物」的總稱是 food，而經常出現在 food 前面的形容詞也相當多，但必須注意的是「固定用語」。例如，「速食」是 fast food，不是 quick food，「垃圾食物」是 junk food，不是 trash/garbage food。如果要形容一個東西「好吃」，除了可以 delicious、yummy、tasty 之外，也可以試試 mouth-watering 這個複合形容詞，字面意思是「令人流口水的」，是不是更加生動了呢？

4. **For question number 4 and 5, please look at Picture C.**

Question number 4: What are these women doing?

（這些女人在做什麼？）

(A) They're selling clothes.（她們正在賣衣服。）

(B) They're putting the clothes in order.（他們正在整理衣服。）

(C) They're choosing something.（她們正在選擇東西。）

答題解說

答案：(C)。圖片上方有 ON SALE（拍賣中）的字樣，顯然這些女士正在挑衣服，準備購買，所以正確答案應為(C)。

破題關鍵

關鍵還是在 ON SALE 的字樣，雖然一名女子拿起一件衣服，但別受到 (A)中 clothes 的誤導，所以她們不可能是在「賣衣服」，也不會是在「整理」衣服。

字詞解釋

put... **in order** 整理　　**choose** [tʃuz] **v.** 選擇

相關文法或用法補充

choose 有「選擇，挑選，決定」的意思，是個不規則變化的動詞（三態為 choose, chose, chosen），而另一個也有「挑選」意思的 select，是個規則變化的動詞。choose 後面可接不定詞（to-V）來表示「選擇／決定（做某事）」，而 select 後面只能接名詞。

5. **Question number 5: Please look at Picture C again.**

   What information is given in this picture?
   （圖片中提供了什麼資訊？）

   (A) They are at a train station.（她們在火車站。）
   (B) These women are housewives.
       （這些女人都是家庭主婦。）
   (C) The clothes are cheaper than usual.（這些衣服比平常便宜。）

   答題解說

   答案：(C)。題目是在問圖片上方 ON SALE 的文字要提供的是什麼樣的資訊。on sale（販售中，減價促銷中）的字樣通常出現在百貨公司或大賣場等地，所以圖片中婦女們正在撿便宜貨。

   破題關鍵

   "What information is given in this picture?" 的問法屬於「綜合」題型，通常要一個個選項去對照圖片內容來作答。train station 是車站，想當然與 ON SALE 沒有任何關係；housewives 是 housewife 的複數，意思是「家庭主婦」，會來撿便宜貨的當然不一定是家庭主婦。

   字詞解釋

   station [ˋsteʃən] n. 車站　　**housewife** [ˋhaʊsˏwaɪf] n. 家庭主婦　　**than usual** 比起平常而言

   相關文法或用法補充

   "than usual" 是經過文字刪減後形成的，在比較級的句子中是很常見的。 "The clothes are cheaper than usual." 這句話可還原成 "The clothes are cheaper than they are in a usual way."

第二部分 問答

6. **May I have your name, please?**（請問尊姓大名？）

   (A) I'm Judy.（我是茱蒂。）
   (B) I'm twelve years old.（我十二歲。）
   (C) I'm from Taiwan.（我來自臺灣。）

   答題解說

   答案：(A)。May I have your name 是用來問對方的名字，等同於 What is your

name?，但屬於比較正式或社交場合的說法。所以答案是(A)。

雖然大家都知道用 What's your name? 來問名字，但 May I have your name? 這個說法也許有些初級程度的人不一定知道，何況是要聽得出來。不過就算不知道這個用法，只要聽出 name，應該就不會答錯了。

字詞解釋

May I..., please? 麻煩可否…？

相關文法或用法補充

在西方國家，人們很注重自己的隱私，其中包括：年齡、婚姻狀況、薪資等個人問題，所以不要隨意問他們這些問題，因為他們會覺得你很不禮貌，很唐突，甚至沒有教養。隨著國際文化交流的加速，這種注重個人隱私的意識在東方國家也漸漸提高，人們在交談中也不會隨意問及別人這些隱私問題，比如不問女士的年齡。

7. **Please spell the word "pen."**（請拼出 pen 這個字。）

(A) Yes, I have a pen.（是的，我有一支筆。）
(B) Pen.（筆）
(C) P-e-n（P-e-n）

答題解說

答案：(C)。題目是 Please 開頭的祈使句，是要請對方拼或寫出一個單字。所以應該是以「念出每一個字母」的方式來回答。

破題關鍵

本題有兩個關鍵點：

1. 聽出 Please 開頭的句子是祈使句，所以不可能用 Yes 來回答。 2. 當然就是要聽出 spell（拼字）這個動詞，而且 spell the word 也是個很常見的用語。如果是 Please "say" the word "pen." 的話，那答案就要選(B)了。

字詞解釋

spell [spɛl] v. 用字母拼（寫）

相關文法或用法補充

題目句中有同位語的用法：the word "pen"。在這個同位語的用法中，the word 是先行詞，而 pen 是對先行詞的補充說明。同位語結構很單純，就是「先行詞 + 補充／修飾用語」，兩者必須「同詞性」。一般來說，同位語一般由名詞或名詞

短語來充當，例如：

1. Shanghai, the economic center of China, is very attractive to foreign investors.（上海，中國的經濟中心，對外國投資者非常有吸引力。）
2. Tom, the tallest boy in our class, is good at sports.（湯姆，是我們班上最高的男生，他運動體育非常棒。）

8. **Is your mother in?**（你媽媽在家嗎？）

(A) Yes, she is cooking in the kitchen.（是的，她正在廚房煮飯。）
(B) No, she is in her room.（不，她在她的房間裡。）
(C) Yes, she is in her office.（是的，她在她的辦公室。）

答題解說

答案：(A)。題目句屬於 Yes-No 的疑問句，因此三個選項均符合正確的回答方式，但題目要問的是「你媽媽在家嗎？」，所以只有(A)是正確的回答。

破題關鍵

本題關鍵在於句尾的 in，因為是屬於「功能性」字眼，在收聽錄音時不容易聽得出來，而且這裡的 in 後面沒有名詞，所以它並不是介系詞，而是個副詞，表示「在家，在屋子裡」，相當於 at home，與它相反意思的是 out。

字詞解釋

kitchen [ˋkɪtʃɪn] n. 廚房　　**office** [ˋɔfɪs] n. 辦公室，營業處所

相關文法或用法補充

英文裡有一些「長得像介系詞，但其實是也可以當副詞」的字，例如：above, over, beyond, around, below, down, in, along, near, off, on, inside, outside, round, past 等，後面接受詞時，它們就是介系詞，否則就是副詞，例如：

1. Come in, please.（請進！）→當副詞
   They are studying in the classroom.（他們在教室念書。）→當介系詞
2. Don't look around in class.（上課時不要東張西望。）→當副詞
   The host showed us around his new house.（主人帶我們四處參觀他的新居。）→當介系詞
3. We'll go on with the next lesson.（我們繼續學習下一課。）→當副詞
   The article is on the subject of peace.（這篇文章的主題是關於和平的議題。）→當介系詞

9. Are you and Jenny classmates?（你和珍妮是同班同學嗎？）

　　(A) No, we are not.（不，我們不是。）
　　(B) No, they are not classmates.（不，他們不是同學。）
　　(C) Yes, we are not.（是的，我們不是。）

答題解說

答案：(A)。題目句屬於 Yes-No 的疑問句，因此三個選項均符合正確的回答方式，但題目這個問句的主詞是 you and Jenny，所以 (B) They...明顯錯誤；而 (C) 既然是回答 Yes,...，後面卻有否定的 not，顯然前後矛盾，所以也是錯誤的。

破題關鍵

本題的關鍵就在題目這個疑問句的主詞：you and Jenny，對方問「你和某某人」怎樣時，回答當然不可能是用 they，而要用 we。另外，有基本文法概念的話，應該可以只看選項就知道要踢除 (C) 了。

字詞解釋

classmate [ˋklæsˏmet] **n.** 同班同學

相關文法或用法補充

classmate 是由 class（班級）與 mate（伴侶）構成的，類似的名詞還有 roommate（室友）、schoolmate（校友）、teammate（隊友）…等，也有像是 soul mate（精神伴侶）這種分成兩個字的情況。另外，知道為什麼 coffee mate 叫作「奶精」了吧！所以不一定 -mate 結尾的單字都跟「人」有關喔！

10. Have you drunk this before?（你喝過這個嗎？）

　　(A) I'm not ready.（我還沒準備好。）
　　(B) Yes, I think I am a bit drunk.（是的，我想我有點醉了。）
　　(C) No, but I can give it a try.（沒有，不過我可以試試。）

答題解說

答案：(C)。題目句子問「是否喝過」，回答「還沒準備好」和「我想我有點醉了」很明顯都是答非所問，只有 (C) 的「可以試試看」的回答是比較合邏輯的。選項 (B) 試圖以相同字彙 drunk 來誤導答題。

破題關鍵

首先要知道題目句子屬於 Yes-No 問句，且與「過去的經驗」有關。所以只有 (C) 是可以用來回答過去是否有特定經驗。

字詞解釋

drunk [drʌŋk] v. 喝酒（**drink** 的過去分詞）adj. 喝醉的　**give it a try** 嘗試看看

相關文法或用法補充

drunk 與 drunken 當形容詞都有「(酒) 醉的」意思，但 drunk 通常放在 be 動詞或 get 等連綴動詞之後。例如：

1. He got very drunk on only two glasses of wine.（他才喝了兩杯酒就爛醉了。）
2. There was a drunken man lying on the ground.（地上躺了一名醉漢。）

11. **What time is it by your watch?**（你的錶上顯示幾點？）

(A) I go to school at seven thirty in the morning.（我早上七點半去上學。）
(B) I had no time to watch it.（我沒有時間看。）
(C) It's ten after eleven.（現在是十一點十分。）

答題解說

答案：(C)。這是詢問時間的題目，對於這樣問題，往往都會回答 7 o'clock、「It's + 數字」之類的，也就是準確地回答當時的時間是幾點幾分。不過，可別「看到黑影就開槍」，還是要看清楚選項的意思。(B) 的回答是完全答非所問，且試圖以相同發音的 watch 來誤導；而 (A) 回答的是「平時做某件事情的時間」，但題目問的是「現在幾點」，也是答非所問。所以 (C) 的「11 點過 10 分」是正確答案。

破題關鍵

兩個關鍵：1. 題目句的 "What time is it"（即使沒有 by your watch）就是在問「現在的時間」；2.「數字 + after/before + 數字」的時間表達方式。再強調一次，別看到「幾點幾分」的用語就選了喔！

字詞解釋

What time...? …幾點鐘？　**by your watch** 根據你的錶（所顯示）

相關文法或用法補充

在 by your watch 這個片語中，by 的意思是「根據～」，類似用語如 by hour、by day，意思分別是「按小時計」，「按日計算」，例如：

I am paid by hour, and my friend Tom is paid by day.
我的工作按小時計酬，而我朋友湯姆的工作是領日薪。

12. Where are you going after school?（放學後你要去哪裡？）

(A) I'm going to do my homework.（我要做家庭作業。）
(B) I'm going to the library.（我要去圖書館。）
(C) I'm going on a diet.（我正在節食。）

答題解說

答案：(B)。題目要問的是「放學後去什麼地方」，選項 (B) 的「去圖書館」是最直接的回答。雖然在中文裡，被問到「要去哪裡」時，我們可能會回答「我要去買東西」之類的，但是英文是「問什麼答什麼」的原則，至於 (C) 與 (A) 相同，都是在說明「做某件事情」，答非所問。

破題關鍵

本題三個選項試圖以 "be going" 來混淆視聽，但其實關鍵就是搞清楚「題目要問什麼」即可。這是針對地點提問（Where... ?），所以回答應該與地點有關，選項中只有 (B) 有提到地點（library）。

字詞解釋

after school 放學　**do one's homework** 做作業　**library** [ˋlaɪˏbrɛrɪ] n. 圖書館
diet [ˋdaɪət] n. 節食，減重計畫

相關文法或用法補充

be going to-V 與 will+V 都可以用來表示「未來」要做的事。但 will 表示「將會做某事」，而 be going to 是「現在就要去做某事」。也就是說 I'll... 強調的是「現在的意志」，但事前並沒有這樣的計畫。而 I'm going to... 表示在當下的時間點已決定，也就是事前已計畫好的。所以當我們要表達想幫助的「善意」時，要用 will。不過，如果是要實現答應幫忙的承諾時，要說 "Yes, I know. I'm going to help you."（是的，我知道。我這就過去幫你。）會比較「有誠意」一點。

13. What date is it today?（今天是幾月幾號？）

(A) It's Friday.（今天是星期五。）
(B) I didn't go to school today.（我今天沒去上學。）
(C) It's September 15.（今天是九月十五號。）

答題解說

答案：(C)。題目問「日期（date）」，所以回答要有明確的「幾月幾日」，答案當然是有 September 15 的 (C) 了。如果是問 What "day" is today?，那麼答案就要選 (A) 了。選項 (B) 試圖以相同的字彙 today 來誤導答題，請勿上當。

破題關鍵

雖然只要知道題目是 "What date" 開頭的，就不會答錯了，但也許有人會問 date 與 day 在聽力測驗中幾乎聽不出來差別，怎麼辦？沒錯，如果只是單字發音，很難聽出來，但如果後面還有單字的話，可以從字與字之間的「連音」來判別："date is" 的發音會是 [de tɪs] 而 "day is" 則是 [de ɪs]，只要仔細聽，還是很容易聽得出來的。

字詞解釋

date [det] n. 日期　　**September** [sɛp`tɛmbɚ] n. 九月

相關文法或用法補充

記住：英文裡的 what time、what day、what date 分別詢問「幾點」（時間）、「星期幾」（星期）以及「日期」，例如：

問：What time is it now? 答：It is 9 o'clock.
問：What day was it yesterday? 答：It was Monday.
問：What date was it yesterday? 答：It was July 20th.

14. **Let's go out for lunch. It's my treat!**（我們出去吃午餐。這頓我請！）

(A) Sounds good.（聽起來不錯。）
(B) Yes, I can see many trees.（是的，我可看見許多樹。）
(C) Lunch isn't ready.（午餐還沒準備好。）

答題解說

答案：(A)。題目是問對方，要不要一起吃午餐，自己要請客。所以只有 (A) 的回答是最正確的，也可以 "Good idea!"、"I'd love to" …等等，來表示願意。選項 (B) 試圖以 tree 與 treat 的類似發音來造成混淆，但其實答非所問。選項 (C) 則以相同字彙 lunch 來誘導選擇錯誤答案。

破題關鍵

Let's + V 的用法常常用來表示提出邀請或建議，而且 Let's 在聽覺上的辨識度頗高，如果事先看過 3 個選項，或是選項一個個去對應看看，應該就能立刻掌握正確的答案。

字詞解釋

treat [trit] n. 請客　　**sound** [saʊnd] v. 聽起來

相關文法或用法補充

"Sounds good." 省略了主詞，在口語中很常用，原本應該是 It sounds good.。

sound 是個「連綴動詞」，像是「看起來（look）」、「聞起來（smell）」、「感覺上（feel）」、「嘗起來（taste）」等也都是。連綴動詞不能單獨存在，後面必須再接形容詞，作為主詞補語，句意才算完整。

15. Hi, Daddy! I just left school.（嗨，爹地！我剛放學。）

(A) Oh, is it still open?（噢，它還開著嗎？）
(B) It's my pleasure.（這是我的榮幸。）
(C) OK. Just take care.（好的。要小心注意喔。）

答題解說

答案：(C)。本題應是孩子在電話裡告訴父親，他／她剛下課。由於孩子可能正踏上回家路，所以選項中只有 (C) 的路上小心注意，比較適合用來回應這句話。其餘 (B) 主要用於一班社交場合，而 (A) 反問「還開著嗎？」是完全不相關的回應。

破題關鍵

在尚未聽到錄音播放前，就本題來說，即使先看過三個選項也無法預測題目會怎麼問，只能在聽過並了解播放的題目句之後，才能正確作答。題目句的 left 是 leave 的過去式，有時候一閃神會不容易聽出，須多加熟練。

字詞解釋

left [lɛft] v. **leave** （離開）的過去式　**pleasure** [ˋplɛʒɚ] n. 愉快，高興　**take care** 保重，小心

相關文法或用法補充

school 這個字可能連很多小學生都會，不過 at school 與 in school 的差別，可能很多人就搞不清楚了。at school 中的 at 表達的是「整個校園的含義，它包括：操場、餐廳、自行車庫和圖書館等，只要是屬於學校的地方都涵蓋在內。在這個校園內所做的任何活動都可以用「at school」表達。而 in school 則表示「正在接受某種教育或學習某個課程的過程中，我們通常表達為「（在）上學」是一種「抽象概念」，而不是在「具體的校園裡」。

第三部分 簡短對話

第 1 回
第 2 回
第 3 回
第 4 回
第 5 回
第 6 回
第 7 回
第 8 回
第 9 回
第 10 回

16. **M: Do you know why Mary's looking so blue?**
    W: Who knows!
    M: Maybe we should go cheer her up.
    W: I think so.

    Question: What does the woman think about Mary?
    (A) She is sick.
    (B) She shouldn't wear blue clothes.
    (C) She has no idea.

    男：你知道瑪麗為什麼看起來這麼憂鬱嗎？
    女：誰知道！
    男：也許我們應該過去給她打打氣。
    女：我也這麼認為。
    問題：女子認為瑪麗怎麼了？
    (A) 她病了。
    (B) 她不該穿藍色衣服。
    (C) 她也不知道。

    答題解說

    答案：(C)。題目問的是女子認為瑪麗可能發生什麼事，所以應注意聽女子的發言部分：Who knows!（誰知道！）這表示女子也不知道她怎麼了，所以答案是(C)。"have/has no idea" = "don't/doesn't know"。對話中沒有提到誰生病了，所以 (A) 是錯的；(B) 試圖以相同字彙 blue 來混淆判斷，且是答非所問。

    破題關鍵

    本題有三個關鍵點：1. 題目問 "the woman" 的看法，2. 這個看法是針對 Mary，3. 理解 Who knows! 的意思。

    字詞解釋

    blue [blu] adj. 憂鬱的　**cheer up** 使（人）振作　**have no idea** 沒有想法，不知道

    相關文法或用法補充

    英文裡，有一些表示顏色的字還有別的意思（或情感色彩）：
    1. white 白色：在西方，白色代表純潔或善意，所以「善意的謊言」叫作 white

lie，而「被寄予厚望的人」叫作 white hope。

2. red 紅色：在英文裡有「脾氣暴躁」以及「害羞」之意。例如：She turned red when she saw the photo.（她看見這照片時，滿臉通紅了。）

3. yellow 黃色：在英文裡，黃色也往往和「色情」聯想在一起，這一點和中文一樣，但也有例外。例如 yellow book 的意思不是「黃色書刊」，而是「黃頁」的意思。

4. blue 藍色：藍色通常表示「憂鬱、心情不好」，但 blue blood 的意思是「高貴的血統」。

5. black 黑色：多為負面意思。英文裡的 black sheep 是「敗類、害群之馬」，而 black 當形容詞也有「生氣的」、「不祥的」、「不名譽」的意思喔！

17. W: You look quite different today! You just got a haircut?

M: That's right. You like it?

W: Sure. It suits you very well.

M: Thanks a lot.

Question: What are the speakers talking about?

(A) The man's new hairstyle

(B) A barber shop

(C) What hairstyle suits the man

女：你今天看起來很不一樣！你剛去剪頭髮嗎？

男：是的。你喜歡這髮型嗎？

女：當然。它很適合你。

男：多謝了。

問題：說話者們在談論什麼？

(A) 男子的新髮型。(B) 某家理髮廳。(C) 什麼髮型適合男子。

答題解說

答案：(A)。題目問的是整篇對話的「要點」，所以必須完整理解對話內容才能作答。女子一開始問，男子是不是去理髮了，因為看起來很不一樣。最後男子謝謝女子對其新髮型的讚美。因此，對話內容主要關於男子的新髮型。

破題關鍵

即使對於會話內容半知半解，但關鍵還是在聽出 haircut 這個字，因為選項中出現兩次 hairstyle，而對話並未提及與 barber shop 有關的字眼，因此 (B) 可直接先排除。而對話中，女子是說「這個髮型很適合你」，但沒有提到「什麼樣的髮型」，因此 (C) 純粹只是想用 hairstyle 與 suit 這個動詞來誤導答題。

第 1 回
第 2 回
第 3 回
第 4 回
第 5 回
第 6 回
第 7 回
第 8 回
第 9 回
第 10 回

字詞解釋

haircut [ˋhɛrˏkʌt] n. 理髮　**suit** [sut] v. 適合　**hairstyle** [ˋhɛrˏstaɪl] n. 髮型　**barber shop** [ˋbɑrbɚˏʃɑp] n. 理髮店

相關文法或用法補充

hair 這個字雖然很簡單，但它有時候以單數出現，且不能加 -s，有時候又會看到 hairs 的用法，而且是一定要加 -s。您知道 hair 字尾加及不加 -s 的差別嗎？其實，hair 用於指整個頭髮或毛髮時，是「集合名詞」，沒有複數形式；但是當 hair 用於表示一根根頭／毛髮時，則是可數名詞。例如：

1. He had his hair cut. （他理了頭髮。）
2. She found two gray hairs. （她找到了兩根白頭髮。）

＊注意：「一根白頭髮」不是 white hair，而是 gray hair 喔！

18. M: Jennifer, you're 15 minutes late.

W: I'm really sorry. I overslept this morning.

M: You must be on time tomorrow. We have an important meeting.

W: I will.

Question: Where did the dialogue probably take place?

(A) In a company　(B) In a classroom　(C) In a barber shop

男：珍妮佛，你遲到 15 分鐘了。

女：真是抱歉。我今早睡過頭了。

男：你明天一定要準時到。我們有個重要的會議。

女：我會的。

問題：這則對話可能發生在何處？

(A) 在公司裡　(B) 在教室裡　(C) 在理髮廳裡

答題解說

答案：(A)。題目問的是對話發生的「地點」，基本上還是得理解對話內容才能作答。首先，男子責備女子遲到，接著女子解釋了原因，然後男子提醒他明天要準時，因為有重要會議要開，顯然兩人在公司裡應是主管與下屬之關係。因此，對話的地點應該是在公司裡。

破題關鍵

整篇對話的關鍵字只有一個：meeting。如果是 (B) 在教室裡，老師當然也會責備學生遲到，但從 We have an important meeting. 來看，顯然不會是發生在教室裡的情境。當然，這對話更不可能是 (C) 理髮廳裡中的對話了。

overslept [`ovɚ`slɛpt] **v.** 睡過頭（oversleep 的過去式）　**on time** 準時
important [ɪm`pɔrtnt] **adj.** 重要的　**meeting** [`mitɪŋ] **n.** 會議

相關文法或用法補充

許多初學者也常常搞不清 in time 與 on time 的差別。on time 可用來表示在訂定好的時間內準時赴約、準時上班、準時上課等。例如：Boss wanted to start the meeting on time.（老闆要準時開始開會。）而 in time 表示「及時」完成，或在某個時間點或期限到之前完成某件事。例如：The ambulance arrived just in time at the accident spot.（救護車及時趕到事故現場。）

19. W: Let's talk about your family. How many children are there in your family?
    M: I'm the only child.
    W: So your parents must expect much of you?
    M: No, they always respect my decision.

    Question: How many brothers or sisters does the man have?
    (A) He has one brother and one sister.
    (B) He has only one brother.
    (C) He doesn't have any brothers or sisters.

    女：我們談談你的家人吧。你家裡有幾個小孩？
    男：我是唯一的小孩。
    女：所以你的父母對你的期望一定很高了？
    男：不，他們總是尊重我的決定。
    問題：男子有幾個兄弟姊妹？
    (A) 他有一位哥哥及一位姊姊。
    (B) 他只有一個哥哥。
    (C) 他沒有任何兄弟姊妹。

答題解說

答案：(C)。本題是問男子有幾位兄弟姊妹，所以應注意聽男子發言的部分。男子的第一次發言提到 I'm the only child.，這表示他家裡面只有他一個小孩。所以正確答案是 (C)。

破題關鍵

首先，注意題目是問數字（How many...），所以要注意：1. 與數字有關的內容；2. 男子的發言部分。聽到男子說 only child 時，答案就出來了。

第 1 回
第 2 回
第 3 回
第 4 回
第 5 回
第 6 回
第 7 回
第 8 回
第 9 回
第 10 回

字詞解釋

expect [ɪk`spɛkt] v. 期望　　**respect** [rɪ`spɛkt] v. 尊敬　　**decision** [dɪ`sɪʒən] n. 決定

相關文法或用法補充

only 可以當形容詞，也可以當（程度）副詞，修飾動詞。但是當 only 與「數字」搭配使用時，必須放在數字前面。例如：

She has only one child.（她只有一個孩子。）

He told the secret to me only.（他只把這個祕密告訴了我。）

I only had a look of his new computer.（我只是看了看他的新電腦。）

20. W: I'm a bit hungry! What do you have to eat?

　　M: What about instant noodles? I bought them last night.

　　W: No, I'm sick of eating instant noodles.

　　M: Then let's eat out, OK?

Questions: Why doesn't the woman want to eat instant noodles?

(A) She ate them last night.

(B) Because she caught a cold.

(C) Because she eats them very often recently.

女：我有點餓了！你有什麼吃的嗎？

男：要吃泡麵嗎？昨晚買的。

女：不，我吃膩了泡麵。

男：那我們出去吃，好嗎？

問題：女子為何不想吃泡麵？

(A) 她昨晚才吃過。

(B) 因為她感冒了。

(C) 因為她最近很常吃。

答題解說

答案：(C)。本題問的是女子不想吃泡麵的「原因」，所以應注意女子有關吃泡麵的發言部分。女子的第二次發言提到，I'm sick of eating instant noodles.，這表示她厭倦了吃泡麵，也就是說她最近可能常吃，所以答案是 (C)。選項 (A) 刻意重複相同字詞 last night 來誤導答題，而選項 (B) 以「感冒（caught a cold）」來與對話中的 sick 作連結，也是刻意誤導。

首先，注意題目關鍵字 instant noodles，以及女子對此發言的部分：I'm sick of eating instant noodles.。be sick of... 是常見的片語，意思是「厭惡了～」，甚至是「對～感到噁心」，所以只有 (C) 比較符合這個意思。

字詞解釋

hungry [ˋhʌŋgrɪ] **adj.** 飢餓的　　**instant** [ˋɪnstənt] **adj.** 立即的，快速的　　**noodle** [ˋnudl] **n.** （常複數）麵條　　**be sick of** 厭惡，非常不喜歡　　**catch a cold** 感冒　　**recently** [ˋrisntlɪ] **adv.** 最近

相關文法或用法補充

sick 和 ill 都有「生病」的意思，但用法不太一樣。雖然兩者都可以用於「主詞 + be 動詞 + 形容詞」的結構，但 sick 不能放在「人」的名詞前作修飾語。例如：

1. Why is Tom absent from class? He is ill / sick.（湯姆為什麼沒來上課？他生病了。）
   →當主詞補語時，sick 與 ill 可互換。
2. The ill old man has to lie in bed all day.（這名生病的老人必須整天躺在床上。）
   →這時候 ill 不可換成 sick。
   不過 sick 可修飾「事物」，表示「感到噁心的」。例如：sick feeling（噁心的感覺）。而 ill 也有別的意思，常作「壞的，不吉利的」解釋，例如 say ill words about others（說別人的壞話）

21. W: Excuse me, where can I find the nearest bank?
    M: There's one just down the road. Go straight about 500 meters and you'll see it beside a gas station.
    W: Thanks a lot.
    M: No problem.

    Question: What does the woman probably want to do?
    (A) Go fishing.
    (B) Draw some money.
    (C) Get something to eat.

    女：請問一下，我可以在哪裡找到最近的銀行？
    男：就這條路過去有一家。直走大約 500 公尺，你會在加油站旁看見它。
    女：非常感謝。
    男：不客氣。

問題：女子可能想要去做什麼事？

(A) 去釣魚。(B) 去領一些錢。(C) 去買東西吃。

第 1 回　第 2 回　第 3 回　第 4 回　第 5 回　第 6 回　第 7 回　第 8 回　第 9 回　第 10 回

答題解說

答案：(B)。本題問的是女子想做什麼事，因此應從女子的發言中找尋線索。女子在找路，所以一開始問男子說 ... where can I find the nearest bank?。這表示她想去銀行。選項中只有 (B) 的「提款」與去銀行這件事有關。

破題關鍵

答案關鍵點除了會出現在女子的發言部分之外，如果有事先看過三個選項，也可以在一開始立即將 bank（銀行）與 money（錢）連結在一起，答案就出來了，即使不懂 "draw money" 就是「提款」，也不影響答題。

字詞解釋

straight [stret] **adv.** 直直地　　**meter** [`mitɚ] **n.** 公尺　　**gas station** 加油站　　**No problem**. 不客氣。（＝ You'll welcome.）

相關文法或用法補充

其實回應對方的謝意時，有時候 You're welcome. 聽起來可能會太過於正式。以下是比較輕描淡寫自己所提供的協助，或是覺得這個幫忙沒什麼，只是舉手之勞，同時也可以拉近彼此的距離：No problem.／No worries.／Not at all.／Don't mention it.／It's nothing.／It's no big deal.

22. M: What a long line! Maybe we'll fail to catch the 1:15 p.m. train.

W: Don't worry. The next one will still arrive in 15 minutes.

M: That way, let's go get something to drink. I'm a bit thirsty.

W: That's what I'm thinking too.

Question: What are they doing?

(A) They're standing in line to buy some drinks.

(B) They're buying tickets.

(C) They're eating lunch.

男：好長的隊伍啊！也許我們無法搭上 1:15 p.m.這班火車了。

女：別擔心。下一班還是會在 15 分鐘之後抵達。

男：這樣的話，我們去買個東西來喝。我有點渴。

女：我也這麼認為。

問題：他們正在做什麼？

(A) 他們正在排隊等候買飲料。

(B) 他們正在買票。

(C) 他們正在吃午餐。

答案：(B)。本題問的是這對男女現在正在做什麼事。可以從男子的第一句話「好長的隊伍啊！也許我們無法搭上 1:15 p.m.這班火車了。」可知，他們正要買車票。因為太多人排隊，這一班車可能趕不上了，所以正打算坐下一班（The next one...），正確應為 (B)。選項 (A) 刻意以「他們正在排隊」來呼應一開始的 "What a long line!" 以達到誤導答題的目的，必須特別注意。

本題屬於「主旨」型的題目，必須確實理解對話內容才能作答。但首先，必須先聽清楚題目是現在進行式，問的是「正在做什麼」（而不是等一下要做什麼）。既然問的是正在做的事」，就必須注意其相關動作的內容。關鍵字句是第一句的 long line 以及 catch the... train。

line [laɪn] n.（等待順序的）行列　　**fail to-V** 無法（做到～）　　**worry** [ˋwɝɪ] v. 擔心　**arrive** [əˋraɪv] v. 抵達　　**thirsty** [ˋθɝstɪ] adj. 渴的　　**in line** adv. 在排隊中

中文常常會用「這小 Baby 真可愛！」、「好好吃喔！」、「天氣好熱！」來特別強調情緒，但英文要如何表達這樣的感嘆語句呢？主要有 3 種方法：

1. What a/an +（形容詞）+ 單數名詞！

   例如：What a lovely day!（真是美好的一天啊！）

2. How + 形容詞 +（主詞+動詞）！

   例如：How cute (the baby is)!（這寶寶真可愛！）

3. （主詞 + be 動詞）Such a + 形容詞 + 單數名詞！

   例如：(It's) Such a good idea!（真是個好點子!）= This idea is so good!

23. M: I can't open the door. I think I left it in my office, along with my wallet.

    W: You always make such a mistake. What can we do now?

    M: Let's call a locksmith.

    W: But do you have money? Where's your wallet?

    Question: Where are the man and the woman?

    (A) On a train

(B) In the living room
(C) Outside a house

男：我無法打開門。我想我把鑰匙，連同我的皮夾留在辦公室了。
女：你總是犯這樣的錯誤。我們現在怎麼辦？
男：我們打電話叫鎖匠吧。
女：你有錢嗎？你的皮夾呢？
問題：這對男女在哪裡？
(A) 在火車上　　(B) 在客廳裡　　(C) 在房子外

答題解說

答案：(C)。本題問的是這對男女現在正在什麼地方，所以我們可以從男子的第一句話「我無法打開門。」得知，他們正要進入房子裡，但因為男子把鑰匙忘在公司了，所以暫時無法進到屋內，至於後面的對話，就與答題沒有關係了。正確答案應為「在房子外。」

破題關鍵

基本上，本題是屬於「聽懂對話內容才知道答案」的題目，不過既然是問地方，只要注意相關的對話內容即可。即使對話中可能有些字聽不出或超範圍（例如 locksmith），只要抓住關鍵字句是一開始的 "can't open the door"，答案就出來了。

字詞解釋

wallet [ˋwɑlɪt] n. 皮夾　　**mistake** [mɪˋstek] n. 錯誤　　***locksmith** [ˋlɑkˌsmɪθ] n. 鎖匠

相關文法或用法補充

介系詞 inside 與 outside 分別表示「在～裡面」和「在～外面」，既可用於表示地點，又可表示界限、領域、範圍等。例如：

Wait inside/outside the office（在辦公室內／外等待）
Live somewhere inside/outside the city of Taipei（住在台北市內／外的某處）
Be inside/outside one's field（在某人的專業範圍內／外）
Be inside/outside my power to help you（在我幫助你的能力範圍內／外）
A child born inside/outside marriage（婚生／非婚生子女）

24. M: Mary, you look so terrible. Are you O.K.?
   W: Not really. I didn't sleep well last night.
   M: What's the matter? Still worried about that project?

W: Right. I don't think our boss will accept it.

M: Just cheer up! You've made a great effort.

Question: What's wrong with the woman?

(A) She's feeling unhappy.

(B) She doesn't want to go to work today.

(C) She doesn't make much effort on the project.

男：瑪麗，妳看起來很糟。妳還好吧？

女：不怎麼好。我昨晚沒睡好。

男：怎麼了嗎？還擔心那個專案？

女：是啊。我不認為老闆會接受它。

男：還是開心點吧。妳已經很努力了。

問題：女子怎麼了？

(A) 她感到不快樂。

(B) 她今天不想工作。

(C) 她沒有很努力在那個專案上。

答題解說

答案：(A)。本題問的是女子「發生什麼事」，我們可以從女子的兩次發言中得知，「她昨晚沒睡好。」以及「她擔心老闆不接受她提的專案。」顯然，她正處於心情低落狀態，故正確答案應為 (A)。由於對話情境可以看出兩人是在公司中，所以 (B) 是錯誤的。最後男子也鼓勵她說「妳已經很努力了。」，因此 (C) 也是錯誤的。

破題關鍵

這一題要用最傳統的「刪去法」來作答會比較快。先將三個選項的敘述牢記之後，在聽對話的過程中，一個一個比對出「她在和同事對話，所以不是不想上班」以及「同事說她已經很努力了」，自然可以確認最適當的答案。

字詞解釋

terrible [ˈtɛrəbl] **adj.** 糟糕的　**matter** [ˈmætɚ] **n.** 事情，問題　**worried** [ˈwɝɪd] **adj.** 擔心的　**project** [ˈprɑdʒɛkt] **n.** 計畫，企劃　**accept** [əkˈsɛpt] **v.** 接受　**cheer** [tʃɪr] **v.** 歡呼，喝采　**effort** [ˈɛfɚt] **n.** 努力

相關文法或用法補充

如果要用英文表達「我認為約翰不用功。」應該怎麼說呢？若照中文字面翻譯就是：I think that John doesn't study hard.。但其實英文是不這麼說的，因為如果把

not 放在 that 子句中，也就是在 John 後面加 does not，感覺上是直接否定約翰的努力，顯得太過於直接而可能傷及他人自尊心。這種情況，外國人都會這麼說：I don't think（that）John studies hard.。因為把 not 放在整句主詞後面，成為 I don't think，感覺上比較沒有太直接地去批判 John，這是比較和緩且適當的說法喔。

25. M: Don't forget about the meeting with Mr. Chang this afternoon.
 W: Thanks for reminding. I have an interview at 2 p.m. It'll take about 90 minutes. Then I'll go to the meeting room right away.
 M: That's fine. I'm going out in 10 minutes to visit a client.
 W: OK. See you then.

Question: What time will the meeting with Mr. Chang begin?
(A) 2:00 p.m.　(B) 2:30 p.m.　(C) 3:30 p.m.

男：別忘了今天下午要和張先生開會。
女：謝謝提醒。我下午 2:00 有個面試。它大約 90 分鐘就會結束。然後我會立刻進會議室。
男：那沒問題。我十分鐘後要出去拜訪一位客戶。
女：好的。到時候見。
問題：與張先生的會議幾點開始？
(A) 下午兩點　(B) 下午兩點半　(C) 下午三點半

答題解說
答案：(C)。題目問的「會議幾點開始」，所以必須注意提到會議有關的內容。女子第一次發言時提到，她下午 2:00 的面試將進行約一個半小時，結束後她會直接進會議室，顯然這場會議的時間是下午 3:30。故正確答案應為 (C)。

破題關鍵
通常問時間（幾點）的題目，或是問「數字」的題型，不會是直接在對話中聽到的幾點幾分，而是必須稍作推論的，所以答案不會是(A) 2 p.m.。本題關鍵在於 2 p.m.、90 minutes 以及 "go to the meeting room right away"，掌握其意思之後，自然答案就出來了。

字詞解釋
meeting [ˋmitɪŋ] n. 會議　**remind** [rɪˋmaɪnd] v. 提醒　**interview** [ˋɪntɚˏvju] n. 面試，面談　**right away** adv. 立刻　**client** [ˋklaɪənt] n. 客戶

「in + 一小段時間」，很多人都會以為是「在～時間之內」，但其實是「在～（一段時間）之後」的意思。例如，I'll be back in 5 minutes.，不是「我 5 分鐘之內回來。」而是「我 5 分鐘之後回來。」如果要表示「在～時間之內」，要用介系詞 within。例如：The building will be done within 2 years.（這棟大樓會在兩年內建造完成。）

第四部分 短文聽解

For question number 26, please look at the three pictures.

Question number 26: Listen to the following talk. Which picture best describes the talk?

Today when I was on my bus heading to school, I saw a bicycle rider hit by a bus on the roadside. Some people stopped and watched the accident. Luckily, the bicycle rider did not get too hurt, and he was able to stand up by himself and bring his bicycle back. However, my bus arrived late and I failed to take the first class.

請看以下三張圖。並仔細聆聽播放的廣播內容。這則談話最適合描述哪一張圖？今天我在上學途中的巴士上，看見一名腳踏車騎士被一輛公車撞倒在路邊。有些人停下來看著這場意外事故。所幸，腳踏車騎士沒有太嚴重的傷，且他能夠自行爬起，並將他的單車扶起。然而，我的公車晚到了，我也未能趕上第一堂課。

答案：(B)。題目問的是談話內容是在敘述哪一張圖，首先，三張圖都有腳踏車騎士，但內容提到這位腳踏車騎士「被一輛公車撞倒（hit by a bus）」，所以到這裡，第一張圖就可直接排除了；第三張圖雖然也有腳踏車騎士倒在地上，但他是自撞路樹，所以也不是答案。

破題關鍵

這則談話內容的最快速解題方式就在於，你只要注意到「被公車撞」就行了，因為當中的 hit by a bus on the roadside 應該不難聽得出來。

字詞解釋

rider [ˋraɪdə] n. 搭乘者　**roadside** [ˋrodˏsaɪd] n. 路邊　**accident** [ˋæksədənt] n. 意外　**by oneself** 靠某人自己　**arrive** [əˋraɪv] v. 抵達　**fail to-V** 未能（做到）

相關文法或用法補充

所謂「知覺動詞」就像是 see、hear、watch、feel... 等，而部分知覺動詞也可以用於「S+V+C」的句型，像是 look、sound、feel... 等。但不同的是，知覺動詞運用於 S+V+O+OC 的句型，就像是「使役動詞」用法，其後接受詞後，可接原形動詞或分詞作為受詞補語。例如：

I heard her cry/crying out loudly at midnight.（我半夜聽見她哭得很大聲。）
至於用 cry 或 crying 的差別在於，只聽到一聲，用 cry，如果是聽到「一直在哭」，就要用 crying。

For question number 27, please look at the three pictures.

Question number 27: Listen to the following live sport report. What ball game are they playing?

Now let's get back to the game.The ball is going straight toward the base, and the player seems ready to hit it this time. Yes, he hit the ball with his bat... It is flying so high, and so far that two players on the field cannot catch it in time.

請看以下三張圖。並仔細聆聽以下球賽現場直播。什麼球賽正在進行？
我們現在回到比賽現場。球直接往壘包進來，而這名球員這次似乎已準備好要把球打出去了。是的，他用棒子擊中了球，球飛得如此高、如此遠，使得場上兩名球員無法及時接到球。

答題解說

答案：(C)。這則報導前半段的內容都沒有在三張圖片上顯示出來，所以必須再

仔細往下聽到後面的部分才行。最後提到，球員用棒子（bat）把球擊得很遠，使得場上兩名球員無法及時接到球。顯然這是棒球場上外野常見的畫面。

破題關鍵

雖然三張圖都有「兩個球員」，以及「沒有接到球」的畫面，但只要注意聽到一些關鍵字（base、hit、bat），即可知道這是棒球比賽。

字詞解釋

straight [stret] **adv.** 直接地　　**toward** [tə`wɔrd] **prep.** 朝向　　**base** [bes] **n.** 壘包　　**bat** [bæt] **n.** 球棒　　**field** [fild] **n.** 運動場，場地

相關文法或用法補充

「so + adj. / adv. + that...」的用法具有「強調」的功能，表示「如此～以致於～」，so 與 that 的中間要放形容詞或副詞，以加強形容詞的強度。例如：I am so tired that I might pass out.（我是如此的疲累，以致於我可能會昏倒。）

另外，也有 so that 當連接詞的用法，相當於「強化版」的連接詞 so（所以）。例如： I worked overtime this week so that I can take time off next week.（我這禮拜加班工作，這樣一來我下禮拜才能補休。）

For question number 28, please look at the three pictures.

Question number 28: Listen to the following announcement. At what place might you hear this announcement?

Welcome to Happy Mall, and we need your attention, please. A customer is looking for her 4-year-old son, who is wearing a pair of blue jeans and white shoes. Once you happen to see him around, please kindly guide him to our information counter on the first floor. We appreciate your help, and wish you a wonderful shopping experience today.

中文翻譯

請看以下三張圖。並仔細聆聽以下公告內容。你可能在什麼地方聽到這個廣播？
歡迎來到「樂購商城」，我們要麻煩您注意一下。一名顧客正在尋找她四歲的兒

第 1 回
第 2 回
第 3 回
第 4 回
第 5 回
第 6 回
第 7 回
第 8 回
第 9 回
第 10 回

子，他穿著一件藍色牛仔褲、白色鞋子。若您正好有在附近看見他，請好心引導他到一樓的服務台這邊來。我們感激您的協助，並祝您今天購物愉快。

答題解說

答案：(A)。首先，題目句一定要聽懂，這是個「問地方（At what place ＝ Where）」的題目，所以即使聽不出 announcement（公告廣播），看看三張不同場景的圖，大概也知道要問的是「播放內容的場景是在哪裡？」接著，仔細聽錄音播放內容，即可了解這是什麼地方的廣播內容。其中提到「引導他到一樓的服務台這邊來」以及「祝您今天購物愉快」，這樣應該不難知道這是什麼地方了吧。

破題關鍵

這則廣播內容的關鍵字詞，除了最後的 information counter、wonderful shopping experience 之外，其實一開始的 "Welcome to Happy Mall" 就已經告訴你答案了。

字詞解釋

mall [mɔl] n. 購物中心　**attention** [ə`tɛnʃən] n. 注意　**customer** [`kʌstəmə] n. 顧客
look for 尋找　**jeans** [dʒɪnz] n. 牛仔褲　**happen to-V** 恰巧　**guide** [gaɪd] v. 引導
counter [`kauntə] n. 櫃檯　**appreciate** [ə`priʃɪ͵et] v. 欣賞，感激　**wonderful**
[`wʌndəfəl] adj. 極好的　**experience** [ɪk`spɪrɪəns] n. 體驗

相關文法或用法補充

我們穿在身上的衣物經常是由相同的兩部分組成的。例如一對袖子、兩條褲管。
運用這個概念就能輕鬆記住一些成雙成對出現的衣物該如何「數」：
clothes 衣服由一塊一塊布料（cloth）組成
pants 長褲（美式）　trousers 長褲（英式）
jeans 牛仔褲　pajamas 睡衣　shorts 短褲
這些成雙成對的名詞已經是複數，所以：
(X) My pants is too tight. │ (O) My pants are too tight.
如果想表達「兩件褲子」，可加上單位：a pair of（一雙；一對）。例如：a pair of jeans、two pairs of jeans。

For question number 29, please look at the three pictures.

Question number 29: Listen to the following message. What will the parents do next?

Hi, darling, your grandmother is going to leave the hospital this afternoon. Daddy and I have to go there to pick her up. Because today is Saturday, the traffic could be busy on the road, and we need to go out as early as we can. Then we'll get home, along with Grandma, at about 6:00 p.m. to cook dinner. Can't wait to see her, right? See you later. Love you.

請看以下三張圖。並仔細聆聽以下的留言。這對父母接下來會做什麼？
嗨，親愛的！你的奶奶今天下午要出院了。爹地和我必須過去那裡接她。因為今天是星期六，路上可能會塞車，所以我們必須盡可能早點出門。然後我們，還有奶奶，大約會在晚間六點回到家煮晚餐。等不及要見到她了，是吧？晚點見。愛你。

答題解說

答案：(C)。題目問的是這對父母「將要做什麼事」，所以必須注意聽相關播放的內容。其中提到「然後我們，還有奶奶，大約會在晚間六點回到家煮晚餐。」（Then we'll get home, along with Grandma, at about 6:00 p.m. to cook dinner.）表示他們接下來要做的事是，回到家後煮晚餐。圖(A)是兩夫妻在吃早餐，牆上時鐘指著六點，顯然要刻意與文中的 6:00 p.m. 呼應來誤導答題。圖(B)是兩夫妻在車上，後座載著小孩，但這並非留言者接下來要做的事，而且他們要去載的人是個老人家，不是小孩。

破題關鍵

像這類「接下來會做什麼」（What... do next?）或是「可能會去做什麼」（What... probably do?）的題型，因為是與未來計畫有關的事，答案通常會出現在中後半段，而且要注意特定關鍵字句。這篇的關鍵字句是 Then we'll...to cook dinner.。

grandmother (= **grandma**) [ˋɡrænd͵mʌðɚ] n. 祖母，外祖母　　**hospital** [ˋhɑspɪtl̩] n. 醫院　　**pick** (**sb.**) **up** v. 接送（某人）　　**traffic** [ˋtræfɪk] n. 交通　　**along with** 與～在一起

as ... as one can 是從「比較句型」延伸而來的用法，表示「某人盡力去做某事」，這裡兩個 as 中間可能是形容詞、副詞或名詞，而 one 要隨主詞的「人稱」而變化，而 can 要隨「時態」的不同作變化。例如：

1. To get a good command of English, you need to read as many English articles as you can.（英文要強，你必須盡量多看英文文章。）
2. Take as much exercise as you can.（要盡可能多做運動。）

For question number 30, please look at the three pictures.

Question number 30: Listen to the following response. Which picture best describes the man?

Yes, sir. I did see him in front of the 7-11 convenience store. The man lives alone on the 3rd floor. That day he wore a white shirt and blue jeans. Besides, he was wearing a pair of sunglasses and was smoking when I saw him. I guessed he was waiting for someone there.

請看以下三張圖。並仔細聆聽以下的回答。哪一張圖最能夠描述這名男子？
是的，阿 sir。我的確有在那間 7-11 便利商店前面看到他。這名男子獨自住在三樓。那天他穿著一件白襯衫以及藍色牛仔褲。此外，我看到他時，他戴著一副墨鏡而且正在抽菸。我猜想他正在那邊等人。

答案：（C）。題目問的是哪一張人物圖是談話中描述的男子。前兩句與答題沒有任何關係，重點要從第三句開始聽起：他穿著一件白襯衫⋯此外⋯他戴著一副墨鏡。至於藍色牛仔褲（blue jeans）以及正在抽菸（was smoking）也和答案無

關。掌握以上兩個線索（shirt 以及 sunglasses），就可選出正確答案了。

像這類「描述人物」的題目，要特別注意播放內容中提及「外表、穿著、舉止」等的敘述。如果有仔細先觀察過三張人物圖，就可以去注意兩個點：穿什麼、戴什麼眼鏡。不過，這邊要特別注意 shirt（襯衫）與 T-shirt（圓領汗衫）、glasses（眼鏡）與 sunglasses（墨鏡）都有類似發音的部分，必須特別仔細聆聽。

convenience store 便利商店　**alone** [əˋlon] **adv.** 獨自　**shirt** [ʃɝt] **n.** 襯衫　**jeans** [dʒinz] **n.** 牛仔褲　**sunglasses** [ˋsʌnˏglæsɪz] **n.** 太陽眼鏡　**guess** [gɛs] **v.** 推測

front 雖然也是個簡單到不行的單字，不過它最常出現的片語 in the front of 和 in front of 用法，是有區別的。in the front of... 表示某個「空間內的前面部分」，而 in front of... 表示在某建物（外面）的前面。例如：

❶ There was a cat in front of the car, so the driver had to avoid hitting it.
（車子前面有隻貓，所以司機必須避免撞到牠。）

❷ There is a cat in the front of the car, and the little girl held it in her arms.
（車子前座有隻貓，且這個小女孩正抱著它。）

❸ Miss Li was giving her lecture in the front of the classroom. （李老師正站在教室前面講課。）

There is a big tree in front of the post office. （郵局前有一棵大樹。）

以上兩句的 in front of 以及 in the front of 不能互換，否則就不合邏輯了，因為老師不可能站在教室外面講課，而樹也不可能長在郵局裡面。

第
1
回

第
2
回

第
3
回

第
4
回

第
5
回

第
6
回

第
7
回

第
8
回

第
9
回

第
10
回

第一部分 詞彙

1. **I do not have a motorcycle, _____.**（我也沒有摩托車。）

 (A) too　(B) either　(C) neither　(D) only

答題解說

答案：(B)。題目這句是個否定句（I do not have...），而逗號後面空格要填入的是表示「也不」的副詞，要用 either，不能用 too。選項中的 (C) neither 是用於「附和句」中，相對於 neither 的是 so（請參考「附和句」的相關文法）。而 only 和 not 連用時，都是以 not only... 的形式出現，意思是「不僅，不只是」

破題關鍵

本題關鍵字是 not 這個否定詞。其考點是「肯定／否定句中表示『也』的區別」，也就是 too 與 either 的使用時機必須掌握住。

字詞解釋

motorcycle [`motəˌsaɪkl] n. 摩托車　**either** [`iðə] adv. 也不　**neither** [`niðə] adv. 也不

相關文法或用法補充

either 和 neither 皆具有名詞和形容詞性質：

❶ either 當名詞時，是指「（二者之一的）任一」，在句中可作主詞、受詞，為單數的概念。例如：
 Either of the plans is equally dangerous.（這兩項計畫中不論哪一個都同樣有危險。）

❷ 當形容詞時，修飾單數名詞，例如：
 He could write with either hand.（他左右手都能寫字。）

❸ neither 和 either 用法相同，但意思相反，表示（二者之中）沒有任何一個」，例如：
 I tried on two dresses, but neither fit me.（我試了兩套衣服，但沒一套合適。）
 For a long time neither spoke again.（很長一段時間，他倆沒有再說過話。）
 Neither of my friends has come yet.（我（兩個）朋友一個也沒來。）

2. **Miss Wang asked her students _____ their books.**（王老師要求她的學生們打開他們的書本。）

(A) opened　(B) to open　(C) opening　(D) and opened

答題解說

答案：(B)。這題要考的重點是「要求某人去做某事」的用法，其慣用句型是「ask/require/demand someone to do something」。因此，空格應填入不定詞的 to open。

破題關鍵

本題關鍵就在 asked 這個動詞，接受詞之後必須接不定詞作為「受詞補語」（OC）。就文法觀點來說，ask 當「要求」時，是「不完全及物動詞」，所以必須有個受詞補語讓這個動詞要表達的意思趨於完整。

字詞解釋

ask sb. to-V 要求某人去做～

相關文法或用法補充

當然，ask 也有「完全及物動詞」的意思。例如：I ask to talk to your manager.（我要和你們的經理說話。）因此，ask 後面的受詞如果是「行動、動作」時，必須用不定詞，而非動名詞（Ving）。

3. **Jerry has one brother, but he doesn't have _____ sisters.**（傑瑞有一個兄弟，但是沒有任何姐妹。）

(A) some　(B) many　(C) no　(D) any

答題解說

答案：(D)。any 意思是「任何」，常用於否定句中，且符合題意。some 意思是「一些」，可以修飾可數名詞，也可以修飾不可數名詞，常用於肯定句中；many 意思是「很多」，只能修飾可數名詞，一般情況下用於肯定句中；no 既可作副詞，亦可當形容詞，後面接名詞，表達否定意思，但前面已有否定詞（doesn't），所以 (C) 也是錯誤的。

破題關鍵

本題的考點在於幾個表示「數量」的形容詞用法，重點在於 some 和 any 的區別。前者一般用於肯定句，後者用於疑問及否定句。掌握這一點的話，就能很快選出正確答案。

相關文法或用法補充

＊no 是形容詞，none 是代名詞，兩者皆為否定詞（形成否定句）。例如：

❶ I have no maps. I had one before I moved into the new house.（我沒有地圖。在我搬進新家之前有一張。）

❷ None of them can answer the question.（他們當中沒有人能回答這個問題。）

❸ I hoped for letters from him, but none came.（我希望收到他的信，但一封也沒有。）

＊另外，some, any, no 可以和 one, body, thing 構成合成代名詞，像是 somebody、anybody、nobody、someone、anyone、no one、something、anything、nothing...。這些代名詞都是單數，表示「某人」、「某物」等，可在句中作主詞或受詞：

❶ Someone is asking for you on line.（有人打電話找你。）

❷ Nobody likes to be laughed at.（沒有人喜歡被嘲笑。）

❸ Anybody has his own strength and weakness.（每個人都有其優點和缺點。）

❹ It seems there is something wrong.（好像有什麼不對勁。）

❺ That's nothing.（沒什麼。）

4. It's hard to say how to get there. Let me draw a _____ for you.
（很難說明如何到那兒。我畫一張地圖給你看吧。）

(A) sight　(B) map　(C) photo　(D) line

答題解說

答案：(B)。如果單就「draw a _____」來看，四個名詞的選項都是符合句構的，所以還是必須根據整體句意來判斷。句子大意是「要到那兒去，很難用說的，所以畫一張_____給你看」。顯然答案應該是「地圖（map）」。其餘選項均不符句意與邏輯。

破題關鍵

本題關鍵是「how to get there（如何到那裏）與 map（地圖）的連結」。其餘的 sight（風景）、photo（照片）以及 line（線）都是不相關的選項。

字詞解釋

draw [drɔ] v. 畫　**sight** [saɪt] n. 風景　**map** [mæp] n. 地圖

相關文法或用法補充

「疑問詞（5W1H）＋不定詞（to-V）」其實是從「疑問詞＋S＋助動詞＋原形動詞」簡化而來，當名詞用，在句中扮演主詞或受詞的角色。例如：

where to go（到哪兒去）when to do it（什麼時候做這件事）
how to do it（如何做這件事）what to do（做什麼）
whom to talk to（要跟誰説話）which to buy（要買哪一個）

5. David was not _____ to the party last weekend.（大衛上週末沒有被邀請
   來參加這個派對。）

   (A) invited　(B) invented　(C) interested　(D) increased

   答題解說

   答案：(A)。四個選項都是不同意思的及物動詞，均可用於被動語態中，不過，
   將各選項套入空格中的話，可立即發現，因為主詞是人（David），所以 (B)
   invented（發明）與 (D) increased（增加）是完全不合邏輯的，而 (C) interested
   （感興趣的）似乎可行，不過「對於～感興趣」是 be interested in...，介系詞用
   in，所以 (C) 也是錯誤的。

   破題關鍵

   首先，主詞是「人」的這一點，必須先掌握。英文裡有些詞語，無論是動詞或形
   容詞，都是由「人」來發動，或是用來修飾「人」的。既然主詞是單一個人，那
   麼這個人當然不可能「被增加」或是「被發明」；再者，空格後介系詞為 to 是
   最後二選一時的最主要關鍵了。

   字詞解釋

   invite [ɪn`vaɪt] **v.** 邀請　**invent** [ɪn`vɛnt] **v.** 發明　**interested** [`ɪntərɪstɪd] **adj.** 感興趣
   的　**increase** [ɪn`kris] **v.** 增加

   相關文法或用法補充

   invite 當「邀請」的意思時，其後受詞為「人」，後面常接「to + 地方／活
   動」。例如：invite some friends to the show（邀請幾個朋友去看表演）。而 invite
   後面的名詞也可能是「事物」，表示「徵求、招致」，例如：invite questions
   from you all（請大家提出問題）、invite accidents（招致意外事件的發生）。

6. I work in a _____, where a lot of furniture is made every day.（我在一家
   工廠上班，那裡每天生產很多傢俱。）

   (A) factory　(B) garden　(C) hospital　(D) museum

   答題解說

   答案：(A)。四個選項都是不同意思的可數名詞，因此必須依照句意去判斷正確

的選項。句子大意是「我在一家 _____ 工作，這裡每天生產很多傢俱。」因此，一個生產傢俱的地方當然不會是「花園」、「醫院」或「博物館」，所以答案應該是(A)工廠。

破題關鍵

本題關鍵詞語是空格後的 furniture is made，更確切說，看到後面的 furniture 應該可以直接聯想到 factory 這個字。

字詞解釋

furniture [ˋfɝnɪtʃɚ] n. 傢俱　**factory** [ˋfæktərɪ] n. 工廠　**garden** [ˋgɑrdṇ] n. 花園　**hospital** [ˋhɑspɪtḷ] n. 醫院　**museum** [mjuˋzɪəm] n. 博物館

相關文法或用法補充

furniture 是個不可數名詞。在英文裡，不可數名詞指實質或概念無法分割的名詞，既然不可數，也就無單、複數可言。不可數名詞包括物質名詞、抽象名詞和專有名詞等。例如：news（新聞）、advice（諮詢、忠告）、information（資訊）、work（工作）、travel（旅遊）、weather（天氣）、luggage（行李）、progress（進展）、love（愛）、money（金錢）、furniture（傢俱）、homework（作業）、water（水）、bread（麵包）、milk（牛奶）、wealth（財富）、attention（注意力）、electricity（電）... 等。

7. **After that accident, he didn't work _____.**（在那次意外之後，他就不再工作了。）

(A) anyway　(B) anymore　(C) anything　(D) anytime

答題解說

答案：(B)。依照句意，動詞 work 表示「工作」，為不及物動詞，因此四個選項中，先排除掉只能當名詞用的(C) anything，其餘皆可當副詞，都可以用來修飾動詞 work。但句子的意思是「他發生意外之後，無法再工作了」，所以正確答案應為(B) anymore。

破題關鍵

有些題目可以直接看選項，判斷「考點」為何，然後掌握與它連結的關鍵字，答案就出來了。本題的連結關係是：accident→didn't work anymore。

字詞解釋

accident [ˋæksədənt] n. 意外事故　**anyway** [ˋɛnɪˏwe] adv. 無論如何，反正　**anymore** [ˋɛnɪmor] adv. 不再，再也不　**anytime** [ˋɛnɪˏtaɪm] adv. 在任何時候，總是

anyway 和 any way 的差別，看起來就是一個有空格，一個沒有空格而已，是這樣嗎？當然不是。anyway 是個副詞，它可以是「儘管如此」、「即使這樣」的意思。例如：My mother had told me about that, but I forgot it anyway.（我媽老早就跟我說過了，但儘管如此，我還是忘了。）

any way 是由 any 和 way 兩個字組成，any 是「任何」的意思，是個形容詞，而 way 可以指「方法」、「途徑」，是個名詞，所以兩個加起來是「任何方法／途徑」的意思。例如：I'll help in any way I can.（我會用盡辦法幫忙。）

8. _____ the help of each of you, we're not able to finish the task in time.
（若沒有大家的幫忙，我們無法及時完成這項任務。）

(A) With　(B) Without　(C) For　(D) From

答題解說

答案：(B)。四個選項都是介系詞，均可置於空格中而不影響文法句構。不過，若將各個介系詞套入「_____ 大家的幫忙，我們無法…」中的句意，即可立即選出正確答案是(B) Without。其餘三個選項均不符句意。

破題關鍵

「With/Without the help of...」是常見的用語，表示「（因為）有了／（如果）沒有～的幫忙」，是簡化假設語氣的用法。就本題來說，必須注意的是主要子句是「肯定句」還是「否定句」，如果是「否定句」，那麼就應與 without 搭配。

字詞解釋

finish [ˈfɪnɪʃ] v. 完成　　**task** [tæsk] n. 任務，工作　　**in time** 及時

相關文法或用法補充

help 雖然是個很初級的單字，但它可當動詞或名詞，且和它有關的片語及用法相當廣泛，所以經常是考題的常客。以下列舉一些常見用法：

1. help+(sb. to) + 原形動詞：
   She helped her (to) sit up in bed.（她扶她在床上坐起來。）
2. help 搭配 with
   My parents help me with my bank loan.（我她父母幫我還了一些銀行貸款。）
3. help yourself →請自便：
   A: May I look around the house? B: Sure. Please, help yourself!（A：我可以四處看看這房子嗎？B：當然，請自便！）
4. can't help but 忍不住，不得不：

He couldn't help but shed tears when he saw this photo. （他看到這張照片時，忍不住流了淚。）

9. **The basketball player is taller than _____ of us.** （這名籃球選手比我們任何人都還要高。）

　(A) that　(B) these　(C) much　(D) any

　答題解說

答案：（D）。句子意思是「這名籃球選手比起我們任何一個人都還要高」。所以正確答案應為（D）any。雖然四個選項都是代名詞，但 that、these 不能用來指「人」（如果是 those，則為正確答案），而 much 用來表示「不可數名詞」（如果是 many，則為正確答案）。

　破題關鍵

any 當代名詞時，可以用來指「人」或「物」，也就是 anyone（anybody）或是 anything，表示單數，這是基本的文法概念。

　字詞解釋

basketball player n. 籃球選手

　相關文法或用法補充

一般來說，any 當形容詞時：

1. 用於否定句／疑問句。例如：Have you got any related information?（你有任何相關資訊嗎？）、I don't have any carry-on luggage.（我沒有任何手提行李。）

2. any 後面可以接不可數名詞或可數名詞複數形。例如：Do you have any white shirts?（你有任何白色襯衫嗎？）、Is there any cheese in it?（這裡面有起司嗎？）

　不過，當 any 表示「任一」時：

　可以用在肯定句裡。例如：Any kid can do this.（任一個小孩都能做到這件事。）、Raise your hand if you have any questions.（如果你有任何問題的話，請舉起手來。）

10. **She's always willing to help _____ people with the same problems.** （她總是願意幫助其他有相同問題的人。）

　(A) other　(B) the other　(C) others　(D) the others

第 1 回
第 2 回
第 3 回
第 4 回
第 5 回
第 6 回
第 7 回
第 8 回
第 9 回
第 10 回

答案：(A)。句子大意是「她願意幫助 _____ 的人」，顯然空格應填入一個形容詞，修飾 people。所以 (C)、(D)可直接排除掉。至於 (B) the other 是用來修飾「特定範圍」的人或物，但題目這句的 people 顯然是沒有限定範圍的，故正確答案應為(A)。

只要稍有文法基本概念，應該不會去選 (C) 或 (D)，因此本題重點是在 other 與 the other 的區別。顯然兩者差別在 the 這個定冠詞。意即，有 the 就表示「有限定範圍」。另外，也要看得出來「help 人＋ with 事」的用法，所以 people 後面的 with... problems 並非其修飾語，所以這裡的 people 是沒有限定範圍的。

be willing to-V 願意去做某事

其實 the other 是 other 的延伸，要注意的是，other 沒有限定，但是 the other 是有指定「另外那個」或「另外那些」的。例如：

1. Some boys like to play basketball, and the other boys (the others) enjoy playing football.（有些男孩喜歡打籃球。其他男孩喜歡踢足球。）
2. One of his sons lives in Taipei. The other one lives with him in Hsinchu.（他其中一個兒子住在台北。另一個兒子跟他一起住在新竹。）

   另外，**the other** 可當代名詞用，表示單數，而 the others 表示複數。例如：

   She wore different colored socks today. One was red, and the other was blue.

   （她今天穿不同顏色的襪子。一隻是紅色，另一隻是藍色。）

第二部分 段落填空

Questions 11-14

Grace does not like to read, **but** she enjoys listening to music, especially when she takes a bath every night. Her favorite song goes like this: "Oh, I like **to travel** around the world, but I'm just a passing traveller to the world. I'll tell you where I'm from, what I like to eat and that I'm very happy to be here."

One day, however, she found that she was bored with listening to the same music over and over **again**. She wanted to listen to different styles of songs. So, she went online to search for rock music. But it sounded too noisy. **Then she continued to look for some country music.** She thought it might help her fall asleep, but actually she dislikes such a style.

中文翻譯 葛瑞絲不喜歡閱讀，但是她喜歡聽音樂，尤其當她每天晚上在洗澡的時候。她最愛的歌曲是這麼唱的：「噢，我喜歡到世界各地旅行，但我只是這個世界的過客。我會告訴你們我來自何處、我喜歡吃什麼以及我很高興來到這裡。」

不過，某一天，她發現她厭倦了一而再再而三地聽著相同的音樂。她想聽點不同風格的歌。因此，她上網去搜尋搖滾樂。但它聽起來太吵了。然後她繼續找些鄉村音樂。她認為鄉村音樂對她入睡也許有幫助，但事實上她不喜歡這種風格的。

答題解說

11. 答案：(B)。空格前後為意思相反的完整句，因此應填入 but。

12. 答案：(C)。四個選項都是同一個動詞衍生的不同詞類。重點在於動詞 like 後面，可接 to-V 亦可接 Ving，所以應選 (C)。(A) 的 travel 無論作動詞或名詞，在此均不符文法規則。

13. 答案：(D)。空格這個字與前面的 over and over 形成 over and over again 這個副詞片語，意思是「一而再再而三地」，相較於單一字的 again，更具強調作用。

14. 答案：(B)。這是要挑選一個句子、子句或句子的一部分放入空格後，確認空格

新題型 前後和空格句之間的連接關係，是否讓句意顯得自然通順，所以必須對照上下文或根據整段文章的意旨。空格後面句子提到「她認為『它』對她入睡也許有幫助，但事實上她不喜歡這種風格。」這裡的 it，以及空格前一句的 it，雖然不是指同樣的東西，但都是指某種音樂類型，所以選項中只有 (B)「然後她繼續找些鄉村音樂。」最能夠連接前後兩句且符合句意。以下是其餘選項句子的翻譯：

(A) 所以她試圖看些有趣的書籍。

(C) 此外，她總是有許多新衣服要試穿。

(D) 如今，音樂很容易從許多網站上下載。

破題關鍵

11. 雖然知道要填入的是連接詞，但若能迅速掌握關鍵字詞，就能快速解題：看到前面是 does not like，後面是 enjoys，應該就能知道要填入 but 了。

12. 「一個句子不得有兩個動詞」的基本文法概念一定要牢記，再來就是有些動詞後面只能接不定詞（to-V），有些只能接動名詞（Ving），有些則是兩者皆可。like 就是屬於兩者皆可的動詞。

第 1 回

第 2 回

第 3 回

第 4 回

第 5 回

第 6 回

第 7 回

第 8 回

第 9 回

第 10 回

13. over and over again 為常見固定用語，如果有學過就能立即作答，其餘選項完全不需考慮。

14. 從後面這句提到的 "might help her fall asleep" 以及關鍵字 style 可知，空格要填入一個有提到某種「幫助入眠的音樂」的句子。

take a bath 洗澡　**especially** [əˋspɛʃəlɪ] **adv.** 尤其　**favorite** [ˋfevərɪt] **adj.** 特別喜愛的　**passing** [ˋpæsɪŋ] **adj.** 經過的，短暫的　**traveller** [ˋtrævlɚ] **n.** 旅客　**bored** [bord] 感到乏味的　**over and over again** 一而再地　**search** [sɝtʃ] **v.** 搜尋　**rock music** 搖滾樂　**continue** [kənˋtɪnjʊ] **v.** 繼續　**look for** 尋找　**country music** 鄉村音樂　**fall asleep** 入睡　**actually** [ˋæktʃʊəlɪ] **adv.** 實際上　**nowadays** [ˋnaʊəˌdez] **adv.** 現今，時下　**download** [ˋdaʊnˌlod] **v.** 下載

11. 對等連接詞是用來連接句子中的字、片語或子句。這種連接詞所連接的兩端必須是對等的；「字」和「字」、「片語」和「片語」、「子句」和「子句」。

12. 有些動詞後面一定是接「不定詞」，例如：want、need、decide、learn、plan、would like…；有些動詞後面一定是接「動名詞」，例如：enjoy、finish、practice、keep... 等。有些動詞後面可接「不定詞」或「動名詞」，且意思差不多。這類動詞有 begin、start、try、like、love、hate ... 等，而有些動詞接「不定詞」或「動名詞」意思完全不同。由於篇幅有限，請先記得這樣的基本概念即可。

13. again 表示「再一次」，也許很多初級程度者也都知道了。不過有時候在文章中為了強調作用，也會有 again and again、again and over again 等的用法，必須特別注意。

14. 選項 (C) 的 try on 在這裡也很可能被誤選為正確答案，因為它有「嘗試」的意味，不過 try on 通常指「試穿衣服」，這裡的 on 與 put on（= wear）的 on 有相同的作用。

Questions 15-18

Yesterday my nephew Sam visited me. He told me that his mother **would** be away for a while, and he didn't know where to spend his boring afternoon. So he decided to come to my place to kill time. Actually I knew that he only wanted to play the video games that I had just bought last week.

I took him to my room and showed him **how** to play the newest games. He looked so excited that he almost forgot it was time to go home. **Then his mother made a**

call to me and she asked me to **bring** his son home. Anyway, I always like to help people. But the problem is, Sam was still unwilling to leave my room.

中文翻譯 昨天我姪兒山姆來找我。他告訴我說，他媽媽會暫時不在，而他不知道要在哪裡度過他無聊的下午時光。所以他決定來我這邊消磨時間。事實上我知道他只是想來玩我上週剛買的電動玩具。

我帶他到我房間，然後讓他看看最新的遊戲怎麼玩。他看起來多麼興奮，以致於他幾乎忘了該回家的時間了。後來他母親打電話給我，並拜託我帶他兒子回家。沒關係，我總是樂於助人。但問題是，山姆還是不願意離開我房間。

答題解說

15. 答案：(C)。四個選項都是同一個助動詞的不同時態，且有肯定、否定之別。首先，前面句子提到「山姆來找我」，因為他母親不在家，所以應以 will 或 would be away 來表示，接著是選擇適當的時態。因為一開始就提到是昨天（Yesterday...）發生的事，所以不能用 will。故正確答案應為 (C)。

16. 答案：(B)。四個選項皆為疑問詞，用於「疑問詞 + 不定詞（to-V）」的表達，而 to-V 後面有受詞了，所以 (A) what 不可選。其餘 (C) where 及 (D) when 均不符句意。

17. 答案：(A)。這是要挑選一個句子、子句或句子的一部分放入空格後，確認空格前後和空格句之間的連接關係，是否讓句意顯得自然通順。空格前一句提到「他看起來多麼興奮，以致於他幾乎忘了該回家的時間了。」而後面這句說「…並且她拜託我帶他兒子回家。」顯然空格這一句應該是跟小孩子的母親做了什麼動作有關，故 (A) 的「後來他母親打電話給我（並拜託…）」最符合句意。以下是其餘選項句子的翻譯：

(B) 所以我很開心有他在這裡
(C) 我想他母親還沒到
(D) 也許我應該打電話給他母親

18. 答案：(D)。四個選項皆為不同意思的動詞，應理解前後文句意才能做答。句意是「他母親要求我帶他兒子回家」，這裡的「帶」應用 bring，而非 take，因為「要求者」不在現場。其餘 (B) ask 及 (C) call 均不符句意。

破題關鍵

15. 本題考的是「動詞一致性」的問題。由於主要子句動詞（told）為過去式，that 子句中也應用過去式。

16. 「疑問詞 + 不定詞（to-V）」的用法，必須注意不定詞後面是否有受詞，再來就是考慮符不符合句意的問題。

第 1 回
第 2 回
第 3 回
第 4 回
第 5 回
第 6 回
第 7 回
第 8 回
第 9 回
第 10 回

17. 空格這句是一個「and 連接兩個對等子句」的第一個子句，所以一定會和 and 後面這句有動作上的連帶關係，亦即「她打電話給我而且要求我…」。

18. 這題主要是考 bring 與 take 表示「帶」的用法區別。bring 意思是「帶來」，而 take 意思是「帶走、帶去」。

字詞解釋

nephew [ˋnɛfju] **n.** 姪兒，外甥　**for a while** 暫時　**boring** [ˋborɪŋ] **adj.** 乏味的　**actually** [ˋæktʃʊəlɪ] **adv.** 實際上　**excited** [ɪkˋsaɪtɪd] **adj.** 興奮的　**make a call to**... 打電話給～　**unwilling** [ʌnˋwɪlɪŋ] **adj.** 不願意的

相關文法觀念補充

15. would 在使用上讓很多人困擾，因為 would 有很多用法，would 是 will 的過去式，但也能用在表達「想要」的意思。例如想請求別人幫忙時，可以說 Would you please help me?，雖然也可以用 will，但用 would 會比用 will，更顯得有禮貌多了。

16. 「疑問詞 + 不定詞（to-V）」= 名詞片語，它簡化自「疑問詞引導的名詞子句」。例如 I don't know how I can help you. 可以簡化成 I don't know how to help you.。不過前提是，主要子句與疑問詞子句的主詞必須是同一個人。

17. It is time... 是用來表達「現在是時候做某事了」。例如：It is time to take a break.（現在是該休息一會兒了。）另外也可以在 to-V 前面加「for + 人」：It is time for you to take a break.。當然，也可以用「It is time for + 名詞」表示「該做某事的時候了」：It's time for a break.（現在是時候休息一會兒了。）

18. 如果外國朋友要到國外出差，你想好心地說「我可以帶你去機場。」要怎麼說好呢？如果你說 I can bring you to the airport.，那對方可能會稍微呆滯一下再回過神回答你「Thank you.」吧！為什麼呢？其實這裡正確的用法要用 take 這個動詞才對。bring 是一個帶有方向性的動詞，可以想像是把某個東西「從外面帶過來」，而 take 也是一個帶有方向性的動詞，可以想像是將某個東西「從這邊帶過去」。因為外國朋友的方向是要「過去」機場，並不是要將他從機場「帶過來」說話者（你）這邊，所以這邊要用 take 才對喔。

第三部分 閱讀理解

Questions 19-21

中文翻譯

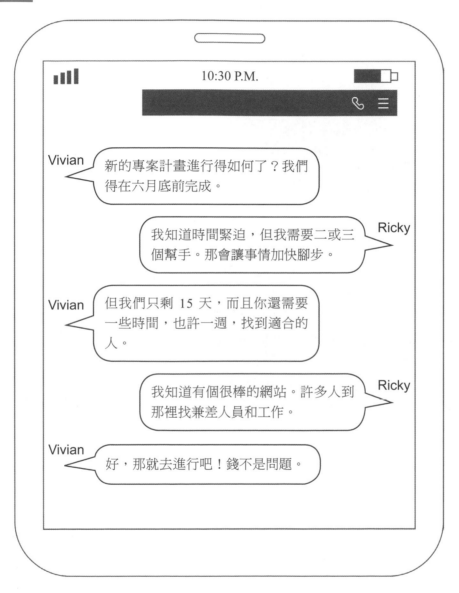

10:30 P.M.

Vivian 新的專案計畫進行得如何了？我們得在六月底前完成。

Ricky 我知道時間緊迫，但我需要二或三個幫手。那會讓事情加快腳步。

Vivian 但我們只剩 15 天，而且你還需要一些時間，也許一週，找到適合的人。

Ricky 我知道有個很棒的網站。許多人到那裡找兼差人員和工作。

Vivian 好，那就去進行吧！錢不是問題。

第 1 回
第 2 回
第 3 回
第 4 回
第 5 回
第 6 回
第 7 回
第 8 回
第 9 回
第 10 回

Ricky 隔天上這個網站，並填寫以下表格。

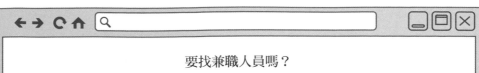

要找兼職人員嗎？

有線上的免費廣告！數萬人及公司正使用我們的網站找到他們完美的幫手了。我們在全國各地都有。填寫以下表格然後送出即可。今天就開始吧！

公司類型：建築公司
工作類型：室內裝潢
需求人數：3 人
聯絡人：Ricky Chang
聯絡電話：0987-888-168
工作地點：台中
時薪：NT$200（一天八小時）

送出

19. 這則廣告的目的為何？
   (A) 幫助人們找到兼職工作。
   (B) 幫助公司或店家為他們的產品打廣告。
   (C) 引導公司寫兼職工作的廣告。
   (D) 鼓勵人們或企業加入一個網站。

20. Ricky 何時上網去找助手？
   (A) 在 6 月 14 日　　　　　　　(B) 在 6 月 15 日
   (C) 在 6 月 16 日　　　　　　　(D) 在 6 月 17 日

21. 他們一天得支付多少雇用短期工人的費用？
   (A) 新台幣 200 元　　　　　　　(B) 新台幣 1600 元
   (C) 新台幣 4800 元　　　　　　　(D) 完全免費。

答題解說

19. 答案：(D)。從標題「要找兼職人員嗎？」可知，這是一家廣告公司針對一些想要找人手的個人或公司，提供一個免費的徵才平台，但這些個人或公司必須先註冊登記（Register by filling out...），也就是要先「加入這個網站，成為會員」。

20. 答案：(C)。本題需要整合與歸納兩篇文本的資訊並比對多項訊息才能夠得到正確的答案。題目問的是 Ricky 何時上網去找助手，首先，在聊天訊息中 Vivian 提到 "We need to get it done at the end of June."（我們得在六月底前完成。）以及 "we only have 15 days left"（我們只剩 15 天）顯然這則聊天訊息的時間是在 6 月 15 日的晚間 10:30（時間顯示於訊息最上方）。接著，在進入網頁內容之前有一句說明：Ricky went to the site the following day...（Ricky 隔天上這個網站…）因此，我們可以推知 Ricky 是在 6/16 上網登入資料來找兼差工人。

21. 答案：(C)。本題需要整合與歸納兩篇文本的訊息與資訊，才能夠得到正確的答案。首先，一定要看清楚題目要問什麼：「每日總共要支出的雇用工人費用」。雖然第一篇的對話訊息中，Ricky 提到要雇用 2 至 3 人，但沒有一個確切數字還是無法得到答案。所以要繼續看網頁內容：「需求人數：3 人」以及「時薪：NT$200（一天八小時）」，所以每一日總費用是 200 x 8 x 3 = 4,800。此外，別被「免費使用網站（Free advertisement online）」的文字給誤導而去選了（D）喔！

破題關鍵

19. 題目要問的是「廣告的目的」，這種「主旨型」的題型其實是可以留待後面兩題答完之後再回過頭來解題，因為你只要大略了解內容即可輕易答題。

20. the following day 可以當作副詞用，表示「在隔天」。following 當形容詞表示「接下來的」。

21. 題目中的 "pay for" 意思是「為了～付錢；支付～的費用」，而 short-time hired workers 就是指網頁上方的 part-timers。

字詞解釋

project [`prɑdʒɛkt] n. 專案，計畫　**tight** [taɪt] adj.（時間、空間）緊湊的　**helper** [`hɛlpɚ] n. 助手，幫手　**get... in place** 使～就定位　**speed up** 加快　**part-time** [`part`taɪm] adj. 兼職的　**go ahead** 繼續進行　**part-timer** [`part͵taɪmɚ] n. 兼差工作者　**advertisement** [͵ædvɚ`taɪzmənt] n. 廣告，宣傳　**perfect** [`pɝfɪkt] adj. 完美的　**helper** [`hɛlpɚ] n. 助手，幫手　**available** [ə`veləbl] adj. 可用的，可得的　**nation-wide** [`neʃən͵waɪd] adv. 在全國　**register** [`rɛdʒɪstɚ] v. 登記，註冊　**fill out** v. 填寫　**purpose** [`pɝpəs] n. 目的　**advise** [əd`vaɪz] v. 建議，勸告　**building** [`bɪldɪŋ] n. 建築（物）**indoor** [`ɪn͵dor] adj. 室內的　**decoration** [͵dɛkə`reʃən] n. 裝飾，裝潢

相關文法或用法補充

❶ 英文沒有「萬」這個字，而是以 ten thousand 來說。所以 tens of thousands of... 這個片語就是「數以萬計的～」意思。這是由片語 tens of..（數十～）加上 thousands of...（數千～）而成的。

❷ 字尾 -er 通常指「人」，例如這則廣告中的 helper（幫手），通常表示「動作的發動者」。另外字尾 -ee 也是指某種「人」，但它代表「動作的接受者」。例如：employer（雇主）vs. employee（雇員）、interviewer（面試官）vs. interviewee（面試者）、examiner（審查員）vs. examinee（受檢查者）…等。

❸ 字尾 -wide 是個代表「整體範圍」的字尾，通常可當形容詞或副詞用，例如 nationwide/countrywide（全國性的；在全國）、worldwide（遍及全球的；在世界各地）、citywide（全市的）…等。

Questions 22-24

中文翻譯

（電話鈴聲響起…）

茱莉亞：午安，這裡是周醫師辦公室。有什麼可以為您效勞的？

胡太太：我是胡太太。我想要預約健檢的時間。

茱莉亞：讓我查看一下預約紀錄。請稍候。

（幾秒鐘之後…）喂。胡太太嗎？感謝您的等候。

胡太太：我在。不客氣！

茱莉亞：您的檢查將安排在七月十五日週五來進行。您應於上午九點前到醫院。這時間對您來說是否方便呢？

胡太太：沒問題！

茱莉亞：可以請問您的電話幾號嗎？

胡太太：當然。0-9-7-2-3-4-9-1-7-6

茱莉亞：謝謝。對了，我想提醒您一下，從當天凌晨 12:00 起，不可以再吃或喝任何東西。

胡太太：我知道。謝謝您的提醒。

茱莉亞：如果您想更改預約時間，請盡快打電話給我。

胡太太：好的，非常感謝您。

茱莉亞：到時候見。

胡太太：再見！

22. 胡太太為什麼打這通電話？
    (A) 她想和茱莉亞講話。
    (B) 她想要去拜訪周醫師。
    (C) 她想要了解她的健康狀況。
    (D) 她想要取消她的約診。

第 1 回
第 2 回
第 3 回
第 4 回
第 5 回
第 6 回
第 7 回
第 8 回
第 9 回
第 10 回

23. 茱莉亞可能是做什麼的？

(A) 她是個家庭主婦。

(B) 她是個護士。

(C) 她是個飯店員工。

(D) 她是個餐廳女服務生。

24. 胡太太被告知要做什麼？

(A) 盡速支付帳單。

(B) 如有需要，取消預約。

(C) 如果想要做任何變更，打電話給周醫師。

(D) 記住禁食的規定。

答題解說

這是一則醫院護士與想做健檢的民眾之間的對話。

22. 答案：(C)。對話中胡太太說的第一句話（I would like to make an appointment for my health checkup.）就點出了她打這通電話的原因：她想預約做健康檢查，亦即她想要了解她的健康狀況。

23. 答案：(B)。題目問的是「茱莉亞可能是做什麼的」，也就是她的職業，所以從整篇對話內容可知，胡太太打電話進來預約健檢，然後茱莉亞幫她完成預約，並提醒健檢注意事項，所以她的職業可能是護士。

24. 答案：(D)。題目問「胡太太被告知要做什麼？」所以應該從茱莉亞的說話當中去找線索。她最後提醒胡太太健檢前應禁食的規定（I'd like to remind you that... do not eat or drink anything.）所以答案為 (D)。

破題關鍵

22. 一般來說，答案選項中的用字很少會和短文中的一模一樣，所以往往必須注意「換句話說」的對照考法。如本題：make an appointment for my health checkup 與選項 (C) 的 "know what's going on with her health" 都是在表達同一件事情。

23. 其實整篇對話只要抓到一個關鍵字 hospital，答案就出來了。因為茱莉亞對胡太太說 "You should be in the hospital before 9:00 a.m."。

24. 茱莉亞最後提醒了胡太太兩件事情：1. 她說「從當天凌晨 12:00 起，不可以再吃或喝任何東西。」以及 2.「如果你想更改預約時間，請盡快打電話給我。」所以選項中只有「記住禁食的規定」是符合題目要問的。

字詞解釋

ring [rɪŋ] v.（鐘，鈴等）鳴響 **appointment** [ə`pɔɪntmənt] n.（會面的）約定 **health** [hɛlθ] n. 健康 **checkup** [`tʃɛk͵ʌp] n.（體格）檢查 **arrange** [ə`rendʒ] v. 安排 **carry out** v. 進行，實施 **hospital** [`hɑspɪtl] n. 醫院 **convenient** [kən`vinjənt] adj. 方便的

by the way adv. 順道一提　**remind** [rɪ`maɪnd] v. 提醒　**from... on** 從～開始
reminder [rɪ`maɪndə] n. 提醒（的人事物）

❶ appointment（約定，約會）這個字常用於「make an appointment with + 人」（與某人有約）。例如：If you want to see someone important in a company, you should make an appointment first.（若想要見公司的某重要人物時，你應該事先預約。）另外，在英文裡，男女朋友或戀人之間的約會，通常會用 date 這個字。例如：I have a date with my wife tonight.（我今晚要和我太太約會。）

❷ as soon as possible 的意思是「儘快」，當副詞用。「as +形容詞／副詞 + as possible」是個常用的片語，例如：I will return your notebook as soon as possible.（我會儘快還筆記本給你。）、She finished her homework as quickly as possible.（她儘快地做完了家庭作業。）、I tried to read as many books as possible when I was at school.（我上學時盡可能多讀書。）、We should try our best to save water as much as possible.（我們應該努力多節約水。）

Questions 25-27

　　如今，智慧手機已成為我們日常生活中的必需品。我們用它來看電視和電影、繳費、獲知最新消息與資訊，而且我們不會再迷路，因為有 Google 地圖。所以現代的年輕人很難想像以下的故事會發生。

　　瓊斯先生是一個鄉下的老實人，他通常都在田野工作。他不喜歡用太多電子產品。他沒有智慧手機，因為他覺得它太複雜了。不過他有一支舊式行動電話。反正，他對於自己的簡單生活感到滿足。某日，他想要到某城市裡的百貨公司。於是他在報紙上找到了地址、進了他的車，並開往這座城市。他開了很久，卻迷路了，所以他停下來找人來幫忙他。

　　一位女士告訴他：「沿著這條路直走一公里，然後當你看到轉角有一間郵局，就右轉，然後走左邊的第二條路」。半個小時以後，瓊斯先生終於到達了百貨公司，但是已經打烊了。

25. 這篇短文應該給個什麼標題？
　　(A) 智慧手機可以如何給你協助
　　(B) 發現電子產品對健康有害
　　(C) 並非每個人都使用智慧手機
　　(D) Google 地圖幫你很多忙

26. 為什麼瓊斯先生要找人幫他？

    (A) 他不知道地址。   (B) 他在意外中受傷了。

    (C) 他的車在路上拋錨了。   (D) 他迷路了。

27. 當瓊斯先生看到郵局時，他應該做什麼？

    (A) 右轉。(B) 左轉。(C) 停車。(D) 繼續直走。

答題解說

這是一篇說明兼記敘文，內容講述一位沒有智慧手機的男子，辛苦找路的結果。

25. 答案：(C)。題目問的是本篇短文的標題，雖然一開始提到智慧手機已成為我們日常生活中的必需品，但第一段的最後一句出現重要轉折點：所以現代的年輕人很難想像以下的故事會發生。接著第二段開始敘述瓊斯先生沒有使用智慧手機，所以正確答案是(C)的「並非每個人都使用智慧手機」。

26. 答案：(D)。題目要問的是瓊斯先生要找人幫他的原因為何。短文中有個片語 got lost 告訴我們，瓊斯先生因為迷路了，所以要找人幫忙。

27. 答案：(A)。根據短文中那位指路的小姐回答的話，瓊斯先生在看到郵局時應該向右轉彎，所以正確答案是(A)。

破題關鍵

25. 文章或故事主旨的部分，只要從各段主題句下手，即可大致掌握全篇的要點所在，通常第一段一開始就會點出主旨，但出現在最後一句也是常有的情況："...it is difficult for young people now to imagine such a story..."。

26. 在短文中找線索：「但是他迷路了，所以他停下來找人來幫忙他。（...but he got lost, so he stopped and asked somebody to help him.）」

27. 短文中那位指路的小姐說「當你看到轉角有一間郵局，就右轉（Then turn right when you see a post office on the corner.）」其中 turn right 正好與 (A) 的 Take a right turn. 是一樣意思。

字詞解釋

smartphone [ˋsmɑrt͵fon] **n.** 智慧型手機   **necessary** [ˋnɛsə͵sɛrɪ] **adj.** 必需的   **latest** [ˋletɪst] **adj.** 最新的   **thanks to...** 由於〜   **imagine** [ɪˋmædʒɪn] **v.** 想像   **as follows** 以下所示   **honest** [ˋɑnɪst] **adj.** 正直的   **complex** [ˋkɑmplɛks] **adj.** 複雜的   **mobile phone** 行動電話   **satisfied** [ˋsætɪs͵faɪd] **adj.** 感到滿意的   **usually** [ˋjuʒʊəlɪ] **adv.** 通常   **address** [əˋdrɛs] **n.** 地址   **lost** [lɔst] **adj.** 迷路的   **straight** [stret] **adv.** 直接地   **post office** 郵局   **corner** [ˋkɔrnɚ] **n.** 街角   **arrive** [əˋraɪv] **v.** 抵達

❶ get hurt 的意思是「受傷」，其中 get 是「連綴動詞（不完全不及物動詞）」，其後要接主詞補語（名詞或形容詞），而 hurt 是過去分詞當形容詞用。動詞 hurt 的過去式、過去分詞都是 hurt。

❷ right 和 left 可以用做形容詞（表示「左／右的」），也可以用做副詞（表示「向左／向右」）。例如：Turn right（向右轉）= take a right turn；Turn left（向左轉）= take a left turn 向左轉。另外，如果要表示「迴轉」，可以用 Take a U-turn。

❸ 一個小時是 an hour，半個小時是 half an hour，須注意 half 放在不定冠詞 an 前面，而非 a half hour。另外，half 亦可當名詞用，其複數形為 halves。

Questions 28-30

中文翻譯

寄件人	janet_chen@tpa.edu.gov
收件人	grace_liu@goodmail.com
主旨	回覆：近來可好？

親愛的 Grace：

　　真是抱歉，這麼晚才回覆你上一封信。最近這些日子我一直忙著準備入學考試，而且我總是很晚才從圖書館回到家。我每天晚上留在那裡念書一直到 9:30。入學考試將於七月二日舉行，而且只剩下約一個月的時間。在那之後，我將會知道我過去一年來學了多少、念了多少東西。

　　其實，我一直承受很大的壓力。我父母希望我可以進入第一名的學校且他們期望我成為一位醫師。他們說，他們有信心我可以做得到。那或許對我來說是鼓勵的話，但我懷疑我參加這考試要幹嘛。大學的學歷對我而言沒有任何意義，雖然我大部分同學都決定無論如何都要取得大學學位。

　　那麼，我會在考試結束之後盡快跟你聯絡。屆時我們可以好好東聊西聊。我知道在我家附近有一家很棒的咖啡廳。我們還可以享受那裡的美麗海景。

期待再見
Janet

第 1 回
第 2 回
第 3 回
第 4 回
第 5 回
第 6 回
第 7 回
第 8 回
第 9 回
第 10 回

28. Janet 的這封電子郵件目的為何？
    (A) 為了決定一個相聚的日期
    (B) 為了取消一個重要的約會
    (C) 為了告知近況
    (D) 為了計畫一趟海外之旅

29. Janet 最有可能的身分是？
    (A) 教師
    (B) 學生
    (C) 圖書館員
    (D) 上班族

30. 以下關於 Janet，何者為非？
    (A) 她擔心即將到來的考試。
    (B) 她的父母希望她進入最好的學校。
    (C) 目前她想要賺錢。
    (D) 大學學位對她來說很重要。

答題解說

這個題組是一封電子郵件，內容主要關於 Janet 回覆 Grace 目前的近況。

28. 答案：(C)。題目要問的是這封電子郵件的目的（或主旨），可以先從第一段找線索：最近這些日子我一直忙著準備入學考試…（These days I've been busy preparing for the entrance exam...）顯然是要告訴對方最近在忙什麼，所以這麼晚才回覆。故正確答案為 (C) 為了告知近況（To tell about current situation.）

29. 答案：(B)。題目要問的是 Janet 最有可能的身分，雖然第一段提到 "These days I've been busy preparing for the entrance exam..."，但也不能百分之百確定她是學生。可以從第二段最後的 "...most of my classmates decided to..." 確認 Janet 目前還不是上班族，包括老師及圖書館員。故正確答案為 (B) A student。

30. 答案：(D)。(A) 的部分可以從第二段一開始的 "In fact, I have been under much pressure." 得知；(B) 的部分可以從這段的 "My parents hope I can enter the No.1 school..."；(C) 的部分並未提及。只有 (D) 是不符合短文內容的，因為 "The college degree doesn't mean anything to me..." 的部分已告訴我們，大學學位對她來說並不重要。所以正確答案為 (D)。

破題關鍵

28. 信件最上方，在收件人與寄件人下面都會有個「主旨」欄位，這是找尋信件主旨的第一線索。 "How's it going?" 是問對方「近來如何？」的常見話語。

29. 一個人的「身分」或是「職業」，通常可從內容中提及他／她「目前正在做以及想要做的事」來判斷。Janet 目前正在準備考試，但她想要開始工作賺錢，這是本題的關鍵線索。

30. 「何者為真」或「何者為非」的題型，都屬於內容細節型的題目。必須了解每一個選項的內容，然後對照短文中提及的相關內容才能作答。

this adv.【口】這麼，這樣地　**prepare** [prɪ`pɛr] v. 準備　**entrance** [`ɛntrəns] n. 進入，入學　**in fact** adv. 事實上　**pressure** [`prɛʃɚ] n. 壓力　**expect** [ɪk`spɛkt] v. 預料，預期　**confident** [`kɑnfədənt] adj. 有信心的　**make it** 做得到　**encouraging** [ɪn`kɝɪdʒɪŋ] adj. 令人鼓舞的　**doubt** [daʊt] v. 懷疑　**take an exam** 參加考試　**college** [`kɑlɪdʒ] n. 大學　**degree** [dɪ`gri] n. 學位，程度，等級　**anyway** [`ɛnɪ,we] adv. 無論如何，反正　**by then** adv. 到時候，屆時　**view** [vju] n. 景觀　***get-together** n. 聚會　**cancel** [`kænsl̩] v. 取消　**current** [`kɝənt] adj. 目前的　***situation** [,sɪtʃʊ`eʃən] n. 狀況　**overseas** [`ovɚ`siz] adj. 海外的　**likely** [`laɪklɪ] adv. 可能地　***librarian** [laɪ`brɛrɪən] n. 圖書館員　**worried** [`wɝɪd] adj. 擔心的，發愁的　**coming** [`kʌmɪŋ] adj. 即將到來的，接著的

❶ 「there be + 名詞 + 分詞」屬於 there be 的延伸句型。現在分詞表示主動（某動作正在進行；呈現一種狀態），過去分詞表示被動，譯為「有～（正在做某事）」。

1. There is someone waiting for him.（有人在等他。）
2. There is a door leading to the garden.（有一座門通往花園。）
3. There is nothing written on it.（上面沒寫東西。）
4. There were ten people killed in the accident.（事故中有 10 人喪生。）

❷ 「未來進行式」表示某個動作將在或可能在未來某一時刻進行或持續進行中，通常帶有表示未來時刻的副詞片語或子句，如 At this time tomorrow, next Monday... 等。例如：We'll be leaving early tomorrow morning.（我們明天一早就離開。）

3

GEPT
全民英檢

初級初試
中譯＋解析

第一部分 看圖辨義

1. **For question number 1, please look at Picture A.**

   Question number 1: Who should pay attention to this sign?（誰應該要注意這個標誌？）
   (A) Bus drivers（公車司機）
   (B) Factory workers（工廠工人）
   (C) Waiters or waitresses（男或女服務生）

   ### 答題解說
   答案：（B）。Electric Shock 表示「觸電」，接著再看到底下的 "Turn power off when doing repairs."（進行維修時請關閉電源。）顯然不可能是給公車司機或餐廳服務生看的，所以最有可能是給「工廠工人」看的標誌。

   ### 字詞解釋
   pay attention to... 注意　**waiter** [ˋwetɚ] n.（男）侍者，服務生　**waitress** [ˋwetrɪs] n. 女服務生

   ### 相關文法或用法補充
   ❶ pay attention to... 當中的 to 是介系詞，後面接名詞，來表示「應被注意的人事物」。attention 這個名詞衍生自動詞 attend。因此，attend 除了有「參加」的意思之外，還有「注意、傾聽」的意思。例如：She did not attend to the warning sign.（她沒有注意這個警示標誌。）
   ❷ 字尾加 -ess 都是「女性」，例如：hostess（女主人）、princess（公主）、goddess（女神）、actress（女演員）、waitress（女服務員）、heiress（女繼承人）、mistress（女主人）、stewardess（空姐）。

2. **For question number 2 and 3, please look at Picture B.**

   Question number 2: How many policemen are there?
   （有多少個員警？）
   (A) One（一個）　(B) Two（兩個）　(C) Three（三個）

第 1 回
第 2 回
第 3 回
第 4 回
第 5 回
第 6 回
第 7 回
第 8 回
第 9 回
第 10 回

答題解說

答案：(B)。本題問的是有多少個員警，數一下圖中有幾個穿員警制服的人，就可以選出正確答案。

破題關鍵

在英文裡，「警員」有幾種說法：police officer(s)、policeman（複數是policemen）。不過以本題來說，即使聽不出 -man 或 -men，至少要把 police 聽出來，就不會答錯了。

字詞解釋

policeman [pə`lismən] n. 警員

相關文法或用法補充

how many + 可數名詞複數，how much + 不可數名詞。例如：

❶ How many eggs are there in the basket?（籃子裡有幾個蛋？）
❷ One can't tell how much hair he has.（沒有人知道自己到底有多少根頭髮。）

3. **Question number 3: Please look at Picture B again.**

   What happened to the man in trouble?
   （這名遇到麻煩的男子發生什麼事？）
   (A) He was ticketed for speeding.（他因為超速被開罰單。）
   (B) He had a car accident.（他出了車禍。）
   (C) His car was stolen.（他的車被偷了。）

答題解說

答案：(B)。本題問「遇到麻煩的男子」發生了什麼事，也就是指用手摀著額頭的這名男子。圖片上方有兩部車對撞，顯然是他發生了車禍（car accident），故正確答案為(B)。

破題關鍵

"the man in trouble" 就是指「遇到麻煩的男子」，而 accident 是指「意外」。選項(A)中的 ticket 當動詞表示「對～（某人）開出交通違規罰單」，而 speeding 是「超速」的意思。

字詞解釋

in trouble phr. 處在困境、麻煩中　***ticket** [`tɪkɪt] v. 對～（某人）開罰單
speeding [`spidɪŋ] n. 超速行車　**accident** [`æksədənt] n. 事故，意外事件

happen to 是個常見的動詞片語，然而它有兩個截然不同的含意：

1. 表「發生在～（某人）身上」，這裡的 to 是介系詞。例如：A bad accident happened to the family.（那一家人發生了不幸。）
2. 表「正好，碰巧，偶然～」，此處 to 是不定詞的（to-V）to。例如：If you happen to meet your friend, give him these.（要是你剛好遇到你朋友，把這些東西給他。）

4. **For question number 4 and 5, please look at Picture C.**

   Question number 4: Where are these people swimming?（這些人在哪裡游泳？）
   (A) In a swimming pool（在游泳池）
   (B) In a lake（在一個湖泊）
   (C) By a riverside（在河邊）

答題解說

答案：(B)。圖中顯示有 3 個人在湖邊（或河邊釣魚），兩個人在游泳。題目問的是「在哪裡游泳」，所以最接近的答案是「湖泊」了。另外，因為有人在釣魚，所以這地方不可能是（A）游泳池。而 riverside 是指「河邊」，它的概念是「河岸邊的陸地」，所以當然不會是游泳的地方了。

破題關鍵

riverside 是 river（河）+ side（邊）的合體字，記住它是「陸地（land）」的概念，介系詞 by 表示「在～旁邊」。

字詞解釋

pool [pul] **n.** 水池　　**lake** [lek] **n.** 湖泊　　**riverside** [ˋrɪvəˏsaɪd] **n.** 河岸邊

相關文法或用法補充

介系詞 by 可以表示「在～旁」、「靠近～」。例如：The hotel is by/beside the river.（那家飯店在河邊。）在這個用法中，by 可以用 beside 取代。又例如：Come and sit by/beside me.（過來坐在我旁邊。）

5. **Question number 5: Please look at Picture C again.**

   What information is given in this picture?

   （圖片中提供了什麼資訊？）

   (A) There are three men swimming. （有三個男人在游泳。）

   (B) There is one man wearing a hat. （有一名男子戴著帽子。）

   (C) There are three men standing at the riverside.

   （有三名男子站在河岸邊。）

第 1 回
第 2 回
第 3 回
第 4 回
第 5 回
第 6 回
第 7 回
第 8 回
第 9 回
第 10 回

   答題解說

   答案：(B)。這是根據圖片內容判斷「何者為真」的題型，所以必須仔細聽清楚每一個選項的內容。在游泳的有兩個人，所以 (A) 是錯的；釣客中有「一名男子戴著帽子。」，所以 (B) 是正確的；三名釣客「坐在」河岸邊釣魚，所以 (C) 也是錯的。

   破題關鍵

   三個選項均運用「There + be 動詞 + Ving.」的句型，通常關鍵會出現在 Ving 這部分。

   相關文法或用法補充

   「There + be + N + Ving.」表示「有～主動進行某個動作」。這個句型是簡化自形容詞子句：

   There is a dog which is catching a ball in the park. （公園裡有隻狗在接球）

   = There is a dog catching a ball in the park. → which + be 動詞可以省略

第二部分 問答

6. **How are things going now?** （現在事情進行得如何了？）

   (A) I think I did a great job. （我想我做得很棒。）

   (B) I did many things. （我做了很多事情。）

   (C) I don't agree with you. （我不同意你的説法。）

   答題解說

   答案：(A)。題目問的是「現在情況如何？」，(B) 試圖以相同的字彙 things 來誤導答題，但其實答非所問，(C) 也是不相關的回答，只有 (A) 是問題的合理回答。

題目屬於 "How... going?" 的句型，針對人事物的狀況如何來提問。如果是問「人」，就是指「過得好不好、過得如何」，如果是問「事情」，就是問「進展得如何」。

agree [əˋgri] v. 同意

that 的副詞用法也很重要，例如：

I can't really eat that much.（我無法吃那麼多。）
We haven't got that much time.（我們沒剩下那麼多時間了。）
Is the problem that easy?（這問題有那麼簡單嗎？）

7. **That's a really nice movie.（那真是一部好電影。）**

(A) There are still other movies.（還有其他的電影。）
(B) It sure looks bad.（它看起來真的很糟。）
(C) But I don't like it.（但是我不喜歡它。）

答案：(C)。題目這句話是在讚美一部電影，(C) 的回答表示不以為然，也是一種正常的回答。而 (A) 回答「還有其他電影」顯然語意不明，應該再補充說「還有其他電影更好」才合乎邏輯。至於 (B) 中的 sure（的確）是一種「肯定對方的話」的表達，後面卻又說「看起來很糟」，與題目內容自相矛盾。

關鍵在於聽懂題目句 "That's a really nice..." 是對於某事物，發表個人的看法或意見，就可確定底下選項只有 (C) 也是用來發表個人的喜好意見。

movie [ˋmuvɪ] n. 電影

副詞 sure 意思是「的確」，表示「肯定」。它置於 be 動詞後，一般動詞前，就像本題選項 (B) 的用法。形容詞 sure 則常用於 I'm sure. 等表達中，表示對自己的話或表現很有信心、立場明確、不容懷疑，其確信程度比只是回答 "Sure!" 更高。

第 1 回
第 2 回
第 3 回
第 4 回
第 5 回
第 6 回
第 7 回
第 8 回
第 9 回
第 10 回

8. **May I use your toilet?**（我可以借用一下你的廁所嗎？）

(A) Maybe in the future.（也許在未來。）
(B) Of course. This way, please.（當然。這邊請。）
(C) You're welcome.（不客氣。）

答題解說

答案：(B)。這題的情境是，到別人家裡要借用洗手間的說法。只有 (B) 的回答是合乎邏輯的。(A) 的回答是要告訴對方，也許未來可以讓你用廁所，完全不合邏輯，而 (C) 通常是針對對方表達感謝時的回應。

破題關鍵

May I...? 通常就是在當下提出請求、詢問許可的問句，了解這個概念之後，很容易判斷 (A) 與 (C) 都是答非所問的回答。

字詞解釋

toilet [ˋtɔɪlɪt] n. 廁所　　**future** [ˋfjutʃɚ] n. 未來

相關文法或用法補充

很多人借廁所都會說成 "May I borrow your toilet/restroom?"，這是完全錯誤且會鬧笑話的說法，因為 borrow 是指把東西拿走的「出借」，如果用在這邊，不就「想把人家的廁所搬走」了嗎？所以記住，要說 May I use your toilet/restroom? 才行。

9. **Have a good time.**（祝你玩得愉快。）

(A) It's twelve o'clock.（現在是十二點鐘。）
(B) Thanks. I will.（謝謝，我會的。）
(C) I'm fine. Thank you.（我很好。謝謝。）

答題解說

答案：(B)。題目句是祝福對方「玩得愉快」，當對方表達對你的美好祝願時，最直接的回答就是感謝之類的話語，所以 (B) 為正確答案。另外，雖然 (C) 有 Thank you. 的話語，但重點是前面這句 I'm fine.，通常用來回應對方的問候（Ex. How are you?）話語，所以別被誤導了。

破題關鍵

題目句是原形動詞 Have 開頭，加上後面的 good time，很容易判斷是一句「祝福」的話語。

good time n. 美好時光

英文裡常見的祝福語，除了常見到 Have 開頭，May you...、Wish you... 也很常用。另外，以 Good、Happy 開頭的短詞也是一開始學英文時會接觸到的。例如：

Have a good trip! 旅行愉快！　　Have a nice day! 祝你有愉快的一天！
Happy New Year! 新年快樂！　　Merry Christmas! 聖誕快樂！
Good luck! 祝你好運！　　Congratulations! 恭喜！
May you succeed! 祝你成功！

10. **Can I help you?**（要不要我幫忙？）

(A) It is my luggage.（這是我的行李。）
(B) That's very kind of you.（你人真好。）
(C) Never mind.（別放在心上。）

答案：(B)。題目這句是對方要向自己提供幫助時所說的話，通常以「感謝」或「讚美對方好心」的話來回應，再根據自己的實際需要決定接不接受對方的幫助。故正確答案是 (B)。(A) 與 (C) 的都是答非所問。選項 (A) 的問句可能是 What is it?（這是什麼？）或者 Whose luggage is it?（這是誰的行李？）選項 (C) 的問句是用於寬慰別人，當別人不小心做錯了什麼事，給自己帶來不便或麻煩時，你就可以說 Never mind 來安慰對方，讓對方寬心。

聽到 Can I help you? 或是 Man I help you? 時，最直接的回應是 Thank you. 等感謝用語，然後視自己有無需要幫助，再做回應。如果選項中沒有感謝用語，就是找「你人真好。」這類讚美的話。雖然 Can I...? 似乎是 Yes-No 的問句，但回答可不一定會有 Yes/No 這種直接性的回答。

luggage ['lʌgɪdʒ] n. 行李　　**mind** [maɪnd] v. 介意

＊英文裡主動向人提供幫助的表達方式有：
　　Can I help you? 我能幫上忙嗎？

What can I do for you? 我能為你做什麼嗎？

Is there anything I can do for you? 有什麼需要我幫忙的嗎？

＊ 向別人請求幫忙的表達方式有：

Can you do me a favor? 你能幫我一個忙嗎？

Can you help me? 你可以幫助我嗎？

Would you mind doing...? 你介意幫我做……嗎？

I would appreciate it if you could...? 要是你能……，我將非常感激。

I'm obliged if you could...? 要是你能……，我不勝感激。

11. What would you like to take in your tea?（你想在茶裡加什麼？）

(A) I like to drink hot tea.（我喜歡喝熱茶。）

(B) Milk and sugar, please.（麻煩加糖和牛奶。）

(C) Well-done.（全熟。）

答題解說

答案：(B)。這是詢問對方想在茶裡面加什麼的題目，對於這種問題，往往都會直接回答要加的東西，也就是牛奶或糖之類的添加物。所以 (B) 是正確答案。

破題關鍵

本題可採用刪除法來解答。What... take in tea?（要加什麼在茶裡面？）是對事物（What）的提問，回答時自然要具體說出是什麼東西。選項中只有 (B) 符合正確的回答方式，所以可以刪除其他兩個選項。

字詞解釋

would like to-V 想要～　　**milk** [mɪlk] n. 牛奶　　**sugar** [`ʃʊgɚ] n. 糖　　**well-done** [`wɛldʌn] adj.（牛排等）全熟的

相關文法或用法補充

Well done 可以用於兩種場合：在西餐廳吃飯時，當服務生詢問你牛排要幾分熟時，你可以說 Well done（全熟）、Medium-Well（七分熟）、Medium（五分熟）、Medium-Rare（三分熟）、Rare（一分熟）；它還可以用於表揚別人的工作做得出色，相當於 You did a great job.。

12. Sorry, I'm late.（對不起，我遲到了。）

(A) Yes, that's right.（是，沒錯。）

(B) No, that's nothing to do with me.（不，那和我無關。）

(C) That's all right.（沒關係。）

第 1 回
第 2 回
第 3 回
第 4 回
第 5 回
第 6 回
第 7 回
第 8 回
第 9 回
第 10 回

答案：（C）。題目句是某人遲到而向你道歉，這時你可以說 "It's okay."、 "Never mind."、 "That's all right."（沒關係，不要緊），故正確答案是（C）。

破題關鍵

選項（A）和（B）是一般 Yes/No 疑問句的回答；而當別人向你道歉時，你可以說 "That's all right."，要對方不要感到內疚難過。That's nothing to do with me 意思是「那和我無關。」和它意思相反的是 That's something to do with me（那與我有點關係。）或是 That's much to do with me（那和我有很大的關係）。

字詞解釋

late [let] **adj.** 遲到的　　**nothing** [ˈnʌθɪŋ] **n.** 沒什麼

相關文法或用法補充

That's right 和 That's all right 的區別在於：前者的意思是「對的」、「是這樣沒錯」，相當於 That's correct.；後者意思是「沒關係、不要緊、不客氣」，相當於 It's okay./ Never mind./ Not at all.，例如：

Is your mother at home? Yes, that's right.（你媽媽在家嗎？是的，在家。）
Is that the way you did it? Yes, that's right.（你是那樣做的嗎？是的，沒錯。）
I'm sorry to bring you trouble. That's all right.（很抱歉給你帶來麻煩。沒關係。）

13. **It's a nice skirt.**（這裙子真漂亮。）

(A) Thanks.（謝謝。）
(B) May I help you?（我能幫上什麼忙嗎？）
(C) How much is it?（這多少錢？）

答題解說

答案：(A)。題目句 It's a nice skirt. 相當於 "Wow! Nice skirt."，當別人對自己或自己的穿著等事物表示誇獎或稱讚時，最直接的回應當然就是感謝之類的話了。所以正確答案是（A）。

破題關鍵

本題 3 個選項都是日常生活中常聽到的。(A) 是用於回應對方的讚美或施予時，所表達最簡單的謝意。(B) 則用於主動提供協助的場合，(D) 是購物情境中的基礎用語，用於買東西詢問價格的時候。先了解各選項可能的使用情境，在聽錄音播放時心裡先有個底，答題時就會更有把握。

字詞解釋

skirt [skɝt] n. 裙子

相關文法或用法補充

對於別人的讚美或恭維，說完 Thank you.、Thank you so much.、Thank you very much.、Thanks a lot. 之外，還可以接著怎麼說呢？以下提供您參考：

It's very sweet of you! / It's very nice of you! 你真貼心！／你真好！
I'm deeply moved / touched. 我好感動。
Oh, you shouldn't have. 喔，你太客氣了！

14. **Ted, this is my brother, David.**（泰德，這是我的弟弟大衛。）

(A) Nice to meet you, David.（大衛，很高興認識你。）
(B) Let's go, David.（大衛，我們走吧。）
(C) How are you today?（你今天好嗎？）

答題解說

答案：(A)。本題的情境是介紹某人給朋友認識，因為是第一次見面，在英文裡通常會說 Nice to meet you.（很高興認識你。）所以正確答案為 (A)。(C) 是問候語，看似正確答案，不過題目是「向對方介紹第三者」，如果只是回答 How are you today?，問候的對象是說話的人，而不是被介紹的人，所以是錯誤的選項。

破題關鍵

注意題目句尾的人名 David，可立刻推知這句是「介紹第三者」的話語。所以回應時，也一定會有人名 David。

字詞解釋

Nice to meet/see you. 幸會。　　**Let's go**. 走吧。

相關文法或用法補充

Nice to meet you. 是最常見的見面問候語，比較正式的說法還有 "Pleased to meet you."、"It's a pleasure to meet you."。另外，一般熟識朋友間的打招呼用語也要學起來喔！像是 Hi!、Hello!、What's up?、How are you doing?、How's everything?、What's new?、Long time no see. 等。

15. **Have you met Jack?**（你曾見過傑克嗎？）

(A) Jack is a doctor.（傑克是一位醫生。）
(B) Yes, I had a good time.（是的，我玩得非常愉快。）
(C) No, I haven't.（沒有，我沒見過。）

答案：(C)。本題是問對方是不是曾見過某人，(A) 回答他是個醫生，完全答非所問，(B) 如果改成 Yes, "we" had a good time. 也是正確的回答。(C) 的「不，我沒見過」，是直接針對問題回答的正確答案。

破題關鍵

本題是一般的 Yes/No 疑問句，三個選項中 (B) 和 (C) 符合這個要求，但問題句是用現在完成式，所以正確答案是 (C)。

字詞解釋

have a good time 玩得開心

相關文法或用法補充

「S + have/has/had a good time」如果刪去主詞（S），就會變成一個祈使句的祝福用語：Have a good time.（祝你玩得愉快。）類似用語還有 Have a good jurney.、Have a good trip.（旅途愉快。）

第三部分 簡短對話

16. M: Wow! You look so cool!

W: What do you mean?

M: This skirt makes you totally different.

W: That's very sweet of you.

Question: What are the speakers talking about?

(A) The woman's new style.

(B) A skirt is on hot sale.

(C) The weather becomes cool.

男：哇喔！你看起來好酷啊！

女：你是指什麼？

男：這件裙子讓你看起來完全不同了。

女：你的嘴巴真甜。

問題：說話者們在談論什麼？

(A) 女子的新風格

(B) 一件裙子正在熱賣。

(C) 天氣變得涼爽了。

第 1 回
第 2 回
第 3 回
第 4 回
第 5 回
第 6 回
第 7 回
第 8 回
第 9 回
第 10 回

答題解說

答案：(A)。題目問男女在談論什麼，其實就是指「對話的內容是關於什麼」。首先，男子對於女子的外表表示讚美（"look so cool"），後面又說裙子讓她看起來很不同（也許女子平時很少穿裙子），所以是在談論她的穿著新風格，所以答案是(A)。

破題關鍵

本題有兩個關鍵點：男子對女子說 "look so cool" 以及 "makes you totally different"，表示對於女子外表的看法，所以顯然「裙子正在熱賣」與「天氣狀況」都是不相關的答案。

字詞解釋

mean [min] v. 意指　**totally** [`totlɪ] adv. 完全地　**different** [`dɪfərənt] adj. 不同的
style [staɪl] n. 風格，（衣服等的）流行款式

相關文法或用法補充

1. look 是個「連綴動詞」，像是「聽起來（sound）」、「聞起來（smell）」、「感覺上（feel）」、「嚐起來（taste）」等也都是。連綴動詞不能單獨存在，後面必須再接形容詞，作為主詞補語，句意才算完整。
2. make 是「使役動詞」用法，在受詞之後，可接原形動詞、分詞或形容詞（本篇對話中的 "totally different"）作為受詞補語。

17. M: I go swimming on Thursdays.

    W: Can I join you?

    M: Of course. Have you got a swimsuit?

    W: No. Where can I buy it?

    Question: How often does the man go swimming?
    (A) Once a week　(B) Every day　(C) Every other day

    男：我每個星期的週四都會去游泳。
    女：我可以跟你一起去嗎？
    男：當然可以。你有泳裝嗎？
    女：沒有。哪裡可以買得到？
    題目：男子多久去游泳一次？
    (A) 一星期一次　(B) 每天都去　(C) 每隔一天去一次

答案：(A)。男子第一句話說「我每個星期的週四都會去游泳。（I go swimming on Thursdays.）」其中 on Thursdays 就是指「在每個星期的週四」，也就是一星期去一次。故正確答案為(A)。

破題關鍵

即使對話內容沒聽懂，題目句的 "How often..." 應該很容易理解，所以可以採用反推法來解答。從選項可以反推出問題對時間頻率提問，問多久去遊一次泳。on Thursdays（每逢週四）這個片語告訴我們，他每個星期去游泳一次。

字詞解釋

Of course adv. 當然　**swimsuit** [ˋswɪmsut] n. 泳衣　**go swimming** 去游泳　**once** [wʌns] adv. 一次，一回　**every other day** adv. 每隔一天

相關文法或用法補充

once 的意思是「一次」，twice 的意思是「兩次」，它們常常和表示一段時間的詞彙連用，表示事情發生的頻率，動詞要用現在式，例如：

She takes exercise twice a week.（她每星期運動兩次。）

My mother goes to a supermarket to do shopping twice a month.（我媽媽每個月去兩次超市買東西。）

The boy is allowed to watch TV only once a week.（這個男孩每星期只被允許看一次電視。）

We celebrate the new year once a year.（我們每年慶祝一次新年。）

18. M: May I speak to Mary, please?

    W: Speaking.

    M: This is John, your classmate.

    W: Oh, John. What's going on?

Question: What are the speakers doing?

(A) They are studying in a classroom.

(B) They are talking on the phone.

(C) They are eating dinner in a restaurant.

男：請問瑪麗在嗎？

女：我就是。

男：我是約翰，你的同學。

女：喔，約翰。什麼事？

第 1 回
第 2 回
第 3 回
第 4 回
第 5 回
第 6 回
第 7 回
第 8 回
第 9 回
第 10 回

題目：說話者們正在做什麼？
(A) 他們正在教室裡念書。
(B) 他們正在講電話。
(C) 他們正在一家餐廳吃晚餐。

答題解說

答案：(B)。男子第一句話說 "May I speak to...?"，接著女子說 Speaking.。顯然他是打電話要找某人，所以正確答案是 (B) 的 "They are talking on the phone."。

破題關鍵

其實這一題只要有先看過三個選項，然後在對話中聽到 May I speak to...、Speaking、This is... 等「電話用語」的關鍵字詞，答案就出來了。

字詞解釋

What's going on? 有什麼事？／發生什麼事？ **on the phone** 在電話中
restaurant [ˋrɛstərənt] n. 餐廳，餐館

相關文法或用法補充

電話用語與一般日常對話不同。通常打電話要找某人時，開頭的第一句話會說「May I speak to + 人？」如果接電話的人正好就是對方要找的人，就可以說「This is...（某人）speaking.（或是 Speaking）」或是 This is he/she.。但如果要問對方的身分，不可以說 Who are you?，而是說 "Who's calling?"。

19. M: How may I help you?
　　W: I'd like a table for three.
　　M: This way, please.
　　W: Thanks.

　　Question: What is the woman going to do?
　　(A) She is going to buy some new clothes.
　　(B) She is going to have dinner with two friends.
　　(C) She is going to book a hotel room.

男：有什麼可以為您效勞的？
女：我們有三人要用餐。
男：這邊請。
女：謝謝。
題目：女子打算要做什麼？

(A) 她打算去買一些新衣服。

(B) 她打算去和朋友一起吃晚飯。

(C) 她打算訂飯店房間。

答案：(B)。男子一開始說「有什麼可以為您效勞的？（What may I help you?）」。顯然他是一位店員或服務員，準備服務顧客。接著女子說「我要一張三人桌（I'd like a table for three.）」，也就是說「我們有三人要用餐。」所以正確答案是(B)。

破題關鍵

本題的關鍵就是女子 "I'd like a table for three." 這句話，然後再看過三個選項，不論是「去買衣服」或是「訂飯店房間」，都不可能說「我要一張三人桌」吧！

字詞解釋

would like + N. 想要～   **a table for three** 一張三人坐的桌子   **this way** 這邊（走）   **book** [bʊk] v. 預訂

相關文法或用法補充

have 當動詞時，主要有三種用法：

1. 表示「擁有」，相當於 own。例如：
   I have a computer.（我有一部電腦。）
   He has had this car for five years.（他擁有這輛車已經五年了。）

2. 表示「吃（飯）」，相當於 eat。例如：
   I have breakfast at 7 o'clock.（我七點鐘吃早飯。）

3. 表示「舉辦（派對等）」，相當於 hold、give。例如：
   We are having a party this Sunday.（這個星期日我們將舉行一個聚會。）

20. M: Wow! You're getting so wet!

   W: I forgot to bring an umbrella.

   M: You always forget about something!

   W: Maybe that's because I'm getting old.

   Question: How's the weather now?

   (A) It's raining.   (B) It's a cloudy day.   (C) It's windy.

   男：哇，你濕透了！
   女：我忘了帶傘。

男：你總是忘東忘西的。

女：也許是因為我年紀大了。

題目：現在天氣如何？

(A) 正在下雨。(B) 現在陰天。(C) 現在風很大。

第 1 回
第 2 回
第 3 回
第 4 回
第 5 回
第 6 回
第 7 回
第 8 回
第 9 回
第 10 回

答題解說

答案：(A)。題目問的是「現在天氣如何」，所以應注意聽一些和天氣有關的用語。男子說「你濕透了！」然後女子回答「我忘了帶傘。」所以可以推斷出他們說話時正下著雨。

破題關鍵

首先，注意聽到題目關鍵字 weather，然後與對話中相關字詞作連結，包括 "getting so wet" 以及 umbrella，答案就出來了。(B) 的 cloudy（多雲的）來自名詞 cloud（雲），而 (C) 的 windy（颱風的）來自名詞 wind（風）。其他類似的衍生還有 sun → sunny（晴朗的）、fun → funny（有趣的）……等。

字詞解釋

umbrella [ʌmˋbrɛlə] **n.** 雨傘　　**forget** [fəˋgɛt] **v.** 忘記　　**weather** [ˋwɛðɚ] **n.** 天氣
cloudy [ˋklaʊdɪ] **adj.** 多雲的，陰天的　　**windy** [ˋwɪndɪ] **adj.** 颱風的，風大的

相關文法或用法補充

so 的副詞及連接詞用法如下：

1. 用作副詞時，位於形容詞和副詞之前：
   It is so hot that the factory stops producing.（天氣熱到這家工廠停產了。）
   He runs so fast that nobody can catch him.（他跑得快到沒人能追上他。）
2. 用作連接詞時，位於它所引導的子句之前：
   I got up late this morning, so I was late for class.（今天早上我起床晚了，所以上課遲到了。）
   The teacher is very kind, so his students like him very much.（這位老師非常親切，所以學生很喜歡他。）

21. M: Excuse me, are there any more chairs upstairs?

   W: Yes, there are some. What do you need them for?

   M: We didn't expect so many people to come.

   W: Got it. But I'm not sure if they're enough.

   Question: What is the man probably doing?

   (A) Preparing for a birthday party.

(B) Studying for an entrance exam.

(C) Cooking for dinner.

男：請問一下，樓上還有多的椅子嗎？

女：是的，還有一些。你要它們做什麼？

男：我們沒預期到會有這麼多人來。

女：了解。但我不確定是不是足夠。

題目：男子可能正在做什麼？

(A) 準備一場生日派對。

(B) 為入學考試在念書。

(C) 煮晚餐。

答案：(A)。本題問的是男子可能正在做什麼事，因此應從男子的發言中找尋線索。男子一開始時就詢問是不是還有多餘的椅子，後來又說「沒預期到會有這麼多人來」。這表示他正在準備一場聚會，而參加的人數比其原先預計還要多。因此，(A) 是比較有可能的答案。

答案關鍵點除了會出現在男子的發言部分之外，如果有事先看過三個選項，也可以清楚分辨這是三種完全不同的「情境」，然後再仔細聽對話內容，尤其是 "so many people to come"（這麼多人來），就可以了解這跟「準備考試」以及「煮晚餐」是完全扯不上邊的。

upstairs [ˋʌpˋstɛrz] **adv.** 在樓上　　**expect** [ɪkˋspɛkt] **v.** 預期　　**prepare** [prɪˋpɛr] **v.** 準備

entrance [ˋɛntrəns] **n.** 進入；登場　　**dish** [dɪʃ] **n.** 菜餚；盤

1. Excuse me 的意思是「打擾一下，請原諒」，常常用在句子的開頭，要請求他人協助或引起他人注意時，例如：Excuse me, could you tell me how to get to the nearest post office?（打擾一下，你能告訴我怎麼去最近的郵局嗎？）

2. need 用法概述：

① 一般來說，need 當及物動詞時，後面必須接名詞、不定詞（to-V）作為受詞，不可接 Ving。例如：

❶ I need to review my lesson this afternoon.（今天下午我需要複習功課。）

❷ How much money do you need? I need $ 10.（你需要多少錢？我需要十美元。）

② 不過 need 後面如果接不定詞的被動式，則可替換為動名詞。例如：

　❶ This pair of shoes needs repairing/ to be repaired. （這雙鞋需要修修了。）

　❷ The sheet needs washing/to be washed. （這床單需要洗洗了。）

③ 當情態動詞時，後面接動詞原形，可用於否定句或疑問句：

　Need I finish the work today? No, you needn't. （我今天必須把這項工作做完嗎？不用，你不必今天做完。）

22. M: We are five minutes late.

　W: Just take it easy. It's OK we'll take the next bus.

　M: What about taking a taxi? The boss told us yesterday that the meeting is very important.

　W: I know that, but he always says so.

Question: What happened to the speakers?

(A) Their bus just left five minutes ago.

(B) They have missed an important meeting.

(C) They didn't have money to take a taxi.

男：我們晚了五分鐘。

女：放輕鬆點。我們搭下一班巴士也沒關係啊。

男：我們去搭計程車好嗎？老闆昨天和我們說過這場會議很重要。

女：我知道啊，但是他總是那樣講的。

題目：說話者們發生了什麼事？

(A) 他們的公車五分鐘前剛開走。

(B) 他們已錯過一場重要的會議。

(C) 他們沒有錢搭計程車。

答題解說

答案：(A)。本題問的是這對男女發生了什麼事。可以從一開始男女各自的的第一句話找到答案。首先，男子說「我們晚了五分鐘。」而接著女子說「沒關係，我們搭下一班巴士吧。」在此，我們就可以推測，他們沒趕上公車，因為公車在他們抵達車站的五分鐘前就開走了。所以(A)是正確答案。

破題關鍵

本題屬於「內容細節」型的題目，基本上是要理解整段對話內容才能作答，不過只要可以在一開始時掌握到與題目（發生什麼事？）有關的敘述或內容，即可迅速作答：「我們晚了五分鐘（We are five minutes late.）」→「他們的公車五分鐘前剛開走（Their bus just left five minutes ago.）」。

take it easy 放輕鬆　**meeting** [`mitɪŋ] **n.** 會議　**important** [ɪm`pɔrtn̩t] **adj.** 重要的
happen to... 發生在～（某人身上）**miss** [mɪs] **v.** 錯過

相關文法或用法補充

「搭乘交通工具」可以用「ride/take/drive＋冠詞＋交通工具」來表示，後面可以再接「to＋地方」。當然，動詞必須依照交通工具的類型而有所變化：

1. ride 用於可跨坐式或搭乘的交通工具。如：腳踏車、機車以及馬（bike, bicycle, scooter, motorcycle, horse...）等

2. take 用於一般可搭載乘客的交通工具。如：train, bus, HSR, MRT, taxi, car, plane, boat... 等。

3. drive 是「駕駛」的意思，也就是自行操作方向盤的概念，像是 truck, car, taxi, bus... 等。

23. M: How come your eyes look red? Are you all right?

    W: I'm OK, but I just feel quite sleepy, because my son hasn't been able to sleep well.

    M: I see. I hope things will be a bit better tonight.

    W: I hope so.

    Question: How does the woman feel today?

    (A) She dislikes young kids.

    (B) She doesn't feel any pain.

    (C) She feels tired.

男：妳的眼睛怎麼看起來紅紅的？妳還好嗎？
女：我還好，只是覺得很想睡覺，因為我兒子一直無法睡好。
男：我了解。希望今晚可以好一點。
女：但願如此。
問題：女子今天覺得如何？
(A) 她不喜歡幼兒。(B) 她沒感覺到任何痛苦。(C) 她覺得疲累。

答題解說

答案：(C)。本題問的是「女子覺得如何」，我們可以從男子的第一句話「妳的眼睛怎麼看起來紅紅的？（How come your eyes look red?）」以及女子的回答「覺得很想睡覺（feel quite sleepy）」得知，比較接近的答案應該是 (C)「她覺得疲累。」

破題關鍵

基本上，針對「女子覺得如何」的問題，第一個思考點就是從她說過的話來判斷。因此我們可以從女子發言中的關鍵字 sleepy（想睡的），在三個選項中找到對應的字：tired，答案自然就出來了。

字詞解釋

how come 何以……，為什麼……　**all right** adj.（健康）良好的　**sleepy** [`slipɪ] adj. 想睡的，睏倦的　**dislike** [dɪs`laɪk] v. 厭惡　**pain** [pen] n. 痛苦　**tired** [taɪrd] adj. 疲倦的

相關文法或用法補充

1. How come 其實就是 Why（為什麼）的意思，屬於較為不正式或口語上的慣用語。若在商務、正式社交或公開場合，還是避開如此口語的用法較為妥當。另外，必須注意的是，How come 後面要接「直述句」的語法（沒有助動詞），而 Why 後面須接疑問句的語法。例如：Why do you take the bus? = How come you take the bus?

2. 文法裡有所謂「連綴動詞」，look 就是其中之一，另外像是「聞起來（smell）」、「感覺上（feel）」、「嘗起來（taste）」等也都是。連綴動詞不能單獨存在，後面必須再接形容詞或名詞，作為主詞補語，句意才算完整。但 lock 等連綴動詞只會以「連綴動詞＋形容詞」的結構使用。

24. M: Wow! That'll be very exciting! I love Tom Cruise.
    W: But I don't like that loud sound. My ears will be hurt.
    M: Come on! You need the loud music for the action scenes!
    W: Maybe you're right.

    Question: What are the speakers talking about?
    (A) A concert　(B) A famous book　(C) A film

男：哇！那會相當令人興奮！我喜歡湯姆‧克魯斯。
女：可是我不喜歡那麼大的聲音。我的耳朵會痛。
男：別這樣！那些動作場景就是需要大聲的音樂啊！
女：也許你是對的。
問題：說話者們在談些什麼？
(A) 一場演唱會
(B) 一本有名的書籍
(C) 一部電影

答案：（C）。本題問的是「對話內容」為何，首先，男子提到「某個東西」very exciting 以及 Tom Cruise，接著女子表示不喜歡很大的聲音。接著男子又說，大聲的音樂才能搭配 action scenes（動作場景），至此，我們可以知道他們談論的是一部電影。

破題關鍵

雖然題目要問的是「對話內容」。但如果有先看過三個選項（演唱會、書籍、電影），在聽播放內容時就可以去注意相關字詞。對話中其實有幾個關鍵字詞，只要聽出其中之一，很容易可以猜出正確答案，那就是 Tom Cruise（湯姆・克魯斯）以及 action scenes（動作場景）→ 直接與「電影」（film）連結在一起。

字詞解釋

exciting [ɪk`saɪtɪŋ] **adj.** 令人興奮的　**loud** [laʊd] **adj.** 大聲的　**hurt** [hɝt] **adj.** 疼痛的　**action** [`ækʃən] **n.** 行動　**scene** [sin] **n.** （電影，電視的）一個鏡頭　**concert** [`kɑnsɚt] **n.** 音樂會，演奏會　**famous** [`feməs] **adj.** 著名的　**film** [fɪlm] **n.** 電影

相關文法或用法補充

1. exciting 是「令人興奮的」意思，用來修飾「事物」，如果是 excited 的話，表示「感到興奮的」，用來修飾「人」。-ed 與 -ing 的差別，是很多類型考試的最愛之一。只要記住一點：-ed 表示「感到～」，-ing 表示「令人～」；是「人」才會「感到～」，是「事物」才會「令人～」。

2. 電影的類型很多，像是「動作片（action film）」、科幻片「（science fiction film）」、「驚悚片（thriller film）」、「war film（戰爭片）」、「動畫片（animated film）」、「romance film（愛情片）」、「documentary（紀錄片）」、「情色片（erotic film）」、「恐怖片（horror film）」、「武俠片（martial arts film）」……等。

25. M: I have a meeting with Mr. Wang at 3:00.

    W: Well, I'm still busy with a project. If I can leave around half past one, then I can pick you up around 2:30.

    M: OK. I'll wait here for you. It'll only take fifteen minutes to our office.

    W: OK. See you then.

    Question: What time will they arrive at their company?
    (A) 2:30 p.m.　(B) 2:45 p.m.　(C) 3:00 p.m.

    男：我 3:00 和王先生有個會議。

女：嗯，我還在忙一個專案。如果我可以在一點半左右離開，那我可以在大約兩點半去接你。

男：好的。我會在這裡等你。到我們辦公室只要 15 分鐘的時間。

女：好的。那就到時候見了。

問題：他們幾點會到達他們的公司？

(A) 下午兩點半。(B) 下午兩點四十五分。(C) 下午三點。

答題解說

答案：(B)。題目問的是「幾點到達公司」，所以必須注意對話內容中提到與「時間」有關的內容。女子第一次發言時提到，她可以在大約兩點半去接男子（I can pick you up around 2:30），接著男子說，到我們辦公室只要 15 分鐘的時間（It'll only take fifteen minutes to our office.）。因此，從這兩個線索可以得知，他們可能在 2:45 抵達他們的公司。

破題關鍵

通常問時間（幾點）的題目，或是問「數字」的題型，不會是直接在對話中聽到的幾點幾分，而是必須稍做推論的。本題第一個關鍵是將對話中的 office 與題目句的 company 連結在一起，第二個關鍵是「到辦公室只要 15 分鐘」以及「兩點半去接人」，因此答案就是 2:30 再加 15 分鐘，也就是 2:45。

字詞解釋

meeting [ˋmitɪŋ] **n.** 會議　**be busy with**... 忙於～　**project** [ˋprɑdʒɛkt] **n.** 方案，企劃　**pick up** 接送（某人）　**arrive** [əˋraɪv] **v.** 到達

相關文法或用法補充

表達的時間若是「整點」時，其句型為：「It's＋數字（＋o'clock）.」。例：It's twelve.（現在十二點。）＝It's twelve o'clock.＝It's 12:00.。如果是要表達幾點幾分時，代名詞用 it，「時」與「分」各以數字表示。「分」若為兩個英文字的數字時，中間要加上連字號「-」，如 thirty-five（35 分），但「時」與「分」之間不用連字號。若「分」為個位數，常會在前面加英文字 O（代表「零」），如 10:06 唸作 ten O six。另外，英文不會用 24 小時制來表達時間，所以要更明確的表達時間在一天中的哪一個時段，可在時間後加 a.m. / p.m. 或加上時間副詞。另外，表達「某事在幾點」發生時，需用介系詞 at，其句型為「主詞＋be 動詞＋at＋時間.」。例：The party is at seven o'clock.（派對在七點鐘開始。）而詢問「某事在幾點」發生時，其句型為「What time＋be 動詞＋主詞?」，其中主詞為「某事」。例：What time is the movis?（電影在幾點）最後，以下是一些表達時間的特殊表達方式：

❶ It's 4:15. = It's a quarter past four.
❷ It's 3:30. = It's half past three.
❸ It's 7:03. = It's three past seven.
❹ It's 8:40. = It's twenty to nine.
❺ It's 2:45. = It's a quarter to three.

第四部分 短文聽解

For question number 26, please look at the three pictures.

Question number 26: Listen to the following talk. Who is Michael?

Here's my boss, Michael. He is a middle-aged and friendly man. He wears glasses and always wears a business suit. Besides, he likes to smile at everyone. However, he seems very busy and seldom stays in office in the morning.

請看以下三張圖。並仔細聆聽播放的談話內容。哪一位是 Michael？
這是我的老闆，Michael。他是一位中年且友善的男人。他有戴眼鏡且總是穿西裝。此外，他喜歡逢人便給予一個微笑。然而，他似乎非常忙碌且早上的時候很少待在辦公室中。

答題解說

答案：（A）。題目問的是談話內容是在敘述哪張圖的人物。其中提到「中年男子（middle-aged）」、「穿西裝（business suit）」、「戴眼鏡（wears glasses）」。在觀察這三張圖後可以發現，只有 (A) 這張圖是符合這三項要件的。

破題關鍵

首先觀察三張圖後，可以發現三張圖的男子都有戴眼鏡，所以這則談話內容的最快速解題方式就在於哪一張符合「中年」+「穿西裝」。「中年」→ 刪除沒有鬍子的 (C)；「穿西裝」→ 刪除穿襯衫的 (B)。那麼答案就是 (A) 了。

第 1 回
第 2 回
第 3 回
第 4 回
第 5 回
第 6 回
第 7 回
第 8 回
第 9 回
第 10 回

字詞解釋

boss [bɔs] **n.** 老板，上司　**middle-aged** [`mɪdl`edʒd] **adj.** 中年的　**friendly** [`frɛndlɪ] **adj.** 親切的　**glasses** [`glæsɪz] **n.** 眼鏡　**business suit** [`bɪznɪs`sut] **n.** 西裝　**seldom** [`sɛldəm] **adv.** 不常，很少

相關文法或用法補充

middle-aged 如其字面意思，就是「中年的」意思。像這樣由兩個字組成的形容詞，稱為「複合形容詞」。「複合形容詞」在英文裡有多種形式，常見的有：

① 「名詞 - 現在分詞 / 過去分詞」：man-eating（吃人的）、snow-covered（被雪覆蓋著的）

② 「形容詞 / 副詞 - 現在分詞 / 過去分詞」：good-looking（好看的）、never-ending（永無休止的）、well-done（做得好的）

③ 「形容詞＋名詞」：last-minute（最後一刻的）

④ 「數字＋單位」：14-year-old（14 歲的）、10-mile（10 英里的）

⑤ 用連字號把片語變成一個字：all-too-common（很常見的）

For question number 27, please look at the three pictures.

Question number 27: Listen to the following announcement. Where can you hear this talk?

  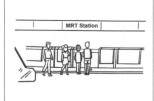

May I have your attention, please! The next train to Hualien station is arriving in three minutes. Please stay behind the waiting line until the train comes to a complete stop. Besides, please keep away from the platform edge at all times to avoid any possible danger. Watch your step and the narrow gap between the platform and the train when boarding the train. Thank you and have a nice trip.

請看以下三張圖。並仔細聆聽以下的廣播公告。你會在哪裡聽到這樣的談話？
請大家注意一下！下一班前往花蓮車站的列車即將在三分鐘之後抵達。請留在等候線後面，直到列車進站且完全停止。此外，無論何時請遠離月台邊緣，以避免危險發生。請在上車時小心腳下並留意月台與列車的間隙。感謝您，祝您旅途愉快。

答案：(A)。首先，我們知道這是在一個公共場所的廣播內容。雖然第一句「May I have your attention, please!」尚無法確定是哪裡的廣播，但接著重點就來了：The next train to Hualien station is arriving in three minutes.（下一班前往花蓮車站的列車即將在三分鐘之後抵達。）到這裡，你一定不會去選 (B) 這張圖的，至於圖 (C)，只要注意到圖中的 MRT 三個字樣，就知道這是捷運，而捷運不會開到花蓮去吧！所以答案就是 (A) 了。

在聽錄音播放之前，先看過三張圖，很容易可以看出「火車站」、「電影院」「捷運站」這三個地方。然後只要注意聽短文中的關鍵字詞，像是 train、Hualien station，答案自然就出來了。

attention [əˋtɛnʃən] **n.** 注意　**arrive** [əˋraɪv] **v.** 抵達　**keep away from**... 遠離～ **platform** [ˋplæt͵fɔrm] **n.** 月台　**edge** [ɛdʒ] **n.** 邊緣　**waiting line** 等候線 **complete** [kəmˋplit] **adj.** 完全的，徹底的　**at all times** 一直　**avoid** [əˋvɔɪd] **v.** 避免　**narrow** [ˋnæro] **adj.** 狹窄的　**gap** [gæp] **n.** 間隙　**board** [bord] **v.** 上（船、車、飛機等）

搭火車之前，要確定是要買單程票（one-way ticket）還是來回票（return ticket）？然後是車種，包括區間車（local train）、快車（express train），包括自強號（Tze-Chiang）及莒光號（Chu-Kuang）。另外還有專跑西部的太魯閣號（Tilting Train）、專跑東部的普悠瑪號（Puyuma），這兩種被稱為觀光列車（tourist train）。此外，要看懂時刻表（time table），因為它能指引我們找到對的「月台」（platform）。

For question number 28, please look at the three pictures.

Question number 28: Listen to the following message. Where could Jeff probably go after hearing this message?

Hello, Jeff. This is Jack. Where are you now? I've been calling you for the past few hours. Brown had a car accident this morning on the highway, and is now in the operating room. Please call me back as soon as you hear this message. I'll let you know where we are.

第 1 回
第 2 回
第 3 回
第 4 回
第 5 回
第 6 回
第 7 回
第 8 回
第 9 回
第 10 回

中文翻譯

請看以下三張圖。並仔細聆聽以下的訊息內容。傑夫在聽到這則訊息之後可能會去哪裡？

喂，傑夫。我是傑克。你現在人在哪？我在過去幾個小時一直在打電話給你。布朗今天早上在快速道路上出了一場車禍，他現在正在手術室中。請你一聽到這則訊息之後立即回電話給我。我會再告訴你我們在哪裡。

答題解說

答案：（C）。首先，要知道題目問的是「傑夫在聽到訊息之後可能會去哪裡？」，而留言的對象就是傑夫。其中提到，某個人早上出了一場車禍（had a car accident），現在正在手術室中（now in the operation room）。以及後面提到「我再告訴你我們在哪裡。（I'll let you know where we are.）」這表示留言的對象在聽到訊息之後，會過去和留言者會面，而且從上述的「車禍」及「手術室」可知，一定是去醫院了。

破題關鍵

這則留言內容的關鍵字詞：accident 以及 operation room。特別要注意後者，因為如果只是聽懂 accident，還是可能選到 (B) 的警察局這張圖了。

字詞解釋

accident [ˈæksədənt] n. 意外事故　**highway** [ˈhaɪˌwe] n. 快速道路；高速公路
operation [ˌɑpəˈreʃən] n. 手術

相關文法或用法補充

完成進行式就是「完成式」與「進行式」的組合。進行式是表示「某動作在某段時間內持續進行」，而完成式則表示「到某時間點為止已經做了某事」。因此完成進行式就是用來強調「在某段時間前一直持續的動作」，結構是「have + been + 現在分詞（V-ing）」。而現在完成進行式表示某行為從過去到現在一直持續著。例如：到目前為止 Ken 已經持續閱讀了兩個小時，可以說 "Ken has been reading for two hours." 這表示表示 Ken 從兩個小時前就一直在閱讀，直到現在說話的當下仍在閱讀。

For question number 29, please look at the three pictures.

Question number 29: Listen to the following news report. Which picture best matches the talk?

Breaking news! A man wearing a mask was pointing a gun at a clerk in Public Bank about one hour ago. He was pushing them to hand out a lot of money, or else they would be shot dead. Finally, he successfully robbed about 5 million dollars and quickly rode a stolen motorcycle away. The police are now going all out to find the man.

請看以下三張圖，並仔細聆聽以下的新聞報導，哪一張圖最符合這則談話的內容？
新聞快報！一名戴口罩的男子大約一個小時之前在民眾銀行裡用槍指著一名行員。他逼迫她交出很多錢，否則她會被擊斃。最後，他成功地搶了大約了五百萬元，然後很快地騎著一輛偷來的摩托車逃走了。警方目前正全力找尋這名男子。

答題解說

答案：(A)。題目問的是哪一張圖最符合談話內容，所以基本上要大致聽懂其內容在講什麼。第一張圖是「戴口罩的男子用槍指著一名女行員」，第二張圖是「戴口罩的男子在戶外用槍指著一名女子」，第三張圖是「警察用槍指著戴口罩的男子」，但談話內容一開始說「一名戴口罩的男子大約一個小時之前在民眾銀行裡用槍指著一名行員。（A man wearing a face mask was pointing a gun at a clerk in Public Bank about one hour ago.）」所以正確答案應為(A)。

破題關鍵

圖 (A) 與 (B) 的差別只有「被槍指著的人」，通常這樣的題目設計，就是要給你「二選一」，答案不是 (A) 就是 (B) 了，至於第三個選項（圖 (C)）通常只是陪襯用，一定不會是答案。所以只要聽到關鍵的 "pointing a gun at a clerk"。如果還認為圖 (B) 是可能答案，只要注意到接下來的 in Public Bank，就不會去選 (B) 了。

第 1 回
第 2 回
第 3 回
第 4 回
第 5 回
第 6 回
第 7 回
第 8 回
第 9 回
第 10 回

字詞解釋

breaking news 新聞快報　**mask** [mæsk] n. 面具，口罩　**point... at...** 用～指著～　**clerk** [klɝk] n. 辦事員，職員　**push** [pʊʃ] v. 逼迫　**hand out** 交出　**shoot sb. dead** 將某人射死　**successfully** [səkˋsɛsfəlɪ] adv. 成功地　**rob** [rɑb] v. 搶劫，劫掠　**stolen** [ˋstolən] adj. 被偷了的　**go all out** 盡全力

相關文法或用法補充

分詞片語是由現在分詞或過去分詞結合其他字所形成。分詞片語都是當作形容詞，用來修飾名詞或代名詞。像是這裡的 "A man wearing a mask was pointing a gun..."，"wearing a mask" 就是一個分詞片語，修飾主詞 A man。

For question number 30, please look at the three pictures.

Question number 30: Listen to the following message. How does the woman get to Peter's company?

Hello, Peter. This is Mary, and I'd like to say sorry that I'm running a bit late. I'm already on my way, and I should be there in 30 minutes. By the way, I wanna make sure that your address is No.233, Beiping E. Rd. and your company is at the 7th floor, right? I need to tell the driver. Thanks. I'll see you soon.

請看以下三張圖，並仔細聆聽以下留言訊息，這名女子如何前往彼得的公司？
哈囉，彼得。我是瑪麗，我要說聲抱歉，因為我會晚一點到。我現在已經在路上，而且我應該三十分鐘之後可以到達那裡。對了，我想確認你的地址是北平東路 233 號，你的公司在七樓，對嗎？我必須告訴司機。謝謝。等會兒見。

答題解說

答案：(A)。題目問的是女子如何前往彼得的公司。這段訊息後半段提到 your company 的地址，然後一說「我必須告訴司機。」顯然她應該是搭計程車去的，所以正確答案是 (A)。

破題關鍵

這三張圖示已經告訴我們，題目要問的是女子所使用的交通工具，只要注意相關

的敘述，答案就出來了，而關鍵句 "I need to tell the driver." 已經明顯點出答案。

on one's way（**to**...）在某人（前往某地）的路上　**by the way** 順道一提　**make sure** 確定～（一件事）　**address** [əˋdrɛs] n. 地址

running 是 run 的現在分詞，本來是「跑步」的意思，常引申為「運作」或「流動」，"I'm running a bit late." 這一句中不能直譯，因為 running late 要視為一個形容詞，表示「來不及了」或「遲到了」的意思。它的意涵是，某人時間不夠用而用跑步的，但還是晚了。通常是用來告知對方，我會晚點到或事情在預計時間內做不完。直譯的話就是「我運作上遲了。」其他類似用法：

1. My nose is running. 不是「我的鼻子在跑」，而是「我在流鼻水」。

2. My refrigerator is running fine. 不是「我的冰箱跑得很好」，而是「我的冰箱運作正常」。

第一部分 詞彙

1. **We are going to have a picnic _____ Saturday.**（我們打算下星期六去野餐。）

   (A) on the　(B) last　(C) next　(D) on next

   答題解說

   答案：(C)。表示「星期幾」的專有名詞，其前不加冠詞 the。此外，當它前面有形容詞（例如 this、last、next... 等）修飾時也不加任何介系詞，所以正確答案是 (C)；另外，(B) last 錯誤的原因是，前面有 are going to-V 表示「未來」。

   破題關鍵

   掌握本題兩個考點：1. 只有「on + 星期幾」或是「形容詞 + 星期幾」的用法。2. be going to-V（= will）表示「未來」，答案就出來了。

   字詞解釋

   have a picnic 去野餐

   相關文法或用法補充

   「時間介系詞」要用 in、at 還是 on，總是讓人傻傻分不清！以下就為您稍作整理：

   1. 在季節、月份、年份、世紀等比較長的時段，要用 in。例如：in spring（在春天）、in September（在九月）、in 1993（在 1993 年）和 in 18th century（在 18 世紀）。
   2. 在星期幾、日期、或節日等確切的日子，前面會搭配的介系詞是 on。例如：on Thursday（在星期四）、on Thanksgiving（在感恩節）、on July 27th（在 7 月 27 日）。
   3. at 是加在某個確切「時間點」前面的介系詞，如：at 7:30 a.m.。

2. **Look at the _____! It's the last day of this month.**（看日曆！今天是這個月的最後一天了。）

   (A) clock　(B) channel　(C) calendar　(D) computer

   答題解說

   答案：(C)。本題的考點是要根據前後文句來選出較恰當的用字。我們可以根據

第二句的 "It's the last day of this Month." （今天是這個月的最後一天了。）來判斷，說話者當時正看著日曆。選項中的 clock、channel 及 computer 的意思分別是「時鐘」、「頻道」、「電腦」。

破題關鍵

有時候選項中的單字，你不一定都知道意思，但只要從題目句子中找到相對應，或是有相關的「連結」，就可以找到答案，因為答案的用字絕對不會超出英檢初級的範圍。例如本題，"last day of this month" 與 calendar 就有很強烈的「連結關係」。

字詞解釋

channel [ˈtʃænl] **n.** 頻道　　**calendar** [ˈkæləndɚ] **n.** 日曆　　**computer** [kəmˈpjutɚ] **n.** 電腦

相關文法或用法補充

祈使句有命令、建議、請求等語意，祈使句沒有主詞，通常以原形動詞開頭。例如：

Turn down the radio!（把收音機的聲音調小點！）
Take care! There is a car coming.（當心！有輛車開過來了。）
Don't believe in that liar!（不要相信那個撒謊的人！）
上面舉的例子語氣比較強硬，為了緩和語氣，可以加上 please，或者降低語調，如：
Please be patient!（請耐心點！）
另外，還可以用　will you?、Would you?、Can you?、Can't you?　等使語氣更委婉，更容易讓人接受，如：
Would you please close the door?（麻煩你關上門好嗎？）
Can you get me another apple?（可以麻煩你再給我一顆蘋果嗎？）

3. **My father did not go home early _____ he worked late.**（我爸爸沒有很早回家，因為他工作到很晚。）

(A) so　(B) because　(C) before　(D) after

答題解說

答案：(B)。空格前面是「我爸爸沒有很早回家」，後面是「他工作到很晚。」顯然前後兩句有「因果」關係，前面是「果」，後面是「因」。所以應填入 because。選 (A) 或 (C) 的話，都會造成不合理的句子，而 after 主要強調「事件的時間先後」，放在本句中也是不恰當的。

第 1 回

第 2 回

第 3 回

第 4 回

第 5 回

第 6 回

第 7 回

第 8 回

第 9 回

第 10 回

破題關鍵

從空格前後的 early 與 late 兩個相反意思的用字，即可直接判定要用 because。

字詞解釋

go home 回家　　**work late** 工作到很晚

相關文法或用法補充

go home、come home 都是「回家」的意思，兩者看似相同，但實則差很大。go home 是指說話者人不在自己的家 但是他／她想要回家的時候。例如： I feel like going home now.（我現在想要回家了）而 come home 是指某個人（已經在家裡等你的人）希望你回家的時候。例如：Hey honey, today is our boy's birthday. Can you come home a bit earlier tonight?（喂，親愛的，今天是我們兒子的生日。你今晚可以早點回家嗎？）

4. I want ＿＿＿＿＿ of you to listen carefully. This is quite important.（我要你們所有人都仔細聽。這件事很重要。）

(A) all　(B) every　(C) much　(D) none

答題解說

答案：(A)。第一句的意思是「我要你們……仔細聽。」這裡的 you 顯然不是單數的「你／妳」，而是複數的「你們」，所以 (C) much 可直接排除；而如果是「你們每一位」，要填入 each，而非 every（不能當代名詞用）；如果填入 (D) none，變成「我要你們都不要仔細聽。」加上後面這句「這件事很重要。」，顯然就不合邏輯了。所以正確答案應為 (A) all。

破題關鍵

代名詞的考題要注意「可數、不可數」的問題。在 of you 之前的代名詞，一定是「可數」（因為「人」是可數的）。接著是考量「符合語意」的部分（所以 none 是錯的）。

字詞解釋

carefully [ˋkɛrfəlɪ] adv. 小心地，仔細地　　**important** [ɪmˋpɔrtṇt] adj. 重要的

相關文法或用法補充

all 是個無所不在的字，像是 all the... 、all my... 、all of... 、all but 、...not at all 、after all... 等等。這裡繼續為 all of... 進行延伸學習。all 當不定代名詞時，所指稱的名詞可能是可數，也可能是不可數名詞。例如：

He brought gifts for all of us.（他為我們所有人帶了禮物。）

All of this has to go out into the rubbish bin.（這些全部都必須放入垃圾桶。）

5. **Is the world safer ＿＿＿＿ it was a year ago?**（這個世界比一年前更安全嗎？）

(A) after　(B) than　(C) and　(D) then

答題解說

答案：(B)。空格前後是完整句子，應填入一個連接詞，所以 (D) then 應直接排除。第一個子句意思是「這個世界更安全」，第二個子句是「它一年前」，而 (A) 與 (C) 填入空格的話，都會形成不合邏輯的句意。故正確答案應為 (B)。

破題關鍵

空格前是一個比較級形容詞，如果稍有文法上的敏感度的話，應該可以直接聯想到 than 這個搭配比較級的連接詞。如果不確定是否要填入 than，只要把其他兩個連接詞選項（after 與 and）填入空格試試，也很輕易就能看出是不合邏輯的句子。

相關文法或用法補充

認識形容詞比較級的「變化」，是學「比較級」文法的第一步。以下是形容詞「原級」改為「比較級」的方法整理：

1. 規則變化：

單音節：原級加 -er	舉例：small→smaller、strong→stronger
形容詞字尾為 e，原級加 -r	舉例：wise→wiser、cute→cuter
形容詞字尾是「短母音＋子音」，重複字尾子音加 -er	舉例：hot→hotter、thin→thinner、big→bigger
形容詞字尾是「子音 -y」，去掉原級字尾 y，加上 -ier	舉例：busy→busier、easy→easier、heavy→heavier
多音節形容詞，在形容詞前加上 more 或 less	舉例：beautiful→more beautiful、expensive→more expensive、important→more important

2. 不規則變化：

原級	比較級	原級	比較級
good	better	bad	worse
many 或 much	more	little	less

6. **If you want your English to be better, just _____ practicing.**（如果你要自己的英文更進步，就持續練習吧。）

   (A) keep　(B) to keep　(C) keeping　(D) keeps

   答題解說

   答案：(A)。空格前有個逗號（,），在逗號前是個 If 開頭的條件句，因此逗號後面應為主要子句，但因為選項是動詞 keep 的各種類型，顯然沒有主詞，也就是要用「祈使句／命令句」來取代主要子句，所以正確答案應為原形動詞的(A)。

   破題關鍵

   「祈使句／命令句」不一定都是用「原形動詞」開頭，前面可能會加上 Please、just... 等副詞，甚至還會有副詞子句來干擾你的判斷。因此，只要能夠看出整個句子的結構（框架），就能輕易解題。

   字詞解釋

   better [ˋbɛtɚ] **adj.** 更好的　　**practice** [ˋpræktɪs] **v.** 練習

   相關文法或用法補充

   V-ing 如果當「動名詞」，功用就跟名詞沒有兩樣，所以這時的 Ving 就具備名詞特有的「存在性」及「持久性」，所以當我們表達一種「持續」的狀態、事實或習慣等，要用 Ving。比如這裡的 keep practicing（持續練習）。常見後面接動名詞的動詞還有：admit 承認、mind 介意、miss 想念、quit 戒除、avoid 避免、enjoy 享受、can't help 忍不住、risk 冒……的風險、consider 考慮、keep 保持、practice 練習、suggest 建議…等。

7. **My mom cooks dinner sometimes, but _____ my dad does it.**（我媽有時候會煮晚餐，不過通常都是我爸煮的）

   (A) ever　(B) never　(C) usually　(D) seldom

   答題解說

   答案：(C)。四個選項都是頻率副詞，所以應根據句意來選出正確答案。首先，對等連接詞 but 前面是「我媽有時會煮晚餐」，後面是「我爸煮晚餐」，顯然前後句有相反的意味，所以應填入 (C) usually（通常）。

   破題關鍵

   空格前的 but 是關鍵，因為是要填入頻率副詞，前面是 sometimes（有時候），選項中只有 usually 可以和 sometimes 形成相反意義的對照。

usually [ˈjuʒʊəlɪ] **adv.** 通常　　**seldom** [ˈsɛldəm] **adv.** 不常，很少

相關文法或用法補充

助動詞 do、does、did 可以形成一般疑問句以及否定句，例如：Do you speak English?（你說英文嗎？）還有 He didn't eat anything for lunch.（他中午什麼都沒吃。）但是助動詞的妙用可不只有這樣喔，它還可以代替已經出現過的動詞，例如題目這句：My mom cooks dinner sometimes, but usually my dad does it.。如果把同樣的 cooks dinner 再重複一次會使得整個句子冗贅，因此可以把後者以 does 來替換。

8. **I saw her parents at the school fair, but I didn't see _____.**（我在學校園遊會上看見了她的父母，但我沒看到他的父母。）

(A) them　(B) his　(C) that　(D) it

答題解說

答案：(B)。連接詞 but 前後句子大意分別是「我看見了她的父母」與「我沒看到……」，而 but 前後句有比較的意味，而四個選項都是代名詞，看下來只有 his（he 的所有代名詞，等於 his parents）是最正確的答案。如果填入 (A) them，則前後矛盾，(C) 與 (D) 皆所指不明，故不可選。

破題關鍵

對等連接詞前後兩個句子都是「S+V+O」，第一句的 O 是 her parents，因此第二句的 O 也應對應第一句，所以只有 his（= his parents）是最正確的。

字詞解釋

fair [fɛr] **n.**（熱鬧的）市集　　**school fair** 學校園遊會

相關文法或用法補充

「所有格代名詞」是用來代替人稱代名詞的所有格及其所修飾的名詞，也就是「所有格 + 名詞」。人稱代名詞的所有格（my, our, her...）後面一定要有名詞，而所有格代名詞（mine, ours, hers...）後面則不能再有名詞。例如：

my book = mine／your pen = yours／his parents = his／her dog = hers／its fate = its／our house = ours／their car = theirs

9. **Andrew grew up in Taiwan, but he _____ born in Japan.**（安德魯在台灣長大，但他出生在日本。）

(A) is　(B) was　(C) has been　(D) will be

第 1 回
第 2 回
第 3 回
第 4 回
第 5 回
第 6 回
第 7 回
第 8 回
第 9 回
第 10 回

答題解說

答案：(B)。對等連接詞 but 前面這句用的時態是過去式（grew up），所以 but 之後這句也應用過去式。故正確答案應為 (B) was。

破題關鍵

這一題的答案其實不必考慮 "Andrew grew up in Taiwan" 這句，只要看空格後到關鍵的 born，答案就是「過去式 be 動詞」，因為任何人的「出生」都是過去已經發生的事，其餘時態皆不必考量。

字詞解釋

grow up 長大

相關文法或用法補充

出生指的是你出生當下的時間點，通常使用這個詞時都是使用「過去式」。要注意的是，born 的動詞三態變化是 bear-bore-born。另外，born 後面搭配不同介系詞時，會產生不一樣的意思。例如，「出生在有錢人家」要用 into：Tim was born into a rich family.（Tim 出生在有錢人家。）；「天生就是～」要用 for：Lisa was born for the job of singing.（Lisa 天生就是唱歌的料。）；「某人所生的」要用 to：Jerry was born to Mary.（Jerry 是 Mary 親生的。）但是記住：沒有 "is/am/are born" 的說法喔！

10. **The fried chicken is so _____ that so many people are willing to stand in line for it.**（這炸雞是如此地美味，難怪這麼多人願意為它來排隊。）

(A) amazed　(B) foreign　(C) expensive　(D) delicious

答題解說

答案：(D)。句子的意思是「炸雞如此…以致於許多人願意為它來排隊」。(C) 是最明顯的錯誤選項，可直接排除。(A) amazed 須搭配「人」的主詞，而非「事物」（若改成 amazing 也會是個正確答案）；(B) foreign 通常置於名詞前，而非 be 動詞後面當補語，且不合邏輯。故正確答案應為 (D)。

破題關鍵

本題答題關鍵在於：1.「主詞補語（用來修飾主詞）的概念」。英文裡有些形容詞只能修飾名詞；2. -ed（形容「人」）與 -ing（形容「事物」）形容詞的認知。

字詞解釋

fried [fraɪd] **adj.** 油炸的　**stand in line** 排隊　**amazed** [əˋmezd] **adj.** 感到驚奇的

foreign [ˋfɔrɪn] **adj.** 外國的　**expensive** [ɪkˋspɛnsɪv] **adj.** 昂貴的　**delicious** [dɪˋlɪʃəs] **adj.** 美味的

相關文法或用法補充

「so + adj. / adv. + that」是個很常考也很好用的句型。它具有「強調」的功能，強調前面是「如此……以致於……」，所以中間加上的是形容詞或副詞，加強形容詞的強度。例如：

I was so tired that I might fall asleep at that time.（我當時是如此地疲累，以致於我可能會睡著。）

第二部分 段落填空

Questions 11-14

　　Susan was an office lady a few years ago. Although she was always busy, she kept the habit of learning some languages. After Susan got off **work** at six o'clock, she went to an evening class to study English three days a week. It was such a wonderful course that she enjoyed more and more learning English. Besides, she had wished her GEPT grades could improve a lot **so that she might get a pay raise**.

　　However, sometimes she forgot to do her homework and she did not remember to bring her textbooks needed for the class. She wanted to avoid making such mistakes, which **had caused** her much trouble. As a result, she always tried to remind herself **of** putting it in her bag before she went to bed every night. Besides, she would do her homework right after arriving home.

中文翻譯 數年前蘇珊是一位女性上班族。雖然她總是忙碌，她仍保持著學習一些語言的習慣。蘇珊在六點下班之後，她一週有三天會去上一個學習英文的晚間課程。那是如此棒的課程，以致於她越來越喜歡學英文了。此外，她一直希望她的英檢成績能夠進步很多，那麼她就可能獲得加薪。
　　然而，有時候她會忘記做功課，也不記得要帶上課要用的課本。她想要避免繼續犯這些錯誤 — 已經帶給她許多麻煩了。所以，她總是試著提醒自己，要在每天晚上睡覺之前將課本放進她的包包中。此外，她一回到家就會馬上做作業。

答題解說

11. 答案：(D)。四個選項都是名詞，所以應依照前後文的句意判斷。第一句說「數年前蘇珊是一位上班族。（Susan was an office worker a few years ago.）」而 get off 是「離開」的意思，所以不會是「下課」或「放學」，而「下班」的正確說法是 get off work。

12. 答案：(B)。這一題是要挑選一個句子、子句或句子的一部分放入空格後，確認空格前後和空格句之間的連接關係，是否讓句意顯得自然通順。前面句子提到「她越來越喜歡學英文了」，所以答案不會是 (D)；空格前半句提到，她希望她的英檢成績能夠進步，但這跟她英文說得好不好沒有直接關係，所以 (A) 也是錯誤的；至於 (C) 的交很多好朋友也與前後文不相關。故正確答案為 (B)「那麼她就可能獲得加薪」，因為英文檢定考試在實務上確實可能與加薪有關係。以下是其餘選項句子的翻譯：

　　(A) 因為她的英文可以說得更好

　　(C) 而且她可以結交許多好朋友

　　(D) 但是她還是無法喜歡英文

13. 答案：(D)。四個選項是同一個動詞（cause）的不同時態。由於整段都在敘述過去的事情，所以不可能用現在式、未來式或現在進行式。

14. 答案：(C)。四個選項都是介系詞，顯然是在考「搭配某個動詞的介系詞」。看到空格前的 remind，以及空格後的 Ving（putting）應直接聯想到 remind... of... 的動詞片語。

破題關鍵

11. 「下班」的英文說法是 get off work，沒有 get off office 的用法，也不是 get out of work（失業）喔！

12. 先看過四個選項，了解答案是一個副詞子句或對等子句，且後面的 "she had wished her GEPT grades could improve a lot"（她當時一直希望她的英檢成績能夠進步很多）這句話會是主要參考指標。

13. 「動詞時態」的考題必須考慮當下的「時空背景」，因為整篇都是敘述過去的事情，所以如果不是用過去式，當然也可以用過去完成式來表達。

14. 動詞 remind 常用於「remind + 人 + of N./Ving」或是「remind + 人 + 不定詞（to-V）」的用法。

字詞解釋

office worker 上班族　**language** [ˈlæŋgwɪdʒ] n. 語言　**get off work** 下班　**wonderful** [ˈwʌndɚfəl] adj. 極好的　**course** [kors] n. 課程　**improve** [ɪmˈpruv] v. 改進，改善　**textbook** [ˈtɛkstˌbʊk] n. 教科書，課本　**avoid** [əˈvɔɪd] v. 避免　**make a mistake** 犯錯　**as a result** 因此，所以　**remind** [rɪˈmaɪnd] v. 提醒，使想起　**go to**

bed 上床睡覺   **arrive** [əˋraɪv] v. 到達

11. 「上班」是 go to work，「下班」是 get off work，所以當然還是要用到 work。另外，「加班」叫作 work overtime。

12. so that 被視為是一個副詞連接詞，相當於連接詞 so（所以）的意思，前後子句需有因果連帶關係。

13. 當我們想要表示一件事情從過去的時間點發生，並且一路持續到現在的時候，我們會用現在完成式。而「過去完成式」使用時機是：從過去某時間點持續到過去另一個時間點的事件或動作。

14. 動詞 remind 還有個用法：「remind ＋ 人 ＋ that 子句／wh-子句」。例如：The photo reminded me how we had spent time together.（這照片使我想起我們在一起的日子。）、These letters remind me that we once loved each other.（這些信件使我想起我們曾經彼此相愛。）

Questions 15-18

Nowadays many people are used to shopping online. You will be considered out-of-fashion if you do not know how to buy things online. Just by a click of the mouse, you can buy whatever you're interested in **without** going outdoors. You can avoid getting tired and being trapped in the crowds or busy traffic. You can save a lot of time. Besides, you can choose from more varieties of goods whose prices are generally lower.

Every coin has its two sides. Shopping online could cause some troubles or unhappy experiences, because you could buy things **different** from the pictures you see on the Internet. **Furthermore**, it may cause people to buy goods that are not badly needed. That's a waste of money.

如今許多人已習慣上網購物。如果你不知道如何上網買東西，你可能被視為落伍的人了。只要用滑鼠點一下，你不必出門就可以買到你有興趣的任何東西。你可以避免勞累以及困在人群或繁忙的交通中。你可以省下許多時間。此外，你可以選擇各式各樣的物品，基本它們的價格都是比較低廉的。

一個銅板都有兩面。網購可能造成一些麻煩或不愉快的經驗，因為你可能買到和你在網路上看到的圖片不一樣的東西。此外，它可能使得人們去購買不是很迫切需要的東西。那是在浪費錢。

第 1 回
第 2 回
第 3 回
第 4 回
第 5 回
第 6 回
第 7 回
第 8 回
第 9 回
第 10 回

答題解說

15. 答案：(B)。這一題是要挑選一個句子、子句或句子的一部分放入空格後，確認空格前後和空格句之間的連接關係，是否讓句意顯得自然通順。後面句子提到，如果你不知道如何上網買東西，你可能被視為落伍的人（You will be considered out-of-fashion if you do not know how to buy things online.）。顯然這句話應該和「線上購物已普及化、受歡迎」等說法有關，故正確答案為 (B)。以下是其餘選項句子的翻譯：

(A) 有時候你線上購物時要小心。

(C) 線上購物有它的優缺點。

(D) 有些長者可能不太了解線上購物。

16. 答案：(D)。因為內容主要是關於「網購」，意思就是「不用出門」就可以買東西，所以根據句意，答案應為 without。

17. 答案：(A)。可以採用「刪除法」：空格前是完整句子（有動詞），所以不可能再填入動詞（differ）。(B) difference、(C) differently 皆不合邏輯或不符句意，正確答案應為形容詞 different。

18. 答案：(B)。前文提到網購的一個缺點，後面提到「使得人們去購買不是很迫切需要的東西」，顯然是在講另一個缺點。因此應選「此外（Furthermore）」最為恰當。其餘選項 (A) 首先、(C) 簡言之、(D) 因此，皆不符句意。

破題關鍵

15. 空格句子出現在文章開頭的第一句，表示這句話很可能是全篇文章的主旨。因此，只要再往下看個一兩句，大致上可以決定要選哪一個答案了。

16. 掌握段落篇章的「意旨」（網路購物，不必出門就能買東西）就能正確解題。

17. 形容詞的「後位修飾」是來自於「形容詞子句的簡化」，應建立起這樣的文法概念。

18. 從四個選項來看，要填入的是一個副詞的「轉折語」，所以只要對照前後文句意（列舉「網購的缺點」）去判斷，很容易找出正確答案。

字詞解釋

be used to... 習慣於～　**consider** [kən`sɪdɚ] v. 認為　**out-of-fashion** [`autəv`fæʃən] adj. 落伍的　**click** [klɪk] n. 卡嗒聲　**outdoors** [`aut`dorz] adv. 在戶外　**avoid** [ə`vɔɪd] v. 避免　**trap** [træp] v. 使落入圈套　**crowd** [kraud] n. 人群　**variety** [və`raɪətɪ] n. 多樣化　**goods** [gudz] n. 商品，貨物　**generally** [`dʒɛnərəlɪ] adv. 一般來說　**cause** [kɔz] v. 導致　**waste** [west] n. 浪費；濫用　**differ** [`dɪfɚ] v. 產生不同

相關文法觀念補充

15. 並不是看到 used to 就以為後面都要接 Ving 喔！如果是 "used to" 單獨出現，那就是個「助動詞」，表示「曾經」，後面必須接原形動詞。例如：He used to run

very fast before the accident took place.（在這場意外之前，他曾經跑得很快。）

16. without 也常用於「假設語氣」，表示「要不是～，如果沒有～」。例如：I wouldn't have passed the exam without your help.（要不是你的幫忙，我沒辦法通過考試。）

17. 對於初學英文的人來說，「後位修飾」雖然聽起來有點複雜，但其實它就是把本來的形容詞子句的關係代名詞以及 be 動詞刪除而已。

18. furthermore 這個副詞通常出現在句首，其後所要陳述的內容應該要和前面提到的有「一致的觀點」。

第三部分 閱讀理解

Questions 19-21

中文翻譯

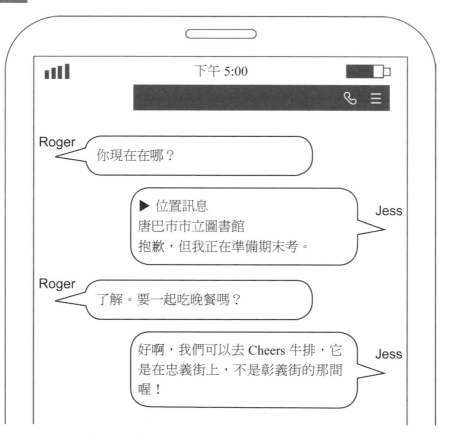

第 1 回
第 2 回
第 3 回
第 4 回
第 5 回
第 6 回
第 7 回
第 8 回
第 9 回
第 10 回

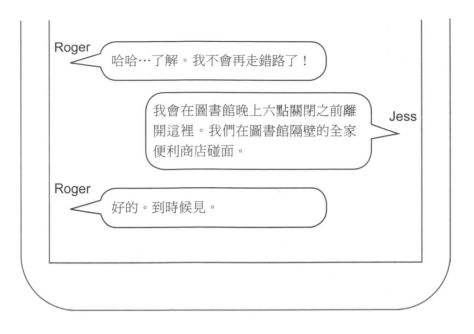

Roger 哈哈…了解。我不會再走錯路了！

我會在圖書館晚上六點關閉之前離開這裡。我們在圖書館隔壁的全家便利商店碰面。 **Jess**

Roger 好的。到時候見。

Roger 上這個圖書館網站去確認它的地址。

市立圖書館開放時間
平日：上午 10 點至晚上 9 點
週六：上午 10 點至下午 6 點

來享受閱讀與自修吧！您將在此發現並可借走想閱讀的書籍，而且這是個非常安靜、您可準備大考的地方。此外，我們不僅提供書籍，還有雜誌、DVD、期刊，甚至電腦遊戲。

※ 週日及例假日不開放。
※ 地址：唐巴市光復二街 77 號
※ 電話：1569-6852

19. 這則 LINE 訊息的發生時間是在星期幾？
    (A) 在週一　　　　　　　　(B) 在週五
    (C) 在週六　　　　　　　　(D) 在週日

20. 關於人們可以使用圖書館的時間，何者為真？
   (A) 人們每週七天，一天 24 小時都可以去這間圖書館。
   (B) 圖書館週日開放到下午 6:00。
   (C) 圖書館週一是從是早上 10:00 開門。
   (D) 圖書館週六於晚間 9:00 以後關門。

21. 根據談話訊息，全家便利商店在哪裡？
   (A) 在忠義街　　　　　　　　　(B) 在彰義街
   (C) 在光復二街 77 號　　　　　 (D) 在光復二街 75 號

答題解說

19. 答案：(C)。本題需要整合與歸納兩篇文本的資訊並比對多項訊息才能夠得到正確的答案。題目問的是這則對話訊息的時間。可以從 Jess 最後一次發言中的 "And I'll leave here right before the library closes at 6:00 P.M." 訊息中得知，當天圖書館關閉時間是 6:00 P.M.，接著再看網頁上方圖書館開放時間（Public Library Open Hours）的資訊顯示 "Saturdays: 10 A.M. - 6:00 P.M."，所以當天對話的時間是星期六。

20. 答案：(C)。關於圖書館的開放時間，可以從標題 Open Hours 下方的文字內容找到答案。首先 (A) 當中的 24/7 可不是七月二十四日的意思，而是「每週七天，一天 24 小時」，顯然是錯誤的；另外，沒有提到週日（Sunday）的開放時間，所以 (B) 是錯的；而週六僅開放到下午 6 點，所以 (D) 也是錯的。weekdays 就是指「週一至週五」的平日，所以答案是 (C)。

21. 答案：(D)。本題需要整合與歸納兩篇文本的訊息與資訊，才能夠得到正確的答案。首先，Jess 在對話訊息的最後一次發言中提到 "Let's meet at the Family Mart convenience store next to the library."，表示「全家便利商店」是在圖書館隔壁，而網頁資訊中顯示圖書館地址是 "No.77, Guanfu 2nd St"，所以最有可能的答案是 (D) On No.75, Guanfu 2nd Street。

破題關鍵

19. 詢問時間或日期的題型通常不會在篇章／文本中直接顯示，本題既然問「星期幾」，就必須現在注意到提及「星期幾」的 "Saturdays: 10 A.M. - 6:00 P.M." 下方資訊，然後再與對話訊息中的 6:00 P.M. 連結在一起，答案就出來了。

20. 掌握選項中的 24/7、open until...（開放至～）、open from...（從～開始開放）的意思，就能輕易解決此題了。

21. 既然題目要問的是便利商店的位置，那麼就應先注意提及便利商店的資訊：Family Mart convenience store next to the library。next to... 意思是「緊鄰～，在隔壁～」，了解之後再去找圖書館地址，答案就出來了。

第 1 回

第 2 回

第 3 回

第 4 回

第 5 回

第 6 回

第 7 回

第 8 回

第 9 回

第 10 回

字詞解釋

final [ˋfaɪnl] adj. 最終的　**steak** [stek] n. 牛排　**convenience store** 便利商店　**next to...** 在～隔壁　**library** [ˋlaɪˌbrɛrɪ] n. 圖書館　**weekday** [ˋwikˌde] n. 平日，工作日　**borrow** [ˋbaro] v. 借，借來（用）　**prepare** [prɪˋpɛr] v. 準備　**provide** [prəˋvaɪd] v. 提供　**periodical** [ˌpɪrɪˋɑdɪkl] n. 期刊　**public holiday** 國定假日

相關文法或用法補充

❶ 口語說「我懂了」、「我明白了」，往往不會用 I understand，而會說「I get it.」或「I've got it.」。首先，get 在這類表達中指「懂得、明白、理解」，在對話中，詢問他人是否明白你說的話，是否理解某個觀點、笑點的時候，會用 Do you get it ?來詢問對方。而 Do you understand? 這個問法，雖然語意上沒錯，但在外國人聽起來有一種質問和不耐煩的感覺，更接近於「你到底懂不懂啊？」這樣的含義，有些不禮貌和不友好。而 Got it. 是 I've got it. 的縮簡用法，表示「本來不明白，經過一番思考後明白了、豁然開朗」的狀態，所以用了現在完成式。

❷ 基本上 not only... but also... 是個「對等連接詞」，可以連接對等的單字、片語或子句。例如網頁中這句：Besides, we provide not only books but also magazines, DVDs, periodicals, and even computer games.，連接 books、magazines、DVDs、periodicals 四個名詞。又例如：She is not only beautiful, but she is (also) kind.（她不止漂亮，而且善良。），連接 beautiful、kind 兩個形容詞。

Questions 22-24

中文翻譯 許多人，尤其是超過 40 歲者，都不容易入睡。每個人所經歷這問題的理由可能不盡相同。但對我而言，那是因為我家裡有人在睡覺時會打呼。這問題有時候還挺嚴重的，因為沒有人可以睡得好，除了正在打呼的那個人之外。
那麼我們要怎麼做才能在睡覺時避免打呼呢？有一個方法是睡前不要吃大餐。睡覺時改變姿勢也會有幫助。對於像我這樣因為噪音而無法入睡的人來說，戴耳塞是另一個方法。但如果還是沒有用，你就得把打呼的這個人叫醒。告訴他／她，是時候該他們看著你睡覺了。

22. 說話者為何無法入睡？
　　(A) 因為他聽見有人呼吸地很吵。
　　(B) 因為他通常入睡時會一直打呼。
　　(C) 因為他睡覺前吃太多東西。
　　(D) 因為他不知道如何戴耳塞。

23. 第二段第一行中 resist 這個字的意思較接近 _____ 。
    (A) 輕鬆看待～　　　　　　　　　(B) 遠離～
    (C) ～不當一回事　　　　　　　　(D) 擅長～

24. 以下何者「不是」真實的？
    (A) 人們可以戴耳塞避免吵雜聲。
    (B) 人們可以改變睡覺的姿勢來停止打呼。
    (C) 如果你聽見有人打呼，你會做噩夢。
    (D) 如果你睡前吃太多，你睡覺時可能會出現呼吸地很吵。

答題解說

這是一篇說明文，內容講述中年人常遇到的睡眠問題，並舉出一些因應之道。

22. 答案：(A)。題目要問的是說話者無法入睡的原因，我們可以從一開始的「每個人所經歷這問題的理由可能不盡相同。但對我而言，那是因為～（There can be quite different reasons for each person to experience this trouble. But for me, that is because...）」找到答案：我家裡有人在睡覺時會打呼。選項 (A) 以 breathe noisily (while one is sleeping) 來取代 snore 這個動詞。

23. 答案：(B)。resist 這個字所在的句子是 "One way is to resist eating a big meal before going to bed." →「一個方法是睡前——吃大餐。」把四個選項的動詞片語套入空格內，可以清楚知道只有「(B) 遠離～」是最符合語意的答案。

24. 答案：(C)。第二段提到「睡前不要吃大餐。」、「對於像我這樣因為噪音而無法入睡的人來說，戴耳塞是另一個方法。」、「睡覺時改變姿勢也會有幫助。」所以只有 (C) 是沒有提到的。

破題關鍵

22. 本題關鍵句當然是 But for me, that is because there was someone in my family who snores while he is sleeping.（但對我而言，那是因為我家裡有人在睡覺時會打呼。）但如果不知道 snore 這個動詞的意思也無所謂，只要在第二段找到這句 For people like me who can't fall asleep with noise...，應該就可以推斷 snore 就是「打呼」的意思。

23. 直接針對關鍵字 resist 在短文中找線索：前文是「一個方法是…」，後面是「吃大餐」，而本段落探討的是「如何避免睡覺打呼」，因此可以直覺認定為「睡前避免吃大餐」。

24. 這是屬於細節性的綜合考題，通常是解決完這個題組的其他題目之後再作答。

字詞解釋

especially [ə`spɛʃəlɪ] adv. 特別，尤其　**fall asleep** 入睡，睡著　**reason** [`rizn] n. 理由，原因　**experience** [ɪk`spɪrɪəns] v. 經歷　*****snore** [snor] v. 打鼾　**serious** [`sɪrɪəs] adj. 嚴重的，嚴肅的　**except** [ɪkˋsɛpt] **prep**. 除～之外　**avoid** [əˋvɔɪd] **v**. 避免 ***resist** [rɪˋzɪst] **v**. 抗拒　**position** [pəˋzɪʃən] **n**. 姿勢　***earplug** [ˋɪr͵plʌg] **n**. （常複數）耳 塞　**wake up** 叫醒

相關文法或用法補充

❶ have trouble/difficulty/a hard time 表示「有困難」，後面常接 (in) V-ing，表示「做 ～有困難」。在此句型中，trouble/difficulty 皆用單數表示，其前面可加上 some、 great、little... 等修飾語，例如本篇這句：Many people, especially at the age of over 40, have difficulty falling asleep.

❷ way 當主詞時，其 be 動詞後面的補語，必須用不定詞（to-V），類似用法的名詞 還有 goal、plan... 等表示「未來計畫、目標、方法…」等名詞。例如本篇這句： One way is to resist eating a big meal before going to bed.。

❸ work 除了「工作」以外，還可作為「有效」的意思。例如本篇的這句：But if it doesn't work, you need to wake up the one who is snoring.。

Questions 25-27

中文翻譯

　　大衛在義大利長大，且從他還是個小學生時，就已經學過英文了。然而，他在 英文課堂上並沒有很認真念書。他經常忘記做家庭作業，且這個科目的成績很差。 隨著時間過去，他當時變得很害怕講英文。

　　他在 25 歲時，前往美國到一家國際公司上班。在他上班第一天，他搭乘公車去 公司時，他需要知道他應該在哪一站下車。坐在他旁邊的小姐是個漂亮的美國人， 留著長金髮，戴著一頂時尚的帽子。當他用很破的英文和她說話時，她卻用義大利 語回答他。她在大學時曾學過兩年的義大利語。而且他們一見鍾情。他們在一年後 結婚了。

　　現在大衛的英文說得好多了 — 而且更有自信，幾乎比他五歲的兒子要好了。

25. 這篇故事應該給個什麼標題？
　　(A) 一見鍾情：大衛和他的妻子
　　(B) 英文這個語言的重要性
　　(C) 大衛如何與他的妻子相遇
　　(D) 大衛的英文是如何進步的

26. 大衛何時開始學英文？
　　(A) 在 25 歲時。
　　(B) 當他遇見他的妻子時。
　　(C) 當他上小學時。
　　(D) 在他去美國工作時。

27. 以下何者為真？
   (A) 大衛的兒子英文無法說得比他爸爸好。
   (B) 大衛在 26 歲時結婚。
   (C) 大衛的妻子義大利語說得比英文好。
   (D) 大衛是義大利人，而他的妻子是美國人。

答題解說

這是一則記敘文。內容敘述從害怕說英文到能夠自信地侃侃而談的轉變過程。

25. 答案：(D)。選項 (A) 的「一見鍾情」只是第二段中提到的「小插曲」，不是本篇主旨；同樣，(C) 的「大衛如何與他的妻子相遇」也是。因為整篇從一開始提到大衛何時開始學英文，接著是前往美國工作認識了現在的妻子，後來英文慢慢進步，顯然跟「英文的重要性」沒有關係，故 (B) 也是錯的。故正確答案應為 (D)。

26. 答案：(C)。本篇一開始提到「從他還是個小學生時，就已經學過英文了。（he had studied English there since he was an elementary school student.」。故正確答案應為 (C)。

27. 答案：(B)。最後提到，「幾乎比他五歲的兒子要好。」「幾乎」表示「快要但還未」的程度，所以 (A) 是錯誤的；另外，只有提到「當他用很破的英文和她說話時，她卻用義大利語回答他。」，但並未提及他的妻子義大利語說得比英文好，所以 (C) 是錯誤的。而第一句說「大衛在義大利長大（David was brought up in Italy）」，這並不表示他是義大利人，所以 (D) 也是錯誤的。故正確答案是 (B)。

破題關鍵

25. 本篇短文一開始就提到大衛學英文的事情，而最後以「大衛的英文說得好多了（David can speak English much better）」作結尾，顯然主旨應該和「大衛的英文」有關。

26. primary school 是 elementary school 的另一種說法。

27. 第二段一開始時提到，他在 25 歲時，前往美國工作（At the age of 25, he left for the United States...），而且「在他上班第一天（On his first day of work...）」他遇見他未來的妻子，以及「一年後他們結婚了（They got married one year later.）」，所以表示他是在 26 歲時結婚的。

字詞解釋

bring up 把（某人）帶大　**elementary school** 小學（=primary school）　**grade** [gred] n. 成績　**subject** [ˋsʌbdʒɪkt] n. 科目，學科　**as a result** 因此，所以　**be afraid of...** 害怕　**leave for...** 前往　**destination** [ˌdɛstəˋneʃən] n. 目的地　**next to...** 在～旁邊　**broken** [ˋbrokən] adj. （語言）拙劣的，不流利的　**instead** [ɪnˋstɛd] adv. 反而，卻

at first sight 在第一眼時　**get married** 結婚　**importance** [ɪm`pɔrtn̩s] n. 重要性
improve [ɪm`pruv] v. 改進，改善

相關文法或用法補充

❶ hard 可以當形容詞或副詞。當形容詞表示「硬的，困難的」，例如：The wood is as hard as rock.（這木頭像石頭一樣硬。）、He is hard to get along with.（喬治很難相處。）當副詞可表示「努力地」，如：study hard（用功念書）或 work hard（努力工作）。另外，副詞 hardly 是完全不一樣的意思，表示「幾乎不」。例如：He has hardly any money.（他幾乎沒有錢。）、It hardly snowed at all last winter.（去年冬天幾乎沒下雪。）

❷ 說某種「語言」，動詞要用 speak，例如 speak English、speak Chinese。而「說話」要用 say，例如 say something、say goodbye、say "Thank you."。

Questions 28-30

中文翻譯

寄件者	Jason Fried Chicken@surmail.com
收件者	不具名收件人
主旨	慶祝活動與特別優惠

親愛的顧客們：
　　為慶祝我們首年營運的成功，我們將於九月一日提供您一些特別套餐。為了給我們的老顧客一個大驚喜，如果您購買一份有編號的炸雞餐，您可免費獲得一份蔬菜三明治及一份玉米濃湯。此外，若您購買三支炸雞棒腿或三支雞翅，則可再加送一支。請注意，免費的炸雞腿或雞翅必須與購買的價格相同或更低。您只要出示您的會員卡即可享有這些優惠。
當日首次光顧的客人們將可獲得所有炸雞餐九折的優惠。

　　備註：任何時候透過 UberEats 或 Foodpanda 的 APP 訂購餐點 250 元以上的話，可享有八八折優惠以及免運費服務。

Jason 炸雞店

28. 這封電子郵件的目的為何？
   (A) 為了邀請顧客參加一場活動
   (B) 為了增加會員人數
   (C) 為了宣傳線上訂購及運送服務
   (D) 為了鼓勵顧客買東西

29. 寫這封電子郵件的人可能是誰？
   (A) 餐廳員工
   (B) 常來光顧的客人
   (C) 俱樂部會員
   (D) 外送員

30. 關於特別優惠，何者為真？
   (A) 顧客僅於 9/1 當天才可享有免運費。
   (B) 第一次光顧的顧客無法享有「買三送一」的優惠。
   (C) 顧客只能在店內購買炸雞餐。
   (D) 第一次來的顧客可以享有所有炸雞餐八折優惠。

答題解說

這個題組是一封電子郵件，內容主要關於某家炸雞店為慶祝開幕滿周年而進行的一些促銷活動。

28. 答案：(D)。題目問的是電子郵件的目的（或主旨），可以先從第一段找線索：To celebrate our first successful year in business, we are going to offer you some special deals on September 1. （為慶祝我們首年營運的成功，我們將於九月一日提供您一些特別優惠。）顯然這是一般餐廳藉由周年慶推出一些優惠吸引顧客的廣告郵件，目的當然是鼓勵顧客前來消費，故正確答案為 (D) To encourage customers to buy something。

29. 答案：(A)。從 "From: Jason Fried Chicken@surmail.com" 以及 Jason Fried Chicken Shop 可得知，這是以該餐廳或店家名義寄出的優惠措施內容，因此絕對不會是「常來光顧的客人」、「俱樂部會員」或「外送員」所寫的，只有 (A) 餐廳員工是最有可能的答案。

30. 答案：(B)。(A)、(C) 的部分可以從最後的 PS. 內容中 "... and free delivery... at any time." 得知，皆為錯誤的敘述；(B) 的部分可以從第二段一開始到中間部分的 "To give our regular customers a big surprise... buy three fried drumsticks or three chicken wings, you can get another one free." 得知，這是給「常客」（regular customers）的優惠，而不是給第一次來的顧客，所以答案就是 (B)。(C) 的部分可以從 "when you order through UberEats or Foodpanda app at any time." 的內容得知，可以透過 app 訂購餐點。至於選項 (D)，第三段提到「第一次來的顧客」可獲得所有炸雞餐九折的優惠，所以也是錯誤的。

第 1 回
第 2 回
第 3 回
第 4 回
第 5 回
第 6 回
第 7 回
第 8 回
第 9 回
第 10 回

破題關鍵

28. 信件最上方，在收件人與寄件人下面都會有個「主旨」欄位，這是找尋信件主旨的第一線索。從這封郵件的 "Subject: Celebration and Special Offer" 即可知，「鼓勵消費」是它的主要目的。

29. 題目要問的是寫這封電子郵件的人是誰，基本上，從標題的「寄件者」以及信件末的署名可以得知，但通常答案選項不會與篇章中的文字一模一樣，因此仍必須參考整體信件內容。

30. 「何者為真」或「何者為非」的題型，都屬於內容細節型的題目。通常都是擺在最後一題再作答。在了解每一個選項的內容之後，對照信件中提及的相關內容，然後用刪除法自然能夠得到正確答案。

字詞解釋

celebration [ˌsɛləˋbreʃən] n. 慶祝活動　　**offer** [ˋɔfɚ] n. 提供的事物，折扣優惠 v. 提供　　**customer** [ˋkʌstəmɚ] n. 顧客　　**successful** [səkˋsɛsfəl] adj. 成功的　　**deal** [dil] n. 交易（方式或條件），待遇　　**regular** [ˋrɛgjələ] adj. 固定的，正常的　　***numbered** [ˋnʌmbɚd] adj. 有編號的　　**fried** [fraɪd] adj. 油炸的　　**vegetable** [ˋvɛdʒətəbl] n. 蔬菜，青菜　　**corn soup** 玉米濃湯　　***drumstick** [ˋdrʌmˌstɪk] n.（煮熟的）雞棒腿　　**chicken wing** n. 雞翅　　**membership** [ˋmɛmbɚˌʃɪp] n. 會員身分（或地位、資格）　　***discount** [ˋdɪskaʊnt] n. 折扣　　**order** [ˋɔrdɚ] n. 訂貨，訂單　　***delivery** [dɪˋlɪvərɪ] n. 投遞，交付　　**invite** [ɪnˋvaɪt] v. 邀請　　**increase** [ɪnˋkris] v. 增加　　**advertise** [ˋædvɚˌtaɪz] v. 廣告，宣傳　　**encourage** [ɪnˋkɝɪdʒ] v. 鼓勵，慫恿　　**employee** [ˌɛmplɔɪˋi] n. 員工　　**buy-three-get-one** 買三送一

相關文法或用法補充

❶ offer 在英檢初級程度範圍內，僅學習其動詞用法，意思是「提供」。它和 give 一樣，是個「授予動詞」，後面接兩個受詞。例如信件中這句：We are going to offer you some special deals on September 1.（我們將於九月一日提供您一些特別優惠。）另外，offer 當名詞也很常用，建議初級程度者可為未來「更上一層樓」預先學習喔！一般來說，原則上它就是「提供」的意思，但通常我們在翻譯時，看不到「提供」的字眼。例如：Thank you for your kind offer of help.（感謝你想給予幫助的好意。）、The house is on offer.（房屋待售中。）又例如本篇信件中的 special offer 就是指餐廳「特別提供的優惠」。

❷ 在英文裡，「of + 抽象名詞」等於「形容詞」，請記住這樣的概念。例如本篇信件中的 "...free fried drumstick or fried wing has to be of the same price of the one bought or lower." 這裡 "of the same price" 解釋為「相同價格的」。又例如：Can I be of any help?（我可以幫得上忙嗎？）= Can I be helpful?

學習筆記欄

4

GEPT 全民英檢

初級初試
中譯＋解析

第一部分 看圖辨義

1. **For question number 1, please look at Picture A.**

   Question number 1: Where would you most likely see this sign?（你最有可能在哪裡看見這個標誌？）
   (A) In a park（在公園）
   (B) In a theater（在電影院）
   (C) In a night market（在夜市）

   答題解說

   答案：(B)。最上方的文字當中有 cinema（電影院），如果知道它的意思就可以直接答題。否則至少應該知道中間 SHOWING 吧！show 原本是「演出、放映」的意思，NOW SHOWING 就是「現在上映」的意思。

   字詞解釋

   cinema [ˋsɪnəmə] n.（英式）電影院　　**theater** [ˋθɪətɚ] n. 劇場；電影院　　**night market** 夜市

   相關文法或用法補充

   有時候在電影院外面看到標示寫 theater，但有時候又是 cinema，同樣都指電影院，用法上有沒有不一樣呢？基本上來說 theater 是美式英語的用法，而英式英語通常用 cinema 指電影院，有時候英式英語也會用 theatre 指劇院，但是要注意結尾從 -er 改成了 -re 喔！

2. **For question number 2 and 3, please look at Picture B.**

   Question number 2: What pet doesn't the girl have?
   （這女孩沒有養什麼寵物？）
   (A) Rabbit（兔子）　　(B) Dog（狗）　　(C) Bird（鳥）

   答題解說

   答案：(A)。本題問的是「女孩沒有養什麼寵物？」只要聽出「否定」的助動詞 doesn't，再看看圖中的三種動物（鳥、貓、狗），就知道裡面沒有兔子，所以正確答案是(A)。

要是一時分心沒聽到 doesn't，不確定題目是要問「有」還是「沒有」，從三個選項中也可以知道只有「(A) 兔子」是沒有出現在圖中的動物。

字詞解釋

pet [pɛt] n. 寵物　　**rabbit** [`ræbɪt] n. 兔子

相關文法或用法補充

回答「否定問句」時，yes 是「不」的意思，no 是「是」的意思，因為 yes 或 no 要與後面句子的肯定或否定一致，例如：

Q: Don't you want to go with us?（你不想跟我們一起去嗎？）
A: Yes, I do.（不，我要。）
A: No, I don't.（是的，我不要。）

3. **Question number 3: Please look at Picture B again.**

   What are her pets doing?（她的寵物們在做什麼？）
   (A) They are eating something.（牠們正在吃東西。）
   (B) They are taking a rest.（牠們正在休息。）
   (C) They are having a fight（牠們正在打架）

答題解說

答案：(B)。本題問題目圖片中那些小動物們在幹什麼。我們將問題和圖片聯繫起來，圖中貓和狗正趴在地上睡覺，而籠中的鳥耷拉著腦袋，很容易猜出它也正在睡覺，所以本題正確答案是 (B)。

破題關鍵

"take a rest"是「休息」的意思，相當於 rest 的不及物動詞用法。而 fight 也可以當名詞，表示「打架；爭吵」，常見於"have/get a fight"的用法中。

字詞解釋

rest [rɛst] n. 休息，休養　v. 休息　　**fight** [faɪt] n. 打架，爭吵　v. 爭鬥

相關文法或用法補充

rest 當名詞還有個很常見的意思：「剩下的部分／東西」，通常與 the 連用。例如：You can take away the rest of the apples.（你可以帶走剩下的蘋果。）

4. **For question number 4 and 5, please look at Picture C.**

    Question number 4: What is Jenny going to do on July 5th?（珍妮七月五日要做什麼？）
    (A) Go jogging（跑步）
    (B) Go to see a friend（去見一個朋友）
    (C) Buy some fruits and vegetables（買些蔬果）

    答題解說

    答案：(C)。圖中顯示一本筆記本，以及七月五日這一欄的行程。(A) Go jogging. 以及 (B) Go to see a friend. 都不在顯示的行程內容中，而選項 (C) 正符合 10:00 a.m. 的「go to the supermarket」。

    破題關鍵

    通常這種「文字對照」的考題，不會完全與選項的文字一模一樣。本題只要聽出 "Buy some fruits and vegetables."，就能與圖片中的 supermarket 連結在一起了。

    字詞解釋

    supermarket [`supɚˌmɑrkɪt] n. 超市　**grandma** [`grændmɑ] n. 奶奶，外婆　**jog** [dʒɑg] n. 慢跑　**vegetable** [`vɛdʒətəbl] n. 蔬菜

    相關文法或用法補充

    「Go+Ving」很常見，它表示「從事某活動」。例如：go shopping（去購物）、go hiking（去健行）、go mountain climbing（去爬山）、go bowling（去打保齡球）、go camping（去露營）、go cycling（去騎單車）、go dancing（去跳舞）、go picnicking（去野餐）、go skating（去溜冰）、go sightseeing（去觀光）、go surfing（去衝浪）、go fishing（去釣魚）、go skiing（去滑雪）、go swimming（去游泳）、go traveling（去旅行）……等。

5. **Question number 5: Please look at Picture C again.**

    What information is given in this picture?
    （圖片中提供了什麼資訊？）
    (A) She'll go swimming after buying something.
    　　（她將於購物後去游泳。）
    (B) Her grandma is not available in the morning.
    　　（她祖母早上沒空。）
    (C) This is a calendar book.（這是一本行事曆。）

答題解說

答案：(C)。這是根據圖片內容判斷「何者為真」的題型，所以必須仔細聽清楚每一個選項的內容。根據圖片文字顯示，早上 8:30 去游泳，10:00 去超市購物，所以 (A) 是錯的；另外，行程表中僅顯示上午 11:15 去拜訪祖母，並沒有說祖母上午沒空，所以 (B) 也是錯誤的；圖片是一本行事曆，故 (C) 是正確答案。

破題關鍵

calendar 的意思是「日曆；行事曆」，從圖中 "July 5" 以及 Sat. 的字樣，即可知道這是一本行事曆。

相關文法或用法補充

英文裡，很多形容詞的意思都會根據其修飾的對象是「人」或「物」，而有不同的解釋。available 如果適用在「人」身上，是「有空的」意思，如果是用在「東西」上，就是「可取得的；可用的」意思。

第二部分 問答

6. **This drink is good. Don't you think so?**（這飲料不錯。你不覺得嗎？）

   (A) I got it.（我懂了。）
   (B) Don't drink and drive.（別喝酒開車。）
   (C) It sure tastes good.（確實嚐起來不錯。）

   答題解說

   答案：(C)。說話者覺得飲料不錯，然後詢問對方是否認同。所以回答應針對「詢問意見」來回應。(A) I got it. 有「我拿到了」或是「我了解了」的意思，而 (B) 是警告對方時的用語，都不是針對「詢問意見」來回答。只有 (C) 是正確的回應。

   破題關鍵

   雖然題目的關鍵句 Don't you think so? 是個否定 Yes/No 疑問句，但並沒有直接以 Yes 或 No 來回答的選項，因此應直接判斷這是在詢問對方對於特定食物的意見或感受。

   字詞解釋

   drink [drɪŋk] n. 飲料　　**taste** [test] v. 嚐起來

連綴動詞（look 看起來、sound 聽起來、taste 嚐起來、smell 聞起來、 feel 感覺起來）後面要接形容詞，也接「like + 名詞」。例如：

1. You look tired.（你看起來很累）
2. The story sounds like fun.（這故事聽起來很有趣。）

7. **How many cats does Helen have?**（海倫有多少隻貓？）

(A) There are two cats running and playing.（有兩隻貓在奔跑玩耍。）
(B) Her cats are beautiful and smart.（她的貓漂亮又聰明。）
(C) She doesn't have any.（她沒有貓。）

答題解說

答案：(C)。以 how many 開頭的問句通常是對數字提問，回答的時候要回答具體數字，如果沒有就回答 none/not... any，這裡回答的是 "not... any"，所以答案是 (C)。

破題關鍵

只要聽懂這是 How many... 的問句，再與三個選項中 (C) 的 any 作連結，因為 any 可以當「代名詞」，也可以用來表示數量。

字詞解釋

beautiful [`bjutəfəl] **adj.** 漂亮的　　**smart** [smɑrt] **adj.** 靈巧的；聰明的

相關文法或用法補充

how 除了用來問「方法」，另一個常用到的是詢問「程度」，如「遠近、量的多寡、速度」等等，可以運用以下句型：

1. How far / How much / How many / How fast / How long + 助動詞 + 主詞 + 原形動詞？
2. How far / How much / How many / How fast / How long + be 動詞 + 主詞 + 過去分詞／現在分詞？

8. **Hi, I'm Jack.**（嗨，我是傑克。）

(A) Same here.（我也是。）
(B) Hi, I'm Sean. Nice to meet you.（嗨，我是夏恩。幸會。）
(C) Oh, I'm so sorry.（噢，我很抱歉。）

第 1 回
第 2 回
第 3 回
第 4 回
第 5 回
第 6 回
第 7 回
第 8 回
第 9 回
第 10 回

答題解說

答案：(B)。這題的情境是：遇到對方跟你打招呼時，你要如何回應。只有 (B) 是正確的回答。(A) 的回答是要告訴對方，我的想法跟你一樣。而 (C) 是用來表達歉意。

破題關鍵

Hi, I'm... 是很簡單易懂的打招呼用語，可以用同樣的 Hi, I'm... 來作回應即可。

字詞解釋

Same here. 我也是。／我同意。

相關文法或用法補充

只會用 Nice to meet you. 嗎？可以試試用其他說法：

I am happy to meet you.（我很高興認識你。）
It's my pleasure to meet you.（很高興遇見你。）
I'm glad / delighted to make your acquaintance.（很高興認識你。）
*make one's acquaintance 是指「認識某人」。
Hi / Hello, there！（嗨，你好！）
How's everything going?（最近好嗎？）

9. **What a nice shirt!**（這襯衫真棒！）

(A) Thanks.（謝謝。）
(B) That's too bad.（那太糟糕了。）
(C) How much is it?（這要多少錢？）

答題解說

答案：(A)。題目句是稱讚對方的穿著，因此最直接、簡單的回答就是表達感謝的話語，所以 (A) 為正確答案。(B) 與 (C) 是完全雞同鴨講的回答。

破題關鍵

「What a + 名詞」是感嘆用語，通常用來對於某事物的「美」或「好」表示讚美。

相關文法或用法補充

Wh- 開頭的句子一定都是問句嗎？那可不一定。它也可能是感嘆句，以驚嘆號（！）結尾。中文常常會用「這隻小狗真可愛！」、「天氣真好！」、「真好吃！」來特別強調某種情緒，而用英文來表達的話，主要有兩種方式：

1. What a/an + 形容詞 + 單數名詞！例如：

   What an inspiring talk! 真是激勵人心的演講啊！

   What a lovely day! 今天真美好啊！

2. How + 形容詞 +（主詞 + 動詞）！

   How 的後面接形容詞或副詞，而 What 接名詞。

   How lovely（the baby is)!（這寶寶真可愛！）

   How smart!（真是聰明啊！）

10. **May I have your name, please?**（可以請問您的名字嗎？）

(A) Yes, this way please.（是的，請往這邊來。）
(B) Brian Chang is my father.（布萊恩・張是我父親。）
(C) Brian Chang.（布萊恩・張）

答題解說

答案：(C)。題目這句是要問對方的名字，相當於 What's your name?，所以回答就直接講自己的名字即可，故正確答案是 (C)。選項 (A) 是指引對方行走的方向，通常用於餐廳服務生指引客人入座時用。而 (B) 的回答完全是雞同鴨講了。

破題關鍵

"May I have your name?" 是 What's your name? 的委婉問法，因為在有些正式場合直接問對方的名字是唐突且不禮貌的，此時就可以用 May I... 這句，會顯得比較客氣與尊重。

相關文法或用法補充

May I...? 通常是在當下提出請求、詢問許可的問句，但它跟 Can I...? 有何差別呢？比方說，Can I help you？或 May I help you?，其實兩者意思都一樣，而差別在於，May I... 的語意較婉轉、客氣及有禮貌，所以後者較為常見，也就是說 May 是比較客氣有禮貌的用法。而 Can 是比較直接的表達！

11. **Have you seen John?**（你有看到約翰嗎？）

(A) Yes, he was here a moment ago.（有，他不久之前還在這。）
(B) No, I wasn't very busy.（不，我當時不是很忙。）
(C) No, thanks.（不用，謝謝。）

答題解說

答案：(A)。本題是一般疑問句，原則上以 Yes/No 來回答，三個選項都符合這個要求，但選項 (B) 與 (C) 都沒有針對問題回答。所以本題正確答案是 (A)。

破題關鍵

本題可採用刪除法來作答。選項 (B) 回應過去某時是否忙碌，而 (C) 則可能是對方要幫助你時表示不需要幫忙，皆非針對題目問題的回答。

字詞解釋

moment [`momənt] **n.** 片刻

相關文法或用法補充

簡單過去式與現在完成式的比較：

一般過去式表示過去發生的事情，而現在完成式也多表示發生在過去的事情，但兩者的重點不同。一般過去式只是單純敘述過去發生的事情，而現在完成式則強調過去發生的事持續到現在，或是對於現在造成的影響，主要把重點放在說明現在的情況。例如：

1. I have read the book. → 強調對書的內容是瞭解的

   I read the book when I was in middle school. → 強調過去讀過這本書

2. Father has turned off the television. → 說明電視機從關上到現在都沒打開

   Father turned off the television about ten minutes ago. → 說明關閉電視機的時間

12. **How long does it take you to go to work in the morning?**（你早上上班要花多久時間？）

(A) It's been ten years.（已經十年了。）
(B) Usually about 45 minutes.（通常大約四十五分鐘。）
(C) It won't be long.（不會很久。）

答題解說

答案：(B)。題目問「上班花多久時間」，只有 (B) 是符合語意與邏輯的答案。另外，題目句的時態是現在簡單式，而 (A) 的回答卻用現在完成式，因此不可能是正確答案。

破題關鍵

本題可以用刪除法來解。當聽到題目是以 How long... 開頭時，應直接反應：這是問「多久時間」的問句，所以答案內容應是「時間長度」（多久時間）。(C) 是可直接排除的選項；而 (A) 的回答則不合邏輯（去上班不可能花十年的時間）。

字詞解釋

take [tek] **v.** 花費　　**how long** 多久　　**usually** [`juʒʊəlɪ] **adv.** 通常

take 雖然是個基本動詞，但它在不同場合可以有很多意思。其中之一是「花費（時間）」的用法。在「It takes + 人 + 時間長度 + to-V」的句型中，It 是「虛主詞」，代替後面的「真主詞」，也就是不定詞（to-v）片語。例如：It takes me an hour to go through the article.（我花了一個小時仔細看完這篇文章。）

13. **Let's go now. Or it'll be too late.**（我們現在就走。否則會太晚。）

(A) Here you go.（這給你。）

(B) Thanks a lot.（非常感謝。）

(C) Good idea.（好主意。）

答題解說

答案：(C)。本題情境是，時間不早了，應該立即啟程或離開。因此應針對「現在就離開」這件事來回應。(A) 是針對對方要你出示文件或票券之類的東西所做的回應，而 (B) 是表達感謝之意，這兩句皆非針對此題目問句回答。而 (C) 是對於對方所說的話表示認可，故為正確答案。

破題關鍵

Let's... 開頭的祈使句通常有「提出建議」之意，Good idea. 可以表達對方的建議是可以接受的。

相關文法或用法補充

有時我們會聽到 Here you go. 或 There you go.，這是口語說法，和 Here you are. 或 There you are. 沒有分別，只是語氣較為不正式。
請留意以 here 或 there 開頭的句子，通常以倒裝句呈現，即動詞置於主詞之前。不過，假如主詞是代名詞，則句子仍用一般的「主詞在前，動詞在後」的結構，例如：Here are Tom and Mary.（= Here they are. 他們在這裡。）

14. **How well do you know Bill?**（你和比爾有多熟呢？）

(A) He is a writer.（他是個作家。）

(B) He lives in New York.（他住在紐約。）

(C) Not very well.（不是很熟。）

答題解說

答案：(C)。how well 的意思是「……程度有多～？」，只有 (C) 這個選項是直接針對問題來回答。無論回答某人的身分或住在哪裡（(A)「他是個作家。」或 (B)「他住在紐約。」）顯然都沒有針對問題來回答。

第 1 回
第 2 回
第 3 回
第 4 回
第 5 回
第 6 回
第 7 回
第 8 回
第 9 回
第 10 回

破題關鍵

聽到 How well...? 時，只要了解這是在問某事的發展或進展的「程度」，通常可以使用 Very well.（非常好）/ Just so so.（馬馬虎虎）/ Not so well.（不太好）等表達來回應。

字詞解釋

know [no] v. 認識　**writer** [ˈraɪtɚ] n. 作家

相關文法或用法補充

well 可以作程度副詞，例如：John and I have been friends for years, and we know each other very well.（我和約翰是多年朋友，我們彼此很熟。）而 well 在少部分情況下，也可以當形容詞，通常用來形容身體狀況，例如：My grandmother is 70 years old, and she is well.（我奶奶七十歲，她身體很好。）

15. You can't come home too late this evening.（你今晚不能太晚回家。）

(A) Not at all.（一點也不。）
(B) Why not?（為什麼不能？）
(C) Good luck.（祝你好運。）

答題解說

答案：(B)。題目句是要求對方晚上不能太晚回家，也許是父母對孩子說的話。所以當對方要求你「不能」做一件事，而你想詢問原因，就可以用選項 (B) 的 Why not? 來反問。(A) 是當別人向你表示謝意時的回應，而 (C) 是對方臨走之前可以向對方說的話，都不是針對本問題該有的回應。

破題關鍵

You can't... 很明顯是「對方要求你不能怎樣」的情境，也可以改為使用祈使句的 "Don't come home too late..."。因此，在理解這個關鍵點自然能夠選到 Why not? 這個答案。

字詞解釋

evening [ˈivənɪŋ] n. 傍晚，晚上

相關文法或用法補充

一般來說，祈使句會省略主詞，但有時為了指明是向誰說，也可以不省略主詞，但動詞皆使用原形動詞。例如：

1. Somebody go and get some chalk.（誰去拿些粉筆來。）
2. You, clean the blackboard, and John, clean the window.（你，擦黑板，約翰，擦窗戶。）

3. Everybody, go outside the classroom. （大家，都到教室外面去。）
4. Take a seat, Mr. Johnson. （請坐，詹森先生。）
5. You don't take the book out of the library. （你不能把書帶出圖書館。）
6. You mind your own business. （你管好你自己就好了。）

第三部分 簡短對話

16. W: Oh! There's blood dropping to the ground!

M: I just cut vegetables and hurt one of my fingers.

W: Why are you always so careless?

Question: What happened to the man?

(A) He hurt his foot.

(B) He hurt his hand.

(C) He couldn't find the vegetables to cook dinner.

英文翻譯

女：噢，有血滴到地上！

男：我剛剛切菜時切到我一根手指了。

女：你怎麼總是這麼不小心？

問題：男子發生什麼事？

(A) 他傷到腳。

(B) 他傷到手。

(C) 他找不到蔬菜來煮晚餐。

答題解說

答案：(B)。題目問男子發生什麼事，應從男子的發言中去找尋線索。首先，女子發現地上有血，男子回答她，剛才切菜時切到手指，因此 (B) 的 "He hurt his hand." 為正確答案。

破題關鍵

本題關鍵字是 fingers（手指），手指是手的一部分，傷了手指等同於傷了手。

字詞解釋

blood [blʌd] n. 血　**drop** [drɑp] v. 滴下，落下　**ground** [graʊnd] n. 地面
vegetable [`vɛdʒətəbl] n. 蔬菜　**hurt** [hɝt] v. 使受傷　**finger** [`fɪŋɡɚ] n. 手指
careless [`kɛrlɪs] adj. 不小心的，粗心的

第 1 回

第 2 回

第 3 回

第 4 回

第 5 回

第 6 回

第 7 回

第 8 回

第 9 回

第 10 回

相關文法或用法補充

hurt 可以當及物動詞、不及物動詞以及名詞。另外還要注意，hurt 的過去式和過去分詞都是 hurt：

1. 當及物動詞時，是指使（自己或某人、身體的某個部位、動物等）受傷或受肉體痛苦、使（某人）精神痛苦或傷（某人）心。例如：

   She hurt her back when she fell off the bike.（她從自行車上摔下來時背部受傷了。）

   What he said hurt her ego deeply.（他的話深深地傷了她的自尊心。）

2. 當不及物動詞時，意思是「（身體部位）疼痛」。例如：

   It hurts when I move my leg.（我的腿一動就疼。）

3. 當名詞時，意思是精神上的痛苦或創傷，為不可數名詞，但若指肉體上的傷害或痛苦，是可數名詞：

   His parents' divorce left him with a feeling of deep hurt.（父母離異給他的心靈留下嚴重的創傷。）

   The sharp knife gave him a serious hurt in his thumb.（鋒利的小刀在他的拇指上留下了一道嚴重的傷口。）

17. **W: Tea or coffee, sir?**

    M: Coffee, please.

    W: So how do you take your coffee?

    M: Milk and sugar, please.

    Question: Where could you probably hear this dialogue?

    (A) In a movie theater　(B) On an airplane　(C) On a bus

英文翻譯

女：先生，要茶還是咖啡？

男：咖啡，謝謝。

女：那麼您的咖啡要加什麼嗎？

男：牛奶及糖，謝謝。

題目：你可能會在哪裡聽到這則對話？

(A) 在電影院裡　(B) 在飛機上　(C) 在巴士上

答題解說

答案：(B)。對話中女子問男子要茶或是咖啡，以及咖啡要加什麼，顯然是服務員與客人之間的對話。因此，三個選項中只有「(B) 在飛機上」是最有可能的情境（空服員與乘客之間的對話）。

如果在聽到錄音播放之前有先瞄過三個選項,大概可以知道本題是要考你「對話場合」,然後再聽到前兩句(Tea or coffee, sir? /Coffee, please.),應該就可以從容地寫下答案了,即使你不知道 "How do you take your coffee?" 的意思也沒有關係。

字詞解釋

sugar [ˈʃjugə] n. 糖　　**movie theater** n. 電影院

相關文法或用法補充

"How do you take your coffee?" 不是問你要怎樣「拿」你的咖啡,而是問你:「要不要加糖或奶精?」。take 在這裡的不是「拿;帶」的意思。英文裡加糖、加奶精,這裡的「加」,英文就是用 take 這個動詞。例如:I don't take sugar in coffee.(我喝咖啡不加糖。)另外, "How do you take your coffee?" 有時候會簡單說成 "How do you take it?"。

18. M: Your shoes look cool. Are they new?

W: Yes, I just bought them yesterday at the new shop over there.

M: Were they expensive? How much?

W: NT $5,000. So cheap, right?

Question: What are the speakers talking about?

(A) A new shoe shop

(B) How the woman got a good deal

(C) The woman's new shoes

英文翻譯

男:你的鞋子看起來很酷。是新的嗎?

女:是的,我昨天才在那邊那家新的店買的。

男:貴嗎?多少錢?

女:五千塊。多便宜啊,是吧?

題目:說話者們正在談論什麼?

(A) 一間新開的鞋店

(B) 女子如何買到划算的東西

(C) 女子的新鞋

答題解說

答案:(C)。題目問的是「對話內容」的主旨。基本上,這樣的題目必須了解對

整篇對話在講什麼。從男子兩次的發言可知，都是在問女子穿的鞋子，所以正確答案是 (C)。

第 1 回
第 2 回
第 3 回
第 4 回
第 5 回
第 6 回
第 7 回
第 8 回
第 9 回
第 10 回

破題關鍵

基本上本篇對話的第一句（Your shoes look cool.）就已經點出「主旨」，也就是他們的對話內容。

字詞解釋

expensive [ɪk`spɛnsɪv] **adj.** 高價的，昂貴的　　**cheap** [tʃip] **adj.** 便宜的，廉價的
good deal 划算的交易（或買賣之物品）

相關文法或用法補充

over there（或是 over here）為「目視距離內」的指示之意，通常也可在其前加上強調副詞 right，形成 right over there/here（就在那裡／這裡）。此外，我們也可以將 over 省略，形成 right there/here，但這時候就完全沒有距離的含意，而是表達「就是那裡／這裡」的意思。

19. M: I've looked in all the shops nearby, but none of them had a closet I wanted.

   W: Maybe you can go online for it.

   M: Thanks. I'll do that this afternoon.

   W: Good luck.

   Question: What is the man trying to do?

   (A) Buy some furniture

   (B) Surf the Internet

   (C) Sell a closet

英文翻譯

男：我已經找過附近所有店，但沒有一家有我要的櫥櫃。
女：也許你可以上網找找。
男：謝謝。我今天下午會做這件事。
女：祝好運。
題目：男子試圖要做什麼？
(A) 購買某種家具
(B) 上網
(C) 賣廚櫃

答案：(A)。男子一開始表示他找過所有「商店」（shop），但找不到他要的櫥櫃。顯然他是打算要買儲櫃，所以正確答案是 (A)。注意題目是問「男子打算要做什麼」，雖然他確實會「上網」，但上網並非他的最終目的，所以答案不是 (B)。

破題關鍵

本題的關鍵有二：1. 男子一開始發言中的 shop；2. 題目要問的是「男子試著要做什麼」。掌握這兩點之後就能選出正確的答案。

字詞解釋

closet [ˋklɑzɪt] n. 櫥櫃　　**surf** [sɝf] v. 上網瀏覽　　**furniture** [ˋfɝnɪtʃɚ] n. 家具

相關文法或用法補充

some 當形容詞表示「一些的」，後面接可數名詞。但 some 後面也可以接不可數名詞或單數名詞，表示「某種、某個」，因此這裡的 some furniture 就是指 closet。以下是一些常見的不可數名詞：

furniture 家具、luggage 行李、food 食物、clothing 服裝、garbage 垃圾、equipment 設備、money 金錢、weather 天氣、advice 忠告、energy 能源、happiness 幸福、information 資訊、knowledge 知識、truth 真相、work 工作、rice 飯、bread 麵包、coffee 咖啡、mathematics 數學、news 新聞、tennis 網球…。

20. M: Excuse me. I'm meeting Mr. Wang at 10.

W: Are you Mr. Hsu?

M: Yes, I am.

W: OK. Please take a seat here and wait a moment. He'll be with you in 10 minutes.

M: Thank you.

Question: What will the woman do next?

(A) Have some tea　　(B) Speak to Mr. Wang　　(C) Have a meeting with Mr. Hsu

英文翻譯

男：抱歉。我十點和王先生有約見面。

女：您是許先生嗎？

男：是的，我是。

女：請在這裡坐一下，並請稍候。他十分鐘之後會過來找您。

男：謝謝妳。

題目：女子接下來會做什麼？
(A) 喝點茶　(B) 告知王先生　(C) 與許先生開會

答題解說

答案：(B)。題目問的是「女子接下來會做的事」，所以應注意聽女子發言的部分。首先，男子表示在十點鐘與王先生有約，接著女子確認其身分（Are you Mr. Hsu?），接著請他稍候片刻，並表示王先生十分鐘之後會過來。顯然她接下來會去通知王先生，他約的人已經來了。所以正確答案應為 (B)。

破題關鍵

從女子第二句（Please take a seat here and wait a moment. He'll be with you in 10 minutes.）就可以了解，她接下來會去通知 Mr. Wang。

字詞解釋

take a seat 就座　**moment** [`momənt] **n.** 片刻　**meeting** [`mitɪŋ] **n.** 會議

相關文法或用法補充

Excuse me. 在日常對話中出現的頻率極高，它雖然有「抱歉、對不起」的意思，但並非你真的做錯什麼，而是用於「請求、拜託或打斷別人說話」時。例如：

1. 問路或提問時：Excuse me, does this bus go to the zoo?（請問一下／不好意思，這公車到動物園嗎？）
2. 要打斷別人說話時：Excuse me, but what you said was wrong.（不好意思，您說錯了。）
3. 從別人面前經過時：Excuse me. Could I get past?（不好意思。借過一下。）
4. 禮貌地詢問某事或請求允許：Excuse me, Miss Gao. What's this in English?（高老師，請問一下。這個用英文要怎麼說？）

21. M: May I take your order, please?

 W: Sorry, but my boyfriend is still on the way. I need to wait for him to come.

 M: No problem. I'll be back later.

 W: Thanks for your patience.

Question: What does the man do?

(A) He is a waiter.

(B) He is a taxi driver.

(C) He is a policeman.

第 1 回
第 2 回
第 3 回
第 4 回
第 5 回
第 6 回
第 7 回
第 8 回
第 9 回
第 10 回

男：請問可以點餐了嗎？

女：抱歉，我男友還在路上。我得等他過來。

男：沒問題。我稍後回來。

女：感謝您的耐心。

題目：男子是的職業是什麼？

(A) 他是一位服務生。

(B) 他是一位計程車司機。

(C) 他是一位警察。

答題解說

答案：(A)。本題問的是男子的職業，可以直接從他的發言內容去找尋線索。如果知道第一句（May I take your order, please?）的意思，答案應該就很明顯了。到餐廳要開始點餐時，通常服務生（waiter/waitress）會問：May I take your order?。

破題關鍵

take one's order 就是「替某人點餐」的意思，有時服務生會說 "What would you like to order?"

字詞解釋

waiter [ˋwetɚ] n. 男服務生　**policeman** [pəˋlismən] n. 員警　**order** [ˋɔrdɚ] 訂購；訂單

相關文法或用法補充

may 當助動詞可以表示：

❶ 允許：

① You may smoke in that room.（你可以在那個房間吸菸。）

② May I have a look at your note?（我可以看看你的筆記嗎？）

③ May I use your computer? Yes, of course you may.（我可以用你的電腦嗎？當然可以。）

④ 而 may not 則用來表示「拒絕」或「禁止」：People may not park here.（這裡不允許停車。）

❷ 祝願：

① May you have a nice weekend.（祝你週末愉快。）

② May you succeed.（祝你成功。）

22. M: How can I help you?

W: I would like a hamburger and a cup of milk.

M: For here or to go?

W: To go, please.

Question: What is the woman doing?

(A) Eating something

(B) Making a hamburger

(C) Ordering a meal

英文翻譯

男：有什麼能為您效勞的？

女：我想要一個漢堡及一杯牛奶。

男：內用還是外帶？

女：外帶，謝謝。

題目：女子正在做什麼？

(A) 吃東西

(B) 做漢堡

(C) 點餐

答題解說

答案：(C)。本題問的是女子正在做什麼，可以從女子的發言中找到線索。首先，男子問她「有什麼能為您效勞的？」女子回答說「我想要一份漢堡及一杯牛奶。」顯然男子是店員，女子是顧客，且正在點餐。所以 (C) 是正確答案。

破題關鍵

其實從男子說的第一句話 "How can I help you?" 就可以知道，男子是個店員，因為這句話多半是店員服務顧客時說的話。

字詞解釋

hamburger [ˋhæmbɝɡɚ] n. 漢堡　　**milk** [mɪlk] n. 牛奶　　**to go** 外帶　　**order** [ˋɔrdɚ] v. 點（菜或飲料）

相關文法或用法補充

「For here or to go?」是在國外速食店點餐時最常聽到店員問的一句話，而在歐洲國家中則比較常聽到「eat in or take away?」意思都是「內用還是外帶？」，在英文裡還有其他片語也可以表示：

1. 內用：for here、eat in、dine in

2. 外帶：to go、take out、take away

23. W: Hi, may I help you?

　　M: Yes, I'd like to register.

　　W: Have you been here before?

　　M: No, this is my first visit.

　　W: Please fill out this form.

Question: Who could be the woman?

(A) A doctor　(B) A nurse　(C) A waitress

女：嗨，有什麼能為您服務呢？

男：是的，我要掛號。

女：您之前來過嗎？

男：沒有，這是第一次來。

女：請填寫這張表格。

問題：女子可能是誰？

(A) 醫生　(B) 護士　(C) 女服務生

答題解說

答案：(B)。本題問的是「女子的身分」，也就是她的「工作／職業」，所以應從她的發言中找尋線索。首先，從女子第一句話「may I help you」就可以知道，她是個服務人員，所以 (A) 可直接先剔除。女子第二句話說「Have you been here before?」（您之前來過嗎？），餐廳服務人員不一定會說這句話，接著女子第三句話說「Please fill out this form.」（請填寫這張表格。）綜合她第二、第三句話可推知，女子最有可能是診所的護士。

破題關鍵

本題答題關鍵其實是男子第一次發言中的 register（掛號；登記），如果知道這個字的意思，那就可以知道答案了，否則也可以從女子說的第三句話中找出答題關鍵，也就是請對方寫表格（Please fill out this form.）這句話。

字詞解釋

register [ˋrɛdʒɪstɚ] v. 登記；掛號　**fill out** 填寫　**form** [form] n. 表格　**nurse** [nɝs] n. 護士　**waitress** [ˋwetrɪs] n. 女服務生

相關文法或用法補充

雖然 in 跟 out 是相反意思，但 fill in 跟 fill out 用於表單或申請表時，都同樣是「填寫」的意思！若是硬要分，fill in 比較偏向將小的空格填滿，而 fill out 的範圍比較大，像是整張申請表或是問卷。

24. M: I just heard from the radio that it'll drop to 22 degrees this afternoon.

W: That's good. Not too hot.

M: But it'll get colder later in the evening.

W: So I need to bring a coat, right?

Question: What will the weather be like this afternoon?

(A) Cold (B) Warm (C) Hot

英文翻譯

男：我剛剛聽廣播說今天下午的溫度會降到 22 度。

女：那很好啊。不會太熱。

男：不過晚上晚一點會變得比較冷。

女：所以我得帶件大衣，對嗎？

問題：今天下午的天氣會如何？

(A) 冷 (B) 溫暖 (C) 熱

答題解說

答案：(B)。本題問的是「今天下午的天氣狀況」。首先，男子第一句提到「今天下午的溫度會降到 22 度」，女子回答說「不會太熱。」聽到這裡，應該可以從三個選項「冷、溫暖、熱」選出正確答案了。

破題關鍵

本題只要有先看過三個選項，然後在聽到女子第一次發言時說的 "That's good. Not too hot."，應該很容易可以選出正確的 (B) Warm 這個選項。

字詞解釋

drop [drɑp] v.（價格或溫度等）下降 **degree** [dɪˋgri] n. 度，度數 **coat** [kot] n. 外套，大衣

相關文法或用法補充

詢問「天氣狀況」的說法，最常見的就是 What's the weather like? 以及 How's the weather?，其後可接地方／時間副詞。必須注意的是，用疑問詞 How 為首詢問天氣時，weather 之後不加 like。例如：

What's the weather like in your hometown?（你家鄉的天氣如何？）

= How's the weather in your hometown?

第 1 回
第 2 回
第 3 回
第 4 回
第 5 回
第 6 回
第 7 回
第 8 回
第 9 回
第 10 回

25. W: Hi, John. Are you available to go over today's English exam together after school?

M: Yes, I can, but I have to go home to throw away trash first and the garbage truck arrives at 6:30. Then I'll eat dinner. It'll take about half an hour.

W: That's OK. Let's meet in the library after you finish dinner.

M: OK. See you then.

Question: When will they meet?

(A) Before 6:30 p.m.　(B) Between 6:30 and 7:00 p.m.　(C) After 7:00 p.m.

【英文翻譯】

女：嗨，約翰。你放學後有空一起複習一下今天的英文考試嗎？

男：有，我可以，不過我得先回家丟垃圾，垃圾車 6:30 到。然後我會吃晚餐。大約要半小時的時間。

女：那沒問題。你吃完晚餐後，我們就在圖書館見。

男：好的。到時候見。

問題：他們何時會碰面？

(A) 晚間六點半之前　(B) 晚間六點半至七點之間　(C) 晚間七點之後

【答題解說】

答案：(C)。題目問的「他們何時會碰面」，所以答案應該在男子說「到時候見。（See you then.）」之前。在這之前，女子說「你吃完晚餐後，我們就在圖書館見。」所以我們再往前推，男子表示，他 6:30 倒垃圾，然後吃晚餐要花半小時，所以是 7:00 之後前往圖書館。故正確答案為 (C)。

【破題關鍵】

通常問時間（幾點）的題目，或是問「數字」的題型，答案不會是直接在對話中聽到的幾點幾分，而是必須稍做推論的。本題第一個關鍵是女子說 "Let's meet in the library after you finish dinner."，第二個關鍵是男子說 "... 6:30. Then I'll eat dinner. It'll take about half an hour."。綜合這兩句話，答案應該就很明顯了。

【字詞解釋】

go over 溫習，複習　**after school** 下課，放學　**throw** [θro] v. 扔，丟
garbage truck 垃圾車　**arrive** [əˋraɪv] v. 抵達　**library** [ˋlaɪˏbrɛrɪ] n. 圖書館

【相關文法或用法補充】

go over 這個動詞片語可以當及物或不及物動詞，在這則對話中是當不及物動詞，意思是「複習」、「重溫」、「檢視」。例如：Let's go over the rules again.

（我們再複習一下那些規則。）而 go through 有兩個意思，第一個意思跟 go over 一樣。例如：Let's go through the rules again.。

但 go through 也可以指「經歷」，這些經歷通常是指是不好的經驗。例如：He has gone through so much in the past few years.（他過去幾年經歷過很多事。）

第四部分 短文聽解

For question number 26, please look at the three pictures.

Question number 26: Listen to the following talk. What is Bill's favorite hobby?

Last summer Bill took a trip to Japan, and he joined a surfing group. That was the first time he enjoyed the pleasure of skiing on the waves at a very beautiful beach. Though he fell over a few times at the sea, he still really enjoyed the experience. When he came back to Taiwan, he decided to take a surfing lesson. Now he goes surfing every Saturday or Sunday afternoon.

英文翻譯

請看以下三張圖。並仔細聆聽播放的談話內容。比爾最愛的嗜好為何？
去年夏天比爾前往日本旅行，而且他加入了衝浪團。那是他第一次在一個非常美麗的海灘，享受在波浪上滑行的樂趣。雖然他在海上摔了幾次，他還是很喜歡這樣的體驗。當他回到台灣時，他決定去上衝浪課。現在他每個週六或週日下午都會去衝浪。

答題解說

答案：(C)。注意聽題目問的是比爾最愛的嗜好。第一句就提到「去年夏天比爾前往日本旅行，而且他加入了衝浪團。（Last summer Bill took a trip to Japan, and he joined a surfing group.）」。後來又提到他很喜歡這樣的體驗、上衝浪課以及每週六或週日下午都會去衝浪等，在在顯示他最愛的嗜好是 (C) 圖所指的衝浪。

第 1 回
第 2 回
第 3 回
第 4 回
第 5 回
第 6 回
第 7 回
第 8 回
第 9 回
第 10 回

先看過題目的三張圖,可以發現是三種不同活動,然後仔細聽短文中出現的許多關鍵內容,包括 joined a surfing group、skiing on the waves、beach、sea……等。這些都可以讓你輕鬆選出正確答案。但須注意的是,別聽到 skiing 就選了 (A) 喔!

字詞解釋

take a trip to... 去〜旅行　**surfing** [`sɝfɪŋ] n. 衝浪　**pleasure** [`plɛʒɚ] n. 樂趣
ski [ski] v. 滑雪;滑行

相關文法或用法補充

這裡的 every Saturday or Sunday afternoon 也可以用 on Saturday or Sunday afternoons 來表示,但重點是,every 後面必須接單數名詞。例如:every day、every morning、every Saturday……等,但名詞前如果有大於 1 的「序數」,那麼名詞單複數就必須跟著這個序數來決定。例如「每兩天」(every two days)、「每三天」(every three days)、「每兩個月」(every two months)…等。

For question number 27, please look at the three pictures.

Question number 27: Listen to the following message. Which convenience store should Susan meet David at?

Hello, Susan, this is David. I just rang you but you fail to answer your mobile phone. I guess you were riding the motorcycle on your way home. But did you forget to meet me at the convenience store across from a fancy restaurant? Or did you get the times mixed up? We agreed that we meet at six-thirty. So, when you get this voice message, please call me back as soon as possible. See you later.

英文翻譯

請看以下三張圖。並仔細聆聽以下訊息。蘇珊應該在哪一家便利商店與大衛碰面?哈囉,蘇珊,我是大衛。我剛打電話給妳,但妳沒有接電話。我猜妳正在騎摩托車回家的路上。但是妳是不是忘記我們要在一家高檔餐廳對面的便利商店碰面了?或者妳把時間給搞混了?我們約好 6:30 碰面的。所以,當妳收到這通語音訊息時,請盡快回電給我。待會兒見。

答題解說

答案：(A)。題目問的是「哪一家便利商店」是大衛與蘇珊要碰面的地點。重點只有一句：" ... meet me at the convenience store across from a fancy restaurant"（在一家高檔餐廳對面的便利商店碰面）。對照三張圖的便利商店位置，正確答案是(A)。

破題關鍵

這段訊息的前面大半部分都與答案沒有關係，所以先仔細看過三張圖片是很重要的，因為三張圖的共同點都有「便利商店」（convenience store），只是位置上的差異。因此只要掌握到關鍵字句（the convenience store across from a fancy restaurant）即可輕鬆解題。across from... 表示「在～對面」。

字詞解釋

ring [rɪŋ] **v.** 打話給～ **fail to-V** 未能～（做到…） **on one's way home** 在某人回家路上 **convenience store** 便利商店 **across from...** 在～對面 **fancy** [ˋfænsɪ] **adj.** 高級的，高貴的 **get... mixed up** 把～搞混了

相關文法或用法補充

❶ 在英文裡，「接電話」的「接」這個動作要用動詞 answer 或是動詞片語 pick up，而不是用 accept。另外，get through to somebody 則是「把電話轉接給某人」的意思。例如：

You should answer your mom's calls, or she'll keep calling until you go back home.（你最好接一下你媽的電話，不然她會一直打到你回家為止。）

❷ across from... 是「在～對面」的意思，也可以在前面加 directly 或 right，來表示「正」對面。例如：The bus stop is right across from the gas station.（公車站牌就在加油站正對面。）

For question number 28, please look at the three pictures.

Question number 28: Listen to the following broadcast. Where could you probably hear it?

Good afternoon. This is RT-Mart service counter at the 1st floor. We have a lost young kid here. He said his name is Brian, and he's a 5-year-old boy. He's wearing a red coat and blue shorts. He's waiting here for his mother to come. If you hear this, please come here as soon as possible. Thank you for your attention. RT-Mart Mall wishes you a wonderful shopping day.

中文翻譯

請看以下三張圖。並仔細聆以下廣播內容。你可能可以在什麼地方聽到這樣的廣播？

午安。這裡是 RT-Mart 一樓的服務櫃檯。我們這裡有一位迷路的小孩。他說他叫布萊恩，他是個五歲的小男孩。他穿著一件紅色外套以及藍色短褲。他現在在這裡等他的媽媽來。如果您聽見這則廣播，請盡速前來。感謝您的關注。RT-Mart 商城祝您今日購物愉快。

答題解說

答案：（C）。首先，題目句一定要聽懂，這是個「問地方（At what place ＝ Where）」的題目，然後再看看三張不同場景的圖，有警察局、停車場以及百貨公司，所以應該可以知道要問的是「廣播內容的場景是在哪裡？」接著，仔細聽錄音播放內容，即可了解這是什麼地方的廣播內容。最後一句提到 "RT-Mart Mall wishes you a wonderful shopping day."，這樣應該不難知道這是什麼地方了吧。

破題關鍵

這則廣播內容的關鍵句當然是最後一句，不過如果可以更精準抓到錄音內容其中的 shopping 這個字，答案就出來了。

字詞解釋

counter [ˋkaʊntɚ] n. 櫃檯　**floor** [flor] n.（樓房的）層　**coat** [kot] n. 外套　**shorts** [ʃorts] n. 短褲　**attention** [əˋtɛnʃən] n. 注意　**mall** [mɔl] n. 購物中心　**wonderful** [ˋwʌndɚfəl] adj. 極好的

相關文法或用法補充

lost 是 lose 的過去是式及過去分詞。在本題當中 "a lost young kid"（迷路的小孩）的 lost 是「分詞當形容詞」的用法，意思是「迷路的、丟失的」。當然，分詞包括「現在分詞」與「過去分詞」。其他常見例子還有：breaking news（新聞快訊）、broken bike（壞掉的腳踏車）、sleeping baby（熟睡的嬰兒）、burnt toast（燒焦的土司）、stolen money（被偷的錢）、missing girl（失蹤的女孩）……等。

For question number 29, please look at the three pictures.

Question number 29: Listen to the following short talk. What do people in the club usually do?

Johnson and some of his good friends are members of The Great Whale Club. They go hiking in the mountains every month. They pick up trash along the way and put it in a garbage bin or a large plastic bag. They have kept a good habit of protecting the environment. Besides, they sometimes get together watching some interesting short films about their favorite activity on weekends.

英文翻譯

請看以下三張圖。並仔細聆以下簡短談話。此俱樂部裡的人通常會做什麼？
強森以及他的幾位好友都是大鯨魚俱樂部的會員。他們每個月都會去登山健行。他們會沿途撿起垃圾，然後把垃圾放進垃圾桶或是大塑膠袋中。他們一直保持著維護環境的好習慣。此外，他們有時會聚在一起觀賞一些有趣的、關於他們最愛的週末活動的短片。

答題解說

答案：(A)。題目問的是「此俱樂部裡的人通常會做什麼」，也就是他們從事的活動內容。從第二句 "They go hiking in the mountains every month."（他們每個月都會去登山健行。）即可正確選出 (A) 這個答案了。雖然因為最後一句有提到 "...they sometimes get together watching some interesting short films about their favorite activity on weekends"（他們有時會聚在一起觀賞一些有趣的、關於他們最愛的週末活動的短片）而似乎 (C) 也是正確答案，不過必須注意到電視畫面所顯示的並非「登山健行」的活動。

破題關鍵

掌握關鍵字 hiking 即可，因為 hike 本義是「徒步旅行、遠足、健行」的意思，簡單說就是用兩隻腳在走路，而符合這個概念的只有(A)圖了。

字詞解釋

whale [hwel] n. 鯨　**hike** [haɪk] v. 徒步旅行，健行　**along the way** 沿途

garbage [ˋgɑrbɪdʒ] **n.** 垃圾　**bin** [bɪn] **n.** 垃圾箱　**plastic** [ˋplæstɪk] **adj.** 塑膠的　**protect** [prəˋtɛkt] **v.** 保護，防護　**environment** [ɪnˋvaɪrənmənt] **n.** 環境　**favorite** [ˋfevərɪt] **adj.** 最喜愛的　**activity** [ækˋtɪvətɪ] **n.** 活動

相關文法或用法補充

mountain 意思是「山，高山」，指的是高度較高、佔地較大、坡度較陡的大山、高山或山脈（mountain range），如 The hunters went walking in the mountains.（獵人在山裡行走。）而 hill 是指「山丘，丘陵」，通常指高度較低、佔地較小、坡度較緩的小山、小丘，如 Professor Lee and his students finally climbed to the top of the hill.（李教授和他的學生終於爬上了小山的山頂。）此外，mountain 也是「山」的通稱，所以一般登山或爬山叫作 mountain climbing（= mountaineering），登山客叫作 mountain climber（= mountaineer），而不是 hill climbing 或 hill climber。

For question number 30, please look at the three pictures.

Question number 30: Listen to the following message. What time will they go to the night market?

Hi Dad, I kept calling you but you didn't answer the phone. I just wanna tell you that I won't be back home until 12:00 a.m., because Mary and I will go see a movie that will start at 8:30 p.m. The movie is about one hour and half an hour long. Then we'll go to Shilin Night Market, which is just next to the movie theater, to enjoy some famous and delicious dishes. See you later.

英文翻譯

請看以下三張圖。並仔細聆聽以下訊息。他們將在幾點前往夜市？
嗨，爸爸，我一直打電話給你，但你沒有接電話。我只是要告訴你，我凌晨十二點才會回到家，因為瑪麗和我要去看晚上八點半的電影。這部電影的長度大約一個半小時。然後我們要去士林夜市，它就在電影院隔壁，要去享受一些有名的美味佳餚。晚點見。

答題解說

答案：（B）。題目問的是幾點前往夜市。我們可以先找到 "Then we'll go to Shilin Night Market..."（然後我們要去士林夜市）這一句後，往前找尋線索。其中提到，這部電影大約一個半小時，而電影是八點半開始（...go see a movie that will start at 8:30 p.m.）而且就在電影院隔壁（just next to the movie theater），所以他們應該大約在十點會前往夜市。

破題關鍵

像這類「詢問時間」的題目，通常答案不會直接出現在內容中，所以答案不會是 12:00，也不會是 8:30，那麼剩下那一個就是答案了。但若要確實解題，只要將出現的時間與相關的敘述結合即可，比如這一題："... starting at 8:30 p.m. ...about one hour and half long. Then we'll go to Shilin Night Market…"，只要結合「8:30 p.m.」與「one hour and half」，答案就出來了。

字詞解釋

not... until... 直到～才～ **night market** 夜市 **theater** [ˋθɪətə] **n.** 電影院（= **movie theater**） **famous** [ˋfeməs] **adj.** 著名的 **delicious** [dɪˋlɪʃəs] **adj.** 美味的 **dish** [dɪʃ] **n.** 一盤菜，菜餚

相關文法或用法補充

❶ keep 當「保持、繼續」的意思時，相當於 continue、go on，後面接動名詞（Ving）。例如：Just keep moving forward and do what you have to do.（只要繼續向前邁進並做你該做的事。）

另外，keep 也常用於「keep + 受詞 + Ving」的句型。例如：I'm sorry to have kept you waiting.（抱歉讓你久等了。）

❷ see a movie 和 watch a movie 都是「看電影」，但兩者的意思不盡相同喔！see a movie 是指在電影院看電影，而 watch a movie 則是在電視上、電腦上或其他可觀賞影片的裝置上看電影。所以，我們可以說 watch movies/videos online（看線上影片），但不能說 see movies/videos online。至於「去（電影院）看電影」最道地且標準的講法是 see a movie 或 go to the movies。這裡的 the movies 是指「電影院」，即 movie theater，因為現在的電影院在同一時間都不會只上映一場電影，所以 movie 要用複數。

第一部分 詞彙

1. I can't read the _____. I need to find someone to ask for directions.（我不會看地圖。我得找個人來問路。）

　　(A) picture　(B) list　(C) map　(D) newspaper

答題解說

答案：(C)。題目第二句的意思是「我得找個人來問路。」所以可以推知，需要找人問路的原因是「不會看地圖」，因此正確答案應為 (C)。

破題關鍵

本題關鍵字是 directions，四個選項中與「方向」有關的，當然就是「地圖（map）」了。

字詞解釋

map [mæp] n. 地圖　**ask for...** 要求取得～　**direction** [dəˋrɛkʃən] n. 方向，方位，方向指引　**list** [lɪst] n. 列表

相關文法或用法補充

本題當中「看地圖」的「看」，跟「看書」、「看報紙」、「看雜誌」一樣，都用 read 這個動詞。在英文裡，「看電視」用 watch TV 表示，而不用 see TV，甚至是 look at TV。因為 see 屬於一個比較「被動接受」的動詞，只要張開眼睛，事物自然會出現在眼前，無意或有意的進入眼睛，因此我們就會用 see 來表達「看到東西」或是「不經意地注意到」，只是單純、沒有意圖的「看」。

而 watch 屬於比較「主動」性的動詞，因為它代表「集中注意力、專心地『看』某個東西」，與 look 的意涵很接近，但 watch 更強調「看一段時間」。

所以 look 也是主動性動詞，也是「集中注意力、朝著目標看」、「注意看」、「注視」的意思。看著某人、某物，look 後面要加介系詞 at，如果只用 look 的話，指的是「看起來」，屬於連綴動詞的用法。

最後 read 與上述幾個動詞的含意差異性較大，read 本來是「讀」的意思，例如，「看書」、「看雜誌」、「看報紙」這些有文字的東西，比較著重於「看了之後理解內容」的意思。

2. **Although Rebecca has a wide _____, she is unable to spell many words.**（雖然瑞貝嘉字彙量很大，但她沒有辦法拼出很多字。）

(A) knowledge (B) activity (C) vocabulary (D) information

答題解說

答案：(C)。空格後面的主要子句意思是「有許多單字她都不會拼」，顯然前面表「讓步」的 although 副詞子句要表達的是「雖然她認識很多字彙」。所以正確答案為 (C)。

破題關鍵

本題關鍵就在句尾 words 這個名詞，四個選項中與「單字」有關的，當然就是「字彙（vocabulary）」了。另外，也可以從 spell（拼字）這個動詞聯想到正確答案。

字詞解釋

knowledge [`nɑlɪdʒ] n. 知識　**activity** [æk`tɪvətɪ] n. 活動　**vocabulary** [və`kæbjəˌlɛrɪ] n. 字彙　**information** [ˌɪnfɚ`meʃən] n. 資訊

相關文法或用法補充

vocabulary 這個名詞的意思，並不是指學英文時要記的「一個一個的單字」，而是「一個人所擁有的字彙量」，是一個聚集的概念，原則上是個「不可數名詞」。例如：Reading broadly helps to increase your vocabulary.（大量閱讀有助於你提升單字量。）、How big is your vocabulary?（你的字彙量有多少？）

不過，如果想要強調「多少個單字」的話，可以在 vocabulary 後面加上 word。例如：I learned so many new vocabulary words today.（我今天學到了很多新單字。）

3. **John did not _____ a college in the country after graduating from senior high school.**（約翰高中畢業後沒有在國內上大學。）

(A) meet (B) prepare (C) imagine (D) enter

答題解說

答案：(D)。句子大意是，約翰高中畢業後沒有～大學，所以空格要填入的動詞應該是要表達「上大學」、「念大學」的概念。故正確答案應是 (D) enter。enter 本義是「進入」，enter a college/university 表示「進入大學就讀」的意思。另外，如要選 (B) prepare，則 college 後面須再加 exam 這個字。

本題其實只要關注「_____ a college」這部分就可以了，然後再把四個選項一一套入空格內，很容易發現只有 enter 是符合句意的。

相關文法或用法補充

以下，來認識一下「各種教育階段」的英文說法吧！

＊幼稚園：kindergarten/preschool

＊國小：elementary/primary school

＊國中：junior high school/middle school/intermediate school

＊高中：senior high school

＊高職：vocational high school

＊五專：junior college

＊大專：institute/college

＊大學：university

＊研究所（碩、博士）：graduate school/graduate institute

＊碩士班：master's program

＊博士班：doctoral program

4. **George's favorite _____ is collecting coins and stamps.**（喬治最愛的嗜好是蒐集錢幣與郵票。）

(A) habit　(B) hobby　(C) housework　(D) health

答題解說

答案：(B)。如果單就「favorite _____」來看，四個名詞選項都是符合句構的，所以還是必須根據整體句意來判斷。句子大意是「喬治最愛的 _____ 是蒐集錢幣與郵票。」顯然答案應該是 hobby（嗜好）」。其餘選項均不符句意與邏輯。

破題關鍵

本題關鍵是空格後的「collecting coins and stamps（蒐集錢幣與郵票）與 hobby（嗜好）的連結」。其中 habit（習慣）指的其實是不知不覺、不經思考而養成的行為，不適用來表達「蒐集錢幣與郵票」。

字詞解釋

favorite [ˈfevərɪt] **adj.** 最喜愛的　**collect** [kəˈlɛkt] **v.** 收集，蒐集　**stamp** [stæmp] **n.** 郵票　**habit** [ˈhæbɪt] **n.** 習慣　**hobby** [ˈhɑbɪ] **n.** 癖好，嗜好　**housework** [ˈhaʊsˌwɝk] **n.** 家事　**health** [hɛlθ] **n.** 健康

相關文法或用法補充

be 動詞後面的主詞補語有時候要用 to-V，有時候卻是用 V-ing，必須依照主詞本身的性質來判斷使用：

1. be + to-V 具有「未來、計畫、目的、作為」等意思。例如：

   ❶ The best way to learn is to ask questions.（最好的學習方法是問問題。）

   ❷ My hope is to enter a good college.（我的期望是進入一所好的大學。）

2. be + V-ing 是指陳述事實、事件、狀態，比如說某事就是發生了，不是刻意要達到這樣的結果。例如：

   ❶ His hobby is reading comic books.（他的嗜好是看漫畫。）

   ❷ Her excuse is, again, getting up too late.（她的藉口又是起床太晚。）

5. **It was raining so hard that we couldn't go _____.**（當時雨下得大到我們哪裡都不能去。）

   (A) anything　(B) anyway　(C) anyone　(D) anywhere

答題解說

答案：(D)。空格前的句子結構是完整的，因為 go 是個不及物動詞，所以後面不需再接受詞（名詞／代名詞），所以 (A)、(C) 可直接排除掉。(B) anyway 原意是「反正，無論如何」，但套入空格中是不符合語意的。句子大意是，因為下大雨，所以哪兒都去不成。故正確答案應為 (D) anywhere。

破題關鍵

本題除了可以用「刪除法」（以文法結構與句意為基礎）來解題，其實只要將 raining so hard 與 couldn't go 作因果關係的連結，自然可以選出正確的 anywhere。

字詞解釋

so... that... 如此～以致於～

相關文法或用法補充

「so + adj. / adv. + that 子句」的用法具有「強調」的功能，強調「原因是如此地……，所以造成……的結果」。依照主要子句動詞是 be 動詞或一般動詞，so 與 that 中間會加上形容詞或副詞。例如：I am so tired that I might pass out.（我太累了，所以可能會昏倒。）

另外，"so that" 是個「副詞連接詞」，相當於一個字：so，只是更具有強調的語意。例如：I worked overtime this week so that I can take time off next week.（我這禮拜加班工作，所以我下禮拜能補休。）

6. **My aunt is busy _____ in the kitchen.**（我阿姨正在廚房忙著做飯。）

(A) cook　**(B)** to cook　**(C)** cooking　**(D)** for cooking

答題解說

答案：（C）。「忙於做某事」的固定用法就是 be busy（+ in）+ Ving。另外，（A）cook 當名詞是「廚師」之意，但 cook 是可數名詞，所以 busy 前面要再加 a；若要表示「為了／因為某事而忙碌」介系詞要用 with，而非 for，"be busy with..." 表示「忙於～」。

破題關鍵

關於不定詞（to-V）與動名詞（Ving）有個很基本的概念，那就是 to-V 表達的是「前後不同時間的動作或事件」，而 Ving 表示「同時發生」。所以，「忙著做某事」的意思是「忙碌」與「做某事」是同時發生的，而不會是先產生忙碌的狀態，才去做某事。有了這樣的基本概念，就不會選到（B）這個選項了。

字詞解釋

kitchen [ˋkɪtʃɪn] n. 廚房　　**cook** [kʊk] n. 廚師

相關文法或用法補充

當你正忙著工作、忙著家事或其他事，除了用 "busy doing something" 或是 "be busy with something" 來表示之外，還可以怎麼表達自己十分忙碌呢？你還可以說 I'm as busy as a bee.（我像蜜蜂一樣忙碌。= 我忙壞了。）、I've got a lot to do.（我有很多事情要做。）

另外，「今天好忙！」可別說成 "Today is so busy!"，因為「忙碌」是指「人」的感受，不可用來修飾事物名詞。

7. **Tom speaks good English, _____ John doesn't.**（湯姆英語說得很好，但約翰說得不好。）

(A) and　**(B)** when　**(C)** while　**(D)** before

答題解說

答案：（C）。空格前的第一句是「湯姆的英文說得很好」，而第二句是「約翰（英文）說得不好」，顯然中間的連接詞應表達相反意思的轉折，所以只有 while（= but）符合語意。

破題關鍵

基本上，英文裡的對等連接詞主要有三個：and、but、or。而當 while 作「然而，但是」解時，相當於 but，視為對等連接詞。

第 1 回
第 2 回
第 3 回
第 4 回
第 5 回
第 6 回
第 7 回
第 8 回
第 9 回
第 10 回

相關文法或用法補充

省略句是我們在學習英語過程中能不斷體驗到收穫和趣味的一種慣用表達方式，無論是說話還是寫作，都要求生動活潑，簡明扼要。就像本題中，doesn't 後面省略了 speak good English，這是為了避免重複的表達方式。省略句的範圍相當廣泛，無法在此一一介紹，以下僅列出幾個例子供參考：

1. The child wanted to play in the street, but her mother told her not to.（這孩子想在街上玩，但她母親告訴她不行。）→ 最後一個字 to 後面省略 "play in the street"

2. I like red wine better than white.（相較於白酒，我較喜歡紅酒。）→ 最後一個字 white 後面省略 wine

3. John is a lawyer, while his wife a cleaner.（約翰是一位律師，而他太太是個清潔人員。）→ his wife 後面省略 is

8. **David looked so excited because he _____ get a ticket to the concert.**
（大衛看起來相當興奮的樣子，因為他能拿到那場演唱會的門票了。）

(A) has (B) should (C) could (D) won't

答題解說

答案：(C)。四個選項是不同形式的動詞，所以須兼顧句義與時態的合理性。空格位於 because 後方表原因，主要句子則說「大衛相當興奮」，因此表示「能夠」，且時態可以與 looked 相對映的 could 為合理且正確的答案。

破題關鍵

這題是考「句義通順」與「時態一致」。基本上主要子句與 because 引導的副詞子句時態應一致。所以可以直接把答案鎖定在 should 跟 could，再依照前後句義即可刪除 should 而選擇正確答案 could。

字詞解釋

excited [ɪkˋsaɪtɪd] **adj.** 興奮的   **concert** [ˋkɑnsɚt] **n.** 音樂會，演奏會，演唱會

相關文法或用法補充

-ed 與 -ing 的差別，是多類考試的最愛之一。只要記住一點：-ed 表示「感到～」，-ing 表示「令人～」；是「人」才會「感到～」，是「事物」才會「令人～」。例如：

① I am interested in this film because it seems interesting.（我對這部電影很有興趣，因為它似乎很有趣。）

② He kept doing that annoying sound, and I left feeling very annoyed.（他一直發出那種惱人的聲音，讓我最後覺得非常厭煩。）

③ I'm quite satisfied because I ate a satisfying meal.（我現在感到很滿足，因為我吃了一頓令人滿足的大餐。）

9. **John studied hard. He thought getting good grades _____ very important.**（約翰用功念書。他認為拿到好成績很重要。）

(A) was　(B) were　(C) will be　(D) is

答題解說

答案：(A)。四個選項是不同時態的 be 動詞，所以必須參考前後文的句意來判斷應用何種時態。首先，空格位於被省略 that 的 that 子句中，而第一句的動詞與第二句主要動詞都是用過去式，因此空格應填入一個過去式 be 動詞，而且 that 子句的主詞是動名詞片語（getting good grades），應視為第三人稱單數，故正確答案應使用單數 be 動詞的 was。

破題關鍵

從空格前 studied 以及 thought 兩個過去式動詞來看，答案是過去式 was 的機率當然是最大的。如果不放心，只要確認句意即可。另外，雖然空格前有 grades 這個複數名詞，但主詞是 getting good grades 這個動名詞片語，應視為第三人稱單數，所以 (B) were 不可選。

字詞解釋

grade [gred] **n.** 等級；分數　　**important** [ɪmˋpɔrtn̩t] **adj.** 重要的

相關文法或用法補充

動名詞（Ving）具有「名詞的性質」。在句子中可以擺放名詞的位置都可以放動名詞：

① Eating fruit is good for health.（吃水果對健康很好。）
　→ 動名詞片語 Eating fruit 當主詞，後面的 be 動詞是單數 is。
　* 若加上 and doing exercise 變成兩個動名詞片語當主詞，後面的 be 動詞要變成複數 are。

② Listening to music makes me happy.（聽音樂讓我很開心。）
　→ 動名詞片語 Listening to music 當主詞，後面的一般動詞是單數 makes。

③ My hobby is collecting stamps.（我的興趣是集郵。）
　→ 動名詞片語 collecting stamps 放在 is 後面作主詞 My hobby 的補語。

④ Don't be afraid of making mistakes.（不要害怕犯錯。）

→ 動名詞片語 making mistakes 接在介系詞 of 的後面當受詞。

* 介系詞後面要接名詞類的單字或詞組

10. **It is sure _____. Remember to bring an umbrella.**（肯定會下雨。記得帶把傘。）

(A) of raining　(B) to rain　(C) raining　(D) rains

答題解說

答案：(B)。就合乎邏輯的語意來說，本題應該是「肯定是會下雨。記得要帶傘。」所以正確答案應為 (B) to rain。(A) sure of 只用於主詞是「人」時，It 是主詞，表示「天氣」。但是「天氣」是不會「確信的」，因為天氣並不像人有思考能力。(C) raining 錯誤的原因是，如果「現在正在下雨」，那跟第二句請對方「記得」帶傘就有矛盾了；(D) 無論是當動詞或名詞，均不符文法規則。

破題關鍵

(C) 與 (D) 都是明顯錯誤的選項，因此關鍵就在考生對於 "be sure to-V" 與 "be sure of..." 的認知。前者為「我認為」會下雨，後者是「天氣認為它會下雨」的意思，後者顯然不合邏輯。

字詞解釋

remember [rɪˋmɛmbɚ] **v.** 記得　　**umbrella** [ʌmˋbrɛlə] **n.** 雨傘

相關文法或用法補充

英文和中文是兩種大相逕庭的語言，有時候英文有的概念中文不一定有，因此在學習上會遇到困難。像「帶某個東西」的「帶」，你會用 bring 還是 take？這兩個動詞又差在哪裡呢？本題中的 bring 如果改成 take 可以嗎？事實上，如果用 take，意思會變成「我這邊有傘，你可以『帶走』」如果是 bring，意思就是「（你人在家裡，現在要出門）把傘帶在身上」。但因為第二句是 Remember 開頭，顯然是第二種情況，所以這裡用 take 是不適合的。

第二部分 段落填空

Questions 11-14

Once upon a time when people gathered and lived together in a common society, they **made** different rules and laws. Some jobs they had done were aimed at keeping the people in the same society safe, **healthy**, and orderly. In addition, people had to have some basic things, such as food, clothes, and houses. **They had other needs, too.** They needed streets, sidewalks, streetlights, hospitals, shops, markets, and even garbage areas. So they elected their government to provide **them** with what they would need in the future. We can say that the government is a group of people whom these people chose to run their society.

中文翻譯 很久以前，當人們聚集並住在一個共同的社會裡，他們制訂不同的規則與法律。他們所做的一些工作旨在維護在這個相同社會中人們的安全、健康及秩序。此外，人們必須擁有一些基本的東西，例如食物、衣服和房子。他們也還有其他的需求。他們需要街道、人行道、街燈、醫院、商店、市場，甚至是垃圾場。於是他們選出他們的政府，來提供他們未來會需要的東西。我們可以說，這個政府就是人們所選出來的一群要來經營他們這個社會的人。

答題解說

11. 答案：(A)。本題應依據前後文來判斷應該填入哪個動詞。句意是，當人們生活在一個共同社會裡，他們自然會制訂行為準則，也就是規則、法律等。這是為了維護治安、保障人民的生活安全和利益，所以本題正確答案是(A)。

12. 答案：(C)。本題考的是與 keep 這個動詞相關的用法。「keep + 人 + 形容詞」是一個慣用語，表示「讓人保持～」，所以正確答案為(C)。

13. 答案：(A)。本題須挑選一個句子、子句或句子的一部分放入空格後，再確認空格前後和空格句之間的連接關係，是否讓句意顯得自然通順。前一句說「人們必須擁有一些基本的東西，例如…」，顯然空格所在的這句要表達的是「他們還有其他需求」，而這是個肯定句，正確答案為(A)。以下是其餘選項句子的翻譯：
(B) 那些是他們最需要的。
(C) 他們已花很多時間製造這些基本的東西。
(D) 在當時，生活相當艱苦。

14. 答案：(B)。空格前是及物動詞 provide，所以要填入一個「受格」的代名詞。(B)、(C)、(D) 均為可能答案。(D) theirs 是所有格代名詞，是一種省略用法，但其前並無對應的名詞，故亦可直接排除。至於 them 與 themselves 要選哪一個，只要知道空格前不定詞 to provide 這個動作是誰做的就行了，顯然是government，所以這裡的「他們」是指「人們」，正確答案為(B) them。

破題關鍵

11. 若單純以「_____ different rules」來看，再看過四個選項動詞，顯然只有(A) made 與(B) broke 是可能搭配的動詞，一個表示「制定法律」，一個是「違反法律」。那麼再根據句意去判斷，答案就出來了。

12. 即使你沒學過「keep + 人 + 形容詞」這個慣用的表達方式，也可以直接從「safe, _____, and orderly」這個結構，也可以輕鬆判斷這裡要填入一個形容詞。orderly（有秩序的）和 friendly 一樣，都是字尾 -ly 的形容詞。

13. 解答此類題型時，應先大致看過前後兩句，再觀察四個選項的句子，自然可以找出一個最能夠通順地連接前後兩句的句子。從前面一句提到的 "basic things, such as food, clothes, and house" 以及後一句提到的 "streets, sidewalks, streetlights..."，可以知道這些都是「需求」，只是前面是「基本需求」，後面是「其他需求」。

14. 本題的考點是人稱代名詞的受格形式。這句話的意思是「他們選出他們的政府，來提供他們未來會需要的東西。」空格處要填入的「他們」是指「人們」，所以正確答案應為 they 的受格形式 them。

字詞解釋

once upon a time 很久以前　**gather** [ˋɡæðɚ] **v.** 聚集　**common** [ˋkɑmən] **adj.** 共同的，常見的　**society** [səˋsaɪətɪ] **n.** 社會　**be aimed at**... 以～為目標　**healthy** [ˋhɛlθɪ] **adj.** 健康的，健全的　**orderly** [ˋɔrdɚlɪ] **adj.** 守秩序的，有條理的　***in addition** 除此之外　**for example** 例如　***sidewalk** [ˋsaɪd͵wɔk] **n.** 人行道　**streetlight** [ˋstrit͵laɪt] **n.** 路燈　**garbage** [ˋɡɑrbɪdʒ] **n.** 垃圾　**government** [ˋɡʌvɚnmənt] **n.** 政府　**provide** [prəˋvaɪd] **v.** 提供

相關文法觀念補充

11. 若要表示「遵守法律（law）／規則（rule）」，可以用 follow 或 obey 這兩個動詞。另外 make it a rule to do something 也是很常用的慣用語句，意思是「依照慣例去做某事，養成～的習慣」。例如：I make it a rule to be in bed by 10pm.（我養成 10 點前睡覺的習慣。）

12. 「keep somebody/something + 受詞補語」，意思是「使～（受詞）維持～（某種狀態）」，其中受詞補語可以是形容詞、分詞或介系詞片語，例如：

❶ We made a fire in order to keep the room warm.（我們生火來保持房間暖和。）

❷ The teacher kept the students waiting for an hour.（老師讓學生等了一個小時。）

13. too 是個副詞，置於句尾，也可以替換成 also，置於動詞前。例如：The teacher tells his students how to be a good student, and tells them how to be a good man, too.（這個老師教導學生如何成為好學生，還教他們如何成為一個好人。）

＝The teacher tells his students how to be a good student, and also tells them how to be a good man.

14. provide 的用法：

❶ provide somebody with something　提供某人某物
The school provides him with a house.（學校提供他一間房子。）

❷ provide something for/to somebody　提供某物給某人

The park provides a good place to do exercise for/to the residents.（這座公園提供一個運動的好地方給居民們。）

Questions 15-18

When the sun rises and **shines** in the early morning, it produces a bright light and we usually feel the warmth. **Then part of the sea water travels into the air in very small drops.** Later, they will come together to form clouds. Some clouds form as the air warms up near the Earth's surface and **rises**. When the warmed air rises, its pressure and temperature would drop, causing very small water drops to stay together forming clouds.

Several types of clouds form in this way. And then the water in the clouds falls down again, like rain or snow, to the ground and the sea. All this water will turn into springs, rivers and lakes, and at last runs **back** into the sea.

中文翻譯

　　當太陽在一大清早升起並照耀時，它製造明亮的光且我們通常會感受到溫暖。然後部分海水會以非常微小的顆粒進入空氣之中。之後，它們將凝聚在一起形成雲朵。有些雲會在當靠近地球表面的空氣變暖且升起時。當變熱的空氣上升，它的壓力與溫度會下降，導致微小水滴凝聚成雲。

　　有些類型的雲是這樣形成的。然後雲裡面的水會再次降下，就像雨和雪，落到地面及海中。這全部的水會流入泉水、河流和湖泊裡，然後最後回到大海裡。

答題解說

15. 答案：(B)。四個選項是不同意義的動詞，故應依照句意來判斷。大意是「當太陽在一大清早升起並～時，它產生明亮的光……」，我們可以從後面的「產生明亮的光」推斷正確答案應為 (B) shines（照耀）。

16. 答案：(D)。題目要求挑選一個句子、子句或句子的一部分放入空格後，確認空格前後和空格句之間的連接關係，是否讓句意顯得自然通順。前一句提到，太陽在一大清早產生明亮的光，通常我們會感受到溫暖；後面這句是「隨後，它將凝聚在一起形成雲朵。（ Later, it will come together to form clouds. ）」因此空格這句應該是和雲朵形成的「過程」有關，故正確答案為「(D) 然後部分海水會以非常微小的顆粒進入空氣之中。」以下是其餘選項句子的翻譯：

(A) 有些熱空氣會停留在海平面上方。

(B) 雲朵可以許多種不同的形狀呈現。

(C) 通常我們知道炎熱夏季已近在咫尺。

17. 答案：(C)。就句子結構與時態而言，應填入一個現在式動詞，故 (A)、(D) 可直接排除掉。接著應就 "as..." 這個副詞子句來看，主詞是 the air，所以動詞用第三人稱單數的 warms up，那麼空格這個動詞當然也應用第三人稱單數，故正確答案應為 (C) rises。

18. 答案：(C)。空格要填入的是一個副詞，而四個選項均可當副詞，故應依照句意來判斷。句意是「水會流入泉水、河流和湖泊裡，然後最後回到大海裡。」所以正確答案應為 (C) back（返回）。其餘選項均不符合句意與邏輯。

破題關鍵

15. 也可以從空格前的主詞 the sun，想到 sunshine（陽光）這個字（下一段也出現了這個字），很容易將 shine 與 sun 連結在一起。

16. 後面這句中的代名詞 they 應該是指空格這句的某個東西，而能「凝聚在一起形成雲朵」的東西，根據常識判斷，就是 (D) 中的「微小的顆粒（small drops）」。

17. 本題兩個關鍵點：動詞時態與單複數。and 前面用的主詞是單數，動詞是現在式，所以答案當然就是現在式、單數的 rises 了。

18. 若直接單就 "runs _____ into the sea" 這部分來看，將四個選項分別套入空格中，也只有 "run back" 符合邏輯，因為 run out（耗盡）、run up（升上去）以及 run over（輾過）均不合邏輯。

字詞解釋

produce [prəˋdjus] **v.** 生產，製造　**bright** [braɪt] **adj.** 明亮的　**cloud** [klaʊd] **n.** 雲　**warm up** 變暖；熱身　**surface** [ˋsɝfɪs] **n.** 表面　**pressure** [ˋprɛʃɚ] **n.** 壓力　**temperature** [ˋtɛmprətʃɚ] **n.** 溫度　**ground** [graʊnd] **n.** 地面　**flow into** 流入　**shine** [ʃaɪn] **v.** 照耀

相關文法觀念補充

15. 世界上獨一無二的東西，如太陽、地球、月亮、世界、天空、宇宙……等名詞，通常要加定冠詞 the。

16. trip 和 travel 雖然都有旅行的意思，但 trip 作旅行之義時只有名詞的用法，指的是時間上較短，距離上也比較近的旅程，像是當天來回，或是三天兩夜的小旅行；而 travel 則是作為動詞用法時，意味著包含了多個目的地，為期較長且距離較遙遠的旅行。例如：Join our fishing trip this weekend!（這個週末跟我們一起釣魚之旅吧！）、travel to New York on business（前往紐約出差）

17. rise 和另一個長得很像的動詞 raise，最大的不同就是 rise 是不及物動詞，後面不用加上任何受詞。另外，也要注意 rise 是不規則動詞，過去式是 rose，過去分詞是 risen。rise 的常見意思是「上升、升高」，舉個例子：The sun rises in the east.（太陽從東邊升起。）另外，rise 也可以用來形容「站起來；起床」，也能用來

替換 stand up 和 get up 喔！例如：She rose to her feet to give a speech.（她站起來發言。）

18. run 既是動詞也是名詞，且無論是單獨使用或者搭配（介）副詞、介系詞，都能變出百般花樣。以下補充幾個初學階段必須要會的、與 run 有關的表達：
going out for a run（出去跑個步）、run a business（經營一間公司／一門生意）、run a company（經營一家公司）、run around（東奔西跑，四處奔忙）、run away（逃離，逃避）、run into（偶遇；陷入）、run over（輾過）、run out（用完）、Time is running out.（快要沒時間了。）

第三部分 閱讀理解

Questions 19-21

中文翻譯

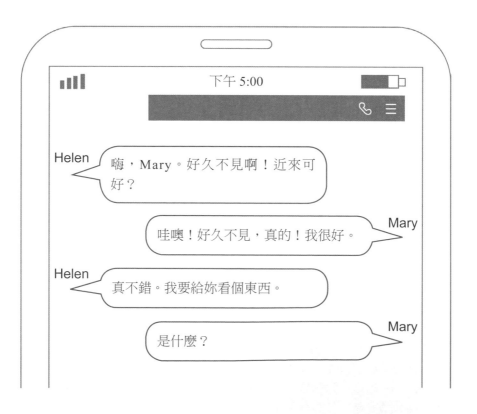

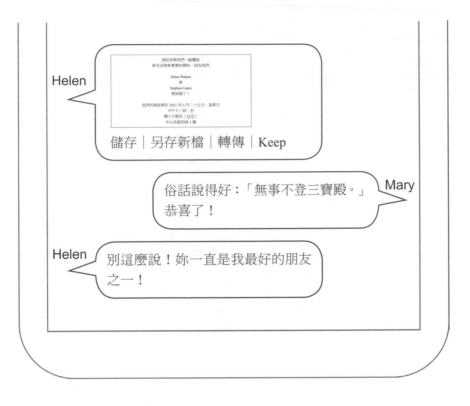

Helen 點開 Mary 傳送的圖片來看。

請前來與我們一起慶祝
新生活與新愛情的開始，因為我們

Helen Parken
與
Stephen Gates
要結婚了！

我們的婚宴將於 2021 年七月二十五日，星期日
中午十二時，於
圓山大飯店（台北）
中山北路四段 1 號

19. Helen 為何傳送這些訊息給 Mary？
    (A) 為了請她幫個忙
    (B) 為了過去的錯誤而致歉
    (C) 為了邀請她參加一項活動
    (D) 為了請她吃大餐

20. 以下關於 Helen，何者為真？
    (A) 她已婚。
    (B) 她恭喜 Mary 要結婚了。
    (C) 7 月 25 日是她的生日。
    (D) Parken 是她的姓氏。

21. Helen 寫 "One never goes to the temple for nothing." 是什麼意思？
    (A) 她 2021 年 7 月 25 日不會有空。
    (B) 她可能是在抱怨某事。
    (C) 她對於她們的友誼感到很開心。
    (D) 她們曾一起去廟裡祈求愛情。

答題解說

19. 答案：(C)。題目問的是 Helen 為何發訊息給 Mary，看似僅針對第一個文本（對話訊息）的內容提問。但其實本題還是需要看過第二個文本的大致內容才能夠得到正確的答案。Helen 在對話訊息中說 And let me show you something. 之後，傳了一張圖給 Mary，而這張圖的內容（第二個文本）就是她發訊息給 Mary 的主要目的。因為第二個文本是一封婚宴邀請函，所以正確答案為 (C) 的「為了邀請她參加一項活動」。

20. 答案：(D)。同樣地，本題也是需要整合與歸納兩篇文本的資訊並比對多項訊息才能夠得到正確的答案。了解 Helen 傳給 Mary 的是婚宴邀請函的照片之後，(A) 當然是錯誤的，另外，要結婚的是 Helen，不是 Mary，所以 (B) 也是錯的。我們知道，第二個文本是一封婚宴邀請函，所以上面的日期（七月二十五日）當然是婚宴的日期，所以 (C) 是錯誤的。(D) 是正確的，因為邀請函上顯示的新娘名字是 Helen Parken。

21. 答案：(B)。中文所謂「無事不登三寶殿」，英文就是 "One never goes to the temple for nothing."，這句話通常帶有貶抑意味，暗指對方特別聯繫一定是別有目的。所以正確答案應為 (B)。

破題關鍵

19. 本題關鍵在對話訊息中的 show you something，並了解第二個文本是一封「邀請卡（invitation card）」的內容，即可正確作答。

20. 英文名字第一個字是「名」，也就是 first name，第二個字是「姓」也就是 last name 或 family name。

21. 就算不了解這句英文諺語的意思，也可以從下一句 Helen 的回答 "Come on! You're always one of my best friends!" （別這麼說！妳一直是我最好的朋友之一！）來推斷 Mary 是在小小抱怨。

字詞解釋

century [ˋsɛntʃʊrɪ] n. 世紀；百年　**saying** [ˋseɪŋ] n. 諺語，格言　**temple** [ˋtɛmpl] n. 廟宇　**congratulation** [kən͵grætʃəˋleʃən] n. 恭喜　**click on** （用滑鼠）點擊　**celebrate** [ˋsɛlə͵bret] v. 慶祝　**freshness** [ˋfrɛʃnɪs] n. 新鮮；新的氣象，新的開始　**wedding** [ˋwɛdɪŋ] n. 婚禮　***reception** [rɪˋsɛpʃən] n. 接待會，宴會（衍生自動詞　**receive**）　**grand** [grænd] adj. 雄偉的，堂皇的　**favor** [ˋfevɚ] n. 幫助，恩惠　***apology** [əˋpɑlədʒɪ] n. 道歉　**invite** [ɪnˋvaɪt] v. 邀請，招待　**treat** [trit] v. 請客，對待　**upcoming** [ˋʌp͵kʌmɪŋ] adj. 即將來臨的　**complain** [kəmˋplen] v. 抱怨，發牢騷　**pray for** 祈求

相關文法或用法補充

❶ 跟別人打招呼可以說 How are you?、How's (it) going 或 What's up? 一般回答時可以說 Pretty good. How about you?。或者不想多說的話，只要回他一個字 Good. 就此結束話題即可。假設你 Good. 完了不加 How about you?，美國人會理解為你不想回話。至於課本上教的 I am fine. Thanks you. How are you?，感覺是極 old-fashioned 的。

❷ show 這個動詞有「授予動詞」的用法，後面接兩個受詞。本篇對話訊息中的 show you something（給妳看個東西）就是這種用法。但要注意的是，show 後面的「物」並非什麼東西都可以放。比方說，要送客時千萬別說 Let me show you the door！中文想說的是「我送你到門口。」但這句英文的意思會變成「大門就在那裡」，這是下逐客令、要別人滾出去的意思。你應該說 Let me show you to the door. 或 Let me walk you out.。

第 1 回
第 2 回
第 3 回
第 4 回
第 5 回
第 6 回
第 7 回
第 8 回
第 9 回
第 10 回

中文翻譯

寄件者	library_service@surmail.com
收件者	不具名收件人
主旨	請注意

親愛的圖書館使用者：

　　本圖書館將於接下來四天的中秋連假期間關閉，且將於 9/24 重新開館。在此期間若要歸還書籍，請使用在「假日室」前門的「歸還」箱。倘若您借閱的書籍會在此期間逾期，您最遲可延後於 9/24 歸還，且不會有任何罰款。

　　對於延遲歸還的書籍、雜誌或期刊，我們有新的規定。您每逾期一日將被罰款 NT$10，直到將所有刊物歸還為止。此外，您的借閱權將於您未歸還逾期品項且未繳罰款的三日後暫時取消。因此請務必在您所借閱的品項逾期前歸還。我們也會在借出物逾期的三日前發送通知給您。

全體中央圖書館員工祝您佳節愉快。

中央圖書館服務中心

22. 這封電子郵件的主要目的為何？
　(A) 告訴圖書館使用者一場特別的活動。
　(B) 讓書館使用者知道一個新的規定。
　(C) 要求圖書館使用者追蹤逾期未歸還的借閱物。
　(D) 通知圖書館員工接下來的休假日。

23. 關於中央圖書館，何者為非？
　(A) 現在是關閉的。
　(B) 它將在 9/24 後開館。
　(C) 圖書館員工在這期間不上班。
　(D) 你可以在這期間內歸還借閱物。

24. 「overdue 的書籍」所指為何？
　(A) 它是指你應該歸還的書籍。
　(B) 它是指你可以從圖書館借走的書籍。
　(C) 它是指已經絕版了的書籍。
　(D) 它是指無法借出的書籍。

答題解說

這個題組是一封電子郵件，內容主要關於圖書館於中秋連假期間關閉及歸還書籍的新相關規定。

22. 答案：(B)。從第一句 "The library will be CLOSED during..." 可知，這則通知是要告訴民眾圖書館不開放的消息。接下來提到不開放的期間如果要歸還書籍的一些注意事項，故正確答案應為 (B)。

23. 答案：(A)。一開始提到，The library will be CLOSED ... and will re-open...，從兩個未來式動詞即可知，(A) It is closed now. 是錯誤的答案。

24. 答案：(A)。overdue 這個字所在的句子是：If the book(s) you borrowed will be overdue during this period, you can return it/them...，表示如果從圖書館借走的書籍在此期間逾期，則最晚可以在 9/24 歸還，因此是「借閱期限過了」必須歸還，故正確答案應為 (A)。

破題關鍵

22. 此類通知的主旨或目的，如果無法從標題看出，通常會出現在一開始的句子或文本的前一、兩句。此外，這種「主旨型」的題型其實是可以留待後面兩題答完之後再回過頭來解題，因為你只要大略了解內容即可輕易答題。

23. 如果前一題答對的話，知道這則通知的目的是告訴圖書館使用者接下來的連假期間不開放的消息，那麼發出通知的「現在」這時候，當然不會是關閉的狀態。

24. 其實只要記住：這是一則圖書館的公告，over- 本身又有「超過～」的意思，很容易可以聯想到：從圖書館借出的書，逾期則應該歸還。

字詞解釋

upcoming [ˋʌpˌkʌmɪŋ] adj. 即將來臨的　**Mid-Autumn Festival** 中秋節　**return** [rɪˋtɝn] n. 歸還，返回　***overdue**[ˋovɚˋdju] adj. 逾期的　**period** [ˋpɪrɪəd] n. 期間　**fine** [faɪn] n./v. 罰款　**cause** [kɔz] v. 導致，引起　**periodical** [ˌpɪrɪˋɑdɪk!] n. 期刊　**rule** [rul] n. 規則，規定　**right** [raɪt] n. 權利　**cancel** [ˋkæns!] v. 取消　***for the time being** 暫時　**fail to-V** 未能做到　**notice** [ˋnotɪs] n. 通知　**staff** [stæf] n.（全體）職員　**follow up** 追蹤～（然後採取進一步行動）　**on time** 準時　***inform** [ɪnˋform] v. 通知

相關文法或用法補充

❶ 介系詞 during 意為「在～期間」，指某事件、活動，從頭到尾的整段時間或期間。例如：Don't speak during the meal.（吃飯時別說話。）另外，during 不可用來表示「持續一段時間」，而是要用 for。例如：

Roy was out of the office for three days last week.
（羅伊上週有三天沒來上班。）（○）
Roy was out of the office during three days last week.（✗）

❷ fine 當形容詞時表示「好的」，如 It's a fine day.（今天是個好日子。），當動詞或是名詞時，意思是「罰款」。例如：The truck driver paid a NT$2,400 fine for speeding.（貨車司機因超速行駛付了兩千四百元的罰鍰。）

Questions 25-27

中文翻譯

　　麗莎去年夏天跟團到歐洲旅行。一天，當他們在飯店登記入住之後，導遊讓他們自由活動，以便他們可以到附近任何地方去，但她要求他們必須在晚餐時間之前返回飯店。

　　晚餐的供應時間是六點至八點。麗莎獨自一人到外面走走。她看見了一棟舊式建築，覺得相當興奮。她想要進去裡面參觀一下，但一些當地人告訴她，當天沒有開放民眾參觀。所以她只能在建築物前面拍了幾張她自己的照片。

　　當她看著她的智慧型手機上顯示的時間時，她對自己說：「糟糕！已經六點十五分了。晚餐的時間到了！我最好現在立刻回去。」

25. 麗莎應該在何時回到飯店？
　　(A) 六點前。　　　　　　　　　(B) 八點前。
　　(C) 六點十五分之後。　　　　　(D) 就寢時間前。

26. 麗莎在自由時間裡沒有做什麼？
　　(A) 她四處走走。
　　(B) 她和一些當地人交談。
　　(C) 她用智慧型手機自拍了幾張照片。
　　(D) 她進入一棟老建築裡面並拍了一些照片。

27. 以下何者正確？
　　(A) 麗莎當天下午外出散步。
　　(B) 這棟舊式建築在當天下午六點前關閉了。
　　(C) 她請一些當地人幫她自己拍照。
　　(D) 麗莎在晚餐時間之前回到了飯店。

答題解說

這是一篇記敘文，內容關於 Lisa 在一趟跟團旅行中所發生的一些事情。

25. 答案：(A)。題目要問的是麗莎「應該」在何時回到飯店。請注意重點不是「何時回到飯店」。「應該何時回到飯店」的意思就是「導遊要求的時間」。第一段最後一句提到 "she asked them to be back to the hotel before dinner time."（她要求他們必須在晚餐時間之前返回。）而下一段又說 "Dinner was served from six to

eight."（晚餐的供應時間是六點至八點。），所以正確答案應為 (A) Before six.。

26. 答案：(D)。題目要問的是麗莎自由時間時「沒有」做什麼。相關資訊都在第二段的部分。其中提到：She wanted to go inside to look around, but some locals told her it wasn't open to the public that day.（她想要進去裡面參觀一下，但一些當地人告訴她，當天沒有開放民眾參觀。）所以 (D) 是麗莎沒有也沒辦法去做的事。另外，選項 (C) 中的 selfies，從 self- 就可推斷，它一定和「自己」有關，它是「自拍」的意思。

27. 答案：(A)。第二段提到 "Lisa went out alone for a walk."，正好與 (A) 是相符合的。而這段又提到 "it wasn't open to the public that day"（當天沒有開放民眾參觀），所以 (B) 是錯誤的；(C) 錯誤的原因在於 "So she could just take some photos of herself..." 這句。至於 (D) 的部分在第三段：Oops! It's fifteen to six thirty. Time to have dinner!，而前面提到過 dinner time 是六點開始，因此她並沒有在晚餐時間開始前回到飯店。

破題關鍵

25. 直接針對關鍵字詞 should come back 在短文中找線索：asked them to be back... before dinner time。

26. 從題目關鍵字詞 NOT do... free time 在短文中找線索：She wanted to go inside to look around, but...。

27. 這種概括式的題目，通常都會在解決了該題組其他題目之後才作答。比方說，本題選項與前一題的選項有重疊的地方：Lisa went out for a walk in the afternoon that day. 等於前一題選項 (A) 的 She took a walk around.。

字詞解釋

tour group 旅行團　**check in** 登記入住　**tour guide** 導遊　**allow** [əˋlaʊ] v. 允許　**take a break** 休息一下　**serve** [sɝv] v. 供應（飯菜等），端上　**alone** [əˋlon] adv. 獨自地　**look around** 四處看看　**local** [ˋlokl] n. 當地居民，本地人　**be open to**... 開放給～參觀　**take a photo of**... 拍～（某人）的照片

相關文法或用法補充

❶ 中文都是「旅行」，但 trip、travel、tour 這三個字的差別你都清楚嗎？
　　① travel 當不可數名詞時意思是「移動」，強調從一個地方到另一地的移動過程。例如：rail travel 搭火車的旅程
　　② trip 意味著造訪某個地方，可能是旅遊觀光或者其他目的，強調「旅程」本身。例如：take a business trip to Japan（去日本出差）。
　　③ tour 是「參觀、遊玩」為主的旅遊，歌手或樂團巡迴演出也是用 tour 這個字。例如：a sightseeing tour（觀光旅遊）、be on tour（正進行巡迴演出）

❷ from... to... 的意思是「從～到～」，可以填入時間或地點，例如：How long does it take from here to the airport?（從這裡到機場要多長時間？）、The holiday is from Monday to Sunday.（假期是從星期一到星期日。）

❸ not... anymore 意思是「不再～」，和 not... any longer 一樣意思，例如：I don't go swimming in a river anymore.（我不再去河裡游泳了。）、She doesn't want to see her ex-boyfriend any longer.（她不想再見到她的前男友了。）

Questions 28-30

中文翻譯

　　當你準備到遠方旅行時，你通常會選擇住在什麼樣的地方？曾經住過昂貴、卻讓你覺得不值得花這筆錢的旅館嗎？或者住過和其他陌生人共享一室的廉價旅舍嗎？如果這兩種經驗都讓你覺得很糟，這裡推薦您一項選擇：度假公寓。

　　比起一般飯店或旅舍，度假公寓可以讓你擁有更大的空間。在這公寓中的所有東西你都可以使用，包括客廳、廚房、書房，當然還有浴室。有些公寓甚至還有很棒的花園、健身房、游泳池、KTV、桌球室……等。在度假公寓你會感覺像是在自己家裡。

　　最棒的是，一般來說度假公寓的住宿都很平價。它是以整間公寓為單位計價，而非以人頭計價。所以基本上很適合一個 3 至 5 名成員的家庭或友人成團出遊住宿。當然，也有度假公寓是為夫妻或情侶們設計的，且價格比一般飯店便宜。如果您是和朋友或家庭出遊的話，度假公寓將是您的最佳選擇！

28. 我們可以從這篇讀物中了解到什麼？
　　(A) 去哪裡找到一間好的度假公寓
　　(B) 如何選擇一間好的度假公寓
　　(C) 為何我們應該選擇度假公寓
　　(D) 如何將房子轉為度假公寓

29. 關於度假公寓，以下何者為真？
　　(A) 它們主要是為兩人以上一起出遊設計的。
　　(B) 你必須支付額外費用以使用健身房或泳池。
　　(C) 人們住在度假公寓時可以結交新朋友。
　　(D) 它們大部分都在鄉下。

30. 本文提到度假公寓的住宿是「affordable」，意思是什麼？
　　(A) 你可以擁有更多個人空間。
　　(B) 你到處都可以找到它們。
　　(C) 你不必花太多錢在度假公寓上。
　　(D) 你可以使用裡面的所有東西。

答題解說

這是一篇說明文,內容講述度假公寓可能會是旅遊住宿的好選擇。

28. 答案:(C)。本篇一開始以兩個「反例」作為對照,最後說「推薦您一項選擇:度假公寓」,接下來兩段說明「度假公寓」優點與特色,也就是告訴讀者「為何我們應該選擇度假公寓。」正確答案應為 (C)。

29. 答案:(A)。(A) 的部分可以從 "Therefore, it is basically suitable for a family or friends traveling in a group of 3 to 5 persons. Of course, there are also holiday apartments designed for couples or lovers..." 得知 (A) 為正確答案;文中並未提到使用健身房或泳池等公共設施必須支付額外費用,所以 (B) 是錯誤的;(C) 的「可以結交新朋友」以及 (D) 的「大部分都在鄉下」也都是未提到的錯誤選項。

30. 答案:(C)。affordable 這個字所在的句子是 "The best thing is, stay in holiday apartments is generally affordable. "→「最棒的是,一般來說度假公寓的住宿都很平價。」其中 affordable 是「可負擔得起的」的意思,所以只有 (C) 的 "You don't have to spend much on them." (你不必花太多錢在度假公寓上。) 是最符合語意的答案。

破題關鍵

28. 本題屬於了解文章內容大意之後,判斷選項中何者正確的主旨型考題。首段最後一句 "here is one recommended choice : holiday apartments." 即點出以下內容是要「介紹度假公寓」。

29. 「何者為真」或「何者為非」的題型,都屬於內容細節型的題目。通常都是擺在最後才作答。在了解每一個選項的內容之後,對照文章中提的相關內容,然後用刪除法就自然能夠得到正確答案。

30. 就算不知道 affordable 的意思,也可以參考後面 "they are cheaper than ordinary hotels. "這句,即可知道 (C) 是最適當的答案。

字詞解釋

prepared [prɪˋpɛrd] **adj.** 有準備的   **travel** [ˋtrævl] **v.** 旅行   **choose** [tʃuz] **v.** 選擇
expensive [ɪkˋspɛnsɪv] **adj.** 昂貴的   *__worth__ [wɝθ] **adj.** 值得～的   **hostel** [ˋhɑstl] **n.** 旅舍(尤其指青年旅舍)   **stranger** [ˋstrendʒɚ] **n.** 陌生人   **experience** [ɪkˋspɪrɪəns] **n.** 經驗   **terrible** [ˋtɛrəbl] **adj.** 可怕的   *__recommended__ [ˏrɛkəˋmɛndɪd] **adj.** 推薦的
choice [tʃɔɪs] **n.** 選擇,選項   **compare** [kəmˋpɛr] **v.** 比較   **space** [spes] **n.** 空間
study [ˋstʌdɪ] **n.** 書房   **lovely** [ˋlʌvlɪ] **adj.** 可愛的,美好   **gym** [dʒɪm] **n.** 健身房   **table tennis** 桌球   **feel at home** 感覺像在家裡一樣自在   **generally** [ˋdʒɛnərəlɪ] **adv.** 一般來說   **affordable** [əˋfordəbl] **adj.** 負擔得起的   **entire** [ɪnˋtaɪr] **adj.** 整個的   **design** [dɪˋzaɪn] **v.** 設計   **ordinary** [ˋɔrdnˏɛrɪ] **adj.** 平常的,普通   **reading** [ˋridɪŋ] **n.** 讀物
change... into... 將～變成～   **countryside** [ˋkʌntrɪˏsaɪd] **n.** 鄉下

❶ stay 當「留宿，過夜」的意思時，在英美的用法上大致都相同。住在旅館用 stay at，而住在朋友或其他人家裡則用 stay with。例如，We're staying at a hotel.（我們住在一家旅館裡）；My mother is staying with us this week.（我母親這星期來我們家住）。

❷ hotel 在台灣一般稱為「飯店」或「旅館」，並以旅客住宿為主要營收來源。相較於 hotel，hostel 是設備比較簡樸、有時住客要合用衛浴設備，且通常是年輕人為了省錢才會住的地方，有時會被稱為 youth hostel（青年旅館），而 hotel 是指設備比較完善、收費較高、服務較好的地方。

5

GEPT
全民英檢

初級初試
中譯＋解析

第一部分 看圖辨義

1. **For question number 1, please look at Picture A.**

   Question number 1: Where would you most likely see this sign?（你最有可能在哪裡看見這個標誌？）
   (A) Near a hospital（在醫院附近）
   (B) On a highway（在高速公路上）
   (C) Near a kindergarten（在幼兒園附近）

   答題解說

   答案：(C)。最上方的文字 SLOW（慢）是告訴駕駛人車速要放慢，而下方的 Children Are Playing（有孩童在玩耍）是說明為何要放慢車速的原因 — 因為可能有孩童突然跑出來。所以最有可能看到此標誌的地方是幼兒園大門口或附近。

   字詞解釋

   hospital [`hɑspɪtl] **n.** 醫院　　**highway** [`haɪ͵we] **n.** 快速道路，公路　　**kindergarten** [`kɪndɚ͵gɑrtn] **n.** 幼稚園

   相關文法或用法補充

   就如同「上學（go to school）」、「上高中（go to senior high school）」、「上大學（go to college）」「上幼稚園」要用 go to kindergarten，不可加冠詞 the 或 a → go to a/the kindergarten（X）。

2. **For question number 2 and 3, please look at Picture B.**

   Question number 2: What is the woman doing?
   （這名女子正在做什麼？）
   (A) She is playing soccer.（她正在踢足球。）
   (B) She is cooking.（她正在煮飯。）
   (C) She is building the camp.（她正在搭帳篷。）

   答題解說

   答案：(B)。本題是對正在做的事情（what）提問，問女子在做什麼。從圖片中可以清楚看到，有三個人，遠處一名女子正在做飯，兩個男孩在踢足球，而帳篷

已經搭好了。所以正確答案是(B)。

第 1 回 第 2 回 第 3 回 第 4 回 第 5 回 第 6 回 第 7 回 第 8 回 第 9 回 第 10 回

破題關鍵

基本上從三個選項的「She is V-ing」句型就知道，題目是要問「某人正在做什麼」，且只要聽到題目句的 woman 或三個選項的 She，答案就出來了。

字詞解釋

soccer [ˋsɑkɚ] n. 足球　　**cook** [kʊk] v. 烹煮　　**build** [bɪld] v. 建造，構築　　**camp** [kæmp] n. 營地，帳篷

相關文法或用法補充

play 表示「參與（某種球類運動或棋牌類活動）」時，其後不加冠詞 the，直接接球類運動名稱或棋牌類活動名稱，可根據實際情況譯成「打、踢、下…」等。例如：play football（踢橄欖球）、play badminton（打羽毛球）、play cards（打牌）、play Mahjong（打麻將）。

3. **Question number 3: Please look at Picture B again.**

Where are the boys playing?（男孩們在哪裡玩耍？）
(A) Near a campground（在營地附近）
(B) Near a tent（在帳篷附近）
(C) In a sports center（在運動中心）

答題解說

答案：(B)。本題問「在哪裡（where）」，即使未聽出 where，至少三個表達地方或位置的選項可以輕易聽出來吧！圖片中兩個男孩在帳篷（tent）附近踢球玩耍，所以正確答案是(B)。另外，雖然看得出來他們在露營，但千萬別聽到 campground 就選了(A)。(A)要改成 On a campground 才是正確答案。

破題關鍵

對於表地方的介系詞要有基本的概念。near 是「在～附近」，所以不可能「在營地（campground）的附近」露營。tent 是英檢初級範圍內單字，閱讀時也許不難認出，但要聽得出來就得多加練習才行。

字詞解釋

campground [ˋkæmpˏgraʊnd] n. 營地　　**tent** [tɛnt] n. 帳篷　　**sports** [spɔrts] adj. 運動的

相關文法或用法補充

sport 和 sports 都可以當作形容詞，但在指服裝「非正式的、輕便的」時，往往是

用 sport，如 sport shirt（運動衫）、sport coat/jacket（運動上衣或便裝外套）。但若是用於「運動類」的表達，通常用 sports。例如 sports center（運動中心）、sports reporter（體育記者）、sportsman（運動員）。而「跑車」的說法通常 sport/sports car 都有人用。

4. **For question number 4, please look at Picture C.**

   Question number 4: What happened to the man?
   （男子發生什麼事了？）

   (A) A phone call stopped him from sleeping.
   　　（一通電話中斷了他的睡眠。）
   (B) He has been lying sleepless the whole night.
   　　（他整個晚上一直躺著無法入眠。）
   (C) He was woken up by an alarm clock.（他被鬧鐘吵醒了。）

   答題解說

   答案：(A)。從圖片中可以看到電話突然響起，使得男子從睡夢中吵醒了，所以並非「一直躺著無法入眠」，而圖中也沒有鬧鐘（alarm clock），故正確答案是 (A)。

   破題關鍵

   圖片內容清楚告訴我們，窗外有月亮，晚上 11 點半電話鈴響了，男子迷迷糊糊地看著電話，由此我們聯想到他是被電話鈴聲吵醒了。

   字詞解釋

   happen to... 發生在（某人身上）　　**stop... from**... 使得…（某人）無法…（做某事）　　**lie** [laɪ] v. 躺，臥（lie→lay→lay）　　**sleepless** [ˋsliplɪs] adj. 失眠的，不眠的　　**wake up** 將…（某人）叫醒（wake → woke → woken）　　**alarm clock** 鬧鐘

   相關文法或用法補充

   wake up 當及物動詞是「將～（某人）叫醒」的意思，也可以當不物動詞，意思是「醒來，起床」。例如：

   ① The noise woke me up.（嘈雜聲吵醒了我。）
   　　→ 當受詞為人稱代名詞時，須擺在 wake 與 up 中間。
   ② Jerry usually wakes early.（傑瑞通常早起。）

5. **For question number 5, please look at Picture D.**

Question number 5:

How do the ladies like the man?

（女士們覺得這名男子如何？）

(A) They think he's a gentleman.（她們覺得他是個紳士。）

(B) They think he's a good singer.（她們覺得他是個好歌手。）

(C) They think he's making noises.（她們覺得他在製造噪音。）

答題解說

答案：(C)。本題問的是女士們對這位男士的看法。圖片中有兩位女士，一位瞪著眼睛看著他，另一位趴在桌子上，一副難以忍受的樣子，她們倆本來是在看書的。由此我們可以知道她們都不喜歡他此時唱歌，既然不喜歡當然就覺得他很吵。故正確答案應為(C)。

破題關鍵

How do you like...? 意思是「你覺得～怎麼樣？」，常用來詢問別人的觀點或看法，例如：

A: How do you like the movie?（你覺得這部電影怎麼樣？）

B: I think it is very interesting.（我覺得非常有趣。）

字詞解釋

gentleman [ˋdʒɛntḷmən] n. 紳士，男士

相關文法或用法補充

以 that 引導的名詞子句相當常見，許多動詞如 say, think, see, suggest, believe, agree, hope, wish, explain, hear, feel, wonder, know, note, mean... 等，其後都可以接 that 引導的名詞子句作為其受詞。如：The teacher said that there would be a test next week.（老師說下週會有考試。）

第二部分 問答

6. **Would you like to join us?**（你要和我們一起來嗎？）

(A) You look so cool.（你看起來很酷。）

(B) Just enjoy yourselves.（你們好好玩吧。）

(C) Very funny.（非常有趣。）

第 1 回
第 2 回
第 3 回
第 4 回
第 5 回
第 6 回
第 7 回
第 8 回
第 9 回
第 10 回

答案：(B)。題目是邀請對方一起來參加或是從事什麼活動，但 (A) 的「你看起來很酷。」以及 (C) 的「非常有趣。」顯然都是答非所問，所以只有 (B)「你們好好玩吧。」可以間接表達無法一起去的意思。

本題屬於一般 Yes-No 疑問句，但其實不一定要用 Yes 或 No 來回答。有時候「間接性」的回答聽起來比較婉轉而不失禮，(B) 的 Just enjoy yourselves. 表示請對方盡情玩樂，就表示自己無法前去參加。

enjoy oneself 玩得開心

enjoy oneself 可單獨使用，表示「請自便、玩的開心」，相當於 have a good time、have fun。例如：We enjoyed ourselves at the beach.（我們在海邊裡玩得很開心。）另外，「enjoy + V-ing」也相當常見。例如：I enjoy fishing with my father.（我喜歡和父親釣魚。）

7. **I really love your hat.**（我好喜歡你這帽子。）

(A) I wear it only once a week.（我一星期只戴一次。）
(B) Thanks. It's a present from my boyfriend.（謝謝。那是我男友送的禮物。）
(C) I got a headache yesterday.（我昨天頭疼。）

答案：(B)。題目這句話是在讚美對方的帽子，(A) 回答說「我一星期只戴一次。」以及 (C) 的「我昨天頭疼。」都是明顯的、不知其所以然的回應。而 (B) 先表示感謝之後，說明這是某人送的禮物，是合乎常理的回應。

當有人對你說 "I love your xxx"（我喜歡你的…）時，一定要知道對方是在讚美你的某個東西，最直接的回應當然就是「感謝」了。

once [wʌns] adv. 一次，一回   **present** [ˋprɛznt] n. 禮物   **headache** [ˋhɛdˏek] n. 頭痛

英文裡表示「讚美」的話，除了很常聽到的 You did a good job.、You're so nice...

等 You 開頭的說法，你也可以說 I love...。藉由「我喜歡你的…」的說法，其實更能夠拉近彼此的距離喔！例如，在和對方聊天的最後，可以用「I love talking with you.（我喜歡跟你聊天。）」來表達相談甚歡的意思。

8. **What did you do last Sunday?**（你上週日做了什麼？）

(A) Nothing. I just stayed home.（沒什麼。我就待在家裡。）
(B) How about you?（你呢？）
(C) I need to make an important call.（我得打一通重要的電話。）

答題解說

答案：(A)。本題是針對「做什麼」（what）提問，選項 (B) 反問對方「你呢？」並沒有回答對方的提問，而 (C) 回答必須去做某事，也是答非所問。(A) 的 Nothing.（沒做什麼。）已經直接回答對方的問題了。

破題關鍵

既然 What... do? 是要問「做什麼？」，就要回答具體的事件，如果沒做什麼事，就用 Nothing. 來回答即可。

相關文法或用法補充

need 可作情態助動詞，也可以作一般動詞：

	情態助動詞	一般動詞
用於肯定		He needs to work overtime.
否定式	He needn't work overtime.	He doesn't need to work overtime.
用於肯定疑問	Need he work overtime?	Does he need to work overtime?
用於否定疑問	Needn't he work overtime?	Doesn't he need to work overtime?

9. **Would you mind turning off the radio?**（麻煩你關掉收音機好嗎？）

(A) She's going to turn up.（她快到了。）
(B) You're welcome.（不客氣。）
(C) Not at all.（當然好。）

答題解說

答案：(C)。題目這句也是屬於 Yes/No 的問句，本來對方麻煩或請求你做某件事，通常我們會回答 Yes/No problem/No... 等來表達願意或不願意，因此 (A) 與

(B) 很明顯都是答非所問。而 (C) 的 Not at all.（一點也不介意。）是針對 Would you mind...（你介意～嗎？） 來回答，所以「一點也不介意」的意思就是樂意幫忙了。

英文裡表示「請求」的說法有很多種，"Would you mind...?" 就是其中之一，而且是屬於比較客氣、委婉的問法。mind 表示「介意」，所以如果你願意幫忙，要「否定」回答（No...），要是不想幫忙，要用「肯定」（Yes, ...）回答。

mind [maɪnd] v. 介意，注意　**turn off** 關閉（電器等設備）　**turn up** 出現，現身

我們每天都會用到很多電器，開關微波爐、電燈、電風扇等等，這些「開開關關」，英文中可不是用 open 和 close，而是 turn on/off 喔！另外，還有 switch on/off 也可以用來開啟或關閉一般家電設備，而 power up/off 通常用於電腦等「機器設備」，如果是電燈的開關就不會這樣用。而 shut off / shut down 通常用於關閉引擎、機器等。

10. **Excuse me. Where can I find the restroom?**（請問一下。洗手間在哪裡？）

(A) You can try it on in the dressing room.（你可以在更衣室試穿。）
(B) Turn around, and let me take a look.（轉過身來，讓我看一下。）
(C) Go straight ahead, and you'll find it.（往前直走就會看到。）

答案：(C)。題目這句 Where can I find...? 常聽到的「問路」用語，因此回答要有具體的「路線指引」，然後可以再補上一句 you'll find it（你就會看到了）。故正確答案應為 (C)。(A) 試圖以相同字彙 room 來混淆，而 (B) turn around 是「（原地）轉身」的意思，答非所問。

本題可採用「刪除法」來快速解答，因為是針對地點提問（where），回答時要具體指明這個地點的方位，比如說，是直走還是轉彎，是向左轉還是向右轉，要盡可能地讓對方更容易地找到。而選項中只有 (C) 可用來表達指路。

restroom [ˈrɛstrum] n. 洗手間　**try on** 試穿　**trun around** 轉身，迴轉　**straight** [stret] adv. 挺直地，直接地

第 1 回
第 2 回
第 3 回
第 4 回
第 5 回
第 6 回
第 7 回
第 8 回
第 9 回
第 10 回

相關文法或用法補充

Excuse me. 本來是「對不起，原諒我」的意思，但日常會話中主要用來引起他人注意，這是因為可能打擾他人，如打斷別人談話、在人群中推擠別人（借過）或無法認同他人意見時。例如：Excuse me, could you tell me the way to the post office?（對不起，請問郵局怎麼走？）

若要表達「歉意」時，可以用 sorry 或 I beg your pardon.，例如：

I'm so sorry that I hit you on the head.（真是抱歉，我打到你的頭了。）

要是沒聽清楚某人剛才說的話，而請對方再說一次時，可以說 Pardon?、Sorry? 或 Pardon me.，例如：Pardon? I didn't catch you.（對不起，請再說一遍。我沒聽清楚你說的話。）

11. Can I watch a movie now?（我現在可以看一齣電影嗎？）

    (A) Yes, I like it.（是的，我喜歡。）

    (B) Yes, if you like.（可以，如果你要的話。）

    (C) This is Henry speaking.（我是亨利。）

答題解說

答案：(B)。本題的「我現在可以看一齣電影嗎？」是個一般疑問句，基本上要用 Yes/No 來回答，所以 (C) 可直接排除掉。(A) 的「是的，我喜歡。」無法用來回答對方的問題「可以看一齣電影嗎？」所以正確答案應為 (B) 的「可以，如果你要的話。」

破題關鍵

情狀助動詞 Can/May 常用於表達「請求允許」的問句中，所以聽到 Can I...? 時，應給予對方明確的 Yes 或 No 的回答。最後再透過刪除法來找到正確的答案。

相關文法或用法補充

「This is + 人 + speaking.」是常見的電話用語，無論是撥打出去或是接電話，都可以用來表明自己的身份。例如：

① A: May I speak to Miss Lee? B: Sorry, she is unavailable now.（A：請找李小姐。B：抱歉，她現在不在／不方便接電話。）

    → 不能說：I'm not Miss Lee.

② Hello, this is Andy Lee (speaking). Who is that?（你好，我是李安迪。您哪位？）

    ❶ Who is that? 不能說成 Who are you?

    ❷ This is Andy Lee (speaking). 不能說成 I'm Andy Lee.

12. Hey, you don't look very good.（嗨，你看起來臉色不太好。）

(A) What's wrong with you?（你怎麼了？）
(B) I must be catching a cold.（我肯定是感冒了。）
(C) How much does it cost?（這個東西多少錢？）

答題解說

答案：(B)。題目這句的情境是，當對方看到你臉色不太好，可能認為你生病了，或是心情不好，於是想關心你的狀況所說的話，可以直接說明臉色不太好的原因，故選項 (B) 是正確的回答。

破題關鍵

在回答對方的關切之意時，說明自己的狀況就是最直接的回應。本題亦可用刪除法來作答，因為 (A) 反問對方怎麼了，以及 (C) 問某物值多少錢，都是明顯答非所問。

字詞解釋

catch a cold 感冒

相關文法或用法補充

must be... 常用來表示猜測，意思是「肯定是～」。例如：A: Where is John? B: He must be studying in the classroom.（A：約翰在哪裡？B：他肯定正在教室念書。）

13. Who's the principal of the school?（這間學校的校長是誰？）

(A) He's coming here soon.（他就快到這裡了。）
(B) I don't care.（我不在乎。）
(C) I have no idea.（我不知道。）

答題解說

答案：(C)。題目是問「這間學校的校長是誰」，但選項中沒有出現人名，如果「不知道是誰」，回答「我不知道。」也是正確的回答，所以正確答案應為 (C)。I have no idea. = I don't know.。另外，選項 (B) 的 I don't care.（我不在乎。）似乎也是可能的回答，但比起「我不知道是誰。」的直接回答，是比較不恰當的，因為對方並非問你「你的感受」。

破題關鍵

針對 Who...? 的問句，就是兩種可能：第一，直接指出人名；第二，表達自己不知道是誰。

字詞解釋

principal [`prɪnsəpl] **n.** 校長；**adj.** 主要的

相關文法或用法補充

I don't care. 意思是「我不在乎。」在日常交際生活中常用到這個句子。例如：

A: I'm sorry to tell you that you failed the exam.
（我很抱歉要告訴你，這次考試你沒有通過。）

B: It doesn't matter. I don't care.（沒關係。我不在乎。）

14. **Are you still teaching English?**（你還在教英文嗎？）

(A) I haven't seen you for a long time.（我好久沒見到你了。）
(B) Not anymore.（已經不教了。）
(C) Neither am I.（我也沒有了。）

答題解說

答案：(B)。本題屬於是「是不是還在做某事」的問句，原本最直接的回答應該要有 Yes 或 No，但選項似乎看不到，所以必須仔細看每一個選項的敘述。(B) 的 Not anymore. 表示「不再教了。」是符合題意的回答。另外，如果沒聽清楚選項 (A) 的 "seen you"，只聽到 for a long time 的話，可能會誤以為是「已經很久沒教了」，必須特別注意。(C) 的 neither 表示「也不」的意思，是附和對方的話而非回答，因此也不是答案。

破題關鍵

聽到一開始的 Are you... 時，應該直覺反應這是個 Yes/No 問句，所以只要抓到題目與選項中關鍵字詞的搭配（Are you...? → No more./Not anymore），答案就很明顯了。

字詞解釋

neither [`niðə] **adv.** 也不

相關文法或用法補充

① 當你很長時間沒有見到某人，等再次見到時可以說 I haven't seen you for a long time，相當於 Long time no see。

② 否定副詞 neither 置於句首時，句子需倒裝。例如：He can't play the piano. Neither can I.（他不會彈鋼琴，我也不會。）

15. What happened to your hand?（你的手怎麼了？）

(A) I cut my finger.（我切到手指了。）
(B) I caught a cold.（我感冒了。）
(C) That's a good idea.（那是一個好主意。）

答題解說

答案：(A)。本題是問發生什麼（what）事情，因此回答時就要具體說明「發生什麼事」，選項中只有 (A)「我切到手指了。」是符合題意的回答，成為本題的正確答案。不是選項 (B) 的「我感冒了。」因為問的是「手怎麼了」而非「你怎麼了」，小心別被騙了。

破題關鍵

"What happened to...?" 表示「～怎麼了？」，但如果忽略 your hand 的部分，也可能誤選了 (B)，所以應注意 hand 與 finger 之間的連結。

字詞解釋

happen to... 發生在～ catch a cold 感冒

相關文法或用法補充

I'm sorry. 是用來表達「歉意」，但 I'm sorry to hear that. 這句話並沒有道歉的意思，而是指「很難過／很遺憾」聽到什麼消息。通常聽到朋友談及一些不幸的事情，你就可以用 I'm sorry to hear that. 來回應。另外，表示「同情」的用語還有：That's too bad.（太糟糕了。）、How sad!（真令人傷心。）

第三部分 簡短對話

16. M: Wow! Did you get Strawberry's newest model of smartphone?
W: No, Strawberry 11 is the newest, and mine is Ten. It's less expensive.
M: Well, it still looks so nice.

Question: What are the speakers talking about?
(A) A kind of fruit
(B) Several strawberry ice cream
(C) A phone

男：哇噢！你拿到草莓的最新款智慧手機了嗎？
女：不，草莓 11 才是最新款的，我這支是 10。它比較便宜些。

男：嗯，不過它看起來還是很棒。

問題：說話者們在談論什麼？

(A) 一種水果

(B) 幾個草莓冰淇淋

(C) 一支手機

第 1 回 第 2 回 第 3 回 第 4 回 第 5 回 第 6 回 第 7 回 第 8 回 第 9 回 第 10 回

答題解說

答案：(C)。題目問男女在談論什麼，其實就是指「對話的內容關於什麼」。首先，男子看到女子手上的新手機，於是問她是不是最新款的智慧手機（newest model of smartphone），後面兩人談話焦點也都跟這支「草莓」手機有關，所以答案是 (C)。(A) 與 (B) 都刻意使用與 Strawberry 有關的字詞來混淆答題，應特別注意。

破題關鍵

本題主要關鍵點：男子對女子說，妳拿到了 "the newest model of smartphone"，表示對於女子手上的智慧手機感到好奇。

字詞解釋

strawberry [ˋstrɔbɛrɪ] n. 草莓　**model** [ˋmɑdl̩] n. 款式，模型　**expensive** [ɪkˋspɛnsɪv] adj. 高價的，昂貴的

相關文法或用法補充

1. look 是個「連綴動詞」，像是「聽起來（sound）」、「聞起來（smell）」、「感覺上（feel）」、「嚐起來（taste）」等也都是。連綴動詞不能單獨存在，後面必須再接形容詞，作為主詞補語，句意才算完整。

2. 以第一人稱的「我」來說，me = 人稱代名詞受格；I = 人稱代名詞主格；myself = 反身代名詞；mine – 所有格代名詞。所有格代名詞是用來代替人稱代名詞的所有格及其所修飾的名詞。例如：Your dog is so cute, and so is mine.（你的狗好可愛，我的也是。）

17. **M: I'm glad we decided to take a walk.**

    W: I agree.

    M: Look. How clear the sky is, and how pretty those roses are.

    W: That's right. It's almost springtime.

    Question: Where are the man and the woman probably talking?

    (A) In a classroom　(B) At a bus stop　(C) In a park

233

男：我很開心我們決定出來散步一下。

女：我同意。

男：看。天空多麼明朗，還有那些玫瑰多美啊！

女：沒錯。春天差不多已經來臨了。

題目：男女可能在哪裡交談？

(A) 在教室裡　(B) 在公車站　(C) 在公園

答案：(C)。題目問的是對話發生的「地點」，基本上還是得理解對話內容才能作答。首先，男子很開心他們可以出來散步，接著談到天空如此明朗、花兒如此美麗，因此，不會是在室內，也不像是在公車站的對話，對話的地點應該是在公園。

整篇對話的關鍵句是男子第二次發言時：How clear the sky is, and how pretty those roses are.。顯然會是在戶外的公園或花園等地。

decide [dɪ`saɪd] v. 決定　**take a walk** 散步　**agree** [ə`gri] v. 同意　**rose** [roz] n. 玫瑰花　**springtime** [`sprɪŋ͵taɪm] n. 春天（的時節）　**bus stop** 公車站

疑問詞（5W1H）開頭的句子可不一定是問句喔！它也可以引導「感嘆句」，以驚嘆號（！）結尾。主要以兩種句型呈現：

1. What a/an + 形容詞 +單數名詞！例如：

   What an inspiring talk! 真是激勵人心的演講啊！

   What a lovely day! 今天真美好啊！

2. How + 形容詞 +（主詞 + 動詞）！

   How 的後面接形容詞或副詞，而 What 接名詞。

   How lovely (the baby is)!（這寶寶真可愛！）

   How smart!（真是聰明啊！）

18. M: Excuse me. Does this bus go to Taipei 101?

　　W: No. You need to go to the bus stop across the road.

　　M: How can I walk to the bus stop?

　　W: Just take the overpass over there. When you go down from it, keep walking to the 7-Eleven. It's right in front of the convenience store.

　　M: Thanks a lot.

Question: What does the man want to do?

(A) Buy some drinks

(B) Walk to Taipei 101

(C) Take a bus

男：請問一下。這班公車有到台北 101 嗎？

女：沒有。你得到馬路對面去搭公車。

男：我要怎麼走到公車站呢？

女：走那邊那座天橋。你下來之後一直走到 7-Eleven。公車站就在這間便利商店門口。

男：非常感謝。

題目：男子想要做什麼？

(A) 買些飲料　(B) 走到台北 101　(C) 搭公車

答題解說

答案：(C)。男子的第一句話說 "Does this bus go to Taipei 101?"，顯然他就是要搭公車前往台北 101，所以正確答案是 (C) Take a bus。選項 (A) 是想利用 7-Eleven 或 convenience store（便利商店）的內容來混淆答題；而選項 (B) 雖然提到台北 101，但從男子第一句就知道，他並非要走路去。

破題關鍵

本題詢問男子想要去做的事，看似單純且容易，但其實必須完整聽完整段對話，否則很容易誤選了其他兩個選項。但有時候如果你很確定其中一個選項是正確的，那麼其他選項就可以不必考慮。比如我們從男子的第一句話 Does this bus go to Taipei 101? 就可以斷定 (C) 的「搭公車（take a bus）」是正確答案。

字詞解釋

bus stop 巴士站　**across** [əˋkrɔs] 在～對面　**overpass** [͵ovəˋpæs] n. 天橋　**in front of**... 在～前面　**convenience store** 便利商店　**drink** [drɪŋk] n. 飲料

相關文法或用法補充

在英文裡，搭乘交通工具可以用 take、ride，或是單純使用介系詞 on、in、by 等。常見的是：

① by + 交通工具、on/in + a + 交通工具

②（搭乘）take + a + 交通工具

③（騎乘）ride + a + 騎乘的交通工具

例如：

❶ by bus（搭公車）= on a bus = take a bus

❷ by car（開車/搭車）= in a car = drive / take a car
❸ by taxi（搭計程車）= in a taxi = take a taxi
❹ by plane（搭飛機）= on a plane = take a plane
❺ by train（火車）= on a train = take a train
❻ by bike（騎腳踏車）= on a bike = ride a bike
※ take the MRT（搭捷運）

19. **W: Tickets for two adults and three children, please.**
   M: One hundred for each adult; free for children, if no more than 120 cm in height.
   W: Good. Here's a two-hundred-dollar bill.
   M: Wait a minute, please.

   Question: Who are the speakers?
   (A) A taxi driver and a passenger
   (B) A clerk and a customer
   (C) A manager and her employee

女：兩張成人票以及三張兒童票，謝謝。
男：每位成人 100 元；小孩身高不到 120cm 的話免費。
女：好的。這是 200 元紙鈔。
男：請稍候。
題目：談話者是誰？
(A) 一名計程車司機及一名乘客
(B) 一名售票員與一名顧客
(C) 一名經理與其員工

答題解說

答案：(B)。女子一開始說「兩張成人票以及三張兒童票」。顯然她要買票，所以對話場景可能是在遊樂園等售票口，接著男子回答說成人票價格，以及兒童票要價的規定，更可以肯定男子是售票員（遊樂場職員），女子是觀光客（顧客），所以正確答案為 (B)。

破題關鍵

先了解對話可能的場合，就可以輕鬆作答。本題的關鍵就是女子第一句 "Tickets for two adults and three children, please."，顯然這不會是對著計程車司機說的話，也不可能在公司場合！

第 1 回
第 2 回
第 3 回
第 4 回
第 5 回
第 6 回
第 7 回
第 8 回
第 9 回
第 10 回

adult [əˋdʌlt] n. 成人　**height** [haɪt] n. 身高，高度　**bill** [bɪl] n. 鈔票，帳單
passenger [ˋpæsndʒɚ] n. 乘客，旅客　**clerk** [klɝk] n. 職員，店員　**customer**
[ˋkʌstəmɚ] n. 顧客　**manager** [ˋmænɪdʒɚ] n. 經理，主管　**employee** [ˏɛmplɔɪˋi] n.
僱員

a ticket "to" 與 a ticket "for" 都很常見，但含義與用法都不同：

① a ticket to... 表示「一張去…的票」。例如：

He booked a ticket to Washington.（他預訂了一張去華盛頓的票。）

② a ticket for 表示「一張為…的票。」。例如：

Somebody gave me a ticket for a concert.（有人給了我一張音樂會的票。）

20. M: Would you like to go to the movies with me tonight?

W: I'm sorry, but I need to stay home to prepare for an important exam.

M: That's OK. Do you want me to help you review some lessons?

W: No need. Thank you.

Question: Why will the woman stay home tonight?

(A) She is ill.　(B) She needs to study.　(C) A friend will visit her later.

男：妳今晚要和我一起去看電影嗎？

女：抱歉，我得待在家裡準備一個重要的考試。

男：沒關係。你要我幫你複習一些課程嗎？

女：不需要。謝謝你。

題目：女子為何今晚要待在家？

(A) 她生病了。(B) 她必須念書。(C) 一位朋友晚點要來找她。

答案：(B)。題目問的是女子今晚要待在家的「原因」，所以應注意聽與 stay
home 有關的語句。她說「我得待在家裡準備一個重要的考試。」言下之意待在
家裡「是為了念書（study）」所以正確答案是 (B)。

女子要待在家的原因，當然要注意她說的話。如果有聽清楚 "I need to stay home
to prepare for an important exam." 這個關鍵句，不難選出正確答案。

would like to-V 想要，願意～　**go to the movies** 去看電影　**prepare** [prɪ`pɛr] **v.** 準備　**review** [rɪ`vju] **v.** 複審，重新檢討　**ill** [ɪl] **adj.** 生病的

go 後面可以接某些動名詞，形成「go + Ving」的結構，意思是「去（做某事）」，通常與休閒活動或其他非例行性事務有關。例如：go jogging 去慢跑、go shopping 去購物、go hiking 去健行、go traveling 去旅行

21. **W: How are you doing with your homework? You've spent the whole day on it.**
   M: Don't worry. See? Here it is.
   W: Great job!
   M: So can I play the video games now?

   Question: How does the woman like the boy's homework?
   (A) She thinks it's so-so.
   (B) She couldn't believe it's so bad.
   (C) It's well done.

   女：你的作業做得如何了呢？你已經花了一整天在這上面了。
   男：別擔心。看到沒？在這兒。
   女：做得很棒！
   男：所以我現在可以打電動了嗎？
   題目：女子覺得這男孩的作業怎樣？
   (A) 她覺得普普通通。
   (B) 她不敢相信是如此糟糕。
   (C) 做得相當不錯。

答案：(C)。本題問的是女子對於男孩的家庭作業的感覺或看法。一開始似乎很擔心，因為這男孩花了一整天時間在做。不過她第二次發言時說 Great Job!，這表示她很滿意男孩的作業，故正確答案應為 (C)。

Great job. 或 Good job. 是比較簡略的說法，也常說成 You did a great/good job. 用來稱讚對方工作做得好，也可以用 well-done 來表示。例如：How do you think of the work? —Well done.

第 1 回
第 2 回
第 3 回
第 4 回
第 5 回
第 6 回
第 7 回
第 8 回
第 9 回
第 10 回

字詞解釋

spend [spɛnd] v. 花（時間），花費　**worry** [ˋwɝɪ] v. 擔心　**so-so** [ˋsoso] adj. 馬馬虎虎的，普普通通的　**well**-**done** [wɛlˋdʌn] adj. 做得好的

相關文法或用法補充

倒裝句的 Here it is. 與 Here you are. 都有「東西在這；給你」的意思。但在表示「給別人東西」時，Here it is. 著重於東西本身，強調「東西在這裡」，而 Here you are. 著重於對方這個「人」，強調「給你」的這個行為。

22. M: Let me drive you home. It's almost midnight.

　　W: But my boyfriend will come here later and we're going to have a late night meal.

　　M: OK. I'm leaving now. See you tomorrow.

　　W: See you tomorrow.

　　Question: What did the man want to do?

　　(A) Give the woman a ride

　　(B) Have a late night meal with the woman

　　(C) Ask the woman to drive him home

男：我載你回家吧。現在幾乎是午夜了。
女：可是我男友晚一點要來這裡，而且我們要去吃消夜。
男：好的。那我先離開了。明天見。
女：明天見。
題目：男子想做什麼？
(A) 載女子一趟。
(B) 與女子一起去吃消夜。
(C) 拜託女子載他回家。

答題解說

答案：(A)。本題問的是男子想要做什麼。可以從一開始男子向女子提議說「我載你回家」得知，(A) 是正確答案。give somebody a ride 就是「騎車／開車送某人一程」的意思。選項 (B) 與 (C) 都刻意使用對話中相同字詞（late night meal、drive... home）來混淆答題，須特別注意。

破題關鍵

drive 當及物動詞後面接「人」時，可以表示「開車送～（某人）」，相當於「give + 人 + a ride」。但必須注意的是，沒有「ride + 人 + home」的說法，否則

會變成「把某人（當馬）騎回家」的意思了！

字詞解釋

drive [draɪv] **v.** 開車送（人）　　**midnight** [ˈmɪdˌnaɪt] **n.** 午夜　　***late night meal** 宵夜

相關文法或用法補充

當你要跟某人說「我先走了。」千萬別說成 "I go first." 或 "I leave first."，否則外國人會在心裡 OS：「那誰是第二個（second）、第三個（third）要走的。」而是要說 I'm leaving now.。另外，你也可以說 "I have to go/run."、"Gotta go."。另外，如果要禮讓別人先，也別說 "You go first."，而是 "After you."。

23. M: I think the farmers will be happy about the weather.

W: That's indeed good news to them, but our clothes over there are still wet. I can't hang them out.

M: Just use the dryer.

W: I think I have to do so.

Question: How will the weather be?

(A) Sunny　　(B) Cloudy　　(C) Rainy

男：我想農夫們對於這樣的天氣會很高興。

女：那的確對他們來說是好消息，但我們那邊的衣服都還是濕的。我無法拿出去曬。

男：用烘衣機吧。

女：我想也只能這樣了。

問題：天氣會如何？

(A) 晴天　　(B) 陰天　　(C) 雨天

答題解說

答案：(C)。本題問的是「天氣會如何」，可以從前兩句得到答案。男子第一句話說「農夫們對於這樣的天氣會很高興」，接著女子提到，他們無法把衣服拿出去曬。可以推知，答案應該是下雨天。故正確答案應為 (C)。

破題關鍵

基本上，無法從第一句「農夫會喜歡的天氣」去斷定答案是晴天或雨天（但肯定不會是「陰天」）。所以重點還是在「無法曬衣服」。hang... out 是本題關鍵字詞，意思是「將～晾在外面」。

第 1 回
第 2 回
第 3 回
第 4 回
第 5 回
第 6 回
第 7 回
第 8 回
第 9 回
第 10 回

字詞解釋

indeed [ɪn`did] **adv.** 確實，的確　**wet** [wɛt] **adj.** 濕的　**hang out** 把～晾或掛出去
dryer [draɪɚ] **n.** 烘衣機　**sunny** [`sʌnɪ] **adj.** 晴朗的，陽光充足的　**cloudy** [`klaʊdɪ]
adj. 陰天的　**rainy** [`renɪ] **adj.** 下雨的

相關文法或用法補充

hang 這個動詞也算是相當基本的字彙，不過從它衍生出來的動詞片語或其他詞
類，可說是相當廣泛。hang out 就是其中一種片語。此片語有類似及物動詞及不
及物動詞的兩種用法，但意思不一樣：

❶ 及物動詞 → 掛出，伸出。例如：They hung out the national flags from the
window.（他們從窗戶掛出了國旗。）

❷ 不及物動詞 → 出去玩，消磨時間，到外面晃晃。例如：I don't feel like
hanging out tonight.（我今晚不想出去鬼混。）

24. W: Do you want to go mountain climbing with us this weekend?
 M: I have an important English test next Monday, so I need to go to the
 library to study.
 W: Looks like you've studied so hard. You must pass it!
 M: I hope so, but I still don't think I'm well-prepared.

 Question: How does the man look?
 (A) Worried　(B) Confident　(C) Excited

女：你這個週末想和我們一起去登山嗎？
男：我下週一有個重要的英文考試，所以我得去圖書館念書。
女：看起來你非常用功。你一定會通過的。
男：但願如此，但我不認為我已經做好準備了。
問題：男子看起來如何？
(A) 憂心　(B) 自信　(C) 興奮

答題解說

答案：(A)。本題問的是「男子看起來如何」，也就是他當下的心情，所以可以
從他的發言中找到答案。男子第二次發言中提到 "I hope so, but I still don't think
I'm well-prepared."（但願如此，但我不認為我已經做好準備了。）顯然他是憂
心忡忡的，而不會是「自信」或「興奮」。故正確答案為 (A)。

破題關鍵

動詞 prepare 是「準備」的意思，prepared 轉為形容詞用，表示「已做了準備

241

的」，那麼 well-prepared 就是 prepared 的「加強版」，表示「充分準備的」。所以只要聽出 "...don't think... well-prepared"，就可推知說話者是「感到擔憂的」。

mountain climbing 爬山　**library** [ˈlaɪˌbrɛrɪ] n. 圖書館　**well-prepared** [ˈwɛl prɪˈpɛrd] adj. 準備就緒的　**worried** [ˈwɜrɪd] adj. 擔心的　**confident** [ˈkɑnfədənt] adj. 自信的　**excited** [ɪkˈsaɪtɪd] adj. 感到興奮的

相關文法或用法補充

❶ exciting 是「令人興奮的」意思，用來修飾「事物」，如果是 excited 的話，表示「感到興奮的」，用來修飾「人」。-ed 與 -ing 的差別，是很多類型考試最愛考的。只要記住一點：-ed 表示「感到～」，-ing 表示「令人～」；是「人」才會「感到～」，是「事物」才會「令人～」。

❷ Looks like 是 "It looks like" 的簡寫，後面接一個完整的句子，也可以說成 It seems that/It appears that...。例如：It looks like the meeting is going to end soon.（看來會議快結束了。）= It seems that/It appears that the meeting is going to end soon.

25. M: Hello, may I speak to Julia?
    W: Julia? You must have the wrong number.
    M: Oh, I'm so sorry to have bothered you.
    W: That's all right.

Question: Who is Julia?
(A) A friend of the woman
(B) Someone the woman doesn't know
(C) A person who is sitting next to the man

男：哈囉，請找茱莉亞。
女：茱莉亞？你一定是打錯電話了。
男：噢，打擾您了，真是抱歉。
女：沒關係。
問題：茱莉亞是誰？
(A) 女子的一位友人　(B) 女子不認識的人　(C) 正坐在男子旁的人

答題解說

答案：(B)。題目問的是「茱莉亞是誰」，所以必須注意對話內容中提到與 Julia

有關的內容。首先男子打電話來找茱莉亞（...may I speak to Julia?），但女子回答說「你一定是打錯電話了。」顯然這是一通打錯的電話，女子並不認識茱莉亞，故正確答案應為（B）。

破題關鍵

本題關鍵句 "You must have the wrong number." 當中的 number 是指 telephone number（電話號碼），動詞 have 也可以用 dial（撥打）取代。

字詞解釋

bother [ˋbɑðɚ] **v.** 煩擾，打攪　　**all right** 可以的，沒問題的　　**next to**... 在～旁邊

相關文法或用法補充

「打錯電話」可別說成 "wrong phone" 喔！如果接到打錯的電話，也可以問對方打幾號，可以說 What number are you calling?。如果對方撥打的號碼是正確的，但確實沒有這個人，可以說 "That's our number, but we have no one by that name."。又假設對方說 Is that 1234-5678? 但這不是你的電話號碼，你可以說 No, this is 1234-5679.

第四部分 短文聽解

共 5 題，每題有三個圖片選項，請聽光碟放音機播出的題目，並選出一個最適當的圖片。每題只播出一遍。

For question number 26, please look at the three pictures.

Question number 26: Listen to the following news report. Which picture best describes the talk?

Yesterday in Water Park, there was a famous international festival for children. It was such a clear sunny day that so many parents brought their kids to enjoy some popular water sports and activities. Each of the children looked very excited to play with their little friends. Almost everyone, including the parents, though getting all wet, has enjoyed themselves to their hearts' content!

第 1 回
第 2 回
第 3 回
第 4 回
第 5 回
第 6 回
第 7 回
第 8 回
第 9 回
第 10 回

請看以下三張圖。並仔細聆聽以下新聞報導。哪一張圖最能夠描繪這則談話？

昨日在「水公園」有一場有名的兒童國際嘉年華會。當天天氣相當晴朗，因此許多父母帶著他們的孩子來享受一些相當受歡迎的水上運動及活動。每個孩子和他們的小小朋友一起玩樂，大家看起來都相當興奮。幾乎所有人，包括父母，雖然全身都濕透了，都能夠盡情玩樂。

答題解說

答案：(A)。題目問的是談話內容是在敘述哪一張圖。其中提到「許多父母帶著他們的孩子來享受一些相當受歡迎的水上運動及活動（many parents brought their kids to enjoy some popular water sports and activities）」。在觀察三張圖後可以發現，只有(A)這張圖是符合敘述的。

破題關鍵

首先觀察三張圖後，可以發現三張圖都是父母帶著孩子出來遊玩，只是場景不同而已。這則談話內容的最快解題方式就在於哪一張符合「水上運動及活動（water sports and activities）」、「全身都濕透了（getting all wet）」這些描述。很明顯答案就是(A)了。

字詞解釋

famous [ˋfeməs] **adj.** 著名的　　**international** [ˌɪntəˋnæʃənl] **adj.** 國際性的　　**festival** [ˋfɛstəvl] **n.** 節日，節慶活動　　**popular** [ˋpɑpjələ] **adj.** 受歡迎的　　**to one's heart's content** 盡情地

相關文法或用法補充

so...that... 與　such...that... 都是相當常見的句型，兩者都是用來表達「如此地…以致於…」，但兩者在文法上是有差異的。

① so... that... ：so 在此句型中當副詞，其後接形容詞或副詞，表示「原因」，而 that 用來引導表示「結果」的副詞子句。例如：

❶ The speaker spoke so slowly that most of the audience fell asleep. （演說者說話太慢，以致於大部分聽眾都睡著了。）

❷ The suitcase is so heavy that I can't move it. （這個手提箱太重我無法搬動它。）

② such... that... ：such 的後面要接名詞。例如：

Jack drove such a big car that it's hard for him to park it here.
傑克開一部如此大台的車子，因此他很難將車子停在這裡。

③ 當 such 後面的名詞片語含有形容詞，且後面是單數可數名詞時，就可以用 so... that... 句型替換。以上句為例：

Jack drove such a big car that it's hard for him to park it here.
= Jack drove so big a car that it's hard for him to park it here.

For question number 27, please look at the three pictures.

Question number 27: Listen to the following talk. What happened to the speaker?

Yesterday evening, when I drove on my way home, I was sending a message to my girlfriend. All of a sudden, a little cat suddenly showed up in front, and I quickly stepped on the brake to avoid hitting it. Luckily, it was safe and I took a deep breath. I almost had a heart attack! I think I won't use a cellphone next time when I drive.

請看以下三張圖。並仔細聆聽以下談話。說話者發生什麼事？
昨天晚上，當我開車在回家的路上時，我正要傳送訊息給我的女朋友。突然間，一隻小貓出現在前面，然後我很快地踩煞車以避免撞上牠。所幸牠沒事，所以我深吸了一口氣。我幾乎要心臟病發作了！我想我下次開車的時候不會再使用手機了。

答題解說

答案：(A)。首先，說話者提到他在開車時使用手機傳訊息，然後前方出現一隻貓（a little cat suddenly showed up in front），然後緊急踩煞車（quickly stepped on the brake），還好牠沒事（Luckily, it was safe...）。聽到這些敘述，應該就很容易選出正確答案(A)了。

破題關鍵

三張圖都是某人在開車，(A) 與 (B) 的差別只有貓與小孩，而 (A) 與 (C) 差別是有沒有撞到貓。因此，如果有先仔細看過三張圖，將彼此的差異稍微記住，然後在聽到 "a little cat" 以及 "it was safe" 時，就可以立即選出正確答案。

字詞解釋

on one's way home 在某人回家路上 **all of a sudden** adv. 突然間 **show up** 出現 **front** [frʌnt] n. 前方 **step on...** 用腳踩在～ **brake** [brek] n. 煞車 **avoid** [ə`vɔɪd] v. 避開，躲開 **breath** [brɛθ] n. 呼吸，氣息 **heart attack** 心臟病發作

「過去進行式」是指過去某個時刻正在發生或持續的動作。例如這裡的 "Yesterday evening, when I drove on my way home, I was sending a message to my girlfriend." ，這表示在「開車回家的路上」這個時間點，「正在使用手機發送訊息」。但必須注意的是，過去進行式不能「單獨使用」，也就是說，它必須有一個過去的時間參考點才行。所以不能說 "I was doing homework." ，而是應該說 "I was doing homework at three o'clock/when my mother came home..." 。

For question number 28, please look at the three pictures.

Question number 28: Listen to the following announcement. Where could you probably hear it?

Good afternoon, ladies and gentlemen. This is Captain speaking. We're going to take off in 5 minutes. Our flight will take 2 hours and 30 minutes. Please do not turn on your mobile phones and other electronic devices throughout the flight, and the notebook computers are not allowed to be used during take-off and landing. Please stay in your seat and have your seatbelt fastened. Thanks for your attention and have a nice trip.

請看以下三張圖。仔細聽以下廣播。你可能在什麼地方聽到這項廣播？
各位先生女士，午安。我是機長。我們即將在 5 分鐘之後起飛。我們的飛行時間是兩小時三十分鐘。在整個飛行途中，請不要開啟您的行動電話以及其他電子裝置，而筆記型電腦於起飛及降落時也禁止使用。請留在您的座位上，並將安全帶繫緊。感謝您的注意，祝您旅途愉快。

答案：(B)。首先，題目句一定要聽懂，這是個「問地方」的題目，所以即使聽不出 announcement（宣布）這個字，看看三張不同的交通工具，很容易知道要問的是「播放內容的場景是在哪裡？」接著，仔細聽錄音播放內容，即可了解這是什麼地方的廣播內容。其中提到 "Our flight will take 2 hours and 30 minutes."

（我們的飛行時間是兩小時三十分鐘。）這樣應該不難知道這是什麼地方了吧。

破題關鍵

這則廣播內容的關鍵字詞很多，像是 take off（起飛）、flight（班機，飛行）、do not turn on your mobile phones（不要開啟您的行動電話）、during take-off and landing（於起飛及降落時），抓住其中之一都可以輕鬆選出正確答案。

字詞解釋

captain [`kæptɪn] n. 船長，機長　**take off** v. 起飛　**turn on** v. 開啟（電器設備等）　**electronic** [ɪlɛk`trɑnɪk] adj. 電子的　**device** [dɪ`vaɪs] n. 設備　**flight** [flaɪt] n. 班機，飛行　**allow** [ə`laʊ] v. 允許　**landing** [`lændɪŋ] n. 降落，著陸　**seatbelt** [`sitbɛlt] n. 安全帶　**fasten** [`fæsn] v. 紮牢，繫緊　**attention** [ə`tɛnʃən] n. 注意

相關文法或用法補充

在英文裡，主要有兩種「表達未來」的方式：「will + 原形 V」與「be going to + 原形 V」，初學英文的人都會認為兩者沒有差別，但其實它們的使用時機與要表達的意思是不太一樣的，尤其是「做決定的時機」不同：be going to 通常表示「早已經有計畫，已決定好」要去做某件事；但 will 時通常表示在「講話的當下才做這個決定」，或是對於這件事「並沒有明確的計畫」。所以就「時間點」來看，"I'm going to ... (future plan)." 通常指較「短期」的未來，可能馬上就要去做了；而 I will ... (future plan). 通常指較「長期」的未來。例如：

① I will see a doctor.（我將要去看醫生）
　→ 說話當下的決定
② I am going to see a doctor.（我就要去看醫生了。）
　→ 在說話之前就決定好了。

For question number 29, please look at the three pictures.

Question number 29: Listen to the following short talk. What is the speaker going to buy?

 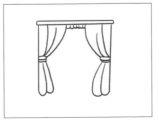 

My wife and I will be moving to a new house next month. My parents said they

will buy us a set of furniture that includes a table and a long couch made of wood. So we are looking for some curtains that go with that furniture. A good friend of ours has suggested we go to a new shop where we can have many excellent items to choose from.

請看以下三張圖。仔細聽以下簡短談話。說話者將要去會買什麼東西？
我太太和我將於下個月搬到一間新房子。我父母說，他們會買一組傢俱給我們，包括一張桌子及一張木製長椅。所以我們正要去找一些搭配那樣家具的窗簾。我們的一位朋友建議我們到一家新開的店看看，那裡有很多很棒的物件可供選擇。

答題解說

答案：(B)。題目問的是說話者「可能會買什麼東西」，內容中提到，說話者的父母會買一組家具給他們（My parents said they will buy us a set of furniture... ），而他們要去買窗簾來搭配父母贈送的傢俱（looking for some curtains that go with that furniture ），所以正確答案就是 (B)。

破題關鍵

本題的設計其實就是刻意用一開始提到的傢俱，包括一張桌子及一張木製長椅，來誤導考生答題。特別是三張圖中，有兩張（A 與 C）是類似的，所以考生可能傾向認為答案不是 (A) 就是 (C)。但是題目問的是「說話者」準備要買什麼，而不是「說話者的父母」要送什麼，所以題目一定要先聽清楚。

字詞解釋

furniture [ˋfɝnɪtʃə] **n.** 傢俱　　**couch** [kautʃ] **n.** 長沙發，睡椅　　**be made of**... 以～做成　　**wood** [wʊd] **n.** 木頭，木材　　**look for**... 找尋　　**curtain** [ˋkɝtn] **n.** 窗簾，門簾　　**go with**... 與～相配　　**excellent** [ˋɛksḷənt] **adj.** 極好的，傑出的　　**choose** [tʃuz] **v.** 選擇，挑選

相關文法或用法補充

go with... 本來是「和～一起去」的意思，因而衍生出幾種不同的意義：

① 與～相配：This pair of shoes really go with your dress. （這雙鞋子真的很配妳的洋裝。）

　　→ 相當於 match、suit

② 伴隨，和～一起存在：Happiness doesn't necessarily go with money. （幸福未必伴隨金錢而來。）

③ 和～約會：I saw Tom go with that girl yesterday. （我昨天看見 Tom 和那個女孩約會。）→ 相當於 date

For question number 30, please look at the three pictures.

Question number 30: Listen to the following talk. What is Jenny going to do on Saturday?

Jenny has a lot of things to do this week. On Monday and Tuesday morning, she has to teach a new table tennis class. From Wednesday to Friday, she needs to leave town to visit some long-lost friends. Yet she has decided to put off a date with her boyfriend Brian on Saturday because there will be a big party at her place the next day, so there is so much to prepare for that.

請看以下三張圖。並仔細聆聽以下談話。Jenny 週六將要去做什麼？
Jenny 這週有許多事情要做。週一及週二早上，她得去教一堂新開的桌球課。而週三至週五，她必須離開城鎮去拜訪一些很久沒見的朋友。不過她已決定將原定週六與男友 Brian 的約會延後，因為隔天在她家要舉辦一個大型的派對，所以有許多事情要準備。

答題解說

答案：(C)。題目問的是 Jenny 週六要做的事情，所以首先應注意內容中提到 Saturday 的部分：Yet she has decided to put off a date with her boyfriend Brian on Saturday...（不過她已決定將原定週六與男友 Brian 的約會延後），所以答案不會是 (B)。接著又說，因為隔天（週日）在她家要舉辦一個大型的派對，所以有許多事情要準備（...there will be a big party at her place the next day, so there is so much to prepare for that.）。顯然大型派對是在週日，而不是週六，所以 (A) 也是錯誤的。圖 (C) 正好符合「有許多事情要準備」（也就是為了隔天的派對而布置家裡）。

破題關鍵

本題最關鍵的一句話當然就是 "...put off a date with her boyfriend Brian on Saturday"。當然，你要知道 put off 的意思是「將～延後」，否則很可能就直接選了 (B)。剩下的「一群人聚會」以及「進行布置」兩張圖，只要聽懂 "a big party at her place the next day"，就可以將 (A) 排除掉了。

table tennis n. 桌球　**long-lost** [ˋlɔŋˋlɔst] adj. 久違的，好久不見的　**decide** [dɪˋsaɪd] v. 決定，決意　**put off** v. 推遲，延後　**date** [det] n. 約會　**place** [ples] n. 住所，寓所　**prepare** [prɪˋpɛr] v. 準備

相關文法或用法補充

morning、afternoon 或 evening 的前面要用 in 還是 on，總是一個令人困惑的問題！為什麼我們用 in the morning、in the afternoon、in the evening，但卻用 on Monday morning、on Tuesday afternoon 呢？其實 in 與 on 在表達「時間點」時，差別就在於「時間點的長短」。因為 in 後面通常接「月份、季節、年、世紀、一段長而非特定的時間」，而 on 後面通常接「特定日期、日子、星期」等比較短的時間點。因為「週一早上」、「週二下午」強調的是「特定的時間」，所以用 on；而「在上午／下午／晚上」都是指幾個小時的不特定時間，所以用 in。至於說 "at night"（在夜晚）又該怎麼解釋呢？因為 at 用在一段「特定」的時刻，而 night 一般是母語人士表示睡前沒事要做的那段「特定時間」，大概就是晚上九到十二點間，所以相較 morning、afternoon 這些範圍較大且較無特定的時間，就用 at night 來表示。

1.　I didn't have a _____ to eat my soup with.（我沒有湯匙可以喝湯。）

　　(A) teapot　(B) dish　(C) plate　(D) spoon

答題解說

答案：(D)。「用湯匙喝湯」、「喝湯要用湯匙」，這是基本的飲食習慣，所以正確答案是 (D)。

(A) teapot 是「茶壺」的意思；(B) dish 與 (C) plate 都有「盤子」的意思。

破題關鍵

本題關鍵語句是 eat my soup。請注意，「喝湯」可不是 "drink one's soup"，別被中文給誤導了。了解這是「喝湯」的意思之後，(D) spoon 當然是最有可能的答案了。

字詞解釋

teapot ['ti,pɑt] n. 茶壺　　**plate** [plet] n. 盤子，碟子　　**spoon** [spun] n. 湯匙

soup [sup] n. 湯

相關文法或用法補充

介系詞 with 常見的意義與用法：

① 表示「伴隨，與～一起」：I often go to the supermarket with my mother on Sundays.（星期天我常常和媽媽一起去超市。）

② 表示「利用～（工具等）」：You are not allowed to fill the form with a pencil.（你不能用鉛筆填寫此表。）

③ 表示「裝滿、填滿」：The roof of the house was covered with snow.（屋頂被雪覆蓋了。）

④ 表示態度上的「贊同，站在同一邊」：I'm afraid I can't agree with you.（恐怕我不能同意你的看法。）

⑤ 表示衣著方面的「穿，戴」：The man with glasses is my Chinese teacher.（那個戴眼鏡的男士是我的中文老師。）

⑥ 表示「附加上去，攜帶」：Students are prohibited to carry mobile phones with them in this school.（這所學校禁止學生攜帶手機。）

2. **I use the electronic _____ if I don't know how to spell a word.**（如果我不知道如何拼寫某個單字時，我就會查電子字典。）

   (A) dictionary　(B) typewriter　(C) newspaper　(D) magazine

   答案：(A)。句子大意是「不會拼字（spell a word）就去查字典」，所以正確答案是(A)。

   (B) typewriter 是「打字機」的意思；(C) newspaper 是「報紙」；(D) magazine 是「雜誌」。

   破題關鍵

   本題關鍵語句是 spell a word，「拼字」肯定和「報紙」或「雜誌」沒有任何關係，但可能與「打字機」有關，所以必須再進一步確認句意是「不知道如何拼字」，才能夠正確選出「字典」這個答案。

   字詞解釋

   electronic [ɪlɛk`trɑnɪk] **adj.** 電子的　**spell** [spɛl] **v.** 拼寫，拼讀　**dictionary** [`dɪkʃən͵ɛrɪ] **n.** 字典　**typewriter** [`taɪp͵raɪtɚ] **n.** 打字機　**newspaper** [`njuz͵pepɚ] **n.** 報紙　**magazine** [͵mægə`zin] **n.** 雜誌

   相關文法或用法補充

   if 是一個從屬連接詞，可以引導條件子句，意思是「假設，如果」。這個條件子句可置於句首，也可以置於句末。if 引導的條件句可用來表達「假設語氣」，也可以用來表達「直述句」。由於「假設語氣」牽涉的範圍較廣且難度較高，在此僅列舉「假設直述句」的例子做說明：

   ❶ I won't go out if it rains tomorrow.（要是明天下雨我就不出門。）
   → 條件句和主句都用現在簡單式時，表示陳述一件事實。

   ❷ If you don't study hard, you won't pass the exam.（如果你不努力，就無法通過考試。）
   → 條件句用現在簡單式，主句用未來式（will、won't），表示「很有可能發生的事」。

3. **Each hand has one thumb and four _____.**（每一隻手有一根拇指及四根手指。）

   (A) feet　(B) teeth　(C) fingers　(D) toes

   答案：(C)。句意是，一隻手有一根拇指（thumb）及四根手指。所以正確答案是

(C) fingers。

(A) feet 是 foot（腳）的複數，(B) teeth 是 tooth（牙齒）的複數，(D) toes 是 toe（腳趾）的複數，置入空格中的話，都會形成不合邏輯或奇怪的句意。

破題關鍵

本題關鍵字是空格前的 thumb，這是初級範圍內的單字，只要知道它是「拇指」的話，自然就能與 finger（手指）連結在一起。toe 是指腳趾頭，它也是可數名詞，其複數形式是 toes。

字詞解釋

thumb [θʌm] **n.** 大拇指　　**finger** [ˋfɪŋɡɚ] **n.** 手指　　**toe** [to] **n.** 腳趾頭

相關文法或用法補充

不定代名詞 each 具有名詞和形容詞的性質，在句子中可作主詞、受詞或形容詞，可以指「人」也可以指「物」，其具體用法如下：

❶ 不定代名詞 each 意思是「每一個」：We each want a complete and happy family.（我們人人想有一個完整幸福的家庭。）

❷ each 後面可以接介系詞 of，of 後面須接複數可數名詞或複數代名詞，且須搭配單數動詞：

① Each of the books is interesting.（每本書都有趣。）

② Each of them made an excellent speech.（他們每人的演講都非常出色。）

❸ each 作形容詞時，修飾單數可數名詞，意思是「每一個的」：

Each book in the library has a number.（圖書館的每本書都有號碼。）

4. **I can't find my keys. Did you see where I put _____?**（我找不到鑰匙。你有看見我放在哪裡嗎？）

(A) they　(B) theirs　(C) it　(D) them

答題解說

答案：(D)。空格要填入的是一個代替前面提到名詞的代名詞，且空格前有及物動詞 put，所以要填入受格的代名詞，(A) 可直接排除。(B)「他們的（東西）所指為何並不清楚；(C) 代替單數名詞，但前一句（I can't find my keys.）並沒有這樣的單數名詞出現。故正確答案為 (D) them 代替的是 keys。

破題關鍵

若先看過四個選項的話，就會知道這題意考的是「代名詞」，然後再看到前一句的 keys 時，即可輕鬆選出 them 這個答案了。

以第三人稱的「他／她／它」來說，he/she/it 是人稱代名詞主格，受格是 him/her/it，為單數；they 是人稱代名詞主格，受格是 them，為複數；himself/herself/itself 是反身代名詞；his/hers/theirs 是所有格代名詞。it 只能指「物」，但是 they/them 可以指「人」或「物」。

5. **Madonna used to be one of the _____ famous singers in the world. Almost everybody knew her.**（瑪丹娜曾是世界最有名的歌手之一。幾乎每個人都知道她。）

(A) every　(B) more　(C) much　(D) most

答案：(D)。空格要填入的是一個修飾其後形容詞（famous）的副詞，且符合「世界最有名的歌手之一」的句意，故正確答案為 (D) most。(A) every 後面不可接複數名詞（singers）；(B) more 不符句意，因為前面有 "one of..."（其中之一），應與「最高級」連用；(C) much 後面須接不可數名詞。

本題只要有注意到關鍵詞彙 "one of... in the world"（世界…之一），應該可以直接聯想到「最高級」是正確答案。

used to-V 曾經～　**famous** [ˋfeməs] **adj.** 有名的

used to-V 的意思是「過去曾經／經常…」（但現在不再做），在這種用法中，use 都用過去式 used，而且後面的 to 是不定詞的 to，所以直接接原形動詞。
另外，"be used to + Ving" 是「習慣於…」，這個用法中的 to 是介系詞，因此後面必須接動名詞，例如：I'm used to drinking a glass of warm water after I wake up.（我習慣在起床之後喝一杯溫水。）但別忘了，use 原本的意思是「使用」，為及物動詞，所以它的被動式（be used to-V）也常常受到混淆。因此，最重要的還是必須看清楚句意。

6. **I can't hear you! Please _____.**（我聽不到你說話。請說大點聲！）

(A) help me　　　　　　(B) speak up
(C) go away　　　　　　(D) lend me some money

答題解說

答案：(B)。空格要填入的是一個動詞片語，且必須與前一句（I can't hear you!）的句意連貫，所以正確答案是 (B) speak up。

破題關鍵

「hear + 人」是「聽見某人說話」的意思，而 speak up 表示「放大音量說話」，從 up（往上）應該很容易判斷 speak up 的意思吧！

字詞解釋

speak up 響亮地說　**go away** 走開

相關文法或用法補充

除了「hear + 人」的用法之外，也要知道「hear from + 人」，以及「hear of/about + 事情」的意思喔！hear from 通常用於書信當中，表示「得到某人的消息」。例如：I haven't heard from you for a long time.（已經很久沒有你的消息了。）

至於 hear of，是指聽說過某人或某物的存在，指的是這個人或物的本身，表示知道世界上有這麼個人或事物。例如：Have you heard of the singer Jay Chou?（你聽過周杰倫這個歌手嗎?）而 hear about... 是指聽說「關於」某人或某物的事，指的是和這個人或物相關的事情。例如：I didn't hear about her accident.（我沒有聽說關於她發生的意外。）

7. **The thief raised _____ of his hands after he was caught by the policeman.**（這小偷被警察抓到後舉起他的雙手。）

(A) each　(B) both　(C) all　(D) two

答題解說

答案：(B)。空格後面是介系詞（of），因此應填入一個代名詞，"------ of his hands" 作為 raised（舉起）的受詞。因為人的手只有兩隻，所以只能選 both（兩者）這個答案。但如果選 (D) two 的話，意思會變成這個賊可能不只兩隻手了。

破題關鍵

看到空格後的 hands 直接聯想到「人只有兩隻手」這個事實，就可直接選出正確的答案了。

字詞解釋

thief [θif] n. 賊，小偷　**raise** [rez] v. 舉起　**caught** [kɔt] v. 抓到（動詞 catch 的過去式、過去分詞）　**policeman** [pə`lismən] n. 警察

raise 和 rise 都有「增加，上升」的意思，兩者最大的不同就是 raise 是及物動詞，後面要接受詞，且主詞通常為「人」（因為人才能做出「舉起、提升」這個動作）而 rise 是不及物動詞，後面不用加上任何受詞。另外，也要注意 rise 是不規則動詞，過去式是 rose，過去分詞是 risen。rise 的常見意思是「上升、升高」。例如：The sun is about to rise.（太陽就要升起。）

8. _____ going, and you'll become better and better.（繼續加油，你會變得越來越好的。）

(A) Keep　(B) Kept　(C) Keeping　(D) To keep

答題解說

答案：(A)。四個選項是 keep 這個動詞的不同形態，因此應先就文法結構的觀點看。首先，and 後面是個完整句子，顯然逗號（,）前是個祈使句，故應填入一個原形動詞，正確答案為 (A)。

破題關鍵

在句子中只要看到 "..., and you'll" 這樣的結構，應立即聯想個祈使句／命令句。

字詞解釋

better [ˋbɛtɚ] **adj.** 較佳的，更好的

相關文法或用法補充

keep 表示「保持，持有，保有」，常用於 keep+Ving（動名詞）及 keep+N（名詞）的結構。例如：

① David keeps asking the teacher questions.（David 一直問老師問題。）
② Tom keeps diary all the time.（Tom 一直都有在寫日記。）

9. I'm about to get off at the next exit, and _____ be there very soon.（我就要在下個出口下匝道了，很快就會抵達那裡。）

(A) would　(B) will　(C) won't　(D) are going to

答題解說

答案：(B)。四個選項都是助動詞，但因為主詞是 I，所以 (D) are going to 可直接先排除掉。句子大意是「就快要下交流道，且即將抵達」，所以 (C) won't 不符句意。而助動詞 would 除了是 will 的過去式，也帶有不確定的臆測意味，也不符

句意。因此答案只可能是未來式助動詞的 (B) will。

第1回 第2回 第3回 第4回 第5回 第6回 第7回 第8回 第9回 第10回

破題關鍵

本題的主要參考指標是前面的 I'm about to...，"be about to-V" 的意思與 be going to 很接近，但是更強調「就要…，即將…」，當然也表示「未來」的時態。

字詞解釋

be about to-V 即將　**get off** 駛離　**exit** [ˈɛksɪt] n. 出口，（快速道路的）匝道

相關文法或用法補充

「be about to」和「will」與「be going to」一樣都是用來表示未來即將、將要做某些事，但又有些不同。比方說，如果你正要打電話給某人，正好這時候對方打電話來問「你怎麼沒打給我？」這時候你就可以說 "Oh! I'm about to call you."，這會比 "I'm going to call you." 的時間差距更短。當然，如果你只是想敷衍對方，可以說 I will call you.。

10. **I lost my pencil. Can you lend me _____?**（我把我的鉛筆弄丟了。你的可以借我一下嗎？）

(A) it　(B) itself　(C) one　(D) yours

答題解說

答案：(D)。第一句意思是要告訴對方，自己的筆不見了；於是第二句接著說，可以借用「你的鉛筆（your pencil）」嗎？所以正確答案是 yours (= your pencil)。(A) it 以及 (C) one 都是用來指提到過的名詞，在此不符合語意與邏輯；反身代名詞的 (B) itself 在此並無指稱之對象，且不合文法規則。

破題關鍵

這是「所有格代名詞」的考題，yours = your pencil，這是為了避免 pencil 這個名詞的重複。

字詞解釋

lend [lɛnd] 借出

相關文法或用法補充

以第一人稱的「我」來說，me = 人稱代名詞受格；I = 人稱代名詞主格；myself = 反身代名詞；mine = 所有格代名詞。所有格代名詞是用來代替人稱代名詞的所有格及其所修飾的名詞。例如：Your car is new, but mine is old.（你的車是新的，但我的是老舊的。）

第二部分 段落填空

Everybody knows that doing exercise is good to health, and there are quite a few ways to do that. Sport games, for some people who like to seek **victory** or championship, may be a choice. Some people, however, do not like sports or team games **because** there must be losers or someone who falls behind or stay in the last place. In my opinion, you can do and enjoy many things in life, and **it is not necessary for you to compete with anybody**. Sometimes you feel unhappy after you play a sport game. You can just go roller-skating, jogging, swimming, hiking, **biking**, or even take a walk with friends along a riverside. Of course, if you are used to staying under pressure, sports might be better to you.

中文翻譯

　　大家都知道運動有益健康，而且運動的方法有許。競賽型運動，對某些喜歡追求勝利或冠軍的人來說，可能是個選擇。不過，有些人不喜歡競賽型運動或團隊比賽，因為一定會有輸家，或落後者或是拿到最後一名的人。就我的意見，你可以去做以及享受生活中許多事情，且你不一定要去和任何人競爭。有時候在你結束一場運動比賽之後，你可能感到不快樂。你可以只是去溜冰、慢跑、游泳、健行、騎單車，或甚至和朋友在河邊漫步一下。當然，如果你習慣處於壓力之下，競賽型運動也許對你而言是比較好的。

答題解說

11. 答案：（C）。空格所在這句的意思是「競賽型運動，對某些喜歡追求-----或冠軍的人來說，可能是個選擇。」（A）與（B）明顯是錯誤的答案，而單就這句話來說，（D）會是可能的答案，不過後面提到，有些人不喜歡競賽型運動或團隊比賽，因為一定會有輸家。所以（D）也是不適合的選項，故答案應為（C）。

12. 答案：（A）。空格前的句子是「有些人不喜歡競賽型運動或團隊比賽」，後面是「一定會有輸家，或落後者或是拿到最後一名的人」前後兩句很明顯是因果關係，所以答案為（A）because。

13. 答案：（A）。這是要挑選一個句子、子句或句子的一部分放入空格後，確認空格前後和空格句之間的連接關係，是否讓句意顯得自然通順。前一句說「你可以去做以及享受生活中許多事情」，而且是用 and 連接，因此空格這一句必須能夠呼應「享受生活中許多事情」這個重點，所以只有（A）的「你不一定要去和任何人競爭」能形成較通順的語意連接。以下是其餘選項句子的翻譯：

　　（B）你總是必須爭取第一名

(C) 運動競賽可能是個好選擇

(D) 你必須更加照顧自己的健康

14. 答案：(C)。本題可以透過「前後對稱」來分析出空格應填入一個 -ing 的詞，因為前面有 roller-skating、jogging、swimming、hiking 等動名詞。故正確答案是 (C)。

破題關鍵

11. 空格後面是 "or championship"（或冠軍），因此這個名詞肯定與 championship 有近似的意義或關係。另外，如果可以真正了解 sport 有「競爭、競賽」的意義在內，也不難選出 victory 這個答案。

12. 空格前這句有 however，顯然是要跟前一句形成對比，說明有些人喜歡的是單純的運動，不喜歡有勝負的感覺介入。了解句意之後自然能夠選出正確的連接詞。

13. 通常三個錯誤選項中會有一個「看似合理」的選項，就像這題的 (D)「你必須更加照顧自己的健康」似乎與 and 前的「你可以去做以及享受生活中許多事情」有相關，這時候你可以再參考後面的句子（繼續在談「運動比賽」），應該就可以消除這個不確定性了。

14. 空格後面的 or 雖然接了個原形動詞 take，但必須注意這個 or 後面的動詞應與前面助動詞 can 後面的動詞 go 對稱，因為句意是「你可以只是去…或是在河邊漫步」。

字詞解釋

exercise [ˈɛksəˌsaɪz] n. 運動，鍛鍊　**quite a few** 許多　**seek** [sik] 追求　***championship** [ˈtʃæmpɪənˌʃɪp] n. 冠軍（的地位、身分、頭銜）　**fall behind**（在比賽中）落後　**first/last place** 第一名／最後一名　**roller-skate** [ˈroləˌsket] v. 溜冰　**riverside** [ˈrɪvəˌsaɪd] n. 河邊　**pressure** [ˈprɛʃə] n. 壓力　**result** [rɪˈzʌlt] n. 結果　**victory** [ˈvɪktərɪ] n. 勝利　**pleasure** [ˈplɛʒə] n. 愉快　**necessary** [ˈnɛsəˌsɛrɪ] adj. 必要的，必需的　***compete** [kəmˈpit] v. 競爭，對抗　**take care of...** 照顧　**bike** [baɪk] v. 騎腳踏車

相關文法觀念補充

11. 「動名詞」當主詞用，一律視為第三人稱單數（有時候動名詞當主詞用時，也可以用「不定詞」代替。）例如： Getting up early every day is really not easy. = To get up early every day is really not easy.。又例如，Planning a lot of trips really takes a lot of time.（計畫許多趟旅行真的要花很多時間。）

12. because 也常見於 because of 的用法，視為一個介系詞。例如：The game was cancelled because of the rain.（這場比賽因雨取消了。）

13. compete 是個不及物動詞，常用來表示競爭或爭奪。例如，「與某人競爭」可以

用 compete with 或 compete against someone 表示：We're too small to compete with a company like that.（我們規模太小，無法與那樣的公司競爭）；「爭奪（某物）」可以用 compete for something 表示：Both teams are competing for the championship.（兩支隊伍將爭奪冠軍。）

14. go+Ving 表示「從事某種活動」，有時也會出現「go + N + Ving」的情形。例如：go bird watching（去賞鳥）、go mountain climbing（去爬山）、go horse riding（去騎馬）…等。

Questions 15-18

Working as a doctor **has been** my first wish even since I was an elementary school student. Every time when I told my parents about this, they just laughed and said, "Keep up the good work and just try your best." With several years **having** passed, however, my goal has never changed. Doctors can save people's lives and help patients recover their health. **What else is more important than helping others keep healthy?** Whether you are rich or poor, and whether you are a famous or an ordinary person, sometimes you get sick. Now I am studying medicine in a university. I feel **more strongly** than ever that I have made a very correct decision to do something meaningful for my future career.

中文翻譯

　　從我還是個小學生時，當醫師一直是我的第一願望。每次當我將這件事告訴我的父母時，他們只是笑著說：「加油，盡你最大能力就好。」然而，幾年過去了，我的目標一直都沒有改變。醫生能夠拯救人們的生命，以及幫助病人恢復他們的健康。還有什麼比幫助人保有健康更重要？無論你是富人還是窮人，且無論你是名人或是平凡人，你有時也會生病。現在，我在大學念醫學。我比從前任何時候都更加強烈感受到，對於自己能夠在未來職涯中做些有意義的事，我已經做了非常正確的決定。

答題解說

15. 答案：(C)。就四個選項來看，空格要填入一個適當的 be 動詞時態，而主要參考指標就是 ever since 引導的子句，表示「自從～以來」，因此主要子句會帶有「一直～」的持續意味，要強調的是從過去到現在持續的一個狀態，因此應選現在完成式的 (C) has been。

16. 答案：(D)。空格所在句子是「With + 名詞片語, 主要子句」的結構，因此從 With 到逗號之前，不是個完整句子，不可填入動詞，所以只有 (D) 是正確答案。

17. 答案：(D)。這是要挑選一個句子、子句或句子的一部分放入空格後，確認空格前後和空格句之間的連接關係，是否讓句意顯得自然通順。所以答題時，必須對

照上下文或根據整段文章的意旨。前一句提到醫生能夠拯救人們的生命，以及幫助病人恢復他們的健康，後面句子以所有人都可能生病，來強化其「想當醫生」的夢想，所以只有 (D) 的「還有什麼比幫助人保有健康更重要？」最能連接前後兩句。以下是其餘選項句子的翻譯：

(A) 你必須早睡早起來保持健康。

(B) 歲月不饒人。

(C) 天助自助者。

18. 答案：(B)。空格後面有比較級用法的 than，所以 (C) 和 (D) 都可以直接排除。另外，可別看到空格前的 feel 就立刻選了形容詞的 (A) stronger，必須注意的是，空格後面有個 that 子句，這是 feel that...（覺得～）的句型，因此應填入的是「副詞」，修飾動詞 feel，表達「強烈地感受到～」之意。

破題關鍵

15. 看到空格後面的 since 應立即想到「完成式」。

16. 「With + 分詞片語」表示附帶條件，屬於分詞構句的一種，請記住它不是完整句子。

17. 掌握全篇「為何想當醫生」的主軸，在看過四個選項，顯然只有 (D) 與醫生的價值有關。

18. 本題關鍵點有二：空格後的 than 以及 that...。前者決定使用比較級，後者決定使用副詞，所以答案是「副詞的比較級」。

字詞解釋

elementary school 小學　**keep up** 保持　**try one's best** 盡力而為　**goal** [gol] n. 目標　**recover** [rɪˋkʌvɚ] v. 重新獲得，恢復　**famous** [ˋfeməs] adj. 著名的　**ordinary** [ˋɔrdṇˏɛrɪ] adj. 普通的，平凡的　**medicine** [ˋmɛdəsṇ] n. 醫學　**correct** [kəˋrɛkt] adj. 正確的，對的　**decision** [dɪˋsɪʒən] n. 決定　***meaningful** [ˋminɪŋfəl] adj. 有意義的　***career** [kəˋrɪr] n. 職業，生涯　***tide** [taɪd] n. 潮汐

相關文法觀念補充

15. 搭配完成式的字詞常見的有 so far（目前為止）、up to now（直到現在）、since（自從）、for + 一段時間、ever/never（曾經／從不）、already（已經）、just（剛才）、recently（最近）…等。

16. 「with + N +V-ing/V-ed」表附帶狀態、條件或原因。例如：

❶ Danny always drives his car with the music playing loud.（Danny 開車時總是把音樂開得很大聲。）

❷ John looked at his daughter's boyfriend, with his arms folded.（John 雙手臂交叉著看著女兒的男朋友。）

17. help 當動詞用時，表示「幫助、幫忙」，其後可以接 to，但通常予以省略。例：She helped her (to) sit up in bed so she could eat the soup. （她扶她在床上坐起來，這樣她就可以喝湯了。）

18. ever 用來強調與「過去」的比較。主要句型為：❶ As + 原級 + as ever（像往常一樣…）、❷ 比較級 + than ever（比以前任何時候都…）、❸ the + 最高級 + ever（有史以來或歷來最…）。例如：

❶ I'm as busy as ever. （我仍像往常一樣忙碌。）
❷ He's worse than ever. （他的病情比以前更嚴重了。）
❸ These are our best results ever. （這些是我們歷來所得到的最好的結果。）

第三部分 閱讀理解

Questions 19-21

中文翻譯

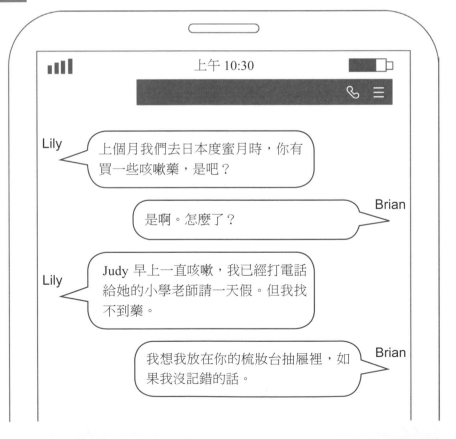

Lily 打開藥盒，看見這個：

用量指示

- 成人及十二歲以上的兒童：每四小時兩匙，二十四小時內不超過十二匙。
- 六至十二歲兒童：每四小時一匙，二十四小時內不超過六匙。
- 六歲以下兒童：請詢求您的醫生建議。

---

19. Lily 為何傳送訊息給 Brian?

 (A) 為了說個祕密

 (B) 為了打一通電話

 (C) 為了找藥

 (D) 為了了解如何吃藥

20. 關於這個咳嗽藥，我們可以得知什麼？

 (A) 它是別人贈送的。

 (B) 它只適合成人使用。

 (C) 孩童若無醫師指示不可吃這種藥。

 (D) Lily 在臥室找到它。

21. Judy 一次可以吃幾匙（的咳嗽藥）?

 (A) 1 匙   (B) 2 匙

 (C) 6 匙   (D) 要聽從醫師建議

第 1 回
第 2 回
第 3 回
第 4 回
第 5 回
第 6 回
第 7 回
第 8 回
第 9 回
第 10 回

19. 答案：(C)。題目問的是 Lily 為何傳送訊息給 Brian，只要針對對話訊息內容即可知道答案。Lily 一開始就問她先生 Brian 上個月在日本買的咳嗽藥，接著在第二次發言最後說 "But I can't find the medicine."，顯然她發送訊息的目的是要「找藥」，故正確答案為 (C) To find medicine.。

20. 答案：(D)。本題屬於「關於…，何者為真？」的題型，需要整合與歸納兩篇文本的資訊並比對多項訊息才能夠得到正確的答案。(A) 的部分可以從 "You bought some cough medicine..." 的內容判斷是錯誤選項；(B)、(C) 的部分皆可以從第二篇的用量指南中得知，是錯誤選項；(D) 的部分可以從 "I think I put it in the drawer of your dresser..." 以及 "Oh, I see it." 的內容確定是正確答案。

21. 答案：(A)。本題也是需要整合與歸納兩篇文本的資訊並比對多項訊息才能夠得到正確的答案。題目問的是 Judy 一次可以吃幾匙咳嗽藥，在第二篇的用量指示中分成三個年齡層，因此首先必須確認 Judy 屬於哪個年齡層。在對話訊息中 Judy 說 "I've made a call to her primary school teacher to take a day off."（我已經打電話給她的小學老師請一天假。）可知，Judy 是個小學生，正好就是「六至十二歲兒童」這個年齡，因此對照其指示的「每四小時一匙」可知，她每次只能吃一匙，故正確答案為 (A)。

19. 發送訊息的目的，其線索會在第一位發言者的談話中找到，因此只要注意第一位發言者的前一、兩次發言內容即可。

20. "the drawer of your dresser" 是「梳妝台抽屜」的意思，基本上梳妝台都是放在臥室（bedroom），所以「Lily 在臥室找到咳嗽藥。」是正確答案。

21. spoon 是「湯匙」的意思，而 spoonful 是「一湯匙的量」。字尾 -ful 多為形容詞，但也有名詞的意思，通常指「～的量」。例如：book → bookful（可編成一本書的量）；bottle → bottleful（一瓶的量）。另外，第二個文本中出現的 dosage 是從 dose（藥物等的一劑）衍生而來，意思是「（藥物等的）劑量」。

cough [kɔf] **n./v.** 咳嗽　**medicine** [ˋmɛdəsn] **n.** 醫藥　***honeymoon** [ˋhʌnɪˌmun] **n.** 蜜月旅行　**primary school** 小學　**take a day off** 請假一天　**drawer** [ˋdrɔə] **n.** 抽屜　**dresser** [ˋdrɛsə] **n.**（附有抽屜的）梳妝臺　***memory** [ˋmɛmərɪ] **n.** 記憶　***dosage** [ˋdosɪdʒ] **n.**（藥的）劑量　***instruction** [ɪnˋstrʌkʃən] **n.** 用法說明，操作指南　**adult** [əˋdʌlt] **n.** 成年人　**spoonful** [ˋspunˌfʊl] **n.** 一匙的量　**advice** [ədˋvaɪs] **n.** 勸告，忠告

❶「吃藥」英文用 take medicine，而不用 eat medicine；eat 的受詞通常為「食物

類」，如：eat a hamburger，而 take 則用在「藥品或保健食品類」之前，如：take vitamins。另外，「喝湯」是 eat soup，而不用 drink soup。

❷ 就像 My job is a teacher. 這種句子一樣，是直譯而又錯誤的中式英文。英文裡沒有 My age is 20 years old.，而應該說 My age is 20.。如果要加上「幾歲以上／以下」的表達，可以用 over 以及 under。

Questions 22-24

中文翻譯

寄件人	採購經理
收件人	所有員工
主旨	簡短通知
日期	2 月 10 日

大家好，

　　當您申請所需要的辦公用品時，請記得遵循辦公室規定並填寫領用表格。這可讓我們定期記錄我們可能固定使用的數量。因此請務必在取走用品之前做到這件事。此外，如果沒有你所需要的物品，且你希望公司購買，你可以填寫辦公室用品採購單，且必須經由你的主管還有我簽名。請牢記在心，否則下次你會受到懲罰。

謝謝

Biob Jesso

採購經理

22. 採購經理為何寫這封電子郵件？
(A) 提醒員工準時上班。　　　　(B) 提醒員工別再犯錯。
(C) 要求歸還辦公用品。　　　　(D) 教導員工如何填寫特定表格。

23. 關於申請辦公用品，這位經理說了什麼？
(A) 有一些規定要遵守。　　　　(B) 要注意特定時間（才能申請）。
(C) 申請變得越來越容易了。　　(D) 請求簽名是很重要的事。

第 1 回
第 2 回
第 3 回
第 4 回
第 5 回
第 6 回
第 7 回
第 8 回
第 9 回
第 10 回

24. 信件當中第一句的 request 所指為何？
(A) 表格填寫的方式。　　　　　　(B) 員工作紀錄的方法。
(C) 員工要求的東西。　　　　　　(D) 員工用來簽字的東西。

22. 答案：(B)。題目問的是採購經理為何寫這封信件，通常這樣的題目可以先從信件上方的「主旨（subject）」找線索。不過這裡的 Quick Note（簡短通知）無法給予明確的訊息，所以應該在內容中找答案。這封 E-mail 主要提醒員工領用及申請購買辦公用品的一些規定，很有可能是之前有些員工未能遵守，因此最後一句又說，請牢記在心，否則會受到懲罰（Please keep this in mind or else you'll be punished next time.）。所以正確答案應為 (B)。

23. 答案：(A)。題目問的是「申請辦公用品（asking for office supplies）」的事，一開始就提到關鍵的 office supplies：Please remember to follow the office rules and fill in the request form...（請記得遵循辦公室規定並填寫領用表格…）也就是「有一些規定要遵守」，故正確答案應為 (A)。

24. 答案：(C)。request 這個字所在的句子是："... and fill in the request form when asking for office supplies you need." 也就是指「員工要求所需要的」→「要申請的東西」，所以正確答案應為 (C)。

22. 從一開始的 "Please remember..." 就可以知道這封 E-mail 是要提醒員工什麼事情，所以只有以 "To remind..." 開頭的 (A)、(B) 是可能的答案。而內容並未提及任何有關準時上班的事情，所以 (C) 是錯誤的。

23. 題目關鍵字詞是 office supplies，指向第一句最後的 "...asking for office supplies you need."，然後再往前看這句講什麼（ ...follow the office rules and fill in...），答案自然就出來了。

24. request form 後面的 "asking for" office supplies 其實已經告訴你答案了，即使你不知道 request 是「要求，申請」的意思，也可以透過句意推測。

staff [stæf] **n.** 全體員工　**purchase** [`pɝtʃəs] **n.** 購買　**fill in/fill out** 填寫（表格等）　**request** [rɪ`kwɛst] **n.** 要求，請求　**ask for** 要求　**supplies** [sə`plaɪz] 生活用品，補給品　**keep a record of**... 記錄　**on a regular basis** 定期地　**unavailable** [ˌʌnə`veləbl] **adj.** 得不到的，缺貨的　**supervisor** [ˌsupɚ`vaɪzɚ] **n.** 管理人，主管　**keep**... **in mind** 將～牢記在心　**or else** 否則　**punish** [`pʌnɪʃ] **v.** 處罰　**remind** [rɪ`maɪnd] **v.** 提醒　**employee** [ˌɛmplɔɪ`i] **n.** 員工　**on time** 準時　**certain** [`sɝtən] **adj.** 特定的　**pay attention to**... 注意　**signature** [`sɪgnətʃɚ] **n.** 簽字

相關文法或用法補充

❶ 除了 that 可以引導名詞子句外，疑問詞（when/what/where/which/who/why/how）引導名詞子句的情況也很常見，在句子裡常扮演主詞或受詞的角色。例如本題短文中：It allows us to keep a record of how many we could use on a regular basis.（這可讓我們定期記錄我們可能固定使用的數量。）→ how many... basis 當介系詞 of 的受詞。以下是當主詞的例子：

What the man did was very dangerous.（這名男子做的事情非常危險。）

❷ buy 與 purchase 都可以當及物動詞，其後可直接加上購買的物品（名詞），在日常生活的口語中比較廣泛使用 buy，而正式場合較常用 purchase。另外，purchase 名詞的用法更常見：

① buy 通常是指日常生活用品等小物或是一般性消費。例如：I bought a pair of pants yesterday.（我昨天買了一件長褲。）

② purchase 用以正式的場合像是商務的合約交易或是金額龐大的消費。例如：He worked very hard to save money for the purchase of a car.（他非常努力工作，為了存錢買一輛車。）

Questions 25-27

中文翻譯

　　當我們洗完澡之後，我們通常用毛巾將自己身體擦乾。不過當你為你的狗洗完澡時，牠只需要迅速搖動身體。根據一項研究，狗的身體濕透時，牠們很自然地可以靠自己，在不到一秒鐘的時間之內甩掉身上一半以上的水。

　　研究發現，動物弄濕時，會從「頭」搖晃到「尾巴」。為了移除水份，體型較小的動物一定會晃得比體型較大的動物更快。此外，在一秒鐘內，老鼠可以搖動 18 次，狗可以搖動 6 次，熊可以搖動 4 次。體型較大的動物雖然晃動次數較少，也能很快地使其身體乾燥。

　　對於某些動物來說，搖晃身體不只是為了讓自己乾燥，也和牠們能否活著有關。如果牠們身上太濕，牠們可能不容易行走甚至跑跳。事實上，他們可能陷入危險中。比方說，如果牠們無法快速移動或奔跑，牠們可能被獵人射死。這就是為什麼「濕狗晃動」成為許多動物一個普遍的習慣。

25. 這篇文章主要關於什麼？
　　(A) 動物讓自己乾燥的速度有多快
　　(B) 為何動物必須讓自己乾燥
　　(C) 什麼動物可以最快地晃動自己
　　(D) 體型較小還是較大的動物才可以活得比較久

26. 關於搖晃，何者為真？
    (A) 不同的動物有不同的搖晃方式。
    (B) 有些動物以搖晃來嚇跑牠們的敵人。
    (C) 寵物型的動物可以搖晃得比野生動物來得好。
    (D) 甩掉身上的水有助於動物們逃離敵人。

27. 何者是閱讀內容中有說明的？
    (A) 動物的尾巴可能阻止牠們逃脫。
    (B) 有些動物搖晃太多次而傷到牠們的頭。
    (C) 體型較大的動物比體型較小的需要較少的搖晃次數。
    (D) 大部分動物學習狗的搖晃動作。

答題解說

這是一篇說明文，內容敘述動物搖晃身體甩掉身上的水其實有另一個重要的目的。

25. 答案：(B)。第一段主要提及狗搖晃身體來甩掉身上的水；第二段主要關於搖晃的方式及不同動物有不同的搖晃次數；第三段提到搖晃更重要的目的是逃離危險。因此，全篇在第三段才點出重點，不在於「搖晃甩水」，而是與拯救自己有關。故正確答案為 (B)。

26. 答案：(D)。第二段提到不同動物搖晃「次數」不同，而非「方式」不同，所以 (A) 是錯誤的；(B)、(C) 都是未提及的事；(D) 的敘述也就是前一題的答案（為何動物必須讓自己乾燥）線索。

27. 答案：(C)。(A)、(B) 都是未提及的敘述。(C) 的部分可以從第二段最後一句 "Larger animals, though shaking fewer times, can quickly dry their bodies." 得知是正確答案。雖然本篇一開始只提到「狗搖晃身體來使自己乾燥」，還有最後也提到 "wet dog shaking" 呼應第一段，但 body shaking 是一種動物的本能，並非學習自狗的行為，故只要根據常識即可判斷 (D) 是錯誤的。

破題關鍵

25. 詢問「主旨」的題型，其線索的位置並非千篇一律，仍應先掌握各段要點才能掌握。本篇的重點在最後一句：This is why "wet dog shaking" has become a common habit of many animals.。

26. 「何者為真」或「何者為非」的題型，都屬於內容細節型的題目。通常必須先看過四個選項的內容，再到文章中找尋線索。

27. 本題也是屬於「以下何者為真」的題型，常必須先看過四個選項內容，再到文章中找尋線索。

字詞解釋

take a shower 洗澡　**towel** [ˋtaʊəl] n. 毛巾　**finish** [ˋfɪnɪʃ] v. 結束　**bathe** [beð] v. 給～洗澡　**shake** [ʃek] v. 搖動　**shake off** 甩掉　**dry** [draɪ] v. 把～弄乾　**have something to do with...** 與～有關　**in danger** 有危險　**common** [ˋkɑmən] adj. 共同的　**scare** [skɛr] v. 使驚嚇　**enemy** [ˋɛnəmɪ] n. 敵人　**wild** [waɪld] adj. 野生的　**explain** [ɪkˋsplen] v. 解釋，說明　**stop... from V-ing** 使得～無法～

相關文法或用法補充

❶ 反身代名詞的字尾是 -self（單數）或 -selves（複數）：

人稱	單數	複數
第 1 人稱	myself	ourselves
第 2 人稱	yourself	yourselves
第 3 人稱	himself、herself、itself	themselves

另外，反身代名詞也有副詞的用法，表示「靠自己、自己一個人」，相當於 alone 的副詞用法。例如：go to the movies myself（自己一個人去看電影）

❷ 「動名詞」的作用跟名詞一樣，具備名詞特有的「存在性」及「持久性」，所以當我們表達一種「持續」的狀態、事實或習慣等，要用 Ving。比如這裡的 finish bathing your dog（幫你的狗洗完澡）。常見後面接動名詞的動詞還有：admit 承認、mind 介意、miss 想念、quit 戒除、avoid 避免、enjoy 享受、can't help 忍不住、risk 冒～的風險、consider 考慮、keep 保持、practice 練習、suggest 建議…等。

Questions 28-30

中文翻譯

　　Adam 最愛的嗜好是閱讀。當他還是個中學生時，他喜歡在一棵大樹底下閱讀，而他大部分同學及朋友都在玩手機電玩遊戲。他最喜歡《塞翁失馬》的故事，因為他被這位總是保持鎮定且對未來抱持希望的老人家所感動。從這故事中，Adam 知道，「在不幸中仍有一線希望。」

　　Adam 的父親不工作且是個爛酒鬼。每當他喝醉時，家裡總會有大爭吵。Adam 的母親，為了保護他，傷心地決定離開他的父親。在當時，對於這對母子來說生活相當困難，因為她必須工作且租個地方來住。即使如此，他仍買給 Adam 任何他有興趣的書籍。她相信閱讀對她兒子來說是好的。

　　Adam 喜歡讀些名人的故事，且對於他們如何成功感到驚訝。事實上，他希望未來成為一位作家，那麼他就可以寫些動人的故事，以幫助可憐的人們改變他們的生活。

28. 這篇故事的主旨為何？
    (A) 喝酒最終會毀了你的家庭。
    (B) 閱讀有助於你成為一個名人。
    (C) 不好的事可能發生，但一定會好轉。
    (D) 雲朵有時候看起來很美麗。

29. Adam 喜歡《塞翁失馬》的故事，因為 _____ 。
    (A) 是關於一隻拯救老人生命的聰明馬
    (B) 它較貼近真實生活中發生的故事
    (C) 他可以從故事中想像美麗的雲
    (D) 它有個美好的結局

30. 關於 Adam 的母親，何者為真？
    (A) 她是個重度飲酒者，但她很照顧她兒子。
    (B) 她窮困，但對 Adam 很慷慨。
    (C) 她過著快樂的家庭生活且她先生很愛她。
    (D) 她希望未來成為一位作家。

答題解說

這是一篇記敘文，內容講述閱讀可以帶給人正向思維的好處。

28. 答案：(C)。本篇故事一開始第一句話說，Adam 最愛的嗜好是閱讀。接著又說他最喜歡《塞翁失馬》的故事。至此，答案就呼之欲出了，因為大家都聽過「塞翁失馬，焉知非福」的諺語吧！故正確答案為 (C)。

29. 答案：(B)。第一段提到，他最喜歡《塞翁失馬》的故事，因為他學習到「在不幸中仍有一線希望。」（every cloud has a silvering lining.）到了第三段，Adam 希望成為作家，寫一些對可憐的人們有幫助的故事。最後顯然呼應了他自己的現實生活。所以正確答案為 (B)。

30. 答案：(B)。(A) 的部分可以從 "Adam's father.... was a heavy drinker" 的內容中得知，是錯誤答案；在第二段內容中可知，雖然母子生活困難，但她仍買給 Adam 任何他有興趣的書籍，所以符合 (B) 的 "She is poor but generous to Adam." 的敘述；由於第二段有 "Every time when he got drunk, there would be a big fight in his home." 的敘述，所以 (C) 是錯的；第三段提到「希望成為一位作家」的是他兒子 Adam，所以 (D) 也是錯的。

破題關鍵

28. 就記敘文的「主旨型」考題而言，答案線索不一定在第一段一開始就看得到，但通常看完第一段都可以掌握要旨。本題要旨有二：❶《塞翁失馬》的故事以及 ❷「在不幸中仍有一線希望。（every cloud has a silvering lining）」這句諺語，

都在第一段出現。

29. 特別注意第一段提到「Adam 最愛的嗜好是閱讀。」以及「他最喜歡《塞翁失馬》的故事」，所用的時態都是現在式，敘述的是現在的狀況，而二、三段都用過去式，顯然利用倒敘法來呼應現在的情況。可以推斷因為自己也生活在不幸的家庭，而《塞翁失馬》的故事讓他樂觀看待人生，所以這故事比較接近他的真實生活。

30. 「何者為真」或「何者為非」的題型，都屬於內容細節型的題目。通常都是擺在最後一題再作答。在了解每一個選項的內容之後，對照信件中提及的相關內容，然後用刪除法自然能夠得到正確答案。

字詞解釋

favorite [ˋfevərɪt] **adj.** 最喜愛的　**hobby** [ˋhɑbɪ] **n.** 嗜好　**middle school** 中學　**video game** 電玩遊戲　**horse** [hors] **n.** 馬　**calm** [kɑm] **adj.** 鎮靜的　**hopeful** [ˋhopfəl] **adj.** 懷抱希望的　**silver** [ˋsɪlvə] **adj.** 銀的，鍍銀的　*****lining** [ˋlaɪnɪŋ] **n.** 襯裡，內襯　**heavy** [ˋhɛvɪ] **adj.** 沉重的，重度的　**fight** [faɪt] **n.** 打架，爭吵　**protect** [prəˋtɛkt] **v.** 保護　**make up one's mind** 下決心　**be interested in...** 對～感興趣　**famous** [ˋfeməs] **adj.** 著名的　**succeed** [səkˋsid] **v.** 成功　**in fact** **adv.** 事實上　**touching** [tʌtʃɪŋ] **adj.** 感人的　**ruin** [ˋrʊɪn] **v.** 毀壞　**imagine** [ɪˋmædʒɪn] **v.** 想像　**wonderful** [ˋwʌndəfəl] **adj.** 極好的，精彩的　**generous** [ˋdʒɛnərəs] **adj.** 慷慨的，大方的

相關文法或用法補充

❶ middle school（初中，中等學校）是美式英語的講法，再往上就是 high school，也都是「高中」的意思；台灣學生一開始都是學 junior high school（國中）、senior high school（高中），有時 school 可省略。

❷ Every cloud has a silver lining. 這句話的字面意思是，每朵雲都有一條銀邊。這比喻有些日子雖看起來很不愉快、很不幸，但終歸都有一條銀邊，即會有好事出現，是一句鼓勵別人常用的的話。常見的翻譯還有「曙光總會出現」、「撥雲見日」、「否極泰來」、「山窮水盡疑無路，柳暗花明又一村」、「黑暗中總有一片光明」…等。

6

GEPT
全民英檢

初級初試
中譯＋解析

第一部分 看圖辨義

1. **For question number 1, please look at Picture A.**

   Question number 1: What does this sign tell us?
   （這個標誌告訴我們什麼？）
   (A) No parking here.（這裡禁止停車。）
   (B) What car can park here.（什麼車可以停在這裡。）
   (C) Stop, watch and listen here.（在這裡要停看聽。）

   答題解說

   答案：(B)。上方的文字 NO PARKING 當然是給駕駛人看的，表示「禁止停車」，而下方 SERVICE CAR ONLY 表示「非施工車輛，請勿停車」，因此正確答案為「什麼車可以停在這裡。」。

   相關文法或用法補充

   only 這個字常出在一些標示牌上，以「名詞 + Only」的格式出現，表示「僅限 XX」。例如 Staff Only 表示「非工作人員，請勿進入」、「員工專用」。另外，在停車場也常看到 Disabled Only（身障人士專用）的標示。

2. **For question number 2 and 3, please look at Picture B.**

   Question number 2: What information is given in this picture?（圖片提供什麼資訊？）
   (A) In front of the building is a parking lot.
       （這棟建築的前面是停車場。）
   (B) Many cars are leaving the parking lot.
       （許多車輛正駛離停車場。）
   (C) The tree is across from the building.（這棵樹在建築物對面。）

   答題解說

   答案：(A)。從圖中可以清楚看到這棟建築是「全家便利商店」，門口就是停車場，有一輛車正駛離該停車場（所以 (B) 是錯誤的）旁邊有一棵樹（所以 (C) 是錯誤的，應改為 next to）。所以 (A)「這棟建築的前面是停車場。」為正確答案。

第 1 回
第 2 回
第 3 回
第 4 回
第 5 回
第 6 回
第 7 回
第 8 回
第 9 回
第 10 回

破題關鍵

掌握這裡表「位置」的介系詞即可。in front of... 表示「在～前面」，across from 表示「在～對面」。

字詞解釋

building [ˋbɪldɪŋ] n. 建築物　　**parking lot** 停車場

相關文法或用法補充

表達「位置」時，可以用「介系詞＋受詞」的結構來表達主詞與受詞之間的相對位置，以下是一些常見的（片語）介系詞：

1. in front of... 在～正前方
2. behind... 在～的後面
3. to the left / right of... 在～的左邊 / 右邊
4. next to... / by... 在～的旁邊
5. close to... 靠近～

3. **Question number 3: Please look at Picture B again.**

   Why do people come here?（為什麼人們會來這裡？）
   (A) To see a doctor（為了看醫生）
   (B) To watch a concert（為了看演唱會）
   (C) To make purchases（為了購物）

   答題解說

   答案：(C)。本題問「為何（why）」，即使未聽出 why，至少連續三個「To ＋原形動詞」的選項可以輕易聽出來吧！圖片中左方的建築物標示著 Family Mart 字樣，顯然這是一間便利商店（convenience store），所以這些人是來購物的。

   破題關鍵

   purchase 是「購物」的意思，可以當動詞或名詞，是比 buy 更為正式的用語，當名詞表示「購物的行為」或「所購買的東西」，常用於 make a purchase 這個片語。

   字詞解釋

   concert [ˋkɑnsɚt] n. 演唱會　　**purchase** [ˋpɝtʃəs] n. 購買，所購之物

   相關文法或用法補充

   purchase（v./n.）常用於正式的場合，像是商務的合約交易或是金額龐大的消費，也常與其他名詞構成複合名詞。例如：purchase order（訂購單）、purchase price（購買價格）、purchasing power（購買力）。

4. For question number 4, please look at Picture C.

Question number 4:

What is the teacher doing?（這位老師正在做什麼？）
(A) She is teaching English.（她正在教英文。）
(B) She is taking an English exam.（她正在考英文。）
(C) She is walking around.（她正四處走動。）

答題解說

答案：（C）。本題問的是這位女老師「正在做什麼」。因為黑板上寫著 English exam 以及考試時間，表示學生正在考試，所以這位老師當然是四處走動在監考。正確答案是（C）。

破題關鍵

知道題目問的是「老師（the teacher）」，並能聽懂 "take an exam" 是「參加考試、去考試」的意思， "walk around" 則是「四處走動」，自然不會選錯答案。

相關文法或用法補充

參加考試，這個參加，其實是「執行、做」，美國人用 take，英國人更直接用 sit 或 sit for，意象鮮明，是坐在那兒寫考題。但千萬別用 join 或是 attend 喔！
（×）I will join/attend an exam tomorrow.
（○）I will take an exam tomorrow.
（○）I will sit/sit for an exam tomorrow.

5. For question number 5, please look at Picture D.

Question number 5: What is the man?
（男子是做什麼的？）
(A) He is a hunter.（他是個獵人。）
(B) He is a farmer.（他是個農夫。）
(C) He is an office worker.（他是個上班族。）

答題解說

答案：（B）。圖中顯示的是一片菜園，一名男子正在用鋤頭工作，顯然他是個農夫。所以正確答案為（B）。

破題關鍵

「What + be 動詞 + 人？」是用來問某人的職業。但即使不了解這個問法，只要聽過三個「He is...」的選項，也知道題目一定是在問工作。

字詞解釋

hunter [ˋhʌntɚ] n. 獵人　　**farmer** [ˋfɑrmɚ] n. n.農夫　　**office worker** n. 上班族

相關文法或用法補充

office 是「辦公室」的意思，而 worker 原意為「工人，工作者」，把這兩個名詞結合成一個複合名詞 office worker，沒有男女之分，表示「在辦公室辦公的人」，所以稱之為「上班族」。如果是在工廠做工的，就不能稱之為 office worker，而是 factory worker，所以 office worker 其實就是指「白領階級」（white-collar class），而 factory worker 是「藍領階級」（blue-collar class）。另外，我們常聽到的 OL 其實是日式英語 office lady，專指「女性上班族」。

第二部分 問答

6. **Have you heard from Sue?**（你有 Sue 的消息了嗎？）

(A) No, her voice is too low.（沒有，她的聲音太小聲。）
(B) Not for a long time.（很久沒有了。）
(C) Yes, I've heard about this girl.（是的，我聽說過這女孩。）

答題解說

答案：(B)。題目問的是「有 Sue 的消息嗎？」，或是「有收到 Sue 的來信嗎？」顯然 (A) 與 (C) 都答非所問，故 (B) 的「很久沒有她的消息了。」是問題的合理回答。

破題關鍵

本題是考你是否了解 hear、hear from 以及 hear about 後面接「人」時的不同。「hear + 人」表示「聽得到某人說話」，「hear from + 人」通常用於書信當中，表示「得到某人的消息」。而「hear about」的後面其實可以接「人」或「事物」，表示「聽說關於～的事情」。例如：I haven't heard about what happened to her. Who told you?（我沒有聽說她發生了什麼事。誰告訴你的？）

字詞解釋

voice [vɔɪs] n. 聲音

相關文法或用法補充

「現在完成式」主要用來表示從過去到現在的「行為、動作、經驗」，且有可能會持續下去。例如：

❶ I have done my work.（我已經把我的工作做完了。）
❷ Have you ever eaten a snake?（你吃過蛇嗎？）
❸ I've lived here for 10 years.（我住在這裡已經十年了。）
→ I have 可以縮寫為 I've。

7. **How long have you been married?**（你結婚多久了？）

(A) It'll take a few months.（要花費幾個月的時間。）
(B) For one year（一年了）
(C) About 10 meters long（大概十公尺長）

答題解說

答案：（B）。How long...? 是關於「時間多久」的問題，回答時要有具體的時間，因此正確答案是（B）。(A) 當中的 take 是「花費～（多久時間）」的意思，所以別只聽到 "a few months" 就選下去了；(C) 回答的是「某物的長度」，並刻意用 long 這個字來混淆答題。

破題關鍵

"how long" 有兩種意義： 1. 時間多久； 2. 長度多長。本題只要聽清楚 married（結婚）這個字，自然不會去選 (C)。至於 (A) 顯然也是答非所問。

字詞解釋

married [ˋmærɪd] **adj.** 已婚的　　**meter** [ˋmitɚ] **n.** 公尺

相關文法或用法補充

long 當形容詞表示長度多「～長」時，須擺在單位詞的後面。例如「一公尺長的繩子」是 "a one-meter-long rope" 或是 "a rope that is one meter long"。如果要表示時間或演講等的「漫長或過久」，須擺在名詞前面。例如 "for a long time"（維持一段長時間）、"a long, boring lecture"（漫長、無聊的講課）。

8. **What are you doing this weekend?**（你這個週末要做什麼？）

(A) I may just stay at home.（我可能只是待在家裡。）
(B) I'm doing the dishes now.（我現在正在洗碗。）
(C) That's a good idea.（那是個好主意。）

答題解說

答案：（A）。本題是在問「未來某個時間點要做什麼」，題目句雖然用現在進行式，但其意義是代替未來，而且是「很短時間內」的未來。所以 (A) 是正確的回

答。(B) 刻意用相同的現在進行式（表示當下正在做什麼）來混淆答題，而 (C) 完全是答非所問。

第 1 回
第 2 回
第 3 回
第 4 回
第 5 回
第 6 回
第 7 回
第 8 回
第 9 回
第 10 回

破題關鍵

「現在進行式」搭配表「未來」的時間副詞時，等同 "be going to-V" 的未來式，了解這個觀念的話，本題就很容易解決了。

字詞解釋

do/wash the dishes 洗碗盤

相關文法或用法補充

may 表示「可能」，但它的「可能性」比 could 與 can 還來得低，可能性最高的是 must。例如：

The news may be true.（這消息也許是真的。）
The news can be true.（這消息可能是真的。）
The news must be true.（這消息一定是真的。）

9. **Let me help you.**（我來幫你。）

(A) I'm so happy.（我很高興。）
(B) It's really nice of you.（你人真好。）
(C) You're welcome.（不客氣。）

答題解說

答案：(B)。題目句是主動提供對方協助，所以對於對方的善意，可以回答感謝或稱讚對方「你人真好」之類的話。(A) 通常用來回答對方問你「過得如何」或「最近好嗎」之類的話語，而 (C) 通常是回應對方的感謝之意。

破題關鍵

「It is + adj. + of + 人」是常見的句型，用來表示「這個人（的人格特質）怎麼樣。」

相關文法或用法補充

常與「It is + adj. + of + 人」做比較的另一個句型是「It is + adj. + to + 原形動詞」，用來形容「做某件事」如何。例如：It is important to study hard.（用功念書很重要。）因此，第一個句型當中的形容詞是用來修飾「人」，而第二個句型當中的形容詞是用來修飾「事情」。

10. Your hairstyle looks so cool!（你的髮型看起來真酷！）

(A) I'm glad you like it.（我很高興你喜歡。）
(B) No, it'll be getting colder.（不，會變得更冷些。）
(C) It is yours.（它是你的。）

答案：(A)。題目這句在稱讚對方的髮型，因此對於對方的讚美，可以回答 I'm glad you like it.。選項(B)刻意以 colder 與 cool 的相關性來混淆答題，而(C)則答非所問。

cool 這個形容詞除了表示「涼快的」，在口語中也常用來讚美人或事物。

hairstyle [ˋhɛrˌstaɪl] **n.** 髮型　　**cool** [kul] **adj.** 涼快的；很棒的；冷靜的　　**glad** [glæd] **adj.** 高興的

「人＋be 動詞＋形容詞＋that 子句」是非常常見的句型，用來表示「某人對於某件事的感受」，所以這裡的形容詞是「人感受（喜怒哀樂）」的形容詞，比如 glad、happy、sad、angry... 等，後面「that 子句」的 that 通常可以省略。

11. Would you care for a cup of coffee?（你要不要來杯咖啡？）

(A) No, I don't care.（不，我不在乎。）
(B) OK. Thank you.（好的。謝謝。）
(C) Just help yourself.（你自己來就好。）

答案：(B)。這是詢問對方要不要喝一杯咖啡，而說話的人會去泡咖啡之類的問句，所以(B)的回答是最正確的。(A)用相同的 care 來混淆答題，實際上是答非所問，(C)就中文來看，似乎也是可行的回答，但英文的 Help yourself. 是「請對方自己來」（不必客氣），那就完全搞錯對象了，你可以說 "Thank you. I'll help myself." 。

care for 的意思是「喜歡，想要」的意思，相當於 would like，所以它跟 care（在意、在乎）完全不同意思。

第 1 回
第 2 回
第 3 回
第 4 回
第 5 回
第 6 回
第 7 回
第 8 回
第 9 回
第 10 回

字詞解釋

care for phr. 喜歡，照料，介意　**help oneself** phr. 隨意取用

相關文法或用法補充

也來熟悉一下 care for 的其他用法：

① 表示「照顧，照料」（相當於 take care of）：He has to care for his elderly parents.（他必須照顧他年邁的父母。）
② 表示「喜歡，深愛」：
　❶ I don't care much for opera.（我不太喜歡歌劇。）
　❷ He cares for his wife deeply.（他深愛著他的妻子。）

12. **Who's your best friend at school?**（在學校，誰是你最要好的朋友？）

(A) My name is David.（我的名字叫大衛。）
(B) I usually walk home after school.（我放學後通常走路回家。）
(C) I don't have one.（我一個都沒有。）

答題解說

答案：(C)。題目是問「誰」是你最好的朋友，通常如果有的話，會回答一個具體的名字，或是說 His/Her name is...，而不會是 My name is...，所以 (A) 是刻意用一個具體的名字來誤導答題，而 (B) 的回答完全是答非所問。(C) 的「我一個都沒有。」是可能的回答情況。

破題關鍵

one 當作「不定代名詞」用來代替面提到過的名詞，這是很常考的文法。這裡是用來代替 "best friend"，這裡的 I don't have one. = I don't have a best friend. 或 I don't have any best friends.。

字詞解釋

at school 上學，在學校（上課）　**after school** 放學

相關文法或用法補充

這裡的 one 也有複數形，而它的複數形也和其它的可數名詞一樣，直接在其後加上 -s 即可，也就是 ones。例如：He has no new jackets. He only has old ones.（他沒有新的夾克。他只有舊的夾克。）

13. **Excuse me. Is this seat taken?**（不好意思。這位子有人坐嗎？）

(A) No, I didn't take any seats.（不，我沒有坐任何座位。）
(B) Yes, you can take it away.（是的，你可以拿走。）
(C) Yes, my friend will be back soon.（是的，我朋友很快就回來。）

答題解說

答案：(C)。當你看到一個空位想坐下來或是想把一張當下沒人坐的椅子拿走時，禮貌上應問對方這位子是否有人坐時，就是用 "Is this seat taken?" 來問。所以只有 (C) 是可能的答案。(B) 的 Yes 應改成 No 才合乎句意。

破題關鍵

當有客人來你家時，可以說 "Take a seat, please."（請坐。）因此，這個問句就是從 "take a seat" 來的。taken 是過去分詞當形容詞用，作為 seat 的後位修飾語。

字詞解釋

seat [sit] n. 座位

相關文法或用法補充

「請坐」也分成較正式與非正式說法。前者是 Please be seated（請就座。）後者則是 Take/Have a seat.，但無論是正式或非正式場合，都不可以說 Please sit down.，因為這是在教室裡，老師請學生坐下的用語，具有命令的語氣。

14. **Who threw the ball?**（誰扔的球？）

(A) My name is David.（我叫作大衛。）
(B) My cousin.（我侄兒。）
(C) I'll be there soon.（我很快就到。）

答題解說

答案：(B)。本題的情境可能是某人被一顆飛來的球打中，於是生氣地問「球是誰扔的？」所以答案如果不是人名就是可以指稱某人的說法，只有 (B) My cousin 是符合句意的回答。

破題關鍵

聽得出 cousin 的話應該就沒問題了。但如果聽不出這個字，也可以用刪除法來作答。題目問 Who，回答 My name is... 或 I'll be there... 都是答非所問。

字詞解釋

threw [θru] v. 投，擲，扔（throw 的過去式）　　**cousin** [ˋkʌzn] n. 堂（或表）兄弟姐妹

相關文法或用法補充

相對於中文的親戚稱呼，英文的親戚叫法則相對簡單很多，許多不同的中文親戚稱呼會在英文中簡化成一個單字。例如，阿姨/叔叔、嬸嬸/伯伯、舅媽/舅舅、姑媽/姑父等等，在英文中只需用 aunt/uncle 來表示。

15. **Let's relax. It's been a long day.**（我們輕鬆一下。今天忙了一整天了。）

   (A) Here you are.（這給你。）
   (B) Today is not my day.（我今天很不順利。）
   (C) That's a good idea.（這想法不錯。）

答題解說

答案：(C)。本題的情境是一起工作累了一天，告訴對方放鬆一下，(C) 的「這想法不錯。」表示同意對方，是最合理的回答。(A) 與 (B) 皆答非所問。(A) 的 Here you are. 是用來回應對方跟你要什麼東西的回答。

破題關鍵

本題只要聽懂第一句 Let's relax. 即可作答，第二句只是補充說為什麼要放鬆一下的原因。

字詞解釋

relax [rɪˋlæks] v. 鬆懈，放鬆

相關文法或用法補充

It has been a long day. 或 It's a long day. 都可以用來表示「我今天很忙。」所以不要只會說 I'm busy today. 了。

第三部分 簡短對話

共 10 題。每題請聽光碟放音機播出的一段對話和一個相關的問題後，再從試題冊上三個選項中，選出一個最適合的答案。每段對話和問題播出一遍。

16. **W: I can't believe it. It's another hot day!**

   M: That's strange. It is usually cool in October.

   W: Maybe that's because of global warming.

   M: I think so. Anyway, would you like to eat some ice cream?

Question: How is the weather today?

(A) It's hot.

(B) It's cool.

(C) It's warm.

女：簡直難以相信。又是一個大熱天！

男：這真是怪。通常十月很涼爽的。

女：也許是因為全球暖化的關係。

男：我想是吧。不管怎樣，要不要去吃個冰淇淋？

題目：今天天氣如何？

(A) 很熱。

(B) 很涼快。

(C) 很暖和。

答題解說

答案：(A)。當女子一開始對男子說「又是一個大熱天！」，男子回答說「這真是怪。通常十月很涼爽的。」表示同意她的說法，今天天氣確實很熱，儘管通常十月很涼爽。所以正確答案為(A)。

破題關鍵

雖然三個選項中的 hot、cool、warm 都出現在對話中，但關鍵還是在女子第一句的 It's another hot day!。

字詞解釋

believe [bɪˋliv] **v.** 相信　**another** [əˋnʌðə] **adj.** 再一個的，另一個的　**strange** [strendʒ] **adj.** 奇怪的　**global warming** 全球暖化　**ice cream** 冰淇淋

相關文法或用法補充

believe 是個及物動詞，後面可以接名詞或代名詞，像是這裡的 I can't believe it.。it 在此是指前面提到的一件事情。believe 後面也可以接子句，例如 I can't believe that this is happening.（我不相信這樣的事會發生。）

17. W: Hey, are you still busy with your project?

　　M: I'm just done with it, and hope I can take a trip to relax a bit. Have any plans this weekend?

　　W: No. What about you?

　　M: Me, either.

Question: What plans does the man have for this weekend?

(A) He'll be busy with his project.

(B) He'll go on a trip to relax a bit.

(C) He hasn't had any plans yet.

女：喂，還在忙你的專案嗎？

男：我剛完成了，而且希望可以去旅行放鬆一下。這個週末有什麼計畫嗎？

女：沒有。你呢？

男：我也沒有

題目：男子這個週末有何計畫？

(A) 他將忙著他的專案。

(B) 他將去旅行放鬆一下。

(C) 他還沒有任何計畫。

答案：(C)。題目問的是男子週末是否有任何計畫，因此應仔細聆聽男子的發言。一開始他表示剛完成一項專案，想去旅行放鬆一下。但並不表示這就是他的週末計畫，所以 (A)、(B) 都是錯誤的。當女子反問他週末是否有何計畫，他的回答是「我也沒有」，所以答案是 (C)。

本題關鍵字是男子最後回答中的 either，它常用於否定句中，表示「也不，也沒」為否定的附和。

project [ˋprɑdʒɛkt] n. 專案，計畫　**be done with**... 完成（= finish）

What about...? 和 How about...? 常用於口語中，且在用法上沒什麼區別。中譯是「～怎麼樣？ 要不要～？」請注意， about 是介系詞，所以後面必須接名詞，或動名詞，但有時亦可接子句。例如：What/How about taking a walk on the beach? = What/How about we go take a walk on the beach?

18. W: What a nice-looking motorcycle! Is it new?

    M: Almost. It's new to me. I bought it from an old friend.

    W: I think it's not cheap, right?

    M: Sure! It cost me half a year's income; it's only two years old. Besides, I can ride it on the highway.

Question: What are the speakers talking about?
(A) The man's income　(B) A motorbike　(C) A highway

女：好漂亮的摩托車啊！是新買的嗎？
男：算是。對我來說是新的。我跟一個老朋友買的。
女：我想應該不便宜，是吧？
男：當然！它花了我半年的收入；它是兩年的車。此外，我可以騎上快速道路。
題目：說話者們在談論什麼？
(A) 男子的收入
(B) 一部摩托車
(C) 快速道路

答題解說

答案：(B)。題目問的是整篇對話的「主旨」，所以必須完整理解對話內容才能作答。女子一開始稱讚男子的摩托車真漂亮，男子回答跟朋友買的，以及花了不少錢、可以騎上快速道路等，話題都圍繞在這部摩托車上，所以答案是 (B)。

破題關鍵

即使對於會話內容一知半解，只要聽出女子的第一句 "What a nice-looking motorcycle!"，即可知道底下的對話與這部 nice-looking motorcycle 有關。

字詞解釋

What's going on? 有什麼事？／發生什麼事？　**on the phone** 在電話中
restaurant [ˈrɛstərənt] n. 餐廳，餐館

相關文法或用法補充

highway、expressway 或是 freeway，哪個是高速公路，哪個是快速道路呢？highway 在國外也是高速公路的意思，在台灣可指穿越不同行政區或縣市的「省道」；「高速公路」的話，台灣政府的定義是 freeway。至於 expressway 是指「快速道路」，以台北為例，環快、水源快速道路或台 64 線等這幾條都是，數年前也開放紅牌及黃牌重型機車上路。

19. W: David, you're half an hour late.
    M: I'm sorry, but I overslept this morning.
    W: You must set your alarm clock. Don't be late next time, or I'll think you cut class.
    M: I won't.

Question: Where did the dialogue probably take place?

(A) In an office　(B) At school　(C) At a train station

女：大衛，你遲到半小時了。

男：真是抱歉，我今早睡過頭了。

女：你要設好鬧鐘啊。下次別再遲到，否則我會認為你要蹺課。

男：我不會的。

問題：這則對話可能發生在何處？

(A) 在辦公室裡　(B) 在學校　(C) 在火車站。

答題解說

答案：(B)。題目問的是對話發生的「地點」，基本上還是得理解對話內容才能作答。首先，女子責備男子遲到，接著男子解釋了原因，然後女子提醒他下次要準時，否則會當作你要蹺課。顯然兩人為學校裡老師與學生的關係。因此，對話的地點應該是在學校。

破題關鍵

整篇對話的關鍵字詞只有一個：cut class。如果是 (A) 在辦公室裡，老闆當然也會責備員工遲到，但從 "...or I'll think you cut class" 來看，顯然不會是發生在公司的情境。當然，這對話更不可能是在火車站的對話了。

字詞解釋

overslept [ˋovɚˋslɛpt] v. 睡過頭（oversleep 的過去式）　**alarm clock** 鬧鐘　**cut class** 蹺課

相關文法或用法補充

「蹺課」可是說 cut/skip (the/one's) class。cut 是「剪掉」，skip 是「略過」，也就是說把上課的那段時間從時間表中「切掉或略過」的意思。

20. W: I'm a bit thirsty. I want something to drink.

　　M: What about iced water? It's the only drink in my fridge.

　　W: No, I'm sick of tasteless drinks.

　　M: Then let me go out to buy some ice cream.

　　W: Good idea.

Questions: Why doesn't the woman want to drink iced water?

(A) Because she wanted some sweet taste.

(B) Because she was sick.

(C) Because she was not thirsty.

第 1 回
第 2 回
第 3 回
第 4 回
第 5 回
第 6 回
第 7 回
第 8 回
第 9 回
第 10 回

女：我有點渴。我想喝點東西。

男：要不要來點冰開水？這是我冰箱裡僅有的飲料。

女：不，我厭倦了沒有味道的飲料。

男：那我出去買冰淇淋。

女：好主意。

問題：女子為何不想喝冰水？

(A) 因為她想來點甜味的。

(B) 因為她生病了。

(C) 因為她並不口渴。

答案：(A)。本題問的是女子不想喝冰水的「原因」，所以應注意女子有關喝冰水的發言部分。女子的第二次發言提到，I'm sick of tasteless drinks.，這表示她厭倦沒有味道的冰水，可以推知她可能比較喜歡「有味道」的飲料或冰品，所以答案是(A)。選項(B)、(C)刻意重複相同字 sick 以及 thirsty 來誤導答題。

首先，注意題目要問的是「不喜歡冰開水」，以及女子對此發言的部分：I'm sick of tasteless drinks.。be sick of... 是常見的片語，意思是「厭惡了～」，甚至是「對～感到噁心」。另外，字尾 -less 表「否定」，雖然 tasteless 可能沒學過，但 taste 是初級範圍內的單字，加上 -less 就是「沒有味道」的意思。

thirsty [ˋθɝstɪ] **adj.** 口渴的，渴求的　**be sick of** 厭惡，非常不喜歡　**iced** [aɪst] **adj.** 冰過的　**fridge** [frɪdʒ] **n.** 【口】冰箱（= refrigerator）　**tasteless** [ˋtestlɪs] **adj.** 沒味道的　**taste** [test] **n.** 味道

21. M: Go straight down the road, and turn right on the next traffic light.

　　W: OK. So, do I need to wait for the green light?

　　M: Sure. I doubt if you've passed the written test.

　　W: Of course I did. I'm just too nervous.

　　M: Just take it easy.

　　Question: What is the woman doing?

　　(A) Asking for directions

　　(B) Taking a written test

　　(C) Learning to drive

男：這條路直走，然後在下個紅綠燈右轉。

女：好的。那我得等綠燈嗎？

男：當然。我懷疑你是不是有通過筆試。

女：我當然有。我只是太緊張了。

男：放輕鬆點。

題目：女子正在做什麼？

(A) 問路

(B) 參加筆試

(C) 學習開車

答題解說

答案：(C)。本題問的是女子正在做什麼事，男子一開始告訴女子這條路直走，然後在下個紅路燈右轉，因此女子有可能在問路，但女子下一句問「是不是要等綠燈（然後右轉）」，男子反問她，我懷疑你是不是有通過筆試。所以男子應該是駕訓班教練，女子正在學開車。因此，(C) 是正確答案。

破題關鍵

如果有事先看過三個選項，也可以清楚分辨三種完全不同的「情境」，然後再仔細聽對話內容，尤其是男子問女子 "I doubt if you've passed the written test."（我懷疑你是不是有通過筆試。）顯然女子正在駕訓班學開車。

字詞解釋

straight [stret] **adv.** 直直地　**traffic light** 紅綠燈　**green light** 綠燈　**written test** 筆試　**nervous** [ˋnɝvəs] **adj.** 緊張的　**take it easy** 放輕鬆　**direction** [dəˋrɛkʃən] **n.** 方向（ex. ask for directions 問路）

相關文法或用法補充

一般來說，if 是「如果」的意思，常用來引導「條件子句」，構成假設語氣。不過這裡的 if 是「是否」的意思，用來引導名詞子句，作 doubt 的受詞，相當於 whether。

22. M: Wow! How big the waves are! I almost can't stand well.

    W: That's because the wind is so strong!

    M: I'm feeling a bit dizzy now. I think I'd better go inside and sit down.

    W: OK. I want to stay here to watch the view.

第 1 回
第 2 回
第 3 回
第 4 回
第 5 回
第 6 回
第 7 回
第 8 回
第 9 回
第 10 回

Question: Where are the speakers?

(A) On an express train

(B) On an airplane

(C) On a boat

男：哇！浪好大啊！我幾乎無法好好站立了。

女：那是因為風很強啊！

男：我現在覺得有點暈眩。我想我最好進去裡面坐下來。

女：好的。我想待在這裡欣賞風景。

題目：說話者們在哪裡？

(A) 在一列特快火車上

(B) 在飛機上

(C) 在船上

答案：(C)。本題問的是說話者在哪裡，只要注意相關敘述及可判斷。男子一開始時說浪好大，幾乎無法站立。其實這第一句話就已經可以判斷是在船上了。而且男子第二句說「我想我最好進去裡面坐下來。」如果是坐飛機或火車，都不可能會有「出來外面、進去裡面」的情況，所以 (C) 是正確答案。

破題關鍵

只要先看過三個選項，就知道是要問地方，然後再找到關鍵字詞 waves 以及 go inside and sit down 答案就出來了。

字詞解釋

wave [wev] **n.** 波浪　　**dizzy** [ˈdɪzɪ] **adj.** 頭暈目眩的　　**view** [vju] **n.** 景色　　**express** [ɪkˈsprɛs] **adj.** 快運的，快遞的

相關文法或用法補充

Wh- 開頭的句子一定都是問句嗎？那可不一定。它也可能是感嘆句，以驚嘆號（！）結尾。中文常常會用「這隻小狗真可愛！」、「天氣真好！」、「真好吃！」來特別強調某種情緒，那麼用英文來表達的話，主要有兩種方式：

1. What a/an + 形容詞 + 單數名詞！例如：

   What an inspiring talk! 真是激勵人心的演講啊！

   What a lovely day! 今天真美好啊！

2. How + 形容詞 +（主詞 + 動詞）！

   How 的後面接形容詞或副詞，而 What 接名詞。

How lovely (the baby is)!（這寶寶真可愛！）
How smart!（真是聰明啊！）

23. **M: What do you think about the movie?**
    W: The acting is no good, and it's so slow. I know what's going on, though it's the first time I watch it.
    M: I think you must watch movies very often.
    W: I do, but my favorite hobby is to go shopping.

    Question: How does the woman feel about the movie?
    (A) She feels tired.
    (B) She feels bored.
    (C) She feels excited.

男：妳覺得這部電影如何？
女：演技不好，且節奏緩慢。我都知道會怎麼演，雖然我第一次看。
男：我想妳一定很常看電影。
女：沒錯，但我最愛的嗜好是購物。
問題：女子今天覺得如何？
(A) 她覺得疲累。(B) 她覺得無聊。(C) 她覺得興奮。

答題解說

答案：(B)。本題問的是「女子覺得如何」，我們可以從她看完電影後的第一句話看出端倪，包括「演技不是很好（The acting is no good）」、「節奏緩慢（it's so slow）」等，可以推知她覺得很「無趣」，故答案應為 (B) She feels bored.。

破題關鍵

tired（感到疲累的）、bored（感到無趣的）以及 excited（感到興奮的）等 -ed 結尾的形容詞，都是用來形容人的感受。

字詞解釋

acting [`æktɪŋ] **n.** 演出，演技　**favorite** [`fevərɪt] **adj.** 最愛的　**hobby** [`hɑbɪ] **n.** 嗜好　**tired** [taɪrd] **adj.** 疲倦的　**bored** [bord] **adj.** 感到無聊的　**excited** [ɪk`saɪtɪd] **adj.** 興奮的

相關文法或用法補充

-ed 與 -ing 的差別，是很多類型考試的最愛之一。只要記住一點：-ed 表示「感到～」，-ing 表示「令人～」；是「人」才會「感到～」，是「人也可以」才會

第 1 回
第 2 回
第 3 回
第 4 回
第 5 回
第 6 回
第 7 回
第 8 回
第 9 回
第 10 回

「令人～」。例如 exciting 是「令人興奮的」意思，用來修飾「事物」，如果是 excited 的話，表示「感到興奮的」，用來修飾「人」。

24. M: I'm afraid we'll be late, if I don't go now. I have an important meeting at three, and it's already twenty past two!

W: I can drive you to your company, and it'll take just fifteen minutes. So don't worry.

M: In that case, let's leave in twenty minutes.

W: No problem.

Question: What time will they leave?

(A) At 2:20 p.m.　(B) At 2:40 p.m.　(C) At 2:45 p.m.

男：如果我現在不走，恐怕要遲到了。我三點有個重要的會議，而現在已經兩點過二十分了！

女：我可以開車載你到公司，只要 15 分鐘就可以到了。所以別擔心。

男：既然這樣，我們二十分鐘後離開吧！

女：沒問題。

問題：他們將在幾點離開？

(A) 在下午 2:20

(B) 在下午 2:40

(C) 在下午 2:45

答題解說

答案：(B)。本題問的是「幾點」啟程離開，因此須注意提到「時間」的相關。首先，男子說現在已經 twenty past two（2:20）了，女子回答說可以載他去，只要 15 分鐘就可以到，所以他們並不是馬上要離開。接著男子說 "let's leave in twenty minutes"（我們二十分鐘後離開），所以他們會在 2:40 離開，故正確答案是 (B)。

破題關鍵

題目關鍵字詞是 they leave，所以對話內容的第一個連結處是 let's leave...，後面接 in 20 minutes，接著只要找到現在是幾點（it's already twenty past two），答案就出來了。

字詞解釋

afraid [əfred] **adj.** 害怕的　　**meeting** [ˋmitɪŋ] **n.** 會議　　**worry** [ˋwɝɪ] **v.** 擔心　　**in that case** 既然這樣，就此看來

第 1 回
第 2 回
第 3 回
第 4 回
第 5 回
第 6 回
第 7 回
第 8 回
第 9 回
第 10 回

相關文法或用法補充

表達時間時，若是整點，一般會用「It's＋數字（＋o'clock).」的句型。表達幾點幾分時，「時」與「分」各以數字表示。「分」若為兩個英文字的數字時，中間要加上連字號「-」，如 thirty-five（35 分），但「時」與「分」之間不用連字號。不過英文裡也會用「幾點過幾分」、「差幾分就幾點」的方式來表達。例如，如果是 20 分之前：It's ten twenty.（現在是十點二十分。）＝It's 10:20.＝ It's twenty past ten.。如果是 20 分之後：It's eight forty.（現在是八點四十分。）＝It's 8:40.＝It's twenty to nine.。

25. M: I'm going out to meet a big boss. If Mr. Wang calls, tell him I won't be in the office until 4:00 p.m., or he can call my cellphone.

W: Got it. What about other people?

M: Ask them to leave a message, and I'll call them back as soon as possible.

W: Yes. Take care.

Question: Who are the speakers?

(A) A manager and a secretary

(B) A doctor and a nurse

(C) A clerk and a customer

男：我要出去見一位大老闆。如果王先生打電話來，告訴他我下午 4:00 才會在辦公室，或者他可以打我的手機。

女：了解。那其他人打來呢？

男：請他們留下訊息，我會盡快回電給他們。

女：好的。路上小心。

問題：談話者是誰？

(A) 經理與祕書　(B) 醫師與護士　(C) 店員與顧客

答題解說

答案：(A)。題目問的是對話中男女的身分（Who），應注意聽一些與職位或身分相關的對話內容。男子一開始說要去見一位大老闆，如果有人打電話找他，告訴對方他何時回來或是留下訊息，他會再回電。這樣的情境，對照選項中三組身分對象，最有可能的答案當然就是 (A) 經理與祕書。

破題關鍵

先看過三個選項，通常只要看到都是職位名稱的話，一定是要問你說話者的身分。然後再注意關鍵字詞（ meet a big boss、leave a message）即可掌握答案了。

message [ˈmɛsɪdʒ] **n.** 訊息　**manager** [ˈmænɪdʒɚ] **n.** 經理　**secretary** [ˈsɛkrəˌtɛrɪ] **n.** 祕書　**clerk** [klɝk] **n.** 店員，銷售員

相關文法或用法補充

在辦公室是 in 還是 at？其實 in 和 at 都對，但意思有些微差別：I'll meet you at the office.（我們在辦公室見。）→ 指地點；I'm in my office.（我正在工作。）→ in 不只是「在辦公室」，而是坐在辦公室裡做事情；好比 in school 是求學，at school 是在學校；in class 是上課，in the office 是辦公。

有時候 in 和 at 用錯了會讓人產生誤解。比如「請打電話到我辦公室給我」→ Please call me _____ the office.，要用 in 還是 at？→ 用 in 才是正確的，當然也可以說 Please call my office，但不要說 Please call me in the office，因為這像是「你在你的辦公室打給我」或「你打電話到我的辦公室找我」，又像是「請你在這間辦公室叫我一聲。」（兩人可能在同一個辦公室），因為 call 也有「呼叫、喊叫」的意思。如此一來，會讓人不知所云！

第四部分 短文聽解

For question number 26, please look at the three pictures.

Question number 26: Listen to the following sports report. Which picture best describes the end of the talk?

Now let's get back. The ball is held by Alex, from the Blue team, and he's ready to throw it in from the side line. Both teams' players are trying hard to catch the ball. It's Charlie... from the White team who gets the ball. Oh, no! David, from the Blue team, pushed Charlie from behind... Luckily he did not fall, and still tried to shoot the ball.

請看以下三張圖。並仔細聆聽播放的運動報導。哪一張圖最能夠表現最後談話內容？

現在我們回到現場。球在藍隊的 Alex 手上，他準備從邊線拋出球。兩隊球員都努力試圖要去爭球。是來自白隊的 Charlie... 接到球了。噢，不！藍隊的大衛，從後方推了 Charlie 一把… 幸好他沒跌倒，還試著要投球。

答題解說

答案：(C)。題目問的是談話內容的最後，在敘述哪一張圖。其中提到「藍隊的大衛，從後方推了 Charlie 一把… 幸好他沒跌到，還試著要投球。」所以只有 (C) 這張圖是符合這項敘述。雖然 (A)、(B) 也都有球員爭球的情形，但都沒有這樣的「犯規」動作。

破題關鍵

首先題目重點要抓到：談話內容的最後。觀察三張圖後，可以發現三張圖都是籃球場上的爭球，但只有 (C) 符合 "...pushed Charlie from behind... Luckily he did not fall..."。

字詞解釋

throw [θro] v. 投，擲，拋　**side line** （運動場上的）邊界線　**from behind** 從背後　**shoot** [ʃut] v. 投射，拋出

相關文法或用法補充

It is/was...that/who... 是「強調」句型。當要強調的部分是「人」時，可用 that，也可以用 who，但指「事物」時，只能用 that，例如：

❶ It was Tom who/that I met last week. （我上週遇見的人是湯姆。）

❷ It is the new bike that his brother wants to buy. （這輛新腳踏車是他弟弟想買的。）

For question number 27, please look at the three pictures.

Question number 27: Listen to the following talk. What dish is available in this restaurant?

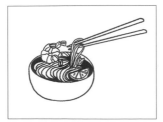  

Here's our menu, Ma'am. We serve the most popular meals in town. For the first dish, you have three choices: fresh shrimp salad, seafood pizza, and onion

rings. So before you make your choice, would you like me to give you any more suggestions, or do you need some time to consider, so I'll be back later?

請看以下三張圖。並仔細聆聽以下談話。這家餐廳提供哪一道餐？

小姐，這是我們的菜單。我們有鎮上最受歡迎的餐點。第一道菜，您有三種選擇：鮮蝦沙拉、海鮮披薩以及洋蔥圈。那麼，在您做決定之前，要我給您更多建議，還是您需要一些時間考慮，我稍後再回來？

答題解說

答案：(B)。這是在餐廳中的服務生對客人介紹三種開胃菜的談話，分別有鮮蝦沙拉、海鮮披薩以及洋蔥圈（fresh shrimp salad, seafood pizza, and onion rings），對照三張圖，只有 (B) 是符合其中之一的鮮蝦沙拉。圖 (A) 明顯可以看到麵食，而圖 (C) 看起來既非沙拉，也不是披薩，更不會是洋蔥圈。

破題關鍵

shrimp、salad、pizza、ring 這些與食物有關的單字，都在英檢初級範圍內，閱讀時也許可以認得出，但聽力的部分，可能要多加練習才可以掌握得到了。

字詞解釋

dish [dɪʃ] n. 一盤菜，菜餚　　**shrimp** [ʃrɪmp] n. 蝦　　**salad** [ˋsæləd] n. 沙拉　　**seafood** [ˋsiˌfud] n. 海產食品　　**pizza** [ˋpitsə] n. 披薩　　**ring** [rɪŋ] n. 圈，環（狀物）　　**suggestion** [səˋdʒɛstʃən] n. 建議，提議　　**consider** [kənˋsɪdə-] v. 考慮，把～視為

相關文法或用法補充

dish 當名詞時有「盤子」，也有「菜餚，（一道）菜」的意思。例如：

❶ Beef noodles is one of Taiwan's famous dishes.
　（牛肉麵是台灣有名的菜餚之一。）

❷ Have you done/washed the dishes?（你洗完餐具沒有？）

For question number 28, please look at the three pictures.

Question number 28: Listen to the following message. What will the speaker probably do tonight?

Hi, sweetheart! It's me. My boss has just called me and said his secretary is feeling sick. He asked me whether I can go with him to meet a very important client tonight. That has a lot to do with our sales next month, so I had no choice to say no. Sorry, but I need to cancel our date tonight. So... would you like to go to a movie tomorrow night? I'll call you later. Bye.

中文翻譯

請看以下三張圖。並仔細聆以下訊息。說話者今晚可能做什麼？

嗨，親愛的！是我。我老闆剛剛打電話給我，並且說他的祕書不舒服。他問我今晚是否可以跟他一起去見一位非常重要的客戶。那跟我們下個月的業績有很大的關係，所以我沒有說「不」的選擇。抱歉，我必須取消我們今晚的約會。那麼…明天晚上要一起去看電影嗎？我晚點打電話給你。再見。

答題解說

答案：(C)。題目問的是說話者「今晚」可能做什麼。其中提到，老闆要求今晚一起去見一位非常重要的客戶，而說話者表示，沒有說「不」的選擇，這表示他一定要去。所以，今晚的情境可能就是「三個人坐下來吃飯」的情況，故圖 (C) 是正確答案。(A) 是看醫生、(B) 看起來是兩人一起去看電影。

破題關鍵

關鍵句是 "... go with him to meet a very important client tonight ... I had no choice to say no."，其中 client 是「客戶」的意思，就算無法理解這個字，至少 go with him... tonight to meet... had no choice 應該要聽得出來，即可掌握正確答案。

字詞解釋

secretary [ˋsɛkrəˌtɛrɪ] n. 祕書　　*client** [ˋklaɪənt] n. 客戶　　**has a lot to do with**... 與～有很大的關係　　**sales** [selz] n. 銷售（額），【口】業務員　　**cancel** [ˋkænsl] v. 取消，廢除

相關文法或用法補充

have to do with... 是「與…有關」的意思，也常看到 have 與 to do 之間加上 something、anything、nothing、a lot... 等字詞。例如：

❶ My question has to do with your being late.（我的問題與你的遲到有關。）

❷ Does his divorce have anything to do with the woman?（他的離婚與這女子有任何關係嗎？）

For question number 29, please look at the three pictures.

Question number 29: Listen to the following talk. Where could you probably hear it?

Ladies and gentlemen, good afternoon and let me have your attention please! Welcome to Japan! My name is Vivian, and I am your tour guide. And this is our young and handsome driver, Mark. Now, we're going to the grand hotel and we'll enjoy our delicious dinner there. Tomorrow, he will take us to Tokyo Disneyland and other scenic areas. You can relax a bit after a long airplane trip.

請看以下三張圖。仔細聽以下簡短談話。你在哪裡可能聽到這則談話？
各位女士、先生，午安！請注意一下我這邊。歡迎來到日本！我的名字是 Vivian，我是你們的導遊。這位是我們年輕又帥氣的司機，Mark。現在，我們將前往大飯店，且我們將在那裡享受我們美味的晚餐。明天，他將帶我們到東京迪士尼樂園以及其他風景區。在長途飛行旅程之後，你們可以放鬆一下。

答題解說

答案：(A)。從 "I am your tour guide. And this is our young and handsome driver, Mark."（我是你們的導遊。這位是我們年輕又帥氣的司機，Mark。）可以聽得出來，這是一位導遊在遊覽車上跟觀光客說的話，所以正確答案是 (A)。圖 (B) 有 "Tokyo Disneyland" 的字樣誤導答題，必須特別小心；圖 (C) 是在觀光巴士旁，導遊小姐對著下車的遊客說話，所以也不是正確答案。

破題關鍵

本題關鍵字詞包括 tour guide 以及 driver，表示說話者在巴士內對著旅客說話，旁邊司機正在開車。

字詞解釋

attention [əˋtɛnʃən] **n.** 注意　**tour guide n.** 導遊　***grand** [grænd] **adj.** 雄偉的，堂皇的　**delicious** [dɪˋlɪʃəs] **adj.** 美味的　***scenic** [ˋsinɪk] **adj.** 風景的　**relax** [rɪˋlæks] **v.** 放鬆　**open country n.** 曠野　**fantastic** [fænˋtæstɪk] **adj.** 極好的

相關文法或用法補充

attention 這個名詞常見於「pay attention to + 名詞」（注意～）、「bring +名詞 + to one's attention」（使某人注意～）、「draw/catch/attract one's attention」（吸引某人的注意）。而這裡的 "May I have your attention?" 是許多公眾場合，主持人或台上的人要請底下觀眾注意聽他／她說話時常用的，是比較客氣、禮貌的請求用語。如果是公司或軍隊中，上對下的場合時。會直接用一個字 Attention!，屬於命令用語。

For question number 30, please look at the three pictures.

Question number 30: Listen to the following recorded message. Which button do you press if you'd like to talk to someone?

 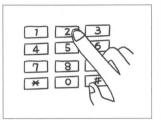 

Asia Mobile customer service hotline. For Chinese service, please press 1. To know about the latest news of offers or good deals, please press 2. For information of different monthly fees, please press 3. To report loss of your SIM card, please press 4. For other services, please press zero. Our customer service staff will be pleased to help you with your problems.

請看以下三張圖。並仔細聆聽以下的錄音訊息。如果你要與人交談，應按哪個按鍵？
亞洲行動客服專線您好。要聽中文請按 1。要知道最新優惠消息，請按 2。要知道不同月租費的資訊，請按 3。要通報 SIM 卡遺失的話，請按 4。如需其他服務，請按 0。我們客服專員將很高興協助您解決問題。

答題解說

答案：(A)。這是行動電話業者的客服語音內容。題目問的是「要與人交談」要按哪個按鍵。應注意聽最後提到「如需其他服務，請按 0。我們客服專員將很高興協助您解決問題。（For other services, please press zero. Our customer service staff will be pleased to help you with your problems.）」所以正確答案是(A)。

英文的「零」是 zero，聽得出這個字的話，基本上作答就沒問題了。就算聽不出來，至少題目 "if you'd like to talk to someone" 要聽懂吧。一般就常識判斷，與客服人員交談不是按 9 就是按 0。

字詞解釋

button [`bʌtn] n. 按鈕，鈕扣　　**press** [prɛs] v. 按，壓　　**customer service** 客服　**hotline** [`hɑtlaɪn] n. 熱線／專線電話　　**latest** [`letɪst] adj. 最新的　　**offer** [`ɔfɚ] n. 提議，優惠　　**fee** [fi] n. 費用　　**zero** [`zɪro] n. 零　　**staff** [stæf] n.（全體）職員　**pleased** [plizd] adj. 高興的，滿意的

相關文法或用法補充

staff 是所謂「集合名詞」，其他像是 family、audience、police、band、crew、public、hair…等都是，如果該集合名詞是當「整體」看，用單數動詞。如果該集合名詞是意指「一群人」，則要用複數動詞。例如：

❶ The family has lived here for at least 10 years.（這家人已經在這裡至少居住了 10 年。）

→ 這裡的 the family 當「整體」看，是全家人的意思，動詞用單數形。

❷ The family have all gone on weekend.（這一家人週末都出門去了。）

→ 這裡的 the family 是指這家的「每一個人」，是一群個體，動詞用複數形。

第一部分 詞彙

1. Is this the answer _____ the question?（這是這個問題的答案嗎？）

(A) to　(B) of　(C) for　(D) from

答題解說

答案：(A)。也許有人會誤選了 (B) of，因為介系詞 of 本來就是「～的」意思，但是在英文裡，看到有「針對」、「解答」、「回應」等意思的字眼時，介系詞必須用 to。雖然「房間的門」可以用 the door of the room，但「門的鑰匙」是 the key to the door。其實，與其去研究文法的問題，不如去「感受」它 — 培養對於介系詞的感覺吧！

破題關鍵

本題的關鍵字有兩個，也就是空格前後的 answer 與 question。在英文裡，「問題的答案」正確說法是 answer "to" the question，這是個常見的固定用法。

字詞解釋

answer [ˋænsɚ] n. 答案，回答　　**question** [ˋkwɛstʃən] n. 問題

相關文法或用法補充

介系詞很多時候都有「固定搭配」用法。雖然必須靠記憶，但其實很多用法也都是「有跡可循」的，也不是一定要死記。例如，to 是「針對／朝向一個目標」的概念：

「問題的解答」：answer to the question、solution to the problem、approach to the issue

「存取的權限」：access to the computer/information/building

「門的鑰匙」：key to the door　「成功的關鍵」：key to success

「演唱會的門票」：ticket to the concert　「對消息的回應」：response to the news

2. Both of the girls are really good. I can't make _____ my mind.（兩個女孩都很好。我沒辦法決定。）

(A) it　(B) up　(C) ready　(D) for

答案：(B)。句子大意是「兩者都很棒，所以沒辦法做決定」。「做決定」的英文就是 make up one's mind。其餘選項的意思是：make it（做得到）、make ready（做好準備）、make for（造成），均不符句意。

破題關鍵

這題純粹考慣用片語。如果有看過或背過 "make up one's mind"，看到空格前的 make 以及後面的 my mind，即可立即選出 up 這個答案了。

字詞解釋

make up 補足，編造，組成

相關文法或用法補充

make up one's mind 後面還可以做延伸。常見用法是：make up one's mind + 不定詞／on + 名詞詞組（就好比 decide to-V / on... 的用法）。例如：I can't make up my mind（on）where to go.（我無法決定要往哪去。）

3. **It makes me _____ to sit there without doing anything.**（坐在那邊沒做什麼事讓我覺得好無聊。）

   (A) bore　(B) boring　(C) bored　(D) to bore

   答題解說

   答案：(C)。空格前是「使役動詞 make + 受詞（me）」的結構，所以應填入受詞補語，選項中的不定詞（to bore）可直接排除。如果選 (A)，因為 bore 當動詞是及物動詞，後面必須有受詞，所以 (A) 也是錯的。bored 與 boring 的差別在於，前者用來形容「人」，後者修飾「事物」。空格前的 me 是「人」，所以應選形容「人」的 bored。

   破題關鍵

   -ed 與 -ing 的差別，是很多類型考試的最愛之一。只要記住一點：-ed 表示「感到～」，-ing 表示「令人～」；是「人」才會「感到～」，是「事物」才會「令人～」。

   字詞解釋

   bored [bord] adj. 感到無聊的　　**boring** [ˋborɪŋ] adj. 令人覺得無聊的

   相關文法或用法補充

   bored 與 boring 都是由及物動詞 bore 衍生而來。例如：題目這句也可以改成：To sit there without doing anything bores me.，但通常主詞過長的話，我們傾向於用虛

主詞 it 來代替。另外，若要表示「對於～感到無聊」可以搭配介系詞 with。例如：I'll be bored with such a movie.（我會對這樣的電影感到無聊。）

4. Mike _____ live with his family when he studied at the university.（Mike 在念大學時沒有和家人住在一起。）

(A) doesn't　(B) didn't　(C) hasn't　(D) hadn't

答題解說

答案：(B)。空格後面是個「原形動詞」，就四個助動詞選項來看，應填入現在式或過去式的助動詞，而完成式助動詞 hasn't 及 hadn't 可直接排除掉。接著，看到 when 子句的時態是過去式，表示主要子句也必定是在描述過去的事情，所以主要子句的助動詞應用過去式的 didn't。

破題關鍵

這題是考「動詞時態的前後一致性」的觀念。基本上 when 就是「同時發生」的概念，所以 when 子句中用什麼時態，主要子句的動詞必須以它作為參考。

字詞解釋

university [ˌjunəˋvɝsətɪ] n. 大學

相關文法或用法補充

同樣表示「大學」意思的 university 與 college 有什麼不同呢？簡單來說是「規模」上的差異，特別是在美國，在一個 university（大學）的校園裡，可能會有文學院、理學院、法學院…等不同的 college（學院），而 college 之所以也被稱為「大學」是因為有些大學只有一個學院，而且在英國，university 與 college 基本上是沒有差別的。另外要注意的是，「上大學」一般會說 go to college，而不會說 go to university。

5. The meeting will begin as soon as the manager _____ in.（等總經理一進來，會議就開始。）

(A) comes　(B) came　(C) will come　(D) is coming

答題解說

答案：(A)。這個句子分成主要子句（The meeting will begin）與副詞子句（the manager _____ in）兩部分。當你遇到這種帶有表示「時間」或「條件」的連接詞，主要子句又是未來式的時候，副詞子句需要用現在式代替未來式，故正確答案應為 (A)。

這題是考「副詞子句中，現在式代替未來式」的觀念。as soon as 就是個「表時間的副詞連接詞」。

meeting [ˋmitɪŋ] n. 會議　**manager** [ˋmænɪdʒɚ] n. 經理

英文中主要有兩種情況，會用現在式代替未來式：表示時間與條件的附屬子句中，要用現在式動詞代替未來式動詞。表示時間的連接詞常見的有：when、while、before、after、as soon as... 等；表示條件的連接詞則有這幾種比較常見：if、unless... 等。例如：He will come if you invite him.（如果你邀請他，他會過來。）

6. **We agreed that Mary _____ on the exam.**（我們一致認為瑪麗考試作弊。）

　　(A) cheats　(B) will cheat　(C) cheated　(D) is cheating

答案：(C)。這個句子分成主要子句（We agreed that...）與附屬子句（Mary _____ on the exam）兩部分。主要子句的動詞時態是過去式，表示「過去的想法」，因此 that 子句中的時態應跟隨主要子句的動詞用過去式。故正確答案應為 (C)。

這題也是考「時態一致性」的觀念。that 也是連接詞的一種，基本上，子句中動詞時態必須跟主要子句的動詞一致。不過當然也有例外，特別是當主要子句的動詞表示「主張、建議、命令…」時，that 子句的動詞要用原形。這部分屬於另外一個層級的文法，在此僅大略提及。

agree [əˋgri] v. 同意　**cheat** [tʃit] v. 欺騙

「對於某事表示同意」，可以用「agree on + 事」，而「同意某人（的說法）」要用「agree with + 人」，而「同意去做某事」是 agree to-V，agree 後面不可接 Ving。

7. Please _____ the lamp and _____ your book to do your homework.
（請開燈並打開書本開始做作業。）

(A) open; close　(B) turn on; turn off　(C) open; turn on　(D) turn on; open

答題解說

答案：(D)。就合乎邏輯的語意來說，應該是「開燈，打開書本，才能開始做作業」，所以有「關閉」意思的 (A) 與 (B) 都可以直接排除。而「開燈」與「打開書」的「開」，英文用的是不一樣的動詞，前者是 turn on，後者是 open。

破題關鍵

看到選項中有 open 及 turn on，就知道這題是考「易混淆動詞」。open 用來表示「打開」箱子、盒子…等有「蓋子」的容器，而 turn on 常表示「開啟」電器類產品，如 TV、radio、lamp... 等。

字詞解釋

lamp [læmp] n. 檯燈　**turn on** 打開　**turn off** 關閉

相關文法或用法補充

我們每天都會用到很多電器，開關微波爐、電燈、電風扇等等，這些「開開關關」，英文中可不是用 open 和 close，而是 turn on/off 喔！另外，還有 switch on/off 也可以用來開啟或關閉一般家電設備，而 power up/off 通常用於電腦等「機器設備」，如果是電燈的開關就不會這樣用。而 shut off/shut down 通常用於關閉引擎、機器等。

8. I'm very surprised that this young little girl is not afraid of _____.（我很訝異的是，這小女孩不怕任何事情。）

(A) something　(B) everything　(C) anything　(D) nothing

答題解說

答案：(C)。句子大意是「小女孩什麼都不怕，令人驚訝。」因此就語意來說，應先排除選項 (D)。再來是從文法觀點來看，something 與 everything 應用於肯定句，因此也都是錯誤的答案，故正確答案應為 (C) anything。

破題關鍵

兩個關鍵點： 1. 什麼樣的代名詞用於肯定句或否定句； 2. 句子的正確語意及邏輯性。

第 1 回
第 2 回
第 3 回
第 4 回
第 5 回
第 6 回
第 7 回
第 8 回
第 9 回
第 10 回

surprised [sə`praɪzd] **adj.** 感到驚訝的 　**be afraid of**... 害怕

形容詞 afraid 後面可以接「of + Ving」或 to-V，但兩者在語意上是有差別的。"afraid of doing..." 是指「擔心、害怕某事發生」例如：He is not afraid of dying.（他不怕死。）而 "afraid to do..." 是指「由於害怕而不願去做某事」，意思較接近 be unwilling to do sth.（because of being afraid of...）。be afraid to do sth. 可以等於 fear to do sth.（害怕做某事）例如：Don't be afraid to ask questions.（不要不敢提問題。）

9. David _____ lots of English magazines when he was a university student.（當大衛還是個大學生時，讀過很多英文雜誌。）

(A) read　(B) reads　(C) was reading　(D) has read

答案：(A)。四個選項都是衍生自動詞 read 的不同形式或時態，所以必須了解這個句子應該用何種時態。首先，當然是先注意「時間點」，可以從 when 子句中的動詞 was 得知，這是發生在過去的事情，所以主要子句應用「簡單過去式」，故正確答案應為 (A) read（read 的動詞三態不變）。(B) reads 為現在式、(C) was reading 為過去進行式、(D) has read 為現在完成式，皆不符合文法規則。

這題是考「動詞時態」的觀念。基本上 when 是「表現時間點」的概念，所以 when 子句中用什麼時態，主要子句的動詞就用什麼時態。

magazine [͵mægə`zin] **n.** 雜誌 　**university** [͵junə`vɝ-sətɪ] **n.** 大學

在英文裡，表示「看」的動詞主要有 look, see, watch, read，但其實「此看非彼看」，每一個「看」所要表達的意義都不同。例如，「看」報紙或雜誌，要用 read，而「看」黑板要說 look at the blackboard；看電視要用 watch TV，去電影院看電影是 see a movie，如果是在家看電視播出的電影，還是要用 watch。

10. Hurry up, or we _____ miss the train.（快點，不然我們會趕不上火車。）

(A) do　(B) will　(C) would　(D) are going to

第 1 回
第 2 回
第 3 回
第 4 回
第 5 回
第 6 回
第 7 回
第 8 回
第 9 回
第 10 回

答題解說

答案：(B)。句子大意是「如果不快一點，會錯過火車」，第一句是祈使句，在這裡具有條件句的作用，所以也可以寫成 If we don't hurry, we _____ miss the train，屬於假設直述句，主要子句助動詞應用未來式的 will。(A) do 表示「的確」，具有強調作用，而 (D) be going to 主要表示計畫或設定好的目標，在此均不符句意；(C) would 用於「與現在事實相反」的假設，亦不可選。

破題關鍵

看到「祈使句／命令句, or (else) / otherwise + S +V...」的句型時，動詞 V 要用未來式，屬於另類的「假設語氣直述法」。

字詞解釋

hurry [`hɝɪ] v. 趕緊，匆忙　　**miss** [mɪs] v. 趕不上，錯過

相關文法或用法補充

表示「否則，不然」的說法有三種：or、or else、otherwise。但必須注意的是，or 是連接詞，otherwise 是副詞。另外，or else 或是 or otherwise 只是 or 的強調說法，所以也是連接詞的作用。所以題目這句可以改寫為：Hurry up, or else/otherwise we will miss the train. 或 Hurry up. Otherwise, we will miss the train.。

第二部分 段落填空

共 8 題，包括二個段落，每個段落各含有四個空格。每格均有四個選項，請依照文意選出最適合的答案。

Questions 11-14

Titan was brought up in the mountains. Every morning, he **needed** to walk down the mountain to a lake where he could collect water. Then he carried two buckets of water on his shoulders and went back up. In this way, he had to go back and forth 4 times a day, before there was enough water needed in a day. In other words, **he had very strong arms and legs**. One day, his cow was injured. So he carried it on his shoulder to a doctor for animals. Everyone in town was **surprised** by what they saw. On the return trip, he noticed a piece of paper on a street wall, which read "Superman Match". He said to himself, "Looks interesting." So he led his cow to the match site. He saw several men lifting large rocks, and others pushing forward very **heavy** objects. When the winner was announced, he clapped loudly and walked to the site.

　　Titan 從小在山上長大。每天早上，他必須走下山，然後到一個湖邊去取水。然後他將兩桶水扛在肩上，再往山上走回去。這樣一天要來回 4 趟，一天要用的水才會足夠。也就是說，他擁有相當強壯的手臂與腿力。有一天，他的牛受傷了。於是他扛著牠去找獸醫。鎮上每個人對於他們所看到的感到驚訝。在回程時，他注意到一張貼在路邊牆上的紙，上面寫著「超人比一比」。他對自己說，「看起來很有趣。」於是他牽著他的牛走到競技場。他看見數名男子舉起大石頭，且其他人往前推著很重的物體。當優勝者被宣布時，他用力鼓掌，並且走進了場內。

11. 答案：(A)。空格後面是不定詞（to walk），所以 (D) finished（後面須接 V-ing）可直接排除。由於後面句子提到 "he had to go back and forth 4 times a day..."（一天要來回 4 趟），所以只有 (A) needed 是符合句意的答案。

12. 答案：(C)。這是要挑選一個句子、子句或句子的一部分放入空格後，確認空格前後和空格句之間的連接關係，是否讓句意顯得自然通順。前文提到「他將兩桶水扛在肩上，再往山上走回去。這樣一天要來回 4 趟」，因此只有 (C) 的 "he had very strong arms and legs" 能夠呼應前文敘述。以下是其餘選項句子的翻譯：
    (A) 他常常摔倒受傷
    (B) 有時候他會懶得做那樣的事
    (D) 他開始厭倦了這樣的生活

13. 答案：(A)。句子大意是「鎮上每個人對於他們所看到的感到驚訝。」（因為他扛著一頭牛到鎮上去找獸醫。）所以正確答案是 (A) surprised。(B) kicked 意思是「踢」、(C) knocked 意思是「敲擊」、(D) lifted 意思是「提起」。

14. 答案：(C)。空格所在的句子意思是「他看見數名男子舉起大石頭，且其他人往前推著很——的物體。」所以只有 (C) heavy 最符合句意。(A) 輕的、(B) 便宜的、(D) 奇怪的都不符句意。

11. 若單就空格所在句子，除了 (D) 之外，其餘選項都是可能的答案。這類題型必須再去前後文找線索。關鍵就在後面提到的，他「必須」提水達到一天足夠的使用量。

12. 本題關鍵是空格前的轉折語 "In other words, ..."，它的意思是「換言之」，這表示前面一句的內容，與空格這一句是相同意義的。所以只有 (C) 可以呼應前面的 "carried two buckets of water on his shoulders"、"go back and forth 4 times a day" 等。

13. 本題關鍵是句子後面的 what they saw（他們所見的），那麼究竟人們是「看到什麼」呢？那就得回推到前一句的 "So he carried it on his shoulder to a doctor for animals."（於是他扛著牠去找獸醫。）相信這一幕應該是讓一般人感到「驚奇」了吧！

14. 空格前有對等連接詞 and，這是本題的關鍵。and 前面這句是 He saw several men lifting large rocks...，既然是 large rocks，當然是非常 heavy 了。

字詞解釋

bring up 將～（人、動物）扶養長大　**collect** [kə`lɛkt] v. 收集，聚集　**carry** [`kærɪ] v. 搬運，攜帶　**bucket** [`bʌkɪt] n. 水桶，提桶　**shoulder** [`ʃoldɚ] n. 肩膀　**back and forth** 來回地　**injure** [`ɪndʒɚ] v. 使受傷，傷害　**return trip** 回程　**notice** [`notɪs] v. 注意到　**match** [mætʃ] n. 比賽，對手　**interesting** [`ɪntərɪstɪŋ] adj. 有趣的　**cow** [kaʊ] n. 母牛　**lift** [lɪft] v. 舉起　**forward** [`fɔrwɚd] adv. 向前　***announce** [ə`naʊns] v. 宣布，發布　**clap** [klæp] v. 拍（手），鼓（掌）　**loudly** [`laʊdlɪ] adv. 大聲地

相關文法觀念補充

11. need 還有助動詞用法，表「必須」，後面接原形動詞，否定形式是「needn't +V」。例如，Need he go so soon?（他這麼快就要走嗎？）此外，need 當助動詞時無人稱之分別，第三人稱單數不加 -s。例如，She needn't have arrived so early, need she?（她不需要那麼早來，不是嗎？）

12. in other words 常置於句首，意思是「換句話說，也就是說」，也可以用 that is to say、that is...等。

13. 空格後面的 what 是「複合關係代名詞」，等於 the thing(s) which。而 what 以及它所引導的子句不是形容詞子句，它的性質是「名詞」，表示一個事物的概念，可當作其前動詞的受詞。例如：My wife knows exactly what I like to eat.（我太太完全知道我喜歡吃什麼。）

14. 在 "He saw several men lifting large rocks, and others pushing forward..." 這個句子裡，可以發現 and 後面並不是個完整句子（沒有動詞），這是一種前後對稱的省略用法，可以還原成 "He saw several men lifting large rocks, and he saw others pushing forward..."。

Questions 15-18

Do you like meat? If yes, you may be interested in the following study results. According to this study, the world's population's need for meat has been **growing**. In 1960, a total of 64 million tons of meat were eaten. At that time, each person ate about 21 kilograms of meat each year. By 2007, this number had climbed to 268 million tons, or about 40 kg per person. Besides, **people's favorite meat also experienced some changes**. In the 1960s, people's favorite meat was beef. Of the meat being eaten, 40% is beef. In 2007, pork was the most popular. However, because people are more concerned about health issues in recent years, poultry meat has increased from 12% to 32%. By the way, do you know which **nation** is the largest meat eater in the world? The answer is Luxembourg! In 2007, every Luxembourger ate about 137 kg of meat! Second only to Luxembourgers are Americans. Every American eats about 126 kilograms! **Next**, let's not talk about the numbers. I will play a song for you. Its title is Currywurst. The singer sang his love for this kind of meat food.

中文翻譯

你愛吃肉嗎？ 如果是，您可能對於以下研究結果感興趣。根據這項研究，全世界人口對於吃肉的需求一直在成長。在 1960 年時，總共有 6400 萬噸的肉被吃掉，在當時，每人每年吃掉約 21 公斤的肉。到了 2007 年，這個數字攀升至 2.68 億噸，每人約 40 公斤。此外，人們喜愛的肉類也產生了一些變化。在 1960 年代時，人們最愛吃的是牛肉。在被食用的肉類中，有 40％ 是牛肉。而在 2007 年時，豬肉是最受歡迎的。但由於近年來人們較關心健康問題，家禽肉類也從 12％ 升至 32％。對了，你知道哪個國家是世界上最大的肉類食用國嗎？答案是盧森堡！在 2007 年，每個盧森堡人吃了約 137 公斤的肉！僅次於盧森堡人的是美國人。每一個美國人大約吃 126 公斤！ 接下來，不談數字了。我將為您播放一首歌，歌名是 Currywurst。其歌手唱出他對這種肉品（咖哩香腸）大餐的熱愛。

答題解說

15. 答案：(B)。空格所在的這個句子意思是「全世界人口對於吃肉的需求一直在-----。」四個選項分別是 (A)「下降」、(B)「成長」、(C)「嚴重的」、(D)「類似的」的意思。所以只有 (A) 與 (B) 是可能的答案。但後面提到 1960 年代到 2007 年的食肉量數字的增加，顯然 (B) 才是符合句意的答案。

16. 答案：(C)。後面提到「在 1960 年代時，人們最愛吃的是牛肉。在被食用的肉類中，有 40％ 是牛肉。而在 2007 年時，豬肉是最受歡迎的。但由於近年來人們較關心健康問題，家禽肉類也從 12％ 升至 32％。」這表示人們喜愛的肉類也產生了一些變化。所以答案是 (C)。以下是其餘選項句子的翻譯：
(A) 我們已改變我們煮肉的方式
(B) 新的肉類已上市
(D) 醫師們一直擔心我們吃太多肉

17. 答案：(A)。空格所在的這個句子意思是「你知道哪個 ----- 是世界上最大的肉品食用國？答案是盧森堡！」所以只有 (A) nation 是最適當的答案。其餘 (B)「公司」、(C)「地區」、(D)「種族」都不符合句意。

18. 答案：(C)。就選項來看，空格要填入一個轉折語，因此前後文句意都應納入判斷。前文提到許多肉食者成長的數字與被喜愛的肉類之變化，都以數字列舉說明，而空格後說 let's not talk about the numbers. I will play a song for you. （不談數字了。我將為您播放一首歌），顯然除了 (C) 之外，其餘選項均不符句意。

破題關鍵

15. 空格所在的句子主詞是 need for meat（肉食的需求），接著再往下看幾行就可以理解文意是「肉食的需求逐漸增加中」。

16. 如果無法從前文句子判斷，那就是從後面句子去推斷。而即使沒學過 poultry（家禽）這個字，至少知道它後面的 meat 吧，再加上前面提到的 beef 與 pork，不難理解這句話要表達的是人們喜愛的肉類有所改變。

17. 本題關鍵當然是 Luxembourg 這個字，但即使不懂它是國家的名字，後面 "Second only to Luxembourgers are Americans" 這句也已經告訴你答案了。

18. 既然後面句子說「不談數字了」，而前面又提到一堆數字，顯然就是要轉移話題了，那麼 next（接下來）當然就是最適合開始轉移重點的用字了。

字詞解釋

following [ˋfɑləwɪn] adj. 下面的，下述的　　**result** [rɪˋzʌlt] n. 結果　　**according to**... 根據～　**population** [ˌpɑpjəˋleʃən] n. 人口　　**a total of**... 總共～　　**concerned** [kənˋsɚnd] adj. 擔心的，關心的　　**issue** [ˋɪʃʊ] n. 問題　　***poultry** [ˋpoltrɪ] n. 家禽　　**increase** [ɪnˋkris] v. 增加　　**by the way** 順道一提　　**second only to**... 僅次於～　**title** [ˋtaɪtl] n. 名稱　　**serious** [ˋsɪrɪəs] adj. 嚴重的　　**similar** [ˋsɪmələ] adj. 類似的　　**hit the market** 上市　　**experience** [ɪkˋspɪrɪəns] v. 經歷　　**worried** [ˋwɝɪd] adj. 擔心的　　**nation** [ˋneʃən] n. 國家　　**race** [res] n. 人種，種族

相關文法觀念補充

15. grow 也是個用法千變萬化的動詞。其動詞三態為：grow → grew → grown。表示「種樹、種花」可以說 grow a tree/flower，此時 grow 是及物動詞。而它當不及物動詞時，表示「成長，增加」，可以表示具體「物」的成長，也可表示「抽象」數字的增加。例如：The tree grew.（這棵樹長大了。）、The population is growing.（人口正在成長。）

16. market 是「市場」的意思，一個產品在市場上開賣，可以用 be on the market 或 hit the market 來表示。

17. meat 是「物質名詞」的一種，諸如 tea（茶）、paper（紙）、water（水）、gold（金）、iron（鐵）、air（空氣）、soup（湯）、oil（油）、beef（牛肉）、food（食物）、milk（牛奶）、bread（麵包）、rice（米）⋯等都是。物質名詞雖然不可數，其前卻可以加上某種單位的名詞來表示數量。例如 a piece of meat（一塊肉）、a cup of water（一杯水）。

18. next 的用法繁多，因為它可以當形容詞、副詞、介系詞及名詞。當副詞時可以置於句首或句尾。例如：What happened next?（接下來發生了什麼事情？）、Next, I'll teach you this.（再來，我要教你這個。）

第三部分 閱讀理解

Questions 19-21

中文翻譯

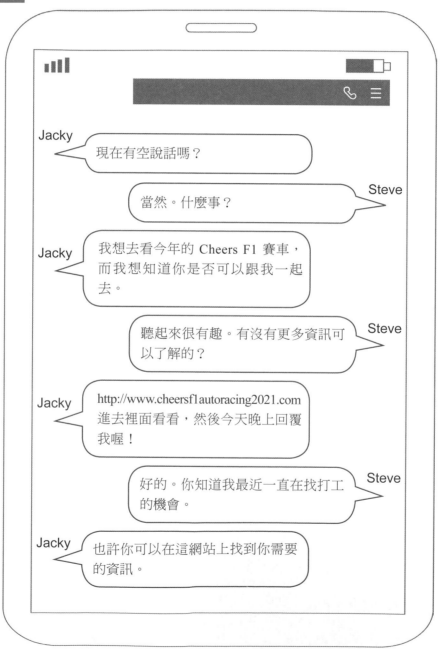

Jacky
現在有空說話嗎？

Steve
當然。什麼事？

Jacky
我想去看今年的 Cheers F1 賽車，而我想知道你是否可以跟我一起去。

Steve
聽起來很有趣。有沒有更多資訊可以了解的？

Jacky
http://www.cheersf1autoracing2021.com
進去裡面看看，然後今天晚上回覆我喔！

Steve
好的。你知道我最近一直在找打工的機會。

Jacky
也許你可以在這網站上找到你需要的資訊。

第 1 回
第 2 回
第 3 回
第 4 回
第 5 回
第 6 回
第 7 回
第 8 回
第 9 回
第 10 回

```
← → C ⌂    Q  http://www.cheersf1autoracing2021.com        _ ⧠ ⊡ ✕
```

還記得去年在 Agogo 市的 Cheers F1 賽車有多令人興奮的嗎？現在可是準備迎接今年在 Trivago 市舉辦的 Cheers F1 賽車的時候了。現在就來看看吧！

➤ 關於 Cheers F1 賽車
  ◎ 歷史　　　　　　　◎ 2021 年賽程　　　　◎ 2021 年競賽隊伍

➤ 關於 Trivago 市
  ◎ 歷史　　　　　　　◎ 交通路線　　　　　　◎ 觀賽地點
  ◎ 找飯店　　　　　　◎ 找美食　　　　　　　◎ 市區購物

➤ 更多資訊
  ◎ 觀賞過去比賽影片　　　　◎ 加入我們的工作團隊
  ◎ 立刻購票　　　　　　　　◎ 寄電子郵件給我們

19. 為何 Jacky 傳送訊息給 Steve？
   (A) 告訴他一個好消息
   (B) 對他表示感謝
   (C) 邀請他一起去參加活動
   (D) 抱怨一些事情

20. Steve 要點擊網頁上的哪裡來了解他要的資訊？
   (A) 觀賽地點
   (B) 加入我們的工作團隊
   (C) 2021 年競賽隊伍
   (D) 2021 年競賽項目

21. 什麼資訊可能不會是令 Jacky 感興趣的？
   (A) 票價多少
   (B) 在 Agogo 市區去哪裡購物
   (C) Trivago 市過去發生的事
   (D) 2021 年競賽隊伍

答題解說

19. 答案：(C)。題目問的是 Jacky 傳送訊息給 Steve，只要看對話訊息內容即可知道答案。Jacky 一開始就問 Steve 是否可以跟他去看 Cheers F1 賽車，所以他想邀請他一起去看賽車，也就是參加一場活動，故正確答案為 (C) To invite him to an activity.。

20. 答案：(B)。題目問的是第二個文本（網頁資訊）中的項目，哪一項會是 Steve 想要點（click）進去了解的。所以需要整合與歸納兩篇文本的資訊並比對多項訊息才能夠得到正確的答案。在對話訊息（第一個文本）中，當 Jacky 邀請他一起去看賽車時，他說「我最近一直在找打工的機會。（I've recently been looking for a part-time job.）」因此我們可以推知，他會想點「Join our work team（加入我們的工作團隊）」。

21. 答案：(B)。本題也是需要整合與歸納兩篇文本的資訊並比對多項訊息才能夠得到正確的答案。題目問的是什麼資訊可能不會是令 Jacky 感興趣的，其實跟前一題的方向是一樣的。從對話訊息中可以了解，Jacky 本身就想去看 F1 賽車，所以基本上在第二個文本的網頁內容都是他感興趣的。但網頁提供的是今年在「Trivago 市」的賽事相關消息，而 (B) 是指在（去年）「Agogo 市」區去哪裡購物」，所以正確答案為 (B)。

破題關鍵

19. 發送訊息的目的，其線索會在第一位發言者的談話中找到，因此只要注意第一位發言者的前一、兩次發言內容即可。

20. 既然是問「令 Jacky 感興趣的」，就要從他的發言內容去找答案。關鍵在 "You know I've recently been looking for a part-time job." 這句話。

21. 本題是考你細心的程度。網頁一開始就提到 "last year in Agogo City" 以及 "this year's Cheers F1 Auto Racing in Trivago City"，所以他不可能對於 "Where to go shopping in Agogo City" 感興趣。

字詞解釋

available [əˋvɛləbl] **adj.** 有空的，可用的　　**auto** [ˋɔto] **n.**【口】汽車（= automobile）
race [res] **n.** 速度競賽　　**wonder** [ˋwʌndɚ] **v.** 想知道　　**check it out** 查看　　**exciting**
[ɪkˋsaɪtɪŋ] **adj.** 令人興奮的　　**history** [ˋhɪstərɪ] **n.** 歷史　　**invite** [ɪnˋvaɪt] **v.** 邀請　　**activity**
[ækˋtɪvətɪ] **n.** 活動　　**complaint** [kəmˋplent] **n.** 抱怨

相關文法或用法補充

❶ Check it out! 是「去查看一下！」的意思，例如對方給你一份參考資訊，你要查看一下，可以說：Let me check it out. 這裡跟 Let me take a look. 的意思差不多。不過單就 check out 來說，還有「結帳退房」的意思，例如 What time did he check out?（他幾點結帳退房的？）

❷ see、look、watch、read 都有「看」的意思，它們的用法有什麼不同呢？
　① see 表示「看見、看到」，也表示「明白、了解」，如：I see.，表示「我了解。」Can you see the taxi coming? We are going to be late.（妳有看到計程車過來嗎？我們快要遲到了。）

② look 表示的是集中目光往目標的方向「看」。如：Look at me when I am talking to you.（我在跟你說話的時候要看著我。）

③ watch 也是集中注意力「看」，但是「看」的時間更長，例如：看電影、看影片、看演出等。如：I usually watch movies on holiday.（我通常在放假時看電影。）

④ read 則是「讀、看」的意思，常見說法有看書、看信、看報紙、看雜誌等。如：Dad always reads English newspapers before breakfast.（爸爸總是在早餐前看英文報紙。）

Questions 22-24

中文翻譯

寄件人	Peter Piper
收件人	Mandy Minor
主旨	大衛的閱讀能力
附件	特別課程.pdf

Minor 太太 您好：

　　我寫這封是要來讓您知道，我真的很擔心您兒子的閱讀能力問題。他在這個班已經有三個月了，而他在所有類型的故事與書籍中都有閱讀上的困難。

　　他的大部分同學都可以讀到七級，而他只能讀到二級。為了協助他更進步些，我建議他去上一個特別的閱讀課程。請打開附件檔案，您會看見一個網站的連結。這項課程以傳統教學方式幫助學生學習及閱讀字的發音。他每天只需要花 20-30 分鐘即可。

　　若您有任何關於這件事的問題，請發電子郵件或直接打電話給我。

謹啟

Peter Piper

閱讀訓練師

22. Piper 先生的電子郵件目的為何？
    (A) 告知 David 的說話能力問題
    (B) 讓這位母親知道她小孩的學習狀況
    (C) 提供學校的最新消息
    (D) 建議這位母親去上一個課程

23. 關於這個特殊閱讀課程，以下何者為真？
    (A) 它專為英文初學者設計。
    (B) 父母們也能夠使用。
    (C) 學生可以每天使用。
    (D) 所有孩童都必須使用。

24. 這裡「attached」的意思最接近 _____？
    (A) 收集　(B) 決定　(C) 包含　(D) 邀請

答題解說

22. 答案：(B)。題目問的是Piper 先生為何寫這封信件，通常這樣的題目可以先從信件上方的「主旨（subject）」找線索。不過這裡的 David's reading 無法給予明確的訊息，所以應該在內容中找答案。這封 E-mail 主要告知 David 的母親，她兒子在閱讀上落後其他同學，並建議他上網去上一個特殊課程。所以正確答案應為 (B) 的「讓這位母親知道她小孩的學習狀況」。

23. 答案：(C)。題目問的是「特殊閱讀課程（special reading course）」有關的「正確」資訊。第二段最後提到 "He only has to spend twenty to thirty minutes on this every day."（他每天只需要花 20-30 分鐘即可。）也就是說學生可以每天使用。所以 (C) 是正確答案。(A) 錯誤的原因是，它是針對初學孩童的閱讀能力，而非英文學習；(B) 錯在「父母」，而 (D) 錯在「必須使用」。

24. 答案：(C)。attached 這個字所在的句子是 Please open the file attached and you'll see the link to a website.，意思是說「請打開附件檔案看一下，您會看見一個網站的連結。」表示這個 file（檔案）是「包含」在這封電子郵件中。所以答案是 (C) 的 included。

破題關鍵

22. 從第一句的 I am writing to let you know... ability to read. 就可以得到線索，ability to read 就是指 her child's learning。

23. 題目關鍵字詞是 special reading course，指向第二段中間部分的 "This course helps students learn and read the sounds of words in traditional teaching methods. He only has to spend twenty to thirty minutes on this every day."（這項課程以傳統教學方式幫助學生學習及閱讀字的發音。他每天只需要花 20-30 分鐘即可。）

24. 即使不知道 attach 的意思，在電子郵件「主旨（Subject）」的下方有 Attachment，根據常識判斷應該也知道是「附件」，也就是「包括」在信件內的文件或檔案（file）。

subject [ˋsʌbdʒɪkt] n. 主題，主旨　***attachment** [əˋtætʃmənt] n. 附屬物，附件　**concerned** [kənˋsɝnd] adj. 擔心的，關切的　**ability** [əˋbɪlətɪ] n. 能力　**in trouble with** 有～麻煩　**level** [ˋlɛvl] n. 等級，程度　**assist** [əˋsɪst] v. 協助　**progress** [ˋprɑgrɛs] n. 進步，進展　**suggest** [səˋdʒɛst] v. 建議　**course** [kors] n. 課程　***attach** [əˋtætʃ] v. 附屬，附加　**traditional** [trəˋdɪʃənl] adj. 傳統的　**directly** [dəˋrɛktlɪ] adv. 直接地　**issue** [ˋɪʃʊ] n. 問題　**design** [dɪˋzaɪn] v. 設計　**beginner** [bɪˋgɪnɚ] n. 初學者　**required** [rɪˋkwaɪrd] adj. 必要的，必需的

❶ ability（能力）是 able（能夠的）的名詞，因為 able 後面常接 to-V（例如 I'm able to speak in English.），所以 ability 後面也會接 to-V，作為其後位修飾語。例如：I have the ability to speak English.

❷ progress（進步）在初學階段，只要知道它的名詞用法即可。常見於 make progress（有進步，前進）或 in progress（進行中）。例如：

① The mountain climbers made slow progress to the top.
　（這些登山客往山頂緩慢前進。）
② She has made great progress in Math.（她的數學已有很大的進步。）
③ The meeting is still in progress.（會議正在進行中。）

Questions 25-27

　　馬塞爾·普魯斯特（Marcel Proust，1871-1922 年）是一位法國偉大的作家，且被認為是 20 世紀最有影響力的思想家之一。他最著名的書是《À la Recherche du Temps Perdu》，一般命名為《追憶逝水年華》。

　　在這本書中，普魯斯特讓我們看到一些有錢人卻總是感到不快樂。這些富人一直認為他們理所當然應該受到歡迎或喜愛。當他們發現自己並非如想像中受歡迎時，他們感到難失望，於是他們努力要讓自己在他人眼中變得重要。這就是為什麼他們總是陷入迷失，且永遠無法享受快樂的生活。

　　相較於他書中這些人的生活，在普魯斯特人生最後十五年中，雖然生活仍然艱苦，他仍然可以找到快樂。在那些年裡，他得了重病。大部分時間他都得在病床上度過。他在病房裡開始寫《À la Recherche du Temps Perdu》。在這寫書過程中他非常快樂，並因為這本書最終成為一位偉大的作家。

25. 關於 Proust，以下何者為非？
    (A) 他在他的作品中寫了關於富有但不快樂的人們。
    (B) 他在他後來的生活中從寫作中獲得很多樂趣。
    (C) 他在他的晚年過著困苦的生活。
    (D) 他在他 15 歲時開始寫《À la Recherche du Temps Perdu》。

26. 關於 Proust 書中的富人，我們可以得知什麼？
    (A) 他們從過去學到教訓。
    (B) 他們試圖得到他們所沒有的東西。
    (C) 他們大多數人始終是健康且快樂地生活。
    (D) 他們有些人經常生病，但仍感到快樂。

27. 最接近第二段第四行 "disappointed" 的含義是什麼？
    (A) 生氣的
    (B) 好笑的
    (C) 傷心的
    (D) 奇怪的

答題解說

這是一篇人物介紹，內容敘述法國一位大文豪的名著及其生平。

25. 答案：(D)。第二段一開始提到普魯斯特讓我們看到一些有錢人卻總是感到不快樂，所以 (A) 是正確的；在第三段中提到在普魯斯特人生最後十五年中，雖然他生活仍然艱苦，他仍然可以找到快樂，所以 (B) 是正確的；同時也提到他在這寫書過程中非常快樂，所以 (C) 也是正確的。而普魯斯特是在他人生最後十五年中開始寫《À la Recherche du Temps Perdu》，所以 (D) 是錯誤的。

26. 答案：(B)。關於 Proust 書中的富人，相關資訊可以從第二段內容得知。其中提到，當他們發現自己並非如想像中受歡迎時⋯他們努力要讓自己在他人眼中變得重要（they try hard to make themselves look important to others）。這表示他們試圖得到他們所沒有的東西。這裡所謂「他們所沒有的東西」就是指「在他人眼中很重要」。故正確答案為 (B)。

27. 答案：(C)。disappointed 這個字所在的句子是 "When they find that they are not as popular as they thought they should be, they feel disappointed, so they try hard to..."，意思是說「當他們發現自己並非如想像中受歡迎時，他們感到 ------」，其實如果單就這個句子來說，四個選項似乎都是可能的答案，不過這段一開始就提到，普魯斯特讓我們看到一些有錢人卻總是感到不快樂。既然是「感到不快樂」，那麼最接近的答案當然就是 (C) sad 了。

破題關鍵

25. 「何者為真」或「何者為非」的題型，都屬於內容細節型的題目。通常必須先看過四個選項內容，再到文章中找尋線索。

26. 「關於…可以得知什麼」，與「何者為真」或「何者為非」的題型都是「內容細節」的問題，只能依據題目關鍵語句，到文本中的相關位置去找線索，然後一項一項檢視何者正確或錯誤。本題關鍵語句是 "rich people in Proust's book" ，所以應從第二段內容去找答案。

27. 本題關鍵點在第二段第一句中的 unhappy 這個形容詞，因此與 unhappy 最接近的是 sad。

字詞解釋

consider [kən`sɪdə] v. 視～為～   *__influential__ [ˌɪnfluˋɛnʃəl] adj. 有影響力的（influence 的形容詞）   **thinker** [ˋθɪŋkə] n. 思想家   **century** [ˋsɛntʃʊrɪ] n. 世紀，一百年   **famous** [ˋfeməs] adj. 著名的   **generally** [ˋdʒɛnərəlɪ] adv. 一般地   *__remembrance__ [rɪˋmɛmbrəns] n. 回憶，懷念（remember 的名詞）   **reasonably** [ˋriznəblɪ] adv. 理所當然地（reason → reasonable → reasonably）   **popular** [ˋpɑpjələ] adj. 得人心的，受歡迎的   *__disappointed__ [ˌdɪsəˋpɔɪntɪd] adj. 失望的   **compare** [kəmˋpɛr] v. 比較   **seriously** [ˋsɪrɪəslɪ] adv. 嚴肅地，認真地   **ill** [ɪl] adj. 生病的   **pleasure** [ˋplɛʒə] n. 愉快，樂趣   **difficulty** [ˋdɪfəˌkʌltɪ] n. 困難   **lesson** [ˋlɛsn] n. 教訓，課程   **strange** [strendʒ] adj. 奇怪的

相關文法或用法補充

❶ 常用的「視…為…」的片語，常搭配 to be 或 as，但有些動詞搭配的 to be 或 as 是可以省略的。例如：
Many people consider Kate Moss's beauty（as/to be）timeless.（許多人視 Kate Moss 的美是永恆的。）
改成被動語態是 Kate Moss's beauty is considered（to be）timeless.
這裡的動詞 consider 可以用 think、see 取代。

❷ with 可以表示原因或理由，多用於與某些動詞、形容詞等的搭配中。例如，He is tired <u>with</u> work.（他對工作厭倦了。）、At the news we all jumped <u>with</u> joy.（聽到這消息我們都高興得跳了起來。）

Questions 28-30

中文翻譯

　　已經快十二點了，李太太有點擔心。發生了什麼事？Mary 原本說她會在十一點之前回到家。李太太不停地打她的手機，但仍然沒人接。她穿上外套，從臥室走出

319

來到客廳。她站在窗前，望著外面。David 走出房間，問他媽媽：「姐姐還沒回來嗎？」「還沒，但我想她正在回家的路上。」David 回到自己的房間念書。他隔天有一場非常重要的考試。

　　李太太心想：「David 一直都是個乖巧的男孩。他小五歲，但他很少讓我擔心。」過了十分鐘，她的手機響了。「你怎麼了？你又讓我擔心了！你在哪？…什麼？好。你就跟 Helen 待在戲院前面就好。我開車過去那裡載你和 Helen 回家。我大約十分鐘後就到。」李太太拿著車鑰匙，馬上就出去了。

28. 這個故事主要告訴我們什麼？
　　(A) 當你在外時不應關閉手機。
　　(B) 孩子不應太晚回家。
　　(C) 父母不應在重要考試前讓孩子外出。
　　(D) 孩子不應讓父母擔心。

29. 以下哪一項是正確的？
　　(A) Mary 會在十分鐘後回家。
　　(B) 李太太不會開車。
　　(C) Helen 是 David 的姊姊。
　　(D) Mary 比 David 大五歲。

30. 瑪麗去了哪裡？
　　(A) 她和海倫一起去了購物中心。
　　(B) 她和海倫一起去看電影。
　　(C) 她和男友約會。
　　(D) 她獨自去了海灘。

答題解說

這是一篇記敘文，內容講述孩子出門在外若要晚歸，應讓父母知道，免得讓父母擔心。

28. 答案：(D)。本篇故事在第二段一開始透過李太太的獨白，點出全篇主旨：「David 一直都是個乖巧的男孩，他小她姊姊五歲，卻很少讓母親擔心。而後面在電話中又再次強調這一點：「你怎麼了？你又讓我擔心了！你在哪？」故正確答案為 (D)。

29. 答案：(D)。第二段提到 "He's five years younger..."，因此可知道「Mary 比 David 大五歲。」故正確答案為 (D)。(A) 錯的原因是，李太太在電話中對她女兒說「我大約十分鐘後就到。」並不表示 Mary 會在十分鐘後回家；(B) 錯的原因是，李太太在電話中對她女兒說「我開車過去那裡載你和海倫回家。」(C) 錯的原因是，David 的姊姊是 Mary，而不是 Helen。

第 1 回

第 2 回

第 3 回

第 4 回

第 5 回

第 6 回

第 7 回

第 8 回

第 9 回

第 10 回

30. 答案：（B）。李太太在電話中對她女兒說「你就跟 Helen 待在戲院前面就好。我開車過去那裡載你…」可見 Mary 和 Helen 去看電影。故正確答案為（B）。

破題關鍵

28. 就記敘文的「主旨型」考題而言，答案線索不一定在第一段一開始就能確定，不過這篇故事中提到 worried 這個字 3 次（Mrs. Lee felt a bit worried、he seldom makes me worried、You made me so worried again!），可見「孩子不應讓父母擔心」是全篇主旨。

29. 「何者為真」或「何者為非」的題型，都屬於內容細節型的題目。通常都是擺在最後一題再作答。在了解每一個選項的內容之後，對照文章中提及的相關內容，然後用刪除法自然能夠得到正確答案。

30. 本題其實是考你「換句話說」，也就是 theater 與 went to a movie 之間的連結。

字詞解釋

worried [ˋwɝɪd] **adj.** 擔心的　**cellphone** [ˋsɛlˏfon] **n.** 行動電話，手機　**put on** 穿上（= wear）　**coat** [kot] **n.** 外套　**on the way home** 在回家的路上　**well-behaved** [ˋwɛlbɪˋhevd] **adj.** 行為端正的，聽話的　**theater** [ˋθɪətɚ] **n.** 戲院　**right away** 立刻，馬上　**turn off** 關閉　**shopping mall** 購物中心　**date** [det] **n.** 約會　**alone** [əˋlon] **adv.** 單獨，獨自

相關文法或用法補充

❶ 動名詞（V-ing）有「同時、持續」的意思，所以當 keep（保持）這個動詞後面要接「一個動作」時，必須接動名詞。例如：The baby keeps crying.（這嬰兒一直在哭。）不過有時候也會看到 keep 後面出現 to，這時候的 to 是個介系詞，"keep to + 名詞" 表示「遵守，堅持」。例如 "We must keep to the rule."（我們必須遵守規定。）

❷ well-behaved 如其字面意思，就是「行為良好的」意思。She behaves well. = She is well-behaved.。像這樣由兩個字組成的形容詞，稱為「複合形容詞」。「複合形容詞」在英文裡有多種形式，常見的有：

① 「名詞 - 現在分詞 / 過去分詞」：man-eating（吃人的）、snow-covered（被雪覆蓋著的）

② 「形容詞 / 副詞 - 現在分詞 / 過去分詞」：good-looking（好看的）、never-ending（永無休止的）、well-done（做得好的）

③ 「形容詞 + 名詞」：last-minute（最後一刻的）

④ 「數字 + 單位」：14-year-old（14 歲的）、10-mile（10 英里的）

⑤ 用連字號把片語變成一個字：all-too-common（很常見的）

學習筆記欄

7

GEPT
全民英檢

初級初試
中譯＋解析

第一部分 看圖辨義

1. **For question number 1, please look at Picture A.**

   Question number 1: What does this sign tell us?
   （這個標誌告訴我們什麼？）
   (A) Cross the rail to take the next train.
   　　（穿越鐵軌去搭下一班列車。）
   (B) The next train will not stop here.（下一班列車不會靠站。）
   (C) The next train will not pass through the station.（下一班列車不會經過本站。）

!	**Next train**

   Next train does not stop
   Please stand behind the yellow platform line.

   答題解說

   答案：（B）。這通常是在車站月台當遇到進站不停的列車時，會打出的警告標誌。就是告訴旅客「下一班列車會直接通過，不會停靠本站。而且不要超出等候線」，所以正確答案是（B）。

   破題關鍵

   即使不知道這是給誰看的標誌，仔細聽過三個選項也會知道這是在火車或地鐵月台的標誌。

   字詞解釋

   cross [krɔs] v. 橫越，穿越　　**rail** [rel] n. 鐵軌　　**pass through** 經過

   相關文法或用法補充

   cross 當動詞表示「穿越」，但別與 across 搞混了。across 是個介系詞，也是「穿越」的意思，常與表「行進」有關的動詞搭配。例如：walk across the street/river（穿越街道／河流）。

2. **For question number 2 and 3, please look at Picture B.**

   Question number 2: What happened to the man?
   （男子發生什麼事了？）
   (A) He couldn't find his keys.（他找不到他的鑰匙。）
   (B) He forgot to bring his keys.（他忘了帶鑰匙了。）
   (C) He lost some money.（他的錢遺失了。）

第 1 回
第 2 回
第 3 回
第 4 回
第 5 回
第 6 回
第 7 回
第 8 回
第 9 回
第 10 回

答案：（A）。圖片中男子手伸進口戴在找東西，而旁邊地上有一串鑰匙，顯然他找不到他的鑰匙。所以正確答案為（A）。

題目中的 "happened to" 是個慣用語，若聽不出來也不影響解題。其實只要聽懂 3 個選項的意思，再對照這張圖，就可以知道男子找不到他的鑰匙。

happen to... 發生在（某人身上）　　**forget** [fɚ`gɛt] **v.** 忘記

happen to 可以當作一個「及物動詞片語」，但須注意的是，它有「發生」以及「恰巧」兩種截然不同的意思。

1. 表示「發生」，to 為介系詞（後接 N.）：主詞必然是「事物」，而受詞必須是「人（或動物等）」。而且主詞通常都是「不好的事、災難、意外」等…。例如：I hope nothing has happened to my friend.（我希望我朋友不會發生任何事情。）

2. 表示「恰巧」，to 為不定詞的 to（後接 V.）：主詞必然是「人」。例如：I happened to meet her at the train station.（我碰巧在火車站遇見她。）

3. **Question number 3: Please look at Picture B again.**

   What is true about the little girl?

   （關於小女孩，何者為真？）

   (A) She looked curious.（她看起來很好奇。）

   (B) She found her keys on the ground.

   　　（她在地上發現她的鑰匙。）

   (C) She told the man she found his keys.（她告訴男子她找到他的鑰匙。）

答案：（A）。圖片中小女孩一臉好奇的表情看著地上的鑰匙，顯然鑰匙不是她的，所以（B）不對，而且她也沒有對著男子說話，所以（C）不對。正確答案為（A）。

curious [`kjʊrɪəs] **adj.** 好奇的　　**ground** [graʊnd] **n.** 地面

「告訴」對方一件事或一個事實，是一種單向的表達，而 tell 後面可以接「事

物」或「人」。像是 tell a story（說個故事）、tell him the truth（告訴他實情）、tell me (that) you love me（告訴我你愛我）。所以當 tell 後面有「人」又有「事物」時（有兩個受詞），tell 是個「授予動詞」。

4. **For question number 4 and 5, please look at Picture C.**

Question number 4: What is the woman doing?
（這名女子正在做什麼？）
(A) She is crying at the dog.（她正對著這隻狗哭泣。）
(B) She is walking her dog.（她正在遛狗。）
(C) She is dancing with her dog.（她正和她的狗在跳舞。）

答題解說

答案：(B)。本題問的是「某人正在做什麼」(what)，聽到問題後立即將圖片與選項連結起來。圖片中女子正在遛狗，所以正確答案是(B)。

破題關鍵

先看過圖片，然後聽出題目要問的對象是 woman，而不是 child 或 kid，那麼就不至於會去選到 crying 或 dancing 這兩個動作了。

字詞解釋

cry at... 對著～哭泣　　**walk** [wɔk] **v.** 陪～走，遛（狗等）

相關文法或用法補充

walk 的意思除了最基本「走路」（為「不及物動詞」）意思之外，還有「陪著～走路」，為及物動詞用法，其受詞可以是「人」或其他「動物」。例如：The mother walked the child along the street.（母親帶著孩子在街上走著。）

5. **Question number 5: Please look at Picture C again.**

What is true about the picture?
（關於這張圖片，何者為真？）
(A) The woman holds the hand of her child.
　　（女子牽著她孩子的手。）
(B) They are watching the sunset.（他們正在觀賞夕陽。）
(C) The young child is sitting and crying on the beach.（這小孩坐在海灘上哭泣。）

答題解說

答案：(C)。圖片顯示女子在海灘上遛狗，而旁邊一個小孩大聲哭泣，且沒有看到夕陽（sunset），所以(A)、(B)都是錯誤的。

第 1 回

第 2 回

第 3 回

第 4 回

第 5 回

第 6 回

第 7 回

第 8 回

第 9 回

第 10 回

破題關鍵

遇到「何者為真」或「何者為非」的題目，就是先仔細觀察圖片後，將三個選項的內容一一對照，是最保險的答題方式。當然，選項中的關鍵字詞一定要聽懂：hold the hand of... 表示「牽著～的手」；sunset 是「夕陽」的意思。

字詞解釋

sunset [ˈsʌnˌsɛt] n. 日落（的景象）

相關文法或用法補充

sunset（日落）這個字是由 sun + set 構成。set 這個動詞意思很多，「復位」就是其中之一。所以「太陽復位」就是太陽回到原來的位置，那就是指「日落」囉！而 The sun is setting. 表示「夕陽西下。」另外，「日出」是 sunrise。

第二部分 問答

6. **May I come in?**（我可以進來嗎？）

(A) Sit down, please.（請坐。）
(B) I'm sorry.（我很抱歉。）
(C) Yes, please.（可以，請進！）

答題解說

答案：(C)。當你要進入別人的房間或辦公室時，禮貌上都會先敲門後，說「我可以進來嗎？」，如果是肯定的回答，可以說 Yes, please come in. 或是簡短的 "Yes, please." 或是 "Come in!"，表示「請進。」另外，(B) 的 I'm sorry. 通常用來表達歉意，如果前面加上 No. 才會是正確的回答。

破題關鍵

"May I...?" 是委婉表達「請求」的用語。通常會直接以 Yes/No 來回答。

相關文法或用法補充

may 是個「情態助動詞」（含不確定的意味），常見用法為：

❶ 表示「猜測」：He may come back home tonight.（他今晚可能會回家）
❷ 表示「允許」：May I use your computer?（我能用你的電腦嗎？）

7. **How does the cake taste?**（這蛋糕味道如何？）

(A) It's very cheap.（它很便宜。）
(B) I'm fine. Thank you.（我沒事。謝謝）
(C) It went sour. When did you buy it?（它變酸了。你什麼時候買的？）

答案：(C)。How... taste? 是問食物味道如何？(A)、(B) 皆答非所問。(C) 的回答是「它變酸了⋯」，表示說話者嘗過後告知這蛋糕已經壞了。所以正確答案是 (C)。

sour 是英檢初級範圍的單字，必須能夠聽得出來。另外 go 也有 become 的意思，go sour 表示「變得臭酸」。但本題也可以用「刪除法」來解。

taste [test] v. 嚐起來　**cheap** [tʃip] adj. 便宜的　**sour** [saʊr] adj. 酸（臭）的

在英文裡，表示「變成」的動詞，除了 become、get 之外，還有其他很基本的動詞也有這個意思，像是 turn、go、grow 等。這些動詞後面要接「主詞補語」（通常是名詞或形容詞）。例如：

❶ He went mad last night when he was drunk.（他昨晚發酒瘋。）
❷ Soon the sky grew dark.（天很快變黑了。）
❸ The weather suddenly turned much colder.（天氣突然變得冷多了。）

8. **You may call later or may I take your message?**（您可以晚點再打來或者要我留個言嗎？）

(A) This is Mr. Lin speaking.（我就是林先生。）
(B) Yes, I'll send messages to him.（是的，我會傳送訊息給他。）
(C) OK. I'll get back to him.（好的。我再打給他。）

答案：(C)。本題考的是電話用語。題目這句通常用於對方要找的人不在或無法接聽電話時，可以做如此的回應。所以只有 (C) 的回答是正確的。(A) 是用來回應自己就是對方要找的人，而 (B) 則是答非所問。

同前一題，聽到 "May I...?" 的問句，可以在選項中找 Yes/No 的回答。不過有時

候會有陷阱，所以還是得仔細聽清楚 Yes/No 後面的句子。而 OK. 的回答也等同於 Yes，後面的 get back to...（回電給～）等於 call... back 的意思。

字詞解釋

later [ˋletɚ] adv. 較晚地，後來　　**message** [ˋmɛsɪdʒ] n. 訊息　　**get back to**... 回電給～

相關文法或用法補充

take a message 以及 leave a message 常用於電話英語中，但意思有點不同。例如，當你打電話到 A 公司要找王先生，而他的祕書告訴你對方正好不在時，你可能問祕書：May I leave a message with Mr. Wang?。這裡的 leave 是「留下」的意思。同樣情境，你也可以詢問來電者：May I take a message?（要我幫您留言嗎？）這裡 take 的意思是「記下口信再轉給某人」。

9. **How do you feel today?**（你今天覺得如何？）

(A) I'm so glad to see you again.（很高興再見到你。）
(B) Cheer up.（振作一點。）
(C) Much better. Thanks.（好多了，謝謝。）

答題解說

答案：(C)。題目問對方身體狀況如何，所以只有 (C) 的回答是正確的。(A) 刻意以 glad（高興的）來讓你以為是正確答案；(B) 是用來鼓勵對方的語句，cheer 有「高興」之意，也是用來混淆答題，這是請對方振作之意，所以是答非所問。

破題關鍵

(C) 的 Much better. 是簡答方式，可還原成 I feel much better.。

字詞解釋

cheer [tʃɪr] v. 歡呼，喝采

相關文法或用法補充

當 much 作副詞時，與 very 是有區別的。very 一般修飾形容詞和副詞，much 常常修飾動詞。例如：

❶ I am very fond of music.（我非常喜歡音樂。）
❷ The news is much talked about these days.（這則新聞最近被廣泛談論。）

另外，much 可以修飾比較級和最高級的形容詞和副詞，而 very 不可以，它只能修飾原級形容詞和副詞：

❶ His English is very good.（他的英文很棒。）

❷ My health is much better now.（如今我的身體更健康了。）

10. Pick up the trash, please.（請把垃圾撿起來。）

(A) You're welcome.（不客氣。）

(B) OK. Sure.（好的。沒問題。）

(C) Here it is.（這給你。）

答題解說

答案：(B)。題目這句是請對方將垃圾撿起來，是個祈使句或命令句，(B) 的回答是認同對方的話，願意去做某件事，所以是正確答案。選項 (A) 是對於別人感謝你時的回答，而 (C) 是當對方請你拿出什麼東西時的回答（也可以解釋成「你要的東西在這。」）

破題關鍵

只要是原形動詞開頭的句子，通常是「祈使句」，客氣一點還可以再加上 please，可置於句首或句尾。不過祈使句會出現在很多情境中，所以還是必須聽清楚對方的意思才能作答。

相關文法或用法補充

「祈使句」在英文的文法中扮演一個相當重要的角色，通常出現在口語會話中。基本上，祈使句省略主詞 you，以原形動詞開頭。

11. What size of cola, sir? Small, medium, or large?（您要多大杯的可樂？小杯、中杯還是大杯？）

(A) That's okay.（沒關係。）

(B) Medium, please.（請給我中杯的。）

(C) I want a large box.（我要一個大箱子。）

答題解說

答案：(B)。題目這句是提出選擇的問句，通常是店員問顧客要「小杯、中杯還是大杯」，所以只有 (B) 是針對問題回答。(A) 是當對方跟你說抱歉時的回答，而 (C) 刻意用同樣的 large 來混淆答題。

破題關鍵

題目句的關鍵在 "Small, medium, or large？"，所以答案必須有這三個字其中之一，那麼 (A) 可直接排除。然後聽到 (C) 的 large box 之後，可以更確定 (B) 是正確答案。

字詞解釋

cola [ˈkolə] **n.** 可樂　　**medium** [ˈmidɪəm] **adj.** 中等的

相關文法或用法補充

「選擇性疑問句」主要有兩種：

❶ 搭配一般疑問句及 or。例如：Do you go to school by bus or by bike?（你搭公車還是騎自行車上學？）或是 Is he in or out?（他在家還是出門了？）

❷ 搭配疑問詞與 or。例如：Which picture do you prefer, the small one or the big one?（你喜歡哪一幅畫，大的還是小的？）、How many pencils do you have? One, two or three?（你有多少支鉛筆？一支，兩支還是三支？）

12. **Jay will hold a singing concert next month.**（Jay 下個月將舉辦一場演唱會。）

(A) Let's call it a day.（今天就到此為止吧。）
(B) How are you lately?（你最近好嗎？）
(C) Would you like to go?（你想去嗎？）

答題解說

答案：(C)。題目這句是告訴對方下個月有一場演場會的消息，所以只有 (C) 反問對方是否想去，是合理的回應。其餘兩個選項都是不相關的回應。

破題關鍵

"call it a day" 是個常見的慣用語，意思是「今天到此為止」；lately 相當於 recently，表示「最近」。

字詞解釋

concert [ˈkɑnsɚt] **n.** 音樂會，演奏會　　**lately** [ˈletlɪ] **adv.** 近來，最近

相關文法或用法補充

「舉辦、舉行」是生活中常見的動詞，而英文中相關的動詞有 hold、host、take place。例如：

❶ We need to hold a meeting to discuss this issue next week.（我們下星期需要舉辦一個會議來討論這個問題。）

❷ Which country is hosting the next World Cup?（哪一個國家會主辦下一屆的世界盃？）→ 要表達「主辦」的意思時，可以用 host。

❸ The concert will take place tomorrow at 7 pm.（這個演唱會將會在明天晚上七點舉行。）→「活動 + take place」不會提到是誰辦的活動。

13. Let's go now. Or we'll be late.（我們現在就走吧。否則會遲到。）

(A) I think so.（我也這麼認為。）

(B) Sorry. I made a mistake.（抱歉。我犯了個錯。）

(C) Ok. There you go.（好的。給你。）

答案：(A)。Let's... 表示「提議大家一起…」，題目這句是向對方提議現在離開，否則會遲到，所以 (A) 選項就是正確的回答，可以還原成 I also think we should go now.（我也認為我們現在應該就走。）選項 (B) 表達歉意，而 (C) 是應對方要求拿出某物給對方，都是不相關的回應。(C) 刻意用相同的 go 來混淆答題。

I think so. 相當於 I agree.，表示「我同意你的說法。」就算不確定它的意思，也可以用刪除法來解答，因為 (B)、(C) 都不是用來回應 Let's... 的適當語句。

join [dʒɔɪn] **v.** 加入　　**coffee** [`kɔfɪ] **n.** 咖啡　　**strong** [strɔŋ] **adj.**（味道，氣味）濃的，強烈的　　**sugar** [`ʃʊgɚ] **n.**（食用）糖

如何用英文提出「邀請或建議」？除了「Let's + 原形動詞」的句型，還有「What/How about + Ving」喔！以下整理三個比較簡單且常用的句型：

❶ Why not + 原形動詞～

　　→ 表示「我們何不～（做某事）吧」，例如：

　　Why not go for a biking trip?（我們何不騎腳踏車出去逛逛？）

❷ What/How about + Ving

　　→ 表示「～（做某事）如何？」，例如：

　　What/How about going for a biking trip?（我們騎腳踏車出去逛逛如何？）

14. Have you ever been to the U.S.?（你去過美國嗎？）

(A) No, I've been here in the U.S. for a year.（不，我已經來美國一年了。）

(B) Yes, that's a good idea.（是的，那是不錯的主意。）

(C) Yes, a few times.（是的。去過幾次。）

答案：(C)。題目是個 Yes/No 的疑問句，而三個選項都有 Yes 或 No，所以必須聽出個選項的意思。要問的是對方過去「去過美國嗎？」所以只有 (C) 的 "a few times"（有過幾次）是正確的回答。(A) 是很明顯的錯誤，因為既然人已經在美國了，就不可能回答 No.；而 (B) 是用來回應對方提出建議，也是錯誤的選項。

破題關鍵

"have/has been to + 地方" 表示「已經去過～」，而且目前說話者本人不在那個地方。

相關文法或用法補充

"have/has been to + 地方" 這個用法常與 "have/has gone to + 地方" 做比較。誠如前面提到，"have/has been to" 是問過去的經驗，而 "have/has gone to" 是問「當下」的狀況，也就是「已經離開往（某地）去了嗎？」

15. **How may I help you, ma'am?**（有需要我幫什麼忙嗎，小姐？）

(A) Can you give me a hand?（你可以幫我個忙嗎？）
(B) Give me the menu, please.（請給我菜單。）
(C) Just help yourself.（自己來吧。）

答題解說

答案：(B)。題目這句通常是在飯店或餐廳等地，服務生對顧客提出協助的問話，也許是要幫對方提行李，或是店員問客人需要什麼。所以只有 (B) 的「請給我菜單。」是符合情境的回答。而對方都已經表達協助的善意了，如果還回答「可以幫我嗎？」不是很奇怪嗎？(C) 這句是當有客人來家裡，端出一些招待的水果或餅乾等時，就可以這麼說。

破題關鍵

give... a hand 字面意思是「給～（某人）一隻手」，就是「幫忙（某人）」的意思。"Help yourself" 是請對方不用客氣（自己動手）的意思。

相關文法或用法補充

How may I help you? 會比 May/Can I help you? 聽起來更客氣一些。無論是公司的接待處或電話接線生，甚至是商店裡的售貨員，看到客人進來時，都會說這句話。另外，give somebody a hand. 是指「幫助某人」，但切勿將 a 改為 my, his, her... 等。如果是 give somebody one's hand. 就只是字面上「把某人的手給某人」的意思而已。

第三部分 簡短對話

16. M: Excuse me. Where can I find the sugar?

W: They are at the Food area. Just go straight toward the end of this way. You'll see it on the right side.

M: Okay. Thanks a lot.

W: You're welcome.

Question: Where are the speakers?

(A) In a parking lot

(B) At a train station

(C) In a supermarket

男：不好意思。我在哪裡可以找到糖？

女：在食品區。只要從這條直走到底。您會在右側看到它。

男：好的。非常感謝。

女：不客氣。

問題：說話者們在哪裡？

(A) 在停車場　(B) 在火車站　(C) 在超級市場。

答題解說

答案：(C)。本題問的是這對男女現在正在什麼地方，我們可以從男子與女子的第一句話「在哪裡可以找到糖？在食品區。」聽出這地方應該是超級市場或大賣場，所以正確答案為 (C)。

破題關鍵

Where are the speakers? 是「簡短對話」出題頻率很高的問題形式。重點是要找出對話中與地方、場合等有密切關聯的字詞。本題線索出現在 "Food area" 這個詞。

字詞解釋

sugar [ˋʃʊgɚ] n. 糖　**straight** [stret] adv. 直接地，直地　**parking lot** 停車場　**station** [ˋsteʃən] n. 車站

相關文法或用法補充

本題選項中的 parking lot 與 train station 都是「名詞+名詞」的複合名詞。而複合名詞還有其他組成結構。例如：

第 1 回
第 2 回
第 3 回
第 4 回
第 5 回
第 6 回
第 7 回
第 8 回
第 9 回
第 10 回

❶ 名詞＋動名詞：horse-riding（騎馬）、book-keeping（簿記）

❷ 名詞＋介系詞：passer-by（路人）

❸ 動詞＋介系詞：break-in（闖入）、take-off（起飛）、warm-up（熱身）

❹ 動名詞＋名詞：washing machine（洗衣機）

17. M: Welcome! How many are there in your party?

W: I'd like a table for four.

M: Let me check... OK, no problem. Please follow me.

W: Thanks.

Question: What is the man going to do next?

(A) Buy some food and drinks

(B) Take the order

(C) Invite some friends

英文翻譯

男：歡迎光臨！你們幾位？

女：我要一張四人座的餐桌。

男：我看一下……好的，沒問題。請跟我來。

女：謝謝。

問題：男子接下來會做什麼？

(A) 買些食物和飲料

(B) 接受點餐

(C) 邀請一些朋友

答題解說

答案：(B)。男子一開始說「你們幾位？（How many are there in your party?）」。顯然他是一餐廳或飯館服務生，準備帶領客人就座服務顧客。所以他接著當然是拿出 menu 準備讓客人點餐，故正確答案是(B)。

破題關鍵

take orders 或 take the order 是「點餐」的意思，服務員常問客人「可以點餐了嗎？」這句話的英文是 "May I take your order?"。另外，「a table for/of ＋數字」表示這一行人有多少位客人。

字詞解釋

party [ˋpɑrtɪ] n.（共同工作或活動的）一行人　　**drink** [drɪŋk] n. 飲料　　**take... order** 點餐　　**invite** [ɪnˋvaɪt] v. 邀請

How many people are (there) in your party?（你們一共幾位？）由於大家太習慣把 party 這個字直接想成「派對」，所以臨時聽到餐廳服務生問這句話，可能會突然很困惑，覺得「我只是來吃飯又不是來開派對」，其實服務生口中的 party 只是指「你們那群人」而已。當然如果是在派對中問這句話，則是真的問「你的派對一共有多少人參加？」所以英文的意思不是死的，要看情境來解釋。

18. W: Who's the pretty lady? Your new girlfriend?

    M: Why do you ask?

    W: No, I just saw you two talk so happily.

    M: Don't put too much thought into that.

    W: Come on! Tell me the truth.

    Question: What are the speakers talking about?

    (A) How to talk happily

    (B) A girl

    (C) The woman's boyfriend

女：那位漂亮的小姐是誰？你的新女朋友嗎？

男：為什麼這麼問？

女：我剛看到你們兩個聊得很開心。

男：別想太多。

女：少來！告訴我實情。

問題：說話者們在談論什麼？

(A) 如何開心暢談

(B) 一個女孩

(C) 女子的男朋友

答案：(B)。女子對於與男子開心暢談的女孩，詢問「漂亮的小姐是誰？你的新女朋友嗎？」男子未直接回應，且接下來的對話也繞著這個 pretty lady 打轉，所以正確答案為 (B)。

本題主要關鍵點：女子一開始問男子的 "Who's the pretty lady? Your new girlfriend?"。(A) 刻意以相同詞彙 talk happily 混淆答題，而 (C) 是完全沒提到的，且刻意以發音類似的 boyfriend，想與 girlfriend 造成混淆，應特別注意。

第 1 回
第 2 回
第 3 回
第 4 回
第 5 回
第 6 回
第 7 回
第 8 回
第 9 回
第 10 回

字詞解釋

put thought into... 思考著～　**truth** [truθ] n. 實情，實話　**thought** [θɔt] n. 想法，見解

相關文法或用法補充

thought 本來是動詞 think（思考，想）的過去式，不過它也可以當名詞用，表示「思考，想法」，不過別跟其他長得很像的 though（雖然）、through（透過～）混淆了喔！

19. W: What's the matter with you? You've kept me waiting for half an hour.

M: I'm sorry, but there's a car accident on the way.

W: Then why don't you give me a call?

M: I left my cellphone at home.

Question: What happened to the man?

(A) He was late.

(B) He had a car accident.

(C) He lost his cellphone.

英文翻譯

女：你怎麼了？你讓我等了半個小時。

男：我很抱歉，只是路上有車禍。

女：那你為何不打電話給我？

男：我把手機留在家中了。

問題：男子發生什麼事？

(A) 他遲到了。

(B) 他出了車禍。

(C) 他遺失手機。

答題解說

答案：(A)。題目問男子發生什麼事，應從男子的發言中去找尋線索。首先，女子問他 "What's the matter with you? You've kept me waiting for half an hour."（你怎麼了？你讓我等了半個小時。）接著男子回答說 "I'm sorry but..."（很抱歉，只是…），顯然他遲到了，因此（A）為正確答案。(B) 與 (C) 都刻意以相同詞彙（car accident 與 cellphone）混淆答題，男子是「遇到車禍」，不是「出車禍」；「手機留在家中」不是「遺失手機」。

本題關鍵語句是女子一開始時間 "You've kept me waiting for half an hour." 。「keep + 人 + Ving」表示「讓某人一直持續做某事」。

matter [ˋmætɚ] n. 事情，問題　　**accident** [ˋæksədənt] n. 事故，意外事件

動詞 keep「保持」的意思，有讓一個動作「持續」的概念，它可以當及物或不及物動詞。比如說，keep going（繼續前進）、keep asking questions（一直問問題）、keep quiet（保持安靜）、keep the kids quiet（讓孩子們保持安靜）…等。

20. W: Hi, John. Do you have time to go shopping with me this afternoon?

M: OK, I'd love to, but I have to eat lunch with my parents at 12:30, and it'll take one hour. Then I'll spend about 15 minutes doing the dishes.

W: That's OK. Give me a call when you arrive near my place.

M: OK. See you then.

Question: When will the man leave home?

(A) At about 1:30 p.m.　　(B) At about 1:45 p.m.　　(C) At about 2:00 p.m.

女：嗨，約翰。你今天下午有時間跟我一起去購物嗎？

男：好的，我很樂意，但是我 12:30 必須和我父母一起吃飯，時間要一個小時。然後，我將花大約 15 分鐘洗碗。

女：那沒問題。你快到我家時打電話給我。

男：好的。到時候見。

問題：男子何時會離開家？

(A) 大約下午 1:30　　(B) 大約下午 1:45　　(C) 大約下午 2:00

答案：(B)。題目問的「男子何時會離開家」，所以應注意男子提到有關時間的部分。他說「我 12:30 必須和我父母一起吃飯，時間要一個小時。然後，我將花大約 15 分鐘洗碗。」所以可以推斷男子會「12:30 + 1 小時 + 15 分」時出門，故正確答案為 (B)。

通常問時間（幾點）的題目，或是問「數字」的題型，不會是直接在對話中聽到的幾點幾分，而是必須稍作推論的。本題第三個關鍵字詞是 at 12:30、take one hour、about 15 minutes。

字詞解釋

do the dishes 洗碗

相關文法或用法補充

如果要打擾別人一下，和他說句話或請他幫忙，就可以用 Do you have time?（你有空嗎？）但如果是 Do you have the time? 呢？它的意思可完全不一樣了。它是用來問人家「現在幾點了？」相當於 What time is it now?。

21. M: Excuse me. How can I get to the Urban Park?

W: It's just over there. You can walk up the stairs there and walk down at the other side.

M: Oh, how high the stairs are! I'm afraid it'll hurt the knees of an old man like me.

W: Then I suggest you take a taxi there.

Question: What does the man want to do?

(A) See a doctor for his knees

(B) Take a taxi

(C) Walk to the Urban Park

英文翻譯

男：請問一下。我要怎麼到都會公園？

女：就在那邊。您可以走那邊的階梯上去，然後往另一側走下去。

男：噢，這樓梯真高啊！恐怕會傷到像我這種老人的膝蓋。

女：那我建議你搭計程車過去。

問題：這個男子想做什麼？

(A) 因膝蓋問題要去看醫生

(B) 搭計程車

(C) 步行到都會公園

答題解說

答案：(C)。題目問的是男子想要做什麼，所以應該先留意他發言的部分。男子第一句話問 "How can I get to the Urban Park?"，但由於男子表示他的膝蓋可能不堪負荷，所以女子建議他搭計程車去。顯然男子一開始時只是想走路到都會公園，故正確答案為 (C)。

本題詢問男子想要去做的事，看似單純且容易，但其實必須理解整段對話，否則很容易誤選了其他兩個選項。但有時候如果你很確定其中一個選項是正確的，那麼其他選項就可以不必考慮。比如我們從女子的第一句話 You can walk up the stairs there... 就可以斷定他是要步行前往。

字詞解釋

get to... 前往～　　*urban* [ˋɚbən] adj. 城市的，都會的　**stair** [stɛr] n. 樓梯，階梯
（慣用複數形）　　**knee** [ni] n. 膝蓋

相關文法或用法補充

high 和 tall 這兩個形容詞都有「高的」意思，但它們所指的「高」卻不太一樣。如果要表示「你好高喔！」應該是 You're so tall.，不會有人說 You're so high! 吧？否則聽起來好像在說對方心情超 high 的樣子！high 表示「高度很高」的話，通常用來形容「物體」從地面算起的高度，且通常形容的對象是無生命的，常見的例子如：high mountains（高山）、high walls（高牆）、high heels（高跟鞋）、high buildings（高聳的建築物）。

22. **M: Two hundred and twenty dollars, please.**

    W: May I use the EasyCard?

    M: Sure. Please put it here... Oh, you don't have enough money in it. Can you pay by cash?

    W: Err... I'm afraid I need to get it from the ATM machine. I'll be back soon.

    Question: Who are the speakers?

    (A) A doctor and a patient

    (B) A shop assistant and a customer

    (C) A judge and a lawyer

英文翻譯

男：這樣是 220 元。
女：我可以使用悠遊卡嗎？
男：好的。請把它放在這裡……噢，你裡面沒有足夠的錢。你可以付現嗎？
女：呃……我恐怕必須去 ATM 提款。我很快回來。
題目：談話者們是誰？
(A) 醫生與病人
(B) 店員與顧客
(C) 法官與律師

答題解說

答案：（B）。從兩人第一句的 "Two hundred and twenty dollars, please." 以及 "May I use the EasyCard?" ，再從三個選項內容可以推知，這是店員與客人之間的對話，所以正確答案為（B）。shop assistant 是「店員」的意思，如果是 shopkeeper 的話，就是指「店主，老闆」。

破題關鍵

先了解對話可能的場合，就可以輕鬆作答。本題的關鍵詞彙是 use the EasyCard?（使用悠遊卡）、pay by cash（付現）等。顯然這不會是醫生與病人，或是法官與律師之間對話會出現的字詞！

字詞解釋

cash [kæʃ] n. 現金　**machine** [mə`ʃin] n. 機器　**patient** [`peʃənt] n. 病人　**assistant** [ə`sɪstənt] n. 助理，店員　**judge** [dʒʌdʒ] n. 法官　**lawyer** [`lɔjɚ] n. 律師

相關文法或用法補充

enough（足夠的）雖然是個很基礎的單字，但它的用法可不簡單。除了修飾名詞或被副詞修飾之外，它常以「enough for + 名詞」或「enough to + 原形動詞」的句型呈現。例如，That's <u>enough for</u> me.（那對我來說足夠了。）、I was stupid <u>enough to believe</u> you.（我真是笨得可以，竟然相信你。）

23. M: Look! Mary is crying. You know what's going on?

W: I think she got into a fight with her boyfriend.

M: Really? What do you think if I go comfort her?

W: I think you'd better leave her alone for a while.

Question: What does the woman suggest the man do?

(A) Make Mary feel comfortable

(B) Do nothing

(C) Ask what happened

英文翻譯

男：看！瑪麗在哭。你知道發生了什麼事嗎？

女：我想她和男朋友吵架了。

男：真的嗎？如果我去安慰她的話你覺得如何？

女：我認為你最好讓她一個人獨處一下。

問題：女子建議男子應該做什麼？

（A）讓瑪麗感到安慰

341

(B) 什麼都不做

(C) 問發生了什麼事

答案：(B)。題目問的是女子建議男子應該做什麼，可以從兩人的第二句話看出端倪。男子問「如果我去安慰她的話你覺得如何？」女子回答 "I think you'd better leave her alone..."（我認為你最好讓她一個人獨處…），也就是說，女子認為男子什麼都不必做是最恰當的，故正確答案為(B)。

既然是問「女子的建議」，只需要從她的發言就可以知道答案：I think you'd better leave her alone for a while.。 "leave someone alone" 就是「讓某人獨自一人」的意思。

fight [faɪt] n. 爭吵　　**comfort** [ˋkʌmfɚt] v. 安慰　　**alone** [əˋlon] adv. 單獨，獨自
while [hwaɪl] n. 一會兒，一段時間　　**comfortable** [ˋkʌmfɚtəbl] adj. 舒適的

英文中 come 或 go 以原形出現，其後接 and 再接另一個原形動詞時，and 可省略，而形成 come 或 go 直接加原形動詞的情況。例如，Come and see me when you have time. = Come see me when you have time.。

24. M: Look, everybody! The building on your right side is the world-famous Conwy Castle.

W: Wow! That's so grand! Do we have a chance to pay a visit there?

M: Yes, but not now. We're going to a fancy restaurant to have lunch. After that, we'll go visit the castle.

W: I'm so looking forward to seeing it!

Question: Who is the man?

(A) A factory worker

(B) A principal

(C) A tour guide

男：大家看一下！右邊的這棟建物就是舉世聞名的康威城堡。

女：哇！好壯觀啊！我們會有機會去那裡參觀嗎？

男：是的，但不是現在。我們正要去一家高檔餐廳吃午餐。之後，我們會去參觀
城堡。

女：我好期待去看看！

問題：這位男子是誰？

(A) 工廠工人

(B) 校長

(C) 導遊

第 1 回 第 2 回 第 3 回 第 4 回 第 5 回 第 6 回 第 7 回 第 8 回 第 9 回 第 10 回

答題解說

答案：（C）。本題問的是「男子的身分（Who）」，也就是他的「工作／職
業」，所以應從他的發言中找尋線索。從男子第一句話「Look, everybody! The
building on your right side is...」就可以知道，他向群眾介紹風景，如果還不確
定，那麼他的第二句話（We're going to a fancy restaurant to have lunch. After that,
we'll go...）應該可以更加確定他是「導遊（tour guide）」了吧！

破題關鍵

本題答題關鍵其實是男子兩次發言中的 "Look, everybody!" 以及出現兩次
"We" 的 "We're going to..."、 "we'll go visit..."，都可以在選項中判斷男子的
身分。

字詞解釋

building [ˋbɪldɪŋ] **n.** 建築　　**castle** [ˋkæsl] **n.** 城堡　　**grand** [grænd] **adj.** 雄偉的，堂
皇的　　**pay a visit** (**to**...) 拜訪，前往～參觀　　**fancy** [ˋfænsɪ] **adj.** 特級的，昂貴的
look forward to... 期待　　**principal** [ˋprɪnsəpl] **n.** 校長　　**tour guide** 導遊

相關文法或用法補充

我們常常會看到 to 後面接原形動詞（形成不定詞），不過 look forward to...（期
待～）中的 to 是介系詞，後面要接名詞或 V-ing。例如：I look forward to David's
English class every week.（我每週都期待大衛的英文課。）、I look forward to
visiting David next Tuesday.（我期待下週二去拜訪大衛。）

25. **M:** Hey, darling! Don't forget to bring the scarf. Besides, you'd better put
on this jacket. The weather is going to change in the evening.

W: Yes, daddy. But I'm not taking an umbrella. The weather report said it
won't rain today.

M: I think you'd better take one. You know, sometimes weather forecasts
can't be trusted.

W: Anything you say.

Question: How will the weather in the evening be?

(A) It'll be rainy and cold.

(B) It'll be cold.

(C) It'll be hot and dry.

男：嘿，親愛的！別忘了帶這條圍巾。另外，你最好穿上這件外套。晚上天氣會有變化。

女：好的，爸爸。但是我不帶傘了。天氣報告說今天不會下雨。

男：我認為你最好帶一枝。你知道，有時候天氣預報是無法信任的。

女：都聽你的。

問題：晚上天氣如何？

(A) 會下雨又冷。

(B) 會冷。

(C) 會又熱又乾。

答題解說

答案：(B)。題目問的是「天氣會如何」，所以應注意聽一些和天氣有關的用語。男子的第一句話說「別忘了帶這條圍巾。另外，你最好穿上這件外套。晚上天氣會有變化。」顯然晚上天氣會變冷，所以正確答案為 (B)。至於會不會下雨，女子表示天氣預報說不會，雖然男子說天氣預報不一定可信，但終究是不確定的事，所以 (A) 不可選。

破題關鍵

首先，注意聽到題目關鍵字 weather，然後與對話中相關字詞作連結，包括 "bring the scarf" 以及 "put on this jacket"，答案就出來了。不過本題因為有 (A) rainy and cold，可以從女子說的 "it won't rain today" 進一步確認。

字詞解釋

scarf [skɑrf] n. 圍巾　　**put on** 穿上，戴上（＝ wear）　　**jacket** [ˋdʒækɪt] n. 夾克，上衣　　***forecast** [ˋforˌkæst] n. 預報，預測　　**trust** [trʌst] v. 信任

相關文法或用法補充

had better 是「最好～（去做某事）」的意思，整個應視為一個「助動詞」，後面須接原形動詞，而且它沒有時態、單複數及人稱的差別，因此沒有 has/have better... 的用法喔！另外，You had better... 可以縮寫成 You'd better。

第四部分 短文聽解

For question number 26, please look at the three pictures.

Question number 26: Listen to the following message. What did Mike get as his birthday gift?

Hi, Auntie Jane. This is Mike. I'm sorry I missed your call because I was not home. And I'd like to say thank you very much for the smartphone. I was wondering how you knew that my old one dropped to the ground and was badly damaged last week. Luckily, I can save back some important photos. I've saved them on my notebook computer. From now on, I will be more careful about using it. Thank you. Bye.

英文翻譯

請看以下三張圖。並仔細聆聽以下訊息。麥克拿到的生日禮物是什麼？
嗨，珍阿姨。我是麥克。抱歉因為我不在家，所以沒接到您的電話。我非常感謝您送我這支智慧型手機。我好奇想問，您怎麼知道我那支舊手機上週掉到地上且嚴重損壞了。幸運的是我可以救回一些重要的照片。我已經將它們存在我的筆記型電腦上。從現在開始，我會更小心使用它。謝謝您。再見。

答題解說

答案：(C)。題目問的是說話者拿到的生日禮物是什麼，所以應注意與生日禮物或贈送有關的內容。其中提到 "I'd like to say thank you very much for the smartphone."（我非常感謝您送我這支智慧型手機。）所以答案是 (C)。訊息內容中刻意出現 call 以及 notebook computer 來誘導考生選擇錯誤的圖 (A)（家用電話）以及圖 (B)（筆記型電腦），應特別小心注意。

破題關鍵

首先，題目句子中的 gift（禮物）要聽得出來，即使聽不出來，前面的 birthday 應該沒問題吧！所以很容易判斷題目要問的是「生日禮物」。接著只要注意聽到 "thank you very much for the smartphone"，應該就不會選錯答案了。

第 1 回
第 2 回
第 3 回
第 4 回
第 5 回
第 6 回
第 7 回
第 8 回
第 9 回
第 10 回

字詞解釋

gift [gɪft] **n.** 禮物　**miss one's call** 未接到某人（打來）的電話　**wonder** [`wʌndə-] **v.** 想知道　**drop** [drɑp] **v.** 掉落　**damage** [`dæmɪdʒ] **v.** 損壞　**notebook** [`not͵bʊk] **n.** 筆記本，筆記型電腦

相關文法或用法補充

我們中文說「玩電腦」，英文不能直接翻譯為 play computer，正確說法是 play on a/the computer。但若 play 的受詞是「遊戲」，比方說，可以用 play computer games 或 play online games。如果是「打電腦」的話，可以用 use a/the computer 來表達。

For question number 27, please look at the three pictures.

Question number 27: Listen to the following talk on the phone. What clothes did the speaker receive?

Hello, I'm making this call to complain about the products I've just received. Last week I went online to purchase a white shirt and a pair of black pants from your shop by credit card. I got them this morning. However, when I opened the package, I found a black shirt and a pair of white pants inside it. What's wrong? Would you please explain about that?

英文翻譯

請看以下三張圖。並仔細聆聽以下電話中的談話。說話者收到什麼？
喂，我打電話來客訴我剛收到的產品。上週我上網以信用卡購買您商店的一件白襯衫和一條黑色褲子。我今天早上收到了。但是，當我打開包裹時，發現裡面是一件黑色襯衫和一條白色褲子。出了什麼事？可以請您解釋一下嗎？

答題解說

答案：(B)。這電話談話內容是關於網購商品後，收到的東西與自己購買的不一樣，而打電話去客訴。其中提到，打開包裹時，發現裡面是一件黑色襯衫和一條白色褲子。所以正確答案為 (B)。

第 1 回
第 2 回
第 3 回
第 4 回
第 5 回
第 6 回
第 7 回
第 8 回
第 9 回
第 10 回

破題關鍵

本題提到兩次襯衫與褲子，第一次是「訂購時」，第二次是「收到時」，所以必須確認「收到」的商品內容為何。所以題目一定要先聽清楚。其中關鍵字詞包括 receive、purchase、found... inside it、shirt、pants 等。

字詞解釋

receive [rɪ`siv] v. 收到　**complain** [kəm`plen] v. 抱怨，投訴　**purchase** [`pɝtʃəs] v. 購買　**shirt** [ʃɝt] n. 襯衫　**pants** [pænts] n. 褲子　**credit card** 信用卡　**package** [`pækɪdʒ] n. 包裹　**explain** [ɪk`splen] v. 解釋，說明

相關文法或用法補充

有一些名詞永遠只能用「複數」形來表示。例如 clothes（衣服）、shorts（短褲）、pants（褲子）、jeans（牛仔褲）、trousers（長褲）、scissors（剪刀）、glasses（眼鏡）、goggles（蛙鏡）、headphones（耳機）、goods（商品）…等，尤其是「成雙成對」的東西。

For question number 28, please look at the three pictures.

Question number 28: listen to the following introduction. Which activity do people NOT have to pay for?

Let me introduce our summer vacation package to you. We offer our members a lot of choices. You can enjoy the beautiful sea view at the beach, go surfing, have a cup of nice tea or coffee, or just lie on a beach chair, letting the sun shine softly on you. But if you want to do some indoor activities, you need to pay extra, because they're not included in the package.

中文翻譯

請看以下三張圖。並仔細聆以下簡介說明。以下哪一種活動「不需」付費？
讓我向您介紹我們的暑假套裝行程。我們為我們的會員提供很多選擇。您可以在海灘上欣賞美麗的海景、沖浪，喝杯美味的茶或咖啡，或者只是躺在沙灘椅上，讓陽光柔和地照在您身上。但是，如果您想做一些室內活動，則必須支付額外的費用，因為它們不包含在套裝行程中。

答題解說

答案：(C)。本題內容是俱樂部員工向顧客說明其提供的活動，有些是會員免費使用，有些需額外付費，而題目要問的是「不需」額外付費的活動為何，所以應注意聽相關內容的部分：如果您想做一些室內活動，則必須支付額外的費用（if you want to do some indoor activities, you need to pay extra），選項中 (A) 與 (B) 皆為室內活動，所以答案是在海灘上做日光浴的圖 (C)。

破題關鍵

第一個關鍵當然是題目要聽清楚 "NOT have to pay for"，接著第二個關鍵是內容提到的 "need to pay extra"（必須支付額外費用）以及 "indoor activities"（室內活動）。

字詞解釋

introduction [ˌɪntrəˈdʌkʃən] n. 簡介 **pay for**... 支付～的費用 **introduce** [ˌɪntrəˈdjus] v. 介紹 **package** [ˈpækɪdʒ] n.（有關聯的）一組事物 **surfing** [ˈsɝfɪŋ] n. 衝浪 **indoor** [ˈɪnˌdor] adj. 室內的 **include** [ɪnˈklud] v. 包括

相關文法或用法補充

indoor 這個形容詞是由 in 與 door 合成，字面意思是「在門內」，也就是「室內的」意思，它的反義字是 outdoor（室外的）。另外，這個字後面加 -s 會變成副詞，表示「在室內」，比如 Stay indoors. It's so hot outside/outdoors.（留在屋內。外面很熱。）

For question number 29, please look at the three pictures.

Question number 29: Listen to the following talk. What does the speaker's brother do first on Saturday mornings?

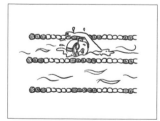  

Every Saturday morning, my elder brother spends nearly one hour to do exercise. First of all, he exercises on the running machine. He would jog or just take a slow walk on it for about 30 minutes. Then he does one hundred slow push-ups. This may take him about 10 minutes. After that, he takes a shower, and he is in very good spirit.

第 1 回
第 2 回
第 3 回
第 4 回
第 5 回
第 6 回
第 7 回
第 8 回
第 9 回
第 10 回

英文翻譯

請看以下三張圖。並仔細聆聽播放的談話內容。說話者的哥哥在週六早晨會先做什麼？

每週六早上，我哥哥都要花近一個小時的時間鍛鍊身體。首先，他在跑步機上運動。他會在上面慢跑或慢走約 30 分鐘。然後，他做一百下緩慢的伏地挺身。這可能要花他大約 10 分鐘。最後，他會去沖澡，而且他會覺得精神煥發。

答題解說

答案：(B)。題目問的是週六早晨會先做什麼？播放內容提到，首先，他在跑步機上運動。他會在上面慢跑或慢走約 30 分鐘（First of all, he exercises on the running machine. He would jog or just take a slow walk on it for about 30 minutes.）。所以正確答案是 (B)。

破題關鍵

本題首要關鍵就在題目這句（What does the speaker's brother do first on Saturday mornings?）本身，其中 "do first" 與播放內容中的 "First of all" 相呼應，"running machine" 就是「跑步機」的意思。

字詞解釋

exercise [ˋɛksəˌsaɪz] n. 鍛鍊，運動　**first of all** 首先　**machine** [məˋʃin] n. 機器　**push-up** [ˋpʊʃˌʌp] n.（體操）伏地挺身　**take a shower** 沖澡　**in good spirit** 精神煥發

相關文法或用法補充

動詞 spend 常見於「人＋spend＋時間／錢＋V-ing」，或是「人＋spend＋時間／錢＋on＋名詞」，表示「某人花了多少錢或時間在做某事」，或「某人花了多少錢或時間在某事上」。其過去式和過去分詞都是 spent。例如：

❶ I am going to spend the whole week preparing for the exam.（我將花整整一週的時間準備這考試。）

❷ I spent 700,000 dollars on this van.（我花了七十萬塊在這部貨車上。）

For question number 30, please look at the three pictures.

Question number 30: Listen to the following talk. What does the speaker want the woman to show?

Sorry, ma'am, but I'm afraid you show me the wrong ticket. This one you just gave me is for you to take a shuttle bus to the airport. It's not for boarding an airplane. Besides, I don't need your passport. If you don't have the right ticket, or if you've lost it, you can't buy anything in this shop. Would you like to make sure whether it is in your bag?

英文翻譯

請看以下三張圖。並仔細聆聽以下談話。說話者要這名女子出示什麼？

抱歉，女士，恐怕您出示的票是錯的。您剛給我的這張是讓您搭乘接駁巴士前往機場的票，而不是用來登機的。另外，我不需要您的護照。如果您沒有正確的票，或者您遺失了，您就無法在這家商店購買任何東西。您要不要確認一下是不是在您的包包中呢？

答題解說

答案：(C)。題目問說話者要這名女子出示什麼，而一開始時，這位女士拿出來的東西是錯誤的，包括接駁巴士（shuttle bus）的車票與護照（passport），所以(A)、(B)皆為錯誤選項，正確答案為(C)。

破題關鍵

本題關鍵語句是 "It's not for boarding an airplane." （它不是用來登機的。）board 當名詞是「板子」的意思，當動詞時可以想像是「登板」之意，可以用來表達「登船」、「登機」。

字詞解釋

wrong [rɔŋ] **adj.** 錯誤的　 ***shuttle bus** 穿梭巴士，接駁巴士　 **board** [bord] **v.** 上（船、車、飛機等）　 **passport** [ˋpæsˏport] **n.** 護照

相關文法或用法補充

sorry 不單只是「對不起」的意思，也可以用來表示「難過、同情」。例如：I'm sorry to hear about that.（很遺憾聽到那樣的事）。另外，如果聽不懂或聽不清楚對方說的話，想要請對方再說一次，可以直接說 "Sorry?"，同時拉高尾音，相當於 "Pardon?／Pardon me?" 的用法。

1. **Kate was sick yesterday, _____ she didn't go to school.**（Kate 昨天生病了，所以她沒有去學校。）

   (A) so　(B) because　(C) that　(D) but

   > 答題解說

   答案：(A)。空格前後為完整句子，所以應填入連接詞，(C) that 可直接排除。接著看句意，第一句是「Kate 生病」，第二句是「她沒有去上學」，顯然互為因果關係，第一句是為因，第二句為果，所以(A) so（所以）是正確答案。

   > 破題關鍵

   從空格前後的句構判斷要填入連接詞，這是第一個關鍵，但主要還是了解語意之後，才能選對答案。至於因果關係的兩句，一定要看清楚哪一句是「因」，哪一句是「果」。

   > 字詞解釋

   go to school 去上學

   > 相關文法或用法補充

   so 當連接詞時，只能放在句中，不能放句首，且 so 前面須有逗點與原因句隔開。例：She was sick, so she didn't go to school today.（她生病了，所以今天沒有去上學）

   because 則可置於句首或句中（不一定要用 , 隔開）。如果是 because of 則為介系詞片語的用法，後面接名詞（片語），而非句子。例如：

   Because I didn't prepare for the test well, I failed the test.（我沒有準備好考試，所以考不及格。）= I failed the test because I didn't prepare for the test well.

   但須注意的是，雖然中文有「因為～所以～」的說法，但在英文中，because 和 so 不得用於同一個句子中。例：

   I didn't do my homework, so my teacher was angry.（○）
   Because I didn't do my homework, my teacher was angry.（○）
   Because I didn't do my homework, so my teacher was angry.（✗）

2. **Sam's dog always _____ loudly at strangers.**（山姆的狗總是大聲地對著陌生人吠叫。）

   (A) answers　(B) barks　(C) jumps　(D) fears

答案：(B)。就合乎邏輯的語意來說，應該是「狗對著陌生人吠叫」，所以正確答案應為 (B) barks。(A) answers 表示「回答」，且其後常連接 to；(C) jumps 表示「跳」，jump at 是「向～撲去」；(D) fears 表示「害怕」，其後常連接 for。

破題關鍵

兩個答題關鍵：(1) 就文法結構來看：空格後有 at，直接剔除 (A) 與 (D)；(2) 就語意邏輯來看：用 loudly 來修飾 jump 的話，不合邏輯。

字詞解釋

bark [bɑrk] v.（狗，狐等）吠叫　**jump** [dʒʌmp] v. 跳起　**fear** [fɪr] v. 害怕　**loudly** [ˋlaʊdlɪ] adv. 大聲地　**stranger** [ˋstrendʒɚ] n. 陌生人

相關文法或用法補充

有一些不及物動詞常與 at 連用，形成「及物動詞片語」，例如：

look at... 看著　stare at... 凝視著 glance at... 看了…一眼

shout at... 對著…喊叫 meow at...（貓）對著…叫著

smile at... 對著…微笑 knock at... 敲著…

3. **My brother helped me _____ my homework.**（我哥哥幫助我做家庭作業。）

(A) for　(B) no　(C) with　(D) in

答題解說

答案：(C)。空格前面有動詞 help，後面是個名詞片語 my homework，顯然它要表達的意思是「幫我做家庭作業」。在英文裡，要表達「幫助某人做某事」時，如果是用 help 這個動詞，就要搭配介系詞 with，其他介系詞都不必考慮。所以本題正確答案是 (C)。

破題關鍵

本題關鍵當然是對於 "help sb. with sth." 這個用法的認知。另外，「幫助某人去做某事」也可能以「動作」表達，那麼其用法就是 "help sb. (to) do sth."，請注意考題亦可能有的變化。

字詞解釋

help... with... 在某事上幫助某人。

相關文法或用法補充

help 可以當名詞，也可以當動詞。當名詞時，為不可數名詞。例如：

❶ Thank you for your help.（謝謝你的幫助。）

❷ The medicine hasn't much help.（這種藥沒太大用處。）

當動詞時，有及物動詞與不及物動詞的用法：

❶ help sb. with sth. 在某件事上幫助某人

Could you help me with this heavy case?（你能幫助我提這個重箱子嗎？）

❷ help sb.（to）do sth. 幫助某人做某事，to 可以省略。例如：

① This book will help you（to）know more about the modern history.（這本書會幫助你瞭解更多近代史。）

② Could you help me（to）carry this case upstairs?（你能幫我把這個箱子搬到樓上去嗎？）

❸ 主詞（事情）+ help（～有所幫助）。例如：Your money helped a lot.（你這筆錢幫了個大忙。）

4. **There are six boys _____ soccer in the park.**（有六個男孩在公園裡踢足球。）

　（A）play　（B）played　（C）playing　（D）to play

答題解說

答案：（C）。空格前是個完整句子（There are six boys），所以空格不可能再放動詞，（A）可直接排除。男孩不可「被足球玩」，所以（B）的 played 也是錯誤的。因為句意是「有六個男孩在公園踢足球」，「踢足球」與「有六個男孩」是「同時發生」的，所以應該用「動名詞（Ving）」來表示。

破題關鍵

本題也是在考一個固定句型：There be + N + Ving（有～在做某事），如果熟知此句型即可直覺反應選出正確答案。否則亦可利用 Ving 與 to-V 的「同時」與「不同時」的概念來解題。

字詞解釋

soccer [`sakə] n. 足球

相關文法或用法補充

　"There be…" 句型是英文裡最常用的句型之一，用來表示「人或事物的存在」或「某地有某物」。There 在此句型中是引導詞，已經沒有副詞「那裡」的含義，be 後面的名詞是句子的主詞，表示「有～」。而 there be 和 have 都可以表示「有」，此時兩者的用法可以相互轉換。如：

There are many small rivers in the ancient town. = The ancient town has many small rivers.

第 1 回
第 2 回
第 3 回
第 4 回
第 5 回
第 6 回
第 7 回
第 8 回
第 9 回
第 10 回

5. Kevin goes jogging _____.（凱文每兩天跑一次步。）

(A) every two day　(B) each two days　(C) each other day　(D) every other day

答題解說

答案：(D)。本題的考點是「每兩天」或「每隔一天」的英文表達用語。(A) 的 day 後面要加 -s，因為前面有 two；另外「每隔～」都是用 every... 來表達，沒有 each 的相關用法，所以正確答案為 (D)。

破題關鍵

看過四個選項後，應該馬上可以知道要考什麼。「每隔～（一段時間）的說法，可以用 every 開頭的片語，接著是 two 後面，一定要接複數名詞，這也是相當基本的概念。有這兩個概念就能刪掉前三個選項，留下答案 (D)。

字詞解釋

go jogging 去慢跑　**every other day** 每兩天，每隔一天

相關文法或用法補充

「每兩天」（every two days）、「每三天」（every three days）、「每兩個月」（every two months）…等，除了在 every 後面加數字，也可以用「序數」的單字，所以前述三個說法也可以用 every second/other day、every third day、every second month 來表示，注意這時候的 day 或 month 後面不可加複數的 -s。另外，「每兩天」也可以用 once in two days 來表示。

6. He is the _____ child in his family.（他是家裡的獨生子。）

(A) each　(B) only　(C) one　(D) just

答題解說

答案：(B)。one 後面雖然可以接單數名詞，但必須有前文的對照才能指稱，而 each 前面不可再加定冠詞 the；所以 (A) 與 (C) 都可直接排除。而 just 當形容詞是「正義的，公平的」，通常用來修飾「事物」，而非「人」。所以正確答案是 (B)。only child 是「獨生子」的意思。

破題關鍵

本題的考點是「獨生子」的固定用語，只要知道這個用語就可以直接選出正確答案。

字詞解釋

only child phr. 獨生子

第 1 回

第 2 回

第 3 回

第 4 回

第 5 回

第 6 回

第 7 回

第 8 回

第 9 回

第 10 回

相關文法或用法補充

only 可以作形容詞和副詞，在本題中是形容詞用法。當副詞時表示「僅僅，只」。例如：Only adults may drink in bars in some countries.（在一些國家只有成年人可以在酒吧喝酒。）、I only slept three hours last night.（昨晚我只睡了三個小時。）另外「only + 單數名詞」的後面如果有「關係代名詞」，要用 that，不可用 who/whom 或 which。例如：He is the only person that knows the truth.（他是唯一知道事情真相的人。）

7. **Tim often eats in McDonald's because he is _____ lazy to cook.**（提姆常常在麥當勞吃飯，因為他太懶了無法煮飯。）

(A) so　(B) very　(C) such　(D) too

答題解說

答案：(D)。本題的考點是 too... to... 的句型，意思是「太⋯而不能⋯」，所以正確答案是 (D)。(A) so 和 (B) very 的意思相近，都有「非常」的意思，但不符句意，會變成「非常懶惰而去煮飯」的奇怪句子。such 後面通常要接名詞，而非形容詞，所以 (C) 也是錯誤選項。

破題關鍵

看到空格後面的不定詞 to cook，應直接聯想到「too... to-V」的句型。

字詞解釋

lazy [ˈlezɪ] **adj.** 懶散的，怠惰的

相關文法或用法補充

too ...to... 句型是初學英文者常遇到的一個句型，而且很容易誤解它的意思，它用來表示否定。to-V 前面通常還可以加上「for + 人」，例如：It was too cold for us to go shopping.（天太冷了，我們不能去買東西。）、The stone is too heavy for him to move.（這塊石頭太重了，他搬不動。）但值得注意的是，當 too 後面接 glad、pleased、willing、happy 等「情緒形容詞」時，那麼句子表示「肯定」，這時 too 可等同於 very 或 so。例如：Mother was too glad to hear from her friends yesterday afternoon.（昨天下午，媽媽收到朋友的來信感到非常高興。）、Tom is too willing to study French.（湯姆很樂意學習法語。）

8. **I couldn't find _____ to stay, because all the hotels nearby were full.**（我找不到任何地方住宿，因為附近所有旅館都客滿了。）

(A) anything　(B) anywhere　(C) anybody　(D) anytime

答案：（B）。find 是及物動詞，空格應填入一個代名詞，所以 (D) anytime（在任何時間）可直接排除掉。根據句子大意，因為所有旅館都客滿，所以無法找到落腳處，故正確答案應為（B）。

破題關鍵

本題關鍵字是空格後面的 stay，表示「停留」，當然必須與表「地方」的 anywhere 搭配在一起。

字詞解釋

nearby [ˈnɪrˌbaɪ] adv. 在附近　**full** [fʊl] adj. 滿的，充滿的　**anytime** [ˈɛnɪˌtaɪm] adv. 在任何時候

相關文法或用法補充

不定詞是動狀詞的一種，它是由動詞演變而來，在句中可扮演名詞、形容詞、或副詞的角色。本題當中的 to stay 屬於哪一種呢？沒錯，就是當形容詞的用法。anywhere 是個名詞，表「任何地方」，“not have anywhere to stay” 表示「沒有『住宿的』地方」。類似用法如，“find something to eat”（找吃的東西）、“have nothing to care about”（沒有在乎的事情）、“There must be somebody to be punished.”（一定要有人被懲罰。）、He's the first to come here.（他是前來這裡的第一個人。）

9. **I got many gifts at the party. Is this the _____ you gave me?**（我在派對上收到很多禮物。這件是你給我的嗎？）

(A) other　(B) another　(C) one　(D) all

答題解說

答案：（C）。第一句意思是「我在派對上收到很多禮物。」而空格所在的這句顯然要表達的是「這是你給我的嗎？」所以只有 (C) one 這個不定代名詞可以用來表達這個意思。而 the other 是指「兩者當中的其中一個」；another 前不會有冠詞 the；all 錯誤的原因在於前面已經提到「許多禮物（many gifts）」，這裡如果要用 all 的話，前面 be 動詞必須用 Are，而非 Is。

破題關鍵

不定代名詞 one 專指前面已提過，而且是沒有限定的「單數名詞」。這裡的 one 代表 one of the gifts I got at the party（我在派對上收到的禮物之一）。

第 1 回
第 2 回
第 3 回
第 4 回
第 5 回
第 6 回
第 7 回
第 8 回
第 9 回
第 10 回

字詞解釋

gift [gɪft] **n.** 禮品，禮物

相關文法或用法補充

one 經常與 the other、another 綁在一起：

❶ one... the other... 是指在「有限的範圍」內列舉兩者。例如：There are only two people at the bus stop. One is an old man; the other is a police officer.（公車站只有兩個人。其中一個是一位老人，另一個則是一位警察。）

❷ one... another... 是指在「沒有限定的範圍」內隨意列舉。例如：There are several books on the table. One is a dictionary; another is a comic book.（桌上有好幾本書。其中一本是字典；另一本是漫畫書。）

10. My uncle is a policeman. He _____ a lot of thieves and robbers.（我叔叔是個警察。他抓過很多強盜及小偷。）

(A) catch   (B) will have caught   (C) has caught   (D) is catching

答題解說

答案：(C)。空格前的主詞為第三人稱單數，應搭配單數動詞，故 (A) 可先排除掉。題目第一句（My uncle is a policeman.）動詞用的是現在式，代表的是一種常態與事實，所以「警察抓小偷或強盜」也是常態的事實，而 (B) 的未來完成式以及 (D) 的現在進行式均非常態的表現，故不可選。正確答案為 (C) 的現在完成式用法。另外，未來完成式不能單獨使用，必須有個未來的時間參考點才行。

破題關鍵

本題是考動詞時態的文法觀念題型。第一句先說明某人是個警察，而第二句接著說他有什麼豐功偉業，因此第二句可以用過去式（caught）、現在式（catches）或現在完成式（has caught）來表達。

字詞解釋

policeman [pə`lismən] **n.** 警察    **thief** [θif] **n.** 賊，小偷    **robber** [`rɑbɚ] **n.** 搶劫者，強盜

相關文法或用法補充

以 -er 結尾的單字，通常表示某種「人」，就像本題中的 robber。它是從 rob（搶劫）這個動詞延伸而來。其他像是：employ（雇用）→ employer（雇主）；manage（管理）→ manager（管理者，經理）；report（報告）→ reporter（記者）

當然也可以表示「物品」，像是：compute（計算）→ computer（電腦）；print（印刷）→ printer（印表機）

第二部分 段落填空

Questions 11-14

In the dark corner, there was a baby mouse hiding around some grasses. His mother collected some dry **leaves** and covered him with them. He lay in this secret place alone, and his mother went to look for some food. He did not move at **all**, during the silent night.

A big cat showed up. The little mouse didn't dare to move his head, and even one of his feet. He was shaken with fear. Luckily, the cat didn't see him and walked past. Shortly after that, a hungry dog came along. **The baby mouse still dared not move.** The dog only caught sight of these dead leaves and walked by.

The mother mouse came back to the secret place. And **it** was safe now for the baby mouse to move and enjoy some food.

◢ dare **v.** 膽敢；still **adj.** 靜止的

中文翻譯

在一個黑暗的角落裡，有一隻幼鼠藏在草叢中。他的母親收集了一些乾葉子，並用這些葉子將他覆蓋住。他獨自躺在這個祕密的地方，而他的母親去找食物。在這寧靜的夜晚裡，他一動也不動。

一隻大貓出現了。小老鼠不敢移動他的頭，甚至一隻腳也不敢動。他因恐懼而發抖。幸運的是，那隻貓沒有看見而走了過去。不久之後，一條飢餓的狗來。幼鼠非常安靜地呼吸。那隻狗只看見這些枯葉就走了過去。

母鼠回到了這個祕密的地方。現在幼鼠可以安全地移動並享用一些食物了。

答題解說

11. 答案：(B)。選項是四個不同意思的名詞，所以應根據句意來判斷：「牠的母親收集了一些乾的 _____，並用這些葉子將他覆蓋住。」(A) 是「空氣」、(B) 是「葉子」、(C) 是「槽；坦克」、(D) 是「樹乾；旅行箱」，所以正確答案為 (B)，因為後面這句說「並用它們將他覆蓋住。」也就是呼應第一句話的 hiding（藏身），其餘選項不是沒有形體，不然就是老鼠無法收集的物體。

12. 答案：(A)。句子大意是「在這寧靜的夜晚裡，他一動也不動。」故正確答案為 (A)。選項 (B) 與空格前介系詞 at 搭配後（at least）意思是「至少」，選項 (C) 與空格前介系詞 at 搭配後（at once）意思是「立即，同時」，選項 (D) 與空格前介

系詞 at 搭配後（at last）意思是「最終」，皆不符句意。

13. 答案：(C)。這是要挑選一個句子、子句或句子的一部分放入空格後，確認空格前後和空格句之間的連接關係，是否讓句意顯得自然通順。空格後面句子提到「那隻狗只看見這些枯葉就走了過去。」，所以答案不會是 (A)、(B)、(D)。只有 (C)「幼鼠依然不敢動。」最能合理地連接前後兩句。因為幼鼠必須不被狗發現，讓狗只看見這些枯葉就走了。以下是其餘錯誤選項句子的翻譯：

(A) 地上的葉子對牠來說，看起來怪怪的。

(B) 牠覺得高興，因為前方有食物。

(D) 那隻貓突然回來爭奪食物。

14. 答案：(C)。句子大意是，現在幼鼠可以安全地移動並享用食物，這是「虛主詞 it」的常見句型：「It + be + adj.（+for + 人）+ to-V」。故正確答案為 (C)。

破題關鍵

11. 本題關鍵字是第一句話（In the dark corner, there was a baby mouse hiding around some grasses.）中的 hiding（hide 的現在分詞）。根據「母鼠將幼鼠藏起來」的文意，當然是用「葉子（leaves）」比較適當。

12. 本題顯然是要考 at 引導的副詞片語，要是沒有看過這些片語，在答題時會容易出現猶豫的狀況。本題關鍵字是前面的 not，not... at all（一點也不～）是常見用語。

13. 這一段前面有提到一隻大貓出現，幼鼠甚至「一隻腳也不敢動」。接著又出現一隻餓犬，所以空格這句應與「一隻腳也不敢動」相呼應，所以只有「依然不敢動」這個選項最符合句意。

14. 空格後看到 for 又看到 to，應該直接聯想到「It + be + adj.+（+for + 人）+ to-V」的句型。

字詞解釋

dark [dɑrk] **adj.** 黑暗的，（顏色）深的　　**corner** [`kɔrnɚ] **n.** 街角，轉角　　**hide** [haɪd] **v.** 躲藏　　**grass** [græs] **n.** 草　　**collect** [kə`lɛkt] **v.** 收集，採集　　**leaf** [lif] **n.** 葉子（複數是 leaves）　　**cover... with...** 用～蓋住～　　**lie** [laɪ] **v.** 躺，臥（動詞變化：lie→lay→lain→lying）　　**not... at all** 一點也不～　　**silent** [`saɪlənt] **adj.** 寂靜無聲的，沉默的　　**show up** 出現　　**dare** [dɛr] **v.** 膽敢　　**shake** [ʃek] **v.** 震動，抖動（動詞變化：shake→shook→shaken）　　**fear** [fɪr] **n.** 害怕，恐懼　　**shortly after...** 在～不久之後　　**breathe** [brið] **v.** 呼吸　　**catch sight of...** 看見～　　**dead** [dɛd] **adj.** 死的，枯的　　**secret** [`sikrɪt] **adj.** 祕密的　　**plant** [plænt] **n.** 植物　　**tank** [tæŋk] **n.** 罐，箱，槽　　**strange** [strendʒ] **adj.** 奇怪的　　**suddenly** [`sʌdnlɪ] **adv.** 突然地　　**fight** [faɪt] **v.** 鬥，打架

11. 英文裡有一些「母音 + f」結尾的名詞，其複數為不規則變化（不是直接加 -s），而是變成 -ves。例如：leaf（葉子）→ leaves；life（生命）→ lives；scarf（圍巾）→ scarves；loaf（一塊麵包）→ loaves... 。

12. "at all" 通常不會單獨出現，且會和 not 連用（亦即用於「否定句」）。另外，"Not at all." 也可用於簡答。例如：A: Are you tired with that?（你對那件事厭倦了嗎？）B: Not at all.（一點也不。）

13. breathe（呼吸）是個動詞，字尾 -the 發 [ð] 的音，而它的名詞是 breath，字尾 -th 發 [θ] 的音。

14. 在「It +be(not) +adj./N +(for sb/sth)+ to-V」的句型中，「真主詞」是 to-V，而其中 sb/sth 是 to-V 這個動作的執行者（意義上的主詞）。

Questions 15-18

Jennifer once thought that the **skinny** old man who lived across from her place was very poor and lonely. She often saw him **dressed** in his same old clothes and sitting alone in the park.

Last Christmas, Jennifer was out for a jog. When passing the park, she saw the old man carrying a big bag on his shoulder. She guessed that he would come over and ask her for money or help. But she was surprised to find that many children followed him. The old man came to her, took out a gift box from the bag and smiled and said to her, "Merry Christmas! I bought gifts for everyone. This is for you." **At that moment, Jennifer felt so moved.** She changed her **mind** about the old man. Since then, she has no longer judged people by how they look. Now she is learning to appreciate others from different points of view.

中文翻譯

　　珍妮佛曾經以為，住在她家對面的那位瘦巴巴的老人非常窮困且孤獨。她經常看到他穿著一貫的舊衣服，且獨自坐在公園裡。

　　去年聖誕節，珍妮佛外出慢跑。她經過公園時，看見老人肩上背著一個大包包。她猜想老人會過來向她要錢或請求幫忙。但她驚訝地發現有許多孩子跟隨著他。老人朝著她走來、從袋子裡拿出一個禮盒，笑著對她說，「聖誕快樂！我為大家買了禮物。這是給你的。」在那一刻，珍妮佛覺得很感動。她改變了對這老人的想法。從那時起，她不再以貌取人。她現在正在學習從不同的視角去欣賞別人。

答題解說

15. 答案：(D)。四個選項都是形容詞，所以必須根據句意來判斷。句子大意是住在她家對面的那位 _____ 的老人非常窮困且孤獨。只有 (D) skinny（瘦巴巴的）

第 1 回

第 2 回

第 3 回

第 4 回

第 5 回

第 6 回

第 7 回

第 8 回

第 9 回

第 10 回

是最適當且符合語意的答案。其餘三個選項意思是：(A) curious（好奇的）、(B) favorite（最受喜愛的）、(C) childish（幼稚的）。

16. 答案：(B)。四個選項是同一個單字 dress 衍生出的不同詞類。句子大意是「她經常看到他穿著一貫的舊衣服…」。dress 當名詞是「衣服」，當動詞就是「穿衣服」的意思。不過當主詞是「人」，要用這個動詞表示「穿衣服」時，要用被動式，也就是「be dressed in + 衣服」的句型。所以答案是 (B) dressed。

17. 答案：(A)。這題是要挑選一個句子、子句或句子的一部分放入空格後，確認空格前後和空格句之間的連接關係，是否讓句意顯得自然通順。空格前面句子提到「聖誕快樂！我為大家買了禮物。這是給你的。」所以答案不會是 (B)、(C)、(D)。只有 (A)「在那一刻，珍妮佛覺得很感動。」最能合理地連接前後兩句。因為老人家的慈愛之心，讓珍妮佛（原本覺得他是個孤獨貧困、需要協助的老人）有不同的感受。以下是其餘錯誤選項句子的翻譯：
(B) 珍妮佛對此表示懷疑。
(C) 然後一個孩子過來抱他的禮物。
(D) 但是，事情並不是那麼簡單。

18. 答案：(A)。句意是「她改變了對這老人的 _____。從那時起，她不再以貌取人。」所以 (A) mind 是正確答案。change one's mind 表示「改變想法／心意」這裡的 mind 也可以用 idea 或 thought 取代。

破題關鍵

15. 本題要選一個形容這位老人家的形容詞，可參考後面的 very poor and lonely，以及 "same old clothes and sitting alone"，呈現的是一名看似可憐的老人家。所以選項中只有 skinny 是最適當的答案。

16. "be dressed in + 衣服" 也等於 "dress oneself in + 衣服"。動詞 dress 是「使～（人）穿衣服」的意思。

17. move 本來是「移動」的意思，過去分詞 moved 當形容詞表示「受到感動的」。從前一句 This is for you. 來看，(B)、(C)、(D) 都是負面的敘述，只有 (A) 呼應 This is for you. 這句話以及後面的句子。

18. "change one's mind (about...)" 為常見用語，呼應下一句的 "Since then, she has no longer judged people by how they look."。

字詞解釋

once [wʌns] **adv.** 曾經 **skinny** [`skɪnɪ] **adj.** 皮包骨的，極瘦的  **across from**... 在～對面  **lonely** [`lonlɪ] **adj.** 孤獨的 (**be**) **dressed in**... 穿著～ **alone** [ə`lon] **adv.** 單獨地  **come over** 過來  **gift box** 禮盒  **moment** [`momənt] **n.** 時刻 **moved** [muvd] **adj.** 感動的 **change one's mind** 改變心意 **no longer adv.** 不再 **appreciate** [ə`priʃɪˌet] **v.** 欣賞，感激  **point of view** 觀點  **curious** [`kjʊrɪəs] **adj.** 好奇的 **favorite** [`fevərɪt] adj. 最喜愛的　**childish** [ˈtʃaɪldɪʃ] adj. 幼稚的，孩子般的　**doubt** [daʊt] n. 懷疑，疑問

15. skin 是「皮膚」的意思，它的形容詞 skinny 就是「皮包骨的」意思，相當於從 bone（骨頭）衍生的 bony（骨瘦如柴的）。

16. dress 雖然也可以當不及物動詞，但後面通常接「穿衣服的風格」，通常譯為「打扮成～」，而不是「穿什麼衣服」。例如 dress in dark colors（穿著深色服裝）、dress as an alien（打扮成外星人）。

17. move 這個動詞也有「使感動」的意思，但通常用於被動式。例如 I was so much moved by this story.（我深深地被這個故事感動了。）

18. mind 當名詞表示「主意，意見，想法」時，常與介系詞 in 搭配。例如，I don't know what's going on in his mind.（我不知道他腦袋在想什麼？）

Questions 19-21

中文翻譯

362

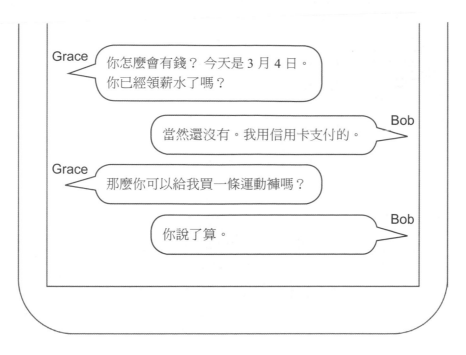

Bob 點開 Grace 傳來的圖片。

Giant 運動用品店

優惠價

僅限 3/8-3/15

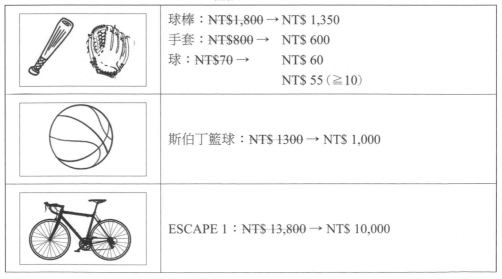

	球棒：~~NT$1,800~~ → NT$ 1,350 手套：~~NT$800~~ → NT$ 600 球：~~NT$70~~ → NT$ 60 NT$ 55（≧10）
	斯伯丁籃球：~~NT$ 1300~~ → NT$ 1,000
	ESCAPE 1：~~NT$ 13,800~~ → NT$ 10,000

第 1 回
第 2 回
第 3 回
第 4 回
第 5 回
第 6 回
第 7 回
第 8 回
第 9 回
第 10 回

	NT$ 4,800 → NT$ 3,600 含兩顆球
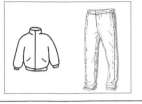	夾克：NT$2,500 → NT$2,000 褲子：NT$~~1,200~~ → NT$ 800

備註：大量訂購另有優惠。請來電詢問更多細節。

19. Grace 為何發訊息給 Bob？
    (A) 建議買什麼給 David 作為生日。
    (B) 問他何時領薪水。
    (C) 告訴他有什麼東西正在特價。
    (D) 邀請他一起去購物。

20. Bob 花了多少錢買 ESCAPE 1？
    (A) 新台幣 10,000 元
    (B) 新台幣 13,800 元
    (C) 新台幣 1,000 元
    (D) 新台幣 4,800 元

21. 關於這家體育用品店，何者為真？
    (A) 它主要販售棒球用品。
    (B) Grace 昨天在這家店買了一條運動褲。
    (C) Bob 得花 NT$ 1,200 買一件運動褲。
    (D) 如果你一次買多一點，會有更優惠的價格。

答題解說

19. 答案：(A)。題目問的是發送訊息（第一個文本）的目的，可以從 Grace 第一次發言中的 "Why not buy David a set of baseball things as his birthday gift?"（何不給大衛買一組棒球用品作為他的生日禮物呢？）得知，Grace 要建議 Bob 買什麼禮物給 David。故正確答案為 (A)。另外，雖然 Grace 發給 Bob 的圖片是關於某運動用品店的特價消息，但這並非她發送此訊息的目的，所以 (C) 不對。

20. 答案：(B)。本題需要整合與歸納兩篇文本的訊息與資訊，才能夠得到正確的答案。題目問的是 Bob 花多少錢買 ESCAPE 1。首先，我們可以在 Giant 運動用品

店的特價清單中看到 ESCAPE 1 原價是 NT$ 13,800，特價是 NT$ 10,000，而上方標示特價期限是 3/8-3/15。接著在對話訊息中，Bob 說他昨天在那家店買了 ESCAPE 1 的自行車，但「昨天」是幾號呢？可以看到 Grace 接著說「今天是 3 月 4 日。」也就是說，昨天是 3 月 3 日，因此 Bob 購買這輛自行車的價錢是 NT$ 13,800。故正確答案為 (B)。

21. 答案：(D)。題目問的是與這家體育用品店（sporting goods shop）有關的資訊。(A) 是錯誤的，因為從清單（第二個文本）可知，它並非主要販售棒球用品；(B) 是錯誤的，因為在對話訊息最後，Grace 問 Bob「你可以給我買一條運動褲嗎？」表示她還沒買。(C) 也是錯誤的，因為 Grace 只是說幫她買褲子，但沒有說什麼時候，而特價是 3/8 才開始，表示 Bob 之後可以用「特價」的 NT$ 800 買到運動褲。最後，從特價清單（第二個文本）的底下這句 "We offer more discounts for large orders." （大量訂購另有優惠。）可知，正確答案為 (D)。

破題關鍵

19. 針對「發送訊息的目的」的題型，通常答案就在發送者一開始所提及的事情或問題上。

20. 從 Bob 發言中的 "Oh, no! I just bought the ESCAPE 1 there yesterday!" 也可以猜到他可能在惋惜錯過特價，所以買的價位可能不是特價的 NT$10,000。

21. 「何者為真」或「何者為非」的題型，都屬於內容細節型的題目。通常必須先看過四個選項內容，再一一從兩個文本中找尋線索。 "better price" 是指「更好、更優惠的價格」，而 large order 是指「大量訂購」。

字詞解釋

why not... 何不～　**How come**... 怎麼會～　**pay** [pe] n. 薪水，收入　**credit card** n. 信用卡　**workout** [`wɝk͵aʊt] n. 運動，鍛鍊　**sporting** [`sportɪŋ] adj. 體育運動的　***goods** [gʊdz] n. 商品，貨物　**bat** [bæt] n. 球棒　**glove** [glʌv] n. 手套　**include** [ɪn`klud] v. 包括，包含　**jacket** [`dʒækɪt] n. 夾克，上衣　**pants** [pænts] n. 褲子　**order** [`ɔrdɚ] n. 訂購，訂單　**\*detail** [`ditel] n. 細節，詳情

相關文法或用法補充

❶ How come 的意思其實就是 Why，也就是「為什麼」的意思，屬於較為非正式，或是口語中較常使用的慣用語。若在商務場合、重大社交場合，或是公開場合，切忌還是避開如此口語用法較為妥當。但 how come 與 why 的差別在於：how come + 直述句、why + 疑問句。

❷ workout 這個名詞是從動詞片語 work out 而來。work out 可當及物或不及物動詞。當及物動詞表示「制訂出～（計畫、辦法等）」，不及物動詞表示「有結果；成功」。而不及物動詞的另一個很特別的意思就是「健身」。因此衍生出 workout 這個名詞，相當於 exercise（運動，鍛鍊）。

第 1 回
第 2 回
第 3 回
第 4 回
第 5 回
第 6 回
第 7 回
第 8 回
第 9 回
第 10 回

Questions 22-24

　　國輝從小在屏東的一個小村莊長大。上個月他和他姊姊來到台南。他們倆住在他們伯父家。他們屏東的房子在一場地震中受到損壞。他們的父母必須留在屏東照顧他們的小弟弟，因為當時他被倒下來的書架撞擊而受傷了。

　　國輝和他的姊姊在台南上同一所學校。學校裡的老師和同學們都對他們很好，但國輝過得並不快樂，因為他們必須在台南待很長一段時間，直到他們的房子修繕完成。他非常想念屏東的同學與朋友。他們是無話不談的朋友。他們會透過電子郵件、LINE 或視訊聯絡他。這使得他感覺好多了。國輝期待能夠早日和他的父母和弟弟住在一起。他也希望能夠回到屏東念書。

22. 關於國輝，以下何者正確？
    (A) 他的父母賣掉了他們的房子。
    (B) 他們家人的房屋在地震中受損。
    (C) 他受傷了且需要更好的醫療照護。
    (D) 他獨自去台南念書。

23. 國輝的父母在哪裡？
    (A) 在大城市。
    (B) 在鄉下。
    (C) 在國外。
    (D) 在醫院。

24. 在第二段中畫底線的 They 是指誰？
    (A) 國輝及其家人。
    (B) 國輝和他在台南的朋友。
    (C) 國輝在屏東的同學和朋友。
    (D) 國輝和他在屏東的同學和朋友。

這是一篇記敘文。內容敘述國輝與其姊姊在地震之後前往台南居住與念書的經過。

22. 答案：(B)。(A) 是錯誤的，因為第一段提到他們屏東的房子在一場地震中受到損壞，而非賣掉房子，所以 (B) 是正確的；(C) 是錯誤的，因為受傷的是他的弟弟（現在還在醫院）；(D) 也是錯誤的，因為第二段一開始提到國輝和他的姊姊在台南上同一所學校。

23. 答案：(B)。題目問的是國輝的父母在哪裡，可以從第一段最後的 "Their parents had to stay in Pingtung to take care of their little brother..." 可以得知，他們現在在屏東，雖然沒有 "in Pingtung" 這個選項，但可以從第一段第一句話 "Guo-hui

grew up in a small village in Pingtung." 得知，正確答案為 (B)。

24. 答案：(C)。題目句中的 They 所在句子是 They would contact him via email, LINE or video call.（他們會透過電子郵件、LINE 或視訊聯絡他。）與前面這句 "They were friends they could talk about everything with him."（他們是無話不談的朋友。）的 They 是一樣的，所以答案會在更前面的這句：He missed his classmates and friends in Pingtung very much.，也就是指 "his classmates and friends in Pingtung"，故正確答案為 (C)。

破題關鍵

22. 「何者為真」或「何者為非」的題型，都屬於內容細節型的題目。通常必須先看過四個選項內容，再到文章中找尋線索。。

23. 選項中的 countryside（鄉下）就是第一句中 village 的意思。就算不知道它的意思，也可以用刪除法得到答案。

24. 本題關鍵語句是 "He missed his classmates and friends in Pingtung very much."，因為想念同學與朋友，所以「透過電子郵件、LINE 或視訊聯絡他」。

字詞解釋

village [ˋvɪlɪdʒ] **n.** 村莊　**elder** [ˋɛldɚ] **adj.** 年齡較大的　**damage** [ˋdæmɪdʒ] **v.** 損害，毀壞　**earthquake** [ˋɝθˏkwek] **n.** 地震　**take care of** 照顧　**fallen** [ˋfɔlən] **adj.** 落下的　**bookshelf** [ˋbʊkˏʃɛlf] **n.** 書架；書櫃　**completely** [kəmˋplitlɪ] **adv.** 完全地　**repair** [rɪˋpɛr] **v.** 修理，整修　**miss** [mɪs] **v.** 想念，惦記　**contact** [kənˋtækt] **v.** 與～接觸／聯繫　***via** [ˋvaɪə] **prep.** 經由，透過　**video call** **phr.** 視訊　**look forward to**... 期待～　***medical** [ˋmɛdɪkl] **adj.** 醫學的，醫療的　**countryside** [ˋkʌntrɪˏsaɪd] **n.** 鄉間，農村　**foreign** [ˋfɔrɪn] **adj.** 外國的　**underline** [ˏʌndɚˋlaɪn] **v.** 在～畫底線，強調　***paragraph** [ˋpærəˏgræf] **n.** 段落

相關文法或用法補充

❶ 英文裡的「稱呼」比較單純，brother 可以指哥哥或弟弟，sister 可以指姊姊或妹妹。另外像伯叔舅（uncle）、姨姑嬸（aunt）或祖父母（grandparents）也都是一個單字可以指好幾種稱呼。但有時候硬要分的話，也可在這些基本字彙前加上修飾語。例如哥哥（older/elder brother）、妹妹（younger sister），或者 grandfather 不知道是爺爺或外公，可以在前面加上 parental 這個字來表示「爺爺」，而「外公」就是 maternal grandfather。

❷ miss 雖然是個很基礎的單字，主要有「錯過」及「思念」兩個完全不同的意思，再從這兩個基本意義，依不同情境衍生出不同解釋：
　　① 「錯過」：miss the train（沒趕上火車）、miss taking the exam（沒來考試）
　　② 「思念」：miss his ex-boyfriend（想念他的前男友）、miss living with his girlfriend（想念和他女友住在一起的時候）

→ 注意：miss 後面接 Ving 作為其受詞。

Questions 25-27

中文翻譯

　　在許多關於殘而不廢的故事中，我們看到許多身體「虛弱」的藝術家在其偉大的藝術品中表現出「強大」的力量。

　　以 Frida Kahlo 為例。她原本是個四肢健全的女孩。她在十八歲時被公車大力撞倒。她的大部分身體受到嚴重損傷，但她仍試圖好好地活著。她熱愛畫畫，而且讓我們欣賞到許多偉大的作品。另一個例子是 Christy Brown。在他出生時，唯一可以移動的部位是他的左腳。然而，他仍然可以非常好地書寫與繪畫。Brown 在他的自傳中寫下了他這輩子所發生的一切，以及他如何開始用他的左腳畫畫。最後，別忘了還有 Steve Wonder。他出生不久後就失明了，但後來他成為一位有名的歌手與作曲家。

　　這些身體狀況比不上一般人的藝術家，以他們堅強的意志力給我們帶來許多美好的事物，以及對於人生的希望。他們的故事告訴我們，生命中最重要的不是我們擁有什麼，而是我們能夠以自己的條件創造什麼。

25. 本文的主要概念應該是？
　　(A) 歷史總是重演。
　　(B) 藝術可以保護脆弱的心靈。
　　(C) 試著善加利用自己的生命。
　　(D) 許多偉大的藝術家都有強大的心靈。

26. 關於本文中三位藝術家，何者為真？
　　(A) 他們出生時都不健康。
　　(B) 他們的身體都有問題。
　　(C) 他們都是受歡迎的畫家。
　　(D) 他們都出生於貧窮的家庭。

27. 畫底線的 autobiography 所指為何？
　　(A) 關於一位名人的電影
　　(B) 某人自己的照片
　　(C) 某人撰寫自己一生的書
　　(D) 關於某人童年的書

答題解說

這是一篇說明文。內容講述殘而不廢的故事，告訴我們即使先天條件不佳，仍可活出精彩人生。

25. 答案：(C)。題目問的是「本文的主要概念」，可以從第二段舉出三位藝術家，先天或後天造成身體狀況不佳，但卻能本著對於藝術的喜好而活出精彩、快樂的人生，告訴我們，人應善加利用自己的生命，故正確答案為 (C)。另外，(B)「藝術可以保護脆弱的心靈」，其中「心靈」若改成「身體」就會是正確答案。(D) 看似正確，但並非本文的主旨。

26. 答案：(B)。關於本文中三位藝術家，可以從第二段的內容找尋線索。(A) 是錯誤的，因為 Frida Kahlo 在十八歲時因為車禍才造成身體殘缺，並非在出生時；(B) 是正確答案，因為本篇主旨就是在講「殘而不廢」的故事；(C) 是錯誤的，因為 Steve Wonder 是一位有名的歌手與作曲家；(D) 是錯誤的，因為文中並未提及任何人生於貧窮家庭。

27. 答案：(C)。autobiography 這個字所在的句子是 "Brown wrote in his autobiography what happened in his life and how he started painting with his left foot."，我們可以直接從中後半段的 "what happened in his life... foot"（他這輩子所發生的一切，以及他如何開始用他的左腳畫畫）知道，autobiography 的內容一定與一個人的生活事蹟有關，而且是用「寫」的，故正確答案 (C)。

破題關鍵

25. 本題屬於「主旨」型的問題，基本上可以綜合各段前一、兩句的大意即可看出端倪。不過本篇第三段第一句 "These artists whose physical condition... bring us many beautiful things, and hope for life." 是關鍵重點。

26. 「何者為真」或「何者為非」的題型，都屬於內容細節型的題目。通常必須先看過四個選項內容，再到文章中找尋線索。本題其實可以從第一段第一句 "those who are unable to use part of their body because of different causes"（由於不同因素造成無法使用其身體某部位）確認 (B) 是正確答案。

27. 如果學過字根的話，知道 auto 是「自己」，bio 是「生命」，graph 是「寫」的意思，就可以知道它是「自己寫下生命（中的事情）」的意思。即使不懂字根，也可從後面的關鍵語句 "...wrote... what happened in his life" 得到答案。

字詞解釋

cause [kɔz] n. 原因　**artist** [`ɑrtɪst] n. 藝術家，藝人　**weak** [wik] adj. 虛弱的　**heavily** [`hɛvɪlɪ] adv. 猛烈地　***injure** [`ɪndʒɚ] v. 使受傷　**paint** [pent] v. 油漆，繪畫　**allow** [ə`laʊ] v. 允許　**appreciate** [ə`priʃɪˌet] v. 欣賞，感激　**wonderfully** [`wʌndɚfəlɪ] adv. 精彩地，極好地　***autobiography** [ˌɔtəbaɪ`ɑgrəfɪ] n. 自傳　**blind** [blaɪnd] adj. 瞎的，盲的　**songwriter** [`sɔnˌraɪtɚ] n. 作曲家　**physical** [`fɪzɪkl] adj. 身體的　**condition** [kən`dɪʃən] n. 狀況，條件　**ordinary** [`ɔrdnˌɛrɪ] adj. 平常的，普通的　***willpower** [`wɪlˌpaʊɚ] n. 意志力　**repeat** [rɪ`pit] v. 重複　**protect** [prə`tɛkt] v. 保護　**make the most use of...** 對～善加利用　**childhood** [`tʃaɪldˌhʊd] n. 童年時期

❶ "those who..." 是常見的用語，相當於 "anyone who..." 、 "Whoever..." ，表示「任何～的人」，須注意的是，those 不能以 these 取代。例如 "Heaven helps those who help themselves.（天助自助者。）

❷ with 這個介系詞的用法之一是用來表示某種特質，通常可以理解成「有著～的」。例如：

① Did you see the girl with red hair?（你看到有著紅頭髮的那個女孩了嗎？）
② I'm looking for books with talking pens.（我在找有點讀筆的書。）

Questions 28-30

中文翻譯

寄件人	sarah1210@yahoo.com
收件人	alicechnag@yahoo.com
主旨	回覆：新生活如何？

親愛的 Alice：

　　坦白說，生活並不容易。身為 Little Angels 裡年紀最大的孩子，你不會感到驕傲。去那裡的人通常想要的是很年幼的孩子，最好是嬰兒，因為他們對於親生父母的記憶甚少，甚至從未見過他們。這讓他們很容易與新的父母有密切的關係。對於可以和新家人離開的人，我為他們感到高興。真的，我做得到，雖然我可能會有點失落。

　　我從沒想過林先生和太太會選擇我。他們說，他們感覺好像已經認識我很多年了。與我交談幾個下午後，他們決定帶我回家。但和一個陌生人住在一起並不容易，至少現在是如此。David 人很好，但是他太客氣了。似乎我只是他家裡的客人。我們很少說話，而只是互相說聲早安或晚安。這方面 Betty 比她哥哥做得好一點。我有自己的房間，而這是現在唯一可以讓我當作是自己家的地方。

　　我試圖讓他們感覺和我在一起是輕鬆的，因為這是我一生中第一次感覺自己屬於某個地方。

祝一切順利，

莎拉

28. 莎拉的這封電子郵件的目的是什麼？
    (A) 抱怨在 Little Angels 的生活
    (B) 談論她的新生活
    (C) 解釋為什麼這對夫妻帶她回家
    (D) 對於離開 Little Angels 表示後悔

29. 關於在 Little Angels 的孩子們，何者為真？
    (A) 他們不與其父母同住。
    (B) 他們常常沒有得到很好的對待。
    (C) 他們大多數有健康問題。
    (D) 他們在那兒出生。

30. 第三段中的 this 所指為何？
    (A) 客氣對待陌生人
    (B) 與陌生人住在一起
    (C) 讓自己感到輕鬆自在
    (D) 為在 Little Angels 的孩子們感到高興

答題解說

這個題組是一封電子郵件，主要關於 Sarah 回覆 Alice 前一封問候「近來如何」的郵件。

28. 答案：(B)。題目問的是電子郵件的目的（或主旨），可以先從第一段找線索：It's not easy, to tell the truth.（坦白說，生活並不容易。）這裡的 It 是指 new life（可以從「主旨」欄得知）。顯然 Sarah 是要告訴 Alice 她的新生活有種種困難，並不容易。故正確答案為 (B) To tell about her new life。

29. 答案：(A)。題目要問的是，有關在 Little Angels 的孩子們的敘述。這部分的線索主要在第一段的內容。(A) 是正確的，因為從第一段內容可以知道 Little Angels 這地方是領養或收養孩童的地方，因此這裡的孩童當然不是跟親生父母住在一起了；(B)、(C)、(D) 都是沒有提及的，而且，只要知道 Little Angels 是個收養中心，按照常理判斷，就知道其餘三個選項是不正確的。

30. 答案：(B)。題目句中的 "this" 所在句子是 "Betty deals with this better than her older brother."（這方面 Betty 比她哥哥做得好一點。）所以必須根據前文判斷：It seems I'm just a guest in his family. We seldom talk, but just say good morning or good night to each other.（似乎我只是他家裡的客人。我們很少說話，而只是互相說聲早安或晚安。）表示 David 尚無法適應與一個陌生人（Sarah）住在一起。而這方面（this）Betty 比她哥哥做得好一點。故正確答案為 (B)。

28. 信件最上方，在收件人與寄件人下面都會有個「主旨」欄位，這是找尋信件主旨的第一線索。從這封郵件的 "Subject: Re: How's the new life?" 即可知，「回覆對方詢問新生活狀況如何」是寫這封信的主要目的。

29. 「何者為真」或「何者為非」的題型，都屬於內容細節型的題目。可以針對題目關鍵語句（kids at Little Angels），及其談論的位置（第一段）即可掌握答題線索。

30. this 是「指示代名詞」，指的是前面提到的一件事情。也可以用刪除法得到正確答案，因為其餘三個選項的敘述都是明顯不相關的。

字詞解釋

to tell the truth 說真的，坦白說　　**proud** [praʊd] **adj.** 驕傲的　　**birth parents** 親生父母　　**sense** [sɛns] **n.** 知覺，感覺　　**loss** [lɔs] **n.** 失去　　**pick** [pɪk] **v.** 挑選　　**stranger** [ˈstrendʒɚ] **n.** 陌生人　　**polite** [pəˈlaɪt] **adj.** 禮貌的，客氣的　　**seldom** [ˈsɛldəm] **adv.** 不常，很少　　**deal with** 處理，對待　　**make oneself at home** 讓自己輕鬆自在　　**for the first time** 第一次，首度　　**belong** [bəˈlɔŋ] **v.** 歸屬（於）　　**complain** [kəmˈplen] **v.** 抱怨　　**explain** [ɪkˈsplen] **v.** 解釋，說明　　**regret** [rɪˈgrɛt] **v.** 後悔，遺憾　　**treat** [trit] **v.** 對待

相關文法或用法補充

❶ 在國中的文法裡，動名詞（V-ing）一定會和不定詞（to-V）一起學習。因為兩者都可以當「名詞」，作為句子裡的主詞或受詞。就像這裡的這個句子：Being the oldest kid at Little Angels isn't something you'd be proud of.。主詞是 "Being the oldest kid at Little Angels"。不過，動名詞與不定詞在「意義」上是有差異的。動名詞表示一種「狀態、存在的事實」，而不定詞指的是一種「目的、未來」的概念，所以如果這句改成 To be the oldest kid at Little Angels isn't something you'd be proud of.，意思會變成「為了成為 Little Angels 裡年紀最大的孩子（這樣的意圖或計畫）不是你會感到驕傲的。

❷ parent 這個名詞如果不加 -s，就表示「父母的其中一方」，一般我們稱為「家長」。而「生父」和「生母」的英文是 parental father 以及 parental mother。「親生父母」可以說 birth parents 或 natural parents 或是 biological parents。「養父母」則是 foster parents。

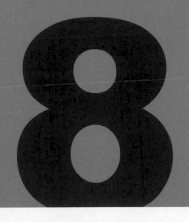

8

GEPT
全民英檢

初級初試
中譯＋解析

第一部分 看圖辨義

1. **For question number 1, please look at Picture A.**

Question number 1: What does this sign tell us?
（這個標誌告訴我們什麼？）
(A) You can't fish here.（你不能在此釣魚。）
(B) You're not allowed to swim here.（你不能在此游泳。）
(C) Be careful of fast-running water when you swim here.
　　（在此游泳時要留意水流湍急。）

答題解說

答案：(B)。這是在河邊或湖邊的標誌，告訴人此地「禁止」游泳，通常是為水深或湍急的原因。

破題關鍵

(B)、(C) 都和游泳有關，但 (C) 顯然刻意以 swim 來誤導答題，應特別注意。

字詞解釋

fish [fɪʃ] v. 釣魚　　**allow** [əˋlaʊ] v. 允許　　**be careful of**... 小心注意～

相關文法或用法補充

careful 是「小心的」意思，除了「be careful of/about/with + 名詞」的用法之外，也常用於「be careful + that 子句」中。

2. **For question number 2 and 3, please look at Picture B.**

Question number 2: What is the man going to do?
（這名男子將要做什麼？）
(A) He is going to take a walk.（他將要去散步。）
(B) He is going to take exercise.（他將要去運動。）
(C) He is going to take medicine.（他將要吃藥。）

答題解說

答案：(C)。從圖中可以清楚看到一位女士正想餵藥給躺在床上生病的男人吃，所以這名男子接下來要做的事應該是吃藥，所以 (C) 為正確答案。

第1回
第2回
第3回
第4回
第5回
第6回
第7回
第8回
第9回
第10回

從圖中我們可以看到有人在餵男子吃東西,而男子一副精神不振的樣子,由此可以猜測出他生病了,正準備吃藥。take a walk 與 take exercise 很明顯都不會是他接下來要做的事。

take a walk 散步　　**exercise** [ˋɛksəˌsaɪz] n. 運動　　**medicine** [ˋmɛdəsn] n. 藥

「be going to + 原形動詞」是用來表達「未來式」的一種方式。表示主詞即將進行的一個動作。這個動作通常是經過預先考慮並含有已經做好準備的意思。注意:一般不常把動詞 go 和 come 用於 be going to 結構中,而常用現在進行式來代替 be going to 結構,即通常不用 I'm going to go 而用 I'm going,不用 I'm going to come 而是用 I'm coming。

3. **Question number 3: Please look at Picture B again.**

   What is true about the picture?(關於這張圖,何者正確?)

   (A) The woman is sick.(女子生病了。)
   (B) The woman uses a bowl to feed the man.
   　　(女子用碗來餵男子。)
   (C) The man is lying on the bed.(男子正躺在床上。)

答案:(C)。圖片中男子病懨懨地躺在床上,而女子用湯匙(spoon)準備餵他吃藥,而不是用碗(bowl)。所以正確答案為(C)。

lie(躺)的動詞變化是 lie → lay → lain → lying。

bowl [bol] n. 碗　　**feed** [fid] v. 餵食　　**lying** [ˋlaɪɪŋ] v. 躺(lie 的現在進行式)

lying 也可以當形容詞,表示「橫臥的」或「說謊的」。The lying child was punished.(這說謊的孩子受到懲罰。)

4. **For question number 4 and 5, please look at Picture C.**

Question number 4: What is the little girl doing?

（小女孩在做什麼？）

(A) She's playing the piano（她正在彈鋼琴。）

(B) She's playing the guitar.（她正在彈吉他。）

(C) She's dancing.（她正在跳舞。）

答題解說

答案：(C)。圖片的小女孩所做的動作，不難看出是在跳舞吧。所以正確答案為
(C)。

破題關鍵

piano、guitar 以及 dancing 都是初級程度的字彙，只要聽出選項中的這三個字就
能輕易作答。

字詞解釋

piano [pɪˋæno] n. 鋼琴　　**guitar** [gɪˋtɑr] n. 吉他　　**dance** [dæns] n. 跳舞

相關文法或用法補充

為什麼「玩樂器」要用「play the + 樂器」表示，而「打球」則是「play + 球」
呢？例如：play the guitar、play baseball。可以這樣記憶：彈奏樂器，就是針對
「特定的樂器」在把弄，所以得加定冠詞 the。而打球的重點不在球本身，而是
在於「玩的過程」，所以不需要 the。如果加上 the，比較像是「玩這顆球」的意
味，也許是想辦法要從它身上變出點什麼似的。

5. **Question number 5: Please look at Picture C again.**

What is true about the picture?

（關於這張圖片，何者為真？）

(A) The old man is playing the piano.

（這位老男人正在彈鋼琴。）

(B) There's a floor lamp in the corner.（角落有個落地燈。）

(C) Everyone is dancing on the floor.（大家都在地板上跳舞。）

答題解說

答案：(B)。正在「彈吉他」的是老婦人，所以 (A) 是錯誤的；角落有個燈，(B)
是正確答案；正在「跳舞」的是小女孩與老人家，而非所有人，所以 (C) 也是錯
誤的。

遇到「何者為真」或「何者為非」的題目，就是先仔細觀察圖片後，將三個選項的內容一一對照，是最保險的答題方式。當然，選項中的關鍵字詞一定要聽懂：playing the piano... 表示「彈鋼琴」；floor lamp 是「立燈」的意思。

字詞解釋

lamp [læmp] n. 燈　　**corner** [ˋkɔrnɚ] n. 角落

相關文法或用法補充

corner 也可以當形容詞，表示「在角落的」，例如：I'm sitting at a corner table.（我們坐在一張放在角落處的桌旁。）

第二部分 問答

6. **How's the weather today in Taiwan?**（今天台灣天氣如何？）

(A) Once a week（一星期一次）
(B) It's a long story.（說來話長。）
(C) It's warm.（天氣暖和。）

答題解說

答案：(C)。以 How 開頭的問句，主要是問「～如何？」，（例如 How are you?），也可能是問「交通工具」例如：How do you go to the supermarket?（你如何到超市？），或者是問「天氣狀況」，例如：How is it/the weather in...?（在～（某地）的天氣如何？）。本題屬於這裡的最後一種問法，因此回答要和「天氣」有關，故 (C) 是正確回答。

破題關鍵

題目這句只要聽出 weather 即可選出正確答案。(A) 的回答是針對 How often... ?（多久一次～？）的提問，而「問天氣」是可以立即回答的問題，不會是用「說來話長。」來回答。

相關文法或用法補充

詢問「天氣」的句型主要有：❶ How's the weather（＋地點＋時間副詞)? 以及 ❷ What's the weather like（＋地點＋時間副詞）?。回答時，可以用 It，例如：It's hot in Canada in summer.（加拿大夏天很熱。）

7. **I failed the test.**（我考試不及格。）

(A) I felt much better. Thanks.（我覺得好多了。謝謝。）
(B) I love fall, too.（我也喜歡秋天。）
(C) I didn't pass, either.（我也沒考過。）

答題解說

答案：(C)。fail the test 是指「考試沒過」，因此當聽到這句話時，回答通常跟「考試」有關。答案可能是 pass（通過）或是 fail（沒過），在否定句中，要用 either（也不），不能用 too（也）。

破題關鍵

本題的解題關鍵在於聽懂 failed the test，就能知道如何回答。很容易聽錯，聽成 feel、felt 或 fell。也可以直接從 3 個選項分析。(A) 用 felt 類似發音，來誤導答題。此類回答和身體不適或探病有關聯，與題目不相關。(B) 喜愛秋天這個季節，也和題目無關。

字詞解釋

fail [fel] **v.** 失敗　**either** [ˈiðɚ] adv. 也不

相關文法或用法補充

either 分為幾種詞性，不同詞性有不同的解釋：
❶ either of you （你們兩者之中一個）→ 當代名詞。
❷ Either you or she... （你或是她…）→ 當連接詞
❸ He won't agree, either.（他也不會同意。）→ 當副詞。

8. **How did you go to Kaohsiung?**（你搭什麼交通工具到高雄？）

(A) By airplane.（搭飛機。）
(B) I went there yesterday.（我昨天去的。）
(C) I felt bad.（我感覺很糟。）

答題解說

答案：(A)。How... go? 用來詢問「搭乘何種交通工具」，回答時要有具體的「交通工具」，因此本題正確答案是(A)。

破題關鍵

本題的破題關鍵在於抓到一開頭的 how 和動詞 go。how 開頭是問「如何」，若有聽到 go 等動詞，就知道是詢問「搭乘何種交通工具」。

第 1 回
第 2 回
第 3 回
第 4 回
第 5 回
第 6 回
第 7 回
第 8 回
第 9 回
第 10 回

字詞解釋

airplane [ˈɛrˌplen] **n.** 飛機　　**yesterday** [ˈjɛstɚde] **adv.** 昨天

相關文法或用法補充

how 用法很多，詢問對方搭乘交通工具可用：How do you go to + 地點？回答用「I go there by + 交通工具」有時候可直接說「By + 交通工具」。How 開頭的問話主要有幾種：how old 詢問年紀、how often 詢問多久一次、how tall 詢問身高、how many/much：詢問數量

9. **I would like to speak to Mrs. Pitt, please.**（麻煩請找彼得太太。）

   (A) Speaking.（我就是。）

   (B) Have fun.（玩得愉快。）

   (C) I am not she.（我不是她。）

答題解說

答案：(A)。本題考的是電話用語。「I would like to speak to... = May I speak to...」表示「請問某人在嗎？」這是打電話過去找某人的第一句話。如果是本人接的，可以用 Speaking. 或 This is he/she speaking. 來回答。

破題關鍵

如果不甚了解 Speaking. 的用語，也可以試著用刪去法。因為 (B) 與 (C) 的回答皆為非所問，所以 (A) 肯定是正確的。

字詞解釋

would like + **to**-V 想要～

相關文法或用法補充

如果對方要找的人不在，可用 I am sorry but ＋人＋ be＋unavailable now. 來回答。但不可用 Who are you? 詢問，這是不禮貌的回話。若是來電者要找的人在，可用 Just a moment, please. 或 Wait a second, please.（請稍等。）回答。

10. **How many times do you play basketball a week?**（你一星期打幾次籃球？）

   (A) I am good at playing basketball.（我擅長打籃球。）

   (B) Only once.（僅一次。）

   (C) I am fifteen years old.（我十五歲。）

答案：(B)。How many times... 是詢問「多少次」。題目是問「一星期打幾次籃球」，以三個選項來分析，(A) 選項的 I am good at... 和題目沒有關聯，而 (B) 選項的 once 就是正確答案。選項 (C) 的 I am fifteen years old. 是用來回應詢問年紀，答非所問。

破題關鍵

time 除了是「時間」的意思之外，也可用來表示「次數」，而 once 等於 one time（一次）。

字詞解釋

once [wʌns] **adv.** 一次，曾經

相關文法或用法補充

time 當「時間」的意思時，是不可數名詞，但是當「次、回」時，為可數名詞。例如，I have no time to watch TV.（我沒有時間看電視。）、I have been to Hong Kong three times.（我去過香港三次。）

11. **A girl just called you. Who's she?**（有個女孩打電話找你。她是誰？）

(A) She's my sister.（她是我妹妹。）
(B) She's sad.（她很難過。）
(C) She's doing her homework.（她正在做功課。）

答題解說

答案：(A)。題目的第一句話不影響答題。只要聽懂第二句 "Who's she?"，知道是 Who 的問句即可。選項 (A) 提到是妹妹，就是回答身分，為正確答案。而 (B) 是表達情緒，通常用 how 詢問，選項 (C) 則是回應 "What is she doing?" 的句子。

破題關鍵

疑問詞（5W1H）開頭的問句在考試中一定會出現，而且是在問句開頭第一個字，一定要聽清楚。而有時候題目會有先來一句不影響答題的直述句擾亂你的聽力，須特別注意。

相關文法或用法補充

do one's homework 是「寫作業」的意思，不是 write one's homework 喔！do 常見於許多慣用語中。例如 do me a favor（幫我個忙）、do/wash the dishes（洗碗）、do the trick（奏效）、do... good（對～有好處）、do a good job（做得好）。

12. Excuse me, coming through. （不好意思，借過一下。）

(A) Good idea.（好主意。）
(B) You're welcome.（不客氣。）
(C) Oh, sorry!（噢，抱歉。）

答題解說

答案：(C)。無論是在大眾運輸工具上、夜市或其他擁擠的場合，都可能說出「（請）借過。」這句話，英文裡的「借過。」是 Coming through.，但其實你也可以只說 Excuse me. 或是 Sorry. 即可，但記得語氣要客氣一點喔！另外，可別說出 borrow 或 lend 的字眼！至於回答的部分，通常如果不是說「抱歉。」（因為你擋到人家的路了），就是直接移動位置讓人家過，而不作任何回應。所以本題正確答案是 (C)。

破題關鍵

through 是「通過，經過」之意。即使不知道 Coming through 的意思，至少Excuse me 應該要知道吧！這通常是是用來「拜託」別人做某事或請求幫忙的第一句話，(A) 與 (B) 顯然都是不相關的回答。

相關文法或用法補充

除了 Excuse me, coming through. 之外，「借過一下」也可以用 "Could you please let me through?"、"Could you please move." 。要是在一些私人場合，因為生氣或急著離開，可以說 "Get out of my way." 或 "Move!" 。

13. How old is your dog? （你的狗幾歲了？）

(A) He's very old.（他很老了。）
(B) He is still a puppy.（他還是一隻小狗。）
(C) He's almost 10.（他快十歲了。）

答題解說

答案：(C)。How old...? 常用來詢問「多大，幾歲」，回答時必須有確切的數字，而不是「很老、年紀很大、還小…」等的回答方式，故正確答案為 (C)。

破題關鍵

關鍵在於聽到 how old 的問句，要想到答案會有「數字」即可。

字詞解釋

puppy [ˈpʌpɪ] n. 小狗，幼犬

如何用英文詢問「年紀」和「回答」？以下整理幾種說法：

❶ How old＋ be V＋主詞？→ 表示「某人幾歲？」。如：How old is your neighbor?（你鄰居幾歲？）

❷ 回答歲數：S＋be V＋數字＋year(s) old. 或是 S＋be V＋數字.

補充：S＋be V＋數字-year-old＋ n.。例如：She is a 20-year-old student.（她是個 20 歲的學生。）

What/How about going for a biking trip?（我們騎腳踏車出去逛逛如何？）

14. How much did the shirt cost you?（你花多少錢買這件襯衫？）

(A) Neil loves it very much.（尼爾超愛這件襯衫。）

(B) It's my favorite.（它是我的最愛。）

(C) About NT$ 2000（大概兩千元左右）

答題解說

答案：(C)。How much 可以用來詢問「多少錢」，再加上 cost（花費），可以推知答案是跟價格有關，所以選項 (C) 的「大概兩千元左右。」就是最正確的回應，其他兩個選項都是不相關的回答。

破題關鍵

how much 對於初學英文的人來說，相信耳熟能詳，可能是問「價格、重量、或是程度」，本題只要掌握住 how much 和 cost，再與選項中的 NT$2000 作連結，就可以確定答案了。

字詞解釋

shirt [ʃɝt] **n.** 襯衫　**favorite** [ˋfevərɪt] **n.** 特別喜愛的人事物

相關文法或用法補充

日常生活對話中，常會聊到各種衣物服飾，有可能會出現在聽力或閱讀考題中，如果聽不出來，會影響作答的信心！以下是一些重要衣物相關的說法：pants 長褲、 shorts 短褲、uniform 制服、suit 西裝 、vest 背心、sweater 毛衣、jeans 牛仔褲、coat 大衣、jacket 夾克、T-shirt T 恤、stockings 絲襪、dress 洋裝、skirt 裙子、socks 襪子。另外，「穿～衣服」的動詞可用 wear 或是 put on。

15. It's cool today. Let's go on a picnic.（今天天氣涼爽。我們去野餐吧。）

　　(A) Sounds great.（聽起來不錯。）

　　(B) I will pick him up later.（我晚點去接他。）

　　(C) Today isn't my day.（我今天不走運。）

答案：(A)。本題有兩句話。第一句（It's cool today.）要表達的天氣很涼爽，而第二句是表達「提議」（Let's go on a picnic.）。選項中只有 (A) 表示「聽起來不錯。」可以回應這件事情。

基本上，本題第一句話與答題沒關係，有時候題目的第一句話只是想誤導你作答。通常要注意聽的是第二句。Let's... 有「提議做某事情」之意，回答不一定是 Yes/No，也有可能是 Sounds good. 或是 Good idea. 等。

picnic [ˋpɪknɪk] n. 野餐　　**sound** [saʊnd] v. 聽起來　　**later** [ˋletɚ] adv. 更晚地

❶ let 是使役動詞，後面接原形動詞。Let's 是 Let us 的縮寫。例：Let's go shopping tomorrow.（我們明天去逛街吧。）

❷ pick someone up 是指「接送」。如果受詞是代名詞，要擺在 pick 與 up 之間。例：He doesn't want to pick him up.（他不想去接他。）

第三部分 簡短對話

16. M: You were late again this morning, Molly.

　　W: I am sorry, Mr. Thomas.

　　M: Don't do it again, or you'll be fired.

　　W: I will be early from tomorrow on.

　　Question: Where are probably the speakers?

　　(A) In a classroom

　　(B) In an office

　　(C) On a bus

男：茉莉，妳今天早上又遲到了。

女：我很抱歉，湯瑪士先生。

男：別再遲到了，否則你會被炒魷魚。

女：我從明天起早點到。

問題：說話者們可能在哪裡？

(A) 在教室裡

(B) 在辦公室中

(C) 在公車上

答題解說

答案：(B)。這篇對話與「遲到」有關，當女子對於自己遲到表示抱歉之後，男子說「別再遲到了，否則你會被炒魷魚。」因此推知，這是在工作場合。所以答案是(B)。

破題關鍵

既然題目問的是對話者所在地點，那麼就應注意與地點相關的發言內容。本題關鍵字只有一個：fire。當動詞表示「使辭職」。

字詞解釋

fire [faɪr] v.【口】解僱，開除　**from... on** 從～開始

相關文法或用法補充

❶ be early to + 地點 ＝ 提早到某地。

　　如: Sean is early to the meeting room. (史恩提早到會議室。)

❷ be late for + 地點 ＝ 晚到某地。

　　如: We will be late for the party. (我們會晚點到派對。)

❸ on time ＝ 準時

17. W: Excuse me, sir. Do you know where the Happy Restaurant is?

　　M: Yes. It's five blocks from here.

　　W: It's a little bit too far.

　　M: Yes. You'd better go there by bus.

Question: What is the woman doing?

(A) She is waiting for the bus.

(B) She is taking an order in a restaurant.

(C) She is asking for directions.

第 1 回

第 2 回

第 3 回

第 4 回

第 5 回

第 6 回

第 7 回

第 8 回

第 9 回

第 10 回

英文翻譯

女：不好意思，先生。你知道「快樂餐廳」在哪裡嗎？
男：知道。離這裡五個街區。
女：有點太遠了。
男：對啊。你最好搭公車去那裡。
問題：女子正在做什麼？
(A) 她正在等公車。
(B) 她在餐廳接受點餐。
(C) 她在問路。

答題解說

答案：(C)。本題是 Do you know where.... (你知道～在哪裡？) 的問題。由 five blocks（五個街區）可知，女子正在問路，所以男子建議她「搭公車去」，所以她不是在「等公車」，(A) 是錯誤的；而選項 (B) She is taking an order in a restaurant. (她在餐廳接受點餐。) 顯然也是錯誤的答案。

破題關鍵

只要注意聽出男子說的 "It's five blocks from here"，這是本題關鍵處，所以別被 (A) 選項的 bus、(B) 選項的 restaurant 誤導了。

字詞解釋

restaurant [ˈrɛstərənt] n. 餐廳　**block** [blɑk] n. 街區　**take an order**（在餐廳中）接受點餐　**direction** [dəˈrɛkʃən] n. 方向

相關文法或用法補充

與「問路」有關的說法，除了「Do you know where + 地點 + is?」之外，也可以說「Do you know how to go/get to... ?」或是「Where can I find the...?」。例如，Do you know how to go to the MRT station?（你知道捷運站怎麼走嗎？）= Where can I find the MRT station?

18. W: Are you ready to order now, sir?

M: Yes, I'd like to have fried rice and an onion soup.

W: Would you like anything to drink?

M: Yes, I'd like a cup of coffee, please.

Question: Who is the woman?

(A) An office worker

(B) A restaurant waitress

(C) A supermarket clerk

女：先生，您現在準備好要點菜了嗎？

男：是的，我要炒飯和洋蔥湯。

女：您想喝點什麼嗎？

男：是的，請給我一杯咖啡。

問題：女子是誰？

(A) 上班族

(B) 餐廳女服務生

(C) 超市職員

答案：(B)。題目問的是女子的身分，所以應注意女子發言的部分。一開始女子說「先生，您現在準備好要點菜了嗎？（Are you ready to order now, sir?）」，所以她應該是餐廳的服務生。故正確答案為 (B)。(A) 是「辦公室上班族」；(C) 是「超市職員」都是明顯錯誤的答案。

本題關鍵字詞除了 order（點餐）之外，女子第二句話說 "Would you like anything to drink?"（想喝點什麼嗎？），也可推知她的身分。

order [`ɔrdɚ] n. 點餐　**onion** [`ʌnjən] n. 洋蔥　**restaurant** [`rɛstərənt] n. 餐廳　**bank** [bæŋk] n. 銀行

anything 常用於以下情況：

❶ anything +單數動詞。例如：Anything is possible.（任何事都有可能。）

❷ anything + 形容詞。一般而言，形容詞放在名詞前面修飾，但如果遇到 anything/something/nothing... 時，則形容詞放在後面。例如：anything good in life（生活中任何美好事情）

❸ 常用於疑問句和否定句。例如：The police officer didn't say anything.（警察一句話都沒說。）

19. M: It's so cold today.

　　W: Yes. It snows heavily outside.

　　M: Are you going to visit your uncle this Saturday?

　　W: I'm afraid not. It will continue to snow until Sunday.

　　M: I see.

Question: What will the weather be like this Saturday?

(A) It will be cloudy.

(B) It will be sunny.

(C) It will be snowy.

英文翻譯

男：今天超冷。

女：是啊。外面下大雪了。

男：這個星期六你要去拜訪你叔叔嗎？

女：恐怕不去了。這場雪將持續到星期天。

男：了解。

問：這個星期六天氣會如何？

(A) 陰天。

(B) 晴天。

(C) 下雪天。

答題解說

答案：(C)。題目問的是「本週六的天氣狀況」，提到 Saturday 的是 "Are you going to visit your uncle this Saturday?"（這個星期六你要去拜訪你叔叔嗎？）回答說 "I'm afraid not. It will continue to snow until Sunday."（恐怕不去了。這場雪將持續到星期天。）所以週六還是個下雪天。故正確答案為 (C)。

破題關鍵

對話中出現與天氣狀況有關的關鍵字只有一個：snow，它的形容詞是 snowy（下雪的）。即使不是下雪的天氣，也不能說一定就是 cloudy 或 sunny，何況對話中也沒提及這兩個字。

字詞解釋

heavily [ˋhɛvɪlɪ] adv. 猛烈地　**visit** [ˋvɪzɪt] v. 探望　**continue** [kənˋtɪnju] v. 繼續

相關文法或用法補充

未來簡單式的用法：

❶ S + will + V. + ... + 未來的時間副詞.（某人在…時候將會…）例如：Gary will take a trip this weekend.（蓋瑞將在周末去旅行。）

　→ will 可以用 be going to 取代，不過意思並非完全相同。

❷ 表「未來」的時間副詞，像是 tomorrow、tomorrow morning...、「next + 年/月/星期」、「in + 一段時間」（如 in three days 三天之後）。

20. W: May I help you?

M: Yes, I'm looking for a sweater that's able to keep me warm.

W: What size are you?

M: Large.

W: This way, please.

Question: What does the woman do?

(A) She's a clerk.

(B) She's a waitress.

(C) She's a coach.

女：有需要什麼嗎？

男：是的，我正在找一件可以讓我保暖的毛衣。

女：您穿幾號？

男：大號。

女：這邊請。

問題：女子是做什麼的？

(A) 她是個店員。

(B) 她是個女服務生。

(C) 她是個教練。

答案：(A)。題目問的是女子的職業，可以從她的發言中找尋線索。從第一句的
"May I help you?" 可以斷定 (C) She's a coach.（她是個教練。）是錯誤的；女子
第二句話說 "What size are you?" （您穿幾號的？），顯然這不會是餐廳服務生
說的話，所以 (B) 也是錯的。故正確答案為 (A)。clerk 可用來表示各種營業、販
售場所的「職員、店員、銷售員」。

從三個選項內容可以推知，題目要問的是職業。接著要知道是問「誰」的職業，
然後從女子或男子的發言中自然可以找到關鍵字詞或語句。本題關鍵是 May I
help you? 以及 What size are you?。

large [lɑrdʒ] **adj.** 大的 　**clerk** [klɝk] n. 店員　**waitress** [`wetrɪs] n. 女服務
生　**coach** [kotʃ] n. 教練

第 1 回
第 2 回
第 3 回
第 4 回
第 5 回
第 6 回
第 7 回
第 8 回
第 9 回
第 10 回

相關文法或用法補充

常見衣服尺寸（size）的英文字母有 S、M、L、XL，它們所代表的英文單字是 small、medium、large、extra large。另外，如果是只有一種尺碼的，就標示 F，表示 free size。

21. M: Excuse me. I'd like to know how long an international mail will take to arrive.

W: To which country?

M: New Zealand.

W: That'll need 7-10 days, by airmail.

M: Then how much is a stamp for that?

Question: What is the man going to do?

(A) Board an airplane

(B) Send a letter

(C) Receive a mail

英文翻譯

男：請問一下。我想知道國際郵件需要多久時間送達。

女：送去哪個國家？

男：紐西蘭。

女：這需要 7 到 10 天，航空郵件。

男：那郵票要多少錢？

問題：男人將做什麼？

(A) 登上飛機

(B) 寄信

(C) 收郵件

答題解說

答案：(B)。題目問的是「男子將要做什麼」，可以從男子的發言中找線索："I'd like to know how long an international mail will take to arrive."（我想知道國際郵件需要多久時間送達。），以及 "Then how much is a stamp for that?"（那郵票要多少錢？），由此可判斷，男子正要寄信。

破題關鍵

本題最關鍵的一句就是男子問 "how much is a stamp...?"，只有要寄信（send a letter）時才會問要買多少錢的郵票。

389

international [ˌɪntɚˋnæʃənl] **adj.** 國際的　**arrive** [əˋraɪv] **v.** 到達　**airmail** [ˋɛrˌmel] **n.** 航空郵件　**stamp** [stæmp] **n.** 郵票　**board** [bord] **v.** 登上（船、車、飛機等）

相關文法或用法補充

郵局常用的幾個單字，你不可不知喔。

❶ 動詞：mail（郵遞）、send（寄送）。

❷ 名詞：postman（郵差）、postage（郵資）、parcel（包裹）、package（包裹）、mailbox（郵箱）、registered mail（掛號）、international express mail（國外快捷件）、domestic mail（國內郵件），express（快捷郵件）、postcard（明信片）

22. M: You have dark circles! Loss of sleep?

    W: I didn't go to bed until 4 a.m.

    M: Why? What were you busy with?

    W: I'm preparing for my math test. I can't fail it again.

    Question: How is the woman feeling now?

    (A) She's feeling excited.

    (B) She's feeling tired.

    (C) She's feeling bored.

英文翻譯

男：妳有黑眼圈！失眠嗎？

女：我到凌晨四點才睡覺。

男：為什麼？妳在忙什麼？

女：我在準備數學考試。我不能再考不及格了。

問題：女子現在感覺如何？

(A) 她覺得興奮。

(B) 她感到疲倦。

(C) 她感到厭煩。

答題解說

答案：(B)。題目問的是女子感覺如何（How is... feeling?），可以從男子與女子的第一句話 "You have dark circles! Loss of sleep?／I didn't go to bed until 4 a.m." 推知，女子因為熬夜而有黑眼圈（dark circles），當下應該覺得很累了，故正確答案為 (B)。

即使不知道 dark circles 的意思，應該可以知道 "Loss of sleep" 是「失眠」吧！但無論女子是否「失眠」，至少我們從她說的 "I didn't go to bed until 4 a.m." 知道，tired 會是最接近的答案。sick 是「生病」，bored 是「無聊、厭煩」，皆與 "go to bed until 4 a.m." 無關。

***dark circle** 黑眼圈　**loss** [lɔs] n. 喪失　**prepared** [prɪ`pɛrd] adj. 準備好的　**fail** [fel] v. 不及格，失敗　**excited** [ɪk`saɪtɪd] adj. 興奮的　**tired** adj. 疲倦的

excited/exciting 都是「情緒形容詞」，但意思與用法是完全不同的：

❶ excited 是指「（人）感到興奮的」。句型：S + be + excited + about/that ...。例如：Kelly is excited about the coming party.（凱莉對將到來的派對感到興奮。）

❷ exciting 是指「（事物）令人感到興奮／刺激的」。句型：S + be + exciting...。例如：The basketball game was exciting.（籃球比賽很刺激。）

23. **M: Where's Mom?**

W: She is cooking in the kitchen.

M: What do we have for dinner?

W: Beef noodles.

M: Again? Give me a break.

Question: Is the man satisfied with his dinner?

(A) Yes, he likes noodles.

(B) No, he wants to take a break before dinner.

(C) No, he isn't.

男：媽媽在哪裡？

女：她在廚房煮飯。

男：我們晚餐吃什麼呢？

女：牛肉麵。

男：又是牛肉麵？饒了我吧。

問題：男子對晚餐滿意嗎？

(A) 滿意，他喜歡吃麵。

(B) 不，他想在晚餐前休息一下。

(C) 不，他不滿意。

答案：(C)。本題是 Yes-No 的問題。題目問的是「男子對晚餐滿意嗎？」，最後一句是重點：「又是牛肉麵？饒了我吧。」，由此推測出男子此刻並不想吃牛肉麵。所以答案就是 (C) 了。選項 (B) 是刻意提到 break 來混淆答題。

break 有「中途休息」、「喘息」之意，但可別以為 Give me a break. 是「讓我休息一下。」喔！這句話常用於口語中，表達「夠了；饒了我吧」。

kitchen [`kɪtʃɪn] n. 廚房　**dinner** [`dɪnɚ] n. 晚餐　**break** [brek] n. 休息，破損　**satisfied** [`sætɪsfaɪd] adj. 滿意的

如果是在開會開了很久時，想向大家提議休息一下，千萬別說 Give me a break!，雖然你想說的是「讓我休息一下」，但其實別人會聽成「閉嘴吧你，休息一會兒」。正確說法是 Let's take a break.。

24. M: What do you do in your free time, Sally?

W: I spend a lot of time playing the piano. How about you, Ken?

M: I love playing tennis.

W: Me too.

Question: What are they talking about?

(A) How to make use of their free time

(B) Their hobbies

(C) Their favorite sports

男：妳有空時都做些什麼，莎莉？

女：我花很多時間彈琴。肯，你呢？

男：我喜歡打網球。

女：我也是。

問題：他們在討論什麼？

(A) 如何利用他們的空閒時間

(B) 他們的嗜好

(C) 他們最愛的運動

第 1 回
第 2 回
第 3 回
第 4 回
第 5 回
第 6 回
第 7 回
第 8 回
第 9 回
第 10 回

答題解說

答案：(B)。題目問的是對話的內容為何，所以建議先看過選項，再仔細聆聽對話，以便正確作答。首先，男子第一句話就說「妳有空時都做些什麼？」而女子回答她花很多時間彈琴。之後男子說「我喜歡打網球。」女子回答「我也是」，所以 (B) 是正確答案。

破題關鍵

男子第一句話中的 do in your free time 是最大的關鍵點，平常喜歡做的事情，可以推測出和「嗜好」有關。順道一提，spend 除了可用在「花錢」，也可用於「花時間」上。

字詞解釋

spend [spɛnd] v. 花費　**piano** [pɪ`æno] n. 鋼琴　**tennis** [`tɛnɪs] n. 網球　**hobby** [`hɑbɪ] n. 嗜好

相關文法或用法補充

與球類運動相關的單字，像是 football（足球）、soccer（足球）badminton（羽球）、basketball（籃球）、badminton（羽球）、baseball（棒球）、golf（高爾夫球）、tennis（網球），皆用於「play + 球類」的句型。例如：We play baseball twice a month.（我們一個月打兩次棒球。）

25. W: Good morning. You look good in the shirt.

　　M: Thank you.

　　W: How much does it cost?

　　M: One thousand dollars.

　　W: It should be a little more expensive than it looks.

Question: What are the speakers mainly discussing?

(A) Why the man bought the shirt

(B) What the man wears today

(C) A very expensive shirt

英文翻譯

女：早安。你穿這件襯衫很好看。

男：謝謝。

女：這襯衫多少錢？

男：1000 元。

女：看起來應該要更貴些。

問：說話者們主要在討論什麼？

(A) 男子為何買這件襯衫

(B) 男子今天穿的衣服

(C) 一件非常昂貴的襯衫

答案：(B)。題目問的是「對話內容主要關於什麼事」，雖然問題的答案不會直接出現在對話中，但可以從對話內容去判斷，屬於「推論」型。從女子「稱讚男子的襯衫」，和「詢問襯衫多少錢」，都跟「男子今天穿的襯衫」有關，所以答案就是 (B)。(A)、(C) 中皆出現 shirt 這個字，以及 (C) 的 expensive 都是刻意誤導答題的設計，因為對話並未提到男子為何買這件襯衫，而且從 "It should be a little more expensive than it looks." （看起來應該要更貴些。）可知，這件襯衫是物超所值的。

首先，題目句中的 mainly 要聽得出來。而選項中 "What the man wears today" 就是指女子第一句話 "You look good in the shirt." 當中的 shirt。介系詞 in 常與衣服的名詞搭配，例如 the girl **in** a pretty skirt（穿著漂亮裙子的女孩）。

cost [kɔst] **v.** 要價　　**expensive** [ɪk`spɛnsɪv] **adj.** 昂貴的　　**discuss** [dɪ`skʌs] **v.** 討論

cost 用於花費「金錢」，主詞有兩種可能情形，其後若有第二個動詞，則只能用「不定詞」形式。其慣用句型為：

❶ It + cost(s) ＋ 人 ＋ 金錢 + to-V → 買（某物）花了某人多少錢。例如：It cost(s) me two thousand dollars to buy a doll.（買洋娃娃花了我兩千元。）

❷ 物 + cost(s) ＋ 人 ＋ 金錢 →（物）花了某人多少錢。例如：The dresses cost her five thousand dollars.（這洋裝花了她五千元。）

請注意，cost 的三態皆為 cost，因此 it costs 跟 it cost 都是對的，但意思有點不同，it costs 是表示「花了多少錢」的「事實」（現在簡單式），而 it cost 是表示「當時花了多少錢」（過去簡單式）。

第四部分 短文聽解

For question number 26, please look at the three pictures.

Question number 26: Listen to the following talk. What place is Uncle Frank?

Yesterday evening I was so hungry, and I called my friend Fiona. I asked her whether she can go with me to Uncle Frank. I have been there for many times because its meals are so delicious. Besides, they are not expensive, as compared to those of other places in the neighborhood. By the way, we haven't seen each other for a long time, and we really enjoyed a very happy night there. I ordered seafood noodles, a pig blood cake, a few dumplings, and a bowl of egg & vegetable soup, while Fiona just ordered a bowl of beef noodles.

英文翻譯

請看以下三張圖。並仔細聆聽以下談話。Uncle Frank 是個什麼樣的地方？
昨晚我肚子餓時，我打電話給我朋友費歐娜。我問她是否可以跟我去 Uncle Frank。我去過那裡很多次，因為它的餐點相當美味。此外，相較於附近地區其他地方的餐點，它們並不貴。順道一提，我們已經許久沒見面，且我們在那裡享受了非常愉快的夜晚。我點了海鮮麵、豬血糕、幾個餃子，以及一碗蛋花湯，而費歐娜則點了一碗牛肉麵。

答題解說

答案：(C)。題目問的是 Uncle Frank 是個什麼地方，所以要注意聽播放內容中提及 Uncle Frank 的內容：I asked her whether she can go with me to Uncle Frank.，但重點還是在第一句 "Yesterday evening I was so hungry..."，這表示要去「吃飯的地方」，所以 (A)、(B) 的 supermarket（超級市場）、mall（購物中心）都不會是正確答案。雖然購物中心內可能也有吃飯的地方，但從 "I have been there for many times because its meals are so delicious."（我去過那裡很多次，因為它的餐點相當美味。）可推知，這個地方純粹就是用餐的地方。故正確答案為 (C)。

本題必須綜合兩個關鍵句才能確認答案：　"Yesterday evening, I was so hungry..."
以及　"I have been there for many times because its meals are so delicious."　。

hungry [`hʌŋgrɪ] adj. 飢餓的　**meal** [mil] n. 餐點　**delicious** [dɪ`lɪʃəs] adj. 美味
的　**expensive** [ɪk`spɛnsɪv] adj. 昂貴的　**compare** [kəm`pɛr] v. 比較　**seafood**
[`si͵fud] n. 海鮮　**noodle** [`nudl] n.（常複數）麵條　**pig blood cake** 豬血
糕　**dumpling** [`dʌmplɪŋ] n. 餃子　**bowl** [bol] n. 碗　**vegetable** [`vɛdʒətəbl] n. 蔬
菜，青菜　**soup** [sup] n. 湯　**order** [`ɔrdɚ] v. 訂購，點菜　**beef noodle** 牛肉麵

指示代名詞 that 與 those 可以用來指「前面提到過的事物」，以避免用字的重
複。例如：

❶ Sales this year has increased by 20% as compared with those of last year.
　（今年的業績比去年成長了百分之二十。）

❷ The toys John has are as many as those owned by David.
　（約翰擁有的玩具和大衛的一樣多。）

For question number 27, please look at the three pictures.

**Question number 27: Listen to the following message. Where is Mark
probably going in the evening?**

Hi, Emma. It's Mark. I'm going to play baseball with some good friends this
afternoon. After that, we can have dinner together. Do you want me to pick you
up after you get off work? At 6:30 p.m.? I know a good place to eat. It is close
to my apartment. If you can't make it, just give me a call. Or see you later.

請看以下三張圖。並仔細聆聽以下訊息內容。馬克晚上可能會去哪裡？
嗨，艾瑪。我是馬克。今天下午我要和一些好朋友一起去打棒球。之後，我們可

以一起吃晚飯。你要我在你下班之後去接你嗎？約晚間 6:30？我知道一個吃飯的好地方。它靠近我的公寓。如果你不行的話，給我打個電話即可。或者稍後見。

答題解說

答案：(C)。題目問的是晚上（in the evening）Mark 可能會去哪裡，答案可以從 "At 6:30 p.m.?" 後面的內容得知：I know a good place to eat. It is close to my apartment.（我知道一個吃飯的好地方。它靠近我的公寓。）所以正確答案為 (C)。(A) 是錯誤的，因為從頭到尾沒提到去籃球場；另外，雖然有提到去打棒球（play baseball），但時間是在下午（... with some good friends this afternoon.），所以 (B) 也是錯誤的。

破題關鍵

首先題目中的 "in the evening" 是第一個關鍵點，接著播放內容中的 "At 6:30 p.m.?" 是第二個關鍵，而且 6:30 p.m. 通常是吃晚餐的時間，答案應該是很好選了。

字詞解釋

pick [pɪk] **v.** 接　**close** [klos] **adj.** 接近的　**apartment** [ə`pɑrtmənt] **n.** 公寓　**give someone a call** 打電話給某人

相關文法或用法補充

close 當形容詞有幾種用法：

❶ Meg is close with money.（Meg 很吝嗇。）→ 表示「吝嗇的」
❷ The shopping center is close to the station.（購物中心靠近車站。）→ 表示「接近的」
❸ That will be a close tennis game.（那將會是場勢均力敵的網球賽。）→ 表示「勢均力敵的（尤指比賽）」
❹ Thcy are really close friends.（他們真的是摯友。）→ 表示「（關係）密切的」

For question number 28, please look at the three pictures.

Question number 28: Listen to the following self-introduction. What does the man usually do on weekends?

My name is Willy Chang. I am the only son in my family, and I live with my parents at present. We watch TV together in the evening every day. On weekends, my parents often go hiking at the mountain area. Sometimes I go with them, but usually I play tennis with my friends. I love to sweat a lot and take a comfortable bath later. That really puts me in high spirits.

中文翻譯

請看以下三張圖。並仔細聆聽以下播放的自我介紹。男子週末時通常做什麼？
我叫張威力。我是家中的獨子；目前我和我父母住在一起。我們每天晚上一起看電視。我父母經常在周末去登山健行。有時候我會和他們一起去，但通常我會和朋友去打網球。我喜歡流很多汗，然後洗個舒服的澡。那會讓我的精神很好。

答題解說

答案：(A)。題目問的是男子週末時通常會做什麼，談話中提到：On weekends, my parents often go hiking at the mountain area. Sometimes I go with them, but usually I play tennis with my friends.，由此可見，男子週末時通常會「和朋友去打網球」，故正確答案為(A)。

破題關鍵

首先應注意題目句的關鍵字詞「通常」（usually）及「週末時」（on weekends）。雖然圖 (B) 的「登山健行」及圖 (C) 的「一起看電視」都有在談話中提到，但請注意「行為者」與「時間點」的不同。

字詞解釋

at present 目前　**go hiking** 去健行　**mountain** [`maʊntn] n. 山，山脈　**sweat** [swɛt] v. 出汗　**comfortable** [`kʌmfɚtəbl] adj. 舒適的　**in high spirits** 精神狀況良好，神采奕奕

相關文法或用法補充

every day 與 everyday 其實是不一樣的，every day 是時間副詞，指「每天」，與現在式動詞連用。例如：He washes the dishes every day.（他每天都洗碗。）everyday 是形容詞，指「每天的，日常的」。例如：everyday business of the office （辦公室的日常業務）

For question number 29, please look at the three pictures.

Question number 29: Listen to the following phone message. Where is Gary making a phone call?

Hi, Meggy. This is Gary. It's 7:30 now. I've kept making phone calls to you for about 10 minutes, but you failed to answer your phone. Where are you now? Have you forgotten that we agreed to study together on Sunday afternoons? I've been here waiting for you for half an hour. I'll go first and wait for you to come. Please called me back as soon as you hear my message.

英文翻譯

請看以下三張圖。並仔細聆聽以下電話留言。蓋瑞正在哪裡打電話？
嗨，梅姬，我是蓋瑞。現在已經 7:30 了。我一直打了大約 10 分鐘的電話給妳，但妳都沒有聽電話。妳現在在哪裡呢？妳忘了我們同意每週日下午一起去念書嗎？我已經在這裡等了妳半個小時。我先走一步，然後等你過來。聽到我的訊息之後，請即刻回電話給我。

答題解說

答案：(A)。題目問的是蓋瑞正在哪裡打電話，雖然留言訊息中沒有提到在什麼地方，但可以從「做什麼事」來判斷。其中提到 "Have you forgotten that we agreed to study together on Sunday afternoons? I've been here waiting for you for half an hour."（妳忘了我們同意每週日下午一起去念書嗎？我已經在這裡等了妳半個小時。）因此從三張圖上顯示的 LIBRARY（圖書館）、RESTAURANT（餐廳）以及圖(C)的在床上，可以推知最有可能的答案是(A)。

破題關鍵

詢問「說話者在哪裡」的題目，如果沒有聽到確切的地點名稱，就要注意說話者「正在做某事」，然後從「做某事」來判斷在什麼地方。本題應從 study（念書）來判斷是在 library（圖書館）。

字詞解釋

forget [fəˋgɛt] v. 忘記（過去分詞 forgotten）　　**make a phone call** 打電話
as soon as... 一～就～

第 1 回
第 2 回
第 3 回
第 4 回
第 5 回
第 6 回
第 7 回
第 8 回
第 9 回
第 10 回

注意 forget（忘記）和 remember（記得）後面接 to-V 和 V-ing 的意思完全不同：

❶ forget（忘記）

　① S + forget + to-V...（某人忘記去做某事。）例如：He forgot to bring his wallet.（他忘記帶皮夾了。）

　② S + forget + V-ing...（某人忘記已做某事。）例如：Emily forgot buying the same coat before.（Emily 忘了之前已經買過同樣的大衣。）

❷ remember（記得）

　① S + remember + to-V...（某人記得去做某事。）例如：Wendy remembered to turn off the light.（Wendy 記得去關燈。）

　② S + remember + V-ing...（某人記得已做過某事。）例如：I remember buying the same desk.（我記得已經買過同樣的書桌。）

For question number 30, please look at the three pictures.

Question number 30: Listen to the following story. Which picture best describes the story?

Last year Lisa was still a college student. One day, she went on a picnic with her two classmates, Kenny and Fiona. It was cloudy and cool. They had a happy chat, about their teachers, studies, families and their future plans. Kenny was especially very excited about such an activity. Lisa prepared some drinks. Sometimes they lay quietly on the grass. That day, they had a lot of fun.

請看以下三張圖。並仔細聆聽以下故事。哪一張圖最能夠描述這個故事？

去年，麗莎還是個大學生。有一天，她和兩個同學肯尼和菲奧娜去野餐。當天是個多雲的天氣且涼爽。他們愉快地聊著天，聊到他們的老師、學業、家庭以及他們的未來計畫。肯尼對這項活動特別感到興奮。麗莎準備了一些飲料。有時他們安靜地躺在草地上。那天，他們玩得很開心。

第 1 回

第 2 回

第 3 回

第 4 回

第 5 回

第 6 回

第 7 回

第 8 回

第 9 回

第 10 回

答題解說

答案：(C)。播放的內容提到，那天是陰天，且天氣涼爽（ it is cloudy and cool），準備三明治和飲料（ ... prepared some sandwiches and drinks. ）。所以他們在陰天的天氣狀況下野餐，並吃著三明治，正確答案當然就是(C)了。

破題關鍵

題目要問的是故事內容符合哪一張圖，三張圖氣候和地點都不同，所以關鍵在於是否可以聽出「不同之處」。第一點內容提到「陰天」，所以圖 (B) 是錯誤。第二點，內容提到「草地」，故圖 (A) 涼亭則不符圖，根據以上兩點可確定圖 (C) 是正確答案。

字詞解釋

plan [plæn] v. 計畫　**luckily** [ˋlʌkɪlɪ] adv. 幸運地　**cloudy** [ˋklaʊdɪ] adj. 陰天的，多雲的　**prepare** [prɪˋpɛr] v. 準備　**sandwich** [ˋsændwɪtʃ] n.三明治　**grass** [græs] n. 草

相關文法或用法補充

除了 be excited about（對～感到興奮）的用法，excited 後面也可以接不定詞（to-V）。例如，He was excited to hear the news.（他聽到這消息很興奮。）

1. **The restaurant has many delicious dishes. Jack often _____ there on weekends.**（這家餐廳有許多美味的餐點。傑克經常在週末去吃。）

   (A) go　(B) went　(C) has gone　(D) goes

   答題解說

   答案：(D)。四個選項是同一個動詞（go）的不同詞類，因此應依照前後文關鍵字詞去判斷。本題第一句用現在簡單式表達「這家餐廳有許多美味的餐點。」第二句有頻率副詞 often，顯然也必須用現在式來表達「傑克經常在週末假日時去那裡。」另外，因為 Jack 是第三人稱單數，所以 (A) 是錯誤的。

   破題關鍵

   雖然看到 often 或 on weekends 時，直覺句子應該要用現在簡單式。不過很多時候在短文或文章中，也可能依照上下文內容而使用過去式，因此本題第一句用現在式就是告訴你，第二句也要用現在式。

   字詞解釋

   delicious [dɪˋlɪʃəs] **adj.** 美味的　　**dish** [dɪʃ] **n.** 一盤菜，菜餚

   相關文法或用法補充

   in, on, at 都是很基本的時間介系詞，其後要接的各有不同：

   ❶ at：一個準確、特定的時刻。例如：
   at 07:11、at 10'clock、at noon、at noon yesterday、at night、at midnight、at the same time

   ❷ in：月份、季節、年、世紀、一段長而「非特定」的時間
   in the morning、in the afternoon、in the evening、in January、in February、in March, 2020、in the spring、in the summer、in the fall、in the winter、in 2020、in the past year、in the 18th century、in the week、in the past、in the future

   ❸ on：特定日期、星期
   on Monday、on Tuesday morning、on Wednesday afternoon、on Thursday evening、on Friday night、on 28, April、on New Year's Day、on Christmas Day、on the weekend

2. **Can you _____ me the way to the train station?**（你可以告訴我到火車站怎麼走嗎？）

(A) give　(B) tell　(C) keep　(D) take

答題解說

答案：(B)。句子大意是「可以告訴我前往～的路嗎？」，所以正確答案是 (B)。
(A) 的「給」、(C) 的「保持」 以及 (D) 的「帶」置入空格中的話，都會形成不合邏輯或奇怪的句意。

破題關鍵

tell 也是個「授予動詞」，後面可以接兩個受詞（間接受詞 + 直接受詞），"tell somebody something" 表示「告訴某人某事」。另外，也可以改成 "tell... about..." 的說法。

相關文法或用法補充

由於 tell 有授予動詞的用法，因此 "tell somebody something" 可以改成 "tell something to somebody"。例如：

❶ He told the news to the whole village.（他把這個消息告訴全村的人。）
❷ I swear I'll never tell the secret to the third person.（我發誓不會將這個祕密告訴第三人。）

3. **The teacher won't _____ her students come in if they are late.**（如果學生遲到了，這位老師不會讓他們進教室。）

(A) put　(B) order　(C) let　(D) need

答題解說

答案：(C)。句子大意是，如果學生遲到，老師將「不讓他們進來。」所以正確答案是 (C)。
(A) 的「擺放」、(B) 的「訂購、命令」 以及 (D) 的「需要」置入空格中的話，都會形成不合邏輯或奇怪的句意。

破題關鍵

"let somebody in" 就是「讓某人進來」的意思，相當於 "allow... in..." 的意思。在英文中，有些動詞後面接受詞後必須再接「受詞補語」，而這個「受詞補語」可能是原形動詞（而非不定詞）或是形容詞，所以這裡的 in 不是介系詞，而是個形容詞，表示「在裡面的」。

order [`ɔrdɚ] v. 命令，指揮，訂購

let 和 make、have 一樣，都是「使役動詞」，接受詞可接原形動詞。例如：

❶ My father let me turn down the radio.（爸爸讓我把收音機聲音調小。）

❷ The sister made her younger brother clean the house.（姐姐讓弟弟打掃房子。）

❸ I'll be glad to have you come here.（能把你請過來這裡的話，我會很開心的。）

4. **Her mother is the _____ of a clothes shop.**（他媽媽是一家服裝店的經理。）

(A) teacher　(B) baker　(C) sailor　(D) manager

答案：(D)。四個選項都是不同意思、與「人」有關的可數名詞，因此必須依照句意去判斷正確的選項。句意是「他媽媽是一家服裝店的 _____。」因此，答案應該是 (D) 經理。

本題關鍵字是空格後面的 clothes shop（服飾店），teacher（老師）、baker（麵包師傅）或 sailor（水手）都跟「服飾店」扯不上關係。

baker [`bekɚ] n. 麵包師傅　　**sailor** [`selɚ] n. 水手　　**manager** [`mænɪdʒɚ] n. 經理

介系詞 of 有很多種意思，以下列舉一些常見的用法：

❶ 表達「屬於」：One leg of the table is broken.（這張桌子的一隻腳斷了。）

❷ 表達「特徵」，解釋為「～的」：The issue of unemployment is of much importance to government.（失業問題對政府來說非常重要。）

❸ 表達「材料」，解釋為「由～做成」：The table is made of wood.（這張桌子是木頭做成的。）

❹ 表達「產生」的概念，解釋為「～到」，與某些動詞連用：What are you thinking of?（你在想什麼？）、I have never heard of him.（我從來沒有聽說過他。）

❺ 表達「對於～」的概念，與某些形容詞連用：My sister is fond of music.（我的姐姐喜歡音樂。）

5. **Last night, Helen was hit by a car. She was taken to the _____.**（海倫昨晚被車撞到。她被送到這家醫院去。）

(A) restaurant　(B) hospital　(C) apartment　(D) museum

答題解說

答案：(B)。句子大意是「…昨晚被車撞…被送到醫院去。」"was hit by a car" 為「因」，「被送去到醫院」為「果」，符合題意。

破題關鍵

「詞彙」題目中若有兩個句子，通常無法直接從空格所在句子去判斷答案，而另一句一定會有關鍵線索。本題的關鍵線索是 hit by a car 與 taken to the hospital 的連結關係。

字詞解釋

hit [hɪt] v. 擊中，碰撞　　**hospital** [ˋhɑspɪtḷ] n. 醫院

相關文法或用法補充

"be taken to the hospital" 當中的 taken（take 的過去分詞）也可以用 sent（send 的過去分詞）取代。而 hospital 前面的 the 如果去掉，意思就變成「送醫（治療）」。"be sent/taken to hospital" 等於 be hospitalized。

6. **The movie was so _____ that many people fell asleep.**（這電影如此無聊，所以很多人都睡著了。）

(A) bored　(B) to bore　(C) boring　(D) bores

答題解說

答案：(C)。四個選項是同一個單字的不同詞類，且 "so _____" 形成主詞（The movie）的補語，所以要填入一個可以被副詞 so 修飾，且可修飾「事物（The movie）」的形容詞，因此只有 (C) boring（令人感到無聊的）是正確答案。(A) bored 用來修飾「人」，表示「感到無聊的」。

破題關鍵

本題關鍵是對於 -ed 與 -ing 形容詞概念的掌握。-ed（過去分詞）修飾「人」，-ing（現在分詞）修飾「事物」。

字詞解釋

bored [bord] adj. 感到無聊的　　**boring** [ˋborɪŋ] adj. 令人感到無聊／無趣的

bored 與 boring 由及物動詞 bore（使～感到無趣）衍生而來。所以如果題目改成 I am ＿＿＿＿＿ with this movie.（我覺得這部電影很無聊。）則答案就要選 bored 了。注意形容詞本身修飾的對象是「人」或「物」。不過，在此要舉一個特例。如果說 He is such an interesting person.，用 -ing 修飾「人」時，那就不是這個人「感到有興趣」的意思，而是這個人「被物化」，表示「這人很會搞笑」的意思。

7. **The manager ＿＿＿＿＿ a lot of time holding meetings every day.**（經理每天都花很多時間在開會上。）

(A) costs　(B) spends　(C) pays　(D) takes

答題解說

答案：（B）。句子大意是「花很多時間在開會」，主詞是「人」（The manager），所以「花時間」的動詞要用 spend。故正確答案應為 (B)。

破題關鍵

本題關鍵是主詞 The manager，以及考表示「花費」的動詞。「人＋ spend ＋時間＋ Ving」＝「It takes ＋人＋時間＋ to-V」。

字詞解釋

manager [ˋmænɪdʒɚ] n. 經理　　**meeting** [ˋmitɪŋ] n. 會議

相關文法或用法補充

「會議」的英文是 meeting，而「開會」的「開」，動詞可別用 open 喔！最常用的除了 hold 之外，也可以用 call、have。

8. **Lisa ＿＿＿＿＿ in the U.S. since 1998.**（麗莎從 1998 年起就住在美國。）

(A) lives　(B) lived　(C) has lived　(D) will live

答題解說

答案：（C）。本題考的是現在完成式。由 since 1998（從 1998 年起）可推知動詞應用現在完成式，故正確答案應為 (C)。

破題關鍵

本題關鍵字就是 since（自從～），看到這個字應直覺選擇「完成式」。

相關文法或用法補充

當我們在使用現在完成式時，如果考量的是動詞的持續時間，就以「for + 一段時間」來定義持續時間的長短；如果考量的是動作開始的時間點，就用「since + 一個時間點」即可。例如：

❶ I have worked here for five years.（我已在這裡工作五年了。）

❷ I have worked here since June, 2018.（我從 2018 年六月起就已在這裡工作了。）

9. **Vicky's daughter is not always early to school. She is _____ late.**（薇琪的女兒並非總是早到學校。她有時候會遲到。）

(A) usually　(B) sometimes　(C) often　(D) never

答題解說

答案：(B)。第一句提到：is not always early to school（並非總是早到學校），第二句的空格後面是 late，not always 是指「並非總是…」，就等於是「有時候…」的意思。所以正確答案是 (B)。

破題關鍵

這種題目很常見，看到 not always 應直接聯想到 sometimes，不管題目多長或是單字不懂，答案一樣可以迎刃而解。

字詞解釋

daughter [ˋdɔtɚ] n. 女兒　**always** [ˋɔlwez] adv. 總是

相關文法或用法補充

如果「早到（early）」或「遲到（late）」後面要接「到哪裡」的話，early 要接介系詞 to，而 late 要接介系詞 for。例如：He was late **for** school.（他上學遲到了。）、I will be early **to** the meeting place.（我會提早到會面的地方。）

10. **Either you or your sister _____ to wash the dishes tonight.**（今晚不是你就是你妹妹要洗碗。）

(A) have　(B) has　(C) had　(D) having

答題解說

答案：(B)。空格前面的主詞（either you or your sister）是 either A or B 的結構，是指「不是你就是你姊姊」，句子動詞須依最接近動詞者，所以正確答案為 (B) has。(C) had 錯誤的原因是句子後面有時間副詞 tonight，不可用過去式。(D) having 並非動詞，故為錯誤答案。

動詞的考題應根據「人稱→時態→單複數」的順序來掌握答案。本題是「Either... or...」當主詞,動詞須依據「是接近的主詞」來決定形態的考法,搭配時間副詞,應選現在式。

字詞解釋

either [ˈiðɚ] conj.(通常與 or 連用)或者　　**dish** [dɪʃ] n. 盤子,碟

相關文法或用法補充

Either A or B（不是 A 就是 B）的用法重點整理如下:

❶ 句型:Either A or B + V ...（不是 A 就是 B…)
Either you or I am going to camping.（不是你去露營,就是我去。）

❷ 動詞根據 B:Either he or I have to pay the bill.（不是他就是我必須要付帳單。）→ 動詞依 I,所以用 have。

❸ either of...（…其中之一）:Either of us is going to the beach.（我們其中一人要去海邊。）

第二部分 段落填空

Questions 11-14

Stanley and William have been good friends for many years. Stanley is planning a trip to Seattle with William. Stanley's uncle lives there, so they will **stay** at his uncle's place. In fact, Stanley **has been** to Seattle for three times. He really loves this city. There are many **famous** places, such as Pike Market and the first Starbucks. When they visit the market, they might also have a good chat at a coffee shop while enjoying the fantastic view. Seattle is a beautiful city. **They are sure they will have fun.** William can't wait to go there after hearing what Stanley said.

中文翻譯

　　史丹利與威廉是多年的好友。史丹利正計劃與威廉一起去西雅圖旅行。史丹利的叔叔住在那裡,所以他們將住在叔叔的居處。實際上,史丹利已經去過西雅圖三次了。他真的很喜歡這座城市。這裡有很多著名的地方,例如派克市場和史上第一間星巴克。當他們參觀這個市場時,他們可能也會在咖啡店裡好好聊個天,同時欣賞絕佳的美景。西雅圖是一座美麗的城市。他們認為他們一定會玩得開心。聽到史丹利說的話之後,威廉等不及要去那裡了。

答題解說

11. 答案：(A)。四個選項是不同意思的動詞，所以應根據前後文句意判斷。句子大意是「他們將住在叔叔的居處。」空格後是地方副詞（at his uncle's place），所以 (A) stay（留宿，停留）是正確答案。(D) visit 雖然也符合句意，但 visit 是「及物動詞」，後面須直接接受詞。其餘的 (B) celebrate（慶祝）及 (C) remember（記得）皆不符句意。

12. 答案：(B)。句子大意是「已經去過西雅圖三次」，故正確答案為 (B) has been。"have/has been to + 地方" 表示「已去過某地」。而 "have/has gone to + 地方" 表示「已去了某地」。故正確答案為 (B)。

13. 答案：(C)。四個選項是不同意思的形容詞，所以應根據前後文句意「這裡有很多——的地方，例如派克市場和史上第一間星巴克。」判斷，正確答案應為 (C) famous。(A) boring 完全前後文句意不符；從後面的地名與「第一間星巴克」可知，(B) new 也是錯誤的選項；(D) glad 僅用來形容「人」，且一般不置於名詞前修飾。

14. 答案：(D)。這是要挑選一個句子、子句或句子的一部分放入空格後，確認空格前後和空格句之間的連接關係，是否讓句意顯得自然通順。空格前面句子提到「西雅圖是一座美麗的城市。」後面句子提到「聽到史丹利說的話之後，威廉等不及要去那裡了。」顯然填入「他們確定他們會玩得開心。」是最能合理地連接前後兩句的答案。以下是其餘錯誤選項句子的翻譯：
    (A) 他們可能會取消這趟旅程。
    (B) 史丹利昨天已出發前往機場。
    (C) 威廉的錢已經用完了。

破題關鍵

11. 看到某人的住處，可推知動詞不外乎 stay，live 等等，根據句意選出正確答案。

12. 本題關鍵語句是句尾的 "for three times"，這是在陳述一種「經驗」，而非過去或現在的單一行為，所以應選擇 "have/has been to + 地方" 表示「已去過某地」。

13. 本題亦可用「刪除法」來確認答案，因為除了 (C) famous 之外，其餘三個選項都是明顯不符句意或文法的選項。

14. 空格這句話的前後文主要關於他們對於西雅圖旅遊的美好幻想，因此掌握這一點之後，即可確認「他們會玩得開心。」這個答案。

字詞解釋

stay [ste] v. 留宿，停留　**place** [ples] n. 住處　**in fact** 事實上　**famous** [ˋfeməs] adj. 著名的，出名的　**fantastic** [fænˋtæstɪk] adj. 極好的，驚人的　**view** [vju] n. 景色　**have fun** 玩得開心　**can't wait to-V** 等不及要…　**probably** [ˋprɑbəblɪ] adv. 或

許，可能　**cancel** [ˋkænsl] v. 取消　**leave for**... 出發前往⋯　**run out of**... 用完⋯

11. 通常旅遊、出差等在某處住宿或短暫停留，常用 stay 來表示，若要表示「和某人」在某處停留，可搭配介系詞 with。

12. "have/has been to + 地方" 這個用法常與 "have/has gone to + 地方" 做比較。誠如前面提到，"have/has been to" 是問過去的經驗，而 "have/has gone to" 是問「當下」的狀況，也就是「已經去了（某地）」

13. such as...（例如⋯），後面名詞（所舉之例子），也可以用 for example 或 for instance 取代。

14. "can't wait" （無法等待）常在口語中用來表示對於某件事情的「迫不及待」，其後須接不定詞（to-V）。例如：He can't wait to get back to work.（他迫不及待要回去工作。）

Questions 15-18

Alan is a senior high school student. He studies hard and does his homework after dinner on weekdays. But on weekends, **he plays basketball with some good friends.** Sometimes he **goes** fishing with his father on Sundays. Still, basketball is his favorite hobby. Maybe that's **because** he likes to move and run, not always to sit somewhere and think about something. When he shoots a layup and scores, he feels so excited and happy. Even if he gets a grade that is not so satisfactory, or he has a fight with his girlfriend, he will feel very relaxed and forget about anything unpleasant **after** leaving the basketball court.

中文翻譯

　　艾倫是一名高中生。他用功念書，且平日在晚餐後會做作業。但是在週末，他會和一些好朋友一起打籃球。有時他在週日會和父親一起去釣魚。不過籃球還是他最喜歡的嗜好。也許那是因為他喜歡移動和奔跑，而不是總是坐在某個地方想事情。當他上籃得分時，他會感到非常興奮和快樂。即使他的學校成績不是那麼令人滿意，或是和女朋友爭吵，他也會在離開籃球場後感到非常放鬆且會忘記任何不愉快的事情。

第 1 回
第 2 回
第 3 回
第 4 回
第 5 回
第 6 回
第 7 回
第 8 回
第 9 回
第 10 回

答題解說

15. 答案：(C)。這是要挑選一個句子、子句或句子的一部分放入空格後，確認空格前後和空格句之間的連接關係，是否讓句意顯得自然通順。空格前面是 "But on weekends," ，從 But 開頭可推知這一句與前一句是有反意關聯的。前句提到，他用功念書，且平日在晚餐後會做作業。所以只有 (C) 最能夠適當地連接前後兩句。以下是其餘錯誤選項句子的翻譯：

(A) 他喜歡在家玩電動

(B) 他總是很晚起床

(D) 他和一個好朋友去圖書館

16. 答案：(A)。句子大意是「有時他在週日會和父親一起去釣魚。」只要知道 「去釣魚」是 go fishing 即可選出正確答案。

17. 答案：(C)。前文提到，Alan 雖然有時在週日會和父親一起去釣魚，但籃球還是他最喜歡的嗜好，所以這句應該是「那是因為他喜歡移動和奔跑」，故正確答案為 (C)。

18. 答案：(C)。就句意而言，選項中的 for 和 when 可直接排除，因為本題型考前後相關行為。由於之前提到，Alan 感到非常放鬆且會忘記任何不愉快的事情，所以這樣的感覺是在離開籃球場後「之後」，故正確答案是 (C)。

破題關鍵

15. 空格前面這句的句尾有 weekdays（平日），而空格前又看到 But 與 weekends 這裡個關鍵字，顯然空格這句要談論的不會是「念書」或「做功課」，而是「運動」等嗜好。

16. 在英文裡，很多與「嗜好」有關的片語，都和動詞 go 有關。例如：go jogging、go hiking、go swimming、go dancing... 等。

17. 空格後的 "he likes to move and run" 與前一句 "basketball is his favorite hobby" 正好形成前後因果關係，故 because 是最符合語意的答案。

18. 刪去最不可能的答案 (B) for 和 (D) when 之後，剩下 (A) before 和 (C) after，語意剛好相反。就「離開籃球場」和「感到放鬆」，兩者誰先誰後，答案就出來了。

字詞解釋

different [ˋdɪfərənt] **adj.** 不同的　　**senior** [ˋsinjə] **adj.** 高年級的　　**basketball** [ˋbæskɪt͵bɔl] **n.** 籃球　　**relaxed** [rɪˋlækst] **adj.** 放鬆的　　**homework** [ˋhom͵wɝk] **n.** 功課　　**difficult** [ˋdɪfə͵kəlt] **adj.** 困難的　　**distant** [ˋdɪstənt] **adj.** 遠的

相關文法或用法補充

15. 若要表示「每逢～」時，可以用「on + 複數名詞」表示，相當於「every + 單數名詞」。例如：每逢週日是 on Sundays（= every Sunday）。

16. go + Ving 這種用法，如果字面中有需要使用到名詞，此時名詞擺中間。例如：go bird watching（去賞鳥）、go mountain climbing（去爬山）…。

17. 連接詞 because 通常用來引導一個副詞子句，但 because 的子句也可能作主詞補語，其性質為形容詞。例如：That/It is because he is foolish.（那是因為他太蠢了。）

18. 「分詞構句」是從副詞子句簡化而來。其簡化方式是先將副詞子句連接詞與副詞子句的主詞省略掉，然後動詞改為 V-ing 的形式。但有時省略掉會讓語意不明顯，因此會保留副詞子句連接詞。例如本題這句：...he will feel very relaxed and forget about anything unpleasant **after leaving** the basketball court.

Questions 19-21

中文翻譯

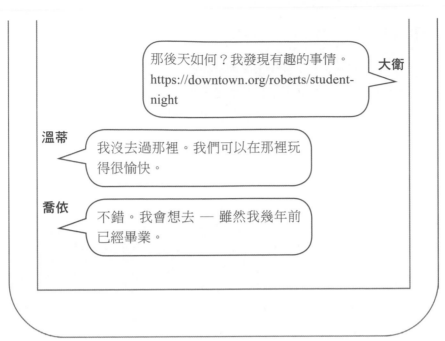

大衛：那後天如何？我發現有趣的事情。
https://downtown.org/roberts/student-night

溫蒂：我沒去過那裡。我們可以在那裡玩得很愉快。

喬依：不錯。我會想去 — 雖然我幾年前已經畢業。

 https://downtown.org/roberts/student-night

羅伯特的學生之夜！
每週四，7:00 P.M.-10:00 P.M.

出示您的學生證就可以免費入場，
並可享有菜單上所有東西半價優惠。

（四人以上同行的話，我們還招待每一位一杯自選的飲料。）

您不是學生嗎？把你的學生制服找出來，並在「學生之夜」時，穿到「羅伯特」餐廳來。我們也免費請您一杯特別的飲料。

預約專線：0960-333-888
LINE：@roberts
Facebook：羅伯特的餐廳

營業時間：5:00P.M. - 10:00P.M.，週一休息。

第1回
第2回
第3回
第4回
第5回
第6回
第7回
第8回
第9回
第10回

19. 關於羅伯特餐廳的「學生之夜」，我們可以了解到什麼？
    (A) 你得穿制服才能去那裡。
    (B) 每一位學生都將獲得一杯免費的自選飲料。
    (C) 羅伯特餐廳在學生之夜當天比其他日子更晚開店。
    (D) 即使你不是學生，也可以在那裡享有免費飲料。

20. 他們的期末考哪一天結束？
    (A) 在星期一
    (B) 在星期二
    (C) 在星期三
    (D) 在星期四

21. 關於談話者們，何者不正確？
    (A) 大衛建議在「學生之夜」去羅伯特。
    (B) 喬依和格蕾絲可以享有一杯免費的自選飲料。
    (C) 溫蒂覺得「學生之夜」會很有趣。
    (D) 喬依現在不是學生。

答題解說

19. 答案：(D)。題目問的是關於羅伯特餐廳的「學生之夜」，可以知道什麼事情，可以直接從第二個文本（網頁內容）找到答案。選項 (A) 是錯誤的，因為其中提到如果不是學生的身分，可以穿舊的學生制服前來，而學生只要出示學生證即可；(B) 是錯誤的，因為四人以上同行（For a table of four or more...），每一位可獲得一杯自選的飲料；(C) 也是錯誤的，因為底下提到營業時間是 5:00P.M. - 10:00P.M.，只是「學生之夜」是 7:00 P.M. 才開始。只有 (D) 是正確答案。

20. 答案：(B)。本題需要整合與歸納兩篇文本的訊息與資訊，才能夠得到正確的答案。題目問的是，他們的大考哪一天結束？在文字對話訊息（第一個文本）中，溫蒂說「今天」大考今天終於結束，接著大衛提議「後天」去羅伯特的學生之夜。而「羅伯特的學生之夜」可以從第二個文本上方看到「每週四，7:00 P.M.-10:00 P.M.」，所以可推知大考是週二結束的。

21. 答案：(B)。本題同樣必須綜合兩篇文本的內容，才能解題。首先文字訊息中大衛張貼羅伯特「學生之夜」的網址，提議大家可以去，所以 (A) 是正確的；喬依和格蕾絲各自提到週末有事情，顯然她們都是學生，然後對照網頁內容：所以如果去「學生之夜」的話，必須四人同行才可以享有一杯免費的自選飲料，但 Grace 並沒有表示要去的意願，所以 (B) 是錯誤的。溫蒂說 " I've never been there. We can have fun there." 這表示她覺得「學生之夜」會很有趣。而喬依說 "though I've graduated for several years"，所以她現在不是學生了。故 (C)、(D) 都是正確的。

破題關鍵

19. 「何者為真」或「何者為非」的題型，都屬於內容細節型的題目。通常必須先看過四個選項內容，再到文章中找尋線索。網頁下方提到 "Not a student? ... We also offer you a special free drink." 。

20. 首先，提到 final exam 的時間點是 today，接著要找出 today 是星期幾。David 提到 "the day after tomorrow" 有 Students' Night，再從網頁內容確認 Students' Night 是在星期四，即可回推 today 是星期幾了。

21. 本題針對四位文字訊息中的 talkers 說過的話，判斷其身分是否仍是學生，再和網頁內容到照，四個選項逐一確認才能找出正確答案。

字詞解釋

finally [ˈfaɪnḷɪ] **adv.** 最後，終於　**relax** [rɪˈlæks] **v.** 鬆懈，放鬆　**date** [det] **n.** 約會　**go shopping** 去購物　**have fun** 玩得愉快　**graduate** [ˈgrædʒʊˌet] **v.** 畢業　**several** [ˈsɛvərəl] **adj.** 幾個的，數個的　**treat** [trit] **v.** 請客　**uniform** [ˈjunəˌfɔrm] **n.** 制服　**business** [ˈbɪznɪs] **n.** 營業，生意

相關文法或用法補充

❶ 一般來說，「現在是該（做）～的時候」會用「It's time to-V／It's time for N」來表達。例如：It's time to get up." 、" It's time for dinner." 。在口語中，也常省略 "It is"，直接以 "Time to／Time for..." 表示。另外，若要在 It's time... 後面接子句的話，要注意這個子句要用過去式。例如：It's time (that) you grew up. （你該長大了。）而不是 It's time (that) you grow up. 。

❷ treat 除了表示「對待」之外，也可用來表示「請客」。這裡的用法是「treat + 人 + 事物」。例如：treat you to dinner（請你吃晚餐）。另外，如果要請對方吃飯或看電影時，也可以說 "How about going to...? My treat!" （要不要去…？我請客。）

Questions 22-24

中文翻譯

　　艾蜜莉昨晚熬夜，因為她必須為今天的一場重要的業務會議準備一份季度報告。如果業務副理約翰昨天早上有如他所承諾提供必要的資訊，那麼她早就可以完成報告了。

　　她到凌晨 2 點才睡覺。她今天早上醒來時，已經 8 點 45 分了，而且她發現她的鬧鐘壞了。她上班快要遲到了，所以決定搭計程車去公司。不過她發現自己把手機留在家裡了。當她抵達辦公室時，已經 9 點 20 分了。會議早在二十分鐘前就已經開始了。Emily 進入會議室時，業務經理擺出一副臭臉。更糟的是，她發現她忘了把昨晚完成的報告帶在身上。艾蜜莉能說的只是「我今天真是倒楣。」

22. 本文最佳標題為何？
    (A) 艾蜜莉的日常生活
    (B) 切勿太常熬夜
    (C) 艾蜜莉今天很不順
    (D) 別太相信他人

23. 業務會議何時開始？
    (A) 它九點開始。
    (B) 它八點四十五分開始。
    (C) 從艾蜜莉走進會議室之後開始。
    (D) 約翰抵達前二十分鐘就開始了。

24. 下列敘述何者正確？
    (A) 艾蜜莉每天都搭計程車上班。
    (B) 艾蜜莉在上班途中打電戶給業務經理。
    (C) 當艾蜜莉走進會議室，業務經理看起來很不悅。
    (D) 約翰準時把必要資料給艾蜜莉。

答題解說

這是一篇記敘文。以第三人稱敘述 Emily 發生的事情，從早上遲到，到忘記帶報告等等不順行為。

22. 答案：(C)。這篇短文敘述 Emily 一早不順遂的經過，但這並非常態「日常生活」的情形，而「切勿太常熬夜」、「別太相信他人」也都不是短文的主旨。故正確答案為 (C)。

23. 答案：(A)。文章中提到，When she arrived at the office, it was already nine twenty. （當她到辦公室時，已經是 9 點 20 分了。）以及 The meeting already started twenty minutes ago.（會議早在二十分鐘前就已經開始了。）由此敘述，可推知會議在九點開始。

24. 答案：(C)。這是個「何者為真」的題型，基本上，應全盤了解整段文章內容之後，以「刪去法」檢視每個選項的敘述。內容中提到 The sales manager pulled a long face when Emily walked into the meeting room.（Emily 進入會議室時，業務經理擺出一副臭臉。）這表示業務經理看起來很不悅，故正確答案應為 (C)。

破題關鍵

22. 題目要問的是「文章標題」，這樣的題型要先看完全文，才能來解題，因為你必須大略了解內容，才能推出此類題型答案。

23. 題目是問「會議幾點開始」，因此找出「會議」和「幾個時間點」，就可以推測答案。如：九點二十到會議室，會議二十分鐘前開始，由此兩點，可推知會議九點開始。

24. "pull a long face" 字面意思是「把臉拉長」，就是「擺出一副臭臉」的意思。

stay up 熬夜　**prepare** [prɪˋpɛr] **v.** 準備　***quarterly** [ˋkwɔrtɚlɪ] **adj.** 季度的　**important** [ɪmˋpɔrtnt] **adj.** 重要的　**meeting** [ˋmitɪŋ] **n.** 會議　**be done with**... 完成　**assistant** [əˋsɪstənt] **adj.** 助理的，副的　**sales manager** 業務經理　**alarm clock n.** 鬧鐘　**fail to-V** 無法做到～　**decide** [dɪˋsaɪd] **v.** 決定　**arrive** [əˋraɪv] **v.** 抵達　**office** [ˋɔfɪs] **n.** 辦公室　**what's worse** 更糟的是　**forget** [fɚˋgɛt] **v.** 忘記

相關文法或用法補充

❶ Today isn't one's day! 是指「某人今天真倒楣。」除了此句，還有其他說法。out of one's luck（某人很倒楣）、what a bummer（真掃興，真倒楣）Just my luck!（還真幸運喔！— 有反諷意味。）

❷ 時間的說法，除了直接照數字說，還有其他方式，可以多多運用：
　① eight forty（八點四十分）
　② 數字＋to＋點鐘（差幾分就…點）如：ten to ten（9 點 50 分）
　③ 數字＋after/past＋點鐘（……點過了幾分）如：ten after ten（10 點 10 分）
　　　（剛好半小時：half ＋ past ＋點鐘
　④ 十五分：a quarter past/after ＋點鐘。如：a quarter past ten（10 點 15 分）

Questions 25-27

中文翻譯

　　幾乎每個人都會作惡夢的經驗。通常，人會在惡夢中或做惡夢後醒來，並且能清晰地記住全部或部分的惡夢。它們是一種讓你感到憂心、害怕或受驚嚇的夢。

　　許多人可能夢到從高處掉下來，而有些人可能夢到考試不及格、失去工作、遺失金錢或看到他們親友死亡。如果你在早晨看到一場車禍，那麼你之後可能會夢到那一場車禍的惡夢。因為你做了不好的夢，所以會睡不好覺。有時候，惡夢不只是惡夢。它們可能會嚴重到讓一個人陷入憂愁，或者可能擾亂一個人的工作、家庭或社交生活。

　　如果您想睡個好覺，可以在睡覺前聽個音樂、喝杯牛奶或看些有趣的電視節目。那可以幫助您睡個好覺。

25. 這篇短文可能來自何處？
　　(A) 旅遊指南　　　　　　　　(B) 使用者手冊
　　(C) 健康雜誌　　　　　　　　(D) 日記

26. 劃底線的 distress 可以改為哪一個字？
　　(A) 安全　　　(B) 懷疑　　　(C) 憂愁　　　(D) 沉默

27. 以下選項何者為非？
  (A) 沒有很多人做過從高處掉下來的夢。
  (B) 如果你在早上看到可怕的事情，你可能會做惡夢。
  (C) 如果想睡個好覺，可以在睡前聽一些好音樂。
  (D) 惡夢可能影響你的社交生活。

這是一篇說明文。內容講述惡夢可能對健康與正常生活造成影響。

25. 答案：(C)。全篇短文都在探討惡夢有關的議題，而第一段最後一句提到 "They are a type of dream that causes you to feel anxious, fearful or scared."（它們是一種讓你感到焦慮、害怕或受驚嚇的夢。）由此可以斷定應該是從「健康雜誌」來的文章。其他選項的「旅遊指南」、「使用者手冊」及「日記」都是不相關的。

26. 答案：(C)。畫底線的這句意思是「它們可能會嚴重到讓一個人陷入——，或者可能擾亂一個人的工作、家庭或社交生活。」這裡的「它們」當然是指惡夢，所以 (C)「憂愁」是最接近的答案。其餘的「安全」、「懷疑」、「沉默」都不會是經常惡夢的後遺症。

27. 答案：(A)。文章中提到「如果你在早晨看到一場車禍，那麼你之後可能會夢到那一場車禍的惡夢。」以及「如果想睡個好覺，可以在睡前聽一些音樂」，以及「有時候，惡夢不只是惡夢。它們可能會嚴重到讓一個人陷入憂愁，或者可能擾亂一個人的工作、家庭或社交生活。」只有選項 (A) 是錯誤的，因為第二段一開始就提到「許多人可能夢到從高處掉下來…」。

25. 題目問的重點是「文章來自何處」，這類題型建議留待後面兩題答完之後，再繼續來解題，因為這類題目很容易得分，只要了解大致上內容，輕易答題沒難度。

26. 本題關鍵是 distress 前的 "so serious that..."（嚴重到…），探討的是噩夢對心理健康與生活造成的影響。「安全」就直接刪除了，「懷疑」與「沉默」都說不上什麼「嚴重」的程度。

27. 「何者為真」或「何者為非」的題型，都屬於內容細節型的題目。通常必須先看過四個選項內容，再到文章中找尋線索。

experience [ɪkˋspɪrɪəns] v. 經驗，體驗　***nightmare** [ˋnaɪtˏmɛr] n. 噩夢　**wake up** 醒來　**remember** [rɪˋmɛmbɚ] v. 記得，想起　**worried** [ˋwɝɪd] adj. 擔心的　**fearful** [ˋfɪrfəl] adj. 害怕的　**scared** [skɛrd] adj. 受驚嚇的　**height** [haɪt] n. 高度　**fail** [fel] v. 沒有通過（考試）　**accident** [ˋæksədənt] n. 意外　**more than...** 不只是…　**serious** [ˋsɪrɪəs] adj. 嚴重的　***distress** [dɪˋstrɛs] n. 苦惱，憂傷　**trouble** [ˋtrʌbl] v. 擾亂　**social** [ˋsoʃəl]

adj. 社會上的　**travel guide** 旅遊指南　**handbook** [ˋhændˏbʊk] **n.** 手冊　**health** [hɛlθ] **n.** 健康　**doubt** [daʊt] **n.** 懷疑　**silence** [ˋsaɪləns] **n.** 無聲，沉默　**terrible** [ˋtɛrəbl] **adj.** 可怕的，嚇人的　**influence** [ˋɪnflʊəns] **v.** 影響

相關文法或用法補充

❶ experience 可當動詞或名詞。當名詞是指「經驗，經歷」。當「經驗」是不可數名詞，若是當「經歷」，則為可數。後面介系詞接 of、in、with。例如：

　① Kenny has no experience with speaking in front of others.（Kenny 沒有在他人面前演講的經驗。）

　② 當動詞，是指「體驗、經歷、感受」。例如：Mr. Smith experienced a lot of difficulty in selling his car.（史密斯在賣車方面，經歷不少困難。）

❷ If + 現在式, S + will + V...，用於表示「單純假設」，未來可能會發生。注意，if + 現在式，主要子句要用未來式。例如：If it is rainy tomorrow, we'll cancel the picnic.（如果明天下雨，我們將取消野餐。）

Questions 28-30

中文翻譯

寄件人	Kelly_huang@gmail.com
收件人	lisa_chen@msn.com
主旨	回覆：計劃中的溫哥華之旅

親愛的麗莎：

　　你最近好嗎？我聽說最近有個強颱襲擊你的國家，且對某些房屋和建築物造成嚴重破壞。希望您和您的家人安然無恙。

　　在上一封電子郵件中，你說正計劃去加拿大旅行，且問到是否可以住我這裡。非常歡迎！現在有可用的客房。此外，我可以給你一些好去處的建議。因此，在決定要停留多長時間後，列出想去的一些有趣或受歡迎的風景名勝。另外，找出你可能感興趣的一些室內或室外活動。最後，不要忘記去了解一下如何給小費的資訊，否則你會感到尷尬的。

　　如果妳已設定好旅行日期，請盡快讓我知道。保持聯繫。

祝安
凱莉
2021 年 6 月 20 日

28. 這封電子郵件的目的是什麼？
    (A) 抱怨強烈颱風
    (B) 提供旅行的點子
    (C) 了解最近的生活事件
    (D) 邀請朋友來家裡

29. 第一段最後的 sound 是什麼意思？
    (A) 聲音
    (B) 精力充沛的
    (C) 健康的
    (D) 自由的

30. 以下哪一項是正確的？
    (A) 麗莎正在旅行。
    (B) 凱利將於夏天到加拿大找麗莎。
    (C) 凱利的家方便讓麗莎留宿天。
    (D) 麗莎已決定何時去拜訪凱利。

答題解說

這個題組是一封電子郵件，主要內容是 Kelly 回覆 Lisa 詢問加拿大之旅期間可否住他家，並給予一些旅行建議。

28. 答案：(B)。題目問的是電子郵件的目的（或主旨），第一段其實只是問候與詢問近況。第二段開始才是這封電子郵件的目的。其中 Kelly 建議 Lisa 列出想去的一些有趣或受歡迎的風景名勝，以及找出可能感興趣的室內或室外活動。最後提醒給小費的事情，都是與旅行有關的事情，故正確答案為 (B)。

29. 答案：(C)。題目句中的 "sound" 所在句子是 "I hope you and your family members are safe and sound." （希望您和您的家人安然無恙。）sound 前有 and，所以 sound 一定跟 safe 是近似意義的，而且這句子以 I hope... （但願）開頭，表示一種祝福語，故正確答案為 (C) Healthy（健康的）。

30. 答案：(C)。這封 E-mail 是 Kelly 給予 Lisa 一些旅行建議，最後提到「如果妳已設定好旅行日期，請盡快讓我知道。」所以 Lisa 的旅行只是正在計畫當中，而非「正在旅行。」(A) 的「正在旅行」、(B) 的「將於夏天到加拿大」、(D) 的「已決定何時去拜訪」都是錯誤的。故正確答案為 (C)，因為第二段提到 "There's a guest room available now."，其中 "guest room" 是「客房」的意思。

破題關鍵

28. 信件最上方，在收件人與寄件人下面都會有個「主旨」欄位，這是找尋信件主旨的第一線索。從這封郵件的 "Subject: Re: Planned Trip to Vancouver" 即可知，「回覆對方計劃中的溫哥華之旅」是寫這封信的主要目的。雖然 Kelly 說歡迎 Lisa 去她家住，但這並不表示 Kelly「邀請」Lisa 去他家住，所以 (D) 是錯誤的。

29. safe and sound 是很常見的用語，表示「安然無恙」的，但即使沒看過這個慣用語，也能從 and 前面的 safe（安全的）去推斷它的意思。

30. 「何者為真」或「何者為非」的題型，都屬於內容細節型的題目。通常必須先看過四個選項內容，再一一從文章內容中確認是否正確。通常放在最後再來做答。如果來不及讀整篇文章，且解完其他題目之後，對於某一個選項的敘述是否正確，還不是那麼確定，那麼就只能再回到文章中去做確認。此外，有些選項的敘述無法直接在文章中找到對應答案。因此，舉一反三很重要。可以用答案反推，找出答案。

字詞解釋

planned [plænd] **adj.** 有計畫的　　**lately** [`letlɪ] **adv.** 近來，最近　　**recently** [`risntlɪ] **adv.** 最近，不久前　　**cause** [kɔz] **v.** 導致　　**serious** [`sɪrɪəs] **adj.** 嚴重的　　**damage** [`dæmɪdʒ] **n.** 損害，毀壞　　**safe and sound** 安然無恙　　**guest room** 客房　　**available** [ə`veləbl] **adj.** 可用的　　**suggestion** [sə`dʒɛstʃən] **n.** 建議，提議　　**scenery** [`sinərɪ] **n.** 風景，景色　　**tip** [tɪp] **v.** 給小費　　**embarrassed** [ɪm`bærəst] **adj.** 尷尬的，難為情的　　**in touch** 有聯絡　　**event** [ɪ`vɛnt] **n.** 事件　　**energetic** [͵ɛnə`dʒɛtɪk] **adj.** 精力旺盛的

相關文法或用法補充

❶ cause 當名詞時，是指「原因」。例如：What was the cause of this accident?（造成這一事故的原因是什麼？）當動詞時，表示「造成，導致」。但是當動詞時有個用法須特別注意，那就是「cause + 人 + 不好的事（名詞）」=「cause + 不好的事（名詞）to + 人」，這時候的 cause 有「帶給／來」的意思，是個「授予動詞」，後面接兩個受詞。例如：This may cause you much trouble. = This may cause much trouble to you.（這可能給你造成很多麻煩。）

❷ bedroom（臥房）、living room（客廳）、storeroom（儲藏室）、dining room（飯廳）、bathroom（浴室）、guest room（客房）、basement（地下室）、attic（閣樓）、balcony（陽台）

學習筆記欄

9

GEPT 全民英檢

初級初試
中譯＋解析

第一部分 看圖辨義

1. **For question number 1, please look at Picture A.**

   Question number 1: What does this sign tell us?
   （這個標誌告訴我們什麼？）
   (A) Only staff can touch the machine.
   　　（僅工作人員可碰觸機器。）
   (B) Turn off the machine before fixing it.
   　　（修理機器前先應先關閉電源。）
   (C) Pay attention to possible personal injury.（注意可能的個人傷害）

   答題解說

   答案：(C)。這通常是工廠內的警告標示，會貼在機器設備表面，針對任何接近此高溫（high temperature）機器設備的人員，有燙傷的危險，所以正確答案為(C)。

   破題關鍵

   圖片中的 CAUTION 是「警告」的意思，即使不知道這個字，看到底下 high temperature（高溫）以及 "Don't touch." 也知道這是警告人不可碰觸，否則會有人身的傷害（personal injury）。

   字詞解釋

   *caution [ˋkɔʃən] n. 警告，告誡　**temperature** [ˋtɛmprətʃɚ] n. 溫度，氣溫　**staff** [stæf] n. 工作人員　**machine** [məˋʃin] n. 機器　**turn off** 關閉（機器、設備等）**fix** [fɪks] v. 修理　**pay attention to** 注意　**personal** [ˋpɝsn̩l] adj. 個人的　**injury** [ˋɪndʒərɪ] n. 傷害

   相關文法或用法補充

   attention（注意，專心）是個不可數的抽象名詞，也常用於人群聚集的公開場合。例如：May I have your attention, please? 或 Attention, please!（麻煩各位注意一下我這邊！）

2. **For question number 2 and 3, please look at Picture B.**

Question number 2: What does the lady probably do?
（這位女子可能是做什麼的？）

(A) She's a nurse.（她是個護士。）

(B) She's a teacher.（她是個老師。）

(C) She's a taxi driver.（她是個計程車司機。）

答題解說

答案：(A)。圖中左方的指示牌上畫著一個「十」的標示牌字，表示前方有一間醫院，既然題目是問「職業」，所以與醫院有關的工作當然就是 (A) 了。

破題關鍵

本題從選項就可以知道是在問職業，而圖中其實有兩個關鍵處：「十」字標示牌以及騎單車女孩頭上的護士帽，只要注意到其中一樣就可以選出答案。

字詞解釋

nurse [nɝs] n. 護士　　**taxi driver** n. 計程車司機

相關文法或用法補充

如果有人問你 "What are you?"、"What do you do?" 或是 "What is your job?"，都是在問你「是在做什麼的？」，不過很多人會錯誤地回答 "My job is a nurse/teacher/taxi driver..."。事實上，job 是一個「東西」，而職位像 engineer、teacher、secretary 或是 manager、director 等，指的是「人」，兩者不對等。因此，別再被中文誤導了。

3. **Question number 3: Please look at Picture B again.**

What is true about the picture?（關於這張圖，何者正確？）

(A) The lady's riding a scooter.（女子正在騎輕型機車。）

(B) A hospital is in front of the lady.

　　（一間醫院在女子的前方。）

(C) She's on her way home.（她正在回家途中。）

答題解說

答案：(B)。圖片中女子正在騎單車，不是輕型機車所以 (A) 是錯誤的；(B) 是正確答案，因為標示牌的十字符號就是指醫院，且箭頭指著前方，表示女子的前方有醫院；從女子的穿著以及醫院的標示牌，可推知女子是護士且正要去上班，所以 (C) 是錯誤的。

「何者為真」的題型,需從三個選項一一確認。而圖片中女子的穿著與左方的標示牌是答題關鍵。

scooter [`skutɚ] n. 速克達(輕型摩托車) **hospital** [`hɑspɪtl] n. 醫院 **in front of**... 在~前方 **on one's way home** 在某人回家的路上

in front of 常與 in "the" front of 做區別。in front of 表示「在~的前面」,指某一範圍以外的前面。而 in/at the front of... 是指某一範圍以內的前面。例如:

❶ Mary is standing at the front of the classroom.(瑪麗站在教室的前面。)→ 指某一範圍內的前面

❷ There is a tall tree in front of the house.(房子前面有一棵大樹。)→ 指某一範圍以外的前面

4. **For question number 4 and 5, please look at Picture C.**

Question number 4: How did these people go to the zoo?(這些人如何去動物園?)

(A) On foot(走路)

(B) By bus(搭公車)

(C) By taxi(搭計程車)

答案:(B)。本題問的是「如何前往」(How),聽到 "How... go to...?" 的問句應立即與 "By + 交通工具" 的答案連結在一起。看到圖中的 "To the zoo $30" 即可知道他們要搭公車去動物園,所以正確答案是(B)。

三個選項中有兩個是「By + 交通工具」,即使你不知道 "On foot." 是「走路」的意思,也可以推知題目要問什麼了。

on foot 步行,走路

表達走路或步行,應該用 on foot,因為「腳」不是交通工具,所以如果用 by foot 的話,會變成「搭乘腳丫子」去上班。另外,「香港腳」的英文可不是

Hong Kong foot，而是 athlete foot。athlete 是「運動員」的意思。

5. **Question number 5: Please look at Picture C again.**

What is true about the picture?（關於這張圖，何者為真？）
(A) These people are standing in line.（這些人正在排隊。）
(B) A bus is passing the stop.（一輛公車正經過這個站牌。）
(C) This stop is at the zoo.（這站是動物園。）

答題解說

答案：(A)。圖片中人們正站在站牌前排隊等公車到來，所以 (A) 是正確的。圖片上並沒有公車，所以 (B) 是錯誤的，因為站牌上有「往動物園（Zoo）」的指示，所以 (C) 是錯誤的。

破題關鍵

對於「何者為真」的題目，先仔細觀察圖片後，仔細聆聽三個選項的內容，尤其是三個句子主詞皆不同時。但只要掌握句子裡的關鍵字詞（standing in line），即可輕鬆作答。本題選項中的關鍵字詞是

字詞解釋

in line 排隊　　**stop** [stɑp] n. 停車站

相關文法或用法補充

stop 與 station 都有「車站」的意思，但其實兩者意思大不相同。station 通常是指有一凍建築物或比較大的車站，而 stop 通常指較小的「（公車）車站」，因此基本上，火車、地鐵或捷運的「站」，不會用 stop，而是用 station。例如，如果你搭公車發現自己過站了，要說 I missed my stop.，如果是搭地鐵或捷運，那就要說 I missed my station.。

第二部分 問答

6. **Mother's Day is coming.**（母親節快到了。）

(A) Yes, she is late.（是的，她遲到了。）
(B) I hope so.（但願如此。）
(C) We'll celebrate it at a fancy restaurant.（我們將在一家高級餐廳慶祝。）

答題解說

答案：(C)。題目這句是「母親節快到了。」(A) 的「是的，她遲到了。」與 (B)

的「但願如此。」都是莫名其妙的回應，只有 (C) 的「我們將在一家高級餐廳慶祝。」是正確的回應。也可以反問 "How are you going to celebrate it?（你們將如何慶祝呢？）" 來回應。

破題關鍵

聽到某節日 "is coming"，就知道不可能回答 "I hope so."，因為那是必然的事情。而選項 (A) 是針對「某人快來了」的回答，但這裡是節日，所以也刪除此選項。所以如果用刪去法，亦可以得到答案。

字詞解釋

celebrate [ˋsɛləˌbret] **v.** 慶祝　　**fancy** [ˋfænsɪ] **adj.**（價格）昂貴的，（食品等）特級的　　**restaurant** [ˋrɛstərənt] **n.** 餐廳

相關文法或用法補充

be coming 是很常見的用法，有 happening soon（即將發生）之意。例如：The train is coming.（火車快來了。）另外，Coming soon. 是指「即將上市，敬請期待」之意。

7. **How would you like your steak?**（請問牛排要幾分熟呢？）

　(A) It tastes better than chicken.（它比雞肉好吃。）
　(B) It is terrible.（牛排很糟糕。）
　(C) Well done, please.（全熟。）

答題解說

答案：(C)。How would you like your steak? 是問「牛排幾分熟」，回答時有「五分熟、七分熟、全熟⋯」幾種說法，不能含糊回答，因此本題正確答是 (C)。

破題關鍵

本題的破題關鍵是 steak 這個字，如果只是聽到 "How would you like..."，會以為是「你覺得～如何？」可能覺得 (A) 和 (B) 都是答案了。這類疑問詞所引導的句子，搭配不同名詞會有完全不同的意思，應特別注意。

字詞解釋

steak [stek] **n.** 牛排　　**chicken** [ˋtʃɪkɪn] **n.** 雞肉　　**terrible** [ˋtɛrəbl] **adj.** 糟糕的，可怕的

相關文法或用法補充

被問到牛排要幾分熟時，有幾種答法：rare（一分熟）、medium rare（三分熟）、medium（五分熟）、medium well（七分熟）、well done（全熟）。

8. **When will you visit your uncle?**（你將於何時探望你伯父？）

(A) No, this Friday.（不是，這個星期五。）
(B) Next Tuesday.（下週二。）
(C) My uncle lives nearby.（我伯父住在附近。）

答題解說

答案：(B)。就三個選項來分析，題目是問「你將於何時探望你伯父？」(A) 選項的「不，這個星期五」，看似相關，但因為多了 No，所以錯誤，而 (C) My uncle lives nearby.（我伯父住在附近。）答非所問。選項 (B) 的 Next Tuesday. 可以還原成 I will visit him next Tuesday.，這是正確答案。

破題關鍵

這是以 When 開頭的問句，基本上不用 Yes/No... 來回答，不過考題會有陷阱，常見的答案都是屬於「間接性」的回答，譬如不會出現 I will visit...這幾個和題目一樣的字。而 (A) No, this Friday.，千萬別看到有「星期幾」，就以為答案是正確的。

字詞解釋

visit [ˋvɪzɪt] **v.** 探望　　**nearby** [ˋnɪrˏbaɪ] **adv.** 在附近

相關文法或用法補充

when 的常見用法：

❶ 當「疑問詞」，引導問句：When did Emma finish her homework?（Emma 何時完成她的作業呢？）
❷ 當副詞連接詞，引導副詞子句：When Jack knocked on the door, Dora was playing the piano.（當 Jack 敲門時，Dora 正在彈鋼琴。）

9. **Which color do you like, blue or pink?**（你喜歡哪種顏色，藍色的或是粉色的？）

(A) This an old color TV.（這是老舊的彩色電視。）
(B) I like both.（兩種我都喜歡。）
(C) Yes, pink is better.（沒錯。粉色比較好。）

答題解說

答案：(B)。which 問的是「哪一個」，再加上句尾有 A or B 兩者擇一，通常回答要明確指出 A 還是 B，或者「兩個都要」、「兩個都不要」。故正確答案為 (B) I like both.。疑問詞開頭問句，不可用 Yes/No 來回答，所以 (C) 是錯誤的。

多熟悉 "Which..., A or B?"（哪一個，A 還是 B？）的問句即可輕鬆解決這一題。

color [`kʌlɚ] **n.** 顏色　**both** [boθ] **pron.** 兩者　**better** [`bɛtɚ] **adj.** 比較好的

color 是「顏色」的意思，它的形容詞是 colorful（彩色的），也有「多采多姿的」意思。例如：colorful life（多采多姿的人生）。不過如果是「彩色電視」或「彩色螢幕」的話，英文是 color TV、color screen，而不是用 colorful 來修飾 TV 或 screen。

10. **You look terrible.**（你看起來很糟。）

(A) I like the movie so much.（我非常喜歡這部電影。）
(B) Yes, I won the basketball game.（是啊。我籃球比賽贏了。）
(C) I failed the exam again.（我考試又不及格。）

答案：(C)。對於「You look terrible.（你看起來很糟。）」這句話，回答不會是 Yes/No 開頭的句子，再加上比賽贏了，看起來不會「糟糕」，所以選項 (B) 是錯的。選項 (A) 回答的是「我非常喜歡這部電影。」這是雞同鴨講，選項 (C) 我考試又不及格，這是針對問題在回答。

關鍵當然在於聽出且聽懂 terrible 的意思。terrible 用來形容「人」的時候，表示「糟糕的，極差的」，所以通常會回答「為何 terrible」的原因，也就是一種負面狀態。

terrible[`tɛrəbl] **adj.** 糟糕的，可怕的　**fail** [fel] **v.** 失敗，不及格

terrible 可以用來修飾「人」或「事物」例如：

❶ Lisa just told him some terrible news.（Lisa 剛剛告訴他一些可怕的消息。）
❷ Stone is a terrible writer.（Stone 不擅長寫作。）

11. Where is the Happy Restaurant?（快樂餐廳在哪裡？）

(A) The Happy Bank is in front of the supermarket.（快樂銀行位於超市前面。）
(B) I go to the Happy Restaurant once a week.（我一星期去快樂餐廳一次。）
(C) It's near my school.（在我學校附近。）

答題解說

答案：(C)。對於題目這句「快樂餐廳在哪裡？」，回答要有具體的地點，所以 (C) 就是正確的回答。(A) 刻意以不同主詞（Happy Bank）混淆視聽，而 (B) 是針對 "How often...?" 問句的回答。

破題關鍵

關鍵在於聽出且了解 Where 用來表達「詢問地點」，答案通常會是「在～路」，「在～附近」或「～前／隔壁」等。或者如果有先看過三個選項，可以馬上判斷出 (A)、(B) 的回答是錯誤的。

字詞解釋

restaurant [ˋrɛstərənt] **n.** 餐廳　　**front** [frʌnt] **n.** 前面　　**supermarket** [ˋsupɚˏmarkɪt] **n.** 超市　　**once** [wʌns] **adv.** 一次

相關文法或用法補充

常見用來表達「位置」的說法：

❶ next to + 地方 → 表示「在～隔壁」，例如：The coffee shop is next to the restaurant.（咖啡廳在餐廳隔壁。）

❷ in front/back of...
→ 表示「在～前面／後面」，例如：The bookstore is in back of the post office.（書店在郵局後面。）

❸ between A and B → 表示「介於 A 和 B 之間」，例如：The gift shop is between the supermarket and the bakery.（禮物店介於超市和麵包坊之間。）

❹ across from A → 表示「在 A 對面」，例如：The bank is across from the mall.（銀行在購物中心對面。）

12. The coat is too big for me.（這外套對我來說太大！）

(A) It looks big enough.（它看起來夠大件。）
(B) Do you want to try a smaller one?（你要不要試穿小號一點的？）
(C) Sorry. We don't have a fitting room.（抱歉。我們沒有更衣室。）

第 1 回
第 2 回
第 3 回
第 4 回
第 5 回
第 6 回
第 7 回
第 8 回
第 9 回
第 10 回

答案：(B)。too big 是指「太大件 …」，因此聽到對方說衣服或褲子等「太大件」，應做何回應呢？當然是要選較小的，因此選項 (B) 的「你要不要試穿小號一點的？」即為最正確的回應，其他兩個選項都是不太相關的回答。

too big for me 其實就是： too big for me to wear，表示「太大件穿不下」，所以店員會建議穿其他尺寸小一點的大衣。

coat [kot] **n.** 大衣　　**enough** [ə`nʌf] **adj.** 足夠　　**fitting room** **phr.** 更衣室

too... for + 人 + to+ V... → 表示「對某人太 ～而不能～」，具有否定意味，例如： The room is too old to for them to live.（這間房間對他們而言太舊，沒辦法住。）如果是 so... that ... 的話，表示「如此～以致於～」，例如：

Gary is so easy to be angry that many people don't like him.（Gary 如此容易生氣，以致於很多人不喜歡他。）

13. May I ask you for a favor, sir?（我可以請你幫個忙嗎，先生？）

(A) What's that?（什麼事？）
(B) Sorry. I don't have one.（抱歉。我沒有。）
(C) You're welcome.（不客氣。）

答案：(A)。題目問「我可以請你幫個忙嗎？」(A) 反問對方「什麼事？」是正確的回答。(B) 錯誤的原因是，對方不是要跟你要什麼東西，而是請你幫個忙。(C) 是針對對方對你表示謝意時的回應。

favor 本意是「恩惠，善行」，是個抽象名詞，而 ask for a favor 是「請求協助」之意。 "May I ask you for a favor?" 等同於 Can you help me? 或 Can you give me a hand?。

favor [`fevɚ] **n.** 幫助，善意的行為，恩惠

相關文法或用法補充

「ask ＋人＋ for ＋事情／事物」表示「向某人要求某事物」，而 ask for 後面可以接「事物」，也可以接「人」，表示「有事要找某人。」例如：A man was asking for you this morning.（今天早上有人來找你。）

14. **Have you ever watched that film?**（你看過那部片嗎？）

(A) No, I've lost my watch.（沒有，我遺失我的錶了。）
(B) Yes, I have.（有啊，我看過了。）
(C) Yes, I've heard of the film.（是的，我聽說過這部片。）

答題解說

答案：(B)。題目問的是「有沒有看過～」，這是個 Yes/No 問句。(B) 的 Yes, I have." 是最直接的回答。(A) 刻意以相同發音 watch（手錶）來混淆答題，而 (C) 雖然也有 film，但題目是問有沒有「看」過，不是「聽」過，所以 (A)、(C) 皆為錯誤回答。

破題關鍵

看電影的「看」可以用 see 也可以用 watch，但場合有所不同。本題並未指出在去電影院還是在家看，所以也能用 seen（see 的 P.P.）來回答。

字詞解釋

film [fɪlm] **n.** 電影　**hear of**... 聽說過～

相關文法或用法補充

「看電影」的英文，可以說 "go to the movies"，這裡 movie 之所以要加 -s，是因為 movies 代表「電影院」，而「電影院」有分不同的「廳」，同時上映不同的片子。但如果是用 see，就要說 scc a movie，沒有 see the movies 的說法。另外如果是在家看電視播出的電影，要用 watch a move。

15. **What are you cooking? It smells nice.**（你在煮什麼？聞起來很棒。）

(A) Cooking is my favorite hobby.（烹飪是我最愛的嗜好。）
(B) Some French fries（一些薯條）
(C) Thanks for your praise.（謝謝你的讚賞。）

答題解說

答案：(B)。本題有兩句話。第一句（What are you cooking?）才是要回答的重點，且回答要有具體的「正在煮的東西」，因此選項中只有 (B) 的「一些薯

條。」可以回應這件事情。(A) 是答非所問的回應；而 (C) 是針對 "It smells nice." 回應，所以是錯誤的。

要聽出題目要問什麼，多餘的句子只是要擾亂你的聽力。只要聽出題目句的 what 與 cooking 的意思即可答對問題。

字詞解釋

smell [smɛl] **v.** 聞起來　　**favorite** [ˋfevərɪt] **adj.** 最喜愛的　　**hobby** [ˋhɑbɪ] **n.** 嗜好
French fries 薯條　　**praise** [prez] **n.** 讚揚，稱讚

相關文法或用法補充

praise 也可以當名詞用，通常作為不可數名詞，表示「讚美，讚揚」，常用於 in praise of...（以讚揚～）的片語。例如：a poem in praise of Taiwan（一首讚美台灣的詩）

第三部分 簡短對話

16. M: What are you going to do on Sunday, Sandy?
    W: I'm going jogging with my friends, and you?
    M: Me too.
    W: Let's go jogging together next time.
    M: Sure. I'd love to.

    Question: Who will the man go jogging with on Sunday?
    (A) The woman
    (B) His friends
    (C) The woman's friends

    英文翻譯
    男：仙蒂，妳星期天要做什麼呢？
    女：我要和朋友去慢跑。
    男：我也是。
    女：我們下次一起去慢跑吧。
    男：當然。我很樂意。
    問題：男子星期天要和誰去慢跑？
    (A) 女子

(B) 他的朋友

(C) 女子的朋友

第1回 第2回 第3回 第4回 第5回 第6回 第7回 第8回 第9回 第10回

答題解說

答案：(B)。題目問的是男子星期天要和誰去慢跑（go jogging），應注意聽男子的發言部分。可以從 Me too.（我也是。）的回答推知，他「也和女子一樣」，星期天要「和朋友去慢跑」。

破題關鍵

本題關鍵句是 "Me, too."，在口語中是相當常見的回應。看到 "Me, too." 之後，從上一句找答案就對了。

字詞解釋

jog [dʒɑg] v. 慢跑　　**nex time** adv. 下次

相關文法或用法補充

❶ 未來簡單式：

① S + will+ V… +未來時間副詞。例：He will move to Boston next year. （他明年將搬到波士頓。）

② S+be 動詞+ going to+V… +未來時間副詞。例：She is going to the gym this afternoon.（下午她將 去健身房。）

❷ 未來進行式：S + will+ be + Ving… +未來時間副詞。例：She will be mopping the floor at 7. （她將在七點時拖地。）

❸ 未來完成式：S + will + have P.P. + 未來時間副詞。例：Next summer, Emma will have lived in New York for 6 years. （明年夏天，Emma 住在紐約將六年之久了。）

17. W: What is today's special?

M: It is fried beef with vegetables.

W: I'd like to order one.

M: OK. It'll be ready in 15 minutes.

Question: Where did the conversation take place?

(A) In a convenience store

(B) In a restaurant

(C) In a farm

英文翻譯

女：請問今日特餐是什麼？

男：炒牛肉配蔬菜。

女：我要點一份。

男：好的。十五分鐘之後就好了。

問題：這則對話可能是在什麼地方？

(A) 在便利商店

(B) 在餐廳

(C) 在農場

答案：(B)。本題提到：today's special 和 beef with vegetables，兩者都和食物有關。(A) 的「在便利商店」以及 (C) 的「在農場」皆不符合對話內容 (B) 的「在餐廳」明顯與和合對話內容相符。

破題關鍵

先看過三個選項內容就會知道題目是要要問「地點」。本題答題關鍵在於對話中的關鍵字詞 today's special（今日特餐）、fried beef with vegetables（炒牛肉配蔬菜）、order（點餐）。

字詞解釋

special [ˋspɛʃəl] **adj.** 特餐，（臨時減價的）特價商品　**beef** [bif] **n.** 牛肉　**order** [ˋɔrdɚ] **v.** 點餐　**convenience store** [kənˋvinjəns] [stor] **n.** 便利商店

相關文法或用法補充

與「餐廳用餐」有關的英文都非常實用，以下語句可以好好學起來：

❶ We have a reservation at + 時間 + for + 人名. （我們～（幾點）有預約，訂位者是～）。例如：We have a reservation at 11:30 for Mr. Roberts.（我們訂了十一點半，訂位者是羅伯特先生。）

❷ Do you have a table for/of + 人數？（你們有～人的位子嗎？）。例如：Do you have a table for/of three?（你們有三人的位子嗎？）

❸ What would you recommend? （有推薦的餐點嗎？）

❹ I'd like (to order) + 食物／飲料／甜點... （我想要點～）例如：I'd like a cup of Mocha.（我要點一杯摩卡咖啡。）

❺ It will come in + 時間. （將在～內上桌。）It will come in 10 minutes.（餐點將在十分鐘後上桌。）

18. M: May I help you?

   W: I bought the dress here. Now I'd like to return it and get my money back.

   M: What seems to be the problem with it?

   W: It is too big for me.

   M: When did you make this purchase?

   Question: Who are the speakers?

   (A) A shopkeeper and an employee

   (B) A manager and an assistant

   (C) A clerk and a customer

英文翻譯

男：我能替您服務嗎？

女：我之前在這裡買了這件洋裝。我現在想要退貨並拿回我的錢。

男：請問衣服有什麼問題嗎？

女：太大件了。

男：你何時買的？

問題：說話者們是誰？

(A) 店主與員工

(B) 經理與助理

(C) 店員與顧客。

答題解說

答案：(C)。本題是問兩位說話者的身分，雖然對話中沒有提到有關身分的名詞，因此必須聽懂對話中男女的談話內容，才能依照邏輯判斷。一開始男子說 May I help you?，顯然男子是個店員或店家，而女子回答說，之前在這裡買了洋裝，現在想要退貨，因此女子是顧客，故正確答案為 (C)。

破題關鍵

本題其實可以用「刪除法」來解題，男子說 May I help you?，此時 (B) 可直接排除，但是當女子說：I bought the dress...和 refund（退款），可知不會是店主與員工的關係，因此確定答案為 (C) 了。

字詞解釋

dress [drɛs] n. 連衣裙，洋裝　　**return** [rɪ`tɝn] v. 退回　　**purchase** [`pɝtʃəs] n. 購買，所購之物　　**shopkeeper** [`ʃɑp͵kipɚ] n. 店主　　**employee** [͵ɛmplɔɪ`i] n. 員工　　**manager** [`mænɪdʒɚ] n. （商店，公司等的）負責人，主任，經理　　**assistant**

[ə`sɪstənt] n. 助理　**clerk** [klɝk] n. 職員，店員，銷售員　**customer** [`kʌstəmɚ] n. 顧客

purchase 意思與 buy 相近，但 purchase 更加正式，一般說購買產業或大批器材或名貴古董的時候用 purchase，如果說買菜，買肉就用 buy。

19. M: Is your telephone out of order?

　　W: I don't think so.

　　M: I tried to call you this morning, but I wasn't able to get through.

　　W: You can call me on my cellphone.

　　M: In fact, I don't have your number.

Question: What is the woman probably going to do?

(A) Give the man her cellphone number

(B) Show the man her new cellphone

(C) Order some food

英文翻譯

男：妳電話壞了嗎？

女：我不這麼認為。（沒壞吧。）

男：我早上試著打電話給妳，但妳的電話一直接不通。

女：你可以打手機給我啊。

男：事實上，我沒有妳的手機號碼。

問題：女子可能會做什麼？

(A) 給男子手機號碼。

(B) 給男子看她的新手機。

(C) 點餐。

答題解說

答案：(A)。題目問的是女子「可能會要去做」的事情，屬於「推論」題型，所以答案絕對不會直接出現在對話中，必須從對話內容去判斷。本題答案線索會出現在女子的回應中。男子一開始問說「妳電話壞了嗎？」注意這裡的「電話」（telephone）是指家用電話，而從三個選項來看，(C) 的「點餐」可以直接排除，而男子最後提到「我沒有妳的電話號碼（I don't have your number.）」可推知答案就是 (A) 的「給男子手機號碼」。

破題關鍵

本題關鍵點有三個：telephone 、cellphone 和 number。須注意的是，對話中出現 get through 是指「電話接通」。

字詞解釋

out of order 故障　**through** [θru] adv.（電話）接通　**number** [`nʌmbɚ] n. 電話號碼　**order** [`ɔrdɚ] v. 點餐

相關文法或用法補充

order 在初學階段，主要必須知道的意思是「命令，點餐，訂單」。另外，「順序」也是很常見的意思。例如：I will answer your three questions in order.（我將一個個回答你這三個問題。）其中 "in order" 表示「依序」，因此，" out of order" 就是「失了次序」，用來形容機器、設備等，也就是「故障，壞掉」的意思。

20. W: Hi. Long time no see. You look different.

M: Oh? How different?

W: Errr... You're thinner and a bit more handsome. How did you make it? Go running every morning?

M: No, I go to the gym every night.

W: How can you spend money on that?!

Question: What does the man do every night?

(A) Go running

(B) Lose weight

(C) Go shopping

英文翻譯

女：好久不見。你看起來不太一樣了。

男：是嗎？哪裡不一樣？

女：呃…你瘦了一些且比較帥一點。你是怎麼做到的？每天早上跑步嗎？

男：我每天晚上去健身房。

女：你怎麼會把錢花在那上面？！

問題：男子每天晚上做什麼？

(A) 跑步

(B) 減重

(C) 購物

答案：(B)。本題是問男子「每天晚上」做什麼，所以應注意男子發言的部分。男子說 "I go to the gym every night."（我每天晚上去健身房。）然後對照三個選項，只有 (A)、(C) 是跟上健身房有關的答案。接著對話中雖然也有提到 (A) 的「跑步」，但那是在女子發言中提到的「每天早上跑步嗎？」所以答案是 (B)。

先注意題目句中的關鍵字詞 every night，接著是女子發言中的 thinner（更瘦了）以及男子的 "I goes to the gym every night."，所以不難選出 (C) Lose weight 這個答案。

different [ˋdɪfərənt] **adj.** 不同的　　**thin** [θɪn] **adj.** 瘦的　　**handsome** [ˋhænsəm] **adj.**（男子）英俊的　　**lose** [luz] **v.** 失去　　**weight** [wet] **n.** 重量

gym 是 gymnasium 的簡寫，意思是「健身房」或「體操館」。隨著現代人對健康的日益重視，gym 這個字在日常生活會話中也經常出現。一般人上健身房的方式，則以繳費當「會員」者居多。例如：I go to the gym four to five times a week.（我每周上健身房四到五次。）→ go to 可以用 hit 取代。

21. W: Excuse me. How can I get to the movie theater?
    M: You can take Bus 101. The bus stop is over there.
    W: How often does a bus come by?
    M: About every ten minutes.

    Question: What might the woman do next?

    (A) Eat lunch
    (B) Buy a movie ticket
    (C) Go to the bus stop

女：請問，我要怎麼到電影院？
男：你可以搭 101 號公車。公車站就在那裡。
女：公車多久來一班？
男：大約每十分鐘。
問題：女子接下來可能會做什麼？
(A) 吃午餐

(B) 買電影票

(C) 去公車站

答題解說

答案：(C)。題目問的是「女子接下來可能會做何事？」，可以從一開始女子詢問男子「到電影院怎麼走？」男子回答她「你可以搭 101 號公車。公車站就在那裡。」推測出女子接下來會「去公車站等公車」所以答案就是 (C) 了。選項 (B) 刻意用 movie 混淆答題。

破題關鍵

關於「接下來可能會做何事？」這種推測型題目，必須要聽清楚前後對話，比較難憑著一個關鍵字可以推測。如本題的 How...? 和 Bus 101 以及 every ten minutes，答案應該就很清楚了，但別被 (B) 選項的 movie ticket 誤導了。

字詞解釋

movie [`muvɪ] n. 電影　　**theater** [`θɪətɚ] n. 戲院　　**stop** [stɑp] n. 公車站
lunch [lʌntʃ] n. 午餐

相關文法或用法補充

考題常會出現一些比較實用的地點單字，像是：bakery 麵包店、bank 銀行、beach 海邊、bookstore 書店、church 教堂、department store 百貨公司、factory 工廠、fast-food restaurant 速食店、fire station 消防站、gym 健身房、hospital 醫院、shopping mall 購物中心、market 市場、museum 博物館、post office 郵局、police station 警局、supermarket 超市、east 東方、west 西方、south 南方、north 北方

22. M: Good morning, Mrs. Pitt. What's wrong?

　　W: I feel sick and tired. I also have a headache.

　　M: How long have you felt like this?

　　W: It started yesterday morning.

　　M: Well. Sounds to me like you have caught a cold. Just take some medicine with water every four hours.

Question: What is the woman doing?

(A) Advising a patient

(B) Taking some medicine

(C) Seeing a doctor

英文翻譯

男：早安，彼德女士。怎麼了？

女：我覺得病了而且很累。我還頭痛。

男：妳這種情況多久了？

女：昨天早上開始的。

男：嗯。在我看來，妳應該是感冒了。每四小時配開水服藥。

問題：女子正在做什麼？

(A) 告誡病人

(B) 吃藥

(C) 看醫生

答題解說

答案：(C)。本題問的是女子正在做什麼，可以從男子問女子「怎麼了？（What's wrong?）」女子回答說「我覺得病了而且很累。我還頭痛。（I feel sick and tired. I also got a headache.）」表示「身體不舒服」發生在她身上，此時還不知道女子正在做什麼。但當男子說最後一句話：「每四小時配開水服藥，可以推斷女子是病人（而男子是醫生），故女子正在看醫生，正確答案為 (C)。

破題關鍵

本題應從男子發言去判斷女子正在做什麼。從 "How long have you felt like this?" 以及 "Just take some medicine with water every four hours." 可知，女子正在看病。

字詞解釋

wrong [rɔŋ] adj. 錯誤的　**tired** [taɪrd] adj. 疲倦的　**headache** [ˋhɛdˌek] n. 頭痛
catch a cold 感冒　**medicine** [ˋmɛdəsn] n. 藥物

相關文法或用法補充

ache 是「痛」的意思，因此英文裡有一些「身體部位-ache」的組合字，像是 headache（頭疼）、backache（背痛）、stomachache（胃痛）、earache（耳痛）、toothache（牙齒痛）... 等。

23. M: Why did you move to Taipei?

    W: I got a job there.

    M: Good. Where do you live?

    W: I live with my younger sister. In Sanchong.

    M: It saves you a lot of money.

    Question: Why did the woman move to Taipei?

    (A) She wants to save money.

（B）She wanted to live with her sister.

（C）She moved to Taipei to work.

第1回
第2回
第3回
第4回
第5回
第6回
第7回
第8回
第9回
第10回

英文翻譯

男：妳為何搬到台北呢？

女：我在那兒找到工作。

男：很棒。妳住哪呢？

女：我和妹妹一起住。在三重。

男：那你可以省很多錢。

問題：女子為何搬到高雄？

（A）她想省錢。

（B）她想要照顧妹妹。

（C）她搬到台北去工作。

答題解說

答案：（C）。本題的對話內容有點繁瑣，三個選項雖然很容易看懂意思，不過還沒聽到錄音播放之前，可以推測出「某種原因」因此，建議先看選項，絕對可以掌握對話中的關鍵字。本題主要關鍵就在是否聽出且聽懂 got a new job（找到新工作），因為這是搬到台北最大的原因。

破題關鍵

本題關鍵語句是 got a job。其餘選項的 "save money" 及 "live with her sister" 都是刻意誤導答題的設計。

字詞解釋

save [sev] v. 節省　**take care of**.... 照顧～

相關文法或用法補充

「找到工作」的「找」，動詞用 get/find/locate。不過要注意的是，「找到」是過去的事情，應用過去式。所以應該說成 I got/found/located a job.。若要表達「我正在找工作」，要說 "I am trying to find a job." 或是 "I am looking for a job."，也不能說 "I am getting/finding/locating a new job."。

24. M: Emma, What's going on between you and Maggie?

　　W: She is always so serious. I found I can't live with her anymore.

　　M: What did you tell her?

　　W: I told her if she could smile more, she could be more popular with people.

M: No wonder she looked blue all day.

Question: What are they talking about?
(A) How to be popular with people
(B) Their friend
(C) Their own plans

男：艾瑪，你和梅姬之間發生了什麼事？
女：她好嚴肅。我發現我無法和她住在一起。
男：妳跟她說了什麼？
女：我告訴她，如果她能多一點笑容，那麼她才會更受人們歡迎。
男：難怪她一整天悶悶不樂。
問題：他們在談論什麼？
(A) 如何受到人們歡迎
(B) 他們的朋友
(C) 他們自己的計畫

答題解說

答案：(B)。本題目是「對話內容的主旨為何」的題型。男子第一句話說「你和梅姬之間發生了什麼事？」接下來的話題還是集中在梅姬身上，包括為何不想跟她住在一起、她太嚴肅、應多一點笑容、她一整天悶悶不樂等。所以正確答案為(B) Their friend。

破題關鍵

本題關鍵語句是男子第一句話 "What's going on between you and Maggie?"。選項 (A) 刻意用 "popular with people" 來混淆答題，而 (C) Their own plans 是完全沒提到的事。

字詞解釋

serious [ˋsɪrɪəs] **adj.** 嚴肅的　　**popular** [ˋpɑpjələ˗] **adj.** 受歡迎的
no wonder... 難怪～　　**blue** [blu] **adj.** 悶悶不樂的

相關文法或用法補充

go on 這個片語有幾種意思：

❶ 繼續：可以用來表示「繼續做」、「繼續討論話題」等等。例如：If he goes on like this, you will lose your job. （如果你繼續這樣做，你工作將不保。）

❷ 流逝：通常對象是「時間」、「經過」等等。例如：They may forget each other as the day goes on. （隨著時間流逝，他們可能會忘了對方。）

❸ 發生：通常表示「事情進行如何」、「發生」。例如：What's going on between Tom and Anna?（Tom 和 Anna 之間怎麼了？）

25. M: I was late for work today.

W: Why is that?

M: I got up late and missed the bus. So I took a taxi.

W: How much did it cost you?

M: Three hundred dollars.

Question: How does the man usually go to work?

(A) By taxi

(B) By bus

(C) On foot

英文翻譯

男：我今天上班遲到了。

女：為什麼？

男：我太晚起床且錯過公車了。所以我搭計程車。

女：那要花多少錢？

男：三百元。

問題：男子通常如何去上班？

(A) 搭計程車

(B) 搭公車去

(C) 走路

答題解說

答案：(B)。本題是問男通常如何去上班（How... usually go to work?），而對話中提到了 bus，也提到 taxi，這是刻意造成混淆的題型設計。當然，選項 (C) 可以先排除掉。男子第二次發言說 "I got up late and missed the bus. So I took a taxi."，表示他平時是坐公車去上班的，今日因為太晚起床且錯過公車，所以搭計程車，故正確答案為 (B)。

破題關鍵

題目句的 usually 是第一個關鍵，第二個關鍵是 "got up late and missed the bus"，「錯過公車」就等於「平時坐公車」的意思。

字詞解釋

late [let] **adj.** 遲到　**miss** [mɪs] **v.** 錯過　**cost** [kɔst] **v.** 要價　**on foot phr.** 步行

第 1 回
第 2 回
第 3 回
第 4 回
第 5 回
第 6 回
第 7 回
第 8 回
第 9 回
第 10 回

常見交通工具（transportation）有 high Speed Rail（高鐵）、car（汽車）、bicycle／bike（腳踏車）、motorcycle/motorbike（摩托車）、taxi（計程車）、bus（公車）、truck（卡車）、van（箱形車）、SUV（休旅車）、airplane／plane（飛機）、train（火車）、subway（地鐵）、MRT（捷運）…等。而搭乘交通工具的表達法，主要是「by + 交通工具」以及「take + 交通工具」

第四部分 短文聽解

For question number 26, please look at the three pictures.

Question number 26: Listen to the following short story. Which picture best describes the short story?

Long ago, Frank and his wife lived in a small village. Their children studied in town and came back home every weekend. He worked as a farmer. He grew some vegetables and carrots on his farm. He kept a dog as a pet. He got up at six and went to bed before 11 p.m. Frank and his wife enjoyed their life very much. He worked hard and felt happy every day.

請看以下三張圖。並仔細聆聽以下簡短故事。哪一張圖最能夠表現出這則小故事？
很久以前，佛蘭克和老婆住在一個小村莊。他們的孩子都在鎮上上學且每個週末會回家。他是個農夫。他在農場上種了一些蔬菜和胡蘿蔔。他養了一隻狗當寵物。他每天六點鐘起床，晚上 11 點之前就寢。佛蘭克和他太太非常享受自己的生活。他每天努力工作，並覺得很快樂。

答案：(A)。題目要問的是故事內容符合哪一張圖，而播放內容主要是關於一對農夫與農婦在田野種蔬菜和胡蘿蔔，且養了一隻狗當寵物，所以圖（A）是最符合

敘述的答案。圖 (B) 乍看之下也很接近答案，但它呈現的是，男子在澆花，女子在種花。圖 (C) 中的男女在溜狗，是明顯錯誤的答案。

第
1
回
第
2
回
第
3
回
第
4
回
第
5
回
第
6
回
第
7
回
第
8
回
第
9
回
第
10
回

破題關鍵

從三張圖可以看出一樣的地方是：一對夫婦在村落（village）中，而不一樣的地方是：「種植什麼」（遛狗的圖 C 可先排除）。如果可以聽出其中的關鍵字詞 "vegetables and carrots"，基本上就不會去選 (B) 了。

字詞解釋

village [`vɪlɪdʒ] n. 村莊　　**farmer** [`fɑrmə-] n. 農夫　　**grow** [gro] v. 種植

vegetable [`vɛdʒətəbl] n. 蔬菜　　**carrot** [`kærət] n. 蘿蔔　　**pet** [pɛt] n. 寵物

enjoy [ɪn`dʒɔɪ] v. 享受

相關文法或用法補充

keep 有「保持，使～繼續」之意，其主要用法：

❶ keep 當「使～繼續」之意。句型：S + keep + O. + O.C.（受詞補語）。例如：He kept Kelly waiting on purpose.（他故意讓 Kelly 一直等。）

❷ keep 當「保持～（做某事）」之意。句型：S + keep + Ving。例如：The student kept asking the teacher silly questions.（這個學生一直繼續問老師一些蠢問題。）

For question number 27, please look at the three pictures.

Question number 27: Listen to the following announcement. Where can you possibly hear it?

Good afternoon ladies and gentlemen, this is the service center. We are looking for a little girl, aged about 5. She wears a white sweater and a black skirt. Her name is Sandy. She came to the amusement park with her parents, and they are now here waiting anxiously for good news. Her father said she was last seen at the Merry-go-round. If you see the girl, please take her to the service center. Or if you, the little girl, hears this, just come here to your parents. Thank you so much.

請看以下三張圖。並仔細聆聽以下宣布內容。你可能在哪裡聽到這樣的廣播？

午安,各位女士及先生,這裡是服務中心。我們正在尋找一位約五歲、穿著白色毛衣及黑色裙子的小女孩。她的名字叫仙蒂。她是和父母一起來遊樂園的,而他們現在正在這裡焦急地等待好消息。她的父親說,最後看見她的地方是在「旋轉木馬」旁。如果您有看到這個女孩,請將她帶到服務台來。或者如果小女來有聽到廣播,請到我們這邊來找你父母。非常感謝。

答案:(C)。題目要問的是「可能在哪裡聽到這樣的廣播?」然後,請仔細看過三張圖之後,在錄音播放內容裡,聽出「關鍵字」就是得分之鑰,包括 service center(服務中心)、amusement park(遊樂園)、Merry-go-round(旋轉木馬)。圖 (A) 是在遊覽車上,不會有 service center,所以可先排除掉。圖 (B) 是在大賣場或超市,即使不知道 amusement 這個字的意思,至少看到 park(公園,園區)應該知道是在室外吧!所以 (B) 也是錯的。那麼答案就是 (C) 了,即使你也不知道 Merry-go-round 是指什麼。

這則廣播內容的關鍵字詞是 park,可以知道不會是在室內,而三張圖只有 (C) 是在戶外,所以答案當然是 (C) 了。

gentleman [ˈdʒɛntlmən] **n.** 紳士　**announcement** [əˈnaʊnsmənt] **n.**通知,宣布
look for 尋找　**sweater**[ˈswɛtə] **n.** 毛衣　**skirt** [skɝt] **n.** 裙子
***anxiously** [ˈæŋkʃəslɪ] **adv.** 焦急地,擔憂地　***Merry-go-round** 旋轉木馬
***amusement park** 遊樂園

「if 條件句 + 祈使句」的用法相當常見,屬於「假設直述」的用法。例如:Pick up the phone if it rings.(如果電話響了就接起來。)這時的 if 也可以用 when 取代。」

For question number 28, please look at the three pictures.

Question number 28: Please Listen to the following short talk. Which country does the speaker plan to visit next year?

Look at this photo. I took it when I was in Rome last year. I had dinner with an Italian friend of mine and it ended at almost midnight. I hope to visit Europe again next year. Both England and France are good choices, but I think I will choose London because I have already been to Paris once.

第 1 回
第 2 回
第 3 回
第 4 回
第 5 回
第 6 回
第 7 回
第 8 回
第 9 回
第 10 回

中文翻譯

請看以下三張圖。並仔細聆聽以下簡短談話。說話者計畫明年去哪個國家？
看這張照片。這是我去年在羅馬拍的。我跟我一位義大利籍的朋友吃晚餐，且幾乎到半夜才結束。我希望明年再去一趟歐洲。英國和法國都是很好的選擇，不過我想我會選擇倫敦。我已經去過巴黎一次了。

答題解說

答案：（C）。題目問的是說話者計畫明年去哪個國家，談話中提到，希望明年再去一趟歐洲…我想我會選擇倫敦。所以正確答案為（C）。

破題關鍵

首先應注意題目句的關鍵詞：「明年」（next year）。雖然圖（B）的「巴黎（Paris）」及圖（A）的「羅馬（Rome）」都有在談話中提到，但這是短文聽解考題慣用的設計方式，要注意題目句的「時間點」。

字詞解釋

next year phr. 明年　　**Italian** [ɪˋtæljən] adj. 義大利的　　**midnight** [ˋmɪd͵naɪt] n. 午夜，子夜　　**Europe** [ˋjʊrəp] n. 歐洲　　**England** [ˋɪŋglənd] n. 英國　　**France** [fræns] n. 法國　　**choose** [tʃuz] v. 選擇　　**London** [ˋlʌndən] n. 倫敦　　**once** [wʌns] adv. 一次，一回

相關文法或用法補充

「照片」可以用 photo 或 picture，而「拍照」要用動詞 take，「幫某人拍照」的介系詞可以用 of 或 for。例如：

❶ Excuse me. Could you take a picture for/of us?
= Excuse me. Could you help us take a picture?（不好意思，可以幫我們拍張照嗎？）

❷ Could you take a photo of me with the Eiffel Tower?（可以幫我跟艾菲爾鐵塔合照嗎？）

For question number 29, please look at the three pictures.

Question number 29: Listen to the following phone message. What is Larry probably going to do later?

Hi, Larry. I've just made several calls to you, but you didn't answer your phone. I thought you should be taking your swimming lesson. I called to hold a birthday party for you. I know today is your big day, and we'll hold a party tonight at Molly's place. You MUST come. It will begin at 7:00 P.M. It's important for you to be there on time. Please give me a call as soon as you hear about this message. Thank you.

英文翻譯

請看以下三張圖。並仔細聆聽以下電話留言。萊瑞接下來可能會做什麼？
嗨，萊瑞。我下午打了幾通電話給你，但你都沒有接聽電話。我想你應該是在上游泳課程。我打電話是要幫你辦個慶生派對。我知道今天是你的大日子。我們在茉莉的家舉辦一場派對。你一定要來。派對會在晚上七點開始。準時出現對你而言很重要。請盡快打電話給我。謝謝。

答題解說

答案：(B)。題目要問的是受話者（Larry）晚點或即將「去做什麼」，播放內容提及有關「生日會」、「盡快打電話給我…」，也就是回電給留言者。圖 (A) 的慶生蠟燭，以及圖 (C) 的游泳，雖然都有在留言訊息中提到，但都不是 Larry 稍後（later）會去做的事。

第 1 回
第 2 回
第 3 回
第 4 回
第 5 回
第 6 回
第 7 回
第 8 回
第 9 回
第 10 回

破題關鍵

最後一句是關鍵：請盡快打電話給我（Please give me a call as soon as possible.）。所以 Larry 接下來要做的事，就如同圖（B）所示，打電話給朋友。

字詞解釋

later [ˋletɚ] adv. 較晚地，後來　　**hold** [hold] v. 舉辦　　**soon** [sun] adv. 即刻
possible [ˋpɑsəbl] adj. 可能的　　**give a call to**... 打電話給～

相關文法或用法補充

as soon as possible 是指「盡速」，非常實用的一個片語。句型是：as... as possible（盡可能…），相關用法還有：as far as possible（盡可能遠的）。但須注意的是，as...as 之間要用形容詞原形，不用比較級。例如：Please send an e-mail to Molly as soon as possible.（請盡速寄這封電子郵件給 Molly。）

For question number 30, please look at the three pictures.

Question number 30: Listen to the following talk. What did Roger buy this morning?

  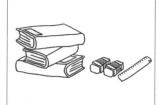

Hi, my name is Roger. I went shopping with Kelly last night. We met at the bookstore at 8 p.m. I bought three books and two erasers. Kelly bought some notebooks and three rulers. Rulers are on sale now, so she bought three. After I went home, I found that I forgot to buy a ruler for my younger sister, so she was angry with me.

英文翻譯

請看以下三張圖。並仔細聆聽播放的談話內容。Roger 昨晚買了些什麼？
嗨，我的名字叫 Roger。昨晚我和 Kelly 一起去購物。我們約晚上八點在書店碰面。我買了三本書和兩塊橡皮擦。Kelly 買了一些筆記本和兩把尺。尺現在有特價，所以她買了三把。回家後，我發現我忘了買尺給妹妹，所以她不太高興。

答案：(A)。談話內容中表示，Roger 昨天買了三本書和兩塊橡皮擦（three books and two erasers）。而 Kelly 買了一些筆記本和兩把尺（some notebooks and two rulers），如圖 (B) 所示。所以顯然答案就是 (A) 了。雖然圖 (C) 中也有橡皮擦（erasers），但 Roger 昨晚並沒買尺，所以圖 (C) 是不正確的。

破題關鍵

首先，第一個關鍵點是題目句的 Roger（而不是 Kelly），接著應注意說話者是以第一人稱的我來發言，所以 I bought... 就成了關鍵要點。

字詞解釋

go shopping phr. 去購物　**bookstore** [`bʊkˌstor] n. 書局　**eraser** [ɪ`resɚ] n. 橡皮擦　**notebook** [`notˌbʊk] n. 筆記本　**ruler** [`rulɚ] n. 尺　**younger sister** phr. 妹妹　**be angry with**... phr. 生～（某人）的氣

相關文法或用法補充

as soon as possible 是指「盡速」，非常實用的一個片語。句型是：as... as possible（盡可能 …），相關用法還有：as far as possible（盡可能遠的）。但須注意的是，as...as 之間要用形容詞原形，不用比較級。例如：Please send an e-mail to Molly as soon as possible.（請盡速寄這封電子郵件給 Molly。）

1. Neil didn't go home until 11 p.m. His parents were _____ about him.
（Neil 昨天晚上十一點才回家。他父母很擔心他。）

(A) worried　(B) embarrassed　(C) glad　(D) sad

答題解說

答案：(A)。由前後語意可以知道是「晚回家造成父母親擔心」的意思，因此 (A) worried（擔心）是正確答案。(B) embarrassed（尷尬）、(C) glad（高興）、(D) sad（悲傷）都與語意不符。

破題關鍵

本題應掌握的關鍵是「因果關係」。第一句是「因」（didn't go home until 11 p.m.），第二句是「果」（...parents were worried...）。

字詞解釋

not... until... phr. 直到～才～　　**worried**[ˋwɝɪd] adj. 擔心

相關文法或用法補充

not until 的意思為「直到～才」，而 "not until" 有「倒裝句」及以 it 當虛主詞的用法。例如：Not until the girlfriend went into the house did Jack leave.（Jack 一直到女友進到屋子後才離開）

2. Christmas is _____ the corner. Let's buy some presents this weekend.
（聖誕節即將來臨。我們這週末去買些禮物吧。）

(A) about　(B) on　(C) around　(D) at

答題解說

答案：(C)。本題大意是「聖誕節 _____ 。」因為後面接著要去買禮物，推知應該「快來了」。片語 around the corner 字面意思是「在角落附近」，也就是指「即將到來」。故選項(C)是正確答案。

破題關鍵

本題關鍵是對於片語 "around the corner" 的認知。而 Christmas 是個抽象名詞，corner（角落）是具體名詞，當然不可能用 on 來表示「在角落」。其餘選項的 about 與 at 都不會與 corner 搭配使用。

Christmas[ˋkrɪsməs] **n.** 聖誕節　　**corner** [ˋkɔrnɚ] **n.** 角落　　**present** [ˋprɛznt] **n.** 禮物

let 是使役動詞，指「令某人做某種行為或動作」。使役動詞一般有：let、make、have、get... 等等。使役動詞重要句型如下：

❶ S + 使役 V + 人 + 原形 V。例：He made her clean the classroom.（他叫她打掃教室。）→ 原形 V 指「受詞主動的行為」

❷ S + 使役 V + 物 + 過去分詞。例：She has her dress washed.（她將她的洋裝送洗了。）→ 過去分詞指「受詞被動的行為」

❸ 人 + be 動詞 + 使役動詞的 P.P. + to-V（使役動詞的被動語態）例：Helen was made to paint the walls.（Helen 被叫去油漆牆壁。）

3. **The manager looked very serious. He had to make a difficult _____.**
   （經理看起來很嚴肅。他必須做出困難的決定。）

   (A) decision　　(B) experience　　(C) wish　　(D) example

答案：(A)。句子大意是「經理看起來很嚴肅，因為必須做出困難的——」，故正確答案應為 (A) decision，來表達「做出困難的決定」。(B) experience、(C) wish、(D) example 意思分別是「經驗」、「希望」、「範例」。

"make a decision" 是常見固定用語，表示「做決定」。

manager [ˋmænɪdʒɚ] **n.** 經理　　**serious** [ˋsɪrɪəs] **adj.** 嚴肅的　　**difficult** [ˋdɪfəˌkəlt] **adj.** 困難的

連綴動詞（look、feel、sound、smell...）後面接形容詞的用法，屬於「S + V + SC」的句型，也就是說，"The manager looked" 是一個不完整的句子，後面一定還要有主詞補語（名詞或形容詞）才行。另外，與連綴動詞概念有些類似的感官動詞則運用於「S + V + O + OC」的句型，例如：He looked at /see David walk into her room.（他看見大衛走進她房間。）以「看」的動詞而言，通常運用在「S + V + SC」的是 look，在「S + V + O + OC」的是 see。同樣，以「聽」來說，前者多用 sound，後者多用 hear。因此，要分辨是連綴動詞還是感官動詞，可由後面接的是主詞補語還是受詞來判斷。

4. Wendy used to be _____ when she was little. She looks a lot slimmer now.（溫蒂小時候身材豐腴。她現在看起來苗條多了。）

(A) slender　(B) chubby　(C) strange　(D) attractive

答題解說

答案：(B)。句子大意是「以前胖胖的，現在——」，所以直覺上應該會選表示「胖嘟嘟的」的答案，故正確答案為(B) chubby；其餘選項的(A) slender、(C) strange、(D) attractive 意思分別是「纖瘦」、「陌生的，奇怪的」、「有吸引力的」。

破題關鍵

關鍵字是第二句最後的比較級形容詞 slimmer（原級是 slimmer），再加上一開始的 "used to-V" 表示「過去曾經～」。顯然空格應是與 slim（纖瘦的）相反意思的形容詞。

字詞解釋

used to-V 過去曾經／習慣～　**a lot adv.** 非常（用來修飾比較級）　**slimmer** [ˋslɪmɚ] **adj.** 較苗條的　**slender** [ˋslɛndɚ] **adj.** 修長的，苗條的　**chubby** [ˋtʃʌbɪ] **adj.** 圓胖的　**strange** [strendʒ] **adj.** 奇怪的，陌生的　**attractive** [əˋtræktɪv] **adj.** 有吸引力的

相關文法或用法補充

除了 chubby、slim、slender 之外，還有哪些單字可以形容身材呢？例如：fat 胖的（通常有貶損意味）、heavy 重的、tall 高大的、short 矮的、charming 迷人的、skinny 皮包骨的、good-looking 好看的、in good shape（曲線窈窕）

5. He thinks eating vegetables _____ good for health.（他認為吃蔬菜對健康有益）

(A) has　(B) have　(C) is　(D) are

答題解說

答案：(C)。主詞是 Eating vegetables（吃蔬菜），為動名詞當主詞，動詞應用單數，所以(B)、(D)可直接排除。空格後的 good 是形容詞，不可能用 has 這個動詞，所以(C) is 是正確答案。

破題關鍵

動名詞當主詞，應視為第三稱單數，這是個重要的文法。本題空格前 vegetables 用複數名詞，刻意誤導考生去選 are。

onion [ˋʌnjən] **n.** 洋蔥　　**potato** [pəˋteto] **n.** 洋芋　　**vegetable** [ˋvɛdʒətəbl] **n.** 蔬菜

「動名詞」當主詞用，也可以用「不定詞」代替，同樣應視為第三稱單數，動詞要加 -s。例如本句的 "Eating vegetables is good for health." = "To eat vegetables is good for health."

6. **The Art Museum _____ soon. We look forward to visiting it.**（藝術博物館即將落成。我們期待去參觀這間博物館。）

    (A) will build (B) is building (C) has been built (D) will be built

答案：(D)。主詞是 Art Museum，所以不會「自己蓋房子」，因此不能用主動，選項 (A) will build 與 (B) is building 可直接刪除。再從時間副詞 soon 來看，當然只有 (D) will be built 是正確的。

從四個選項來看，這是考「主／被動」+「動詞時態」的問題。關鍵是 Art Museum 與動詞 build 的主被動關係，以及 soon 這個時間副詞。

museum [mjuˋzɪəm] **n.** 博物館 **look forward to** 期待

"look forward to"（期待）後面要接 V-ing 作為其受詞，而另一個表示「期待」的動詞，expect，後面要接 to-V。例如： We look forward to visiting it. = We expect to visit it.

7. **Frank looks very happy. He's been _____ by the University of Seattle.**（佛蘭克看起來很快樂。他已經獲得西雅圖大學許可入學。）

    (A) allowed　(B) quit　(C) arrived　(D) accepted

答案：(D)。句子大意是「看起來很快樂，因為已經被西雅圖大學──。」符合句意的是 (A) allowed（准許）以及(D) accepted（接受）。不過 allow 的用法是「allow + 人 + to-V」，轉成被動式的話，後面還是要有 to-V 這部分，但本句「by + N」後面就結束了，顯然不能選 (A)。故正確答案為 (D)。(C) arrived（抵達）沒有被動式的用法。

破題關鍵

本題第一句也是參考關鍵，否則 (B) quit 也會是答案。了解整體句意之後，再根據觀點從 allow 與 accept 這兩個動詞選出最正確的答案。

字詞解釋

accept [ək`sɛpt] v. 接受　**university** [ˌjunə`vɝsətɪ] n. 大學　**allow** [ə`laʊ] v. 允許，准許

相關文法或用法補充

文法中有所謂「完全及物」與「不完全及物」動詞，雖然看似複雜，但基本上是來自「五大句型」的概念。而有些動詞具有這兩種動詞形態的用法，以 allow 這個動詞為例。如果主詞是「事物」，那麼 allow 就是「完全及物」，可直接改為被動式。例如：Swimming is not allowed here.（這裡不可以游泳。）但若主詞是「人」，改為被動式之後，必須再有補語，才能讓語意完整。例如，你就不能說「你不被允許。」因為顯然話還沒講完吧！應該說「你不被允許在此抽菸。」（You are not allowed to smoke here.）

8. The writer _____ name is Beth just bought a new apartment.（這個叫作 Beth 的作家剛剛買了一間公寓。）

   (A) who　(B) whose　(C) what　(D) that

答題解說

答案：(B)。本題考的是「關係代名詞」用法。當然，關係代名詞也有主格、受格、所有格。所以空格後面的單字是主要答題參考指標。空格後 "name is Beth" 是個完整句子（有主詞、動詞、補語），所以空格應填入「關係代名詞所有格」whose。

破題關鍵

先看過四個選項，知道要考關係代名詞，然後看到 writer 和 name 之後，就可以選出 (B) whose 這個答案。

相關文法或用法補充

whose 也可以當疑問詞，引導直接問句或間接問句。但須記得，它的性質為形容詞，後面接名詞。例如：

❶ Whose socks are these?（這是誰的襪子？）
❷ I don't know whose socks these are.（我不知道這些是誰的襪子。）

457

9. **Rita lost her money. She borrowed money _____ her classmate.**（Rita 錢不見了。她向她的同學借錢。）

   (A) to　(B) from　(C) for　(D) by

   答案：(B)。句子大意是「她『向』她的同學借錢」，所以正確答案應為 from。空格後面的名詞為單數（her classmate），是指「被借錢對象」，因此不可能接介系詞 to。另外，選項 (C) 與 (D) 雖然看似沒問題，但不符合語意與邏輯。

   破題關鍵

   這題要考的是關鍵字 borrow 搭配的介系詞。中文說「向某人借錢」，英文的思考方向是「從～借錢」，搭配 from（來自）。

   字詞解釋

   borrow [`baro] v. 借來

   相關文法或用法補充

   「借錢」，也是常考題型之一。關於借錢的重點如下。

   ❶ borrow money from + 人（向某人借錢）。例如：He has borrowed ten thousand dollars from his roommate.（他已經向室友借了一萬元了。）

   ❷ lend money to + 人（把錢借給某人）例如：He lent some money to his girlfriend.（他借了一些錢給女友。）

   → lend 動詞三態：lend/lent/lent）

10. **Vicky found her bicycle _____ this morning.**（薇琪今天早上發現她的腳踏車被偷了。）

    (A) stolen　(B) stealing　(C) stole　(D) steal

    答題解說

    答案：(A)。從四個選項可知，句子大意是「發現她的腳踏車被偷了」，所以過去分詞的 (A) stolen 是正確答案。

    破題關鍵

    關鍵在於 found（發現）的受詞是「物」（bicycle），與「偷」這個動詞之間的語意關連，因為腳踏車不會自己去做偷這個動作，所以應選被動式。

    字詞解釋

    steal [stil] v. 偷竊（動詞三態為 steal/stole/stolen）

相關文法或用法補充

find 這個動詞當「發現」的意思時，後面接「受詞 + 受詞補語」。此時受詞補語可能是 V-ing 也可能是 P.P.。但如果是「找到」的意思，後面接受詞之後語意就算完整了。

第二部分　段落填空

Questions 11-14

Stanley took a three-day trip alone to eastern Taiwan. He **caught** an early train at 8:00 o'clock. When he arrived at his first station, it was already 11:30 A.M. The weather was pretty good. **It was a sunny day.** Then he took a walk to a very famous street vendor and enjoy his **delicious** lunch. It tasted so good and cost only one hundred dollars. After that, he rented a bicycle and rode it carefreely to a hot spot where rice fields were around. There were not many people **because** it wasn't a holiday. He decided to spend the whole afternoon hiding himself in such a beautiful nature.

中文翻譯

　　史丹利獨自去東台灣旅遊三天。他搭乘一早八點整的火車。當他抵達他的第一站時，已經是上午 11 點半了。當天天氣很好，是個晴朗的日子。然後他走路到一家非常有名的攤販並享用他的午餐。口味極佳，卻只要一百元。在這之後，他租了一輛自行車，悠哉地騎到一個四處都是稻田的有名景點。不過當時人不多，因為是非假日的時間。他決定一整個下午將自己藏身在這美麗的大自然中。

答題解說

11. 答案：(B)。空格前是主詞 He，後面動詞的受詞是 an early train at 8:00 o'clock，所以符合本句文意的是 (A) drove 與 (B) caught，但第一句提到 Stanley took a three-day trip alone...，顯然他不是火車司機吧！故正確答案為 (B)。

12. 答案：(D)。這是要挑選一個句子、子句或句子的一部分放入空格後，確認空格前後和空格句之間的連接關係，是否讓句意顯得自然通順。空格前面句子提到「當天天氣很好。」後面句子提到「然後他走路到一家非常有名的攤販並享用他的午餐。」顯然填入「當天是個晴朗的日子。」是最能合理地連接前後兩句的答案。以下是其餘錯誤選項句子的翻譯：
(A) 他看見許多人在那裡騎單車。
(B) 但是他想休息一下。
(C) 但是突然下雨了。

459

13. 答案：(A)。空格後是 lunch，但光從這句仍無法確應用哪個形容詞來形容午餐，因此要繼續往下找線索，下一句提到 It tasted so good and cost only one hundred dollars.（口味極佳，卻只要一百元。）因此要表達的是「美味的又便宜的」，故正確答案為 (A) delicious。

14. 答案：(C)。四個選項是不同意思的連接詞，所以應根據前後文句意判斷。句意是：「…當時人不多，…是非假日的時間」，兩者之間有因果關係，因此正確答案為 (C) because。

11. 從四個選項可知，要填入一個與其後受詞中的 train 搭配的動詞。catch a train 是「趕上火車」的意思，為固定用語。

12. 空格後面的文意是本題的關鍵。其中提到「當時人不多，因為是非假日的時間。」所以 (A) 是錯誤的；而 (B)、(C) 的「他想休息一下」、「突然下雨了」與後面的「享用午餐」、「租了一輛自行車，悠哉地騎到…」都是不自然的連結。

13. 四個選項都能用來形容 lunch。此時，先參考其後句子或最近的句子來判斷，就能找出正確答案。

14. 空格前的 "not many people" 以及空格後的 "it wasn't a holiday" 是關鍵語句，可推知前面是「果」，後面是「因」。

already [ɔl`rɛdɪ] **adv.** 已經　　**weather** [`wɛðɚ] **n.**天氣　　**sunny** [`sʌnɪ] **adj.** 晴朗的　　**street vendor** 街頭攤販　　**delicious** [dɪ`lɪʃəs] **adj.** 美味的　　**famous** [`feməs] **adj.** 著名的　　**restaurant** [`rɛstərənt] **n.**餐廳　　**taste** [test] **v.** 嘗起來　　**rent** [rɛnt] **v.** 租賃　　***carefreely** [`kɛr,frilɪ] **adv.** 自在地，悠閒地　　**hot spot** **phr.** 熱門景點　　**decide** [dɪ`saɪd] **v.** 決定

11. 「搭乘」交通工具的動詞，通常用 take，或是「by + 交通工具」表示，而「catch + 交通工具」是「趕搭～」的意思。

12. 天氣相關表達，除了可用 The weather is ... 之外，也可以用 It is +描寫天氣的形容詞。如 rainy、stormy、snowy、sunny、windy... 等。

13. terrible 可用來形容「食物」，除了可以表達食物「難吃」之外，還可以形容外表「糟透的」、電影「很難看」、服裝「嚇人的」…，算是非常多元化的單字。

14. although（雖然）用來連接語氣轉折的兩句、when（當）用於表示事情發生的同時。if（如果）用於用來表示「條件」，且涉及的「假設語氣」是文法中的一大重點。

第 1 回
第 2 回
第 3 回
第 4 回
第 5 回
第 6 回
第 7 回
第 8 回
第 9 回
第 10 回

Questions 15-18

Many people like to go shopping. It makes them **feel** good, but sometimes there might be bad experience. Some people feel bored during the holidays, so they decide to go shopping in a department store, hypermarket..., etc. **Take Brad's wife for example.** She is a housewife and in fact, she has no hobbies, except window shopping. Sometimes Brad goes with her. Usually he buys things he wants quickly, but his wife spends much time **thinking** about whether to buy something or not. It wastes a lot of time to Brad. Since Brad's wife can't make a **quick** decision, sometimes they argue with each other on the street.

中文翻譯

　　許多人喜歡購物。購物使他們感覺良好，但有時也可能有不好的經驗。有些人在假日時會感到無聊，因此他們決定去百貨公司、大賣場等地方逛街。舉布萊德的太太為例。她是個家庭主婦且其實她沒有嗜好，除了逛街之外。有時候布萊德會跟她一起去。通常他很快就買了想買的東西，但他太太卻會花很多時間考慮要不要買。布萊德覺得那很浪費時間。由於他太太總是無法迅速做出決定，有時候他們會在街上爭執。

答題解說

15. 答案：（C）。本題考的是使役動詞 make 的基本句型：make + 受詞 + 原形動詞。選項中只有（C）feel 是原形動詞。

16. 答案：（B）。這是要挑選一個句子、子句或句子的一部分放入空格後，確認空格前後和空格句之間的連接關係，是否讓句意顯得自然通順。空格前面是「有些人在假日時會感到無聊，因此他們…」，後面這句是「她是個家庭主婦且…」顯然兩句中間必須有個連接「有些人」與「她」的句子。故正確答案為（B）Take Brad's wife for example.（舉布萊德的太太為例。）以下是其餘錯誤選項句子的翻譯：
（A）但布萊德的太太非常愛逛街。
（C）他們可以在那兒撿到一些便宜。
（D）有時候購物是個好嗜好。

17. 答案：（A）。句意是，「他太太卻會花很多時間考慮要不要買」，「花時間做某事」可以用「spend time + Ving」表示，所以應選 Ving 的（A）thinking。

18. 答案：（D）。首先，就結構而言，選項中四個答案都有可能。因此必須在前後文找線索：It wastes a lot of time to Brad.（布萊德覺得那很浪費時間。）所以句意是，因為浪費時間，所以應迅速做決定，故正確答案是（D）quick。make a quick decision 表示「迅速做出決定」。

15. 從四個選項可先判斷要考同一個動詞的不同詞性或時態，接著就是找影響此動詞產生變化的關鍵字詞，也就是使役動詞 make。

16. 空格後的 "She is..." 與空格前一句 "Some people..." 似乎完全沒有任何關聯，所以要將兩個完全沒有關聯的句子連結在一起的，只有「拿…做例子」的（B）是最適合的答案。

17. 從四個選項可先判斷要考同一個動詞的不同詞性或時態，接著就是找影響此動詞產生變化的關鍵字詞，也就是表「花費」的動詞 spend。

18. 從前文的 spend much time 以及 a waste of time 來看，這個句子要表達的是「迅速做決定」。

字詞解釋

experience [ɪk`spɪrɪəns] n. 經驗，體驗　**bored** [bord] adj. 感到無趣的　**\*hypermarket** [ˌhaɪpɚ`mɑrkɪt] 大賣場　**take... for example** 以～為例　**housewife** [`haʊsˌwaɪf] n. 家庭主婦　**in fact** 事實上　**hobby** [`hɑbɪ] n. 嗜好　**window shopping** phr. 逛街　**whether... or not** 是否要～　**waste** [west] v. 浪費　**decision** [dɪ`sɪʒən] n. 決定　**thoughtful** [`θɔtfəl] aj. 深思的，考慮周到的　**similar** [`sɪmələ] adj. 類似的

相關文法或用法補充

15. 使役動詞主要有 have, make, let。對於「使役動詞」的用法，只要記住 Let's go. = Let us go.（我們走吧！）這個句子即可。也就是「使役動詞 + 受詞 + 原形動詞」。

16. 寫作時常需要舉例來為自己的論述佐證，可以用 for example/instance、take... for example/instance、such as、like 來表達。

17. spend 這個動詞的用法是「人+ spend + 時間/錢 + V-ing」，或者「人+ spend + 時間/錢+ on + 名詞」，表示「某人花了多少錢或時間在做某事」，或「某人花了多少錢或時間在某事上」。過去式和過去分詞都是 spent。

18. make a decision 後面可以接不定詞（to-V）來表示「決定～（做某事）」。另外，從這個片語可以衍生 decision-maker 這個複合名詞，意思是「決策者」。

中文翻譯

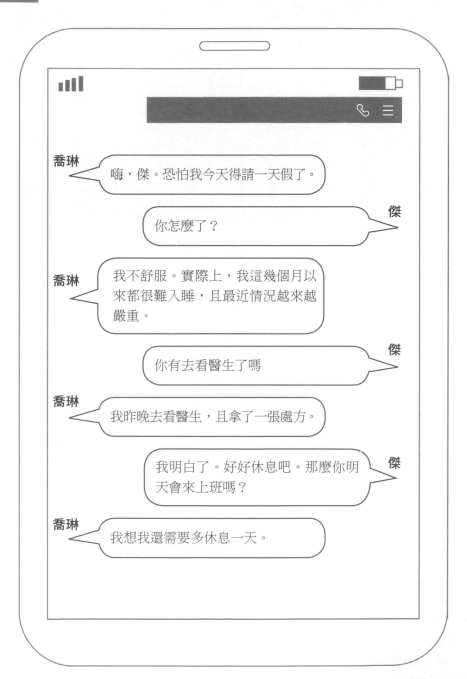

喬琳：嗨，傑。恐怕我今天得請一天假了。

傑：你怎麼了？

喬琳：我不舒服。實際上，我這幾個月以來都很難入睡，且最近情況越來越嚴重。

傑：你有去看醫生了嗎

喬琳：我昨晚去看醫生，且拿了一張處方。

傑：我明白了。好好休息吧。那麼你明天會來上班嗎？

喬琳：我想我還需要多休息一天。

第1回
第2回
第3回
第4回
第5回
第6回
第7回
第8回
第9回
第10回

陳醫師給了喬琳這張一星期藥量的處方籤。

健康醫院

◇ 名字：王喬琳
◇ 年齡：28
◇ 問題：失眠
◇ 藥品：Xychelin
　　每天睡前兩顆，為期一星期
　　只用水服藥
　　服藥後不得開車
◇ 醫師：陳友偉
◇ 日期：10 月 13 日

19. 喬琳為何發送此訊息？
   (A) 為了要去看醫生
   (B) 為了要辭職
   (C) 為了要請假
   (D) 為了要說個祕密

20. 喬琳可能何時才會回去上班？
   (A) 10 月 13 日
   (B) 10 月 14 日
   (C) 10 月 15 日
   (D) 10 月 16 日

21. 喬林拿到多少顆 Xychelin 藥片？
   (A) 2
   (B) 7
   (C) 14
   (D) 28

答題解說

19. 答案：(C)。題目問的是喬琳（Jolin）傳送訊息（給 Jay）的原因（Why），這樣的題型通常可以從文字訊息的第一句話看出線索：Hi, Jay. I'm afraid I need to take one day off today.（嗨，傑。恐怕我今天得請一天假了。）故正確答案為 (C) To ask for leave（為了要請假）。

20. 答案：(D)。本題需要整合與歸納兩篇文本的訊息與資訊，才能夠得到正確的答案。題目問的是喬琳可能何時才會回去上班。首先，從第一個文本的對話訊息中，Jolin 說 "I went to see a doctor last night..."（我昨晚去看醫生…），在第二個文本的醫師處方籤最下方可以看到一個日期是 10 月 13 日，也就是說「今天」是 10 月 14 日。接著我們再回到對話訊息，Jay 問她 So will you come to the office tomorrow?（那麼你明天會來上班嗎？），Jolin 回答說 I think I'll need one more day off.（我想我還需要多休息一天。）也就是說，她「後天」10 月 16 日才會回去上班。故正確答案為 (D)。

21. 答案：(C)。題目問的是喬林拿到多少 Xychelin 藥片（pills），可以在第二個文本的處方籤內容找到答案：Two pills before going to bed every day for a week（每天睡前兩顆，為期一星期），也就是說，一天吃兩片，要吃一星期，所以是拿到 14 片。

破題關鍵

19. take a/one day off 就是「請一天假」的意思，而 leave 也可以當名詞，意思是「離開」，引申為「准假，休假」，表示「離開工作崗位」。

20. 問「日期」的題目，當然不會是直接出現在任何一個文本上的日期，必須透過層層推斷才會得到答案：哪裡出現「日期」（二個文本最後）→ 確認「昨晚」去看醫生 → 後天才會回去上班。

21. 首先，直接判斷本題可以直接從第二個文本的處方籤找到答案，然後尋找關鍵字 pills 的位置，找到 "Two pills... for a week" 這句話，答案就出來了。

字詞解釋

afraid [əˋfred] **adj.** 害怕的　　**take a day off** **phr.** 請一天假　　**serious** [ˋsɪrɪəs] **adj.** 嚴重的　　***prescription** [prɪˋskrɪpʃən] **n.** 處方，藥方　　**take a rest** **phr.** 休息　　***insomnia** [ɪnˋsɑmnɪə] **n.** 失眠症　　**medicine** [ˋmɛdəsn] **n.** 藥，醫學　　***pill** [pɪl] **n.** 藥丸，藥片

相關文法或用法補充

❶ 「請假」的英文經常會用到 leave 這個名詞。大家最熟悉它的意思是「離開」，從而衍生出「准假，休假」，只要把它想成「離開工作崗位」就不難理解了。另外，「病假（sick leave）」、「事假（personal leave）」、「公假（official leave）」、「年假／特休（annual leave）」、「婚假（marriage leave）」、「無薪假（unpaid leave）」…等，也可以順便學起來喔！

❷ 「吃藥」不能直接 "eat medicine"，原因在於 eat 在定義上是將食物「咀嚼」並「吞嚥」的動作，「吃藥」不能用 eat 除了藥不是食物之外，最重要的是口服藥物不需要「咀嚼」。因此，一般多用 take medicine，take some pills 來表示。

Questions 22-24

　　湯米非常喜歡老歌，而且他還在使用錄音帶聽音樂，即使現在許多人已學會如何上網下載 MP3 檔案。

　　他上週從一家跳蚤市場商店買了一台收錄音機。他覺得音質很差，所以他把它帶回到那家店裡。他告訴店員他想退款。但是店員說：「恐怕我們沒辦法辦到喔，但我可以換另一台給你。」湯米非常生氣，他對她大吼。然後，湯米要求見店長。店長很有禮貌，且對他很有耐心。店長說：「很抱歉聽到這個消息。我們不能退錢給您，但是我可以送你一盞燈當禮物。」

　　湯米把燈帶了回家，但數日之後發現它不會亮了。

22. 湯米為什麼要去這間商店？
　　(A) 他想購買收音機。
　　(B) 他想和經理碰面。
　　(C) 他在那裡工作。
　　(D) 他想退掉收錄音機，並把錢拿回來。

23. 第二段中畫底線的 refund 意義為何？
　　(A) 支付更多費用
　　(B) 拿回錢
　　(C) 購買另一項產品
　　(D) 找出問題所在

24. 下列敘述何者正確？
　　(A) 經理非常友善好。
　　(B) 店員對湯米大吼。
　　(C) 湯米最後拿回他的錢。
　　(D) 湯米買了一盞燈。

答題解說

這是一篇記敘文。以第三人稱敘述 Tommy 到跳蚤市場買了一台收錄音機後想退貨的經過。

22. 答案：(D)。題目要問的是 去商店（go to the store）的原因。第二段落提到 He thought the sound quality was terrible, so he brought it back to the store. He told the clerk he wanted a refund.（他覺得音質很差，所以他把它帶回到那家店裡。他告訴店員他想退款。）所以他是因為「想退款」（wanted a refund）才去這家商店。

23. 答案：(B)。題目要詢問 refund 這個單字的意思，由本文最後兩行：We can't give your money back.（我們不能退錢給您。）可知正確答案應為 (B)。

24. 答案：(A)。這是個「何者為真」的題型，基本上，應全盤了解整段文章內容之後，以「刪去法」檢視每個選項的敘述。The storekeeper was polite and patient.（店長很有禮貌，也很有耐心。）故正確答案為 (A)。

破題關鍵

22. 在內容中找尋 go to the store 的關鍵字，注意此關鍵字的前後資訊，答案（he wanted a refund）就出來了。

23. 在內容中找到 refund 的相關字詞。通常答案就在 refund 的前後。不過，本題比較特別，答案離考的單字（refund）比較遠，但還是可以判斷出來，只是增加一點難度。

24. 這一題的答案，可以先看過選項，再看文章選出正確答案。這種「何者為是／非」的題型，建議留到最後再做答，因為它的解題線索，分布比較廣，可能在解其他題目時，就已經出現了。

字詞解釋

video tape 錄音帶　**download** [ˋdaʊnˌlod] v. 下載　*file [faɪl] n. 檔案　*flea market 跳蚤市場　**quality** [ˋkwɑlətɪ] n. 品質　**terrible** [ˋtɛrəbl] adj. 糟糕的　**bring** [brɪŋ] v. 帶來　**afraid** [əˋfred] adj. 恐怕的、害怕的　**mad** [mæd] adj. 怒氣的　**shout** [ʃaʊt] v. 大吼　**manager** [ˋmænɪdʒɚ] n. 經理　**polite** [pəˋlaɪt] adj. 禮貌的　**patient** [ˋpeʃənt] adj. 有耐心的　**lamp** [læmp] n. 燈

相關文法或用法補充

❶ want 後面必須接不定詞（to-V）作為其受詞，而同樣表示「想要」的 feel like，後面必須接動名詞（V-ing）。例如：Wendy wants to buy an apartment before 30. = Wendy feels like buying an apartment before 30.（Wendy 想要在三十歲前買一間公寓。）

❷ bought（購買）是 buy 的過去式，而 buy 也是個「授予動詞」，後面接兩個受詞。例如：He bought his girlfriend a ring. = He bought a ring to/for his girlfriend.（他買了戒指給女友。）

Questions 25-27

減肥絕非易事，因為許多節食計畫會讓您感到飢餓甚至容易憤怒。這就是許多節食者可能難以堅持到底的主要原因。

這裡有三個減重的祕訣，且不會讓您感覺在折磨自己。首先，試著在你的飲食中減少糖分，這可讓你不輕易感到飢餓。第二個祕訣是要睡個好覺。而且如果你經常熬夜，你就很難減肥。最後，你應該每天運動。你可以選擇慢跑、打網球…等。經常運動很重要。如果你每星期只運動一次，你會發現你在減重計畫過程中越來越重。

順道一提，不要不吃早餐。試著每天都要吃早餐。不吃早餐對健康不利。如果早上不吃東西，你很容易感到疲倦。

25. 本文最佳標題為何？
    (A) 好好善用時間
    (B) 三個運動技巧
    (C) 如何健康減重
    (D) 吃早餐的重要性

26. 第二段中 torturing 這個字可以換成何者？
    (A) 注意～
    (B) 將痛苦帶給～
    (C) 造成～受傷
    (D) 背叛～

27. 根據本文，以下何者正確？
    (A) 避免過多糖分會有幫助。
    (B) 減重期間，如果覺得飢餓，就去運動。
    (C) 熬夜讓你容易感到疲倦。
    (D) 若你一星期運動一次，你能輕易的減重。

這是一篇說明文。內容講述如何避免減重期間有自我虐待的感覺。

25. 答案：(C)。題目要問的本文的最佳標題（the best title of the passage）。這段落一開頭就提到 Losing weight is never easy...，之後內容都是和減重有關，並告訴讀者有三個正確減重的祕訣（Here are three tips for weight loss that...）。所以正確答案是 (C) How to Lose Weight Healthily。

26. 答案：(B)。題目要問的是 torturing 這個字可以替換成什麼。通常這個單字一定是考試程度以外的字彙，但一定可以從前後文判斷其意思。第一段一開始提到

Losing weight is never easy, because many diet plans make you feel hungry or even easily angry.（減肥絕非易事，因為許多節食計畫會讓您感到飢餓甚至容易憤怒。）而 torturing（原形是 torture）所在句子是〝Here are three tips for weight loss that won't make you feel you are torturing yourself.〞（這裡有三個減重的祕訣，且不會讓您感覺在──自己。）從「感到飢餓甚至容易憤怒」來看，是導致自己「痛苦」的意思，所以正確答案為 (B) Bringing pain to。

27. 答案：(A)。文章中提到 At first, try to cut back on sugar in your diet plan.（首先，試著在你的飲食中減少糖分。）與選項 (A) 的內容相符，故為正確答案；(B) 錯誤的原因是，內容提到許多減重計畫導致容易飢餓與痛苦，應多加運動有助於建空減重，而不是「如果覺得飢餓，就去運動。」(C) 錯誤的原因是，內容提到的是「如果早上不吃東西，你很容易感到疲倦。」而不是「熬夜讓你容易感到疲倦」(D) 錯誤的原因是，與文章本身所提的正好相反，文章說若每週只運動一次，將會越來越重，而非輕易減重。

破題關鍵

25. 在內容中，提到哪一個重點最多，然後注意前後資訊，答案（How to Lose Weight Healthily）就呼之欲出了。這種題目，需要閱讀技巧，即使有些單字不懂，也能判斷出來。

26. 從四個選項的意思也可很容易判斷正確答案：(A) Paying attention to（注意）、(B) Bringing pain to（將痛苦帶給）、(C) Causing injury to（造成～受傷）、(D) Turning back on（背叛～）。

27. 本題屬於「了解細節內容」的題型，雖然難度稍微偏高，但字詞的使用都在程度範圍內，只要細心地去理解內容，就很容易選出正確答案。另外，此類的解題線索，可能在解答其他題目時看到，因此做完其他題目，比較能理解整篇文章內容。

字詞解釋

diet [ˈdaɪət] n. 節食（計畫）　**hungry** [ˈhʌŋgrɪ] adj. 飢餓的　**angry** [ˈæŋgrɪ] adj. 發怒的，生氣的　**major** [ˈmedʒɚ] adj. 主要的　**reason** [ˈrizn] n. 理由，原因　**dieter** [ˈdaɪətɚ] n. 節食者　**make it** 做得到，成功　**at the end** 在最後　**lose** [luz] v. 失去　**weight** [wet] n. 重量　**tip** [tɪp] n. 祕訣　**skip** [skɪp] v. 跳過　**easily** [ˈizɪlɪ] adv. 容易地　**second** [ˈsɛkənd] adj. 第二的　**stay up** 熬夜　**exercise** [ˈɛksɚˌsaɪz] v. 運動　**tennis** [ˈtɛnɪs] n. 網球　**importance** [ɪmˈpɔrtns] n. 重要性　**injury** [ˈɪndʒərɪ] n. 受傷　**avoid** [əˈvɔɪd] v. 避免　**sugar** [ˈʃʊgɚ] n. 糖

❶ tip 可以當名詞，有「忠告」、「尖端」、「小費」的意思，它也可以當動詞，有「給小費」、「翻倒」、「輕拍」的意思。例如：

① Take my tip and keep a distance from him.（聽我的話，離他遠一點。）

② He walked on the tips of his toes.（他踮著腳尖走路。）

③ I gave the waiter a five-dollar tip.（我給服務生五塊錢小費。）

④ He forgot to tip the waiter, which was very embarrassing to me.（他忘記給服務生小費，我覺得很不好意思。）

⑤ The desk tipped over in the way.（桌子倒了，擋住去路。）

❷ 「the reason why S+V」是個很常見的句型，其中 why 可以省略或以 that 替代，例如：The teacher wanted to know the reason (why/that) Isabel didn't do her homework.（老師想要知道伊莎貝兒為什麼沒寫作業。）

Questions 28-30

中文翻譯

寄件者	dora_hills@gmail.com
收件者	dennis88@msn.com
主旨	莎莉的生日派對

親愛的丹尼斯：

　　一切都還好嗎？我寫這封信是要問你 6 月 25 日晚上 7 點是否有空，有個重要的活動。沒錯。我們將慶祝莎莉的生日。她就要滿 18 歲了。這是人生的一個里程碑，而它需要我們每一個人聚在一起並享受歡樂。我們誠摯地邀請你加入我們。

　　派對上將有很多美味的食物、飲料和甜點。你是莎莉最要好的老友之一，所以你不能錯過這次聚會且這派對有你的加入會很特別。如果您有任何疑問，請回覆此電子郵件與我聯繫。

　　也非常歡迎你的家人或朋友來參加這場晚會。對了，別忘了帶禮物。你知道的，心意比貴重禮物來得重要！

祝安

朵拉・希爾

6 月 18 日

28. 朵拉這封電子郵件主要關於什麼？
    (A) 莎莉將取消聚會。
    (B) 莎莉將為朵拉舉行派對。
    (C) 朵拉想邀請丹尼斯參加派對。
    (D) 丹尼斯將拒絕邀請。

29. 第一段的 milestone 所指為何？
    (A) 大驚喜
    (B) 很棒的經驗
    (C) 重要事件
    (D) 絕佳的消息

30. 以下哪一項是正確的？
    (A) 莎莉邀請丹尼斯參加派對。
    (B) 派對只提供飲料。
    (C) 朵拉要求丹尼斯離莎莉遠點。
    (D) 莎莉即將滿 18 歲。

答題解說

這個題組是一封電子郵件，主要內容是 Dora 詢問 Dennis 是否要來參加 Sally 的生日派對。

28. 答案：(C)。題目問 Dora 這封信主要關於什麼，一開頭就可以看到 "I'm writing to ask if you are available..." （我寫這封信是要問你…是否有空），如果這還不確定，看到本段最後一句 "We are sincere to invite you to join us." 應該可確定答案是 (C) 了吧！

29. 答案：(C)。題目句中的 milestone 所在句子是 "This is a milestone in life, and it needs each of us to get together and have fun." （這是人生的一個里程碑，而它需要我們每一個人聚在一起並享受歡樂。）如果不知道是「里程碑」的意思，將四個選項套入句子裡，也可以選出正確的答案 (C) 重要事件。

30. 答案：(D)。這是個「何者為是／非」的題型，基本上，應全部了解整段內容，以「刪除法」的方式，閱讀每個選項的敘述。(A) Sally invites Dennis to the party.→ 寄件人是 Dora，所以錯誤。(B) The party offers drinks only. → 文中提到 There will be many delicious food, drinks, and desserts at the party...（派對上將有許多美味的食物、飲料和甜點。），所以錯誤。(C) Dora asks Dennis to leave Sally alone. → 剛好相反。第三段第一句：Your family members or friends will be very welcome to this evening party.（也非常歡迎你的家人或朋友來參加這場晚會。）(D) Sally will be 18 years old.→ 正確。信中剛開始提到「要慶祝 Sally 十八歲生日。」因此 (D) 就是正確答案。

28. 這一題比較類似「主旨」的解題方式，通常這種「本篇主旨」題型，大部分會在前一兩句開頭，會有端倪。所以找到「關鍵字詞（I'm writing to...）」之後，通常下一句就會出現答案，或者和答案有關，請注意這種解題小技巧。

29. 第一段第二句後半段其實已經告訴你答案了：when there will be an important event，這裡的 milestone 就是前面提到的 important event。

30. 這是屬於「何者正確」型的題目，有時內容不會直接提及答案線索，而是需要經過融會貫通，才能理解。有時會看到特別明顯錯誤的選項，如：派對只提供飲料。因此建議用答案來回推，答案比較容易找出來。

字詞解釋

available [ə`veləbl] adj. 有空的，可利用的　**event** [ɪ`vɛnt] n. 事件，大事　**celebrate**[`sɛləˌbret] v. 慶祝　**turn**[tɝn] v. 過～（幾歲生日）**milestone** [`maɪlˌston] n. 里程碑　**take place** 舉行　**invite** [ɪn`vaɪt] v. 邀請　**delicious**[dɪ`lɪʃəs] adj. 美味的　**special**[`spɛʃəl] adj. 特別的　**contact** [`kɑntækt] v. 聯繫　**refuse** [rɪ`fjuz] v. 拒絕　**invitation** [ˌɪnvə`teʃən] n. 邀請（函）**excellent** [`ɛkslənt] adj. 出色的

相關文法或用法補充

❶ hold the party 是指「舉辦」派對或活動等等。除了用 hold，還可用 take place（舉行），但須注意的是 hold 前面主詞是「人」，而 take place 的主詞是「活動、事件」等。

❷ alone 表示「獨自」，當副詞，常置於句尾。例如：The shy man likes living alone.（這個害羞男喜歡獨居。）另外，也可表示「僅，只是」，常置於主詞後面。例如：The woman alone needs to solve the problem.（只有這名女子必須解決這問題。）

10

GEPT
全民英檢

初級初試
中譯＋解析

第一部分 看圖辨義

1. **For question number 1, please look at Picture A.**

Question number 1: Who will receive this letter?

（這封信的收件人是誰？）

(A) John Smith

(B) Lily Ho

(C) San Francisco

答題解說

答案：(A)。圖中顯示的是一個已寫上寄件方與收件訊息的信封。左上角部分為寄件方資訊，中間部分當然是收件人資訊。所以答案是 (A)。(C) San Francisco（舊金山）是地名，不是人名。

破題關鍵

本題其實就是考你書信封面的「常識」問題。另外，是要聽出 receive 這個動詞才能解題。

字詞解釋

receive [rɪˋsiv] v. 接收，收到

相關文法或用法補充

通常一個句子要有主詞和動詞，或者再加上受詞或補語。但有些句子會缺少其中一個或數個元素，如此看似不完整的結構，但其實們仍被視為合乎文法且能夠讓聽者理解，因為它們能表達一個比較完整的、獨立的概念，這類句子叫作「省略句」。以下來看看幾個例子：

Any questions? = Do you have any questions?（還有什麼問題嗎？）

Nice to meet you. = It's nice to meet you.（很高興見到你。）

此外，省略句在對話中很普遍。可以簡略回答「重點部位」，也讓話語更為簡潔有力。例如：

① A: What day is it today? B: Monday. = It is Monday.

② A: What time is it by your watch, please? B: A quarter to five. =It is a quarter to five.

③ A: Have you finished your homework? B: Not yet. = I haven't finished my homework yet.

2. **For question number 2 and 3, please look at Picture B.**

Question number 2: What are the men doing?
（男子們正在做什麼？）
(A) They are moving a piano.（他們正在搬一部鋼琴。）
(B) They are playing the piano.（他們正在彈鋼琴。）
(C) They are taking a piano lesson.（他們正在上鋼琴課。）

答題解說

答案：(A)。本題是問男子們正在做什麼。從圖片中可看到兩名男子正在搬一台鋼琴，也許是搬進屋子或搬出屋子，但選項中只有 (A) 是符合正確的敘述。

破題關鍵

只要聽清楚三個選項中的現在進行式動詞（moving、playing、taking a... lesson）即可選出正確答案。

字詞解釋

piano [pɪˋæno] **n.** 鋼琴　　**lesson** [ˋlɛsn] **n.** 課程

相關文法或用法補充

如果要用 lesson 來表示「英文／數學／音樂課…」等，可以用「lesson + in/on + English/math/music...」。）

3. **Question number 3: Please look at Picture B again.**

What is true about the picture?（關於這張圖，何者正確？）
(A) It's a rainy day.（這是個雨天。）
(B) The men are in front of a garage.（男子們在車庫前。）
(C) The piano seems very heavy.（鋼琴似乎很重。）

答題解說

答案：(C)。圖片中兩名男子在一間房子前搬鋼琴，故 (B) 錯誤。從兩名男子相當使勁費力的樣子，表示鋼琴很重，所以 (C) 是正確的。左上方有太陽，表示晴天，故 (A) 錯誤。

破題關鍵

「何者為真」的題型，需從三個選項一一確認。而圖片中的太陽、房子及男子們的動作表情都是答題關鍵。

字詞解釋

rainy **adj.** 下雨的　　**garage** [gəˋrɑʒ] **n.** 車庫　　**heavy** [ˋhɛvɪ] **adj.** 重的

seem（似乎）是個「連綴動詞」，後面一定要接主詞補語，可能是形容詞也可能是名詞，其實把它想成是 be 動詞的一種就行了。例如：He seems happy every day.（他每天似乎都很快樂。）

4. **For question number 4 and 5, please look at Picture C.**

Question number 4: What are these people doing?

（這些人正在做什麼？）

(A) They are broadcasting.（他們正在做廣播。）

(B) They are celebrating.（他們正在慶祝。）

(C) They are taking an exam.（他們正在考試。）

答案：(B)。本題問的是圖片中的人們「正在做什麼」(What)。顯然，這些人在慶祝某人的生日，所以正確答案是(B)。

本提純粹是考「單字辨識能力」，也就是 broadcast、celebrate 以及 exam 三個單字，因此只要是初級程度範圍內的字彙，都要有「聽得出」的能力，而非只是「會認」而已。

broadcast [ˋbrɔdˌkæst] **v.** 廣播，播放　　**celebrate** [ˋsɛləˌbret] **v.** 慶祝

exam [ɪgˋzæm] **n.** 考試

celebrate 的名詞是 celebration，表示某種「慶祝活動或場合」，常用於 "in celebration of..."（為了慶祝～）的用法中。例如：They hold a party in celebration of his birthday.（他們舉辦一場派對，以慶祝他的生日。）

5. **Question number 5: Please look at Picture C again.**

What is true about these people?

（關於這些人，何者正確？）

(A) They're clapping their hands.（他們正在鼓掌。）

(B) They're seated and singing.（他們坐著唱歌。）

(C) They're eating the birthday cake.（他們正在吃生日蛋糕。）

第 1 回
第 2 回
第 3 回
第 4 回
第 5 回
第 6 回
第 7 回
第 8 回
第 9 回
第 10 回

答題解說

答案：(A)。從圖中可以清楚看到四個人站著正在慶祝生日（可能正唱著生日快樂歌），因為桌上有蛋糕，且他們正在拍手，而不是在吃蛋糕，所以 (A) 是正確的。

破題關鍵

基本上這類綜合題型要聽完三個選項的敘述才可以作答，而本題三個選項只要掌握住 clapping（鼓掌，拍手）→ 正確、seated（坐著的）→ 錯誤、eating → 錯誤，這樣答案就出來了。

字詞解釋

clap [klæp] **v.** 鼓掌，拍手　　**seated** [`sitɪd] **adj.** 就座的

相關文法或用法補充

表示「坐」的動詞，最簡單的就是 sit，而 seat 也可以當動詞（名詞是「座位」），表示「使就座」。例如：Can I sit next to you?（我可以坐在你旁邊嗎？）= Can I seat myself next to you?

第二部分 問答

6. **Have you ever been to the U.S.?**（你去過美國嗎？）

(A) Yes, since 2019.（是的，自從 2019。）
(B) Yes, next week.（是的，下週。）
(C) Yes, a couple of times.（是的，去過幾次。）

答題解說

答案：(C)。「have been to + 地方」的意思是「曾經去過～」，詢問「經驗」，所以 (C) Yes, a couple of times.（是的，去過幾次。）是正確答案。

破題關鍵

即使不知道「have been to + 地方」的意思，題目句中的關鍵字 ever 也告訴你這是「詢問經驗」的題目，所以聽到選項中有 "a couple of times" 就知道是答案無誤了。

字詞解釋

have been to... 曾去過…　　**a couple of**... 數個的，一些

"have been to..." 表示曾經去過某地，但現在不在那兒。如：Have you ever been to Greece？（你去過希臘嗎?）如果是 "have gone to..." 就表示「已經去了…」，所以現在不在這裡。例如：He has gone to Greece.（他已經去希臘了。）

7. **Kelly is 14 years old.**（Kelly 今年 14 歲。）

(A) That means she went to the U.S. last year.（意思是，她去年去美國了。）
(B) Where does she go to the elementary school?（她在哪裡上小學？）
(C) So she's a junior high school student, right?（那麼她是國中生，是嗎？）

答題解說

答案：(C)。(A) 的「意思是，她去年去美國了。」聽起來是不相關的回應；(B) 的「她在哪裡上小學？」顯然是錯誤的，因為 14 歲不可能還在上小學；(C) 反問說「那麼她是國中生，是嗎？」就是正確且合乎邏輯的回應。

破題關鍵

對於題目這句「Kelly 今年 14 歲。」，似乎各種回應方式都有可能，不過如果回答是以 "So..." 或 "That means..." 開頭，那就表示前後有因果或換言之的關係，掌握這一點之後，自然不會去選 (A) 了，而 (B) 的 "elementary school" 顯然與 14 years old 不相關。

字詞解釋

mean [min] **v.** 意指　　**elementary school** 小學　　**junior high school** 初中，國中

相關文法或用法補充

常聽到的不同階段的學校說法，例如：public school 公立學校、privates chool 私立學校 kindergarten 幼稚園、elementary school 國小、junior high school 國中、senior high school 高中、college 大學、學院、university 大學、graduate school 研究所

8. **How long is the skirt?**（這條裙子多長？）

(A) It is 23 inches.（它 23 吋長。）
(B) It's been long time.（已經好久了。）
(C) Its only 50 dollars.（它只要 50 元。）

答題解說

答案：(A)。how long... 可以是用來問「某物多長？」，也可以問「時間多久」，回答時都要有具體的「數字」，因此正確答案是 (A) It is 23 inches.。

破題關鍵

本題關鍵就是 How long 問句和「回應確切數字」之間的連結，但除了選項中要有數字之外，它的「單位」也是答題關鍵。所以本題仍必須判斷 inches 和 dollars 何者可用來回應 "How long...?"。

字詞解釋

inch [ɪntʃ] n. 英吋

相關文法或用法補充

買衣服時，會詢問 size 大小。通常有下列幾種說法。例如： extra-large（XL）（超大號 的），large（L）（大號），medium（M）（中號），small（S）（小號）和 extra small（XS）（特小號）。此外還有其他說法，可直接說號碼，例如： size 38 等等。在外國購物 時，還會看到 petite 等字眼，這是指身材嬌小的人適合穿的衣物。

9. **You look very nice today!**（你今天很好看！）

(A) Nice to meet you.（很高興認識你。）
(B) I bought this dress a couple of days ago.（我幾天前買了這件洋裝。）
(C) It's a nice day.（天氣很好。）

答題解說

答案：(B)。look nice 就是指「看起來不錯」，可能是稱讚對方的髮型、氣色、或服裝…等，所以只有 (B) 是正確的回應。(A) 是打招呼用語，而 (C) 的「天氣很好。」也是完全不相關的回應。

破題關鍵

題目中的關鍵字詞 look... nice 是「讚美」的話，而如何回應對方的讚美，相信要選出答案就不難了。

字詞解釋

dress [drɛs] n. 洋裝

相關文法或用法補充

英文裡和「衣物」搭配的動詞主要是 wear 以及 put on，不過根據其後名詞的不同，這兩個字詞也有「戴」的意思。例如：She is wearing an expensive ring.（她戴著一枚昂貴的戒指。）、She is putting on boots.（她正在穿靴子。）

10. It looks like it'll rain soon.（看起來快要下雨了。）

(A) The look is nice.（這表情很不錯。）
(B) Take this umbrella with you.（把這支傘帶在身上吧。）
(C) It's a nice deal.（這很划算。）

答題解說

答案：(B)。題目句說「看起來快要下雨了。」而選項 (A) 刻意以相同字彙 look 來混淆答題，其實是完全不相關的回答；(B) 是正確的，umbrella 常與 rain 同時出現，因為快下雨了，跟對方說「把這支傘帶在身上」，是正確的回應；(C) 的回應是針對買回來的東西，覺得很便宜或划算的回應。

破題關鍵

題目句中的 rain 與選項 (B) 的 umbrella 是相互連結的關鍵字詞，但須注意，如果題目沒聽清楚，有兩個選項出現 nice，就很容易被誤導是要從兩者當中選一個。

字詞解釋

umbrella [ʌmˋbrɛlə] n. 雨傘　　**deal** [dil] n. 交易

相關文法或用法補充

It looks like... 在口語會話中，也常省略 It，以 "Looks like..." 出現。須注意的是， "look like" 和 "feel like" 一樣，後面都可以接句子。

11. How have you been lately?（你最近過得好嗎？）

(A) Yes, I've been there once.（是的，我去過那兒一次。）
(B) I've been great.（我過得很好。）
(C) I'm never late.（我從不遲到。）

答題解說

答案：(B)。題目是問「最近好嗎？」(A) 選項的「是的，我去過那兒一次。」顯然並沒有直接針對問題回應，(B) 的 "I've been great." 是「我過得很好。」的意思，為正確答案；(C) I'm never late.（我從不遲到。）也是牛頭不對馬嘴。

破題關鍵

本題關鍵就在 been 和 lately 這兩個字，另外，I've been great. 也可以直接說 Great!。

字詞解釋

lately [ˋletlɪ] adv. 近來，最近　　**once** [wʌns] adv. 一次，一回

對於 How have you been (lately)?（最近好嗎？）的問候，回答可以用：I've been travelling a lot.（我最近很常旅行。）、Great.（很棒。）、Not bad.（還不錯。）…等。

12. **I'd like to check these books out.**（我想借出這些書。）

(A) Your check, please.（這是您的帳單。）

(B) They are sold out.（它們已經售罄。）

(C) I need your library card, please.（請出示您的圖書館卡。）

答題解說

答案：(C)。以 I'd like 開頭的句子是在表達「我想要做～」，三個選項似乎都有可能。所以關鍵在 check... out 這個用語，在此有「登記～（並借出）」之意，而選項 (A) 表示「這是您的帳單。」通常用於餐廳的場合。選項 (B) 通常用於購物場合。因此答案為 (C) I need your library card, please.（請出示您的圖書館卡。）

破題關鍵

check out 有及物與不及物動詞的意思，在此為及物動詞的用法。check + 書 + out 常用於圖書館「借書（出去）」，而圖書館人員會要求出示「圖書館卡」或「學生證」之類的建。千萬別被相同單字（check），但不同意思而誤導了。

字詞解釋

check... out 登記離開　**library** [ˋlaɪˏbrɛrɪ] n. 圖書館

相關文法或用法補充

check out 除了借書，或是檢查的意思之外，在飯店聽到 check out 則表示「退房結帳」，而 check in 則是「入房登記」的意思。那麼還有哪些用法和飯店有關呢？像是 lobby 大廳、room service 客房服務、front desk 接待櫃檯、booking/reservation 預約、brochure 旅遊手冊。另外，還有各種住宿設施，如 inn 小旅館、hostel 青年旅館、hotel 飯店、resort 度假村…等等。

13. **How are you doing, Steve?**（Steve，最近如何？）

(A) Oh, couldn't be better.（喔，好得不能再好／再好不過了。）

(B) I am doing it well.（我做得很好。）

(C) I am doing my homework.（我正在寫作業。）

答案：(A)。本題考的是常用問候語。問候朋友時，除了可用 How are you?、How is it going? 還可以用 How are you doing?，因此回答 (B) 是錯誤的，並沒提到做什麼事。至於 (C) 的回答則是雞同鴨講，可直接排除掉。答案 (A) Oh, couldn't be better. 雖然沒有直接說 good，但意思是指「再好不過了。」為正確答案。

關鍵當然就在能否聽出 How are you doing...並了解其意思，建議先看選項，對於聽力會有幫助。如果 how 聽成 what，則答案節然不同，就變成了 (C) I am doing my homework.（我正在寫作業。）所以請小心。

better [ˋbɛtɚ] **adj.** 較好的   **homework** [ˋhomˏwɝk] **n.** 作業

答案的 "couldn't be better" 省略了主詞 it，字面意思是「沒有辦法再更好了」，意思就是「已經是最好的狀況了」。it 可以指 My life。

14. **We'd like to take a trip to the beach next Saturday.**（我們下週六將去海邊旅遊。）

　(A) Did you go swimming?（你去游泳嗎？）
　(B) What day are you taking a trip?（你星期幾要去旅遊？）
　(C) That sounds like fun.（聽起來很好玩。）

答案：(C)。本題有兩個重點。第一個是 take a trip，要表達的是「去旅行」，而第二個是下周六（ next Saturday），所以 (A) 用過去式反問是錯誤的，(B) 用 What day... ? 詢問也是明顯錯誤。只有 (C)「聽起來很好玩。」可以用來回應去海邊旅遊的看法。

三個選項中，乍聽之下 (A) 與 (B) 都和題目有點關係，因為有相關的單字，不過這只是陷阱，故意誤導。That sounds good. 常用來回應「建議、提議」等用語。

take a trip phr. 去旅行   **beach** [bitʃ] **n.** 海邊

相關文法或用法補充

sound 或 "sound like" 都有「聽起來～」的意思，差別在於，sound 是連綴動
詞，後面要接形容詞，而 "sound like" 後面要接名詞（因為 like 在此為介系
詞），也可以接子句。例如：It sounds like we're going to be late.（聽起來我們要
遲到了。）

15. **What kinds of things do you like to do?**（你喜歡做什麼事？）

　　(A) I like to sing and dance.（我喜歡唱唱跳跳。）
　　(B) It's very kind of you.（你人真好。）
　　(C) Everything will be fine.（一切都會很好。）

答題解說

答案：(A)。Why kind...? 常用來詢問「種類」，題目這句是向對方詢問「喜歡做
什麼事」，所以 (A) 選項 "I like to sing and dance." 就是正確的回答。其餘 (B)、
(C) 選項的敘述雖然也都出現 kind 和 like 的字眼，但顯然是為了混淆聽者的辨別
能力。

破題關鍵

本題的關鍵字當然就是 kind，我們必須了解 kind 有多種意義，因為聽力的考題
最喜歡用同一個字的不同意思來混淆你答題。另外，選項 (C) 以 Everything... 開
頭來呼應 What kinds of... ? 須特別注意是陷阱選項，一定要聽完並了解
"Everything will be fine."（一切都會很好。）整句其實與 "What kinds of... ?"
完全沒關係。

字詞解釋

kind [kaɪnd] n. 種類；adj. 仁慈的

相關文法或用法補充

kind 當名詞時表示「種類」。例如：

❶ There are many kinds of shirts in the store.（這間商店有很多類型的襯衫。）
❷ Sean is not the kind to tell a joke.（Sean 不是那種會講笑話的人。）

當形容詞時表示「親切的，仁慈的」。例如：

❸ He is very kind to his friends.（他對朋友很好。）
❹ 常用於「It + be 動詞 + kind of + 人 + to-V」的句型：It's very kind of you to
　invite me to the party.（你人真好，邀我去派對。）

第三部分 簡短對話

16. **M: Lucky Airlines. May I help you?**
    W: Yes. Do you have any flights to Japan next Tuesday morning?
    M: Yes. There's one at 6:30 A.M.
    W: That's too early for me. I'll try other airlines. Thank you.

    Question: What is the woman doing?
    (A) Going to the airport
    (B) Buying an airplane ticket
    (C) Boarding a flight

    英文翻譯

    男：幸運航空公司。有什麼地方可以替您服務嗎？
    女：是的。請問下週二早上有飛往日本的航班嗎？
    男：有的。早上 6:30 有一班。
    女：那對我來說太早了。我試著問其他航空公司。謝謝。
    問題：女子正在做什麼？
    (A) 前往機場
    (B) 購買機票
    (C) 登機

    答題解說

    答案：(B)。題目問的是女子正在做什麼，所以應注意聽女子的發言部分：Do you have any flights to Japan next Tuesday morning?（請問下週二早上有飛往日本的航班嗎？），只要聽到這裡，就可以推測出想要買機票。

    破題關鍵

    從選項來看都和航空公司、飛機、航班及機票有關，不過答題線索只有一個："Do you have any flights to..."。另外 (C) 選項的 board 當動詞，表示「登上（船、火車、飛機）」。因為女子說 I'll try other airlines.（我試著問其他航空公司。）所以她絕對不是正在登機。

    字詞解釋

    airline [ˈɛrˌlaɪn] n. 航空公司　**flight** [flaɪt] n. 班機　***board** [bord] v. 登上（船、火車、飛機）

相關文法或用法補充

airline 是「航空公司」，但 airliner 是「飛機」的意思，只是它比一般 plane 或 airplane 大一些，且 airliner 只用來「載客」，一般譯為「大型客機」。）

17. M: How can I help you?

W: It's been 30 minutes since I gave my order. But I haven't received any food or even any drinks yet.

M: I'm sorry. Your order will be on your table within the next 10 minutes.

W: Thank you.

Question: What does the man probably do?

(A) He is a booking clerk.

(B) He is a doctor.

(C) He is a waiter.

英文翻譯

男：有需要服務的地方嗎？

女：我訂餐已經過了 30 分鐘。但我還沒得到任何食物，甚至飲料也沒上。

男：抱歉。您的餐點在 10 分鐘內將會上桌。

女：謝謝。

問題：男子的職業可能為何？

(A) 他是個售票員。

(B) 他是醫生。

(C) 他是服務生。

答題解說

答案：(C)。這題是要問「男子是做什麼的？」應從男子的發言去找線索。從他的第一句 "How can I help you?" 可以直接將 (B) 排除掉。接著他的第二句 "Your order will be on your table within..."，以及前一句女子說 "I haven't received any food or even any drinks yet." 可知，男子應是餐廳服務員。故正確答案為 (C)。

破題關鍵

由對話可以聽到女子在詢問食物、飲料、上桌等等字眼，回答的男子說「抱歉，並確定上桌時間」，推知此人可能是「服務生」。

字詞解釋

order [`ɔrdɚ] n. 點餐，訂餐　**receive** [rɪˋsiv] v. 收到　***booking** [ˋbʊkɪŋ] n.（座位、票子等的）預訂，預約　**clerk** [klɝk] n. 店員，銷售員

現在完成式用法：

❶ 過去某個動作持續到現在（未來也將持續下去）。句型：S + have/has + p.p.。
例如：He has finished mopping the floor.（他剛才把地拖好。）

❷ 維持一段時間的行為或動作。例如：We've lived in London for one year.（我們住在倫敦已經一年了。）

❸ 表示經驗。例如：Sandra has been to Thailand once.（Sandra 曾去過一次泰國。）

18. M: What do you like to do in your free time?

W: I like to play computer games.

M: Me too. I also like to play tennis.

W: That's good. Let's play it after school.

M: OK. Can you call Mary to come together?

Question: What's the man going to do after school?

(A) He's going to play computer games.

(B) He's going to play tennis.

(C) He's going to visit Mary.

英文翻譯

男：你有空時喜歡做什麼？

女：我喜歡玩電腦遊戲。

男：我也喜歡。我也喜歡打網球。

女：打網球有趣。放學後一起玩吧。

男：好啊。你可以找瑪麗一起來嗎？

問題：男子放學後打算做什麼？

(A) 他要去玩電腦遊戲。

(B) 他要去打網球。

(C) 他要去拜訪瑪麗。

答題解說

答案：(B)。本題是問「男子放學後要做什麼？」首先注意「放學後」這個時間點。當男子說 I also like to play tennis.（我也喜歡打網球。）女子回答 Let's play it after school.（放學後一起玩吧。）然後男子回答 OK.，可以確定男子放學後要去打網球。

破題關鍵

首先，題目句中的關鍵字詞 after school，然後對照對話中女子的〝Let's play it after school.〞這句話，it 所指為何？就可以找到答案了。

字詞解釋

free [fri] adj.空閒的　　**computer** [kəm`pjutɚ] n.電腦　　**tennis** [`tɛnɪs] n. 網球（運動）

相關文法或用法補充

回應對方「我也是。」時，應注意對方的話語是肯定或否定，要用 too 或 either。例如：A: I am a singer. B: Me too. (= So am I.)（A：我是個歌手。B：我也是。）如果是否定呢？例如：A: I don't like coffee. B: Me either (= Neither do I./ I don't either.)（A：我不喜歡咖啡。B：我也不喜歡。）

19. M: I'd like to return this blue shirt. I bought it two days ago. This is my invoice.

    W: What seems to be the problem, sir?

    M: It's too small for my younger brother.

    W: Would you like to change it for a smaller size?

    M: No. I just want my money back.

    Question: What did the man try to do?

    (A) Change a shirt

    (B) Have a refund

    (C) Make some money

英文翻譯

男：是的，我想退掉這件藍色襯衫。我兩天前買的。這是我的發票。

女：先生，襯衫有什麼問題嗎？

男：對我弟弟而言太小了。

女：你要換小一點的尺寸嗎？

男：不了，我只想退錢。

問題：男子試圖要做什麼？

(A) 換一件襯衫

(B) 退款

(C) 賺些錢

答題解說

答案：(B)。本題是問「男子試著做什麼」，對話中他提到：「退回購買的襯

衫」，然後重點是 "I just want my money back." 因此，答案是 (B)。但即使不知道 refund 的意思，也可以用「刪除法」確定答案，因為 (A) Change a shirt 及 (C) Make some money 都是很明顯的錯誤答案。

雖然 refund（退款）或 fund（資金）不是初級程度的單字，不過從對話中 I just want my money back. 可以推知，既不是想要「換一件襯衫」，更是與「賺錢」沒有任何關係。至於對話中 invoice（發票）這個字，不知道意思的話也不會影響答題。

字詞解釋

return [rɪˋtɝn] **v.** 退回　*invoice [ˋɪnvɔɪs] **n.** 發票　**change A for B** 以 B 換 A
*refund [ˋriˌfʌnd] **n.** 退款　**younger** [ˋjʌŋgɚ] **adj.** 更年輕的（young 的比較級）

相關文法或用法補充

change 可用作名詞或動詞，常指「改變」、「變化」、「交換」…等。另外當名詞時的「零錢」也很常用喔！例如：

❶ Some things never change.（有些事從來沒有改變過。）
❷ He changed his jobs.（他換工作了。）
❸ He wanted to change his cellphone for my tablet.（他想用手機換我的平板。）
　→ 此時 change 與介系詞 for 連用。
❹ I told the taxi driver to keep the change.（我跟計程車司機說不用找零了。）
　→ "keep the change"（不用找了）是常見的固定用語。

20. M: May I have your ticket, please?
　　W: Here you are.
　　M: Here is your boarding pass. Have a nice flight.
　　W: Thank you.

Question: Where did the conversation take place?
(A) At an airport
(B) At a train station
(C) At a movie theater

英文翻譯

男：可以看一下您的票，謝謝。
女：給你。
男：這是您的登機證。一路順風。

女：謝謝。

問題：請問對話正在哪裡進行？

(A) 在機場

(B) 在火車站

(C) 在電影院裡

第 1 回
第 2 回
第 3 回
第 4 回
第 5 回
第 6 回
第 7 回
第 8 回
第 9 回
第 10 回

答題解說

答案：(A)。本題是問兩位說話者在什麼地方，雖然對話中完全沒提到與地點有關的名詞，可藉由對話中男女的交談內容推推斷。一開始提到「可以看一下您的票，謝謝。」，由於沒提到哪種票，三個選項的地點都有可能。後來男子說：這是您登機證。一路順風，顯然這不會是在「火車」與「電影院」的情境對話。就算不知道 boarding pass 的意思，至少知道 flight（班機）這個初級程度的單字就行了！

破題關鍵

本題關鍵句是 Have a nice flight. ，更確定答案一定是 (A) At an airport。

字詞解釋

ticket [ˋtɪkɪt] n. 票　**boarding pass** 登機證　**flight** [flaɪt] n. 班機　**conversation** [͵kɑnvɚˋseʃən] n. 對話

相關文法或用法補充

"Here you are." 這句話很常聽到，卻讓許多考生搞得霧煞煞！例如，服務生把餐點送到你桌上，會跟你說 "Here you are."；計程車司機載你到目的地時，也會跟你說 "Here you are."（你要去的地方到了。）或同學把東西遞給你時也會說 "Here you are."（這給你。）但除了 "Here you are." 之外，"Here you go." 和 "There you are." 都有類似意義，在很多不同情況下都可用得著。

21. M: Does this sweater fit?

　　W: Good. I think I'll take it.

　　M: How would you like to pay? By cash or with a credit card?

　　W: Do you take an Easy Card?

Question: How does the woman want to pay?

(A) By cash

(B) With a credit card

(C) With an Easy Card

男：這毛衣合身嗎？

女：很好。我想我會買這件。

男：請問您付款方式？現金或信用卡。

女：你們可以用悠遊卡嗎？

問題：女子想用何種方式付款？

(A) 用現金

(B) 用信用卡

(C) 用悠遊卡

答題解說

答案：(C)。本題問的是女子想用何種方式付款。當男子問女子想用現金或信用卡支付時，女子反問是否可以用悠遊卡。所以答案是 (C) With an Easy Card。

破題關鍵

關鍵在於，女子如何回應男子問她 "How would you like to pay？"。女子的回答 "Do you take an Easy Card？" 就表示她希望用 Easy Card 來支付。

字詞解釋

sweater [ˋswɛtɚ] n. 毛衣　　**cash** [kæʃ] n. 現金　　**credit card** 信用卡
Easy card 悠遊卡

相關文法或用法補充

店員（clerk）通常會說 "How would you like to pay？" 來詢問顧客「付款方式」。而顧客如果要「付現」，介系詞要用 by，如果是「卡片」之類的，要用 with。

22. M: Hello. I'm calling to ask about the apartments for rent on Happy Street.

W: Which one are you interested in?

M: I want a three-bedroom apartment.

W: OK. When are you available to take a look at it?

M: What about 4:30 P.M.?

Question: What is the man probably going to do this afternoon?

(A) Rent an apartment

(B) Look around an apartment

(C) Buy an apartment

英文翻譯

男：哈囉。我打電話來是要詢問快樂街上這間公寓的出租事宜。

女：您對哪一間感興趣呢？

男：我想要一間三房的公寓。

女：好的。你什麼時候有空可以去看一下？

男：下午四點半如何？

問題：男子下午可能會去做什麼？

(A) 租一間公寓

(B) 看一間公寓

(C) 買一間公寓

答題解說

答案：(B)。題目問的是「男子下午可能會做什麼？」男子一開始詢問快樂街上這間公寓的出租事宜，所以 (C) 可直接排除。後來女子問他什麼時候有空可以去看一下，男子回答說「下午四點半如何？」所以正確答案為 (B)。另外，(A) 雖然也可能是答案，但事實上要租房子的人會先去看一下，不一定當下就會決定租下來。

破題關鍵

本題有兩個關鍵點：ask about the apartments for rent 以及 When are you available to take a look at it?。選項 (B) 的 Look around 是指「四處看看」，正呼應了對話中的 take a look at it。

字詞解釋

apartment [ə`pɑrtmənt] **n.** 公寓　　**bedroom** [`bɛd͵rʊm] **n.** 臥室

available [ə`veləbl] **adj.** 有空的

相關文法或用法補充

rent 可以當動詞及名詞。無論是租客或房產所有人，都可以用動詞 rent（租入，租出）來表達。例如： Ted rents his apartment from a retired teacher.（泰德的公寓是向一名退休老師租的。）、I can rent (out) two spare rooms.（我可以把兩間空房租出去。）另外，「付房租」可以用 pay one's rent 來表達，而「吉屋出租」是 "The house/apartment is for rent." 。

23. M: Who's the man?

W: Jay Chou. Many of his songs are pleasant to the ear.

M: I agree. Then have you ever been to his concerts?

W: Not yet. My parents won't allow me to go there by myself.

M: Maybe we can go together next time.

Question: What are they talking about?

(A) The woman's parents

(B) A famous singer

(C) When to go to a concert

男：這男子是誰？

女：周杰倫。他的很多歌都好聽。

男：我同意。你去過他的演唱會嗎？

女：還沒去過。我父母不允許我單獨去那裡。

男：或許我們下次可以一起去喔。

問題：他們在討論什麼？

(A) 女子的父母

(B) 一位著名的歌手

(C) 何時去看演唱會

答題解說

答案：(B)。題目問的是對話的內容為何（What are they talking about?），男子第一句話問男子是誰，女子回答說 "Jay Chou. Many of his songs are pleasant to the ear." （周杰倫。他的很多歌都好聽。）到這裡答案已經出來了，他們談論的是一位著名的歌手，故正確答案為 (B)。

破題關鍵

本題關鍵字詞包括 songs 及 concerts（演唱會），可直接先排除 (A)；但究竟重點在 (B) 的 singer 還是 (C) 的 concert，可以從最後一句 "Maybe we can go together next time." 並未敲定「何時」要去看演唱會，可推知 (C) 是錯誤的。

字詞解釋

pleasant [ˋplɛzənt] **adj.** 令人愉快的　　**concert** [ˋkɑnsɚt] **n.** 演唱會

allow [əˋlaʊ] **v.** 允許

第 1 回
第 2 回
第 3 回
第 4 回
第 5 回
第 6 回
第 7 回
第 8 回
第 9 回
第 10 回

相關文法或用法補充

"pleasant to the ear" 從字面意思應該很容易理解，它是「悅耳的，好聽的」意思。當然，可以 "to the ear" 也可以 "to the eye"，只是要注意的是，這裡的 ear 和 eye 都要用單數。

24. M: Where did you live when you just went abroad to study?
    W: I lived in New York.
    M: Where do you live now?
    W: In Boston. But I'll move to Seattle next year.

Question: Where does the woman live?
(A) In New York
(B) In Boston
(C) In Seattle

英文翻譯

男：妳剛出國念書時住在哪裡？
女：我住在紐約。
男：那妳現在住哪裡呢？
女：波士頓。但我明年要搬去西雅圖。
問題：女子現在住在哪裡？
(A) 在紐約
(B) 在波士頓
(C) 在西雅圖

答題解說

答案：(B)。題目問的是女子「目前住在哪裡」，可以從男子問她「妳現在住哪裡」，以及女子回答「波士頓」得知，答案是 (B)。

破題關鍵

本題看似容易，但其實真正要考你的是，注意動詞時態與相關時間副詞。畢竟 "Where did you live..." 以及 "I lived in New York." 這兩句話要聽出「過去式」也不容易。所以要注意的是相關時間副詞，包括 now、next year 等。

字詞解釋

abroad [əˋbrɔd] **adv.** 在國外，到國外

abroad 這個副詞，和 overseas 一樣，都表示「在／到國外或海外」，例如：He's currently abroad on business.（目前他在國外出差。）、She always go abroad in the summer.（她夏天總是到國外去。）

25. M: Why are you looking for a new job?

W: I got fired by my boss last week.

M: Why? You must have argued with your boss, right?

W: No. I was just late for work too often.

Question: What happened to the woman?

(A) She quit her job.

(B) She was let go by her boss.

(C) She argued with her boss and was fired.

英文翻譯

男：妳為什麼在找新工作？

女：我上星期被老闆解雇了。

男：為什麼？你一定是和老闆爭執，對嗎？

女：不。我只是太常上班遲到了。

問題：女子發生了什麼事？

(A) 她辭職了。

(B) 她被老闆辭退了。

(C) 她和老闆爭執並被炒魷魚了。

答題解說

答案：(B)。題目問的是「女子發生了什麼事」，基本上可以先從女子的發言中找線索。女子說她上星期被老闆解雇了，故正確答案為 (B) She was let go by her boss.。let someone go 字面意思是「讓某人走」，就是 "fire someone" 的意思。(C) 錯誤的原因是，女子是因為經常遲到而被辭退，不是與老闆爭執。

破題關鍵

本題關鍵是 "got fired" 是 "was let go" 的意思。即使你不知道 "let go" 的意思，也應該要知道 "got fired" 跟 "quit one's job" 是完全不同的意思，一個是「被動」辭職，一個是「主動」辭職。

字詞解釋

look for phr. 尋找　**boss** [bɔs] n. 老闆　**argue** [ˋɑrgjʊ] v. 爭執

*let go phr. 解雇，辭退

相關文法或用法補充

❶ 「遲到」的說法：be late for + 名詞。例如：Sam was late for school this morning.（Sam 今天早上上學遲到。）

❷ 「早到」的說法： be early to + 名詞。例如：You should be early to work.（你該早點去上班。）

❸ 「準時」的說法：on time。例如：You have to show up the meeting on time.（你要準時出席會議。）

❹ 「及時」的說法: in time。I caught the train just in time.（我及時趕上這班火車。）

第四部分 短文聽解

For question number 26, please look at the three pictures.

Question number 26: Listen to the following announcement. Where does it take place?

 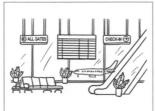 

Ladies and gentlemen. May I have your attention, please? The next train will arrive at Platform 1 at 2:35 P.M. We are sorry to announce that this train headed for New York is delayed about 5 minutes. Please ensure that you have purchased your train ticket before you get on the train. For more information, please go to the service center. Have a nice trip. Thank you.

英文翻譯

請看以下三張圖。並仔細聆聽以下廣播內容。廣播的地點是在哪裡？

各位女士及先生們。請各位注意。下一班火車將在下午兩點三十五分抵達一號月台。我們很抱歉要宣布，這班前往紐約的列車誤點約 5 分鐘。請確認在上車前已購買車票。欲知更多資訊，請前往服務中心。祝您旅程愉快。謝謝您。

答題解說

答案：(A)。首先，這是 where 開頭的問句，即使你若不太了解 take place（發生）之意，看看三張圖，仔細聽廣播內容，也會知道題目是要問你「場景」在哪

裡？例如 "The next train will arrive at Platform 1 at 14:35." 、 "purchased your train ticket" 都可以確定(A)是正確答案。

廣播考題的重點就是抓到內容中的關鍵字，像是 train（火車）、delay（誤點）、train ticket（火車票），get on the train（上火車）等，即使無法聽懂全部意思，亦能推知此為火車站的廣播。

字詞解釋

attention [əˋtɛnʃən] n. 注意　**platform** [ˋplætˌfɔrm] n. 月台　***announce** [əˋnaʊns] v. 通知　**ensure** [ɪnˋʃʊr] v. 保證　**purchase** [ˋpɝtʃəs] v. 購買　**information** [ˌɪnfəˋmeʃən] n. 資訊

相關文法或用法補充

"for more information" 字面意思是「為了更多資訊／訊息」，白話一點就是「如欲取得更多資訊」，後面通常接個 please 開頭的祈使句。類似用法還有 "for your information"（供您參考），在書信中常被簡寫為 FYI。例如： For your information, I attached a list of potential customers.（我附上一張顧客清單，供您參考。

For question number 27, please look at the three pictures.

Question number 27: Listen to the following message. What will Steve probably buy after work?

Hi, Mom. I saw you make a call to me, but I was at the meeting at that time. I couldn't answer your call. I'm still in the office with Steve, and have already had some toast and milk. We plan to leave here at 8:30, and go to Burger King for the second meal. Then I will go home directly. Don't worry about me.

英文翻譯

請看以下三張圖。並仔細聆聽以下訊息內容。史蒂夫下班後可能會買什麼東西？
嗨，媽。我看到妳打電話給我，但那個時候我還在開會。我沒辦法接妳的電話。

我跟史帝夫還在辦公室，而且已經吃了一些吐司跟牛奶。我們計畫在八點半的時候離開這裡，並且到漢堡王吃第二餐。然後我會直接回家。不用替我擔心。

答題解說

答案：(C)。本則訊息的留言者表示 Steve 會跟她一起離開辦公室，並且一起去漢堡王吃第二餐，所以可以推測 Steve 下班後會買漢堡類的食物，圖 (A) 是義大利麵，圖 (B) 是吐司和牛奶，都不可能，而 (C) 雞塊和漢堡，就是正確答案。請注意，中間提到吐司和牛奶是刻意混淆的陷阱。

破題關鍵

當看到三個圖案都跟食物有關時，要先把圖案中食物的單字先在腦中想過一遍，因為之後的短文中可能會提到，不過聽到相關單字要判斷是否為陷阱，雖然提到 toast 但是是「已經吃了」所以這不可能是答案，而另一個提到與圖有關的 Burger 就有可能了。

字詞解釋

make a call to... 打電話給～　　**meeting** [ˋmitɪŋ] n. 會議　　**office** [ˋɔfɪs] n. 辦公室
fast food 速食　　**worry** [ˋwɝɪ] v. 擔心

相關文法或用法補充

worry 可以當動詞或名詞，其過去分詞 worried 也常當形容詞，用來表達「（人）感到憂慮的」：

❶ Don't worry. Everything will be fine. （別擔心。一切會沒事的。）

❷ S+be worried that + 子句 （某人對於～感到憂心）。例如：Emily is worried that she might be fired by her boss.（Emily 擔心會被老闆上司炒魷魚。）

❸ A: I'm sorry to reply so late. B: No worries. I've handled it. （A：抱歉這麼晚回覆。B：沒關係。我已經處理好了。）

For question number 28, please look at the three pictures.

Question number 28: Listen to the following talk. Where is the speaker now?

Hi, Melissa. It' twenty after four. I am waiting for the bus. I'm going to the Happy Department Store. Emma's birthday is coming. I may buy her a watch or a jacket for her as a gift. Maybe we can get together and have dinner after I finish shopping. Please call me as soon as you get this message. See you then.

中文翻譯

請看以下三張圖。並仔細聆聽以下播放的談話內容。說話者現在在哪裡？

嗨，梅麗莎。現在是四點二十分。我正在等公車。我正要去快樂百貨公司。Emma 的生日快到了。我可能會買給她手錶或夾克當禮物。東西買完後，也許我們可以聚在一起吃頓晚飯。聽到留言後，請立刻打話給我。待會見。

答題解說

答案：(C)。說話者表示"I am waiting for the bus."，所以正確答案為 (C)。注意別被"I'm going to the Happy Department Store."（我正要去快樂百貨公司。）誤導而選了(A)。

破題關鍵

題目要問的是男子目前位置，所以要注意聽播放內容中提及關於地點。內容中提到了「百貨公司」，「吃晚餐」，以及「等公車」，此時注意聽這些地點的先後順序，就能選出正確答案。

字詞解釋

department store 百貨公司　　**jacket** [ˋdʒækɪt] n. 夾克　　**finish** [ˋfɪnɪʃ] v. 結束
message [ˋmɛsɪdʒ] n. 留言

相關文法或用法補充

❶ It's +數字+(o'clock). → 可表示「整點」。例：It five.（現在五點整。）

❷ 數字（分）＋ to ＋ 數字（時），表示「差幾分就幾點」。例如：ten to five 是「4 點 50 分」。

❸ 數字（分）＋ past ＋ 數字（時），表示「幾點過幾分」。例如：ten past five 是「5 點 10 分」。

❹ 如果是 15 分，可用 a quarter。半小時則用 half。例如：It's a quarter past eight.（現在 8 點 15 分。）、It's half past seven.（現在 7 點半。）

For question number 29, please look at the three pictures.

Question number 29: Listen to the following talk. Where is the speaker going after work?

My name is Wendy. I work as a clerk in a bakery in town. My working time is 11:00 A.M. to 8:00 P.M., and I have 6 days off every month. I sometimes go to the movies after work if I am not tired. On weekends, I go shopping with my best friend, Maggie. Today is her birthday. I am going to buy a dress for her after work. I hope she can be happy every day.

英文翻譯

請看以下三張圖。並仔細聆聽以下談話內容。說話者下班後會去哪裡？

我的名字是溫蒂。我在市區一家麵包店擔任店員。我的工作時間是上午 11 點到晚上 8 點，且我每個月有 6 天休假。如果我不累的話，我有時候下班後會去看電影。週末時，我會和最好的朋友梅姬去逛街。今天是梅姬生日。下班後我要去買一件洋裝給她。我希望她每天都會很快樂。

答題解說

答案：(C)。題目是問「說話者下班後將要做什麼？」播放的內容提到，她是在麵包店擔任店員（work as a clerk in a bakery），只是在說明平時的工作，所以圖 (B) 的麵包店是刻意誤導答題。另外，還提到平時若不累的話，下班會去看電影，所以圖 (A) 同樣有誤導作用。重點來了：「今天是梅姬生日。下班後我要買一件洋裝給她。（Today is her birthday. I am going to buy a dress for her after work.）」因此，正確答案是 (C) 了。

破題關鍵

第一個關鍵點是題目句中的 "after work"（下班後），然後對照播放內容中的 "I am going to buy a dress for her after work."。大家應該知道「去哪裡買一件 dress」吧！

字詞解釋

clerk [klɝk] n. 店員，職員　**bakery** [`bekərɪ] n. 麵包，麵包店　**working time** 工作時間　**tired** [taɪrd] adj. 疲倦的

第 1 回
第 2 回
第 3 回
第 4 回
第 5 回
第 6 回
第 7 回
第 8 回
第 9 回
第 10 回

常見的「頻率副詞」有 always（總是）、usually（通常）、often（經常）、sometimes（有時候）、seldom（鮮少）、never（從未）等。它們通常放在一般動詞前，和 be 動詞後，搭配現在式動詞。例如：He seldom visits his uncle because he is busy.（他因為很忙，所以鮮少拜訪伯父。）

For question number 30, please look at the three pictures.

Question number 30: Listen to the following short talk. What happened to the speaker today?

I am a junior high school student, and I live a happy school life. My parents say it is the golden time of my life, and they ask me to study hard. To tell the truth, I agree with them, but I still spend much time playing video games. Today I got up a bit late but luckily I caught the bus to school in time. When the first class started, I found I forgot to bring my textbook again. Miss Chen looked at me angrily. Sometimes I don't know what to do about my forgetfulness.

請看以下三張圖。並仔細聆聽以下簡短談話。說話者今天發生什麼事？
我是一名國中生，並且過著快樂的學生生活。我的父母說這是我一生當中的黃金時刻，他們要求我要用功念書。說實話，我同意他們的觀點，但是我仍然花很多時間玩電玩遊戲。今天我起床得有點晚，但幸運的是，我及時趕上了去學校的公車。第一堂課開始時，我發現我又忘了帶課本了。陳老師生氣地看著我。有時我真不知道我的健忘該怎麼辦。

答案：(C)。談話內容中提到 "I caught the bus to school in time."（我及時趕上了去學校的公車。）所以圖 (A) 是錯誤的；接著說 "I found I forgot to bring my textbook again."（我發現我又忘了帶課本了。）而圖 (B) 的桌子上有書本，所以也是錯誤答案。最後是 "Miss Chen looked at me angrily."（陳老師生氣地看著我。）正符合圖 (C)。

破題關鍵

題目句的 "happened to..." 是「發生在～（某人身上）」的意思，所以應先仔細看過三張圖，仔細聽相關「發生的事」。其中 in time 是「及時」的意思，caught 是 catch 的過去式；textbook 是書本，"forgot to bring my textbook" 以及 "looked at me angrily" 都要聽得出來才能夠選出正確答案。

字詞解釋

live a... life 過著～生活　**golden** [ˋgoldn̩] **adj.** 黃金般的　**agree** [əˋgri] **v.** 同意　**in time** 及時地　**textbook** [ˋtɛkstˌbʊk] **n.** 教科書，課本　**angrily** [ˋæŋgrɪlɪ] **adv.** 憤怒地，生氣地　***forgetfulness** [fɚˋgɛtfəlnɪs] **n.** 健忘

相關文法或用法補充

動詞 live（活著）的名詞是 life（生活），「過著什麼樣的生活」可以用 live a... life 來表示。類似用法還有可當動詞或名詞的 dream。「做了一個什麼樣的夢」可以說 dream a... dream，千萬別說成 "do/make a... dream"。

1. **Mrs. Thomas is very busy. She decides to _____ someone as a secretary to help her.**（湯瑪斯女士很忙。她決定雇用一位祕書來幫她。）

   (A) employ　(B) embarrass　(C) encourage　(D) examine

   答題解說

   答案：(A)。句意是「湯瑪斯女士很忙。她決定 _____ 一位祕書來幫她。」四個選項中，以「雇用（employ）」最符合句意。

   破題關鍵

   由 busy（忙碌的）可推知需要「聘請、雇用」人來幫忙。再加上 secretary（祕書）這個單字，推知是職場上的「雇用」關係。

   字詞解釋

   decide [dɪˋsaɪd] v. 決定　**secretary** [ˋsɛkrəˏtɛrɪ] n. 祕書　**employ** [ɪmˋplɔɪ] v. 僱用　**embarrass** [ɪmˋbærəs] v. 使感到不好意思　**encourage** [ɪnˋkɝɪdʒ] v. 鼓勵　**examine** [ɪgˋzæmɪn] v. 檢查

   相關文法或用法補充

   「雇用」他人，除了用 employ 之外，還可用 hire（聘僱）。employ + er 變成名詞，表示「雇用者」、employ + ee 變成名詞，表示「雇員」。employ 相反的意思是 fire／dismiss 是「解聘」的意思。

2. **Alan is only _____ for collecting suggestions. The manager will make the final decision.**（亞倫只是負責彙整建議。經理會做最後決定。）

   (A) responsible　(B) regular　(C) relative　(D) recent

   答題解說

   答案：(A)。本題大意是「亞倫只是 _____ 彙整建議。經理會做最後決定。」四個選項中，以 (A) 的「負責的（responsible）」最符合句意。

   破題關鍵

   本題關鍵就是 make the final decision 這個片語，表示 Alan 不是做決定的人，他「負責」的部分只是蒐集資料。

第 1 回
第 2 回
第 3 回
第 4 回
第 5 回
第 6 回
第 7 回
第 8 回
第 9 回
第 10 回

字詞解釋

gather [ˋgæðɚ] **v.** 蒐集　**suggestion** [səˋdʒɛstʃən] **n.** 建議　**decision** [dɪˋsɪʒən] **n.** 決定　**responsible** [rɪˋspɑnsəbl] **adj.** 負責任的　**regular** [ˋrɛgjələ] **adj.** 正規的，一般的　**relative** [ˋrɛlətɪv] **adj.** 相對的，比較的

相關文法或用法補充

responsible 這個形容詞常用於 "be responsible for..." 「對～負責」的片語中。同樣，它的名詞 responsibility 也搭配介系詞 for，例如 "Alan is only responsible for collecting suggestions." 這句話可改成 "Alan takes responsibility only for collecting suggestions."。

3. **Rose has her teeth checked by a(n) _____ once a month.**（羅絲每個月讓牙醫檢查牙齒一次。）

(A) journalist　(B) artist　(C) dentist　(D) scientist

答題解說

答案：(C)。句子大意是「羅絲每個月讓 _____ 檢查牙齒一次。」故正確答案為 (C) dentist（牙醫師）。其餘選項均不符句意或邏輯。

破題關鍵

本題關鍵字是 teeth（牙齒），從四個表「人」的選項（字尾 -ist）來看，和「牙齒」最相有的當然是「牙醫」了。

字詞解釋

teeth [tiθ] **n.** 牙齒（單數為 tooth）　**check** [tʃɛk] **v.** 檢查　**journalist** [ˋdʒɝnəlɪst] **n.** 新聞記者　**artist** [ˋɑrtɪst] **n.** 藝術家　**dentist** [ˋdɛntɪst] **n.** 牙醫
scientist [ˋsaɪəntɪst] **n.** 科學家

相關文法或用法補充

關於「身體不適」的用字，像是 headache（頭痛）、light-headed（頭暈）、fever（發燒）、chills（發冷）、dizzy（頭暈的）、itch（發癢）、cough（咳嗽）、sneeze（打噴嚏）、runny nose（流鼻水）、toothache（牙痛）、stomachache（胃痛）、pain（痛）等，都是很實用的喔！

4. **Helen paid NT$2,000 _____ the brown jacket.**（Helen 花了 NT$2,000 買這件棕色夾克。）

(A) from　(B) by　(C) of　(D) for

答案：(D)。句子大意是「Helen 花了 NT$2,000 ＿＿＿＿＿ 這件棕色夾克。」顯然答案應該是表「為了～」的 for。「pay + 金額 + for + sth.」表示「為了某物支付多少錢」。

破題關鍵

本題是考「慣用語」：「pay（付款）+ 金額 + for + 物品」。

字詞解釋

brown [braʊn] **adj.** 褐色的，棕色的　　**jacket** [ˋdʒækɪt] **n.** 夾克

相關文法或用法補充

pay 的本意為「付錢」，故其後受詞如果是「物」的話，就只能是「錢」或「金額」。不過 pay 後面也可以接「人」，表示「付錢給～（某人）」，此時的 pay 為「授予動詞」。例如：I paid him three hundred dollars.（我付給他三百元。）那如果是要用 pay 表達「花錢買～（東西）」，可以用 pay for sth.。例如：Let me pay for dinner.（晚餐我買單。）

5. **I apologized for interrupting your talk, ＿＿＿＿＿ I have something important to say.**（抱歉打斷你們的談話，不過我有重要的事要說。）

(A) and　(B) but　(C) or　(D) when

答題解說

答案：(B)。第一句話是「抱歉打斷你們的談話」，第二句是「有重要的事要說」，這兩句之間的關聯為何？顯然是前句是「果」，後句是「因」，不過選項沒有 because，那當然就是表達相反意思的 (B) but 最適當了。

破題關鍵

本題關鍵字是 apologized（道歉），看到它就好像看到 sorry，進而想到 "I'm sorry but..."（我很抱歉，因為…）這句話。所以答案是 but。

字詞解釋

apologize [əˋpɑləˏdʒaɪz] **v.** 道歉，認錯　　**interrupt** [ˏɪntəˋrʌpt] **v.** 打斷

相關文法或用法補充

動詞 apologize 的名詞形式是 apology，常用於 "make an apology"，同樣也是搭配介系詞 for，例如：He made a public apology for what he had said.（他為他說過的話公開致歉）。

6. **This reminds me _____ a story I have ever read.**（這使我想起我曾看過的一則故事。）

(A) with　(B) of　(C) from　(D) for

第 1 回

答題解說

答案：(B)。句子大意是「這使我想起我曾看過的一則故事。」本題考介系詞。空格前有動詞 reminds 和受詞 her，後面是名詞 a story。remind + 受詞 + of... 是指「使某人想起…」，因此，選項(B)為正確答案。

破題關鍵

關鍵字是動詞 remind。看到 remind 應立即想到介系詞 of，也就是「提醒某人某事（remind sb. of sth.）」的慣用語。

字詞解釋

remind [rɪˋmaɪnd] v. 提醒，使想起

相關文法或用法補充

remind 還有其他用法：

❶ remind + 人 + to-V（提醒某人去做某事）。例如：Please remind Tommy to pick up Molly.（請提醒 Tommy 去接 Molly。）

（2）remind sb + of + 名詞（想起…）

❷ remind + 人 + about（提醒某人關於…）。例如：Can you remind Sean about the party on the weekend?（你能提醒一下 Sean 週末的派對嗎？）

7. **Molly is _____ at his decision to move to Seattle.**
（Molly 對於他要搬去西雅圖的決定感到驚訝。）

(A) surprising　(B) surprised　(C) surprises　(D) surprise

答題解說

答案：(B)。從四個選項來看，這是考 surprise（驚訝）的不同類型。句子大意是「Molly 對於他要搬去西雅圖的決定感到 _____。」因為主詞是「人」，所以要表達「驚訝」時，用 surprised（感到驚訝的），因此，選項(B)為正確答案。

破題關鍵

本題目可以直接看選項，判斷「考點」，掌握相關聯的關鍵字。本題的關鍵字是「主詞」Molly，所以要用 surprised 來修飾。如果主詞是「某事或物」，則要用 surprising，表示「令人驚奇的」。

decision 建議　**decision** [dɪˋsɪʒən] n. 決定　**Seattle** [siˋætḷ] n. 西雅圖

我們知道動詞 decide 後面常以不定詞（to-V）作為其受詞，那麼它的名詞 decision 後面，也常以不定詞作為其後位修飾語。例如：She made a final decision to study abroad.（她做了一個出國念書的最終決定。）

8. **Dr. Potter was the smartest man _____ Sally has ever known.**
　（波特教授是莎莉認識的男人當中最聰明的一個。）

　(A) which　(B) that　(C) whose　(D) who

答案：(B)。從四個選項來看，空格要填入的是關係代名詞。空格後面主詞是 Sally，動詞是 has known，缺少的受詞，而先行詞 man 是「人」，所以 (A)、(C) 可直接排除。本題中關鍵點是先行詞 man 前面有「最高級」形容詞，所以不能用 who 或 whom，只能用 that。

本題是考「關係代名詞之先行詞前有『極端』修飾語」時，關係代名詞只有一個選擇，那就是 that。所謂「極端」修飾語包括最高級、序數、only、the very… 等。

ever 是個副詞，主要意為「在（過去、現在或未來）任何時候，曾經，從來都～」，通常用於疑問句，否定句以及表示比較和條件的副詞子句。例如：

❶ Have you ever been to New York?（你去過紐約嗎？）
❷ No such person ever lived here.（這裡沒有住過這樣的人。）
❸ His health is worse than ever.（他的健康狀況比以前更嚴重了。）

9. **Someone knocked at the door _____ he was watching TV.**（當他正在看電視時，有人敲門。）

　(A) because　(B) after　(C) while　(D) although

答案：(C)。句子大意是「_____ 他正在看電視，有人敲門。」故 (C) while (= when) 是最符合句意的答案。

第 1 回
第 2 回
第 3 回
第 4 回
第 5 回
第 6 回
第 7 回
第 8 回
第 9 回
第 10 回

破題關鍵

連接詞的考題，應先觀察前後兩句之間的關聯，是「時間前後」、「因果」、「條件」、「讓步」還是「同時」的關係。

字詞解釋

knock [nɑk] **v.** 敲

相關文法或用法補充

while 可以表示 when（當），也可以表示 although（雖然）。例如：

❶ I found the wallet while he was talking on the phone.（當他正在講電話時，我找到皮夾了。）

❷ While I am interested in the job, I am not satisfied with the salary.（雖然我對此工作有興趣，但我對薪水不滿意。）

10. Larry is _____ taller than his neighbor, Peter.
（萊利比他的鄰居彼得高很多。）

(A) more (B) most (C) very (D) much

答題解說

答案：(D)。本題考的是「修飾比較級的副詞」，故正確答案為 (D) much。沒有 "more taller" 及 "most taller" 這種用法，所以 (A)、(B) 錯誤；(C) 的 very 用來修飾形容詞原級。只有 much 可以用來修飾比較級。

破題關鍵

關鍵字詞是空格後的 taller，再看看四個選項，掌握「考點」是「修飾比較級的副詞」。記住一個觀念：並非所有副詞都可以修飾比較級。

字詞解釋

neighbor [ˈnebɚ] **n.** 鄰居

相關文法或用法補充

常見的「修飾比較級的副詞」有 much, far, still, even, a lot, a bit, a great deal... 等。

第二部分 段落填空

Frank was looking for a new job, and he had an interview this morning. However, He got up too late. When he arrived at the company, the **interviewer** looked at him unhappily and asked him many questions he did not know how to answer. **He knew he had done it badly.** After that, he decided to have lunch near the company. He got a call while he was **waiting for** his food. A stranger said on the phone that his son was kidnapped by them. He asked Frank to prepare one million dollars. Then Frank shouted at him, "Are you kidding? I don't have a kid. I am still **single**."

中文翻譯

　　佛蘭克正在找新工作，且他今天早上有個面試。然而，他太晚起床了。當他抵達這家公司時，面試官不悅地看著他，並且問了他許多他不知如何回答的問題。他知道自己表現很差。然後，他決定在這家公司附近吃頓午餐。他在等食物時，接到一通電話。一個陌生人說他兒子被他綁架了。他要求佛蘭克準備好一百萬元。然後佛蘭克對著他大吼：「你在開玩笑嗎？我沒有小孩。我還是單身。」

答題解說

11. 答案：(C)。前文提到「他今天早上有個面試。」空格要填入的是一個表示「人」的名詞，那麼什麼樣的「人」適合出現在「面試（interview）」的情境中呢？答案很明顯是 (C) interviewer 了。其餘選項的字義是 (A) professor（教授）、(B) policeman（警察）、(D) shopkeeper（店主）。

12. 答案：(A)。這是要挑選一個句子、子句或句子的一部分放入空格後，確認空格前後和空格句之間的連接關係，是否讓句意顯得自然通順。空格前面句子提到「面試官不悅地看著他，並且問了他許多他不知如何回答的問題。」顯然 (A) He knew he had done it badly.（他知道自己表現很差。）是語意上最適合連接前句的答案。其餘選項提到的面試似乎很成功、要求二度面試、聊得很愉快等，都與前一句產生不自然的連結。

13. 答案：(A)。空格後面是 food（食物），只要單就這個句子來看就可以解題了。「等候食物（等上菜）」、「對著食物吼叫」、「以食物為榮」、「對食物生氣」，哪一個比較有可能？當然是 (A) waiting for 了。雖然 (B)、(C) 就中文意思來說似乎也有可能（畢竟面試不順利又遲到嘛！），不過 shout at 和 be mad at 通常後面接「人」的名詞。

14. 答案：(B)。句意是「我沒有小孩。我還是 ＿＿＿＿。」將四個選項 (A) skinny 纖瘦的、(B) single 單身的、(C) sincere 誠懇的、(D) skillful 技巧純熟的，套入空格後可明顯了解只有 (B) 是合乎語意與邏輯的。

破題關鍵

11. 本題關鍵字除了一開始出現的 interview 之後，其實看到空格前的 "When he arrived at the company..."，應可斷定其餘三個選項都跟 company 不相關。

12. 本題主要參考指標是前一句的內容，與後面句子不相關。這類題型的解題基本要點是「觀前觀後」，有時只要觀看前面或後面的句子，答案就出來了，但通常可以在其他問題都解決之後，再回過頭來解這一題會比較順利找到答案。

13. 本題只是考你「動詞＋名詞」的合理性，故以「刪除法」解題也是可行的。

14. 關鍵字當然是 "not have a kid" 了，雖然實際上，單身並不表示一定沒有小孩，但比起其他選項，只有 single 是最合適的答案。

字詞解釋

look for... 尋找　**interview** [ˋɪntə͵vju] n. 面試　**arrive** [əˋraɪv] v. 抵達　**office** [ˋɔfɪs] n. 辦公室　**interviewer** [ˋɪntə͵vjuə] n. 採訪者，面談者　**unhappy** [ʌnˋhæpɪ] adj. 不高興的　**decide** [dɪˋsaɪd] v. 決定　**company** [ˋkʌmpənɪ] n. 公司　**stranger** [ˋstrendʒə] n. 陌生人　**million** [ˋmɪljən] n. 百萬

相關文法或用法補充

11. 從 interview 這個動詞可以衍生出兩個表示「人」的名詞：interviewer 與 interviewee。前者是「面試官，採訪員」，後者則是指「受試者（應徵者）／接受採訪者」。

12 這裡的 "do it badly" 就是指「出包，搞砸了，表現不好」。也可以用 mess up 或 ruin 來表達。例如：He made a mistake and messed up his chance of getting promoted.（他犯了個錯，而且搞砸了可獲得晉升的機會。）

13. wait for 等於 await，後面可以接「人」或「事物」。另外，若要表示「等待做某事」可以用 "wait to-V" 來表達。例如：These people are waiting to board the buy a kind of delicious cake.（這些人正等著要買一種可口的蛋糕。）

14. single 本來是「單一的」，可用來強調「唯一，只要一個…（就夠了）」例如：I can finish the work in a single day.（我可以只用一天就完成這工作。）

Questions 15-18

Everyone has a dream or many dreams. Do you remember what your dream was when you were an elementary school student? **Do you still insist on your past dreams?** Everyone can be successful **no matter** what they are or where they come from, even though some people try their best just to earn a living. It may take a lot of courage to **make** them come true. Although some dreams may look difficult, never say **die**. As an old saying goes, "Men are great for the dreams they have."

　　每個人都有一個夢想或很多夢想。你還記得當你還是小學生時，你的夢想是什麼？你現在還堅持著你的夢想嗎？每個人都可以成功，無論他們是做什麼的或是從哪來的，即便有些人只是為了謀生而竭盡心力。要實現夢想，可能需要很大的勇氣。雖然有些夢想也許看似困難，但絕不要輕言放棄。如同一句諺語：「人因夢想而偉大。」

答題解說

15. 答案：(C)。空格前面是「你還記得當你還是小學生時，你的夢想是什麼？」，後面這句是「每個人都可以成功…」顯然兩句中間這一句一定還是跟「夢想」，而不是「睡眠」或「作夢」有關，因此 (A)、(B)、(D) 皆可直接刪除。以下是其餘錯誤選項句子的翻譯：

(A) 有時候你可能會無法入睡。。

(B) 你對於你做過的夢有興趣嗎？

(D) 你夢到過鬼嗎？

16. 答案：(D)。空格前是個完整句子，後面的 "what they are" 以及 "where they come from" 是名詞子句，所以需要填入的是介系詞或是可與 what 及 where 形成副詞子句的詞彙。因此，(C) as if 可直接排除。句子大意是「每個人都可以成功，無論他們是做什麼的或是從哪來的」，故正確答案為 (D) no matter。(A) in case of…（萬一）與 (B) according to…（根據）皆不符句意。

17. 答案：(A)。空格後面是受格的 them 以及原形動詞 come，應思考什麼動詞可以構成「動詞 + 受詞 + 原形動詞」的結構？顯然是使役動詞 make。故正確答案為 (A)。

18. 答案：(C)。本題純粹考的是慣用語 "never say die"，本意是「絕不要說『完了』」，引申為「絕不放棄」，即使你不知道這個慣用語，從「絕不要說 ＿＿＿＿」這個字面意思，也可以猜出是 die（死亡，完蛋了，殆盡）。

破題關鍵

15. 本題關鍵是前一句中的 "when you were an elementary school student"（當你還是小學生時），因為這句提到「過去」的夢想，最能與「你『現在』還堅持著你的夢想嗎？」前後語意連貫。

16. no matter + wh- 表示「無論～」，是個副詞子句。本題關鍵在於必須了解句意，否則以文法結構來看，很容易選了介系詞的 (A) 與 (B)。

17. 本題只要單就空格所在句子，從文法結構的觀點來看即可答題。關鍵是空格後的 come true（實現）是原形動詞，應直接聯想到使役動詞 make。

18. 考慣用語或俚語的選項，通常可以直接套入空格內去揣摩句意。

第 1 回

第 2 回

第 3 回

第 4 回

第 5 回

第 6 回

第 7 回

第 8 回

第 9 回

第 10 回

字詞解釋

remember [rɪˋmɛmbɚ] **v.** 記得、想起　**elementary school** 小學　**successful** [səkˋsɛsfəl] **adj.** 成功的　**even though conj.** 即使　**try one's best phr.** 盡力而為 **earn a living phr.** 謀生　**courage** [ˋkɝɪdʒ] **n.** 勇氣　**come true phr.**（夢想等）實現 **difficult** [ˋdɪfəˏkəlt] **adj.** 困難的　**saying** [ˋseɪŋ] 諺語，格言　**fall asleep phr.** 入睡，睡 著　**insist** [ɪnˋsɪst] **v.** 堅持　**ghost** [gost] **n.** 鬼，幽靈

相關文法或用法補充

15. insist（堅持）常與介系詞 on 並用。例如：I insist on seeing it.（我一定要見到它。）

16. no matter + wh-（無論～）可引導副詞子句，也可以改成 wh-ever...可置於句首或 句尾。不過 wh-ever... 的形式可作副詞子句或名詞子句。例如：

    ❶ No matter where you go, I'll follow you. = Wherever you go, I'll follow you.（無 論你去哪裡，我都要跟著你。）

    ❷ I'll support whatever you do.（無論你做什麼我都會支持。）

17. 使役動詞主要有 have, make, let。對於「使役動詞」的用法，只要記住 Let's go. = Let us go.（我們走吧！）這個句子即可。也就是「使役動詞＋受詞＋原形動詞」。

18. 「絕不放棄」也可以用 "never give up" 來表示。

Questions 19-21

中文翻譯

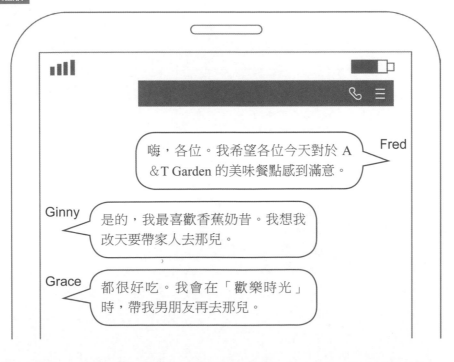

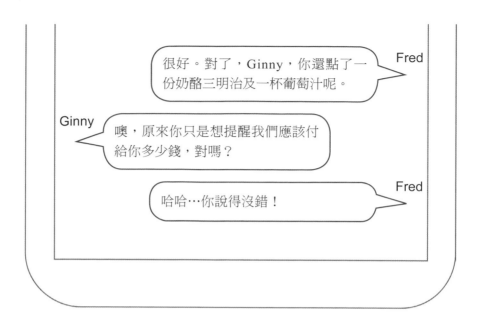

很好。對了，Ginny，你還點了一份奶酪三明治及一杯葡萄汁呢。 —— Fred

Ginny —— 噢，原來你只是想提醒我們應該付給你多少錢，對嗎？

哈哈…你說得沒錯！ —— Fred

這是他們的帳單以及這家餐廳的海報。

A&T Garden			
桌次：2	人數：3	買單者：Fred	13:30 | 12/14
1	蘋果派		NT$250 x3
2	冰淇淋		NT$100 x1
3	奶昔（巧克力）（大）		NT$180 x2
4	奶昔（香蕉）		NT$150 x2
5	雞肉三明治		NT$80 x1
6	雞肉三明治（配奶酪）		NT$90 x1
7	柳橙汁		NT$100 x1
8	葡萄汁		NT$100 x1
		總價：NT$ 1,880	
謝謝惠顧，並期待您下次光臨！			
電話：2882-5252			

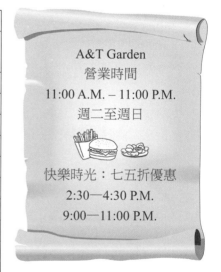

A&T Garden
營業時間
11:00 A.M. – 11:00 P.M.
週二至週日

快樂時光：七五折優惠
2:30—4:30 P.M.
9:00—11:00 P.M.

19. Fred 為何傳送訊息給他的朋友？
    (A) 邀請他們去一家餐廳
    (B) 向他們要錢
    (C) 請他們吃午飯
    (D) 告訴他們一些有趣的事情

20. Ginny 應該為她的食物付多少錢？
    (A) 新台幣三百元
    (B) 新台幣三百二十元
    (C) 新台幣三百四十元
    (D) 新台幣三百五十元

21. Grace 可能何時與她男友去那裡？
    (A) 週三上午 11:00
    (B) 週一下午 3:00
    (C) 週五晚上 8:00
    (D) 週四晚上 10:00

答題解說

19. 答案：(B)。題目問的是 Fred 傳送訊息給兩位朋友的原因（Why）。Fred 一開始時詢問兩位朋友對於當天在 A&T Garden 這家餐廳的食物覺得如何。單從這句話尚無法判斷其發送訊息的目的。接下來他提醒 Ginny 說她還點了什麼，於是 Ginny 似乎恍然大悟說，「原來你只是想提醒我們應該付給你多少錢，對嗎？」於是 Fred 說 "There you go!"，意思就是「你說得沒錯！」所以正確答案為 (B) 的「向他們要錢」。

20. 答案：(C)。本題需要整合與歸納兩篇文本的訊息與資訊，才能夠得到正確的答案。題目問的是 Ginny 應該為她的食物付多少錢。首先，從第一個文本的對話訊息中，Ginny 說，我最喜歡香蕉奶昔，後來 Fred 提醒她還點了一份奶酪三明治及一杯葡萄汁。接著我們可以從第二個文本的帳單中得知香蕉奶昔是 150 元，奶酪三明治是 90 元，葡萄汁是 100 元。所以她應付給 Fred 三百四十元。

21. 答案：(D)。本題需要整合與歸納兩篇文本的訊息與資訊，才能夠得到正確的答案。題目問的是 Grace 可能何時與她男友去 A&T Garden 這家餐廳。首先，在對話訊息中她提到，她會選在「歡樂時光」（Happy Time）時帶她男朋友再去那兒。接著，在第二個文本右方海報（poster）中，可以知道 Happy Time 的營業時間。因此，選項中只有 (D) 的「週四晚上 10:00」是在 Happy Time 的營業時間範圍內。

第 1 回
第 2 回
第 3 回
第 4 回
第 5 回
第 6 回
第 7 回
第 8 回
第 9 回
第 10 回

19. 本題關鍵只有在最後 Ginny 和 Fred 的對話，以及考生對於 "There you go!" （你說得沒錯！）的理解。

20. 本題關鍵是要先知道 Ginny 點了什麼，可以從對話訊息中得知。然後再從帳單中的金額去計算，即可得出答案。

21. 本題要找的兩個線索是：1. 對話訊息中提到 Happy Time；2. 海報中的 Happy Time 兩個時段。然後一一檢視四個選項，即可得到答案。

字詞解釋

satisfied [ˋsætɪsˌfaɪd] **adj.** 感到滿意的　**delicious** [dɪˋlɪʃəs] **adj.** 美味的　**milk shake** 奶昔　**by the way** 順道一提　**sandwich** [ˋsændwɪtʃ] **n.** 三明治　**cheese** [tʃiz] **n.** 乳酪，乾酪　**grape** [grep] **n.** 葡萄　**juice** [dʒus] **n.** 果汁　**remind** [rɪˋmaɪnd] **v.** 提醒，使想起　***poster** [ˋpostɚ] **n.** 海報　**open hour** 營業時間　**expect** [ɪkˋspɛkt] **v.** 期待

相關文法或用法補充

❶ 凡是表達「希望某事發生」，即可使用 hope。hope 後面可接 that 子句，但 that 可省略。例如：I hope (that) I'll pass the test.（我希望考試及格。）至於另一個表示「希望」的 wish，最常見的用法是「wish + 受詞 +（形容詞 +）名詞，表示「祝福」。例如：I wish you a happy new year.（祝你新年快樂。）。另外，wish 後面不接 that 子句，所以不能說 "I wish (that) you have a happy new year."。

❷ "There you go." 有兩個意思：
① 當「別人把東西交到你手中時」會說的一句話。例如：A: How much altogether? B: That's US$28.50, please. A: OK, there you go.（A：總共多少錢呢？B：28.50 元。A：好的，給你。）
② 當「你贊同對方所說的話時」會說的一句話（意思是「就是這麼回事」），相當於 "You're right. / I agree."。例如本題組中對話訊息中的。例如：A: I can't stand the weather there. B: There you go. It was just too hot.（A：我無法忍受那裡的天氣。B：你說得沒錯。實在太熱了。）

Questions 22-24

中文翻譯

　　我母親很不會煮飯。對她來說，煮飯更像是一種令人興奮的體驗。你把一些這個、一些那個放入鍋內，然後等著看會發生什麼事。「沒有嘗試，就沒有結果。」就是當她的結果不佳時她會說的話，而且我聽過很多次了。

　　我父親是個好廚師，他也喜歡煮飯。他經常說，他就是用一桌美味的食物讓我母親嫁給了他，而不是用貴重的戒指。他說，「一個家庭只需要一位好的廚師。」

現在我自己就是個廚師了。而且我有自己的餐廳。我從父親那裡學到如何做菜。從他那裡，我學到了烹飪的藝術。但是我確實從母親那兒學到一件事：她的名言「沒有嘗試，就沒有結果。」

22. 本篇短文的最佳標題應為何？
　　(A) 盡力而為
　　(B) 如何成為一位好廚師
　　(C) 勇於嘗試
　　(D) 烹飪的技術

23. 第一段畫底線的 awful 這個字可以改為 ＿＿＿＿＿。
　　(A) 棒極了的
　　(B) 最喜愛的
　　(C) 一般的
　　(D) 笨拙的

24. 下列敘述何者正確？
　　(A) 你得嘗試多次才能成為一名好廚師。
　　(B) 作者在抱怨其母親的廚藝。
　　(C) 丈夫應幫助妻子煮飯。
　　(D) 作者從父親那裡學到烹飪的技術。

答題解說

這是一篇記敘文。以第一人稱敘述不會作菜的母親嫁給一位廚藝大師，而自己後來也開了餐廳。

22. 答案：(C)。題目要問的是本篇短文的最佳標題。內容提到作者的母親與父親。一位不善於廚藝但勇於嘗試，一位很會做菜，讓作者從中學習到烹飪的藝術。所以 (A)、(B) 可直接排除，至於 (C) 與 (D)，其實我們從第一段與最後一段的內容，提到兩次「沒有嘗試，就沒有結果。」表示作者特別強調的部分為何，故正確答案為 (C)。

23. 答案：(D)。題目要詢問 awful 這個單字可以替換成哪一個字，由本文最後一行：" No tries, no results." is what she would say when her result did not turn out good...（「沒有嘗試，就沒有結果。」就是當她的結果不佳時她會說的話…）可知，這裡的 be awful at... 等於 be not good at 或 be stupid at...（對～不在行），故正確答案應為 (D)。

24. 答案：(D)。這是個「何者為真」的題型，基本上，應全盤了解整段文章內容之後，以「刪去法」檢視每個選項的敘述。從第三段的 From him, I learned the art of cooking. 可知，正確答案為 (D)。

22. 本題關鍵語句是 "No tries, no results." ，且於首段及末段皆出現一次，顯然它是全文的要旨所在。

23. 從 "My mother was _____ at cooking." （我母親對於煮飯很 _____ 。）這樣的語句來看，再參考接下來的內容，很明顯要表達的是「對於煮飯很不行」。

24. 這一題的答案，可以先看過選項，再看文章選出正確答案。這種「何者為是／非」的題型，建議留到最後再做答，因為它的解題線索，分布比較廣，可能在解其他題目時，就已經出現了。

字詞解釋

awful [ˋɔfʊl] **adj.** 極糟的，嚇人的　**exciting** [ɪkˋsaɪtɪŋ] **adj.** 令人興奮的　**experience** [ɪkˋspɪrɪəns] **n.** 經驗　**pot** [pɑt] **n.** 鍋　**result** [rɪˋzʌlt] **n.** 結果　**turn out**... 結果是…　**delicious** [dɪˋlɪʃəs] **adj.** 美味的　**famous** [ˋfeməs] **adj.** 著名的　**try one's best** 盡某人最大力量，盡力而為　**give it a try** 嘗試　**fantastic** [fænˋtæstɪk] **adj.** 極好的，了不起的　**favorite** [ˋfevərɪt] **adj.** 最喜愛的　**general** [ˋdʒɛnərəl] **adj.** 一般的，普通的　**stupid** [ˋstjupɪd] **adj.** 愚笨的

相關文法或用法補充

❶「擅於～」可以用 "be good at / be excellent/skillful in..." 來表示，相反地，「不擅於～，對於～不在行」，只要改變中間的形容詞即可，常見有 bad、lousy、awful... 等。

❷ turn out 的意思是「結果是～」，有時會看到 turn out to be... 的用法，不過 to be 常被省略掉。另外，turn out 後面已可以接「子句」。例如：It turned out you're right. （結果你才是對的。）

Questions 25-27

中文翻譯

　　讀書絕非考試前一晚才做的事。考試前一天晚上不可能讀所有的書。人皆各異，針對不同學生會有不同習慣。因此，養成良好的習慣很重要。這裡有一些重要的讀書技巧。

　　首先，預習和複習。上課前預習。使你在課堂上良好理解。另外，放學後複習當天的課程。第二點，養成每天讀書的習慣。放學後每天應該至少花一小時讀書。不要只有在考試前才讀書，因為這不可能得到好成績。第三點，上課時要做筆記。不要睡著或在課堂上和同學聊天。另一方面，要注意老師在課堂上所言。最後，妥善安排學習時間。有規劃可以節省很多時間。

　　良好學習永遠不嫌太晚。如果你想提高成績，應該遵照這些有用的技巧。相信

自己，可以辦得到。

25. 本文主旨為何？
    (A) 用功讀書的優點
    (B) 一些讀書技巧
    (C) 如何培養良好嗜好
    (D) 做功課的祕訣

26. 劃底線的單字 effective 的含意最接近 _____？
    (A) 有用的
    (B) 容易的
    (C) 特別的
    (D) 有名的

27. 你可能會在哪種雜誌上看到這篇短文？
    (A) 音樂雜誌
    (B) 時尚雜誌
    (C) 旅遊雜誌
    (D) 教育雜誌

答題解說

這是一篇說明文。內容舉出一些良好讀書習慣，並應避免臨時抱佛腳的壞習慣。

25. 答案：(B)。第一段最後提到：it is important to develop good habits. Here are some important tips for study.（養成良好的習慣很重要。這裡有一些重要的讀書技巧。）接著一些讀書祕訣，故正確答案為 (B) Some tips for studying well（一些讀書技巧）。

26. 答案：(A)。通常詢問單字意思的題目，其線索可由所在句子的前後文推知。由後面句子的 "They are useful." 可斷定正確答案為 (A) useful。

27. 答案：(D)。本文內容提到關於「讀書技巧」和「建立讀書習慣」，因此關於這方面的內容，可能會在和「教育」或「學校」方面的雜誌上看到。因此選項(D)就是正確的答案。

破題關鍵

25. 以「說明文」來說，文章主旨通常在首段的一開始或最後。本題關鍵句是第一段最後的 "Here are some important tips for study."。

26. 從本篇主旨「一些讀書技巧」，以及後面的關鍵字 useful 都可以確認正確答案。

27. 這種「出現在何處」的題型，可以留到最後再做，因為它的解題線索或許在解其他題時，會出現端倪，因此建議最後再作答。

第 1 回
第 2 回
第 3 回
第 4 回
第 5 回
第 6 回
第 7 回
第 8 回
第 9 回
第 10 回

quiz [kwɪz] n. 小考　**impossible** [ɪmˋpɑsəbl] adj. 不可能的　**examination** [ɪgˏzæməˋneʃən] n. 考試　**different** [ˋdɪfrənt] adj. 不同的　**develop** [dɪˋvɛləp] v. 發展　**preview** [ˋpriˏvju] v. 預習　**review** [rɪˋvju] v. 複習　**understand** [ˏʌndəˋstænd] v. 了解　**asleep** [əˋslip] adj. 睡著的　**attention** [əˋtɛnʃən] n. 注意、專心　**improve** [ɪmˋpruv] v. 增進、改善　**grade** [gred] n. 成績　***effective** [ɪˋfɛktɪv] adj. 有效的

相關文法或用法補充

❶ tip 可以當名詞，有「忠告」、「尖端」、「小費」的意思，它也可以當動詞，有「給小費」、「翻倒」、「輕拍」的意思。例如：

① Take my tip and keep a distance from him.（聽我的話，離他遠一點。）

② He walked on the tips of his toes.（他踮著腳尖走路。）

③ I gave the waiter a five-dollar tip.（我給服務生五塊錢小費。）

④ He forgot to tip the waiter, which was very embarrassing to me.（他忘記給服務生小費，我覺得很不好意思。）

⑤ The desk tipped over in the way.（桌子倒了，擋住去路。）

❷ kind of 主要有兩種意義：

① 種類。例如：three kinds of drinks（三種飲料）。其他類似片語還有 type of，例如：two types of watches（兩種類型的手錶）。

② 有點。例如：He is kind of tired.（他有點累。）類似用法還有 sort of，也是指「有點」。

Questions 28-30

中文翻譯

先生／女士您好：

　　我寫這封信來是要投訴上週六在您店內所受到的不良服務。我對於貴店店員麗莎的不當行為感到很不滿。實際上，我是您店內的老客戶。已經多次在貴店大手筆的購物。

　　我昨天看中了幾件洋裝。我試穿時，店員正忙著打電話。我認為我挑選的幾件洋裝讓我穿起來不是那麼好看，所以我只買了一件。但是這位店員把那些衣服放回去時，冷淡地又無禮地看著我。她真是太沒禮貌了，讓我不想再去您的商店。我要你們要為我受的待遇而道歉。

　　我希望在下週之前收到您的回覆。

謹啟

Meg Pitt

12 月 12 日

第 1 回

第 2 回

第 3 回

第 4 回

第 5 回

第 6 回

第 7 回

第 8 回

第 9 回

第 10 回

28. Meg Pitt 為何寄這封信？
    (A) 為了感謝善意
    (B) 為了退還已購買的物品
    (C) 為了讚美一名店員
    (D) 為了抱怨服務太差

29. 關於 Meg，何者為真？
    (A) 她買了一些衣服。
    (B) 她買了很多東西。
    (C) 她只買了一件洋裝。
    (D) 她什麼也沒買。

30. 下列敘述何者正確？
    (A) Meg 於 12 月 12 日去這家商店。
    (B) Meg 希望有人對她說聲抱歉。
    (C) 那位店員對她很友善。
    (D) Meg 給 Lisa 寫了這封信。

答題解說

這個題組是一封信件，主要是關於 Meg 在某服飾店受到委屈後，寫信給該店家要求道歉的內容。

28. 答案：(D)。題目要問的是 Meg Pitt 為何寄這封信，一開始答案就出來了：我寫這封信來是要投訴上週六在您店內所受到的不良服務（I am writing to complain about the poor service I received from your store on last Saturday.）。故正確答案為 (D)。

29. 答案：(C)。內容提到，「我只買了一件。（I only took one.）」故正確答案為 (C)，其餘選項皆明顯錯誤。

30. 答案：(B)。這是個「何者為是／非」的題型，基本上，應全部了解整段內容，以「刪除法」的方式，閱讀每個選項的敘述。(A) Meg went to the store on December 12. → 這是寫信的時間，不是去商店購物的時間；(B) Meg wanted someone to say sorry to her. → 最後提到 "I would like an apology for how I was treated."（我要你們要為我受的待遇而道歉。）所以是正確答案。(C) The clerk treated her friendly. → 剛好相反。第二段中間："The clerk, however, looked at me coldly and impolitely..."（但是這位店員冷淡地又無禮地看著我…）。(D) Meg wrote the letter to Lisa. → 信件一開始的 "Dear Sir/Madam,"，所以是錯誤答案。

28. 詢問寫信目的的題型，只要看到 "I am writing to..." 時，大概後面的內容都不用
看了，答案就在這句話的後面。

29. 「何者正確／為真」的題型，通常先看過四個選項，再從內容中的相關位置去找
答案。不過本題四個選項都圍繞在同一件事情打轉，只要你確定其中一個是對
的，那麼其他三個選項就一定是錯誤的。

30. 這是屬於「何者正確」型的題目，有時內容不會直接提及，而是經過融會貫通，
才能理解。

字詞解釋

complain [kəm`plen] v. 抱怨　**receive** [rɪ`siv] v. 受到　**satisfied** [`sæt͵ɪs͵faɪd] adj. 感到
滿意的　**behavior** [bɪ`hevjɚ] n. 行為　**regular** [`rɛgjələ] adj. 固定的，定期的
customer [`kʌstəmɚ] n. 顧客，買主　**purchase** [`pɝtʃəs] v. 購買　***impolitely**
[͵ɪmpə`laɪtlɪ] adv.不禮貌地　**apology** [ə`pɑlədʒɪ] v. 道歉

相關文法或用法補充

❶ 寫信時，如果對象是給不確定對象的名字或是男士或女士，建議開頭用 Dear Sir／
Madam。另外還有個更正式的用語是 "To whom it may concern,"，一般譯為「敬
啟者：」。

❷ 這類信件是屬於「投訴信」，因此信件開頭常見到 "I am writing to complain...，
或是 "I am writing to bring your attention to a serious problem that..." 之類的語句。

正確答案 Answer Key

TEST 01 Listening				
1 (C)	2 (C)	3 (A)	4 (A)	5 (C)
6 (B)	7 (B)	8 (C)	9 (B)	10 (C)
11 (B)	12 (B)	13 (A)	14 (C)	15 (A)
16 (A)	17(C)	18 (A)	19 (C)	20 (B)
21 (C)	22 (C)	23 (B)	24 (A)	25 (B)
26 (A)	27 (C)	28 (B)	29 (B)	30 (C)

TEST 01 Reading				
1 (B)	2 (C)	3 (D)	4 (C)	5 (B)
6 (C)	7 (A)	8 (C)	9 (B)	10 (B)
11 (D)	12 (B)	13 (B)	14 (A)	15 (B)
16 (C)	17(A)	18 (A)	19 (B)	20 (C)
21 (C)	22 (C)	23 (D)	24 (D)	25 (D)
26 (B)	27 (A)	28 (C)	29 (C)	30 (D)

TEST 02 Listening				
1 (B)	2 (B)	3 (A)	4 (C)	5 (C)
6 (A)	7 (C)	8 (A)	9 (A)	10 (C)
11 (C)	12 (B)	13 (C)	14 (A)	15 (C)
16 (C)	17(A)	18 (A)	19 (C)	20 (C)
21 (B)	22 (B)	23 (C)	24 (A)	25 (C)
26 (B)	27 (C)	28 (A)	29 (C)	30 (C)

TEST 02 Reading				
1 (B)	2 (B)	3 (D)	4 (B)	5 (A)
6 (A)	7 (B)	8 (B)	9 (D)	10 (A)
11 (B)	12 (C)	13 (D)	14 (B)	15 (C)
16 (B)	17(A)	18 (D)	19 (D)	20 (C)
21 (C)	22 (C)	23 (B)	24 (D)	25 (C)
26 (D)	27 (A)	28 (C)	29 (B)	30 (D)

TEST 03 Listening					TEST 03 Reading				
1 (B)	2 (B)	3 (B)	4 (B)	5 (B)	1 (C)	2 (C)	3 (B)	4 (A)	5 (B)
6 (A)	7 (C)	8 (B)	9 (B)	10 (B)	6 (A)	7 (C)	8 (B)	9 (B)	10 (D)
11 (B)	12 (C)	13 (A)	14 (A)	15 (C)	11 (D)	12 (B)	13 (D)	14 (C)	15 (B)
16 (A)	17(A)	18 (B)	19 (B)	20 (A)	16 (D)	17(A)	18 (B)	19 (C)	20 (C)
21 (A)	22 (A)	23 (C)	24 (C)	25 (B)	21 (D)	22 (A)	23 (B)	24 (C)	25 (D)
26 (A)	27 (A)	28 (C)	29 (A)	30 (A)	26 (C)	27 (B)	28 (D)	29 (A)	30 (B)

TEST 04 Listening					TEST 04 Reading				
1 (B)	2 (A)	3 (B)	4 (C)	5 (C)	1 (C)	2 (C)	3 (D)	4 (B)	5 (D)
6 (C)	7 (C)	8 (B)	9 (A)	10 (C)	6 (C)	7 (C)	8 (C)	9 (A)	10 (B)
11 (A)	12 (B)	13 (C)	14 (C)	15 (B)	11 (A)	12 (C)	13 (A)	14 (B)	15 (B)
16 (B)	17(B)	18 (C)	19 (A)	20 (B)	16 (D)	17(C)	18 (C)	19 (C)	20 (D)
21 (A)	22 (C)	23 (B)	24 (B)	25 (C)	21 (B)	22 (B)	23 (A)	24 (A)	25 (A)
26 (C)	27 (A)	28 (C)	29 (A)	30 (B)	26 (D)	27 (A)	28 (C)	29 (A)	30 (C)

TEST 05 Listening					TEST 05 Reading				
1 (C)	2 (B)	3 (B)	4 (A)	5 (C)	1 (D)	2 (A)	3 (C)	4 (D)	5 (D)
6 (B)	7 (B)	8 (A)	9 (C)	10 (C)	6 (B)	7 (D)	8 (A)	9 (B)	10 (A)
11 (B)	12 (B)	13 (C)	14 (B)	15 (A)	11 (C)	12 (A)	13 (A)	14 (C)	15 (C)
16 (C)	17(A)	18 (C)	19 (B)	20 (B)	16 (D)	17(D)	18 (B)	19 (C)	20 (D)
21 (C)	22 (A)	23 (C)	24 (A)	25 (B)	21 (A)	22 (B)	23 (A)	24 (C)	25 (B)
26 (A)	27 (A)	28 (B)	29 (B)	30 (C)	26 (D)	27 (C)	28 (C)	29 (B)	30 (B)

TEST 06 Listening					TEST06 Reading				
1 (B)	2 (A)	3 (C)	4 (C)	5 (B)	1 (A)	2 (B)	3 (C)	4 (B)	5 (A)
6 (B)	7 (B)	8 (A)	9 (B)	10 (B)	6 (C)	7 (D)	8 (C)	9 (A)	10 (B)
11 (B)	12 (C)	13 (C)	14 (B)	15 (C)	11 (A)	12 (C)	13 (C)	14 (C)	15 (B)
16 (A)	17(C)	18 (B)	19 (B)	20 (A)	16 (C)	17(A)	18 (C)	19 (C)	20 (B)
21 (C)	22 (C)	23 (B)	24 (B)	25 (A)	21 (B)	22 (B)	23 (C)	24 (C)	25 (D)
26 (C)	27 (B)	28 (C)	29 (A)	30 (A)	26 (B)	27 (C)	28 (D)	29 (D)	30 (B)

TEST 07 Listening						TEST 07 Reading				
1 (B)	2 (A)	3 (A)	4 (B)	5 (C)	1 (A)	2 (B)	3 (C)	4 (C)	5 (D)
6 (C)	7 (C)	8 (C)	9 (C)	10 (B)	6 (B)	7 (D)	8 (B)	9 (C)	10 (C)
11 (B)	12 (C)	13 (A)	14 (C)	15 (B)	11 (B)	12 (A)	13 (C)	14 (C)	15 (D)
16 (C)	17 (B)	18 (B)	19 (A)	20 (B)	16 (B)	17 (A)	18 (A)	19 (A)	20 (B)
21 (C)	22 (B)	23 (B)	24 (C)	25 (B)	21 (D)	22 (B)	23 (B)	24 (C)	25 (C)
26 (C)	27 (B)	28 (C)	29 (B)	30 (C)	26 (B)	27 (C)	28 (B)	29 (A)	30 (B)

TEST 08 Listening						TEST 08 Reading				
1 (B)	2 (C)	3 (C)	4 (C)	5 (B)	1 (D)	2 (B)	3 (C)	4 (D)	5 (B)
6 (C)	7 (C)	8 (A)	9 (A)	10 (B)	6 (C)	7 (B)	8 (C)	9 (B)	10 (B)
11 (A)	12 (C)	13 (C)	14 (C)	15 (A)	11 (A)	12 (B)	13 (C)	14 (D)	15 (C)
16 (B)	17 (C)	18 (B)	19 (C)	20 (A)	16 (A)	17 (C)	18 (C)	19 (D)	20 (B)
21 (B)	22 (B)	23 (C)	24 (B)	25 (B)	21 (B)	22 (C)	23 (A)	24 (C)	25 (C)
26 (C)	27 (C)	28 (A)	29 (A)	30 (C)	26 (C)	27 (A)	28 (B)	29 (C)	30 (C)

TEST 09 Listening					TEST 09 Reading				
1 (C)	2 (A)	3 (B)	4 (B)	5 (A)	1 (A)	2 (C)	3 (A)	4 (B)	5 (C)
6 (C)	7 (C)	8 (B)	9 (B)	10 (C)	6 (D)	7 (D)	8 (B)	9 (B)	10 (A)
11 (C)	12 (B)	13 (A)	14 (B)	15 (B)	11 (B)	12 (D)	13 (A)	14 (C)	15 (C)
16 (B)	17 (B)	18 (C)	19 (A)	20 (B)	16 (B)	17 (A)	18 (D)	19 (C)	20 (D)
21 (C)	22 (C)	23 (C)	24 (B)	25 (B)	21 (C)	22 (D)	23 (B)	24 (A)	25 (C)
26 (A)	27 (C)	28 (C)	29 (B)	30 (A)	26 (B)	27 (A)	28 (C)	29 (C)	30 (D)

TEST 10 Listening					TEST 10 Reading				
1 (A)	2 (A)	3 (C)	4 (B)	5 (A)	1 (A)	2 (A)	3 (C)	4 (D)	5 (B)
6 (C)	7 (C)	8 (A)	9 (B)	10 (B)	6 (B)	7 (B)	8 (B)	9 (C)	10 (D)
11 (B)	12 (C)	13 (A)	14 (C)	15 (A)	11 (C)	12 (A)	13 (A)	14 (B)	15 (C)
16 (B)	17 (C)	18 (B)	19 (B)	20 (A)	16 (D)	17 (A)	18 (C)	19 (B)	20 (C)
21 (C)	22 (B)	23 (B)	24 (B)	25 (B)	21 (D)	22 (C)	23 (D)	24 (D)	25 (B)
26 (A)	27 (C)	28 (C)	29 (C)	30 (C)	26 (A)	27 (D)	28 (D)	29 (C)	30 (B)

台灣廣廈 國際出版集團
Taiwan Mansion International Group

國家圖書館出版品預行編目（CIP）資料

NEW GEPT 新制全民英檢初級聽力＆閱讀題庫大全／國際語言
中心委員會 著. -- 初版. -- 新北市：國際學村, 2020.10
　　面；　　公分
　　ISBN 978-986-454-139-3（平裝附光碟片）
　　1. 英語. 學習 2. 英檢測驗

805.1892　　　　　　　　　　　　　　109012382

🌐 國際學村

NEW GEPT 新制全民英檢初級聽力＋閱讀題庫大全

作　　　者／國際語言中心委員會　　編輯中心編輯長／伍峻宏・編輯／許加慶
　　　　　　　　　　　　　　　　　封面設計／何偉凱・內頁排版／菩薩蠻數位文化有限公司
　　　　　　　　　　　　　　　　　製版・印刷・裝訂／東豪・鴻源・秉成

行企研發中心總監／陳冠蒨　　　　線上學習中心總監／陳冠蒨
媒體公關組／陳柔兮　　　　　　　數位營運組／顏佑婷
綜合業務組／何欣穎　　　　　　　企製開發組／江季珊、張哲剛

發　行　人／江媛珍
法律顧問／第一國際法律事務所 余淑杏律師・北辰著作權事務所 蕭雄淋律師
出　　　版／國際學村
發　　　行／台灣廣廈有聲圖書有限公司
　　　　　　地址：新北市235中和區中山路二段359巷7號2樓
　　　　　　電話：（886）2-2225-5777・傳真：（886）2-2225-8052
讀者服務信箱／cs@booknews.com.tw

代理印務・全球總經銷／知遠文化事業有限公司
　　　　　　地址：新北市222深坑區北深路三段155巷25號5樓
　　　　　　電話：（886）2-2664-8800・傳真：（886）2-2664-8801
郵政劃撥／劃撥帳號：18836722
　　　　　　劃撥戶名：知遠文化事業有限公司（※單次購書金額未達1000元，請另付70元郵資。）

■出版日期：2020年10月　　　ISBN：978-986-454-139-3
　　　　　　2024年3月8刷　　版權所有，未經同意不得重製、轉載、翻印。